"Robert G. Schneider has written a fascinating tale of a young man's quest for enlightenment in the ashram of an Indian guru, revered as a saint by his thousands of followers in the West. This compelling tale of spiritual seduction and betrayal, of ecstasy and trauma, is riveting, surprising, and most importantly, deeply authentic. If you were enchanted by the mystical mystery of the ashram in Eat, Pray, Love, this is the book that describes the other side of such groups – the corrupt, abusive world of the inner circle of a powerful, charismatic, traumatizing narcissist guru. This is the story of the dark side of enlightenment, and it could not be more clearly portrayed or better written."

—DANIEL SHAW, AUTHOR, TRAUMATIC NARCISSISM: RELATIONAL SYSTEMS OF SUBJUGATION, AND PSYCHOTHERAPIST IN PRIVATE PRACTICE IN NEW YORK CITY.

"For me, it is not plot that is compelling, it is good writing, and Robert Schneider's novel, The Guru's Touch, is a beautifully crafted story. It is in many ways a page-turner, which is not to say that it is an "easy read" or that it lacks depth. Rather, it is a story in which the characters come to matter greatly to the reader, and the reader wants to know more. But characters come to matter only because of the writing with which they are created. The reader must marvel at Schneider's writing. I found myself re-reading passages asking myself, How did he do that? The story is told in the style of a memoir, which gives almost every passage, every chapter, the quality of delicately managed irony. The narrator of this book is a solid, highly complex presence who speaks as no other writer I have ever read. This is a remarkable novel."

—THOMAS H. OGDEN, AUTHOR OF THE NOVELS, THE PARTS LEFT OUT AND THE HANDS OF GRAVITY AND CHANCE.

This is a work of fiction. Names, characters, businesses, places, events and incidents are either the products of the author's imagination or used in a fictitious manner. Any similarity to real persons, living or dead, or actual events is purely coincidental and not intended by the author.

First published June, 2017 by Robert G. Schneider
Strange Land Publications

www.robertgschneider.com

Text © Robert G. Schneider, 2017

The author's moral rights have been asserted.

All rights reserved
No part of this publication may be reproduced or transmitted by any means, electronic, mechanical, photocopying or otherwise without the permission of the publisher

Typeset in ITC New Baskerville by Elou Carroll Creative, UK.
Front cover by Marta S. Brody
Author photo by Sophie Bland

ISBN 978-0-692-90027-7
eISBN 978-0-692-90028-4

The Guru's Touch

a novel

Robert G. Schneider

For my mother and father, June and Victor
For my wife, Manette
And for my children, Melissa and Victor

Contents

Prologue 13

PART ONE **15**

1. Who by Fire? 17
2. Everlasting Happiness and
   the Ocean of Infinite Bliss 32
3. New Friends 53
4. The Call From Afar 67
5. A Ripening of Karmic Fruit 81
6. A Warm Welcome 90
7. Angel 106
8. It Burns 120
9. Gossip 136
10. A Precious Gift 152

11.	Initiation	164
12.	The Avadhoot	189
13.	Brothers	210

PART TWO 217

14.	Promised Land	219
15.	Ask No Questions and You Will Hear No Lies	229
16.	Austerities	248
17.	Orphans	261
18.	Wish-Fulfilling Tree	272
19.	A Sacred Mission	280
20.	Superman	304
21.	By Any Means Necessary	313
22.	Pilgrimage	330
23.	The Real Job of the Guru	366
24.	A Divine Plan	377
25.	Confidential	389
26.	What's Mine Is Yours	398
27.	The Man Behind the Curtain	410

PART THREE 421

28.	Exile	423
29.	Sooner is Better than Later	451
30.	Baba's Command	463
31.	The Test	473

32.	Never Go Too Close to a Holy Man	495
33.	Return to Ithaca	512
34.	Above the Law	533

PART FOUR 543

35.	Pezzo di Merda	545
36.	Dull Night of the Soul	553
37.	Fall from Grace	561
38.	A Denial	578
39.	The Secret Path	594
40.	A Change of Heart	615
41.	Satyananda's Letter	637
42.	Trespassers	649
43.	The Guru's Touch	673
44.	The Hymn the Brahmin Sings	688

GLOSSARY OF SANSKRIT AND HINDI TERMS 709
ACKNOWLEDGEMENTS 715
ABOUT THE AUTHOR 717

Out beyond ideas of wrongdoing and rightdoing,
There is a field.
I'll meet you there.
—Jalal ad-Din Muhammad Rumi

Time wounds all heels.
—Groucho Marx

Prologue

GOD WAS SHORTER THAN I thought he'd be. Even though it was quite a warm day for the end of March, he was bundled up as if he were on a visit to the North Pole. Over his orange silks he wore a bulky, bright red down jacket. His head was covered by a knitted orange woolen ski hat, and around his neck was a matching scarf. He was followed out of the limo by the siblings, Suresh and Anjali.

The chant reached a crescendo. Baba Rudrananda entered the building, flanked by his two young Indian disciples. With a wave of his hand, he motioned for the musicians to stop playing. Within a few seconds, the chanting ended. Rudrananda greeted the devotees with folded hands and the call, "Jai Gurudev!"

"Jai Gurudev!" cheered the crowd. Then there was silence, as if everyone in the lobby were holding their breath in anticipation of what the guru might do next.

PART ONE

1.
WHO BY FIRE?

IT WAS THE FALL of 1981. I was sixteen. I brought my boom box to the memorial service at Anabel Taylor Hall and set it down within easy reach on the seat next to me. Professor Braff led the service.

"Is he some kind of rabbi?" Grandma Millie asked, speaking too loudly.

"No Grandma," my sister Melanie whispered for the umpteenth time. "He's a professor at the university. A neighbor."

I remember Braff had asked me to speak, but there was no way I was going to get up in front of all those people to "share my thoughts and feelings." Instead I made a mixtape of all the saddest songs I knew. Ones my mom had loved. The first to be played, "Leaves That Are Green," by Simon and Garfunkel, had the desired effect. Most of the people in the chapel were fighting back tears. Some wept openly.

My mother had not wanted a traditional funeral. She had asked to be cremated and her memorial service to be held at the non-sectarian chapel on the Cornell University campus. She was an avowed atheist her whole life, even at the end. My father, on the other hand, had not had the luxury of time to plan. He was killed in a car crash in the winter of 1969, a week before my fifth birthday. My family lived in New York City at the time and we were driving home from a wedding out on Long Island. Back then, most cars had only lap belts, with no shoulder harnesses. So when the accident happened, there was nothing to stop his head from slamming into the steering wheel.

"Open the damn windows! I'm falling asleep," was the last thing I heard my father say. I must have fallen asleep too, because the next thing I knew the car was upside down and I was on top of my mother, with my left leg through the skylight, pinned underneath the weight of the car. At first I didn't understand why the car had turned upside down. The windshield was broken and both my older brother and younger sister were gone. I can still picture my father. His forehead was against the steering wheel and he wasn't moving.

At the hospital, I shared a room with my brother Jeremy. Like me, he had sustained only minor injuries. I suffered a broken leg, Jeremy a broken arm. But I was worried about my mother and father, and my little sister, Lucy. Where were they? Were they alright? The last time I had seen my father he wasn't moving. I asked a nurse.

"Your mommy and daddy are going to be just fine," the nurse said.

My father hadn't *looked* like he was going to be "just fine."

"My daddy's okay?" I wanted to believe her.

"That's right. You wait and see. He's going to be as good as new. He just needs a little time to rest in the hospital before you can all go home together."

"But where is he? Where's my mommy?" The nurse became flustered and was unable to answer my question.

"They're not here!" my brother cried from the bed next to mine. "They took them to a different hospital."

"With Lucy?"

"Yes."

Jeremy and I weren't roommates for long. My constant crying made it impossible for him to get any rest and my uncle arranged a room change.

The first time I got wind that something was terribly wrong was a couple of days after everybody was back home from the hospital—except for my father. I was in my room playing with blocks and a beloved robot. I heard my brother crying somewhere else in the house, and I knew that something bad had happened. A few minutes later I heard the knock on my door. Stan, a close friend of my father's, entered. "I have some sad news for you, Doug," he said. His face was grim, his tone businesslike.

Stan knelt down on the floor and looked me square in the eye. "Daddy died."

Daddy died. Daddy died. Daddy died. Daddy died.

"But the nurse said he's going to be as good as new. He just needs a little time to rest in the hospital!"

"I'm sorry, Dougie, but it's true—Daddy is never going to come home."

Pins and needles all over my body, a burning sensation on my cheeks.

The next day I threw my toy robot down a flight of stairs, smashing it to pieces. We never saw Stan again. Dad was buried somewhere out on Long Island.

At some point prior to his death, my father had taken out a life insurance policy offering double indemnity in the event of an accident, allowing my mother to receive twice the face value of the policy. With the relative windfall of the insurance money, my mother, a lover of the great outdoors, moved my family from smog-filled Queens to the fresh air of upstate New York.

My mother and father had both fallen in love with Ithaca when they first visited Cornell while college hunting with my older sister Melanie. I can still remember my mother describing to us the town's idyllic green hills and lake, its spectacular gorges and waterfalls. She was in awe of the Cornell campus, with its ivy-covered stone buildings and lofty elm trees. As far as my mother was concerned,

Ithaca embodied the two things she and my father had valued most in this world: nature and higher learning. The fact that Melanie already lived there made it even more appealing.

The Simon and Garfunkel song came to an end. I pushed *STOP* on the boom box.

"Thank you, Douglas, for that beautiful selection," Professor Braff said, gazing down at me with soulful eyes. "I know it was a favorite of Susan's."

Braff was a short, frail-looking man with salt and pepper hair, kind eyes, and thin, red lips. My mother was fond of him, but less so of his wife. She used to say Jonathan Braff was a mensch, but also a bit of a nebbish. He used to mow our lawn and drive my sister and me to school, along with his own kids. I think he felt sorry for my mother because she was a widow. In warmer weather I used to sit with him and his kids on the front stoop of his house while he read aloud to them. I liked the stories, but couldn't help feeling cheated and resentful. It made me angry that all the other kids around me had fathers and I didn't.

"And yes, time does march on," Braff said. "And yes, green leaves do indeed turn to brown. Fall is inevitably followed by winter. And for many of us in this room, it must feel like winter already. But spring will eventually come again."

Oh, really? I thought. I wasn't so sure. I wondered what kind of professor Braff was. I couldn't remember. In any case, he sounded like an idiot to me. I thought of the character Chauncey Gardiner, played by Peter Sellers in the film *Being There*. A simpleton who always speaks in gardening metaphors and is taken by everyone to be a prophet. That's what Braff seemed like to me now—a phony, ridiculous. But what I resented most about him was the way he always poked his nose into my family's business. Before my mother had been diagnosed, he had told me he thought I should do more around the house to help her. *Who the fuck did he think he was?*

I never felt responsible for what happened to my father, but I did blame myself for my mother's illness. After the car accident, I changed overnight from a happy-go-lucky kid to a moody, self-centered, spoiled brat. By the time I reached adolescence, my mom couldn't handle me anymore and gave up trying. I refused to go to school and flew into a rage if I didn't get exactly what I wanted whenever I wanted it. I was convinced that the constant worry and grief I caused my mother had given her cancer. I believed it. I was sure of it. And I was so tortured by feelings of guilt that not an hour went by that I didn't entertain a fantasy of ending my own life.

"Susan was a good neighbor and a dear friend," Braff said, gesturing to a large framed portrait of my mother. "She was a mom to Melanie, Jeremy, Douglas, and Lucy. And she was also a daughter to Millie. All of us came to know Susan under different circumstances, but whether you had the privilege of knowing her because you volunteered with her, played bridge with her, lived next door to her, or were related to her, she touched your life in a deeply positive way."

While Professor Braff sung my mother's praises, I began to tune him out and made a survey of the room to see who had come. I was convinced that everyone there must have thought I was some kind of freak. I certainly felt like one. *Who loses both parents before the age of seventeen?* I was sure it was somehow a bad reflection on me.

My mother's mother, Grandma Millie, looked more angry than sad. She had flown up from Florida, where she lived in a predominantly Jewish retirement community. She was a bitter and cantankerous old woman who had worked her whole life in the labor movement. My great Aunt Gabby, one of Millie's sisters, had also come and brought her middle-aged son Harvey with her.

Looking around the chapel, I couldn't help notice that more of Lucy's friends were there than mine. I obviously went to school with a bunch of assholes. But a few of them had come. Seated in the back row were Mike McFadden,

Stuart Campbell, Elisabeth Jensen, and Eddie Rubenfeld. Eddie and I had been best friends since my family had first moved up to Ithaca, but I hadn't seen much of him lately. These days I saw much more of Mike and Stuart. Eddie was determined to get into the right school—any Ivy League college other than Cornell—and spent virtually all his time studying.

Eddie had also been through a family tragedy, and I think it had changed him. Three winters ago, over the Christmas break, his older sister was hiking and slipped and fell into a gorge. Cornell was notorious for its high suicide rate, and the most popular method amongst its students was throwing oneself into the gorge. But Eddie's sister's death was a complete accident. Eddie had always worshiped and idolized his older sister. I think that when she died, an adventurous, warm, fun-loving side of him died too.

Sitting next to Eddie was Elisabeth. I had recently developed a bit of thing for her. She was a pretty girl with dark blonde hair and a penchant for dressing in tight fitting turtleneck sweaters. She looked amazing in them—the way they accentuated her large, perfectly round breasts. Sadly, despite my advances, Elisabeth seemed determined to remain friends. She hoped to become a psychotherapist one day. Whenever we were together all she was interested in was hearing about my feelings. Maybe she was practicing for her future profession. I hadn't had sex yet, and I wondered if I could use my pathetic situation to finally break down her resistance. And that made me feel seriously messed-up, that at my mother's funeral I was thinking of how I could use her death to get sex.

As various members of the community stood up to share their cherished memories of my mother, I studied the faces of my friends. Mike McFadden looked as though he were attending a lecture on his favorite subject. Eddie Rubenfeld was staring blankly out the window. Stuart Campbell's eyes were red with tears and he couldn't stop rubbing them. Halfway through the service, I noticed he got up and left. I didn't hold it against him—Stuart had always been uncomfortable with displays of emotion.

For some reason, my brother Jeremy was not seated with our immediate family. He sat with his wife Carrie, who was squeezing his limp hand between hers. I liked my brother's wife and so had my mom. She had believed that Carrie was a good influence on Jeremy and that it was thanks to her he had decided to go to medical school. Carrie fit in well with the women in my family, partly because she was so tiny. But her physical resemblance to them ended there. Carrie was not Jewish and she didn't look like us. Everyone in the Greenbaum family had dark hair and eyes, and an olive complexion. Carrie had light hair, blue eyes and fair skin. She had a nervous temperament and a myriad of phobias, but she adored my brother and had been kind to my mother as her illness had progressed, teaching her to meditate and making helpful recommendations for her diet.

Jeremy was seven years my senior and although he had never applied himself at school before college, he was a better student than me. Getting straight A's came naturally to him. While I was plagued with learning disabilities and would be lucky to finish high school, Jeremy sailed through effortlessly and became the second person in my family to get into Cornell. But by then he was introverted and my mom said he was depressed. When he moved into campus housing, there was no indication that he had a single friend. Then one day, without any warning, he brought a girlfriend home for Thanksgiving. He had met Carrie at the Raja Yoga meditation center. The fact that Jeremy was interested in yoga and meditation was news to my family and raised some eyebrows, but everybody, particularly my mom, was pleased he had finally made a friend and seemed happy.

By the spring of 1979, Jeremy and Carrie got engaged. They were married later that summer. My mother welcomed Carrie into the family, but always rolled her eyes at any mention of Raja Yoga or the holy man from India that Carrie called "Baba." Then Jeremy said something the following Thanksgiving that gave everybody pause: "This year I have been doubly blessed: by the grace of God, I have found my soul mate and my true guru."

Although I had always looked up to my brother, at the time I was convinced that he had joined a cult. First of all, we were all atheists. No one in my family ever mentioned the word "God" unless they were swearing or joking. Whenever he and Carrie came over to my mother's house, I mocked him about his new religion. Then one day he had enough of it, and he and Carrie blasted me for my "total lack of respect" for such a "great being like Baba." I never teased him about his religion again.

"Would anyone else like to share any memories or thoughts about Susan?" Professor Braff asked.

"I would," Aunt Gabby said.

"Won't you please stand up and tell us what's on your mind?" Braff said.

Aunt Gabby frowned and shook her head: "I am standing." Almost everybody in the chapel burst out laughing. "Susan was such an extraordinary woman. Words *cannot* describe how wonderful she was."

"Excuse me!" Grandma Millie interrupted, rising to her feet, "I strongly disagree! Susan was *my* daughter and I can tell you myself that words *can* describe how wonderful she was."

"Oh no, but you're wrong," Aunt Gabby said, "Words *cannot* describe her virtues."

"Excuse me, but they *can!*"

"Oh, *no*—they *can't!*"

"Oh, *yes* they *can!*"

By this point, half the gathering was watching the argument between my aunt and grandmother unfold with their mouths wide open in disbelief. The other half was in stitches.

"Then tell us!" Aunt Gabby said. "Describe how wonderful she was!"

"I have nothing to prove to you," Grandma Millie said, folding her arms. Grandma would argue with anybody about anything, anytime, but she was especially fond of contradicting her sister. Millie and Gabby fought with each other at every possible opportunity. It made no difference what the fight was about.

Ordinarily, Cousin Harvey would have been oblivious to the scene Millie and Gabby were making. He was fifty-three years old and had lived his entire life with his mother in her rent-controlled apartment on the Lower East Side of Manhattan. Until recently, when Grandma Millie moved to Florida, he had never lived more than a couple of blocks away from his mother's sister. He was used to their squabbles. But today was different. Harvey had worshiped my mother and was devastated when she died. On any other occasion, he would simply have tuned them out. But today their arguing was making him ill. He kept clutching at his throat, and he was sweating profusely, even though the chapel was cool.

When I was a small boy, Grandma Millie once told me that Harvey had a metal plate in his head. Although she never did explain why he had it or what it was for, I guessed it had something to do with his odd way of speaking, which I later learned was called a "speech impediment." But stuttering was the least of his problems. My mother told me that Harvey was also "severely myopic." The impossibly thick-lensed glasses he wore to help him see made his eyes look huge like an owl's. As if the awkwardness of his speech and the air of perpetual bewilderment caused by his glasses weren't enough to make Harvey seem like a freak, he also wore his pants pulled up practically to his chest.

Despite his strangeness, I was in constant awe of my cousin. He could recite all fifty states and their capitals in under thirty seconds. He could recite Pi up to at least a hundred decimal places. He had encyclopedic knowledge of the Finger Lakes region where we lived, and of the Native American tribes that once inhabited it. He might have known just as much about a lot of other subjects, but I would never have guessed. Whenever he came Upstate to visit us, Native American culture was all he wanted to talk about.

Even though my cousin was obviously some kind of genius, he had never gone to college. My mother said this was because Harvey was probably autistic—what we call nowadays "on the spectrum." Despite this disadvantage, he had managed, somehow, to hold down a job as a city clerk and earn a decent living. Why he never left home was a mystery to me.

I liked Cousin Harvey and always looked forward to spending time with him. He was especially fond of Ithaca's many gorges and enjoyed going on long hikes, for which he was never appropriately attired. Whether he was climbing a gorge trail or attempting to wade across a stream, Harvey never deviated from his standard outfit: polyester slacks, a white button-down shirt, and ten-dollar shoes from Sears.

Although I was not a patient kid by nature, I always managed to find the time to listen to Harvey and to accompany him on his outdoor adventures. I tried not to stand too close to him, however; his breath always reeked of peanut butter, and he tended to spray saliva when he spoke. Interestingly, he didn't stutter nearly as much when we were alone. Of all the strange things about my cousin, the oddest was that he always addressed me as "sir."

"Harvey, why do you call me 'sir?'" I once asked him.

"Because I have the ut—ut—ut—most res-res-spect f-f-f-for you, sir."

Most of the time I went around feeling like a misfit. But spending time around Harvey helped me to feel more "normal" by comparison. I also tended to like myself more when I was around him. Harvey brought out the best in me; it wasn't often that I was kind.

As Professor Braff brought the service to a close, I heard the rain start up again, drops pattering against the windows of the chapel. "Let us conclude with another musical selection from Douglas."

I pressed a button on the boom box and "Who by Fire" by Leonard Cohen began to play. My mother had been particularly fond of this song, and I couldn't stop listening to it after she died. She once told me that its lyrics had been inspired by a Hebrew prayer sung on the Day of Atonement:

> *Who by fire and who by water,*
> *Who by the sword and who by wild beasts,*
> *Who by hunger and who by thirst,*
> *Who by earthquake and who by plague,*
> *Who by strangling and who by stoning?*

The song, like the prayer, lists all the ways someone can die. But at the end of the song, Cohen asks, "Who shall I say is calling?" I didn't believe in God, but I couldn't stop wondering who or what had called my parents away.

The song came to an end. While it was playing, the drizzle had turned into a downpour. In the reception area, a cold buffet of Jewish delicacies had been laid out. I found Grandma Millie still arguing with Aunt Gabby. Absorbed in her debate with my aunt, she was oblivious as Melanie, Jeremy, Lucy, and I formed a receiving line.

My father's brother and his wife were among the first to offer their condolences: "You come down and visit us soon, Dougie," my aunt said crushing me in her arms and kissing me on the cheek. When she pulled away I could see that she was crying. I tasted her salty tears on my lips. I wiped my mouth with the sleeve of my suit jacket and nodded. My uncle looked like he had just been run over by a truck. He took me in his arms and kissed the top of my head. When he released me I waited for him to say something, but he was speechless.

Next it was Eddie Rubenfeld's turn. He weakly shook my hand and made fleeting eye contact. Then he nodded and headed out the door of the chapel and into the pouring rain. As I greeted some other friends from school, Mike McFadden darted past the receiving line on his way to the exit, snapping closed his raincoat. I caught his eye and he turned red. I thanked him for coming with a silent nod of my head. He smiled self-consciously and gave me a shy wave goodbye. Then he escaped out the door as fast as his feet could take him. I couldn't bear another second of this excruciating awkwardness. I was uncomfortable in my dress clothes and my tie was strangling me. I couldn't wait for the reception to be over so I could get home to the safety of my room.

"Hey, Greenbaum, it sucks that your mom is dead," Elisabeth Jensen said. She gently placed a hand on my shoulder. When she hugged me, I felt her large firm breasts push against my chest, and I started to get a stiffy.

"Call you later?" she asked.

I nodded, my eyes following her ass as she walked away. God, what was wrong with me?

After the reception at the chapel, Jeremy and Carrie headed home to Boston instead of coming back to the house with us. My brother was in his last year of medical school at Tufts. My aunt and uncle also returned to Long Island. Much to Melanie's chagrin, however, Grandma Millie would be spending another week with us. We were also stuck with Aunt Gabby and Cousin Harvey for the rest of the afternoon, since their bus didn't leave for the City until evening. It would be a long day.

THE RAIN HAD FALLEN in sheets the day before the memorial service and the streets of Ithaca were littered with soggy masses of brightly colored leaves. The sky, as it was on most days I can remember from my adolescence, was overcast and gray.

My mother's home was a five-bedroom, 1950s-style split-level, located in the quiet residential neighborhood of Belle Sherman, on Ithaca's East Hill. Lucy and I each had our own room, but when my mom got sick and Melanie and her young daughters moved into the house, I claimed the large finished basement as my lair.

When we got home, Melanie and Lucy busied themselves in the kitchen, putting away the prepared food that friends and well-wishers had dropped off for us. Grandma Millie and Aunt Gabby continued to torture Cousin Harvey in the living room, resuming the argument they had begun in the chapel.

I was on my way downstairs from my room to grab a snack in the kitchen when Aunt Gabby called out to me: "Douglas, darling, please join us." She was seated on the sofa between my grandmother and Harvey. I glanced at my cousin—his forehead was beaded with sweat and the color had drained from his face

"Excuse—cuse—cuse—me—me—me, S-s-s-ir," Cousin Harvey said, beseeching me with his eyes.

"Yes, Harvey."

My cousin mopped his brow with a handkerchief. "I was wo—wo—wondering if-f-f-f w-w-w-we could stay the night and catch the b-b-bus for Man—Man—Man—hattan in the mo—mo—morning?"

"Did you ask Melanie?"

Harvey began to answer, but was having an even more difficult time than usual getting his words out. His eyes had a glazed quality, as if he were about to pass out. "I-I-I…"

"Don't worry, I'll talk to her," I said, trying to sound reassuring.

I found Melanie alone in the kitchen with her boyfriend, Herb. She was slumped forward in her chair, resting her forehead against her hand, the way she always did when she was about to get one of her migraines. Herb was sitting next to her, massaging the back of her neck.

Herb was a well-known professor of psychology at Cornell. At least ten years older than Melanie, he was a short, bearded, teddy bear of a man with kind eyes that shined when he smiled. He was good to Melanie, and had been a big support to her when my mother got sick. But for some reason I still don't fully understand, I didn't like Herb. As far as I was concerned, Herb was around much too often, and he got on my nerves. For one thing, he was a know-it-all; whenever I said anything in his presence, which was rare, he would look me in the eye and smile wisely, as if he knew what I were really thinking. When he wasn't analyzing me, he was aggressively trying to win me over. I hated when he said, "I'm here for you, sport, if you ever want to talk." Even more insufferable were his offers to play catch or to throw the football around the yard with me. With all his training as a psychologist, wasn't he perceptive enough to realize that he was the last person I wanted to talk to? Or at least that I hated sports?

"It's you or them," Herb was telling Melanie when I entered the kitchen.

"Harvey wants to know if they can spend the night," I said, interrupting them.

"I know," my sister muttered.

"We're discussing it, Doug," Herb said, glancing up at me and then directing his attention back to my sister. "You're stuck with your grandmother, but having all three of them here together right now is going to do you in. You have to think about *yourself* for a change."

My sister shook her head: "I can't just send them away."

"They'll be fine," Herb said.

Just then we heard loud cries coming from the living room.

"Harvey! My Harvey! Somebody, do something! My Harvey! Help!!!"

Melanie and Herb leapt to their feet and I raced after them into the living room, where we found Cousin Harvey unconscious on the floor. Aunt Gabby was practically on top of him, shaking and slapping him: "Harvey, wake up this instant!"

Herb took one look at Harvey and ran back to the kitchen to call an ambulance. Melanie and Lucy struggled to pull Aunt Gabby off her son. Paralyzed, I stood by my grandmother. Apart from the fact that he was turning blue, I noticed something strange about Harvey's face. At first I couldn't put my finger on it. Then I realized what it was: He wasn't wearing his glasses. I had never seen him without them before.

Within a few minutes, the paramedics arrived on the scene and tried to resuscitate my cousin. But they were too late. By the time they got there, Harvey was already gone.

"My Harvey! My Harvey! My Harvey!" Aunt Gabby wailed as Melanie and Herb barricaded her behind the sofa. "Let me go! Let me go! I need to save him!"

As they lifted Harvey's lifeless body onto the stretcher, Aunt Gabby began hitting herself in the face. "My Harvey!" *Smack!* "My Harvey!" *Smack!* "How can I live without my Harvey!" My aunt was in her mid-eighties and couldn't have weighed more than seventy-five pounds. But Herb and Melanie couldn't hold her down by themselves and they asked for my help. Meanwhile, Lucy ran to the bathroom in search of a Valium.

"My Harvey!' *Smack!* "My Harvey!" *Smack!* "My Harvey!"

"Gabby, you need to stop hitting yourself," Herb said.

"Aunt Gabby please!" Melanie begged. "Dougie, hold her arms!" I grabbed onto my aunt's wrists, but we were unable to subdue her. She fought us off with the strength of an angry bear.

"Let me go! Let me go!"

"Gabby, you need to calm down," Herb said.

"A Harvey!" she cried again, even louder than before. "How can I live without a Harvey?"

2.
Everlasting Happiness and the Ocean of Infinite Bliss

I WAS IN MY junior year of high school. I had been just barely getting by before my mother got sick. Now dragging myself to school was hard enough. Most days I didn't even go. I either hung out in the student lounge or got high with my friends at nearby Lake View Cemetery.

I dreaded the idea of writing college application essays, visiting schools, and being subjected to interviews. Picturing the slew of rejection letters that was sure to follow filled me with anxiety. But what frightened me even more was the realization that even if I somehow did get in somewhere, I would be forced to leave home and live in a place where

I didn't know anyone. I would be all alone and would have to fend for myself. Here in Ithaca I was depressed and miserable, but at least I was depressed and miserable in my own home. I also had Melanie to take care of me.

Melanie was eleven years older than me, and ever since my father died she had been like a second mother to Lucy and me. When we were little, before her daughters Leah and Nicole were born, Melanie showered us with attention. She read to us, helped us with our homework, and took us swimming, boating, hiking, and camping every chance she could find. Now, with my mother gone, she was as determined as ever to not let me fall behind or succumb to depression.

One evening when Herb wasn't around, I summoned the courage to tell Melanie I had no idea what I wanted to do with my life. I found her cleaning up in the kitchen. She assured me that it would eventually come to me, but in the meantime I should focus on finishing high school and getting accepted to college. "Where do you think I could get in?" I asked her, preparing myself for disappointment.

Melanie started the dishwasher and turned around to look me squarely in the eye. "You're going to Cornell."

"Cornell? You must be joking."

"You're very bright, Dougie. And you were getting decent grades before Mommy got sick."

I shook my head ruefully. "I don't have a prayer."

"Your GPA is not that impressive, but your SAT scores are high enough. Anyway, there are extenuating circumstances—the admissions department is going to take them into consideration."

I looked down at the kitchen floor. "I don't know."

"Don't forget, you're also a legacy. *I* went to Cornell. And so did Jeremy." Melanie had gotten both her bachelor's and master's degrees from the Cornell School of Agriculture. Now she owned and operated a wholesale shrub nursery on a fifty-acre farm she had purchased during her last year of graduate school, with a lot of help from my mother.

Technically, I wasn't a legacy. I would have been if one of our parents had attended, but I didn't bother to point this out to her. The conversation was making me uncomfortable. Even if by some miracle I did get in, I didn't want to go to Cornell, or any other college. I didn't want to do anything.

Eventually Melanie convinced me to apply to Cornell's pomology department, only because practically no one wanted to study fruit. She was also "old friends" with the head of the department, which "couldn't hurt."

"With the right application essay, you'll be a shoo-in!" she had said.

I had zero interest in agriculture, and had to look up the word "pomology" in the dictionary after Melanie suggested it to me. "All you have to do is convince them that you're passionate about fruit trees," she had said. I had no idea where to begin. If I was passionate about anything in my junior year of high school, it was masturbation and my vinyl record collection. Fruit trees, or any aspect of agriculture, for that matter, was probably the *last* thing I wanted to study. But Melanie convinced me it didn't matter. "What matters is getting a diploma from an Ivy league university," she said.

Despite my skepticism, I managed to write a compelling essay, with a lot of help from Melanie. I invented a story about how, driven by my love of horticulture, I had spent every summer since the age of twelve helping my sister in her shrub nursery and vegetable garden. "But my dream," I wrote, "is to one day cultivate my own apple orchard."

It was complete bullshit: I hated working outside and refused to work in the garden or nursery almost every time my help was requested. On the rare occasions Melanie managed to talk me into working, I purposefully did an incompetent job in the hopes of never being asked again. As for apples, I was so uninterested in them

I didn't even know the difference between a Red Delicious and a Granny Smith.

But a few months later, somehow, I did get into Cornell. I would be attending the College of Agriculture and Life Sciences in the fall of 1983. And for a few weeks after receiving the acceptance letter, I didn't feel like killing myself.

AT THE END OF June, Melanie dropped a bombshell: she had put our mother's house up for sale. I was terrified when I found out. Terrified and furious. One morning, as she was getting ready to leave the house to take the girls to day camp, I confronted her.

"Where are Lucy and I supposed to live?"

"The market is soft now," Melanie said, slathering sunscreen on Nicole's little arms and legs. "The house might not sell for months, or even years."

"Okay, but what if it *does* sell soon?"

"You can live on campus."

"Oh really. What about Lucy?"

"She's only got one more year of high school. If the house sells before she goes away to college, she can always come live with the girls and me on the farm."

When Melanie and Herb returned home later that evening, I begged my sister to take the house off the market.

"You can't sell mom's house! It hasn't even been a year since she died!"

"We know you're scared, Doug," Herb said. "But the only way to overcome your fears is by facing them."

"No one cares what you think! Get out, asshole!" I shouted, pointing to the door.

"For God's sake, Doug," Melanie said, kneading the back of her neck with her hand. "Herb's just trying to help. You're impossible! I don't know how Mommy put up with you!"

I felt a wrenching pain in my chest. "Go ahead and say it," I shouted. "Say it!"

Melanie's face turned white and she looked confused. "Say what?"

"You know!"

Melanie shook her head. "No, Doug I don't."

"It's my fault she's dead! I'm the one who made her sick!"

Melanie brought a hand to her mouth. "That's not true, Doug. How could you say such a thing?"

Crying now, I ran for the door to the basement. As I stormed down the stairs I heard Melanie call out to me: "Doug! Please come back!"

She followed me into my lair, Herb on her heels.

"Get the fuck out of here!" I squealed.

"Be reasonable, Doug. Even if the house sells soon and you have to leave, it's not like you're going to be out on the street. You'll live in a dorm on campus, and you'll be on a meal plan."

"You'll probably find the experience empowering," Herb added.

I shot him a black look and he remained silent for the rest of the discussion.

"But this is my house too! What right do you have to sell it if I don't agree?"

"I have every right," Melanie answered. "It says so in Mommy's will."

Clearly, I wasn't getting anywhere with my sister. Nothing I said mattered.

A few days later I changed tactics, trying to turn Lucy and Jeremy against her by pointing out that she had made the decision to sell without consulting them. But much to my dismay, neither of them cared. As long as they eventually got their fair share of the proceeds, they were fine with it.

Melanie went ahead with putting the house on the market. But when a real estate agent came by to show the property, I hid in my room and shouted, "Get the fuck out of my house!" at the top of my lungs when they walked in on me. Melanie promised the broker that I would never be in the house during future visits.

At the end of August, when it was time for me to register for classes, I put up more resistance. I advised Melanie that

I had changed my mind, and that I no longer wanted to go to college.

"Okay, fine," my sister said. "So you'd better start looking for a job to support yourself."

"A job? What about my inheritance?"

"Luckily for you, Doug, Mommy's money is locked away in a trust fund. It can only be used to pay for tuition and room and board while you and Lucy are in college."

"That doesn't seem fair," I whined. "It's *my* money. When do I get it?"

"Whatever's left of the trust when Lucy turns twenty-one will be divided between the two of you. Before then, neither of you can touch it."

Fuck, fuck, fuck, and fuck! They had me cornered. Even from beyond the grave my mother was in cahoots with Melanie to stop me from doing anything.

THE WEEK OF REGISTRATION also coincided with a visit from Jeremy and Carrie. My brother was interviewing for internships at hospitals in New York City, and Melanie asked him to stop off in Ithaca on his way back to Boston. She wanted him to talk some sense into me and help me figure out what to take my first semester at Cornell.

I was home alone in the basement listening to The Clash and getting stoned when Jeremy and Carrie arrived. I hid my stash, and then invited them to hang out with me in the playroom while we waited for the others to get home. I was sure they could smell the pot and knew I was high. But my brother was cool; he wouldn't mention it to our older sister.

Jeremy pulled a big, fat paperback book out of his briefcase and presented it to me. "Here, Doug," he said, "this is for you."

The title of the book was *Divine Dance of Consciousness*. On the cover was a picture of a bearded, coffee-colored man in orange silk robes. He had a red dot centered just above the bridge of his nose, and three broad white stripes across his forehead. I was immediately struck by the serenity in the man's smiling face and the kindness in his eyes. I tried to think of something sarcastic to say about him, but nothing came to mind.

"Who's this guy?" I asked.

"That's Baba!" Carrie exclaimed.

"It's Swami Rudrananda. He's a fully Self-realized being," Jeremy said.

I picked up the book and looked more closely at the photo. There was something about the swami's eyes that intrigued me—they seemed to be gazing back at me.

"He has the power to awaken others and guide them all the way to enlightenment," Carrie said, her eyes getting wider as she spoke. "He's like a modern-day Christ."

My brother's gentile wife apparently thought that his being Jesus-like would be a big selling point for me.

I put the book down on the card table. "Why do you call him 'Baba'?"

"Baba means father," Jeremy said, his voice cracking a little. A momentary sadness spread across his face, and he broke eye contact with me.

In an attempt to steer the conversation away from my brother's new religion and back to me, I told Jeremy about my misgivings regarding college and how I had no idea what I wanted to do with my life. His answer was not what I expected.

"You should understand that whatever worldly knowledge you acquire in this life will be lost to you when you die. But what Baba can teach you will stay with you forever." Carrie nodded her head up and down in agreement. There was a zealous gleam in my brother's eyes that I found unsettling.

I cleared my throat. "So, I guess what you're saying is since we're all eventually going to die, college is useless. Do you regret going to medical school?"

"No, of course not," Jeremy said, turning to Carrie for support. She took his hand in hers and stroked it reassuringly.

"What your brother means is that worldly knowledge—a career, money—is not enough to truly be happy.

You, me, Jeremy—we all have tremendous spiritual potential sleeping inside of us. The guru can awaken it with just one touch."

"Far out," I answered, trying not to yawn.

Carrie smiled at me patiently. "Your brother was skeptical at first, too."

"That's right," Jeremy said, nodding. "I was." My brother turned to his wife and they grinned at each other.

Jeremy picked up the book again and put it back in my hands. "Here, just read it," he said. "Your life will change forever."

Jeremy and Carrie returned to Boston the next morning. Before they drove off, I thanked them for the book and promised to read it. Later, when I was back in my room, I tossed *Divine Dance of Consciousness* in my closet and promptly forgot about it.

THE SEMESTER STARTED. MY biggest challenge was finding my classes, especially the ones that had anything to do with my major. When I did finally locate them, I thought I'd die of boredom. So I didn't return. A couple of weeks into the term, I was in the kitchen with Melanie and Lucy when they asked me how school was going. I admitted I had only been to a couple of classes so far, and was having difficulty finding my way around campus.

Melanie shook her head in disbelief. "Doug, you're joking, right?"

Frustrated and embarrassed, I lashed out at her. "How am I supposed to find Goldwin-fucking-Smith Hall?"

"Maybe if you actually *wanted* to find your classes, you'd make more of an effort," she scolded.

Lucy, who was setting the table, rolled her eyes at me. "Hey genius, did you ever think of looking at a *map*? Or asking for directions?"

"Mind your own business, jerk!"

Lucy slammed the silverware drawer closed and stormed out of the kitchen. "Screw you, loser! You set the table for once, you lazy asshole!"

"You'd better get your ass in gear," Melanie said, putting the finishing touches on the table. "If you don't show up for your classes, they'll automatically flunk you."

I didn't want to admit it, but I knew Melanie was right. I wouldn't be able to blow off my classes for much longer. I asked Mike McFadden for help locating them, and it turned out we were both registered for the same required freshman writing seminar. The writing course bored me stupid. I went to a few classes, never did a single assignment, and then stopped attending it, along with all the others. Flunking out of college became a foregone conclusion.

Since I had no intention of returning to any of my classes, the wisest course of action would have been to officially withdraw and ask the university for a deferment. I could have avoided flunking out and would have retained the option of returning to Cornell someday when I was ready. But I couldn't bring myself to do it. Instead, I did nothing. I dreaded the inevitable confrontation with Melanie, but hoped that if I ignored the problem long enough, it would eventually go away.

If I had stayed in the house all day, as I had during the summer, Melanie would have figured out what was going on and forced me to go back to school. Instead, I divided my time between Willard Straight Hall (the student union building) and Collegetown Bagels, where I whiled away my time reading science fiction novels and drawing elaborate maps of dungeons on graph paper to use later for Dungeons and Dragons.

But I didn't seek out Mike's company. Nor did I try to make any new friends. My peers at Cornell appeared to be so full of purpose, and seemed to know the "meaning of life," which for me couldn't have been more obscure. Sometimes I eavesdropped on their conversations or observed them from afar. I was envious of the easy manner with which they related to each other and I wished I could be one of them—smart, happy, self-confident. They were all winners and would enjoy successful careers one day. I was a loser. I felt like a fraud just being in the same room with them. I might as well have been a visitor from another planet; even though I could understand the words they were saying, I was unable to decipher the unspoken communications of their body language and the chummy looks they gave each other. I fantasized about the co-eds, and even about some of the prettier boys. In my mind's eye they were all pleasuring me. Doing whatever I told them, regardless of how degrading or humiliating. In my fantasy life, I was not a loser. I was an irresistible, all-powerful god.

ON MY WAY HOME one chilly day, I rode my bike over Cascadilla Gorge, which separated the university campus from the rest of the town. The deep, spectacularly beautiful ravine called out to me, inviting me to jump: *Now! Do it! You can end it all and finally be free!* How easy it would be to throw myself over the bridge into the abyss. All my problems would be solved and the guilty feelings that tormented me would be gone in an instant. But I couldn't bring myself to do it.

Back home in my room, I wondered how much longer I could hide what was really going on from Melanie. When she found out, she would be furious. But that would be the least of my problems. She would force me to find a job and get a place of my own. I would be poor. How would I manage? The thought of it made me afraid.

The phone rang, and a minute later Lucy knocked on my door. "Jeremy's on the phone. He wants to say hello to you." *Great, now I'll have to lie to my brother too,* I thought.

I picked up the receiver in the hall outside my room. He asked me about school. I told him everything was going "swimmingly."

Then he asked, "Did you start Baba's book?" I heard someone pick up another extension on his end. I was sure it was Carrie. I admitted I hadn't. I blamed it on my "heavy workload" at school.

Next it was Carrie who spoke: "You should read it. Baba's teachings will *help* you with college."

"Let me ask you something about this Baba. How is he different from all the other crazy cult leaders who make their followers sell flowers at airports?"

My brother and his wife laughed. "Baba is a perfected master of Raja Yoga from an authentic lineage," Jeremy answered. "Not some kind of New Age snake oil salesman."

"You said last time you visited that Baba was like Jesus. What did you mean?"

Carrie giggled. "Baba's more like Buddha than Jesus. He wasn't born enlightened. Like Buddha, he had to make a spiritual journey." She was splitting hairs, as far as I was concerned. But Jeremy wasn't exactly an idiot, and neither was his wife, and they believed in Rudrananda. Maybe this guru could help me.

"So what happens when he touches you? I asked.

"He gives you *shaktipat!*" Carrie answered.

"This will awaken the *kundalini* energy dormant inside of you," Jeremy said, "ultimately leading to complete enlightenment, within three lifetimes."

"Kind of like a jump start?" I asked, thinking that three lifetimes was definitely too long to wait for anything.

"That's actually an excellent analogy," Jeremy said.

I took a good look at the cover of the book they had given me, and tried to see the swami with fresh eyes. He was quite handsome for an old man. He had a gentle face, and the way he seemed to be looking back at me made me feel close to him. After getting off the phone, I opened the book and turned to the preface:

Dear One,

Over countless lifetimes you have wandered in the arid desert of mundane existence, looking for love and contentment in the world. You seek this happiness because it is your true nature. It is not wrong to yearn for it.

> *The error, however, is to seek it outside of yourself. There you will find only suffering and pain. True, everlasting happiness, and the ocean of infinite bliss, can only be found within you.*

I already knew it would be impossible for me to find happiness in the world. What had never occurred to me, however, was that other people might be incapable of finding it too. Some of them sure *looked* happy. Maybe they were just fooling themselves.

> *Mired in delusion, you believe that you are your body and that your ego is the center of the universe. Through the grace of God, in the form of the compassionate Guru, you can become free from that delusion and discover your true nature—the blissful, eternal Inner-Self of all.*

My mother had always told me I wasn't the "center of the universe," even if it felt that way at times. I got that—at least intellectually. But that my "true nature" was the "Inner-Self" of everybody? What did that even mean? Was Rudrananda saying that Hitler and I were really the same person and that I just didn't realize it? How could I share the same "Inner-Self" with Melanie, Herb, Ronald Reagan, and Michael Jackson? It didn't make any sense.

I closed the book and again looked at the guru's picture on the cover. Rudrananda really did have compassionate eyes. Again it was as if I were looking at a real person, and not just a photograph. The guru was staring right back at me. He cared. He wanted me to be truly happy. And I wanted to know more about this thing called *shaktipat* that Jeremy and Carrie had spoken of, and how I could get it. *I'm going to read this book*, I decided. *Tomorrow, cover to cover. It just might have some answers.*

I was in high spirits the next morning. I had a new sense of purpose: I was going to read *Divine Dance of Consciousness* and learn all about Rudrananda. I even hummed to myself as I prepared breakfast.

"You're in a good mood this morning," Melanie remarked.

"I guess."

"Interesting class today?"

"Um-hum."

"Which one?"

I had to think fast. "The freshman writing seminar?"

"Right, the one you're taking with Mike. What's the theme?"

"The theme?" I couldn't for the life of me think of it. Then I remembered a title from the course catalogue: "The evolution of fairy tales," I answered. Before the conversation could continue, I quickly finished the last bites of my bagel and cleared my plate from the table.

Eager to get started on the book, I took off on my bike at top speed in the direction of campus and narrowly missed hitting Mike McFadden. He was riding a unicycle in front of his house, and almost fell off when I skidded to a stop a few inches from him.

"Greetings and salutations, Greenbaum!" he said, hopping off his new toy and landing on his feet. "Did you, by any chance, withdraw from the writing seminar?" he asked.

"Um, no. Not exactly..."

A confused expression came over my friend's face. "*C'est ça.* I haven't seen you in class for a few weeks now—"

"Well, yeah, actually, I did drop it. Too boring," I answered, eager to be on my way.

Mike squished his eyebrows together and frowned. "But isn't it required?"

The conversation was becoming irritating. I got interrogated enough at home. Anxious to change the subject, I reached into my knapsack and pulled out Rudrananda's book. "Take a look at this," I said, handing it to him.

"*Dance of Divine Consciousness* by Swami Rudrananda." Mike pronounced *Rudrananda* just the way Jeremy had.

"You've heard of him?"

"No, but judging by his orange frock and the dot between his eyes, I surmise he must be a Hindu holy man of sorts." Mike furrowed his brow and his tongue protruded slightly from his mouth as he continued to study Rudrananda's picture. "From the three stripes of ash on his forehead, I can also tell you that he is a devotee of Shiva, the Hindu god of destruction."

"How do you know so much about Indian religion?"

"I read *Autobiography of a Yogi* by Paramahansa Yogananda when I was thirteen," Mike said with a grin that conveyed superior knowledge. "And my big brother had a brief stint with the Hare Krishnas."

"This Rudrananda guy is my brother's guru. Do you think Jeremy might have joined a cult?"

"Of course he has!" Mike chuckled. "*All* religions are cults!"

"What's that supposed to mean?"

"If they were founded centuries ago we call them *religions*, if they started up ten years ago we call them *cults*."

"Yeah, but what do *you* think?"

"How could I possibly offer a valid opinion by glancing at a book for a few seconds?" Mike said, tossing it back to me.

"Okay, whatever."

I crammed the book back into my knapsack, and then climbed on my bike to leave. Before I rode off Mike invited me to play Dungeons & Dragons with Eddie Rubenfeld and Stuart Campbell at his house on Friday. I told him I'd be there, but was pretty sure I'd change my mind by the weekend.

MAKING MYSELF COMFORTABLE IN the International Lounge at Willard Straight, I opened Rudrananda's book to the foreword by Professor P.J. Mehta.

> *In India there have been many ecstatic beings venerated for their total surrender to God and the unbridled freedom born of such surrender. Holy men and women such as these have passed beyond all*

worldly attachments and concerns. Shree Gurudev Brahmananda was one such extraordinary being and is revered as one of the greatest saints of modern India. Before leaving his physical body to merge with the absolute in 1961, Gurudev passed the mantle of the Raja Yoga lineage to his chief disciple, the author of this book, Swami Rudrananda. Baba, as he is lovingly called by his devotees, has touched and transformed the lives of thousands of people all over the globe, awakening them to the Supreme Truth of their own beings.

I flipped ahead to the first chapter. Rudrananda wrote that he was born into a wealthy and devout family in the village of Surajkot on the Northwest coast of India, in the state of Gujarat, in 1909. Given the name Gopal Rana, he wanted for nothing as a child, and was destined to take his place in the family business. Then one day he encountered a wandering holy man who was passing through his village, and his life changed forever.

I was just a young boy at school when I first encountered my beloved Gurudev. Clad in only a loincloth, his arms outstretched in blessing, he was strolling through my village when my classmates and I first beheld him. His face exuded serenity and wisdom. He moved so gracefully, he appeared not to be walking upon the earth, but upon a cloud in heaven.

The other children and I all loved Gurudev and ran to greet him whenever he appeared outside of our school. At these times, he offered us sweet candy, which he produced out of thin air with a wave of his hand.

On the last day I saw Gurudev as a child, something extraordinary happened. As usual, I waited my turn to receive his blessing, but when I went before him, our eyes met and a beneficent smile played upon his lips. He knelt down in front of me, placed his large powerful hands upon my shoulders, and gazed deeply

> *into my eyes. His stare was so penetrating, I felt he could see into the deepest recesses of my soul.*
>
> *Taking me by the hand, he led me to a quiet place on the outskirts of our village. When we were alone, he stopped, turned to me, and lovingly stroked my face. "We will meet again one day when you are ready," he said. With that, Gurudev touched his head to my head and a ray of blue light emanated from his eyes and entered my own, filling my entire being with its luminance. Surges of blissful energy shot up my spine. My sense of individual self dissolved and I was no longer confined to my body. The illusory distinctions of inner and outer were lifted like a veil. I was one with the Guru, one with the entire cosmos, and one with God.*

The future Swami Rudrananda was so transformed by his first encounter with Brahmananda that he abandoned the comfortable life that awaited him. At the tender age of sixteen, he left his family and his village behind and began a twenty-year spiritual quest that would eventually lead him back to Brahmananda.

During his wanderings, Rudrananda studied yoga and meditation, and all branches of Hindu philosophy. He also met and received the teachings and blessings of many renowned sages and seers, and spent three years in silent retreat in an ashram on the banks of the sacred Ganges. There he took the vows of a renunciant, was given the title *swami*, and the spiritual name *Rudrananda*, after the god *Rudra*, "The Roarer," "Mightiest of the Mighty," sometimes also called "the Wild One" or "the Fierce God."

In 1950, when Rudrananda was forty-one, Brahmananda's prediction came true. Rudrananda met his guru again when his wanderings led him at last to Brahmananda's ashram in the village of Ravipur, in the state of Maharashtra in Western India, where the holy man had settled a decade earlier. Rudrananda wrote:

> *When I was finally reunited with my Guru, I had a burning desire for God-realization. Gurudev arranged*

for me to stay in a secluded hut in the forest where I could live and meditate without disruption.

During my sadhana I had wondrous visions of radiant lights and celestial beings and would sometimes journey to higher realms in my astral body. There I would seek the counsel of divine beings, some of whom once walked the earth as great saints and sadhus. At these times, I felt waves of rapture, love, and ecstasy. My eyes would turn upwards and I would be unable to open them. At other times, I was afraid I was going insane. I encountered corpse-eating demons and had terrifying visions of hell. Images of tortured beings running wildly about screaming, seeking, but never finding refuge from burning ground haunted me. My entire body would ache and burn and I felt that I too was being engulfed by flames. I became obsessed with the most impure and sinful cravings, and my body would begin to move of its own accord. This horrible, confused state of mind would persist for hours, sometimes days at a time.

As I progressed in my meditation, however, the horrifying thoughts and visions subsided. My breathing changed and I was able to hold my breath for long periods of time, remaining in a completely thought-free state of samadhi. All of these experiences were a necessary part of my spiritual journey and happened spontaneously, thanks to the great yogic force that my Guru had awakened within me.

For nine years I remained in the hut in the forest and traveled this path, which culminated in my attainment of enlightenment—the ultimate goal of human existence. I became one with the Godhead, was liberated from all forms of suffering, and was permanently established in a state of absolute bliss. On that fateful day, I went before Gurudev. When he saw me, he knew immediately what had occurred. He sang and danced for joy, declaring that his disciple had become one with the Supreme Being.

Even after attaining the goal of God-realization, Rudrananda wanted nothing but to remain at the feet of his beloved guru as a humble disciple. Despite this wish, Brahmananda gave Rudrananda a small piece of land, which eventually became the site of his own ashram.

In 1961 Gurudev Brahmananda "left his physical body" to attain *mahasamadhi*. According to Rudrananda, when enlightened beings like his guru died, they weren't reborn in another physical body like ordinary people. Instead, they became one with the Godhead and were liberated forever from the vicious cycle of birth and death.

After Brahmananda's passing, devotees began to gather around his successor. Within a few short years, his fame spread and his ashram grew in size, drawing pilgrims from every part of India and seekers from the all over the globe. Strangely, as I read I felt a strong desire to go to this ashram.

I kept reading throughout the afternoon and into the evening. Rudrananda's book was not only a spiritual autobiography, but also contained a wealth of information about the path of Raja Yoga, the "royal" yoga. According to the book, *kundalini* energy was a latent power in the subtle body. When awakened, it travels upward to pierce the six *chakras*, or subtle energy centers in the body, and purifies them. According to Rudrananda, there were only two ways to awaken the *kundalini*: the slow way, through many years of tremendous self-effort and austerities; or the fast way, through the grace of a *shaktipat guru*. A *shaktipat guru* could awaken a seeker's *kundalini* with merely a look, thought, or touch. The awakening happened spontaneously and required no effort on the part of the disciple. The idea of "no effort" appealed to me immediately.

Rudrananda, like his own guru, was a perfected master of Raja Yoga: he possessed the rare ability to give *shaktipat* and awaken the evolutionary energy dormant in his disciples.

Rudrananda wrote:

Dear one, beware: the attempt to awaken the serpent power through your own efforts is fraught with great danger! The supernatural powers you may develop as a result can deceive you into believing that you have already attained the ultimate goal. Moreover, the temptation to misuse these occult powers can become irresistible without the protection of the Guru's grace. Without a genuine Shaktipat Guru to guide you and to control the ascent of the divine energy, you may go completely insane.

I was utterly fascinated, eager to learn more about the ways one could "misuse" these "occult powers." But Rudrananda didn't go into any details. He did say, however, that when the *kundalini* was awakened and guided by a *shaktipat guru*, many people reported mystical experiences almost immediately, and they could expect to reach full enlightenment within only a few years, if they dedicated their lives to spiritual practice.

When I finished the book, I was convinced that having a *shaktipat guru* awaken my *kundalini* and getting on the fast track to God-realization was the way to go.

Up until then, I had never given a thought to religion or spirituality. Both my parents were Jewish, but I was raised as an atheist. Whatever I had gleaned about Judaism from the little I had read didn't appeal to me. It sounded like a lot of meaningless rules to follow. And Christianity seemed even worse, from what I knew about it. The whole crucifixion thing revolted me. And I certainly didn't need anyone to tell me I was a sinner—I already knew it.

The path of Raja Yoga, however, made sense: God was not somewhere up in the sky or outside of me. He dwelled within me *as me*! The story of Rudrananda's personal journey of enlightenment had captured my imagination and I wondered if I might make a similar journey. I was almost eighteen—not much older than Rudrananda when he first met Brahmananda and received the guru's touch. I would have to learn to meditate as soon as possible. The way I saw it, I had wasted countless lifetimes already. I didn't have any time to lose!

That I didn't fit in at Cornell and was clueless about what to do with my life was perhaps not such a bad thing after all. Maybe it was a sign from God that the life of a renunciant was my true calling.

When I arrived home, I went in through the garage entrance so I could avoid Melanie. I needed to call my brother immediately, before dinner. I didn't want to talk about school, or be asked to set the table. I had to find out how I could meet Rudrananda and get *shaktipat* as soon as possible.

I called Jeremy and didn't waste any time on small talk. I told him I had read Rudrananda's book and was blown away.

"Good, good!" my brother said, his voice brimming with approval.

"Jai Gurudev!" Carrie said. She had also picked up the line.

"What does that mean?" I asked.

"Glory to the eternal guru," Jeremy answered. "You'll learn!"

I asked them how I could meet Rudrananda and receive *shaktipat*. They explained that the guru was back in India now, and wouldn't be visiting the States again until the spring. I was disappointed that I'd have to wait to meet the guru, but excited to learn that his main ashram and world headquarters was located right here in New York State, only a few hours from Ithaca.

"Baba will be in residence there for a few months next year," Jeremy said. "You'll have plenty of opportunities to see him."

"But in the meantime, how can I learn to meditate?" I asked.

"You can meet with other devotees at the Raja Yoga center in Ithaca," Jeremy said. "They have *satsang* every Wednesday evening."

When I got off the phone with Jeremy and Carrie, I joined the others upstairs for dinner.

"What are you so happy about?" Lucy asked, eyeing me with suspicion.

"Oh, nothing," I answered, unable to wipe the smile off my face.

I knew my life had changed forever.

3.
NEW FRIENDS

THE RAJA YOGA CENTER was located just west of campus, in a three-story Queen Anne style mansion on Buffalo Street. Even before I saw the sign I could smell the sandalwood incense wafting from its open windows.

I looked for a place to lock up my bike and then heard a voice from behind me say, "You can bring it inside." I turned to see a tall, thin, bespectacled man with serene, ice-blue eyes, impeccable posture, and a perfect haircut. He was dressed in a pale yellow cardigan, freshly pressed khaki pants, and casual dress shoes. He looked to be in his early thirties. "Robert Cargill," he said, holding out his hand.

"Doug Greenbaum."

"Pleased to meet you, Doug." Robert's grip was firm, and I was certain it said something good about his character.

"Are you sure it's okay?" I asked, lifting my bike off the ground to carry it up the steps.

"Yes, of course. Let me help you."

I leaned my bike against the wall in the entranceway, and then followed Robert into the lobby where others were gathered. Hanging on the wall was an enormous framed photograph of a saffron-robed Rudrananda, seated cross-legged on a large cushioned chair. The eyes in the picture were gazing at me and appeared to follow me around the room, just like the portrait on the cover of his book. Beneath the guru's picture was an altar table with a hand bell and a stick of burning incense. Playing in the background was an audio recording of a man—Rudrananda, I assumed—sweetly chanting. His voice was mesmerizing and tugged at my heart. I could have listened to him for hours.

The people I saw in the room were of all ages, but nearly all of them were white. Some were dressed conservatively, like Robert, and others looked like hippies. Some of the women wore red dots painted on their foreheads. Nearly everyone held a folded woolen cloth in their arms. A makeshift boutique at the far end of the room displayed Rudrananda's books, pictures, and audio cassettes, as well as an impressive selection of incense, prayer beads, Indian "Om" shawls, and yoga mats. An austere-looking woman with a frown on her face was tending the boutique. Wrapped in a pale green sari, she was in her late twenties, with tightly cropped dark hair and pocked skin.

Most of the people seemed to know each other and were smiling and talking cheerfully. With no one to talk to, I began to feel uneasy. Maybe I wasn't supposed to come uninvited.

"You must be Doug!" beamed a sturdy young woman dressed in loose fitting white cotton, with a bright orange "Om" shawl draped around her shoulders. She had a red dot on her forehead, prayer beads around her neck, and wore a pendant with a photo of Rudrananda, his hand raised with an emphatic finger pointing upwards.

I extended my hand, but she gave me a big bear hug instead.

"How did you know who I was?"

"You look just like your brother!" she answered. "Shree Ram called to say you'd be coming to *satsang*."

"Shree Ram?"

She smiled sheepishly. "Sorry, I mean *Jeremy*! Shree Ram is your brother's spiritual name. Baba gave it to him! Your sister-in-law's spiritual name is Anshika. Mine is Menaka—I'm the center leader."

I took a good look at Menaka Atkins. She was a Waspy-looking woman in her mid-twenties. She had long mousy hair, big glasses, and bright white teeth. She seemed positively giddy to meet me. *Would I fuck her?* I wondered, before I was able to catch myself.

Menaka motioned for a tall black man to join us. "Alan, I'd like you to meet Doug. He's Shree Ram Greenbaum's brother."

"It's good to finally meet you, Doug," Alan said, shaking my hand firmly, just as Robert had. "I understand you've been through a really tough time. I'm sorry for your loss. Your brother told me about your mom. She seemed like a really fine lady."

I was always clueless how to respond to comments like these. "Thank you very much," I answered.

Alan Jones was no hippie, and I wondered why he didn't have a spiritual name like my brother and the center leader. His hair was closely cropped like Robert's, and he wore a tweed jacket with elbow patches, an olive green cardigan, and black slacks with dress shoes.

"Alan's the manager at the Birchwood Falls ashram," Menaka said proudly.

"*Interim* manager, really," Alan corrected. "Doug, you're a Cornell student, right?"

"Um, yes," I answered, feeling like an imposter. Eager to change the subject, I asked Alan a question. "Why do some people who follow Rudrananda use their given names, while others go by Indian names?"

"In my case, my duties as an ashram manager require me to have a lot of contact with the world. For most of the people I deal with out there, my spiritual name— *Ugrasena*—is hard to say and remember. So I find it easier just to go by Alan."

"Some Raja Yoga managers use the names that Baba gave them," Menaka added. "It's a matter of personal preference."

Just then, the austere-looking woman who had been tending the boutique interrupted us, tapping the face of her watch. "Menaka, it's time."

Following the others into the meditation hall, I removed my shoes like everyone else. I hoped my socks didn't stink. The hall was a large, high-ceilinged room, with beige wall-to-wall carpeting, picture windows, and a boarded-up fireplace. An altar holding another portrait of the guru stood at the front of the room. Next to the altar was a large television set and a video cassette player on a metal rolling stand cart, like the ones used in classrooms. As people filed in, they bowed before Rudrananda's picture, spread their woolen cloths on the floor, and sat cross-legged on top of them. The men sat on one side of the room, the women on the other. Everybody faced the altar.

I found an empty spot toward the back of the hall. Just as I was about to sit, Menaka entered, smiling and waving a cloth at me. Taking care not to tread on anyone, she negotiated her way to where I was sitting.

"Sorry, I almost forgot," she said, handing me the cloth. "You can pay for it later." She gave me a laminated card containing a few texts in a foreign language transliterated into the Roman alphabet. I was taken aback. I wasn't sure I wanted to buy anything. The woolen cloth was padded and had a silk border. I hoped it wasn't too expensive. I only had a few dollars with me.

Returning to the front of the hall, Menaka took a seat behind a musical instrument that looked like a hand-operated pump organ. A young, athletic-looking man sat opposite her, behind a pair of hand drums that I thought were bongos.

"Jai Gurudev!" Menaka exclaimed.

The room responded: "Jai Gurudev!"

She smiled in my direction. "A warm welcome to everyone! Especially to those of you who are here for the first time," she said with a wink.

Menaka played a few introductory notes on the harmonium and the room broke out in a chant based on the words of a poem by someone called "Guru Nanak." The tabla player kept the beat, while others played along with finger cymbals and tambourines. I was immediately struck by the loveliness of the melody and wanted to join in, but it was hopeless. I tried reading the transliteration on the card that Menaka had given me, but the words were too difficult to pronounce. I studied the English translation instead called "Guru Nanak":

> As fragrance abides in the flower, as reflection is within the mirror, so does your Lord abide within you. Why search for Him without? The Guru is my ship to cross the ocean of worldliness. The Guru is my place of pilgrimage and sacred stream. Let no man live in delusion. Without a Guru none can cross over to the other shore!

When I had finished reading the lyrics of the chant on the card, I glanced around the room at the others. They were singing along joyfully with expressions of deep devotion and concentration on their faces. Some twisted and turned their bodies to the music and made odd gestures with their hands as they sang.

When the chant ended, everyone folded their hands in prayer and all eyes were on Rudrananda's photo on the altar. I read along:

> *Guru Brahma Guru Vishnu*
> *Guru Devo Maheshwara*
> *Guru Sakshat Parambrahma*
> *Tasmai Shri Gurave Namah*
>
> *Guru is the creator; Guru is the sustainer; Guru is the destroyer; Guru is verily the Supreme Absolute. To that Guru we bow.*
>
> *Dhyana Moolam Guru Murti.*
> *Puja Moolam Gurur Padam,*

Mantra Moolam Gurur Vakyam,
Moksha Moolam Guru Kripa

The Guru's form is the root of meditation; the Guru's feet are the root of worship; the Guru's word is the root of Mantra; the Guru's Grace is the root of liberation.

By the time I had read through the end of the translation, I began to wonder what the hell I was getting myself into. *These people are all crazy!* I thought, glancing around the room. It was wrong, I told myself, to worship another human being and to attribute that kind of power to him.

I wanted to bolt, but didn't dare. Everyone I had met at the center had been so nice to me. I didn't want to insult them, and I didn't want Menaka or Alan to call Jeremy and tell him I had been rude and left in the middle of the program.

"We have a special treat tonight," Menaka said. "Many of you know Alan from the Birchwood Falls ashram. He has a new video of Baba to show us." There was a round of applause and Alan stood up to start the video. He seemed to be having difficulty getting the player to work, however, and Robert got up to help him. Just then, I felt a tap on my shoulder. I turned around to see a young man around my age. He was smirking.

"Get used to it," he said. "Happens every time they try to show a video here."

I nodded noncommittally. The guy looked like a freak: he had long, matted, yellow hair that fell past his shoulders, and a long, scraggly beard, which he braided under his chin. His small, deep-set eyes were gray, the color of gunmetal. His T-shirt and jeans were dirty, and he reeked of pot.

I heard a sustained, high-pitched tone and turned back around to see color bars being displayed on the TV screen. Everyone clapped again and Menaka dimmed the lights.

The video began with a photo montage of Rudrananda set to Indian instrumental music. I was struck by how different the guru looked from picture to picture. In some, he had a full head of hair and a flowing beard. In others, his head and face were clean shaven. In one photo, Rudrananda wore a knitted red ski hat, dark sunglasses, and a bulky orange winter coat. In another, he was dressed in nothing but a long piece of cloth wrapped around his waist.

Some of the pictures were black and white, from the 1950s and early 1960s. They depicted a younger, dark-haired Rudrananda in different settings with a loincloth-clad Gurudev Brahmananda. In more recent pictures, a smiling Rudrananda appeared with various celebrities, including a Hollywood actress, the governor of California, an English rock legend, a famous athlete, and even an astronaut. In another group of photos, Rudrananda's expression was more solemn and introspective. In one of them he carried a big stick and looked as fierce as a lion.

When the slideshow was over, the video faded to black. It then opened on a wide-angle shot of Rudrananda seated cross-legged on a throne, addressing an audience of hundreds of people, mostly white. He spoke in some Indian language and his words were translated by a radiant young Indian woman standing at his side.

"Everyone in this world is seeking the same thing: happiness. But what is the difference between happiness and true bliss? Mundane happiness has a cause and is temporary." The guru's voice was thin, but not unpleasant. It was rather sweet, rhythmic, and soothing. It had a distant, alien quality to it, as if it were being broadcast from another dimension. In contrast the translator's voice was deep and powerful, her tone cool, detached, and vulnerable, all at the same time.

"For example, you miss a particular friend and are happy when you begin to see him again. But for how long are you happy with this friend? Only a short time. After a while, the same friend who made you happy begins to agitate you. Then you are only happy again when he goes away!" The audience in the video erupted in laughter and so did everyone in the room watching it.

"What kind of happiness is this? The sages call this *mundane happiness* because it has a cause. When the cause disappears, so does your happiness. *Bliss,* on the other hand, is your true nature and has no cause.

"In the pursuit of happiness you eat delicious food, drink the finest wines, and rub your bodies together. But any happiness or satisfaction you may experience as a result of indulging in these sense pleasures is extremely short-lived. The moment you satisfy one desire, another crops up in its place.

"But what happens when you go to bed at night? In the depths of sleep you finally attain peace. In sleep, there is no eating, no drinking, no entertainment, but when you wake up in the morning, you are refreshed and happy. This demonstrates that you can only find true bliss when the senses withdraw from the external world.

"Therefore, if you wish to attain happiness, you should direct your attention inside. Within, there is a vast ocean of peace. When you meditate, you enter into this ocean. You become immersed in it."

As I listened to Rudrananda in the video, I felt a deep connection to him. It was as if he were reaching out through time and space and speaking directly to me.

When the video was over, Menaka led us in a twenty-minute meditation session. She began with instructions on the correct posture, how to breathe, and how to silently repeat the mantra "Om Namah Shivaya" to ourselves: once on the in-breath and once again on the out-breath.

I was incapable of meditating, and for me the session was a complete disaster: my mind raced even faster than usual. Every time I tried to empty it of thoughts, it filled up with them again a moment later. Menaka had said we would be meditating for twenty minutes, but for me it felt like twenty hours.

Om Namah Shivaya. Mmmm...meditating... I'm meditating... Om Namah Shivaya...umm...what is that sound? Is that a clock ticking? It's incredibly annoying...can't open my eyes and look around...people will know I'm not meditating...oh yeah, the mantra.

Before long, it was as though my mind had sprouted little wings and flown away. I forgot I was meditating and started thinking about meditation instead.

How is meditating different from getting high? I wondered. I thought about the last time I had smoked grass with Mike McFadden. Our favorite spot was in front of the Cornell University founder's family mausoleum at Lake View Cemetery. I remembered how Mike had rolled a joint on top of a headstone while I looked around the immense graveyard built on the steepest part of East Hill. I was wishing my mother hadn't been cremated. It upset me to think I would have nowhere to go to mourn her. Her ashes had been scattered to the wind. She was nowhere and everywhere at the same time.

Then it hit me: *Shit! I'm not meditating—I'm thinking! Now, what was that mantra again? 'Om Namah Shivaya?' What did they say it meant? 'I bow to Shiva.' Shiva is the Hindu god of destruction—why worship a god of destruction? Sounds satanic. Satanic.*

A memory of Elisabeth Jensen popped into my head. We were in seventh grade and she was telling me she was a Wiccan. She offered to cast a spell on one of my enemies. Was that what this was? Some kind of Wiccan shit?

Fuck! I'm thinking again! I needed to double down. At this rate, it would take me a thousand lifetimes to reach enlightenment. *Om Namah Shivaya. Om Namah Shivaya. Om Namah Shivaya.*

How long has it been? Om Namah Shivaya. Who's thinking? Om Namah Shivaya. I'm thinking. Om Namah Shivay. Who am I? Om Namah Shivaya. Maybe there is no thinker, only thoughts. Om Namah Shivaya. Hasn't it been twenty minutes yet? I'm hungry? My legs hurt. Who's that snoring?

Just when I thought I couldn't endure one more second of sitting still with my eyes closed, an alarm beeped and Menaka played a sustained note on the harmonium. We chanted a few rounds of the mantra together, and the program came to an end.

Everyone was very quiet. No one said a word until they were outside the meditation hall and had put their shoes back on. They weren't just quiet because they weren't saying anything; I had the impression that their minds were quiet. And despite how agitated I had felt during my first attempt at meditation, my mind was quiet, too. I experienced an unfamiliar internal stillness.

Menaka looked at me expectantly when we had both returned to the lobby. "So, how was it? Did you enjoy the video of Baba?"

"Amazing," I answered, surprised by my own enthusiasm. "What language was the swami speaking?"

"Baba's native language is Gujarati, but he was speaking in Marathi—the language of Maharashtra State, where Baba's ashram is located. Mostly he speaks in Hindi, though—it depends on his audience."

"And who was that beautiful Indian woman translating for him?"

Menaka's eyes twinkled. "Everybody asks that. That's Anjali Bhandary. She's known Baba her whole life and has traveled all over the world with him. Her parents were devotees of Gurudev Brahmananda before Baba succeeded him."

Most of the people who had come to the program were leaving. I noticed the freak who had been sitting behind me in the meditation hall was heading out the door. He was still barefoot. I was also about to leave when Menaka brought me a cup of tea. It was spicy with a lot of milk and sugar already added to it. She said that in India they called it "chai." Back then the word sounded exotic.

"By the way, did you want to pay for the *asana* now?" Menaka asked.

At first I didn't know what she was talking about. Then I realized she was referring to the woolen cloth she had given me to sit on during the program, which was now folded up neatly under my arm. "Oh, yeah," I answered. My face flushed with embarrassment. I knew that I wouldn't be able to afford it. "How much is it?"

"Twenty-five."

I swallowed. That was a lot! My allowance was only ten dollars a week. "Can I pay for it next time?"

"Of course!" Menaka beamed. "Hold on." She left me for a moment to get something from the boutique. "Here, this is for you," she said, handing me a small photograph of Rudrananda. The guru's face was solemn in the picture. He was dressed in red silks with a matching red ski hat, and seated on a plush armchair with two large black dogs prone at his feet.

"How much is this?" I asked, feeling embarrassed. I didn't want Menaka to think I was cheap.

"Don't worry about it!" she laughed. "It's a gift!"

I looked at the photo again. Rudrananda gazed back at me with deep compassion in his eyes. "Thank you. It's beautiful."

Menaka invited me to sit down with her in the kitchen for another cup of chai, and offered me a piece of carrot cake. Robert and Alan joined us. Robert, it turned out, lived above the center and owned the building. Menaka and Lakshmi Dunn—the austere-looking woman who tended the boutique—lived there with him.

"How did you first find out about Baba?" I asked Menaka.

Menaka had heard about Rudrananda three years before, from a college friend of hers who lived at his new ashram in the Catskill Mountains and invited the future Menaka to come hear Rudrananda speak. Birchwood Falls was about a three-hour drive from Ithaca and she had arrived a little late for the afternoon program. By the time she arrived, the hall—a converted hotel ballroom—was already almost full. Menaka's friend, however, had made sure a spot was reserved for her only a few feet from the guru's throne.

"The atmosphere in the ashram was incredibly powerful," Menaka said. "The feeling of being in a space with hundreds of other people, all chanting and meditating together in the presence of a living and breathing saint — it was amazing."

Robert and Alan both nodded and smiled in agreement.

"The subject of Baba's talk that afternoon was love. He spoke about how we're all looking for it, but never in the right places. I had just broken up with a boyfriend at the time, so as you can imagine, Baba's words resonated very deeply with me. I began to sob uncontrollably and at one point Baba looked over in my direction and our eyes met. The love in his eyes was overwhelming, and I melted on the spot.

"When it was time to go up and meet Baba, my friend brought me to the front of the line because she knew I had a three-hour drive back to Ithaca after the program. When she introduced me, Baba tapped me lightly on my head with his wand of peacock feathers and held it there for a moment. Then, for some inexplicable reason, I began to cry. So Baba asked me, 'Why are you so sad?' And I told him: 'I'm not sad, Baba. I'm just very happy to meet you.' Baba's eyes lit up and he began to laugh. Then he took me in his arms and gave me a big hug and asked his assistant to go get something for him. A few moments later, the assistant came back with a beautiful bracelet. And Baba gave it to me."

Menaka pointed to an elegant golden hoop around her wrist.

"After my encounter with Baba, I was overcome with emotion, but didn't notice anything unusual until I was in my car driving back to Ithaca. I began to notice that all the colors around me were incredibly intense. The hills and trees—even the other cars on the road—seemed to be scintillating with energy. Wave after wave of ecstasy passed through me and I felt as though I were one with everything around me on a molecular level."

I was blown away by Menaka's story. "Do you think you received *shaktipat* when you met Baba that first time?"

"Yes, I do, Doug."

Robert, who along with Alan had been listening quietly to Menaka share her story, turned to me. "A *shaktipat guru* can awaken the *kundalini* in anyone with a mere *thought, look, word,* or *touch.*"

"When Baba is in America, he offers weekend *shaktipat* retreats during which you're guaranteed to receive it," Alan said.

I was sold. As soon as I got home I was going to call Jeremy and tell him that I definitely wanted to meet Baba when he was back in New York, and that I wanted to take the *shaktipat* retreat.

I said my goodbyes to Menaka, Robert, and Alan. They told me how much they had enjoyed meeting me and that they hoped to see me again soon. When I went to the door to leave, I noticed that my bike was gone.

"I put your bike outside," Lakshmi said curtly. "Baba's house is sacred space. Visitors are not allowed to bring their bikes into the building."

I felt searing heat in my face. I was mortified for having broken the rules. I glanced over at Robert, hoping he would tell Lakshmi that he had been the one to insist that I bring it inside. Unfortunately, Robert was now standing in a corner finishing a piece of carrot cake.

Despite the awkward end to the evening, I was elated. As I rode home, I thought about the new friends I had made, and the video of Baba. I was excited that in a few months I would have a chance to meet him and take a *shaktipat* retreat. But I also felt disappointed. *Why didn't Jeremy and Carrie bring me to meet Baba while he was still in New York State?*

When I got home I called my brother and told him all about my evening at the center and how much I was looking forward to meeting Baba in the spring. My spirits sank, however, when he told me how much a *shaktipat* retreat cost: two hundred dollars. This was a fortune to me back then. It would have taken me almost two years to save that much money, even if I never spent a dime of my allowance.

"Don't worry about it," Jeremy said. "I'm starting as an intern at NYU Medical Center in the spring and will be earning decent money. I'll pay for it."

As I lay in bed that night, I thought about what Baba had said in the video about people finding happiness in their sleep. I tried to recall a time I had ever woken up feeling particularly happy, but I couldn't. Usually I just felt sad.

As an experiment, I silently repeated the mantra "Om Namah Shivaya" and waited for sleep to take me.

Om Namah Shivaya on the in-breath. *Om Namah Shivaya* as I exhaled. I had never consciously tried to articulate a thought inside my own mind before. The process fascinated me. I "listened" more attentively to the inner sound of the mantra I was forming in my head: *Om Namah Shivaya. Om Namah Shivaya. Om Namah Shivaya...*

WHEN I WOKE UP in the morning I felt much lighter than usual. *What is this unfamiliar feeling?* I asked myself. Then I realized what it was: I felt happy.

4.
THE CALL FROM AFAR

LIFE SUDDENLY HAD MEANING. I had found a goal: the attainment of God-realization.

Over the next month, I became a regular at the Raja Yoga center and began meditating at home twice a day. With the photo of Baba, an incense holder, and a hand bell, I improvised a *puja* altar on top of my dresser. I prayed to Baba with all my heart to allow me to meet him and to receive *shaktipat* as soon as possible. As I gazed at his picture, an all-knowing, infinitely compassionate Baba stared back at me.

The Raja Yoga center became like a second home to me and the other devotees felt like my new family. Every Wednesday night I faithfully attended *satsang*. We would chant, meditate, and listen to talks by guest speakers. Sometimes we were treated to videos of Baba. On Saturday mornings, I attended the recitation of the *Guru Gita*—the sacred, two-hundred-verse Sanskrit text chanted every morning all over the world at Baba's many centers and ashrams. The *Guru Gita* was written by the sage Vyasa in the fifteenth century BC. The text describes a conversation between the Hindu god Shiva and his consort, the goddess Parvati, in which Parvati asks Lord Shiva to teach her about the guru and the goal of God-realization. Shiva answers her by describing the proper methods of worshipping the guru and the benefits of reciting the text.

At the center, I bought a book with the *Guru Gita* and other texts chanted at Raja Yoga ashrams. The texts were in Sanskrit, transliterated into the Roman alphabet and translated into English. In order to perfect my pronunciation of the Sanskrit syllables, I bought an audio cassette of Baba chanting the *Gita* and borrowed a Sanskrit language text from the Cornell library. Since I wasn't attending any classes, I had plenty of time to teach myself how to read and write the language, and to pore over Baba's many books, which I borrowed from the center.

Within a few weeks I was able to read the Devanagari script so well that I no longer had to refer to the Roman transliteration. The *Guru Gita* soon became my favorite chant. I listened to it on my Walkman on my way to and from the Cornell campus, and before I went to sleep at night.

> *Salutations to the Guru, by whom this world is illumined, who perceives all states of consciousness—waking, dreaming, and dreamless sleep—but who cannot be perceived by the mind.*
>
> *Salutations to the Guru who is Truth, whose knowledge of the universe sees through the illusory divisions that split it into fragments, and who perceives no distinction between the universe and the Self.*
>
> *Salutations to the Guru, who is the cause of the universe although appearing as an effect. In truth, the Guru is both the cause and effect.*

> *Salutations to the Guru who reveals that this universe of countless forms is in fact, one undifferentiated whole—a play of cause and effect in which cause and effect are one.*
>
> *Prostrations to the Guru whose lotus feet eradicate the suffering brought by duality and who always protects seekers from all misfortunes and calamities.*

Looking back, I'm not sure why I didn't share my new faith with Melanie. After all, Jeremy was out in the open about it. But I couldn't bring myself to do it. Just as I continued to hide the fact that I had given up on college, I kept my momentous discovery of the meaning of life to myself. She would consider my new enthusiasm for Baba and Raja Yoga as a distraction from school, and I knew she would blame it for my inevitable ejection from Cornell. For this reason, I kept up the charade that I was still attending classes. Every morning I left the house for campus, where I studied Sanskrit and Hindu philosophy and read Baba's books. Later I would return home, just in time for dinner.

Despite my success at deceiving Melanie, I was in a constant state of anxiety. I knew that she would catch on eventually, and one morning in mid-November, it almost happened. Although snow had been predicted that day, Melanie was determined to keep a business appointment in nearby Syracuse. "I'm going to eat out with Herb tonight and the girls are with their father until Monday," she said, zipping up her bulky winter coat. "Lucy and you are on your own for dinner."

"So, you'll be gone all day?" I asked.

Melanie peered out the window and frowned. "I can't believe it's already snowing. It's going to be a *long* winter."

"You'll be in Syracuse all day?" I repeated.

My sister turned to me with a distracted look on her face. "Be sure to shovel the sidewalk and the driveway. They said we could get up to six inches."

"I'll take that as a yes," I said. "I can't shovel the driveway. I have to go to class." I hated it when Melanie ignored me, even though I knew she didn't do it on purpose. The question didn't concern or interest her, so it didn't register. If she couldn't even hear me now, how would she ever be able to listen the day I told her about Baba and Raja Yoga?

Melanie opened the front door and let in a blast of bitterly cold air mixed with powdery snow. "Do it when you get back."

With Melanie out of town and Lucy at school, I decided to spend the day reading at home, and got back into bed with Baba's *Shiva Consciousness: An Introduction to Kashmir Shaivism*. According to Baba, the Hindu philosophy of *Kashmir Shaivism* asserted that *everything* is an expression of Shiva or the Supreme Self. A follower of this school of thought embraced all phenomena, including mental phenomena, as the manifestation of the one all-pervasive being: Shiva.

Halfway through the book, I was about to go downstairs to make myself a sandwich, when much to my horror, I heard the sound of the "Supreme Self" at the front door.

"Hello? Anybody home?" It was Melanie. *Shit, I'm busted!*

I had to think of an excuse, fast. I went to the top of the stairs to greet her.

"Oh hi, Dougie," she said, surprised to see me. "I got all the way to Syracuse and my meeting was canceled. It took me two hours to drive home—the roads are terrible! I'm lucky I didn't end up in a ditch!" Then she regarded me quizzically. "What are you doing home? Shouldn't you be at school?"

"Canceled."

"What? Your classes?"

"Um, yeah."

Melanie looked incredulous as she pulled off her boots. "Canceled? Really?"

Suddenly I remembered about Herb. He was a professor at the university and would almost definitely contradict my story later. "Actually, I don't know if they're canceled," I said rubbing my arm and grimacing in pain. "I hit some ice on Eastwood Ave and fell off my bike. Hurt my elbow."

"Oh, Dougie! That's awful! I guess it wasn't such a hot idea to try to ride your bike in a snowstorm, was it?"

Not as dumb as driving a car in one, I thought. "Guess not."

"You see—when you live on campus, it'll be a lot easier," she smiled. "Can you shovel the driveway now?"

"But my arm!" I whined, rubbing my supposedly sore elbow. "I told you, I'm injured!"

IT WAS ONLY THE beginning of December, but the town of Ithaca was already shrouded in snow. The weather had become too severe to ride my bike, and my commute to campus on foot took much longer.

As the end of the semester loomed, I began to formulate a plan. I knew that once Melanie found out I had been lying to her about school and had flunked all my classes, she would probably kick me out. In anticipation of the inevitable, and as an act of devotion to the guru, I decided to confront my fear of rejection and look for a job.

The first place I checked was Collegetown Bagels. It was owned by the parents of a high school acquaintance, and I hoped that mentioning his name to them might help my dismal chances.

The guy behind the counter at the bagel shop had his back to me. He was wearing shorts with a bright orange T-shirt, and his long blond hair was tangled into a thick mass. It was warm in the store, but outside the temperature was below zero. I wondered how, dressed like that, he had made it to the store without freezing to death. When he turned around I recognized him immediately. On his T-shirt was an image of a smiling Baba Rudrananda in a red ski hat with his index finger raised in the air. His name was Namdev Loman and he was a regular at the Raja Yoga center. He was also a fellow townie and an Ithaca High School dropout.

"Hey, man. Jai Gurudev!"

"Jai Gurudev!"

"It's Doug, right?"

"Yeah. Hey, they don't happen to be looking for any extra help here, are they?"

Namdev reached under the counter, opened a drawer and pulled out a sheet of paper. "Not at the moment, but they will be soon," he said. Then he handed the paper to me, chuckling as if he were in on a private joke. It was an application.

"Oh really, how come?"

"As soon as I save up enough money for a one-way ticket, I'm going to India. Rent is cheap as shit at the Ravipur ashram. They give scholarships and staff positions to devotees who work hard and are willing to do extra *seva*."

Namdev was waiting for a response from me, but I was momentarily swept away by a fantasy of getting on a plane and flying away to Baba's ashram in India. I would learn the native language and become a simple renunciant. I would meditate, chant, study philosophy, and work in the guru's garden all day.

"Doug?"

"*Seva?*" I said, snapping out of my reverie.

"You know," said Namdev, his eyes shining. "Selfless service to the guru—the highest spiritual practice there is!"

I knew very well what *seva* was. I had already done a little at the center, helping to tidy up after *satsang*. According to Menaka, through *seva* one could wash away the sins of countless lifetimes and attain liberation within a few years. Hearing about the staff positions at the Indian ashram made me feel lighter. Maybe there was a way out of my predicament: I could run away to Ravipur and never come back. But the idea also scared me. India was about as far away from home as possible. How would I manage there on my own? What if the ashram didn't take care of me?

"Do they have any *seva* arrangements like that at the Birchwood Falls ashram?" I asked.

"Probably, but I'm sure they're much harder to get," Namdev answered. "And I can't afford to pay rent at a US ashram while I'm waiting to find out."

I felt heavy again. Obviously the rent in Birchwood Falls would not be "cheap as shit."

"If I don't get out of Ithaca soon, I'm gonna go insane," Namdev continued. "All the scriptures say that rapid progress on the path is only possible in presence of the physical guru. If you're serious about your *sadhana*, you've gotta go to the source."

I nodded. I knew he was right. Even if Baba was not in India this spring while Namdev was there, the *samadhi* shrine of Gurudev Brahmananda (Baba's own guru) was in Ravipur. Some of my new friends at the center who had visited the saint's tomb described it as having the *shakti* of a "spiritual nuclear power plant."

"I'm planning on going to Ravipur someday too," I said. "In the meantime, I'm grateful to the guru for the center here in Ithaca."

"The center blows, man. Menaka is a control freak and Robert walks around like he has a stick up his ass. They're both petty dictators. And don't get me started on that bitch Lakshmi. Says she doesn't like the way I chant. Told me I'm not welcome at the center when I'm high! Who the fuck do they think they are? Baba smoked ganja, you know."

The notion that Baba had once smoked "ganja" sounded like the most preposterous thing I'd ever heard.

"James, could you watch your language, please?" said a voice from the back room.

"Sorry, Ira." Apparently they did not refer to Namdev by his spiritual name at Collegetown Bagels. With his back to his boss, Namdev mouthed the word "Asshole."

Just then, the door to the shop opened. A few customers came in from the cold and got in line behind me. "Sorry, man, I can't really talk now. Do you want to order something?"

I ordered a bagel and coffee and sat down to fill out the application. When I returned to the counter to pick up my order, a familiar, friendly voice greeted me.

"Doug?" I turned and could barely recognize the figure who had just entered, bundled up from head to toe. It was Mike McFadden's mom.

"Hi, Professor McFadden."

"How are you holding up, Doug? How's Lucy?" she asked, pulling the hood of her parka down. Her nose and ears were bright red. "I haven't seen you over at the house in months."

"We're both fine," I mumbled, unable to look her in the eye. The truth was, I had no idea how my younger sister was "holding up." The question had never occurred to me.

The professor gave Namdev her order, and then turned to me again. "Mike tells me you're in the same freshman writing seminar together."

Good old Mike, I thought. He hadn't said anything to his folks about my disappearance from the required course. "Um, yeah. It's pretty cool, I guess."

Mike's mom stared at me searchingly and was silent for a moment before speaking again. "Swell!" she said finally, picking up her order. "Hope to see you around the house again soon, Doug. You're welcome anytime. Bring Lucy!"

The conversation with Mike's mom was excruciating. I could tell she was onto me. I had to get out of there before she spoke to me again. I finished filling out my application, gave it to Namdev, and left.

The chimes in McGraw Tower marked the hour. It was ten A.M. I was supposed to be in my *Introduction to Pomology* course, but was on my way to the lounge at Willard Straight Hall instead. Tromping through the snow up College Avenue, I felt gloomy and uncertain and like my legs weighed a ton. The bagel shop had no openings at the moment, but I needed a job *now*. It would take me months to save up for an airplane ticket to India, and even if I managed to get myself to Ravipur, there was no guarantee the ashram would be able to offer me a staff position. I knew I'd be able to meet Baba and take a *shaktipat* retreat with him, because Jeremy had promised to pay for it, but I wanted more than a weekend with the guru. I wanted to live in his ashram and serve him. The world was a cold, dark place, and the sooner I got out of it the better.

As I crossed the bridge over Cascadilla Gorge, I found myself edging closer to the parapet. I stopped to look over the side, down into the gully at the ice-encased stream. *I could be free*, I thought. *I won't have to face Melanie and feel ashamed when she finds out that I'm flunking out. I won't have to look for a job. I won't have to be poor and live alone in a miserable apartment. And I won't have to feel the unbearable guilt anymore.*

I sat down on the parapet. I was about to swing my legs around and dangle them over the side of the bridge when my thoughts turned to Baba. By then I kept a small portrait of him in my wallet. I pulled it out and studied the guru's face. His loving eyes brimmed with compassion. *Baba loves me!* I remembered. *He wants to give me true happiness!* Suddenly I felt ungrateful and ashamed. *What was I thinking?* I got off the parapet, brushed the snow off my jeans, and continued on my way to the student union.

"The guru showers his grace on all those who reach out to him," a guest speaker at the center had said. I decided that through Baba's divine intervention, I would find a way to stay in the ashram and be with him. If I had to suffer in poverty and feel lonely for a while before I become worthy of it, so be it.

What a fool I had been to think that killing my physical body would solve my problems. Hinduism taught that as soon as a soul left its physical body, it was reborn in another body, and then another. The same problems and difficult situations would keep presenting themselves to me, lifetime after lifetime, until I faced them and worked them out. According to the scriptures, that's how *karma*, the law of cause and effect, operated and kept us in bondage. Instead of feeling sorry for myself, I realized, I should feel grateful I had finally found a true guru who could guide me to enlightenment and liberate me from the endless cycle of birth and death.

MELANIE HAD MADE PORK chops for dinner. They looked and smelled delicious, but I had recently committed myself to a vegetarian diet. Baba taught that in order to progress on the path of Raja Yoga, a seeker must avoid eating the flesh of animals and imbibing impure substances.

"Doug?" Melanie said, passing me the pork chops.

"None for me, thanks. Could you pass me the spinach?"

"How's Cornell treating you?" Herb asked, helping himself to mashed potatoes.

"Swell," I answered, avoiding eye contact with him.

Leah, my eight-year-old niece, gave me a penetrating look, narrowing her eyes and tilting her head to one side as if she were trying to read my thoughts.

"Wait!" Lucy said. "Why aren't you having any pork chops?"

"Could *somebody* please pass Corinne the applesauce?" Melanie said, meaning me.

I passed my niece the applesauce, eying her plate as she slopped some on top of her chops. "I've become a vegetarian," I declared.

Lucy rolled her eyes. "This whole family is going nuts. First Jeremy, now the dungeon master!"

"I love vegetarian food," Herb said, through a mouthful of spinach. "Have you ever eaten at Moosewood? It's a vegetarian place in the Dewitt Mall. Wholesome stuff."

Ugh. When would this jackass stop trying to win me over?

"Speaking of nutcases, Grandma Millie and Aunt Gabby are coming to visit," Melanie said.

Lucy kneaded her forehead, as if in pain. "What! Why?"

"When?" I asked.

"Next week," Melanie answered. "Grandma misses us. Don't forget, she's grieving too."

Lucy grimaced. "Okay, but why does Gabby have to come with her?"

"Aunt Gabby needs help tying up Harvey's estate. She and Grandma have become inseparable ever since Aunt Gabby moved down to Florida."

Lucy sighed deeply. "Inseparable? Really? You mean because they *love* each other so much?"

Herb laughed. "It's what's known as a *co-dependent* relationship," the world-renowned psychologist explained.

I wasn't sure what Herb meant by a "co-dependent relationship," but didn't care enough to ask him to elaborate. I was more interested in hearing about Harvey's money.

"Harvey had an estate?"

"Yep," Melanie said, nodding and absent-mindedly offering me the pork chops again. "The man worked his entire life and never spent a dime."

"Lucky Aunt Gabby," Herb said.

"Yeah," Lucy said. "Now she'll finally be able to afford the lifestyle she's always dreamed of: she'll be able to get the early bird special at Bagel World every day for the rest of her life."

WITH THE TRUTH ABOUT college about to come out, I felt burdened by guilt, and one night after *satsang*, as I was helping Menaka straighten up, I told her everything.

Menaka put down the basket of musical instruments she was holding. "Oh, honey, everything's going to be alright."

Tears welled in my eyes.

"You're going through a really rough time, Doug. Don't be so hard on yourself." I followed Menaka into the kitchen, where she poured me a cup of chai. "Maybe this isn't the best time for you to be in school."

I wiped my eyes with the back of my hand. "But I'm throwing away such a great opportunity."

"Baba teaches that the only knowledge we can take with us to the next life is the spiritual kind. Whatever worldly learning we acquire in this life will be lost when we leave our physical bodies."

"That's exactly what my brother said. So college is a waste of time?"

Menaka cut me a slice of zucchini bread. "Not necessarily. It's not that Baba doesn't value education. As a matter of fact, Baba himself is a great scholar of Indian philosophy. He also studied Ayurvedic medicine."

"I just don't know what to do," I said.

"Maybe it's time for you to be with the physical guru. Baba's coming to Birchwood Falls this spring. You could go work with the advance team."

"I don't have any money."

"Didn't your mother leave you anything? You could use that?"

"I can't," I answered, hanging my head low. "It's all tied up in a trust fund until my younger sister turns twenty-one. Until then I can only use it to pay for tuition and room and board while I'm at school."

"Pray to Baba," Menaka said, placing her hand under my chin and lifting my head up so that she could look me in the eye. "Pray to the omniscient *inner guru* and he will give you a sign. Baba can speak to us in many ways, you know. If you pray to him with all your heart, he will show you the way."

When it was time to say goodnight, Menaka wrapped her arms around me and held me close. I could feel her large breasts crush against me through her sweater. I felt an overwhelming urge to touch them. I was getting hard. In my mind's eye I pictured myself sucking on her breasts and then bending her over a chair so that I could do it to her from behind. Then I remembered Baba taught that only those who practiced complete abstinence could attain the ultimate goal:

> *The sexual fluid in an ordinary person flows downward and is lost during sexual relations. But for the master of Raja Yoga, the sexual fluid flows upward toward the sahasrara (the chakra in the crown of the head). Sexual energy and kundalini are one and the same. A yogi needs every drop of this vital fluid to attain the goal. A seeker on the path has no hope of attaining the goal as long as he remains a slave to the senses.*

I put a stop to my impure thoughts with the same technique I had been practicing in meditation: whenever I had distracting thoughts, I would steer my mind gently back to the mantra. Now, instead of picturing Menaka with her clothes off, I began to visualize myself prostrating before Baba, who was seated on a grand throne. *Baba, please take my lust away,* I prayed. A few moments later the urge for Menaka's tits began to subside.

I got home from the center later than usual, and the house was already dark. Melanie's silver station wagon was parked on the street in front of the house, but Herb's car was not. When I got inside, the house was quiet. I assumed everyone had gone to bed. But when I arrived at the top of the stairs I noticed that the door to my room was wide open and the light was on. I entered to find Melanie staring at the altar to Baba on my dresser. "Isn't this Jeremy's spiritual teacher?"

"He's my guru too."

"How long have you been involved with this…group?" my sister asked, her eyes lingering on the photos.

"For a while." I didn't like that Melanie was in my room, invading my privacy. And I didn't like her use of the word "group"—it made Raja Yoga sound like something shady.

Melanie finally took her eyes off the picture and turned to me. "I'm worried about you, Doug. Do you think you might want to talk to someone?"

"Someone? Like a shrink?" I knew where this was going.

"You could talk to Herb."

I wanted to laugh, but controlled myself. "I'm totally fine. Actually, I've never been better. I've been meditating and reading Indian philosophy. It's really helping me."

"Helping you?" Melanie put her hands on her hips. "How?" I could hear the skepticism in her voice.

I was suddenly at a loss for words. I knew Raja Yoga was helping me to attain enlightenment, but I couldn't think of any practical benefits that someone as ignorant as my sister could comprehend. "It's helping me to attain everlasting bliss and to know God."

Melanie rolled her eyes.

I felt a wave of anger rise up inside of me. It was so like her to doubt me.

"It's helping me with...*school!* Meditation improves...*concentration!*"

Melanie pursed her lips and nodded. "I've read that. Listen, Doug, I'm not going to tell you what to think or what to believe. We're all going through a grieving process, but I'm a bit concerned—"

"Concerned about what?" I snapped

"I haven't seen any of your friends over here in months."

"They're away at college—duh!"

Melanie frowned. "Mike's at Cornell with you, isn't he? So are Eddie and Stuart. You can't just study and meditate all day, Doug. You have to find the right balance. You need to have fun, too."

I considered telling her about my new friends at the center, but didn't want to waste my time. And anyway, it was none of her fucking business.

5.

A Ripening of Karmic Fruit

THE CHANT ENDED. ALAN Jones, who was visiting the Ithaca center from the ashram in Birchwood Falls, had a special announcement. "Jai Gurudev!"

"Jai Gurudev!" everyone responded.

"I'm here to let you know the latest word from Ravipur is that Baba will be returning to Birchwood Falls at the end of March."

Alan's announcement was interrupted by a loud round of applause and more cheers of "Jai Gurudev!" My chest buzzed and I had difficulty sitting still. The guru would be here much sooner than expected.

"It will be the first time Baba has ever visited the East Coast in winter," Alan continued, "and we want everyone to know about the many exciting *seva* opportunities coming up. There's a lot of work to be done to prepare the ashram for Baba's six-month stay in New York."

This is a sign from Baba! I told myself. *This is my chance!* As soon as *satsang* was over I approached Alan and asked him if there would be staff positions opening up at the ashram to help with the advance work. "I'm available immediately."

"What about college?" Alan asked.

"I'm dropping out. I don't care about worldly knowledge anymore."

Alan looked dubious. "How old are you?"

"I'll be eighteen at the end of January."

"Look, Doug, I appreciate your enthusiasm," Alan said, pinching his earlobe. "But at the moment, the ashram's only looking for volunteers who can pay their own way. In any case, you would need your legal guardian's signature to stay at the ashram before your eighteenth birthday."

Melanie would never let me go before January. And even if I found a minimum wage job, it would take months to save up enough money to live at the ashram for any length of time. Baba would be back in India by then. I prayed to the guru and asked him to help me understand what he was trying to tell me. Perhaps it was some kind of test of my devotion.

"Cramming for your Sanskrit final, I see," Mike said, startling me. I was in the Uris Hall library, copying the text of the *Guru Gita* into a notebook.

"Quit hovering, McFadden. You're making me nervous."

"You're not actually taking Sanskrit as a freshman in the Ag school, are you?" Mike pulled a chair up to the table and sat down. "Do they even allow that?"

"No, big guy. I'm studying it on my own."

Mike smiled approvingly. "I'm impressed."

"It's easier than it looks."

"Oh, I'm not impressed that you're studying Sanskrit. I'm amazed that you're confident enough to be indulging a pet interest like this right before finals."

Feeling no need to explain myself, I resumed my task.

"My mom asked about you the other day," Mike said. "Wanted to know why I haven't invited you over lately, reached out to you, blah, blah, blah."

"What did you tell her?"

"I told her it's because you're a major asshole."

"Hardy har har."

"But seriously, speaking of indulging pet interests, Eddie and Stuart are coming over tonight to play D&D. Are you in?"

"I don't know. My grandmother and aunt are visiting from Florida, and they just got in this morning. I might have to eat dinner with them or something. Also, I should be studying for finals, as you just pointed out."

"Everybody needs a break sometimes, Greenbaum. Come after dinner. Bring Grandma."

I gave Mike a big sarcastic thumbs-up.

Mike inched closer to me to get a better look at what I was doing. "Your sudden interest in Sanskrit doesn't have anything to do with that book you showed me a while back, does it? You know, the one your brother gave you?"

"It does."

"Would you care to expand on that?"

"Nope."

"Okay, whatever. I'll leave you alone." Mike got up to leave, but then leaned over my shoulder again. "Can you really read that shit?"

"Yep."

"What does *this* say?" Mike asked, pointing to the line of script I had just copied.

"One who speaks to the Guru in a rude or insulting manner or who wins arguments with Him is reborn as a demon in a jungle or in a waterless region."

Mike backed up a couple of feet and raised a trembling hand to his mouth in a mock gesture of fear. "Whoa! That's intense!"

I arrived home to the sound of my grandmother and aunt arguing. Lucy passed me in the front hall on her way to the stairs. "They're back!" she said, rolling her eyes in the direction of the kitchen. "If anyone needs me, I'll be in my room hanging myself."

"My misfortune is greater!" my aunt cried.

"No, I'm sorry, but *my* misfortune is greater!" my grandmother shouted back.

I found Melanie seated at the kitchen table with my grandmother and her sister. Melanie looked like she was going to throw up. I lingered in the doorway trying to decide whether to say hello or escape downstairs to the basement to be by myself.

"I lost my godly son, Harvey!"

"And I lost my only daughter! She was no saint, but she was all I had in this world!"

"I'm very sorry for your loss, but my misfortune is greater!"

"No, mine is greater!"

Just then, Melanie noticed me in the doorway. "Grandma, Aunt Gabby—look who's here. It's Doug!"

Grandma Millie's face lit up. "Oh, hello, darling boy!"

I was always amazed at how quickly she could shift emotional gears. I waved at the two elderly women.

"Who is this handsome young man standing before me?" Aunt Gabby asked. "Have we been introduced?"

This was Aunt Gabby's standard routine—pretending that she didn't know me and Lucy, ostensibly because we had grown so much since the last time she had seen us. But this time I wasn't certain she was joking.

"Hi Aunt Gabby, it's me—Doug."

"Douglas, my boy!" Aunt Gabby said, cupping both sides of her face with her hands and shaking her head back and forth in mock disbelief. "My how you've grown! Have a cookie."

Every time Aunt Gabby came to visit, she brought some of her homemade butter cookies with her. I eyed the open tin. "Mmm! Maybe later."

I would not have one of Aunt Gabby's cookies later. They were a known health hazard. At the age of eighty-three, my aunt was half blind and totally confused. When baking, she almost always mixed up the salt and sugar. Sometimes her cookies were so burnt she presented them as "chocolate," presumably to save face.

Grandma Millie rapped on the table to get my attention. "How's college?"

Her question made me panic. "Um, it's okay, Grandma," I said, taking one of Aunt Gabby's cookies. "I'm going to eat this in my room."

Melanie followed me into the living room. "Dougie, wait."

"What?"

Her shoulders drooped and her arms hung slack at her sides. "You dropped out?"

I felt the blood rush to my face. "Who told you?"

"Mike's mom. She called a few minutes ago."

McFadden!

"I just can't understand why Cornell didn't notify me?" Melanie said, her voice thick with defeat.

"Stop scolding the boy, Susan," Grandma Millie said, coming into the room. "Hasn't he been through enough?"

Melanie winced and covered her eyes with her hands. "Grandma, please."

I let out a long, low sigh. I was out of bullshit excuses. "You weren't notified because I never officially withdrew from my classes. I just stopped going."

Melanie gasped. "Stopped going! The last day of classes was yesterday!"

Suddenly, we heard Aunt Gabby calling to us from the kitchen. "Who's gambling again?"

"Shut up, Gabby!" my grandmother yelled. "This doesn't concern you!"

Melanie's jaw line hardened and she tapped her foot on the floor. "Actually, Grandma, if you don't mind, I'd like to speak to Doug privately."

My grandmother stood up abruptly and scowled at my sister. "Of course, I understand!" Grandma's tone was heavy with sarcasm. "I'll just go back upstairs to my cell. I know when I'm not wanted."

As she climbed the stairs, she continued to mutter to herself about how her opinion wasn't valued. Aunt Gabby followed her.

Melanie propped a cheek on her fist and waited for Grandma to be out of hearing range before speaking again. "Doug, take your boots off and come sit with me."

At first I resisted. Then I decided it was as good a time as any to tell Melanie my future plans. Putting as much space as possible between us, I took a seat at the far end of the room, in what used to be my mother's favorite armchair.

"Okay, I get it," Melanie said. "You can't deal with college right now. That's understandable." Melanie's tone softened. "But why on earth didn't you talk to me about it?"

I felt my gut tighten. "I—"

"If you had officially withdrawn from your classes, we would have gotten most of the tuition money back. Now you'll fail everything. Twelve thousand dollars down the toilet! Do you realize how much money that is? It's Lucy's money too, you know! What were you thinking?"

My head began to throb in pain: "How am I supposed to tell you anything?" I blurted out. "You never listen to me!"

Melanie's jaw dropped. "*I* never listen to *you?*" she said, pointing to herself. "You never listen to a word I say! How many times have I asked you to take out the garbage or do the dishes, only to be ignored?"

As Melanie listed the myriad ways I had failed to obey, I tuned her out. My thoughts wandered to Baba's ashram on the other side of the planet, where all that mattered was meditation and spiritual practice. *In Ravipur I will be free.*

On another level, I knew Melanie was right. I should have officially withdrawn from the classes. Now I would leave Cornell in disgrace, and the money was gone forever. She was also right that I didn't care about Lucy. My only concern was that I might need that money someday to live in the ashram.

"What are you going to do now?" my sister demanded, lowering her chin to look down on me. "You can't stay here. Oh no, sir. You're going to have to find a job and get your own place. Mommy's money can only be used to pay for college."

I felt a pounding in my ears and I exploded: "If I can't stay here, neither can you and Herb! This isn't your house.

If it belongs to anybody, it's rightfully mine and Lucy's! Get the hell out of here and go back to your fucking farm!"

Melanie opened her mouth to shout, but nothing came out. I had her! She couldn't think of a good argument.

Just then, something caught my eye, glimmering on the floor under my mother's stereo system.

"Doug, don't you get it? The house is for sale. We're all going to have to move out. You need to understand that actions have consequences."

As Melanie continued to lecture me, I got up from my seat, walked over to the stereo, and dropped to the floor.

"Doug? Are you listening to me? Doug? What are you doing?"

I reached under the shelving unit and pulled out a pair of impossibly thick-lensed glasses.

Melanie's eyes widened and she covered her mouth with both hands. "Oh my God! Are those what I think they are?"

"I think so," I answered, setting them down on the coffee table. When the paramedics had taken Harvey away, I had noticed he wasn't wearing his glasses.

"Whatever you do, don't let Aunt Gabby or Grandma see them."

I nodded and sat back down in my mother's chair.

"Doug, would you mind telling me what your plans are?" Her tone was more conciliatory now.

I hesitated before answering, and then I looked my sister squarely in the eye. "I want to go to India and study meditation."

"Meditation? In *India*?"

"That's right. I want to eventually take the vows of a renunciant and become a swami."

Melanie threw her hands up in the air. "Oh, terrific! And just how do you plan on funding this lifestyle?"

"Well, I thought the trust would pay for me to go to India because I would be engaged in a course of study."

"Nice try, Doug. The trust is to help you and Lucy to go to *college*. So unless the ashram is an accredited school and can offer a bachelor's degree, no dice."

"But it's *my* money!" I said, banging my fists down on the arms of my chair.

"I'm sorry, but my hands are tied. Even if I wanted to give it to you, Mommy set up the trust to prevent precisely this kind of thing from happening. The last thing she wanted you to do was to squander your money frivolously."

"What the hell is frivolous about wanting to attain the highest goal of life, to attain God-realization and eternal bliss?"

"The answer is no. If you want to go to India, you'll have to get a job and save up for it yourself."

"You suck!" I shouted, springing to my feet. "You do *not* rule my life! I'm going to be eighteen next month, and your days of trying to control everything I do will be over. I serve only one master and his name is Swami Rudrananda Paramahansa!"

My hands were balled into tight fists. My chest felt like it was about to explode.

Melanie stood up, open-mouthed and trembling, holding her hands out toward me in a peace offering. "Dougie, calm down. I'm not—"

"I won't calm down! I knew you wouldn't understand! I hate you, you fucking bitch!"

Crying, I barreled up the stairs and almost knocked over my grandmother and aunt, who had been eavesdropping on my conversation with Melanie from the upstairs hallway.

"Douglas, wait!" my grandmother cried, clutching at her chest with one hand and reaching for me with the other. "I have something very important to tell you—"

Ignoring Grandma Millie, I stormed into my room and slammed the door behind me. To muffle the sounds of my grandmother's voice and the sound of her pounding on my door, I dove into bed, buried my head under a pillow, and sobbed into my sheets.

After a long time, my tears finally subsided, my mind became still, and I was quiet. It was quiet in the house, too.

Baba loves me, I remembered. *He will show me the way.* I got up from my bed, wiped my tears, and blew my nose into a Kleenex. Then I went before the makeshift altar to Baba on top of my dresser and folded my hands. Gazing into Baba's eyes in the photo, I prayed to him as he gazed lovingly back at me.

Oh Compassionate One, please hear my prayer. I only want to be with you, Rudrananda. I only want to serve you. Oh Lord, I long for awakening and your divine grace. Please, Baba—please help me find a way to be with you."

Compassion poured out of Baba's eyes and I was enveloped in his love. I knew with absolute certainty that wherever Baba was, whatever he was doing in that instant, he could hear my prayers and knew what was in my heart. I knew that somehow, some way, the guru would make it possible for me to be with him.

Just then, I heard the sound of something being slid under my door. I looked down at the floor and saw two envelopes. Picking them up, I looked to see who they were from. The first was from Cornell. I ripped open the letter, knowing exactly what it would say. It was a message from the dean's office advising that I would not be matriculated next semester due to my failure to sit for midterm exams. I tossed the letter back on the ground and looked at the second letter. It was from the Law Offices of Klepfish and Stein, and was addressed to Douglas R. Greenbaum. My insides quivered. I didn't have the slightest idea why I would be getting a letter from a lawyer. For a second I thought maybe Cornell had discovered I didn't really have a passion for fruit and was suing me for making false claims in my application essay.

I opened the envelope: the letter was from the executor of my cousin Harvey's will, advising me that I was the *sole beneficiary* of his estate. Enclosed was a check for one hundred and twenty thousand dollars. Payable to me.

6.
A WARM WELCOME

"ONE TICKET TO BIRCHWOOD Falls, New York, please."

"Round trip or one-way?"

"One-way."

I paid for my ticket and Melanie followed me out to the parking lot of the station, where my bus was idling.

"It's not too late to change your mind, Doug." Melanie's posture was bent and the corners of her mouth were turned down. "You could help me in the nursery. I would pay you, of course. Maybe you could take some courses at Tompkins Cortland Community College."

I handed the bus driver my ticket and duffel bag to stow. "I'm sorry, Melanie, but my mind is made up. All I want to do for the rest of my life is serve the guru."

My sister laughed ruefully and wiped the tears from her face with the back of her mitten. "Well, then I hope he has more luck getting you to shovel the snow than I did."

Melanie and I hugged good-bye and I got on board, taking the first empty window seat.

The bus made a loud whooshing noise and pulled out of the station. I waved and a tearful Melanie waved back. The bus turned the corner and she was gone. A lump formed in my throat and my stomach knotted up. *Am I making a terrible mistake?* I asked myself.

This was the first time I had ever left town on my own, and I was anxious. *What if I miss my connection in Binghamton? What if they lose my bag?*

As the bus headed up State Street, the early morning sun stung my eyes. The engine groaned as the bus lunged into third gear. I looked down at my hands. They were trembling. *I could ask the driver to let me off the bus right now, before it's too late.* Despite my mounting anxiety, I knew that I wouldn't do that. I had to be brave.

When I had told everyone at the center about my unexpected windfall, they were overjoyed. Menaka was positively giddy. The money meant that I could finally be with Baba and live in the ashram. Menaka immediately put me in touch with Alan. With his enthusiastic help, I booked a room at the ashram for the next six months—paid in advance. I was elated, of course, but I had some misgivings, too. I called Jeremy and Carrie to talk about them.

"What if nobody likes me in Birchwood Falls?" I had asked.

Carrie giggled. "That's just your ego talking, Doug! It doesn't matter whether others like you or not. Only Baba's opinion matters, and he obviously wants you there. Why else would he have blessed you with all that money?"

My brother also laughed reassuringly. "Believe me, the ashram needs all the help it can get preparing for Baba's visit. They'll be thrilled to have you!"

Somewhere in the back of my mind, I thought they might also be thrilled to have my money.

Even after the phone call, I still had my doubts about whether people would be friendly to me at the ashram. In any case, I was going where no one knew me. People there wouldn't see me as the freak with two dead parents who had just flunked out of college. In the ashram, all that would matter was my devotion to the guru.

Melanie's reaction to the news that I was planning on spending the rest of my life in the ashram had been, as expected, quite different from Jeremy's. While I was packing, she came by my room with a warning.

"When we sell the house, I'm getting rid of everything you leave behind or I'm keeping it for myself," she said, resting her fists on her hips. "I'm not paying for storage for you."

An idle threat, I told myself. At the price Melanie was asking for the house, it wasn't going to sell anytime soon. In any case, the only things I was leaving behind that I cared anything about were my bicycle and my record collection. But what did a swami need with a ten-speed and the complete works of Jethro Tull?

"Fine," I said. "I'm becoming a renunciant. I have no use for material possessions."

Melanie threw her head back and laughed. "No need for material possessions? Then why are you taking *twenty thousand dollars* in traveler's checks with you?"

"I might need the money to go on tour with Baba. He could be heading to Europe or Australia before returning to India." The other reason was that I didn't want to run out of funds. The rest of my small fortune was locked away in a savings account. If I needed cash at any point, I could have the bank wire it to me.

Lucy also made her feelings known to me. "So, you're going to shave your head, put on an orange dress, and dance in the park?" I didn't dignify her question with a response. My spiritually unevolved sisters were pathetic.

My old high school friends' reactions weren't much better. Their suggestions about what to do with the money highlighted the difference between them and my new friends from Raja Yoga.

"I'd take all that money and go live in the Dominican Republic," Stuart said. "The island's crawling with beautiful girls and everything is dirt cheap. You could get high and lie on the beach all day long."

"I'd start my own business," Mike said. "A personal computer in every home, all linked together in a worldwide network. I've got a thousand ideas!"

"A hundred and twenty thousand dollars won't get you very far if you don't invest it wisely," Eddie said. "If I were you, I'd get my shit together and go back to school."

My worldly friends were all deluded, of course. None of them understood the value and true purpose of their precious human existence. I truly thought they were doomed to wander in spiritual ignorance for countless lifetimes.

Elisabeth Jensen was no exception. She was home from Smith for winter break, and we went out for Mexican food to catch up. I had already told her a bit about the guru and Raja Yoga over the phone, but she didn't know I was leaving for the ashram. She was dressed in one of her signature, tight-fitting turtleneck sweaters, and it was all I could do to stop myself from staring at her breasts. I prayed to Baba to rid my mind of impure thoughts.

"You may or may not ever see me again," I said, taking a bite of my vegetarian tostada. Elisabeth was having steak fajitas.

She pursed her lips. "What's that supposed to mean, Doug?"

"I'm embarking on a spiritual journey."

She smirked. "You mean like Larry Darrell?"

"Who's Larry Darrell?"

"He's the protagonist in *The Razor's Edge*. By Somerset Maugham?"

"Never read it."

"Don't bother," she laughed, "it sucked. Anyway, tell me about *your* spiritual quest."

"I'm seeking the ultimate goal of all transmigrating beings."

Elisabeth cut into a thick, juicy strip of meat. "I'm listening."

"The realization that God dwells within us *as us*."

She popped the piece of steak into her mouth and chewed it thoroughly before replying. "Sounds like you realize that already. You sound pretty convinced."

"Well, I grasp it intellectually, of course. But God-realization is a transcendental experience."

Elisabeth pressed her lips into a hard line.

My mind raced, searching for a better answer. I remembered something I'd heard Baba say in a video, and repeated it verbatim: "The ultimate reality of our true nature cannot be grasped through the conceptual mind, nor can it be explained to the uninitiated."

"So, I take it you're one of the initiated."

"I will be after I meet Baba," I answered, trying to stop picturing her naked. "I intend to take an initiation retreat during which the guru will bestow *shaktipat*."

Elisabeth cleared her throat. "*Shaktipat?*"

"The awakening of my *kundalini* and initiation into the path of Raja Yoga."

"I see," Elisabeth said, sipping her Coke. "They charge money for that, I take it?"

I was at a loss. Then I again remembered something I had read in one of Baba's books: "Anything of true value requires an exchange of energy. Only when we are ready to give, are we truly able to receive."

Elisabeth's eyes twinkled and she snorted. "I like that!"

Is she laughing at me? I wondered. My face felt hot.

"So this Swami Rudra character—"

"Swami Rudrananda," I corrected.

"He sounds like he has it pretty good. I mean, he has lots of followers who will do anything for him—travels all over the world—"

"Baba's also ready to do anything for his devotees," I countered. I had never actually heard anyone at the center say that, but I was sure it must be true.

"Does he fly first class?" Elisabeth asked, stabbing a strip of steak with her fork. "I'll bet he flies first class."

I tensed up. "What are you inferring?"

Elisabeth wrinkled her nose. "*Implying*. I'm *implying* that he's taking you and all his other followers for the proverbial ride. Like that other Indian guru out West—what's his name—'Rajneesh' or something—the one with a hundred Rolls-Royces."

I had no idea what so-called "guru" she was talking about, and felt put on the spot. Suddenly I was thirsty. I gulped down some ice water. "Baba's motivations are completely altruistic."

"How do you know that, Doug? I mean, you've never even met this man. Don't you think you're taking a lot on faith?"

I was beginning to wonder if Elisabeth had changed her mind about becoming a psychologist. She didn't sound very supportive.

"First of all, my brother and his wife *have* met Baba and I trust their good judgment. I've also read a lot of his books and I've been studying Hindu philosophy. In any case, *faith* is what it's all about, Elisabeth. A truly spiritual person understands that."

I had been sure that by the end of the evening Elisabeth would want to meet Baba too, but she was as closed-minded as Melanie. Sick of being put on the defensive, I changed the subject. I talked to her about the money I had inherited from Harvey and how unexpected it was.

Elisabeth sat up straight and smiled. "That doesn't surprise me at all."

"What doesn't surprise you? That Harvey had all that money?"

"No," she said. "It doesn't surprise me that *you* were his favorite person and that he wanted to leave you all his money. You're a very special person, Doug, even if you can't see it right now."

I bristled. *Haven't I just spent the last thirty minutes telling her how "special" Baba is? I'm Baba's disciple; that makes me special too.* Then I thought about what Elisabeth had said about my being Harvey's "favorite person." Maybe I was. I had happy memories of all the moments my cousin and I had spent hiking, identifying fossils, and visiting museums together. I hadn't minded listening to his same old stories about the Native Americans of the Finger Lakes region every time he came to visit. I had done those things with him because I enjoyed them, but also because I got an emotional lift out of feeling generous. I just didn't realize it at the time.

Elisabeth asked for the check. "So you're leaving. Your mind is made up?"

"Yes, I'm going to the Birchwood Falls ashram to help with the advance work. Afterwards, I'd like to travel with Baba and eventually return with him to India."

Elisabeth formed a steeple with her fingers and looked pensive for a moment before speaking. "The more I think about it, the more I agree that maybe some mindless work for you is just what the doctor would order right now."

"*Mindless?*"

Narrowing her eyes, she leaned forward and took my hand in hers. My body flooded with warmth. "Doug, you've been through hell. Anyone who doesn't understand that is completely insensitive." *She obviously wants me,* I told myself.

I tried to pay the check, but Elisabeth insisted on splitting it with me. Then I followed her out the door of the restaurant and onto the street.

"Take good care of yourself at the ashram. Don't let anyone take advantage of that good heart of yours."

I had to make my move. It was now or never. My last chance to get laid before taking the vows of a swami. I leaned in to kiss her.

Elisabeth jerked her head back and raised a hand in front of her mouth to block me. "What are you doing?" she said, her eyes wide and her mouth hanging open.

Heat rushed to my face and my skin tingled. I felt like an idiot. "I—um—I—"

"I thought you were all spiritual now?" Elisabeth's eyes twinkled and she let out a bark of laughter. "Men! You're all the same!"

THE BUS PULLED INTO the Greyhound station in Binghamton. My connection for Birchwood Falls was across the street at the Short Line terminal. Even though I had a thirty-minute wait, as soon as the driver retrieved my bag from the hold, I made a run for it. I was completely inexperienced at traveling. I was afraid the bus might leave early without me.

The official name of Baba's American headquarters in Birchwood Falls was Shree Brahmananda Ashram, after Baba's own guru. It was located in the Catskill Mountain region of upstate New York, better known to my family as the "Borscht Belt." Up until the early 1970s, the area had been a popular vacation spot for New York City Jews and was home to numerous upscale kosher resorts. The Raja Yoga Mission in New York had first opened an ashram in a converted brownstone in Greenwich Village. Soon afterward, the Manhattan ashram had proved too small to accommodate the droves of devotees and curiosity seekers who had started coming to see Baba. Almost immediately, the Mission began searching for a larger property Upstate. At the same time, the once flourishing resorts of the "Jewish Alps" were beginning to resemble ghost towns; many of the formerly splendid hotels in the area had closed down and fallen into disrepair. In 1977, the Mission was able to purchase the rundown Danziger Hotel for a pittance. Extensive renovations were begun and devotees started flooding in from all across the globe to volunteer their labor and expertise. Within the space of only a few months, the old Borscht Belt resort was transformed into a "Meditation Mecca." The ballroom was converted into a meditation hall that could seat up to a thousand, its eighteen-hole golf course was transformed into lush gardens, and its Olympic-size swimming pool was filled in and an ornate temple to Baba's guru and a fountain were erected in its place.

I got off the bus in Birchwood Falls and took a taxi to the ashram.

"I'm going to Shree Gurudev Brahmananda Ashram," I told the driver. I was about to give him the address, but he already knew where it was.

On the way to the ashram I saw many dilapidated homes and buildings. But as we drew closer to my destination, I also saw clusters of newer-looking bungalows and structures with what looked like hotel signs written entirely in Hebrew. A group of teenaged Jewish boys with side curls in black hats and long black coats was in the driveway of a building that looked like a schoolhouse. They were boarding a yellow school bus with Hebrew lettering on the side. I admired their obvious commitment to their faith, but thought they were misguided. I believed I was blessed to have found a genuine *shaktipat guru* and to be on a true path to enlightenment.

The driver remained silent the entire trip. I wondered if he realized how lucky he was to live in such close proximity to Baba's ashram.

We turned a corner and passed several acres of grounds surrounded by barbed wire. I was breathless; in the distance I could see a sprawling complex of buildings that I recognized as Baba's ashram, from the many pictures I had seen of it in *Raja Path Magazine*. The gate to the complex was open and the driver turned into a circular driveway in front of what must have been the main building. A sign above the entrance read "Shree Brahmananda Ashram." Tears stung my eyes. I was home at last.

I paid the driver and gave him a big tip. He took the money without comment and popped the trunk open from the dashboard. I got out, grabbed my bag from the trunk, and slammed it shut. Then the driver sped off without so much as a "thank you."

Suddenly, I felt weak in the knees and dizzy. *I'm stranded*, I thought. *What if I don't like it here? What if the people here changed their mind and I won't be allowed to stay? Where will I go?*

I approached the ashram's big glass sliding doors and they opened automatically. As soon as I had crossed the threshold, I felt lighter. On the wall across from the entrance was an enormous photo of a smiling Baba. A sign just beneath it read, "See God in Everyone." Over the sound system, a recording of Baba sweetly reciting the *Om*

Namah Shivaya mantra was accompanied by the light, soothing, almost hypnotic strains of an ektara. It was as though I had entered a higher realm—a celestial space station. I was overcome with gratitude to the guru for bringing me here.

The ashram lobby was vast, immaculate, and fragrant with a mixture of burning incense, flowers, and basmati rice. The lower part of the lobby was lined with benches, all of which were empty. Up a few steps, at the far end of the lobby, some people were going about their business, including a man vacuuming in front of what looked like a reception area. His gaze was cast downward at the wall-to-wall carpeting he was cleaning. The expression on his face was vacant, as if the repetitive motion required by his chore and the unrelenting drone of the vacuum had sent him into a trance. Mounting the steps to the upper lobby, I could now see through the open doors of an enormous cafeteria, with many rows of tables and chairs that looked like they might have originally served in a high school cafeteria. A group of ashramites were setting up a serving line of industrial-size pots. The tantalizing aromas of exotic spices from the kitchen were making me hungry. In the lobby, a line was forming outside the doors to the cafeteria. Luckily, I had arrived just in time for lunch, but I wasn't sure I could eat without checking in first.

I approached the reception area. A sign on the counter said: "Closed." I glanced back at the ashramites waiting in line for lunch. None of them were draped in "*Om Namah Shivaya*" shawls or loose fitting cotton clothing like most of the people who attended *satsang* back home at the center in Ithaca. A couple of men in their early thirties with sawdust in their hair were wearing paint-speckled overalls. Behind them, a contingent of women in their twenties and thirties were drably dressed in boxy blouses and long frumpy skirts. A preadolescent boy and an athletic-looking woman in a pullover top and stretch pants descended a narrow flight of stairs off the dining room, each with what looked like school books under their arms. As I stood in the lobby scratching my head, no one gave me a second look. *Can't any of these people see me?* I thought. *Why hasn't anyone greeted me yet?*

I lingered a little longer in front of the closed reception area, hoping someone would come to my aid. As I waited, I studied the faces of the ashramites converging on the cafeteria. They were of diverse ethnic backgrounds, ages, shapes, and sizes, but I didn't see a single Indian. Some were beautiful, others were homely, but they all glowed with discipline, focus, and devotion to the guru.

The serving line opened and the ashramites working it began to chant "Shree Ram, Jai Ram," one of the thousand Hindu names for God. Their singing was slow and melancholy. If I didn't know better, I would have thought they were chanting a funeral dirge. Just then I noticed a grim-looking man with a shaved head joining the lunch line. He wore orange robes and, like the guru, he had a dot of bright red powder between his eyebrows. Unlike the guru, he was white and, I assumed, American. He was short and stout, with only the suggestion of a neck. Despite an almost grotesque quality about the man, he exuded an air of confidence through impeccable posture and the relaxed manner in which he held his hands behind his back. He looked like he was in his late fifties or early sixties. The orange robes identified him as one of Baba's swamis. *That's what I'm going to look like someday!* I told myself.

As more and more people took their places in line, I felt increasingly like an outsider. I was about to ask the grumpy-looking swami if it would be okay if I ate lunch before checking in, when I felt a tap on my shoulder.

I turned. Alan Jones was standing behind me beaming a smile. "Welcome, stranger." He reached for my hand and shook it firmly. "I saw your name on the list of new arrivals today." Alan was dressed as smartly as ever, in a burgundy turtleneck sweater and charcoal slacks. Hanging from his belt was a large ring of keys and a walkie-talkie. He looked important.

"I wanted to check in, but the reception desk is closed."

"There'll be plenty of time for that later. Come, let's have lunch." With his arm around my shoulder, Alan led me over to the lunch line and stopped to introduce me to the stern-looking man in orange robes. "Swamiji, this is Doug."

The swami's eyes lit up. "Pleased to meet you, I'm sure!" His voice was warm and vaguely flirtatious, incongruous with his solemn countenance.

"Doug, this is Swami Akhandananda. He's one of Baba's senior swamis."

I folded my hands together and lowered my head, in the manner I had seen Indians greet Gandhi in the movie starring Ben Kingsley.

The swami giggled. "Puh-lease! Save your awe and reverence for Baba. I'm very happy to meet you, young Mr. Greenbaum." He knew my last name. I understood that Alan must have told him about me.

Alan gave me an affectionate squeeze on the shoulder.

"Something tells me you're of the Jewish persuasion," the swami said with a comedic gleam in his eyes. "Am I mistaken?"

"I'm of Jewish heritage, yes." My mouth felt dry, and I was getting hot in my winter coat. I wanted to take it off, but I was already carrying a duffle bag and my knapsack.

As if reading my thoughts, the swami glanced down at my bag. "Alan, why don't you take Douglas' bag and coat and put them in your office until he can get settled after lunch."

Alan nodded deferentially and reached for my bag. I removed my coat and handed it to him, and he left me alone in line with the swami. Then he disappeared behind a door next to the reception area that said "Manager."

The swami leaned close, as though he were about to tell me a secret. "I'm an Osmotic Jew, myself," he said softly.

"I beg your pardon, Swamiji?"

"You've heard of Ashkenazi and Sephardic Jews, haven't you?" He gave me the once-over.

I nodded.

"Judging by your last name, I assume that you're of Ashkenazi descent."

"That's right," I said. "But what's an *Osmotic* Jew?" I was beginning to think the swami was pulling my leg—I had never heard of an Osmotic Jew before, and Akhandananda didn't look Jewish.

The swami's face broke into a childlike grin. "After twenty years in Beverly Hills, I'm a Jew by osmosis!" The swami covered his mouth and giggled. I laughed too. I was beginning to like this character.

After Alan returned from the reception area, we entered the cafeteria and I found myself in front of a high stack of hard plastic cafeteria trays. I took one and also grabbed a fork and knife, and then made my way down the serving line. A moderate helping of each prepared dish was carefully ladled into the most appropriate size and shape compartment in my tray. These included a spicy tofu dish, a scoop of brown rice, a wholesome grain and vegetable mixture, plain yogurt, and an apple.

I followed Akhandananda and Alan to a table and glanced around the room. Some of the ashramites sat alone, eating mindfully. Others sat together making lively conversation. Toward the back of the hall, couples sat with small kids. I marveled at the children's extraordinarily good karma. I could imagine how pure and highly evolved they must have been to be born into Raja Yoga and live in one of Baba's ashrams.

As soon as we sat down, I began to devour my food. The swami watched me eat with wide eyes and parted lips. "Everyone's entitled to seconds, you know," he giggled. "And you, young man, need fattening up!"

Akhandananda and Alan spoke about ashram business for a while, and then the swami turned his attention back to me and told me a little bit about his life before Raja Yoga. "When I first met Baba I was an unmitigated hedonist, I'm afraid," he said with a far-away, misty look in his eyes. Then he sighed, shook his head, and smiled a little. "Looking for love in all the wrong places..."

"What did you do before?" I asked. "For a living?"

The swami laughed heartily. "Physician to the stars, my boy!"

"Swamiji's patients included some of Hollywood's biggest names," Alan said.

"That's right," Akhandananda said. "But my life changed forever the day I met Baba."

I loved hearing Baba stories. "What happened?"

"One of my patients, who shall remain nameless," the swami said, winking, "brought me up on the *darshan* line to meet Baba. The look the guru gave me was so penetrating, my entire sense of individuality melted away in an instant. All that remained was an ocean of love. At that moment I knew the only thing I wanted to do for the rest of my life was to learn how to swim in that ocean. I also knew that Baba was the man to teach me. After the program, I went home and I sat down to close my eyes for what I thought was five minutes. When I opened them again and checked my watch, it turned out that I had been in a deep state of meditation for three hours!"

Alan closed his eyes and nodded his head. "Jai Gurudev!"

"Jai Gurudev!" Akhandananda responded. I made a mental note to join in the next time anyone said that.

I asked Akhandananda what the word *darshan* meant and he explained that it was "the opportunity to be in the presence of a great saint." He spoke about his past medical career and I thought of Jeremy. "Swamiji, my brother's finishing medical school now. Do you think he's wasting his time?"

"The life of a renunciant is not for everyone, my boy."

Alan agreed. "Besides, Baba needs doctors for The Mission."

I had seen Alan a few times at the Ithaca center, but had never heard how he had gotten into Raja Yoga. He shared his story with me.

"I met Baba in Cambridge, Massachusetts, in 1974. When I went before him on the *darshan* line, Baba looked me in the eye and said: 'I've been waiting for you. At last you've come.' He tapped me lightly on the head with his wand of peacock feathers, and then he told me: 'We're going to do great things together.'"

Alan's story gave me the chills. "Then what happened?"

The manager shook his head. "Baba didn't speak to me again for five years!" He and Akhandananda burst out laughing and I laughed with them, though I wasn't sure why.

"Why didn't he speak to you?" I asked. My question prompted more laughter from Alan and the swami, and they exchanged knowing glances.

Alan Shrugged. "I guess you could say that was just Baba's way of working on my *huge* ego."

"The guru builds the disciple up, so that he can knock him down," Akhandananda explained. "Now look at him. Alan's the manager of this ashram—Baba's American headquarters."

A flush crept across Alan's cheeks. "Interim manager, technically."

"He's also a swami candidate," Akhandananda added.

I felt a rush of excitement. "You're going to be a swami?" *If Alan can do it, so can I!*

"If that's Baba's will," Alan answered, raising his hands in front of himself.

The swami and Alan were still eating long after I had finished. Akhandananda looked down at my empty tray. "You like our ashram food, I see. Go on, Douglas. Help yourself to seconds."

"Yeah, go get some more to eat," Alan smiled. "You're going to be doing a lot of *seva* around here and need your strength!"

When I returned to the food line only one server remained. He was a short, thin man with dark hair and cold eyes. I guessed he was in his early twenties. He was dressed in high-waisted blue jeans and a tattered red plaid flannel shirt. I held my tray out to him and he looked me up and down, then squinted at me through thick-rimmed glasses. "Name tag?"

"I beg your pardon?"

The young man glared at me disapprovingly and tapped his breast pocket. "Where's your name tag?"

"I don't have one yet."

He pursed his lips and shook his head. "Then I can't serve you."

I glanced down at the man's shirt. He wasn't wearing one either. The young man folded his arms in front of his chest and looked away. I glanced around the cafeteria. Nobody had one.

"You served me before. I'm just coming back for seconds."

"You've got to have a name tag."

"But Swamiji said it was okay."

"Fortunately, Swamiji isn't in charge of the serving line."

Strange, I thought. But rather than make a big deal about it, I just rejoined the swami and Alan at the table, explaining that I wasn't hungry.

7.
ANGEL

AFTER LUNCH, ALAN INTRODUCED me to Mukti at the reception desk, which was now open. Then he left me to my own devices. Mukti was a woman in her late thirties with deep, dark circles under her eyes and a sagging face. Her teeth were crooked and stained, and her hair, which she wore in a tight bun on the top of her head, was an unattractive mixture of yellow and gray.

I filled out the accommodation form and left the departure date blank. When I was finished, Mukti snatched the paper away from me and carefully read what I had put down.

"How long are you staying?"

"I'm not sure," I answered. "Indefinitely?"

"You'll need to pay at least a month's room and board up front."

I swallowed hard. "But I already sent the ashram a check for six months in advance. I arranged it with Alan."

Mukti sauntered through the open doorway of an office behind her, and came back thirty seconds later with another sheet of paper.

"So you have," she said handing me a receipt for twenty-four hundred dollars. "It's nonrefundable, you know."

I nodded my assent.

Mukti reached into a drawer under the counter and pulled out a plastic badge holder and a blank name card that said "Raja Yoga Mission of America" with the Mission's official insignia: a combination of a geometric flower, a Sanskrit "Om" symbol, and something resembling a Greek caduceus.

"Spiritual name?"

"I don't have one—yet."

Mukti wrote "Doug" on the card with a black sharpie, inserted it into the holder, applied a little round green sticker to the upper left-hand corner, and handed it to me.

"Wear this at all times," she said.

I undid the pin on the back of the badge and attached it to my shirt. Mukti turned around to take a key from a panel on the wall.

"You're in *Shiva Shayanagrih*," she said. Then she gave me a pamphlet entitled "Ashram Rules."

"What's *Shiva Shayanagrih*?"

Mukti narrowed her eyes and tapped her fingernails against the counter. "'*Shayanagrih*' means *dormitory*. *Shiva Shayanagrih* is where the men sleep."

I slung my bag over my shoulder and was about to leave in search of my dorm room when Mukti spoke again. "Make sure you read that," she said, pointing to the "Ashram Rules" pamphlet I was holding.

"Of course. Thank you."

"Oh, and Doug—the *seva* desk closes at three."

Massive windows in the lobby framed a view of the snow-shrouded ashram grounds. But the wall on the far end of the lobby was cloaked behind a long gray curtain. I thought about taking a peek behind, but didn't want to be seen poking my nose where it didn't belong.

I knocked before using my key to open the door to my room, in case its occupants hadn't been informed that they would be getting a new roommate. There was no answer.

Inside I was greeted by sunshine blazing through a picture window and the strong smell of recently burnt incense. The room was sparsely furnished, with three crudely-fashioned pine bunk beds, a couple of plywood dressers, and bright orange shag carpeting. I found it hard to believe that I was standing in what was once a room in a luxury resort. Only two of the lower bunks were made up, which meant I had only one roommate. Above each bed, a small shelf was built into the wall. The shelf above one of the made-up beds served as an altar to Baba and Gurudev Brahmananda. The *puja* altar and a thin line of ash from a half-burnt stick of incense were the only signs that I had a roommate. The room was immaculate. Claiming the free bed and empty shelf, I unpacked my pictures of the gurus and set up my own altar.

I took a leak in the bathroom and noticed another sign of life: a bag of toiletries hanging from a hook on the bathroom door. I wondered what it would be like to share the bathroom with five other men. Once Baba arrived there would be few vacancies in the dormitories. I would have to get dressed and undressed every day in front of all those strangers. I would have absolutely no privacy. A wave of homesickness hit. *I have to be strong,* I told myself.

Before unpacking the rest of my things, I sat down on the bed and studied the booklet on *Ashram Rules* that Mukti had given me.

> *All guests are required to follow the entire ashram daily schedule. Participation in all meditation sessions, chants, and public programs is required.*
>
> SEVA
> *Seva (selfless service) is an essential part of ashram life and provides an opportunity for you to participate in the daily chores and maintenance of the ashram. Guests are required to perform at least three hours of seva per day.*

INTOXICANTS
Smoking, the consumption of alcohol, and the use of drugs are strictly prohibited.

MALE/FEMALE
Ashramites and visitors are expected to observe celibacy. Expressions of affection such as hugging and kissing are forbidden.

Men and women must sit in their respective gender-designated areas of the meditation hall and temples.

Male and female dormitories are separate. Men are not allowed in women's rooms and vice versa.

DRESS CODE
Clothing must be modest. Shorts, miniskirts, and tight-fitting or revealing clothing are not permitted.

SILENCE
Guests are asked to observe silence in the cafeteria during meals. Gossip and frivolous conversation are forbidden at all times.

Lights out is at ten-thirty P.M.

When I had finished reading the rules, I faced the altar above my bed and folded my hands in prayer. *Please Baba, help me adjust quickly to my new life in your home. Make me a model ashramite.*

The *seva* desk was across from the reception area, and it was tended by Sita Perkins, a plump, pale-faced, large-breasted woman with a bright smile. She had straight dirty-blonde hair and a pitted complexion.

"Welcome to the ashram, Doug!"

"How did you know my name?"

Sita pointed to the badge pinned to my shirt and let out a guffaw. "It's on your name tag, silly!"

"So it is!" My face tingled with embarrassment. Sita was wearing a name tag too. But instead of a green sticker above her name like mine, she had an orange one.

"I have the perfect *seva* for you, Doug. You'll be working with Madhu Arnold in Housing. He can show you the ropes. He's an old-timer." Sita explained that she was not only in charge of assigning *seva* to ashram guests, but that she also managed the Housing Department. I would be answering directly to her.

"Are there a lot of guests in the ashram?" I asked.

"Not this time of year. Actually, you're the only one." Something caught Sita's eye and she waved. "Oh, here comes Madhu."

Lumbering toward us, with his hands in his pockets and his head hung low, was a deeply tanned young man around my age, with a muscular build and a mop of dark brown hair.

"I thought you said he was an *old-timer*."

Sita laughed. "I meant he's an old-timer in Raja Yoga, silly! His mom has been a devotee of Baba since the first world tour."

"Hand me the screw gun," said Madhu from the other side of the bunk bed we were assembling. Actually, Madhu was doing most of the assembly. My job was to lug whatever hardware I could carry by myself up from the basement.

I rummaged through the toolbox and found a couple of instruments that might qualify as a screw gun. "Which one is it?"

"Boy, you weren't kidding when you said you weren't handy."

"Sorry," I said handing him what I thought might be the screw gun. "I grew up without a father."

"So did I," Madhu said. "He wasn't into Baba." Then he laughed when he noticed what I had passed to him. "That, my friend, is a *glue gun*."

I handed him a different gadget. "Where's your mom now?"

"Yeah, that's the right one," Madhu said. "Don't worry, you'll get the hang of it." The drill made a loud, whirring sound and the screw squeaked as Madhu drove it into a two-by-four, attaching it to a bed platform. "My mom?" he said, putting the screw gun down and standing up to wipe his brow with the back of his sleeve. "She's still in India with Baba. I came back early to take the GED."

"You went to high school in India?"

Madhu chuckled. "Yeah, sort of. But not with Indian kids or anything. Some of the people around Baba used to be teachers. I guess you could say I was home schooled, like all the kids who are raised in the ashram."

Madhu told me he had grown up traveling all over the world with Baba. I was in awe of him. "After you get your high school diploma, are you going to go back to India or travel with Baba?"

"Neither," he said, with a tight-lipped smile. "I've given enough of my life to the Mission. I have big plans. Gonna move out to L.A. Take some acting classes. Maybe do some modeling. I've always wanted to be an actor." Madhu put the screw gun down and glanced at his watch. "Quitting time."

I was shocked, but tried not to let Madhu see it. The way I saw it, here was someone who had practically been born into Raja Yoga, but wanted to throw it all away to pursue an acting career. I couldn't think of anything more antithetical to the spiritual path.

"What happens now?" I asked.

Madhu shrugged. "Dinner's at six-fifteen," he answered. Then his forehead wrinkled in thought. "There's an *arati* in the temple in a few minutes, but almost nobody goes."

We passed through the lobby on our way to return the toolbox to Sita's office, and I asked Madhu what was on the other side of the long gray curtain I had noticed earlier.

"Oh, that's Baba's House."

I gasped and reverently looked back over my shoulder at the curtain.

"Have you ever been inside?" I asked.

"Lots of times. But never when Baba was actually in the ashram. Once I even got to meditate in his bathroom with my mom."

"Why in his bathroom?"

"Cause it's full of *shakti*," he said with an exaggerated roll of his eyes. "Duh!"

I couldn't help wondering why Baba's bathroom would contain more *shakti* than the rest of his house. But Madhu had been in Raja Yoga most of his life. I was sure he knew what he was talking about.

I bundled up and followed Akhandananda and a small group of ashramites to the small Gurudev Brahmananda temple for the evening *arati* ritual. The path had been carefully shoveled and meticulously cleared of ice. The moment I set foot in the temple, I was struck by the deep silence within its walls. A powerful energy pervaded the space, and my mind became still.

Before me was a life-size bronze statue of Gurudev Brahmananda seated in the lotus position on a raised platform. I gazed up at the statue in awe. In most of the photographs of Baba's guru I had seen, he was clothed in a simple loincloth, but the statue of him here was attired in a turban, fine silk and brocade, and adorned with garlands of fragrant flowers.

"This is not a mere statue, my boy," Akhandananda whispered, handing me a laminated card with a translation and transliteration of the chant. "Statues and photographs of great beings and saints are *alive*. They are infused with consciousness. Gurudev *knows* you're here."

I regarded the statue of Brahmananda. His eyes were open, yet they did not appear to be staring back at me the way Baba's pictures did. Gurudev's gaze was directed within.

After taking off their coat and shoes, each person helped themselves to a percussion instrument from a wicker basket near the entrance. Akhandananda prepared a tray of offerings and lit the large multi-tiered *arati* lamp. On the far side of the temple, a rotund, middle-aged man with small eyes, a pug nose, and salt-and-pepper hair wheeled a large drum on its side into the center of the temple, in front of Gurudev's statue. The rest of us stood in silence waiting for the ritual to begin.

The Guru's Touch

At precisely five forty-five P.M., Akhandananda raised the *arati* lamp with his right hand and began to wave it in large clockwise circles in front of the statue, while ringing a hand bell with his left. At the same time, the rest of the temple broke into sound: a tall, athletic-looking man in an aquamarine-colored sweat suit blew into a conch shell, the pot-bellied man beat his big drum, and everybody else shook or struck their musical instruments. *Boom, boom, boom—clang, clang, clang—whoosh, whoosh, whoosh—rattle, rattle, rattle.* I was the only one in the temple not making any noise. The hypnotic motion of Akhandananda's flaming lamp and the rhythmic cacophony of the instruments seemed to go on for ages. I glanced around the temple at the others. All were staring blankly at the statue as they participated in the ritual. Suddenly they reminded me of zombies, and my mood darkened. All the muscles in my body tensed up and, despite the low temperature in the temple, I began to perspire.

While the chants back in Ithaca felt strange at first, they had helped to tame my restless mind and I eventually got used to them. But now I was overcome with fear and doubt. I felt a heaviness in my gut and my insides began to quiver. Unlike the other rituals, this one seemed occult and spooky. The ashramites around me did not look like they were in a state of meditation. They looked like they had entered into a trance. I began to panic, wondering what I had gotten myself into. For the first time in my life, I thought about the Jewish proscription against idol worship. It was taboo in my culture, even if one wasn't religious. I felt ashamed. I was a bad Jew.

I eyed the door and wondered if I could get back to my room, pack my bag, call a taxi, and escape to the bus station before the chant was over and anyone had a chance to notice I was gone.

The drumming and the clashing of cymbals came to an abrupt halt, and the worshippers set their instruments down on the carpeted floor. With folded hands they slowly recited a prayer in Sanskrit. Its melody was melancholic and haunting:

Arati avadhut
Jai Jai
Arati avadhuta...

I tried to follow along but the chanting did little to calm me down. *It's going to be okay. It's going to be okay,* I kept telling myself. I just needed to make it to the end of the ritual. Then I could slip away after dinner.

I glanced down at the English translation:

Hail Hail! I wave lights to you, O Brahmananda
You are the divine lord, present in human form.
You are Manik Prabhu. You are Akkalkot Swami.
You are Sai Baba of Shirdi.
In Kali Yuga you became Gurudev Brahmananda of Ravipur.
In this way you have incarnated yourself for the upliftment of your devotees.

After what felt like an eternity, the chant was over. Before leaving, everyone bowed down before the statue of Brahmananda. Swami Akhandananda waited by the exit and offered everyone a few drops of liquid from a vial, which they received in the palms of their hands. Some drank the liquid, others rubbed it into their hair.

"What is it?" I asked the swami.

"*Prasad.* Rosewater. First it's offered to the guru, and then it's distributed to his devotees in his name. Consider it a gift from Baba."

I held out my hand and waited for Akhandananda to pour a few drops into it.

The swami wrinkled his nose as if he smelled something foul. "The left hand is impure. Never ever accept *prasad* with your left hand, young man." He put the vial down on a small wooden table next to him. "Like so." The swami cupped both hands, placing his right in his left, and held them out as if he were about to receive the *prasad* himself.

I held my hands the way Akhandananda had showed me, and he poured a few drops of rosewater into them.

I didn't drink the rosewater, but rubbed my wet hand into my hair. *Maybe I've been brainwashed,* I thought. *Maybe I have joined a cult after all.*

The Guru's Touch

I stood outside next to the temple, shivering and watching the others return to the main building in silence. I looked up at the night sky and its countless stars. *Am I truly looking up at my own reflection, as Baba teaches? Is my small wretched sense of self merely an illusion? Does my true Self encompass the entire universe?* I wanted to find out. I needed to give the ashram and Baba a chance. I would wait to see how I felt in the morning. If I still felt the same way, I would call Melanie to come take me back to Ithaca.

Suddenly, I felt a strong urge to talk to my sister. Just to check in and to hear her voice. I remembered seeing a bank of payphones down on the basement level. I took a ramp opposite the reception desk that led downstairs. On my way to the payphones, I passed the ashram bookstore. It was closed, but through the windows I could see some lights still on and shifting shadows in a back room. It was almost dinner time, but somebody was still hard at work doing *seva*.

The store had a huge selection of spiritual books, pictures of the guru, and Raja Yoga paraphernalia. On the wall was an enormous framed photograph of Baba. In the picture his face was kind and gentle, and he was staring right back at me with tremendous compassion. I was deeply moved. I remembered that I loved Baba and he loved me. How could I have doubted him, even for a second?

I squeezed into the cramped phone booth, sat down, inserted a quarter, and made my call.

Lucy answered after the second ring: "Doug? Um, how are you? Are you at the monastery yet?"

"Ashram. Yes—I am. Is Melanie there?"

"Doug, what's wrong?" Melanie asked nervously. "Where are you?"

"Everything's fine. I'm in Birchwood Falls."

"Do you have everything you need? Did they feed you? Do you need me to send you anything?"

As I assured Melanie that everything was alright, an ethereal-looking girl with long blonde hair walked past my phone booth and peered in at me through the glass. She smiled at me before disappearing from view. I was breathless. She was, without a doubt, the most beautiful creature I had ever seen.

"If you're not happy there and want to come home," Melanie said, "I have plenty of connections. I'm sure I could help find you a job. No pressure to go back to school right now."

I could hear my sister, but I wasn't listening to her. All I could think about was the angel who had just smiled at me.

The corridor was dimly lit and I had only caught a glimpse of her, but she was magnificent: she had dimples, an upturned nose, and full sensuous lips. There was also something unusual about her eyes that I couldn't pin down. She hadn't lingered long enough for me even to make out what color they were. She was slender, but not too skinny, and the pair of jeans she was wearing were just a tad too tight for the ashram dress code. I guessed she was around my age and height. I was in love.

As Melanie rambled on about my options, I realized that I had allowed my mind to fly away from me. It was occupied with impure thoughts. I stopped myself from thinking about the angel and returned my attention to the conversation I was supposed to be having with my sister.

"—and if you feel like it," Melanie was saying, "you could enroll in a couple of courses at TC3."

"Uh-huh."

"Anyhow, do you want to take down his number?"

"Whose number?"

"The financial advisor."

I didn't have a fucking clue what she was talking about. "Sure, give it to me." Melanie recited the number and I pretended to write it down. "272-3167. Thanks! Got it!"

"Doug, remember, your money should be making money."

I got off the phone with my sister and promised to check in with her again in a few days. I made a mental note to invent something about the financial advisor the next time I spoke to her.

I stepped out into the corridor and heard the angel's voice through the closed door of another phone booth. I hovered for a moment to eavesdrop. "Hi, Mom, it's Gopi! Yes, I just arrived an hour ago. No, the roads were okay—"

I knew from the readings I had done since coming to Raja Yoga that the name Gopi referred to a group of cow-herding girls in the *Bhagavata Purana* famous for their unconditional devotion to Lord Krishna. Baba must have given the angel the name because of her profound devotion to the guru. *Gopi*—a beautiful name for a beautiful girl!

As I waited in line for dinner, all I could think about was the angel Gopi. The crisis of faith I had experienced in the Gurudev Brahmananda temple had ended abruptly. I was definitely staying.

The evening meal was much lighter than what had been offered at lunch: a bowl of bland vegetable soup, two slices of whole wheat bread, and a pat of butter. I thought the petty dictator in charge of the serving line might give me a hard time again, but since I now had a name tag I was as good as invisible to him.

I searched for a table and spotted Madhu sitting with a couple of other young people on the far end. I was about to join him when someone called out to me. "Douglas, over here!" I turned to see Akhandananda beckoning to me. He was seated with Alan again.

"So, how was your first day at the ashram?"

"Wonderful," I answered, briefly remembering the unpleasantness I had earlier experienced in the temple, before putting it out of my mind.

Alan gave me a thumbs up and a tight-lipped smile. "And you haven't even been to the hall yet."

"The hall?" I asked.

"The meditation hall," Alan said. "The devotees did a beautiful job converting the old ball room. It seats a thousand people. You'll see it tomorrow. The *Guru Gita* is at six-thirty."

The swami raised his eyebrows. "And meditation is at five-thirty, Douglas." Then he turned to Alan. "You too, Mr. Manager."

Alan chuckled and blushed a little. "Yes, Swamiji."

Akhandananda carefully brought a scalding hot spoonful of soup close to his mouth and blew. "We want you to feel at home in the guru's house, Douglas." The swami's tone was gentle and soothing. "If you have any questions or problems, you can always come to either Alan or me, you know that, don't you?"

Alan nodded in agreement. "That's right."

"I appreciate that very much, Swamiji, Alan."

Akhandananda's eyebrows pulled down in concentration and he lowered his head so that his almost nonexistent neck vanished. "You've undergone such a great deal of hardship and tragedy in your short life." The swami put his spoon down and reached for my forearm and gave it a light squeeze. Then he gazed deeply into my eyes. "But you know, too much good karma can be an obstacle on the spiritual path."

I was confused. "How could that be?"

"Baba says that *shaktipat* can only occur when a person's negative and positive karmas are balanced. If we have too much good karma, we're too busy enjoying our lives for it ever to occur to us to go looking for the guru. If we have too much bad karma, we are mired in misery and never think to seek him either."

My mind froze. "I find that a little difficult to grasp, Swamiji."

Alan let out a deep laugh and slapped his knee.

Akhandananda abruptly stopped eating with his spoon halfway to his mouth and looked at Alan in disbelief. "It's absolutely true, I assure you."

Alan raised his hands in the air. "I know, I know, Swamiji," he said, still laughing. "It's just the look on Doug's face is priceless."

The swami's expression remained earnest and he gave me another one of his penetrating looks. "You're a perfect example of what I'm talking about, Douglas. In your short life you've suffered tremendous loss and tragedy, but you've also been extremely fortunate."

"Fortunate?" I asked, scratching the back of my head.

"Why, yes. Don't forget the money you just inherited from your uncle."

"Cousin," I corrected. Then it occurred to me that I hadn't mentioned my inheritance to the swami. I realized that Alan must have told him everything about me. I glanced over at Alan, who was now staring into his bowl of soup.

"But how could meeting Baba and getting *shaktipat* be the result of anything but good karma?" I asked.

The swami's face lit up. "My dear boy, ultimate truth transcends all our concepts of how things should or shouldn't be."

Alan looked up and nodded in agreement. "Don't worry, man. You'll get it eventually. The guru will see to that. Baba's *shakti* is relentless." He got up and gave me a pat on the back. "Gentleman, have a blessed evening."

I waited until Akhandananda had finished eating and risen to his feet before getting up myself.

"Douglas, Douglas!" scolded the swami, furrowing his brow and frowning. "You're far too young to be carrying the weight of the world on your shoulders. Stand tall! You look like the Hunchback of Notre-Dame when you slouch."

8.
IT BURNS

AFTER DINNER I RETURNED to my room. Again I found it empty. I thought my roommate might be out of town. But glancing at his *puja* altar, I saw that the line of ash I had noticed earlier on his incense burner had been dusted off. In the bathroom, I found another sign of recent activity: a tablespoon had been left on top of the toilet bowl tank. I tried to imagine what the spoon might have been used for in connection with the toilet, but nothing I could think of made any sense.

I changed into pajamas, got into bed, and read a few chapters of Baba's book, *Where Do I Go Now?* By *lights out* there was still no sign of my roommate. I tried to sleep, but couldn't. I tossed and turned in anticipation of his barging in at any moment and turning on the light. I dreaded the awkward situation of having to introduce myself from bed. I thought again about the strangeness of the *arati* ritual in the temple and I became increasingly restless.

After an hour or so of sleeplessness, I tried to turn my mind toward the teachings. I remembered something

Baba had said in one of his videos: "A practitioner of Raja Yoga should repeat the *Om Namah Shivaya* mantra silently to himself while waiting for sleep to come." But even after following the guru's instructions, repeating the mantra for God knows how long, I still couldn't get any rest. I managed to stop thinking about the *arati*, but I was unable to put out of my head the other sights and sounds I had experienced during the day. I thought about the angel, Gopi: *Is she new to Raja Yoga like me?* I wondered. *Or did she grow up around Baba? If so, is she still a virgin?* I pictured her taking her clothes off.

I started to get turned on, and wanted to do something about it. Then it occurred to me that masturbation was undoubtedly against the ashram rules, even if it didn't explicitly say so in the pamphlet I received. To distract myself from impure thoughts, I decided I was better off worrying about the *arati* again. I replayed the scene of it in my mind a few more times and, after more deliberation, I decided it was a harmless ritual. I was simply too new to Raja Yoga to appreciate its significance. I drifted off to sleep.

I'm in Lake View Cemetery with Mike McFadden, Elisabeth Jensen, and other friends. It's snowing and we are passing a bottle of Cold Duck around. It is twilight. The snow is deep and covers most of the grave markers. Within the walls of the Cornell family mausoleum, my friends and their parents are now waving arati lamps at a life-like statue of the university founder, Ezra Cornell. Some of them carry stacks of cash on trays which they lay at the statue's feet as offerings. Just then, the angel Gopi appears like a spirit. In her hands she holds a large brown paper bag. She tilts the bag toward me so that I can see what's inside. It's full of bagels. I hold out my hands and she places a bagel in them. I hesitate before eating it and begin to caress the bread. It is smooth and yielding to the touch and I become sexually aroused. Suddenly, a large snake springs out of the bag like a jack-in-the box and inserts its head into the hole of my bagel. My sexual tension mounts as I watch the snake thrust its head in and out of the bagel hole. I look up at the angel, who is closing her eyes and puckering her lips in anticipation. I lean toward her, but before I can kiss her, she dissolves into radiant white light and I explode in orgasm.

"Five A.M. Time to wake up. Meditation starts in ten minutes."

An overhead light stung my eyes. I had no idea where I was. When my eyes finally adjusted to the light, I saw a red-faced older man with beady eyes and a pug nose staring down at me. "You have to get up now," he said. The man noisily let himself out of the room and slammed the door behind him.

I hesitantly reached down and felt my underwear. It was sticky and wet. A tingling swept up the back of my neck and across my face. I was mortified and angry with myself. I immediately remembered something Baba had said in one of his books: "The sins committed in the world are washed away at an ashram. But those committed in the house of the Guru cling stubbornly. They are difficult to cleanse."

I was full of shame: *How could I have let this happen?* Since becoming serious about Raja Yoga, I had rarely allowed myself to have any sexual thoughts or feelings at all. This accomplishment, along with the meditation, mantra repetition, and mind training I had been practicing made me feel good about myself. I had been learning self-control and making steady progress on the path, preparing myself to receive *shaktipat*. I considered this a huge setback. From my point of view, I had debased myself, and worse, I had defiled Baba's home. I had been there less than twenty-four hours, but had already committed a sin that might take me the rest of my life to wash away. I prayed to Baba for forgiveness.

I wanted desperately to shower, but there wasn't any time. I hastily cleaned myself off in the bathroom, and changed my underwear. I threw on the sweat suit I normally used for meditation at home, grabbed my *asana*, and rushed to the meditation hall at the other end of the ashram complex. On my way, I passed other ashramites quietly locking their bedroom doors behind them and heading in the same direction.

To get to the meditation hall, I passed through a long windowed corridor. The sun had not come up yet, and the ashram grounds were dark. But the Brahmananda temple was lit up, and I could make out the silhouette of Gurudev's statue within it.

"The statue is alive," I remembered Akhandananda saying. "He knows you're here." *Does Gurudev also know that I just polluted myself and his ashram?* I felt wretched. I prayed to Gurudev to help me to develop self-control and become worthy of living in such a pure, holy place.

To the left of the doors to the meditation hall was an alcove with a huge shoe rack. A sign on the wall said: "Leave your ego with your shoes."

The gigantic, windowless, high-ceilinged hall was majestic, with crystal chandeliers and tiers of sumptuous pale blue carpeting. An aisle down the middle divided the men's from the women's side, and led to a dais holding a throne-like armchair. A large framed portrait of Baba was propped up in it as a surrogate for the guru himself. Above the throne, suspended from the ceiling, was an enormous black and white photograph of a loincloth-clad Gurudev Brahmananda, eyes half closed, seated in the lotus position, absorbed in the supreme state of oneness with the Absolute. On the walls of the hall were large framed photographs of the Indian saints and sages encountered by Baba during his many years of wondering, before he had come to settle down at the feet of his guru in Ravipur. The *shakti* was palpable everywhere in Baba's ashram, but here it was strongest. I had entered the spiritual epicenter of the ashram and was full of reverence.

Down front, close to Baba's throne, a handful of ashramites were seated in perfect meditation posture with ramrod-straight backs. I found a spot toward the back of the group, on the men's side. A harmonium was positioned near the front on the woman's side, but no one was seated behind it. I looked at a clock on the wall. The session would begin in just a couple of minutes.

Although the hall was dimly lit, I could see Akhandananda sitting up front, directly to the right of Baba's throne.

His legs were tucked in under his swami's robes and he was gazing up at Baba's photo in earnest contemplation. I tried to keep my attention on Baba's picture too, but it was hopeless. Despite having already determined that she was not among them, my eyes continually scanned the female meditators seated on the other side of the aisle, in search of my angel. Every time one of the doors opened in the back of the hall, my hope of seeing her was renewed.

As I looked around at the others, it did not escape my notice that I was still the only person wearing a name tag. Sita, who had been wearing a name tag when I reported to *seva* yesterday, was now without one. Just then, the man sitting in front of me shot his arm backwards in my direction, making me start. Then, using the floor for support, he pivoted his body and neck all the way around until he appeared to be looking straight at me. As it happened, the man was my roommate. At first I thought he had turned around to say hello. Then I realized he was doing some kind of *Hatha Yoga* stretch.

Would it cost him something to say good morning or to acknowledge me in some way? I mused. Suddenly, my face, neck, and ears felt impossibly hot, and I thought I would die of embarrassment. I was afraid he might have heard me talk or, God forbid, moan in my sleep. My chest tightened and my breathing quickened.

Maybe he knew I had a wet dream and was disgusted with me. I wanted to disappear into the floor. *If he reports me to Akhandananda or Alan, they might ask me to leave the ashram. Then I'll never meet Baba!*

Regardless of whether my roommate knew about my erotic dream or not, I decided there was nothing I could do to change his perception of me. I resolved to do my best to focus on the mantra during meditation. I would not allow myself to worry about what someone else might or might not be thinking about me.

At five twenty-eight, one of the doors in the back of the hall opened, and a young woman wearing baggy clothes and glasses with her hair pulled back into a tight ponytail walked through. She plodded down the center aisle, spread her *asana* on the floor in front of the harmonium and took a seat. Now that she was closer, I could see that on her forehead was a dot of red kumkum powder, just like Baba's. Draped around her shoulders was a woolen shawl the same shade of orange worn by the Raja Yoga swamis. *What a wannabe!* I thought.

Sitting quietly like everyone else, the gawky-looking girl seemed to be glancing around the darkened hall, perhaps to see who was there. When she noticed I was observing her she seemed taken aback, and arched a single eyebrow at me. Then she turned away and looked solemnly at the photograph of Baba on the throne. A few seconds later she cleared her throat, played a sustained note on the harmonium, and led everyone in a few slow rounds of *Om Namah Shivaya*.

When the chant ended, the lights dimmed until the only light in the hall came from the flickering votive candles on the altars. I assumed the meditation posture I had learned back in Ithaca: legs crossed Indian style, spine erect, stomach in, shoulders back, chin parallel to the floor. My hands, with palms upturned, resting on my legs at the juncture of my thighs and abdominal region. Then I squeezed my eyes shut and continued to repeat the mantra silently to myself.

Om Namah Shivaya. Om Namah Shivaya. Om Namah Shivaya. Om Namah Shivaya. Am I meditating? Om Namah Shivaya. Yes, this is meditating. Om Namah Shivaya. What is thought? Om Namah Shivaya. Om Namah Shivaya. Is thought the same as sound? Am I actually hearing the sounds in my mind? Focus on the mantra. Om Namah Shivaya. Om Namah Shivaya. I have to pee. Om Namah Shivaya. A snake fucking a bagel? Does Baba know our dreams? Where is that angel? Probably sleeping. Didn't see Alan either. Om Namah Shivaya. At least I have enough discipline to make it to morning meditation. Unlike certain old-timers. How long has it been? I wonder what's for breakfast. My legs hurt. Will anyone notice if I change position? I definitely should have gone to the bathroom. Why isn't anything happening?

I wonder how I would look with a shaved head? Shit! I forgot about the mantra! Om Namah Shivaya. Om Namah Shivaya. How much longer do I have to sit here? I have to pee!

Suddenly, my meditation was interrupted by a loud bird sound: *"Brawkk-AWK!! Brawkk-AWK!!"*

At first I thought a chicken had gotten into the meditation hall, or that somebody had gone berserk. Then I remembered reading about this phenomenon. In yogic terms, the sound I was hearing was a manifestation of *kundalini* awakening called a *kriya*. Back in Ithaca, Robert Cargill had told me that after receiving *shaktipat* from Baba, devotees had all kinds of intense spiritual experiences: they saw lights, had visions, attained exalted states of consciousness, and also had these *kriyas*—spontaneous vocalizations and bodily movements of all kinds.

"Brawkk-AWK!!" Someone made the bird sound again. A moment later, a meditator on the women's side began weeping. *How can anybody meditate around here with all these distractions?*

Om Namah Shivaya. Om Namah Shivaya.

Someone else now: *"Hee-haw! Hee-haw!"*

"Brawkk-AWK!!"

Hee-haw! Hee-haw!"

It was hopeless. I opened my eyes. The man sitting next to me was trembling and shaking his head rapidly from side to side. Someone else was muttering what sounded like obscenities in a foreign language.

Since I couldn't get into meditation, I decided I might as well check to see if the angel was in the hall. It was harder to see now because the room was darker, but I was pretty sure she was not among the small group of female meditators. Just then, light spilled into the hall for a moment and then was gone. A latecomer had slipped through a side entrance near the throne. The latecomer was Gopi! I could barely contain my glee. Although I didn't know her, I already felt as though the angel and I had a deep connection. We had probably been husband and wife in a previous life.

In case she looked in my direction, I squeezed my eyes shut again and pretended to be deep in meditation. Two seconds later, unable to resist the urge to look again, I opened my eyes a crack to see Gopi spreading her *asana* on the floor all the way up front next to Baba's throne, directly across from Akhandananda. Sitting down, she formed a perfect X with her legs, then gently placed her hands palms-up on her thighs, curling her index fingers and thumbs so that they touched at the tips.

I tried to meditate for a little while, but then gave up again. Instead I watched Gopi meditate. While everyone else around me seemed to twitch or change the position of their legs from time to time, Gopi never made the slightest move. I was certain that, unlike me, her meditations were deep and silent. By now, she was probably already absorbed in *samadhi*. Her profound serenity was beautiful to behold. I wondered if I would ever attain such a lofty state of consciousness.

After wasting most of the meditation session looking around the room and admiring the angel, I redoubled my efforts to focus on the *mantra*, but I still couldn't get into meditation.

Just when I was about to give up, a sustained note sounded, and the odd woman on the harmonium led us in another few slow rounds of the *Om Namah Shivaya* chant. The chandeliers gradually got brighter and the chanting came to an end. When I got up to stretch my legs I noticed something I never would have expected: despite how distracted I had been, and the randomness of my thoughts during meditation, my mind was still. Stiller than usual, anyway. I felt relaxed and peaceful.

I looked across the aisle at Gopi. She was dressed in a stylish gray sweat suit, her long flaxen hair was tied up neatly in a bun. I tried to catch her eye, but it was useless. Her attention was directed within.

There was a fifteen-minute break between the meditation session and the start of the *Guru Gita*. Leaving my *asana* on the floor, I followed the others into the cafeteria where we observed silence and drank sweet, milky tea from colored plastic cups. It was hard for me to believe that it was still pitch black outside, as I had already been up for over an hour. I relished the peaceful stillness as the hot delicious chai gently stimulated my nervous system.

At precisely six-twenty, everybody got up at the same time, like a flock of birds, and bussed their cups to the dirty dishes station. We hurried back to the meditation hall, where we would spend the next hour and a half chanting the *Guru Gita*. The recitation of this text always felt tedious, but I gave it my full attention. I knew that this chant, in particular, was essential to my spiritual development.

After nearly forty minutes of sitting in the half lotus position, my legs began to ache. I looked around the room to see if anyone else was having difficulty sitting for so long. Everyone else looked perfectly comfortable, like they had practiced sitting that way for years. The same weird woman in the baggy clothes with kumkum on her forehead was behind the harmonium again. She had a powerful singing voice and was definitely the leader of the chant.

The Guru, who is the father, mother, family and Divine Light of devotees, bestows realization of the limitations of worldly existence. Salutations to the Guru.

I glanced across the aisle at the angel Gopi. She held a chanting book in her hands, but didn't seem to be using it. Her eyes were fixed on Baba's portrait. She appeared to be reciting the entire Sanskrit text from memory.

Salutations to the Guru, whose existence brings truth to all beings, through whose form the Divine light—like the light of the sun—shines on everyone, and in whose unconditional love we come to love our family and all beings more and more.

I couldn't tell for sure, but it looked like there were tears in Gopi's eyes. *She is the perfect disciple,* I thought. *The embodiment of purity and devotion, a celestial being in human form.*

Returning my attention to the chant, I soon became acutely aware that my legs hurt. Unable to bear the discomfort a second longer, I shifted position, drawing my legs up and my knees together.

A couple of minutes later I took another break from the chant. Holding my chanting book closer to my face, I pretended to mouth the words while I glanced around the hall. Alan was there now, along with other ashramites who hadn't come for morning meditation. I was disappointed in the ashram manager. *Swami candidate indeed!* I thought. Was I supposed to believe he was meditating in the privacy of his room? Despite my disappointment at Alan's lack of discipline, I still admired him. He had given up a lucrative career as a lawyer, turning his back on the world in order to devote his life to serving the guru. Like all of Baba's devotees who had chosen to live in the ashram, he didn't need a prestigious career to feel successful or material possessions to be happy.

What a relief it was finally to immerse myself in the austere routine of ashram life. I was no longer weighed down by the burden of thinking I had to achieve anything in a worldly sense. Never again would I have to worry about getting a college degree, choosing a career path, or making money. Thanks to Baba, never again would I become the victim of my own ego. After a few years of *sadhana*, enlightenment and eternal bliss would be my reward. And who knew? If Baba willed it, maybe someday I would also become a guru and have my own disciples. I would serve in any way He commanded.

On the breakfast line, the ashramites were again chanting "*Shree Ram Jai Ram,*" and this time I sang along. First I was served a bowl of piping hot porridge that resembled oatmeal, with tiny specks of green vegetables and what looked like chopped onions.

"Nutritional yeast?" the next server asked, offering to sprinkle a heaping tablespoon of bright yellow flakes on top of my porridge.

Yeast? How disgusting, I thought. "Um, yeah, sure."

I recognized the next server. It was the harmonium player with the powerful singing voice from the meditation hall. Even now she was chanting "*Shree Ram Jai Ram*" louder than anybody else. In the bright light of the cafeteria, I could see she had dark red hair and a pallid complexion. Her big round brown eyes monitored the line from behind a pair of horn-rimmed glasses that were held together on one hinge by a strip of electric tape. She wore no makeup except for the smeared, bright red dot of kumkum on her forehead.

"Bitter melon?" she asked, taking a momentary break from the chant. She pointed down to a bowl of jagged, pale green squash in front of her.

"Sounds delicious."

The harmonium player smiled approvingly and scooped a little of the mysterious green vegetable into one of the compartments on my tray. She was wearing a name tag with an orange sticker. It said, "Kriyadevi."

Brilliant sunlight streamed in through the large windows of the cafeteria, but the blinding glare of the snow made it hard to appreciate the view. I looked around for a place to sit. I didn't see Akhandananda or Alan anywhere, so I found an empty table in the back and sat down by myself.

What looked like oatmeal turned out to be a savory blend of grains, onions, coconut, ginger, cilantro, and some spices I didn't recognize. The nutritional yeast was also surprisingly tasty. The so-called bitter melon went well with it too.

"Hey, man." I looked up to see a groggy Madhu in front of me. His bulky flannel shirt was wrinkled and his hair disheveled. He sat down across from me and began shoveling the savory cereal into his mouth, staring down at his food as he ate. Then, with what seemed like a great effort, he glanced up at me.

"Uh—it's Dave, right?"

"Doug," I corrected. "Well, not for very much longer. I'm going to ask Baba for a spiritual name when I meet him next month."

"Cool," Madhu said, yawning.

"I didn't see you at meditation this morning. Or at the *Guru Gita.*"

Madhu stiffened. "Did you need me for something?" His mouth formed a straight, thin line.

"Need you? Um, uh, no. I didn't need you for anything. Doesn't everyone have to go? Isn't that the ashram rule?"

Madhu rolled his eyes. Then he cleared his throat. "They're more like guidelines. Believe me—I know—I've been around Baba since I was a little kid."

I changed the subject. "Your mom's still in India, isn't she? What does she do in the ashram?"

"Kamala? Yeah, she's in Ravipur with Baba. She's the Prasad manager."

I remembered learning the word *Prasad* yesterday from Akhandananda. "They need someone to manage the rosewater?"

Madhu let out a guffaw. "That's a good one!"

I bristled. I didn't like being laughed at. "What's so funny?"

"Sorry, man," Madhu said, stifling another laugh. "*Prasad* just means something that you can eat or drink that's been blessed by the guru—usually something sweet or delicious. It's the guru's grace in physical form. They named the ashram café after it. There's one in all of Baba's ashrams."

"Why does the ashram need a café?"

Madhu glanced around furtively to see if anyone was listening. "Rich people."

"Pardon?"

"Prasad is for rich people," he answered. "The ones who visit the ashram in the summer when Baba's here, or for the staff and tour people who can afford it. During his last visit, Prasad grossed over half a million dollars."

I didn't like what I was hearing and got a heavy feeling in my gut. Madhu was making the ashram sound like a business.

"And of course, The Mission doesn't pay any taxes on that."

"Why would anybody on Baba's staff want to eat in a café when the cafeteria food is so good?"

"Believe me, if you're here long enough, you'll get sick of eating this stuff every day, too."

Out of the corner of my eye I caught a glimpse of blonde hair and a gray sweat suit. I turned to see the angel Gopi carrying a tray in search of a table. Her posture, as it had been earlier during meditation and the chant, was perfect. So was her ass. My eyes followed her as she made her way toward the back of the dining room.

"Forget about her, man," said Madhu, chuckling.

"Forget about who?"

"You know who I'm talking about," Madhu said, gesturing toward the back of the cafeteria with his chin. "That's Gopi Defournier—Raja Yoga royalty. She's off limits."

I didn't know what Madhu meant by Raja Yoga royalty, but I interpreted his words as a warning from the guru himself. The angel was *off limits*. I had to do my best to forget not only about this girl but about all girls, if there was any hope of my attaining God-realization in a single lifetime.

Just then, Kriyadevi, the harmonium player, sat down next to Madhu and poked him in the ribs. "Who let you back in the ashram?" she asked with a straight face.

"Ow! Quit it!" he said, flinching. Kriyadevi bared her teeth and poked him again. I couldn't tell if she was fooling around or not.

Turning to me, Kriyadevi pointed at a spice shaker containing a deep orange powder on the next table. "Could you pass me the cayenne please?"

I passed the spice to Kriyadevi and then watched her dump a ton of it on her porridge. I took a better look at her. I guessed she was about three or four years older than me. Her clothes looked like they came from the Salvation Army.

"So, what are you two talking about?" she asked, glaring at Madhu. "Sharing divine stories of time spent in India in the presence of our beloved guru?"

Madhu sighed heavily for effect, picked up his tray and stood up abruptly. Then he took a pair of dark sunglasses out of his breast pocket and slid them on. "I will see *you* in twenty," he said, pointing to me. I looked at a clock on the wall. It was eight forty-five—morning *seva* started at nine.

Then he playfully jabbed Kriyadevi in the ribs and bussed his tray to the dirty dishes station.

Kriyadevi looked deeply into my eyes, and then glanced down at my name tag. "I feel like I know you, Doug."

I felt exposed again and swallowed. "You mean you're having an experience of déjà vu or something?"

She smiled. "No, it's because you look so much like Shree Ram."

"You know my brother!" I suddenly felt lighter.

"Of course I know Shree Ram," she said, smiling even wider. "When I first saw you in the hall this morning I thought you were him. What's his wife's name again? Wait—don't tell me."

"Carrie."

"Anshika! That's it! Anshika and Shree Ram Greenbaum. How are they?"

"Great! My brother just got an internship at NYU Medical Center in Manhattan. So they'll be up often to see Baba this spring."

Kriyadevi closed her eyes gently, then opened them again and smiled serenely. "I'm so happy. I told them not to worry. I told them Baba's *shakti* would take care of everything, and it did!"

I picked up the spice shaker and was about to add some cayenne to my porridge when Kriyadevi suddenly looked alarmed.

"Careful! It's incredibly hot."

I sprinkled a tiny bit on my porridge and then tasted it, burning my tongue. "I see what you mean."

"So, what brings you to the ashram?" she asked, picking up the shaker and adding even more of the chili pepper.

"I want to know God."

Kriyadevi's big round eyes shone with delight. "Then you've come to precisely the right place! No one can give you a direct experience of the divine faster than a *shaktipat guru*." Then her expression suddenly changed and she looked deadly serious, like an actress in a daytime television melodrama. "But be forewarned, Doug—it burns."

"Burns?" I asked, eyeing her orange-tinged porridge. "What burns?"

"Raja Yoga is not for the faint-hearted. Of course, it's full of many blissful moments spent in the company of the guru, but in order to know God, the ego must be annihilated. All your precious ideas about what you think you know about yourself, the world, and even the guru, must burn in the fire of *sadhana*."

My neck began to hurt and I reached back to massage it. "Um, okay."

"Remember, the ashram is an extension of the guru's mind and body—his *shakti*. You either learn to surrender to the *shakti* or get burned to ashes in the process. That's *sadhana*, Doug. Your *sadhana* encompasses everything that happens to you, even the necessity of putting up with schmucks like Madhu."

I was taken aback by Kriyadevi's vulgar language. Was it okay to use a word like "schmuck" in the ashram?

Kriyadevi screwed her eyes shut and her face contorted, as if in pain. A moment later she began to sing: "*Guru charan kamal balihari re.*"

She sang so loudly that some people at the table in front of us turned around to see what was going on. The melody was sad, and conveyed a feeling of deep yearning.

"That was beautiful," I said. "What does it mean?"

"I offer myself to the guru's lotus feet. Through his grace duality has disappeared from my mind."

I ate another spoonful of the savory porridge. "I heard you playing the harmonium this morning. You're really talented. Is that your main *seva*?"

Kriyadevi finished off her breakfast and drank down the rest of her chai. "*Main seva*? All *seva* is of equal importance, but I spend most of my time in the Audiovisual department. I'm the video editor."

I thought about how amazing it would be to watch film clips of Baba all day. "Lucky you!"

"I also do sound when Baba's in Birchwood Falls—I haven't been on tour yet." Kriyadevi wiped her mouth with a paper napkin, and then turned to look up at the clock on the wall. "Arjuna Weinberg—the cameraman—is in India with Baba right now getting amazing material. He travels with Baba wherever he goes."

"How can I get a *seva* like that?"

Kriyadevi frowned at me, arched an eyebrow, and then stood up. "The savory porridge—it's good with the bitter melon, isn't it?"

"Delicious," I answered, wondering if I had said something inappropriate.

Kriyadevi bussed her tray, and bounded out of the cafeteria with her shoulders back and her chin held high.

9.
Gossip

AFTER BREAKFAST I HURRIED back to change in my room. My roommate was in the bathroom. I didn't hear the shower running and wondered if he might be using the spoon he kept on top of the toilet tank for something. On the dresser next to his bunk was a large ring of keys and a walkie-talkie. Just as I started to take off my sweatpants, the walkie-talkie squawked and made me jump.

"Come in Shivadas. This is Mukti. Do you read me?" I changed into my clothes and the walkie-talkie squawked again. "Come in Shivadas. Do you read me? We have a breach. Over."

The toilet flushed and my roommate stepped out of the bathroom. His brow was wrinkled and his lips were pressed flat. He greeted me with a once over and a curt nod, and then strode to the dresser and picked up the walkie-talkie. "Copy that, Mukti. This is Shivadas. Over." Clipped to his shirt was a plastic badge that said "Security."

"Oh Shivadas, thank Baba you're there! The cross-country skiers are back."

My roommate's eyes widened and his face turned red with anger. "Copy that Mukti, I'll take care of it." Grabbing his key ring, Shivadas stomped over to the door, yanked it open, and slammed it behind him.

Although Baba wasn't arriving until the end of March, work was already in full swing to receive the huge influx of visitors expected to arrive along with him—this year more than ever before. My *seva* assignment was to help Madhu haul newly delivered foam mattresses off the loading dock to the opposite end of the complex, where the dormitories were located. We were told to replace only those that were falling apart.

The mattresses weren't heavy or difficult to carry. What made the job take so long was the sheer number of them.

"If they would only buy better quality mattresses to begin with, we wouldn't have to waste our time replacing them," said Madhu flinging old, half-disintegrated mattresses into the back of a pickup truck. Despite the bright sunshine, it was freezing cold, and neither of us had thought to wear our coats.

On the way to the dump, Madhu suggested we stop off at McDonald's to get some lunch. At first I thought he was joking. "What are we going to eat there, the French fries?"

Madhu shrugged, and then pulled into the drive-through. He ordered a Quarter Pounder with cheese. I was secretly appalled and wondered what Baba would think of Madhu's non-vegetarian meal. I stuck to fries and a milkshake.

In the afternoon, Madhu and I moved furniture. Sita explained that a lot of Raja Yoga VIPs would be traveling from India with Baba, and that the furniture in their rooms needed to be in the best condition possible.

We struggled to lift a heavy oak dresser up a flight of stairs. "What's a Raja Yoga VIP, anyway?" I asked Madhu when Sita was gone. "Like a swami?"

Madhu snorted. "Some of them are VIPs, I guess. She means the tour staff. The people that are really close to Baba."

We hauled the dresser up another flight and then halfway across the ashram. I nearly dropped my end a couple of times. By the time we arrived at our destination, Madhu and I were both dripping with sweat. As we struggled to fit the dresser through the doorway, Sita appeared out of nowhere.

"This is the wrong dresser," she snapped, tapping her foot. Her jaw was clenched, and her usually smiling face was pinched in a frown. Madhu and I carefully set the massive block of wood down. We wiped our brows with the backs of our sleeves. I was one hundred percent sure this was the dresser she had told us to move, and exchanged a knowing glance with Madhu.

"Well, since we already brought it here, can't we—"

"This one has a scratch on it," Sita said, interrupting Madhu. Then she pointed to a tiny mark on the side of the chest of drawers. "This one goes in Parvati's room, in *Devi Shayanagrih*, next to Baba's house."

Madhu glared at Sita. "But that's where we got it from! Anyway, what difference does it make? The scratched side will be up against the wall."

Sita placed her fists on her hips. "Bring it back to Parvati's room. Those are your instructions."

I began to doubt myself. *Maybe I misunderstood her original instructions.* I was upset that she thought I hadn't been paying attention earlier. I wanted so much to make a good impression.

Just then the door to the next room opened, and Swami Akhandananda stepped into the corridor. He had a few books under his arm. He glanced at Madhu who was fuming, and then at me. "Everything alright?" the neckless swami asked, tilting his head to the side.

Sita stiffened and folded her arms across her chest. "Let me handle this, Swamiji."

Akhandananda lowered his chin to his chest and raised his free hand in the air. Then he turned to leave, slowly shuffling his feet as he disappeared around a corner.

"Look, it's no problem, Sita," I said. "We'll bring it back to Parvati's room. Sorry for the misunderstanding."

"Thank you, Doug," the *seva* manager said, beaming at me with approval. "Madhu, you should try to learn something from your new friend here. Doug has only been in the ashram a couple of days and already he has *right understanding*."

Sita frequently asked Madhu and me to lug extremely heavy objects from one end of the ashram to the other, only to tell us later to bring them back to where they came from, or to somewhere else. Sometimes I suspected her of doing it on purpose, for some reason I couldn't fathom. One thing was certain: she was quickly making an enemy out of Madhu. Once, he complained to Alan about her. The next day, Sita assigned Madhu the extra *seva* of keeping the temple path cleared of snow and ice. I volunteered to do it instead of him, but Sita insisted it was now Madhu's responsibility.

One morning, when Sita made us return a heavy desk to the basement after we had carried it all the way upstairs, Madhu decided that we should conduct an experiment: the next time she asked to us to move a piece of furniture somewhere, we would leave it where it was. At first, I didn't want go along with the idea. It didn't strike me as the kind of behavior that Baba would approve of, and I thought it went against the spirit of selfless service. But late one afternoon, after a particularly grueling day, when Sita asked us to move a solid oak bookcase from the basement up to the swami library on the third floor, I gave in. We left the bookcase where it was.

Later after *seva*, when Madhu and I were waiting in line for dinner, I saw a visibly agitated Sita coming out of Alan's office and heading straight toward us. I dreaded this moment.

"Now we're in trouble," I said.

Madhu discreetly elbowed me in the side. "Relax."

"Boys," Sita said, thrusting her chest out. "Tomorrow morning, I need you to take that bookcase back downstairs to storage."

"Oh-kay," said Madhu, sighing heavily for effect. The second she was out of sight, the two of us burst out laughing.

"Now the trick is to see how many times we can get away without doing anything before something actually needs to get moved!" Madhu said.

Just then, someone cleared their throat behind us. I turned around and my face burned with embarrassment. Swami Akhandananda was standing directly behind me.

"Douglas, I'd like to have a word with you," the swami said. He rolled his eyes toward Madhu. "Privately."

After we got our food, I followed Akhandananda to an empty table in the back of the cafeteria. "Douglas, have you ever heard of the spiritual master, Gurdjieff?"

"Um, no."

Akhandananda raised a spoonful of hot soup to his mouth and blew. "Georges Ivanovitch Gurdjieff was an enlightened being who was born in Armenia. About forty years ago, toward the end of his life, he established an institute, much like an ashram, in France. Like the teaching methods of many great masters, Gurdjieff's were difficult for ordinary people like you and me to understand."

The soup was still too hot for me, so I dunked a piece of bread in it, letting it cool a while before trying to eat it. "Like what?"

"He was notorious for putting his most annoying student in charge of his institute when he was away. Later, when he returned, he'd reward her in front of all his other students for her obnoxious behavior." The swami paused for a moment and looked at me, as if he were expecting me to comment. But I had no idea where he was going with this story and how it related to me.

"On one occasion, Gurdjieff asked a new student who had only recently joined his movement to dig a ditch on the grounds of his institute, only later to have another student fill it in."

"What was the point of that?"

"This was Gurdjieff's way of teaching his disciples to drop their egos and to let go. It was his way of teaching them how to perform their *seva* with *right understanding*."

"*Right understanding*—I've heard that expression a lot since I've come to the ashram. What does it mean, Swamiji?"

"*Right understanding* is another way of saying, *right attitude*. All service selflessly rendered to the guru is of equal importance. It's not for us to question the usefulness or logic of what we're being asked to do. When we feel resistance to what is being asked of us, it's a clear indication that the guru is working on our precious egos."

"Yes, but Sita is *not* the guru," I protested.

The swami smiled knowingly. "Isn't she?"

"But—"

"In the ashram, the guru's *shakti* works relentlessly through everyone and everything to cleanse us of our negative karma and to free us from the traps set by our own minds."

"I think I understand what you mean, Swamiji." My soup had cooled down enough for me to eat. It didn't taste good, but I knew it was good for me.

"Baba often tells the story of the great Tibetan Yogi, Milarepa. I think you might appreciate it. Milarepa had been searching for a teacher for many years. When he finally met his guru Marpa, he didn't immediately receive *shaktipat*. Instead, Marpa put his new disciple to work doing manual labor. Determined to be a model disciple, Milarepa performed his *seva* willingly and without any complaints. However, every time Milarepa would complete a task, he'd ask Marpa for initiation. This would send Marpa into a rage. He'd beat his new disciple and then assign him a new chore.

Among the tasks that Marpa asked Milarepa to do was to build him a tower. As soon as construction of the tower was nearly completed, however, Marpa commanded Milarepa to tear it down and to rebuild it elsewhere. Milarepa faithfully did what his guru asked of him, but once again, just as he was about to complete the second tower, Marpa made him knock it down again. Marpa ordered Milarepa to build and destroy many towers, but Milarepa never complained." The swami finished his soup.

"I think I understand," I said. "It was all some kind of test."

The swami buttered his bread. "Correct."

"He wanted to see if Milarepa was willing to let go of his concepts of how things should be and place his trust in him."

The swami licked his lips and batted his eyelashes at me. "Precisely, my boy! In Raja Yoga, we call letting go like this *surrender*. Baba says we should understand Marpa's harshness toward his disciple as a method of burning away all the evil karma Milarepa had created in his past."

"Did Marpa eventually give Milarepa *shaktipat*?"

"Of course! As soon as Milarepa became worthy. How easy Baba makes it for us—all *we* have to do is take the *shaktipat* retreat!" The swami giggled with delight and I laughed too. "Baba says we can learn a lot from the life of this great yogi. Never once while he was building and tearing down all those towers did Milarepa complain about his *seva* or question his guru. After that, Milarepa lived in a cave for the rest of his life, devoting himself to spiritual practice."

I felt full of gratitude and respect for the senior swami. "I think I understand why you told me these stories. I want you to know I'm very thankful for your guidance."

Akhandananda patted my arm affectionately. "Sometimes it's hard to understand everything that goes on in Baba's ashrams, my boy. But never forget, everything that happens to us contains a message from the guru. A big part of our *sadhana* is learning how to listen."

"I understand, Swamiji. I *am* listening."

Akhandananda got up to bus his tray and I followed. "Oh, and one more thing, Douglas," the swami said, turning over his tray and dumping a piece of uneaten bread into the garbage. "Beware the dangers of what Baba calls *bad company*. Not everyone you meet in the ashram has right understanding. Or pure intentions."

The weeks leading up to Baba's arrival passed quickly. My spiritual practice intensified, and my dedication to serving the guru became stronger. In addition to my *seva* with Madhu in Housing, I voluntarily took on extra work. Instead of going to morning meditation some days, I chopped vegetables in the kitchen. After meals, I worked shifts in the dish room, and swept and mopped the dining room floor.

"You're becoming a real pro with that screw gun," Madhu said, passing me a two-by-four. We were assembling our last bunk bed for the morning and were about to quit for lunch. "When you first got here, I'm pretty sure you didn't know what a hammer was."

"Ha, ha." The power tool made a loud grinding noise, encountering some resistance in the wood.

"Hey!" Madhu called over the sound of gun. "Hey!"

I released my finger from the on/off switch and turned to Madhu. "What's up?"

"I'm in the mood for a veggie burger. I'm going to eat lunch at Prasad today. Want to come?"

I thought about it. On principle, I hadn't yet visited the ashram café. *I'm a renunciant,* I told myself. *The cafeteria food should be enough for me.* "I don't know—"

"Come on, even Baba doesn't eat the cafeteria food."

I didn't care for Madhu's irreverent comment about the guru's eating habits, but was curious to see the place. I had only glanced through the windows a couple of times. "Veggie burger, huh?"

"They're nothing like the real thing, of course," Madhu said. "But they're not bad."

We locked up the room we'd been working in and I followed Madhu to Prasad, which was located off the reception area and the cafeteria. I couldn't understand how Madhu, who'd grown up in Raja Yoga, had developed a taste for real hamburgers.

The café didn't bear any resemblance to the dining hall. The tables and chairs were made of teak wood, display cases were filled with an array of appetizing vegetarian sandwiches and baked goods, and a blackboard hanging from the ceiling listed the day's specials. On the wall behind the counters was a mural of palatial structures set amidst fountains, temples, palm trees, and lush, meticulously landscaped gardens. The painting was of Baba's home in India—the Ravipur ashram:

From behind the counter, a fresh faced, wholesome young woman wearing a floaty blouse and a paisley scarf tied around her head took our order. Madhu and I both asked for veggie burgers. For dessert we got sweet yogurt drinks called *lassis*. When our orders were ready, Madhu led me to the far end of Prasad and through a big sliding glass door, where we sat down at a long butcher-block table. On the wall above was a humorous photograph of Baba in the ashram kitchen. He was wearing a big chef's hat and posed in front of an industrial-size pot, with his arms around an attractive Western couple. The man was dressed in paint-splattered overalls and the woman was decked out in a vibrant blue and orange sari.

My veggie burger was topped with grilled onions, tomatoes, crisp lettuce, and a pickle. I took a bite and flavor exploded in my mouth. I decided I needed to start eating at Prasad more often.

"Who's that couple in the photo with Baba?"

Madhu turned to look at the big picture hanging on the wall. "Oh, that's Chamundi and Daniel Groza," he said through a mouthful of food. "She's Baba's personal cook and he's the head of the construction crew. Daniel's also a pretty good singer and guitarist. He wrote a few songs about Baba and he sings the *Guru Gita* in English. They sell his music on cassette in the ashram bookstore."

"What is this room? Why is it closed off from the rest of Prasad?"

"It's the VIP room."

I suddenly felt self-conscious. "Are you sure it's okay we're in here?"

"It's fine."

I wasn't so sure. It felt like we were on display, behind the glass sliding doors.

"Do you see anyone else more important than us around here at the moment?"

I forced a smile. "Why does the ashram even have a VIP room? Doesn't labeling certain people more important than others only puff up their egos and contribute to delusion?"

Madhu shrugged. "I don't know. I never really thought about it." Then his eyes lit up like he was remembering something. "Hey, you know the black guy, Alan Jones?"

"The manager?"

Madhu nodded, swallowed. Then he smirked. "Right, the *manager*. Do you know how he got the job?"

"No, but it sounds like you're going to tell me."

"Gajendra Williams—the *real* manager—got fired. Thrown out of the ashram."

"Why?"

Madhu smiled, with a spark in his eye. "Embezzlement."

"What are you talking about?"

"Stole a small fortune from The Mission. They say that what he didn't spend on Armani suits and expensive restaurants in the City, he locked away in a Swiss bank account. I heard they caught him stealing cash right out of the *dakshina* basket—lots of it."

I didn't know what a *dakshina* basket was, but I had the feeling the money had been meant for Baba's Mission. I got a sinking feeling and looked down at my hands. They were trembling.

Madhu looked over his shoulder for a second, and then turned back to me. An impish grin spread across his face. "You know who else got kicked out?"

Why is he telling me this? I wondered. As painful as it was to hear, I wanted to know all the facts. "Who?" I asked, my voice cracking.

"*Sergio Casto*," he whispered.

"Who's Sergio?"

"He was Baba's tour manager. Now he's no longer welcome at the ashram."

I put my burger down. "What did he do?"

Madhu leaned toward me and whispered, "Raped a sixteen-year-old girl. In his room at the Manhattan ashram."

The room seemed to close in on me. *Rape! Embezzlement! What kind of a place is this?*

"I don't believe that! How is it possible?"

Madhu shrugged. "Yeah, it's nuts," he said, matter-of-factly. "Well, I mean, it wasn't *rape* rape. Cause the girl was going along with it. What's that called?"

I thought I'd throw up. "Consensual?"

"Yeah—I mean *no*," said Madhu, scratching his nose. "Statutory! That's it. They call that *statutory* rape."

"Was he much older?"

Madhu nodded. "Oh, yeah, Sergio's old. He's like thirty or something. Anyhow, The Mission hired a good lawyer and they got him off. But he's not allowed back in the ashram—any ashram. I heard he went back to Sicily. That's where he's from."

My eyes stung and my nose started to run. "Well, if they got him off, maybe the girl was lying." I wiped my nose with my napkin.

The grin disappeared from Madhu's face. His eyes widened. "Hey, you okay, man?"

I stared down at my half-eaten veggie burger. I was unable to speak. Then Madhu said something else about Baba "cleaning house," but I was unable to listen. I stood up too quickly and felt dizzy. Leaving my food and my untouched dessert on the table, I went to the door to let myself out.

"See you later?" Madhu asked, nervously.

"Um, yeah," I muttered, sliding the glass door closed behind me. As I entered the main dining area of the café, I locked eyes with Kriyadevi, who was sitting by herself directly opposite the VIP room. She was eating a pastry.

I walked past her and she followed me with her eyes. "Doug?"

I didn't answer, continuing on my way toward the exit.

"Doug? Are you okay? ...Doug?"

I rushed back to my room and crashed on my bed. I needed to be alone. Dark thoughts about Raja Yoga swirled inside my head. I wanted to run away, but thought maybe I should talk to Swami Akhandananda first and get his perspective. Then it occurred to me that Madhu might be making everything up. The way I saw it, he was the least spiritual person in the ashram, and therefore the least credible. Why should I believe anything he said?

I only had a few minutes before I had to return to *seva*. Doubts about the ashram tormented me: *How can the divine coexist with such evil and corruption?*

I tried to stand up, but felt unsteady on my feet. I sat back down on the bed. Even if Baba had banished the embezzler and the rapist from Raja Yoga, I couldn't understand how an all-knowing and all-powerful guru could allow these things to happen in his ashram in the first place.

I took a framed picture of Baba off my altar and lay down on my bed. I held the photo above me and studied it. As always, Baba was gazing right back with infinite compassion and love. I prayed: *Oh Baba, how could there have been such bad men at your ashram? How could you not have foreseen the evil they'd do?*

From the photo, Baba spoke to me with his eyes. He was deeply sorry for the turmoil I was experiencing, but there was a message in it for me—something I needed to learn in order to progress on the path. I prayed to the guru to help me understand what that message was.

Stepping into the bathroom, I regarded my reflection in the mirror. My face was puffy and my eyes were red. My chest ached and my throat was sore. I needed to go to *seva*, but I didn't want anyone to see me like this. I desperately wanted to get back into bed and pull the covers over my head. I wanted to hide until I could figure out what to think.

I washed my face, pulled myself together, and headed to the *seva* desk to get my afternoon assignment from Sita. I dreaded seeing Madhu again. I was afraid of what he might tell me next.

I mounted the steps to the upper lobby, where I found Kriyadevi talking to Alan. Her expression was deadly serious and her body rigid. Alan also looked tense. As I drew nearer, Kriyadevi noticed me and signaled my presence to Alan with a discreet nod of her head in my direction.

"Oh, Doug," Alan said, raising a hand in the air to get my attention. Kriyadevi took off and headed down the ramp to the basement. "Could I speak to you in my office, please?"

I was afraid I had unknowingly done something wrong or that I might be in trouble for eating in the VIP room. Nervous, I followed Alan into his office.

"I have to report to *seva* in a couple of minutes," I said, glancing at a clock on the wall.

"*Seva* can wait," he said curtly.

There were two chairs in front of Alan's desk. He turned them to face each other. "Take a seat please," he said, gesturing to one. His expression was grim. We sat down and Alan stared at me for a moment before speaking.

"I hear Madhu has been telling you stories about Baba and little girls."

At first I wasn't sure if I'd heard him correctly: *Baba and little girls?* What was that supposed to mean? I was too stunned to respond.

Alan shook his head. "He's got a big mouth on him, that kid."

"What about Baba and *little girls?*" I blurted out.

Alan seemed confused by my question. Then a look of comprehension spread across his face. He closed his eyes, shook his head, and then buried his face in his hands. Looking up at me again, he asked: "What was he gossiping to you about, then?"

"He was telling me about a guy named Gajendra Williams who stole a lot of money from the ashram, and someone named Sergio Casto—Baba's tour manager—who had sex with an underage girl in the Manhattan ashram."

"I want to tell you something, Doug, and I want you to listen very carefully. Anyone who has ever tried to do something truly good in this world has been the target of this kind of character assassination."

"So the stories aren't true?" The words *Baba and little girls* were still reverberating in my head. I couldn't fathom how there could even be a *rumor* like that to begin with. Who could dream up such a horrible lie?

"If everyone were perfect when they came to the ashram, they wouldn't need to do any *sadhana*. Do you understand?"

"I guess so," I lied.

Alan let out a huge breath, smiled tentatively, and then reached for my shoulder. He gave it a weak squeeze. "Everything else okay? How's your room? Are you comfortable?"

"Um, yeah, sure. My room's okay, I guess."

Alan placed a finger on his lips and thought for a while. "Tell you what we're gonna do. We're going to give you a new *seva* assignment. How does that sound?"

It would be a relief not to have to work with Madhu anymore. Clearly he was a perfect example of what Baba would call *bad company*. "I'll serve the guru in any way I'm needed."

Alan got up and went behind his desk. Then he opened a folder and studied its contents. "How'd you like to help out in the Audiovisual department?"

I thought about watching videos of Baba all day, or carrying a light for the crew while they were filming Baba, and got excited. "That would be great!"

"You'll be working in the video library."

The idea of working in a library sounded like it might be boring, but at least I wouldn't have to schlepp furniture around all day. "I'm grateful for any opportunity to be of service."

Alan told me to take the rest of day off. He expressed regret for the "unpleasantness" I had been through. "Oh, and Doug," Alan said as I was about to let myself out. "After today, you won't have to worry about Madhu anymore."

After my talk with Alan, I went outside. Expecting to be cold without my coat, I was surprised by how unseasonably warm it was. The sun was shining and the icicles hanging from the ashram's eaves and gutters were melting. Pools of water were forming beneath them, and the snow on the ground was wet and glistening. Spring was coming soon.

I had faith that once I met Baba, any lingering doubts I might still have about the ashram would be put to rest.

With my afternoon free, I spent some time meditating in the hall. Afterward I visited the ashram bookstore. I pored over the books by Baba I hadn't read yet, and perused the back editions of *Raja Path Magazine*. I loved looking at the stunning pictures of the guru and all the glowing people surrounding him. I looked forward to the day I'd be one of them.

In many of the photographs, two beautiful Indians were at his side. One of them I recognized as Anjali Bhandary, Baba's translator. The other was a handsome, serene looking young man around my age, with the round, pleasant face of a cherub. I guessed they were Baba's closest disciples.

"Excuse me," I said to the woman behind the counter. "I was wondering if you might be able to tell me who this is?" I pointed to the handsome young man.

The woman glanced at the photo and smiled brightly. "That's Suresh Bhandary. He's Anjali's brother. He's known Baba his entire life."

I decided to buy all the back issues of *Raja Path* they had so that I could read them at night before lights out. I also bought a rudraksha bead *mala* that I could wear as a necklace and use to repeat the mantra, an intricately carved wooden incense holder, a dozen pictures of Baba and Gurudev Brahmananda, all the books by Baba I hadn't read yet, and the cassette that Madhu had told me about, of Daniel Groza singing the *Guru Gita* in English. My mouth fell open when the cashier told me how much everything cost. Then I remembered, *I'm rich now. I can buy anything I want.* I added a few more items to my purchases, and paid for everything with traveler's checks.

On my way back to my room, I looked through the large windows of the lobby and noticed a taxi parked in the driveway. I recognized the driver as the guy who had taken me from the bus station to the ashram. He was loading luggage into the trunk. Just then I noticed his passenger was Madhu. I wondered whether he was leaving voluntarily, or if Alan had kicked him out. I thought about going outside to say goodbye, but was afraid he might be angry at me for ratting him out. I moved closer to the window to get a better look. He was laughing and joking with the driver. *Maybe he's happy he's finally going to Hollywood,* I thought.

The rear wheels of the taxi spun on the ice for a few seconds, and then Madhu was on his way. I hoped they had kicked him out. It would serve him right for gossiping. Good riddance.

10.
A PRECIOUS GIFT

THE FOLLOWING MORNING, INSTEAD of reporting to Sita at the *seva* desk, I went directly to the basement and the Audiovisual department. I was warmly greeted by Jake Gooding, the department head, who was expecting me. Jake was a tall, soft-spoken man in his late forties, with kind eyes and graying hair. "Your mission, young man, is to fast-forward and to rewind all the video and audio tapes in the library."

"What's the point of that?" I asked. Then I remembered that questioning one's *seva* assignments in the ashram was frowned upon.

Jake smiled good-naturedly and took a large video cassette off one of the shelves. "Doing that every few months helps prevent creases from forming and causing permanent damage to the tapes."

He popped the cassette into an enormous tape deck, pushed *play,* and a monitor mounted on the wall above flickered on. After about ten seconds of color bars and a high-pitched tone, images appeared of a younger, darker-haired Baba meeting a group of blissed-out hippies at what looked like a farmhouse. The guru's eyes were hidden by dark sunglasses. He wore an extravagant orange knit beret with a large pom-pom, and a red plaid bathrobe over his orange silks. Dressed like that, he reminded me of a funky jazz musician.

"This is footage from Baba's first trip to America in 1970. It was filmed in sixteen-millimeter. Later we transferred it to video. As you can see, the picture quality is excellent. We want to keep it that way."

"Are there a lot of old videos of Baba like this?" I asked, marveling.

"Hours and hours," Jake answered. "But I'm afraid there's no time for you to watch them. Your job is simply to fast-forward them all until the end, and then rewind them back to the beginning again."

The camera zoomed in to a tight shot of Baba's face, then tilted down to a close-up of the guru's quickly changing hand gestures. One moment Baba was pointing upwards toward the sky. The next, his thumb and forefinger curled into an "okay" sign. A moment after that his hand appeared to be raised in blessing. The fluid and graceful movements of Baba's hands were mesmerizing. I could have watched all day.

After giving me my instructions, Jake sat down at a desk on the far end of the room, and left me to work on my own. It took approximately five minutes to fast-forward and rewind each cassette. With nearly six hundred tapes in the library, I figured it would take over two weeks to get the job done.

Most of the videos were of the many talks Baba had given all over the world. The labels on some listed special events, such as "Inauguration of Melbourne ashram" and "Baba meets Governor of California." Others contained miscellaneous footage, like "Ravipur elephant" or "Baba takes ride on golf cart."

While the tapes were rewinding and fast-forwarding, I had a chance to poke around. Adjoining the Audiovisual library was an editing suite. A picture of a wide-eyed Baba with his forefinger raised to his lips was taped to the closed door. From inside I could hear the constant switching between normal playback and the high-pitched, accelerated sound of fast-forward and reverse. Another office and darkroom belonged to someone named Avadhoot Plotnick, who was Baba's personal photographer. Like Arjuna Weinberg, the cameraman, Avadhoot was now in India with the guru. There was also a repair room, with various pieces of broadcast equipment in different stages of disassembly. Inside was young man with acne and a mop of curly blond hair. His name was Mahendra Albright, and he was tinkering with a portable video tape deck.

"What's wrong with it?" I asked the technician.

"Nothing," Mahendra smirked. "I'm retrofitting it with a timecode generator."

"You're an engineer?"

Mahendra laughed. "Well, I don't have an engineering degree, if that's what you mean."

"Mahendra is our resident genius," said Jake. He was standing in the doorway of the repair room. "Completely self-taught. He designed and built that timecode generator himself."

The resident genius giggled. "It lays the code down by cannibalizing the VTR's second audio channel." I had no idea what "timecode" meant, but it sounded impressively technical.

Jake smiled and slowly shook his head. "The ashram should patent that thing. The Mission would make a fortune."

The VTR clicked in the other room, which meant it was time to change tapes. I went back to my station, hit eject, and was about to pop in a new cassette when Sita Perkins suddenly appeared. She stood in the doorway of the library, frowning, with her arms crossed. "Doug, what on earth are you doing down here?"

I felt a tightening in my chest. "Alan told me to report to the video department. He said it was my new *seva*."

Sita tapped her foot on the floor and thrust out her bosom. "Alan is not in charge of the *seva* desk—I am."

Jake came out of the repair room. "What seems to be the problem, Sita?"

Just then the door to the editing suite opened and out came a limping Kriyadevi Friedman on crutches. There was a fresh white plaster cast on her leg. In her hand she clutched a large cassette, and she grinned self-consciously when she saw me.

"Hey, Doug."

I was curious to know what had happened to her leg, but it would have to wait. Sita turned to confront Jake. "Baba's arriving in three weeks. We have fifty plus rooms to prepare and suddenly you need an extra librarian?"

Jake winced and rubbed his brow. He took a deep breath and held it. "Listen, Sita, Alan called me yesterday and asked if I could put Doug to work down here. If you have a problem with that, take it up with him."

"I'm really sorry for the confusion, Sita," I said.

Turning to me, she managed a smile. "Oh, don't worry, Doug. This isn't your fault. Alan hasn't been manager very long and I'm afraid he isn't quite up to the job." Sita scowled at Jake, then left in a huff.

I was about to apologize to Jake, when he raised his hands in front of him and spoke: "Don't worry—Baba's *shakti* will take care of it. For the moment, you work here."

"Nobody ever fights about where I should do *seva*," Mahendra called from the repair room.

"That's because you don't know how to do anything else," Kriyadevi quipped.

Mahendra giggled.

Kriyadevi limped across the room to return the cassette she was carrying to the appropriate shelf. Then she picked out another, and made her way back toward the editing room.

"What happened to you?" I finally asked.

Kriyadevi rolled her eyes. "Oh, yeah—my leg. I had a little accident early this morning before meditation."

Anger flashed across Jake's face. "She slipped on the icy path to the Brahmananda temple—that's what happened."

"I clean the Brahmananda temple and bathe the statue twice a week before morning meditation," Kriyadevi said.

"Kamala's kid—Madhu—he's to blame," Jake said. "It was his *seva* to keep that path clear."

I remembered how warm and wet it had been all day yesterday. The ice had probably formed during the night when the temperature dropped again.

"Just up and left the ashram yesterday and didn't even tell anyone," Jake continued. "We had to take her to the emergency room in Liberty."

Kriyadevi chuckled. "I'm sure there's a message from the guru in it for me!" She gave me a pat on the back. Then she hobbled back into the editing suite and closed the door.

With Baba's arrival only a fortnight away, the ashram was inundated with newcomers. Their name tags were marked with green stickers, like mine.

"Why are there so many new people in the ashram all of a sudden?" I asked Jake. We were bussing our lunch trays to the dirty dishes station.

"God bless 'em," he said. "They're here to help with the final push to get everything ready for the guru. Anyhow, you haven't seen anything yet. Just wait until Baba gets here. The place will be packed every weekend and holiday. In the summer the ashram won't even be able to accommodate all the visitors. Folks will be forced to stay at local motels and camp out."

I wanted to go to my room after lunch, for some quiet time before afternoon *seva*. But the reception area in the lobby was so mobbed with suitcases and people waiting to check in, it'd be impossible to get through without pushing people out of my way. I decided to avoid the crowd by going around the outside of the building. I let myself out through an exit next to the cafeteria and headed toward the main entrance. In the driveway, a couple of taxis were dropping people off. As I drew nearer, a black town car pulled into the driveway and parked directly in front of the sliding glass doors. A uniformed chauffeur got out and opened the door for his passenger. Out stepped a tall, brown-skinned man with jet-black hair. He was wearing dark sunglasses and a long camel hair coat. The driver popped the trunk and set his passenger's suitcases on the curb.

As I walked past the man to go back inside the building, he noticed me and smiled warmly. "Hello," he said, removing his sunglasses.

I gasped, instantly recognizing the man from all the photos I'd seen of him with Baba in *Raja Path Magazine*. "Um—hi. Can I help you with your bags?"

"Yes, thank you," he answered, shaking my hand firmly. "I'm Suresh." His voice was gentle, and his Indian accent soft and lilting.

"I know—I mean, I'm pleased to meet you, Suresh. My name is Doug."

"I know," he said, wiggling his eyebrows.

"You know who I am?"

The Indian smiled puckishly. "You're wearing a name tag."

With Baba's visit just around the corner, I wondered when I could expect a visit from Jeremy and Carrie. I decided to give them a call. They said they wouldn't be at the ashram for Baba's arrival. Jeremy couldn't get away from work that day. They'd be coming soon after, however, and had already registered for the first *shaktipat* retreat of the season.

"You're so lucky to be able to live in the ashram," my brother said.

On another extension, Carrie squealed with delight. "You'll get to see Baba every day!"

"We're so envious!" Jeremy added.

Carrie let out a long sigh. "You see, Doug, you've been through a very tough time, but everything that happens is part of the guru's plan for us."

"Believe me, I know. I thank Baba every day for all of his blessings."

"We can't wait to see him again!" Jeremy said.

"Jai Gurudev!" I exclaimed, beating them to it.

"Jai Gurudev!"

As the date of the guru's arrival approached, Sita became noticeably impressed with my willingness to work long hours and to take orders without questioning them. I could tell she felt this way because she began treating me differently from the others. While their best efforts were met with frowns and disparaging remarks, I could do no wrong. Whatever I did in her presence was met with cheerful smiles and words of praise.

The night before Baba's arrival, Sita found me on the far end of a corridor in the VIP wing.

"I have a special mission for you, Doug!" the *seva* manager called out as she hurried toward me. She told me to take a hand truck from the Housing office and go down to the basement. "On the south end you'll find a large storage unit labeled 'Keep Out'," she said, handing me a key. "Inside are several boxes labeled 'Baba's bedroom.' They need to be delivered to his house right away. Get them and bring them up here."

I was elated. Finally, I would get to see the inner sanctum!

The storage unit was a treasure trove of sacred objects not currently in use: an elaborate but worn throne, a chipped statue of the elephant god Ganesh, and various pieces of furniture of even higher quality than what I had seen in some of the VIP rooms. There was also an array of medical equipment, including a hospital bed, an I.V. pole, a wheelchair, and an examining table with a pair of metal foot supports, which, as an eighteen-year-old male, I didn't recognize as a gynecologist's table.

I wondered who had been sick. *Surely not Baba*, I thought. I was incapable of imagining the guru as an ordinary man in need of medical care. It didn't jibe with my view of Baba as the personification of God on earth. I made a mental note to ask Sita about it.

Next to the furniture, medical equipment, and personal effects of the guru's closest disciples, was a stack of boxes labeled "Baba's Bedroom." When I came upstairs with the boxes, Sita was waiting for me at the top of the ramp, across from the reception area. She asked me to set the boxes down on the floor so she could check their contents.

"Good work, Doug," Sita said, smiling brightly. "Now bring these boxes to Baba's house with me."

Sita led the way and I pushed the hand truck behind her. In the lobby, we passed several new arrivals. Some were carrying suitcases in through the front entrance, and others were standing around talking, waiting for the reception to open so they could check in. Two or three of them did double takes when they noticed the labels on my load. From their expressions of awe, you would've thought they were seeing Baba himself.

When we arrived at the long gray curtain at the end of the lobby, Sita pulled a section aside and we stepped behind it. On the other side was a windowless wall. There was just enough space for us to stand between it and the curtain. Directly in front of us was a vault-like metal door and an intercom. Sita pressed the *talk* button, and then spoke into an intercom box: "It's *me*."

A few seconds later, the bolt was pulled, the heavy door opened wide, and we were greeted by Baba's young Indian disciple, Suresh. We followed him through a corridor, up a sweeping staircase, and into a spacious duplex apartment, where we heard the steady drone of a vacuum cleaner.

Baba's house was lavishly decorated with plush white wall-to-wall carpeting and black lacquer furniture. *So this is where God lives when he's on the East Coast*, I thought. From where we stood on the upper level, I could see a large living room below. At the bottom of the stairs, a lithe young woman with blonde hair was busy vacuuming. Suresh helped me to unload the boxes from the dolly. The girl looked up at me and smiled. When I realized who she was, I almost fell over. It was the angel Gopi! I wasn't sure who I envied more: Gopi, for having the honor of cleaning Baba's house, or Suresh, for being lucky enough to get to hang out with her. Then foolish thoughts filled my head: *What is the most beautiful girl in the ashram doing alone in Baba's house with Suresh? Is Gopi his girlfriend?*

"Do you need any help bringing the boxes to Baba's bedroom?" I asked Suresh. I glanced at Gopi, staring at the curves of her gray sweat suit.

Suresh wiggled his head a little and smiled kindly. "No, thank you." Then he escorted Sita and me back to the lobby entrance, gently closing the heavy metal door behind us.

When we were alone again in the darkened space between the wall and the curtain again, Sita let out a long sigh and clutched her hands to her breast.

"Well, that was exciting, wasn't it?"

I nodded, distracted by thoughts of Suresh and Gopi alone together. Sita lifted the curtain out of her way and stepped back into the lobby. I was about to follow her when something odd caught my attention: pinpricks of light in the fabric of the curtain. I lingered for a moment to look at them.

"Doug, are you coming?"

The tiny holes were at my eye level. They weren't large enough to notice from the well-lit lobby side of the curtain. I thought they might have been made by moths, but they were spaced apart at regular intervals. No, these were definitely man-made.

The door to Baba's house opened again. A man in paint-splattered overalls came out, carrying a drill and a toolbox. I recognized Daniel Groza immediately—from the photo of Baba with Daniel and his wife in the Prasad VIP room—and moved out of his way.

I was relieved: Suresh and Gopi hadn't been alone together after all.

"Doug?" Sita called from the other side of the curtain. "We have work to do."

As I followed Sita to my next assignment, I thought about the holes in the curtain. They had been put there deliberately, I decided. They looked like peepholes.

By late afternoon, the ashram was mobbed. The line of people waiting to check in stretched all the way down to the curtain in front of Baba's house. There were also quite a few men and women in orange robes settling in, some of

Baba's East Coast-based swamis. Like Akhandananda, they were all white.

On my way through the lobby to Sita's office, I counted at least five different languages being spoken. I also recognized a few celebrities, including a folk rock singer-songwriter and two movie stars. One of the celebrities was the Academy Award-winning actress Sylvia Preston. She had been a favorite of my mother's. Her husband Richard Foxman, the famous film director, was standing by her side.

"Hey Doug!" called someone. "Over here!"

I turned to see Menaka Atkins, Robert Cargill, and Lakshmi Dunn among the crowd waiting to check in. I marched up to them and Menaka gave me a big hug. I tried to hug Lakshmi, but she cringed and I backed off. *Still a bitch!*

"Is this the Ithaca contingent?" I said, proud of my status as a resident of Baba's American headquarters.

Menaka looked me up and down. "Look at you—*the ashramite!* You look taller!"

"Well, I suppose I could still be growing."

A knowing smile spread across Robert's lips. "It's your posture, Doug. You're definitely standing up straighter."

Menaka hugged me again, and Lakshmi turned away, frowning.

"Excited to finally meet Baba?" Menaka asked me.

"Totally psyched!"

Seeing Menaka and the others in line waiting to check in was oddly gratifying. It was as though they were in *my* territory now. But the instant the thought took shape in my mind, I shot it down. *Sinful pride rearing its ugly head again.*

"Excuse me," someone said, tapping me on the shoulder. I turned around to be confronted by Sita. Her hands were on her hips and the tight-lipped smile on her face looked forced. "Doug, could I please see you in my office?"

I thought about introducing her to my friends from Ithaca, but Sita didn't give me a chance. She quickly did an about-face and headed in the direction of the lobby. I followed closely behind. *Am I in trouble for something?*

"Take a seat, Doug," my *seva* supervisor said, gesturing to an empty chair in front of her desk. I racked my brain, trying to think of what I might have done wrong. Sita leaned against the edge of her desk and stared down at me. "Doug, I want you to know how much I appreciate all the great *seva* you've been doing since you arrived at the ashram."

I let her words of praise wash over me. I was relieved I wasn't in any trouble. I took a deep breath. "The purpose of my life is to serve the guru in any way I possibly can."

Misty-eyed, Sita went to a cabinet behind her desk and took out a tiny glass bottle containing a clear liquid.

"I want you to have this, Doug," she said, handing me the vial. "This is Baba's bath water."

"Oh, Sita! I don't know what to say!" Tears welled in my eyes and a feeling of warmth spread through my entire body. As far as I was concerned, it was the nicest thing anyone had ever given me. "Thank you so much!"

Sita smiled brightly and wrinkled her nose. "Use it *sparingly*."

"I will!" I promised. I admired my gift and tried to imagine how much pure *shakti* it contained.

"Save it for difficult times."

"Okay—but what should I do with it?"

"Well, whenever you feel you could use an extra boost of guru's grace, just sprinkle a few drops of it on your head."

Her suggestion sounded good, but I had other plans for Baba's bath water: I was going to drink it.

Sita took my hand in hers and looked into my eyes. "Alan told me about what a hard time you've been through. I was so sorry to hear about your mother passing away."

I eyed Sita's chubby fingers as she stroked the back of my hand. "That's very kind of you to say, Sita," I said. Then I gently pulled my hand out of hers and rose to my feet.

Sita stood up too. "You do realize, of course, that Baba is the only parent you'll ever need."

"I know that, Sita, and I'm so grateful to be one of his children."

Sita moved closer to me. Then she pulled me toward her, cradling my head with her hands and holding my face against her bosom. "You're a member of Baba's family now. You don't need anyone else."

"Yes, yes," I answered, my voice muffled. I had no control over what happened next. Sita was holding me so closely, with my dick coming into contact with her hip, that I found myself getting hard.

Sita suddenly tensed up. She pulled away from me, and furtively glanced at my crotch. A smirk spread across her lips. She folded her arms in front of her chest. In that moment, I wanted to disappear.

Sita took a seat at her desk. She took some papers out of a folder and began to study them, pretending I wasn't there. After an excruciatingly long silence, she finally spoke. "You can go now," she said without looking up.

With my head hung low, and my hard-on rapidly shrinking, I left her office. I prayed to Baba for forgiveness, and then went to the cafeteria in search of my friends from Ithaca.

11.
INITIATION

THERE WAS A CONSTANT drumming in my chest. I felt like dancing. I couldn't stand still for more than a second. Baba's limousine would be pulling into the driveway of the ashram any minute. Throngs of devotees had gathered in the lower lobby and were trying to get as close to the door as possible, hoping to catch a glimpse of Baba when he made his big entrance.

My roommate Shivadas and several other men wearing security badges and clasping walkie-talkies were working to keep them at bay. I'd finished *seva* early, and had already staked out a good place to stand. From my vantage point on the steps to the lobby, I'd be able to see everything.

The guru's flight had landed at JFK hours ago. Most of the people who had flown from India with him had already arrived at the ashram. When their buses had pulled up earlier, I'd been working in the lobby, hanging an enormous "Welcome home Baba!" banner. I watched through the windows as they filed out of the coaches. Some of the new arrivals were more of Baba's orange-clad male and female swamis. Others were ordinary devotees who were returning home after spending time in Baba's ashram in Ravipur. But most of them, Shivadas explained, were members of Baba's entourage who traveled with the guru all over the world.

"How can you tell who the tour people are?" I asked.

Shivadas chuckled. "They're the really good-looking ones in nice clothes."

He was right. "*Baba's* people," as he referred to them, were not difficult to spot. They strode around the ashram with their shoulders back and their heads held high, giving orders to the year-round residents. I expected to see more Indians among them, but despite their Indian-sounding spiritual names, the vast majority of them were from Western countries and lily white—like the swamis. They exuded poise and self-confidence, and gave the impression that each of them had been specially chosen by Baba for a unique and important *seva*.

As we waited in the lobby for the guru to arrive, their faces were radiant with devotion and spiritual fervor, and they were dressed in a way that befitted their VIP status. The men wore stylish blazers, ties, and slacks, and the women were dressed in vibrantly colored saris of the finest silk. Among them was a group of teenaged girls and young women in their early twenties. They had flowers in their hair and were adorned with strings of pearls and golden jewelry. They were gathered just inside the sliding glass door in the lobby, positioned so that they'd be the first to greet Baba. They were in front of all the other tour people and VIPs, including the swamis and celebrities.

My breath hitched when I saw the angel Gopi among them. Her face glowed with serenity and love for the guru, and she was stunning in her jewels and elegant turquoise sari. The other girls were hugging her and showering her with kisses as though they had just been reunited with their best friend. Her radiance and beauty filled me with yearning. She was almost too painful to look at.

"Who are all those girls in saris near the entrance?" I asked Shivadas, cupping my hand around his ear and speaking loudly to make myself heard over the hubbub.

His eyes lit up. "Those are Baba's princesses—*darshan girls*. They're always up front and close to the guru, especially when he's on the throne."

"What's *darshan*?"

He grinned. "That's when all the devotees get a turn to bow down to the guru in person, and offer him a token of their gratitude."

"What do the girls have to do with it?"

Shivadas' mouth opened slightly, but no words came out. "I'm not sure actually," he laughed. "They're not too hard on the eyes though, are they?"

"How come so few of the people on tour with Baba are Indian?"

Shivadas shrugged and scratched the back of his head. "I don't know. I never really thought about it. Maybe they don't like to travel."

There was a squeal of feedback over the din of the crowd, and Shivadas went back to work. I turned to see Alan standing on top of one of the benches, struggling with the controls of a megaphone. A tall, well-groomed man with wet hair, dressed in a dark suit and shiny black shoes, was standing on the floor next to him. The man's arms were folded and he was frowning.

"Jai Gurudev!" Alan said, his voice distorted by the megaphone.

"Jai Gurudev!" the crowd cheered.

"Welcome to Shree Brahmananda Ashram, everybody! I just received word that our beloved guru will be arriving shortly."

The lobby erupted in applause and more calls of "Jai Gurudev!"

"I want to remind everyone that while we're all excited to see Baba, we should be mindful—" Alan had more to say, but everybody was talking amongst themselves again and nobody was listening.

Irritated at Alan's ineffectiveness, the man in the dark suit hopped up onto the bench, snatched the megaphone from Alan's hand, and motioned for him to step down. After adjusting the controls, he addressed the devotees: "Quiet, everybody. Listen up!" The crowd was instantly silent and all eyes were on the frowning man. "Everybody needs to back a few feet away from the entrance."

Even though everyone was happily complying with the frowning man's instructions, ashram security sprang into action. Shivadas and the other security officers started herding everybody backward, knocking down an elderly man and a toddler in the process. Only the *darshan* girls, VIPs, and swamis were allowed to remain where they were.

"We need to keep a passage clear for Baba here," the frowning man said, indicating with his hands the most direct path between the main entrance and the big gray curtain. His tone was harsh and the cranked-up volume of the megaphone distorted his voice. "*Do not* cross this line," he warned, pointing to where security was laying down a strip of yellow tape. "I repeat, *do not* cross this line."

The main entrance door slid open automatically and a handsome young man with light brown hair in a button-down shirt, khaki pants, and Birkenstock sandals came in. He was carrying a pair of Indian drums called tablas. I recognized him. His name was Poonish Davidson and he worked in the kitchen. He was around my age and had already traveled to India with Baba and had spent a year in the Ravipur ashram. He was accompanied by an attractive young woman wrapped in an elegant purple and green sari. She was carrying a basket full of tambourines and tiny cymbals. A moment later, the door slid open again and Kriyadevi Friedman and Jake from the video department walked through. Kriyadevi was still on crutches and was wearing a frumpy, shapeless, red and white polka dot dress. Her plaster leg cast was now covered with messages and drawings. Jake was dressed in a navy blue coat with gold buttons, tan slacks, and a dark red tie, and was carrying a harmonium. They were met by the frowning man, who showed Kriyadevi and Poonish where to set up near the entrance. The young woman carrying the basket of musical instruments distributed them to the princesses, and then took her place among them. Kriyadevi sounded a note on the harmonium. Then she and Poonish led everyone in a chant of "Om Guru Om." In no time, the devotees were clapping hands and singing.

While everybody else chanted ecstatically, Shivadas and the other security guards looked grim. Despite the fact that no one had yet set foot over the line of yellow tape on the floor, they obsessively monitored the crowd and pounced on anyone who came within an inch of the line, demanding they move to the back of the lobby. The frowning man who had taken the megaphone away from Alan also looked agitated. He darted from one end of the lobby to the other, barking commands into a walkie-talkie.

With everyone else I clapped my hands and sang at the top of my lungs:

"Om Guru, Om Guru, Om Gurudev! Jai Guru, Jai Guru, Jai Gurudev!"

There were shrieks of excitement when a sleek black limousine pulled up just outside the ashram main entrance. It was followed by a smaller black town car and van. The chant got louder and picked up speed. Arms were lifted heavenward. Tears of devotion streamed down frenzied faces.

A tall thin man in a chauffeur's uniform jumped out of the limo and scrambled to the other side to open the door. I couldn't believe I was about to see Baba in the flesh.

And there he was: the creator of the universe in human form.

God was shorter than I thought he'd be. Even though it was quite a warm day for the end of March, he was bundled up as if he were on a visit to the North Pole. Over his orange silks he wore a bulky, bright red down jacket. His head was covered by a knitted orange woolen ski hat, and around his neck was a matching scarf. He was followed out of the limo by the siblings, Suresh and Anjali.

The chant reached a crescendo. Baba Rudrananda entered the building, flanked by his two young Indian disciples. With a wave of his hand, he motioned for the musicians to stop playing. Within a few seconds, the chanting ended. Rudrananda greeted the devotees with folded hands and the call, "Jai Gurudev!"

"Jai Gurudev!" cheered the crowd. Then there was silence, as if everyone in the lobby were holding their breath in anticipation of what the guru might do next.

AFTER ENTERING THE BUILDING and greeting his devotees, Baba approached the *darshan* girls to offer his blessing. They swooned and beamed smiles at him. When he reached Gopi, he lingered to chat with her. They were soon joined by an older, gray-haired couple. The physical resemblance between Gopi and the couple was strong, and I figured they must be her parents.

"We're so grateful to you, Baba, for taking such good care of our little girl," said the man who I assumed was Gopi's father. When the conversation was finished, the angel's mother knelt down to touch the guru's feet.

Already deviating from the path anticipated for him by security and indicated by the yellow tape on the floor, Baba approached the musicians and stopped in front of Kriyadevi, who was now standing up and leaning on her crutches.

"*Aapake pair ko kya hua?*" Baba said.

"What happened to your leg?" Anjali translated.

"I slipped on the ice, Baba."

Anjali translated Kriyadevi's answer for Baba. The guru responded in the same Indian language. "You should chant when you chant, eat when you, eat, and walk when you walk," Baba's translator said. "Like this, you will not have accidents." Everyone within earshot burst out laughing and Kriyadevi blushed.

"What is all this writing on your plaster?"

"These are messages from my friends wishing me well, Baba," Kriyadevi said. Everyone laughed again. The conversation struck me as funny too: Baba was like a superior being from another planet who was trying to make sense of our primitive customs.

"*Aacha, aacha!*" Baba said.

"Good, good," Anjali translated. The guru said something else to Anjali while making a writing motion with his hand. Then she turned to face Alan and Gajendra, who were standing nearby.

"He needs something to write on this," Anjali said, pointing at Kriyadevi's cast.

A look of comprehension flashed across Alan's face. He shot up the steps past me in the direction of the manager's office, pushing people out of his way as he ran.

Baba turned his attention to Sylvia Preston and the other celebrities who were assembled near the entrance. The guru was all smiles, and so were his famous devotees.

Directing his gaze toward the upper lobby now, I felt as though Baba were staring directly at me. Just then, Alan dashed by me again on his way back to the lower lobby. He was out of breath. When he was once again in front of Baba, he extended a hand containing a marker. The guru took it and then turned his attention to Kriyadevi's broken leg. Removing the cap from the marker and handing it to Suresh to hold, Baba bent over and scribbled something in bold red ink on Kriyadevi's cast. When he finished, the crowd erupted in applause. A blushing Kriyadevi beamed a smile of pure delight and reverently folded her hands.

"What does it say? What does it say?" a woman asked from the back of the crowd.

An amused Anjali called back to her: "Baba signed his name!"

This was followed by more applause.

Moving on, Baba made his way in my direction, toward the upper lobby. Shivadas and another guard rushed ahead of the guru in order to clear a path for him. This was unnecessary, however, as everyone was happy to step out of Baba's way without being asked. As the guru drew nearer,

I had the strong impression that he was headed straight for me. I held my breath as he came within inches of where I stood. Then, when he was right in front of me, he suddenly stopped.

The spiritual force he radiated was undeniable. I felt every particle in my body pulsate, as though I were standing next to an immensely powerful electromagnet. Looking deeply into my eyes, he reached for my hand and took it in his, squeezing it tenderly. I felt completely naked and exposed before him, as though his gaze penetrated the armor of my individual identity and he could see directly into my innermost being.

"Ahh, how are you?" the guru said to me in English. I melted.

My head fell back and I closed my eyes. Tears welled up behind my eyelids and began to stream down my face. I knew then and there that I would be eternally grateful to the guru for this tremendous act of compassion. I'd never doubt him again.

Baba let go of my hand, smiled lovingly at me, and then patted me on the back. Then he turned around and headed back in the direction of his apartment. When he reached the entrance, he turned around and waved one last time to his adoring followers.

"Jai Gurudev!" the guru exclaimed, folding his hands in salutation.

"Jai Gurudev!" the devotees roared in response.

Then he disappeared behind the long gray curtain.

WITH THE GURU IN residence, the energy in the ashram ramped up to a higher level. Every evening, Baba gave talks and greeted visitors. He also made unexpected public appearances nearly every day. It was not usual to see him outside on the grounds taking his dogs for a walk, or riding through the ashram gardens on a golf cart, with a few close disciples sprinting behind him to keep up.

I noticed he was usually accompanied by the same small circle of people. Anjali, Baba's Indian translator, went with him almost everywhere, and so did her younger brother, Suresh. Baba would often show up halfway through the morning recitation of the *Guru Gita* to see who was in attendance. You never knew when Baba might suddenly emerge from behind the long gray curtain in the lobby.

I wasn't the only devotee to spend their breaks from *seva* and chanting by hanging out near the entrance of his apartment in the hope of crossing paths with him. When I did, I kept wishing he'd stop to speak to me again, like he had on the day of his arrival. But he never seemed to notice me. After a couple of weeks around the guru, I was beginning to think my brief exchange with him was a once-in-a-lifetime event.

I reached the top of the ramp connecting the basement to the lobby, and a familiar voice called out to me: "Doug! Over here!" I turned to see my brother and his wife waiting in line at the reception. They were up from the City to see Baba and take the first weekend *shaktipat* retreat of the season. Carrie was waving and smiling at me. I rushed over to them and my sister-in-law gave me a big hug and squealed with joy. Jeremy, as always, was more understated in his display of affection. He embraced me politely and gave me a perfunctory pat on the back.

"There's a free bunk where I am," I said. "You should ask them to assign you to my room."

Jeremy took a step back. "We already requested one of the bungalows across the street for married couples. We always stay there."

Carrie giggled and squealed again. "Excited for your big day tomorrow, Doug?"

"I sure am!"

My brother squished his eyebrows together. "What big day?"

Carrie playfully socked Jeremy in the arm. "Tomorrow is Doug's *diksha* day, silly! He's going to receive *shaktipat* from Baba."

I tingled all over just thinking about it.

Jeremy's mouth fell open a little. Then he smiled. "Oh, that's right! You've been in the ashram for so long now, I totally forgot you only just met Baba."

"After tomorrow, nothing will ever be the same for you," said Carrie, looking more serious now. "The entity known as Douglas Greenbaum will cease to exist."

I was excited to be taking the *shaktipat* retreat because, after months of waiting, my kundalini would finally be awakened. But I was also looking forward to it for another reason, one I kept to myself: anyone taking the weekend retreat was excused from *seva*. Since coming to the ashram two and a half months earlier, this would be my first break from work.

After *seva*, I met up with Jeremy and Carrie in the cafeteria for dinner. I told them all about my life in the ashram over the past months. Then, as my brother and his wife exchanged awestruck glances, I told them all about how Baba, on the day of his arrival, had crossed the lobby for the sole purpose of greeting me. I wondered if they'd heard those rumors about Baba and the people close to him. But I didn't ask them about it.

Instead I asked, "If you've already received *shaktipat*, why do you keeping coming to the retreats?"

My brother and his wife laughed. "You can never have too much *shakti!*" Jeremy answered. "Only a fraction of the people here for the retreat are attending it for the first time."

Jeremy and Carrie again told me how envious they were—how lucky I was to be able to live in the ashram and to be with Baba. "Life in the world is mundane and joyless," Carrie said, slumping forward in her chair.

"Isn't your internship interesting?" I asked my brother. "You're finally a doctor."

Jeremy shrugged half-heartedly. "Sure. But what Carrie and I are really looking forward to are the weekends we'll be spending here with Baba this summer."

Carrie's eyes lit up suddenly and her mouth formed an "o" shape like she had forgotten something. "And *satsang* at the Manhattan ashram with Swami Satyananda, of course!"

Jeremy agreed. "Oh yeah, Satyananda is great. He's one of Baba's most highly evolved swamis. He's got tremendous *shakti*. He's here in Birchwood Falls this weekend and will be the master of ceremonies for the retreat."

"You should visit us in the City sometime," Carrie said. "We'll introduce you."

I smiled and told them I was looking forward to it. But inwardly I thought about how absurd they sounded: *Who would ever leave Baba and the ashram for even a second?*

On the morning of the first day of the retreat, the line to get into the meditation hall stretched all the way past the cafeteria and back into the lobby. Young, impeccably dressed male and female ushers—members of Baba's tour staff—showed the retreatants to their places. I had hoped to be given a seat up front, near Baba's throne. Jeremy had urged me to get in line as early as possible. And I did, as soon as the *Guru Gita* ended. But the closest spots were reserved for Baba's swamis, *darshan* girls, and VIPs. I was shown to a place on the men's side in the second tier of the vast, dimly-lit hall.

As we waited for the rest of the retreatants to be seated, a recording of Baba chanting the *Om Namah Shivaya* mantra played softly over the loudspeakers. The air in the room was fragrant with Nag Champa incense and the carpet smelled faintly of a citrusy perfume. I couldn't help feeling envious of the people who had places reserved for them up front near Baba's throne. *This is my first shaktipat retreat,* I thought. *Shouldn't I get to sit at the guru's feet?* I'd been observing the tour people closely over the week since the guru's arrival. Not only did they get to sit up front during the programs and chants, but they also had special accommodations in the main building next to Baba's house. They didn't keep regular *seva* hours; at any time of the day or night I'd see them dart in and out of the ashram offices with clipboards in hand, or disappear behind the long gray curtain at the end of the lower lobby. Whenever they spoke to each other, it was in hushed tones, as though they were discussing something urgent and confidential. I wondered how I could become one of them.

After everyone was seated, the doors to the hall were closed and Satyananda—Jeremy and Carrie's swami from the Manhattan ashram—addressed the retreatants. He was tall and lanky, with a pleasant face and a shaven, oval-shaped head. His voice was calm and soothing. As he spoke, he frequently paused to let his words sink in. Listening to him, I found myself disconnecting from my body and my surroundings, letting go of my petty concerns about how close to the guru I sat, and preparing myself mentally to receive initiation.

"According to the Yoga Upanishads," Satyananda began, "*kundalini*, the 'serpent power,' lies coiled and sleeping at the base of the spine in an ordinary person. Once awakened, it purifies the subtle body and eventually bestows a state of divine union with God. While many systems of yoga focus on awakening this power through meditation, breathing exercises, and chanting, only a fully realized master of Raja Yoga has the power to effortlessly awaken it for you through *shaktipat*. And only a perfected master, like Baba, can control the *kundalini* once it is activated."

As the swami described what I was about to experience, I got the chills, and goosebumps formed all over my skin.

"The process of *kundalini* awakening affects everyone differently. The divine energy courses through the body and removes physiological, mental, and emotional blockages that stand in the way of enlightenment. Some may find themselves spontaneously performing yogic postures or hand gestures, called *mudras*. They might recite mantras or make strange sounds. Breathing patterns may change. Some may also see lights, have visions, or hear inner music. These reactions to the *shakti* are called *kriyas*. They are a natural part of the purification process and should not be feared."

Feelings of tremendous gratitude to God for having led me to Baba rose up inside of me. I realized that all the pain and suffering I'd been through was for a reason. Without it, I may never have developed a yearning to know the Supreme Self, and would've been doomed to an empty, meaningless existence. Instead of living in a holy place like the ashram, I'd be running after sense pleasures, knowing only dissatisfaction. Now, thanks to Baba, I was about to hit the spiritual jackpot.

After Satyananda's introduction, the lights were dimmed, and the swami took a seat behind an empty spot on the men's side, directly beneath the guru's throne. Kriyadevi played a sustained note on the harmonium, then led us in a slow recitation of *Om Namah Shivaya*. Despite my best efforts to focus, I kept opening my eyes to see if Baba had joined us yet, if he was sitting on his throne. Finally, I gave up trying to get into the chant and kept a watchful eye for the guru's entrance. Just when I thought he'd never come, everyone around me began to straighten their meditation posture. Light pierced the darkness from a door opening in the back of the hall. I immediately recognized Baba's distinctive silhouette and confident stride. Two figures followed closely behind him. Anjali and Suresh.

As he made his way down the middle aisle that separated the men's side from the women's, all eyes were on Baba. Before sitting down, he honored his own guru by lowering his head and folding his hands in prayer beneath the enormous photograph of Brahmananda hanging above his throne. After the guru took his seat, a sharply-dressed young man seated up front jumped up from behind an audio mixer to adjust a stand next to the throne, so that a microphone was positioned directly under the guru's mouth. His voice amplified now, Baba led us in another few rounds of the mantra. When the chanting had come to an end, the hall was thick with silence. Once again I tried to meditate. Within a few moments, my efforts were interrupted by the gentle sound of Anjali's voice over the sound system:

"Baba will give *the touch* now."

Despite my best efforts to turn my attention inward and rid my mind of distracting thoughts, it was impossible to ignore what was going on around me. The deep stillness in the hall was quickly replaced by a cacophony of bizarre vocalizations, weeping, and hysterical laughter. People all around me broke into repetitive body spasms, as if half the retreatants had suddenly been afflicted with Tourette's syndrome. I knew there was nothing wrong with them, of course. Like Satyananda said, they were experiencing *kriyas*.

Unable to meditate, I peeked at Baba as he gave initiation. Wending his way up and down the rows of meditators, he bopped each one on the head with his wand of peacock feathers. Occasionally he'd hover over someone and pinch the bridge of their nose, or stroke their face. One person would begin shaking and jerking and making strange sounds, followed by others in their immediate vicinity responding in kind. In this way, Baba's *shakti* spread out from him in waves throughout the entire assembly.

Looking around the hall as discreetly as possible, I could make out the silhouettes of people getting into what looked like hatha yoga postures or making strange hand gestures, exactly in the way Satyananda had described. Some people's breathing became affected; a man next to me suddenly exhaled powerfully, and then began breathing in and out forcefully, as though he were hyperventilating. I could hear others doing the same thing all over the hall.

As Baba drew nearer I detected a strong, heady fragrance like sweet hay. It became increasingly powerful as the whooshing sound of Baba's wand striking the heads of other retreatants grew louder. The next thing I knew, Baba was touching the man seated behind me.

Whack! The feathers come down on my head. Baba's grassy scent fills my nostrils. *Whack, whack!* The feathers again come down on my head. Baba seizes the top of my nose, just below the bridge, and shakes my head from side to side. One of his fingers presses firmly into my forehead, in the space between my eyebrows. I exhale forcefully. Baba moves on to the next devotee. I feel intense heat, and then a piercing sensation at the base of my spine. It's as if a fuse has been lit and a small flame travels up my spine, triggering tiny explosions along the way. First at the root of my sex organ. Then a burst of energy at my navel. A moment later, there is heat and a sensation of popping in my solar plexus. The flame continues its way up my back until it feels like a bomb is detonated in my chest. My heart is blown wide open. More popping at my throat, and lastly, a burst of energy in the space between my eyebrows, where Baba touched me with his hand. Searing heat radiates throughout my entire body, followed by wave after wave of ecstasy. The muscles in my arms and legs are twitching, and a tiny blue light appears behind my closed eyelids, hovering for a while before fading away.

On one level, I am aware that I am seated in meditation. I feel the usual ache in my legs and the pressure of my butt against the floor. I am cognizant of the weeping, laughing, and strange sounds around me, of Baba's fragrance lingering in the air, but there is a shift in my awareness: I, the perceiver, am also the perceived. I hear, but I am also the sound. I smell, but I am also the fragrance. The distinction between subject and object, inner and outer, experiencer and what is experienced has been dissolved. I have entered into a state of non-dual awareness, which feels familiar and without beginning. My mind is quiet, void of thought. All that remains is luminous, blissful awareness.

A long sustained note on the harmonium signaled the end of the meditation session. Seated on his throne again, Baba led us in a few rounds of *Om Namah Shivaya* and the lights in the hall gradually came back on. Although the meditation session was over—I wasn't even sure how long it had been—one hour? Two?—my mind remained still, deeply peaceful. I looked down: the muscles in my arms and legs were still twitching with the movements of the *kundalini-shakti*.

Baba began to speak in Hindi and, although I didn't understand him, I was mesmerized by the musical rise and fall of his voice, the odd circular motions of his hands, and his frequent, seemingly random gestures.

"All who received the touch this morning have been initiated into the path of supreme Raja Yoga," translated Anjali. I had come to think of Anjali's voice as Baba's "English voice," and the sound of it moved me deeply. "Some of you may have been given a glimpse of the supreme truth, but there is still much work to be done. Do not fall into the trap of imagining that you are already enlightened. Now that your *kundalini* has been awakened, the guru will continue to guide it on its upward journey through the *sushumna nadi*, until it has completely purified both the subtle and physical bodies and opened all seven *chakras*. This will culminate in the opening of the *sahasrara chakra* at the crown of the head. When this occurs, the disciple attains *nirvikalpa samadhi*—complete absorption of the individual consciousness into the godhead. In this state, nothing remains but pure awareness, and nothing detracts from its wholeness and perfection. The disciple becomes unshakably established in the knowledge of his true identity as the *supreme Self*, and is thereby liberated, attaining a permanent and uninterrupted state of bliss and freedom from suffering."

Baba went on to explain that the guru had bestowed his grace upon us, but that it was now up to us to put forth effort. He emphasized that a daily practice of meditation, chanting, devotion, and service to the guru was absolutely essential to keep the *shakti*— the awakened *kundalini*— active within us. He warned us not to weaken the guru's gift through negative actions, such as keeping bad company and idle gossip.

"But above all, you must not squander your vital energy, rubbing your bodies together like beasts in heat," Baba said, wrinkling his nose and frowning. "The sexual fluid produced in the physical body is another form of the divine *kundalini-shakti*. It must be conserved."

As I listened to Baba's talk, I felt as though I were still in a state of meditation. My awareness was detached from both the sensations in my physical body and the mental processes of my own mind, as though I were a witness. This person called "Doug" only existed on the periphery of my consciousness. It was as though my sense of *Self* had expanded to encompass everyone and everything around me. Looking around at other devotees, I felt as though I were in a hall of mirrors. Everyone—even Baba—was simply a reflection of my innermost being.

Baba drew his talk to a close, and at one point he seemed to be staring in my direction: "Some disciples receive *shaktipat* and make swift progress on the path. Others are initiated but cannot evolve because of their pride and inability to follow the guru's commands. The worst of these is the intellectual. The intellectual believes he knows everything and has nothing to learn from a guru. He is unable to receive initiation. On the other hand, even if a disciple is a wretched sinner, if he has a pure heart and obeys his master faithfully, he will attain everything."

Baba's remark about intellectuals stung. My chest tightened and I suddenly felt too hot. My consciousness contracted until my sense of individuality reasserted itself. First Baba had said that everyone who was present today, without exception, had received *shaktipat.* Now he was saying that intellectuals were unable to receive initiation. *Was Baba talking about me?* I wondered. *Am I an intellectual?* I felt my chest tighten. I hated the idea that Baba might disapprove of me.

Unable now to focus on what Baba was saying, I tried to remember the experience of receiving *the touch.* I had definitely felt the *kundalini* awaken within me, travel up my spine, and pierce my lower three *chakras.* My experience matched Baba's description of the process, as well as other accounts I'd read of *kundalini* awakening.

Baba ended his talk with a prayer to Gurudev Brahmananda. Uncrossing his legs, he leaned forward and smiled lovingly at Gopi. She blushed and beamed an adoring smile back at him. As Baba stood up to leave, Suresh and Anjali also rose to follow him. But with a wave of his hand, the guru motioned for them to sit back down.

Baba made his way up the center aisle. Everyone stood up, folded their hands in prayer, and bowed their heads in his direction. At the exit, a tall man in a white cowboy hat and a leather jacket seemed to be waiting for him. I expected to see security spring into action any second, to pull him out of the guru's way, but they never came. Instead, Baba greeted the eccentrically dressed man with an affectionate pat on the back. The man opened the door for Baba, and they left the hall together.

That man bothered me. *He's obviously someone close to the guru*, I thought. *Why doesn't Baba tell him to take off that stupid hat?*

After a short break, Satyananda announced that the next part of the program was for *sharing*—a time when anyone who wanted to talk about what they had experienced during the meditation session was invited to stand up and speak. As the retreatants took turns sharing, a *darshan* girl and one of the male ushers ran between them with cordless microphones. A chubby middle-aged man in the back of the hall raised his hand and shared that after Baba had tapped him on the head with the peacock feathers, he saw golden-white light, and became completely absorbed in it. "The light spread out from my body and filled the entire hall."

A young woman dressed like a hippie told of hearing bells and having had a vision of Christ, who then changed form into Lord Krishna, and then again into Gurudev Brahmananda.

"I saw flashes of blue light, followed by a feeling of deep peace," a man in a lime green sweat suit said.

Satyananda nodded approvingly. "All of these—classic examples of *kundalini* awakening."

An older Asian woman shared: "I had an experience of deep inner peace and a feeling of being enveloped in Baba's love." Then she broke into tears and sat down again.

Another man who looked like a college professor spoke of Sanskrit letters appearing before him and forming syllables, which he could simultaneously see and hear.

A large, buxom lady took the microphone. "I had a vision of myself in a previous life, as a member of Baba's court in his incarnation as a maharaja."

As I listened to these people share their stories of *kundalini* awakening, I was disappointed that my own experience hadn't been as dramatic. I began to doubt whether I had actually received *shaktipat*. But then a person spoke of having seen a tiny blue light, exactly like the one I'd seen, and Satyananda's explanation reassured me.

"You have had a vision of the *supra-causal* body—what Baba calls the 'radiant blue pearl,'" the swami said. "Baba says that despite its minute size, the blue pearl contains the entire cosmos latent within it."

When the sharing session was over, Satyananda thanked all those who had spoken and announced that it was time for lunch. He reminded everyone to observe silence in the cafeteria, in order to help retain what we had received from Baba.

I ate with Jeremy and Carrie. No one spoke. The only sounds we heard were the clink of utensils against cafeteria trays, and the sliding of chairs across the floor. By the looks of mild frustration on their faces, I could tell they were as eager to hear about my *kundalini* awakening as I was to talk about it. But for now we had to make do with smiles and knowing looks.

After lunch, I went back to my room for some alone time before the program resumed. As I lay in bed staring up at the plywood platform of the upper bunk, I tuned out my roommates and silently repeated the *Om Namah Shivaya* mantra to myself. Instead of letting my mind get caught up in thinking, I tried to be aware of my thoughts as ripples in consciousness. Before long I noticed a sporadic quivering in different muscles all over my body. The guru's *shakti* was doing its work.

Swami Paramananda was a slender, austere-looking woman in her mid-thirties. She had shortly-cropped light brown hair and small, dark eyes, and spoke with an British accent. She was the spiritual director of Baba's London ashram, but would be in residence here in Birchwood Falls for the duration of the guru's visit. On Sunday morning, she gave the first talk of the day. The subject was devotion.

"The relationship between the guru and his disciple is sacred," the swami began. "A true disciple considers the guru to be God in human form. According to the *Guru Gita*, devotion to the guru is the highest virtue. Those whose minds are impure or unfit are unable to understand or experience it.

"The seeker becomes receptive to the master's grace only after he's surrendered at the lotus feet of the guru. This kind of self-surrender means that the disciple no longer has any will other than that of his guru. His only wish is to please the guru through his thought, speech, and deeds. Knowing that everything the master does is for the seeker's welfare, the seeker should serve him with humility and complete obedience. Above all, the disciple must never find fault with the guru.

"The master works tirelessly to help the disciple overcome his ego and attain liberation. For this reason, the disciple is forever indebted to the guru."

In the afternoon we again meditated with Baba, but he didn't give the touch. Although I didn't feel explosions of energy in my spine, or see any lights, I slipped effortlessly into meditation as soon as the lights were dimmed. Gone, for now, were the distracting thoughts and restlessness that had previously plagued me.

Before the end of the weekend, everyone who was registered for the retreat was given the chance to approach Baba and receive his blessing. Suresh spoke a few words directed at those who were meeting the guru for the first time: "Whenever one receives the *darshan* of a great saint, one should always make a symbolic offering." He explained that a *dakshina* stand had been set up at the back of the cafeteria, where they sold fruit and small bouquets of flowers that we could lay at Baba's feet. "Remember, whatever is given to the guru will be returned to the gift-bearer ten-fold in the form of good karma."

I looked around for Jeremy, hoping he'd introduce me to Baba. I found him on the way to the *dakshina* stand in the cafeteria.

"It's better if you meet Baba yourself," he said, furrowing his brow. My brother's words stung. They felt like a rejection. *Why wouldn't he want to introduce me to the guru?* I'd heard countless stories about devotees who'd brought friends and relatives up to meet Baba. I began to wonder if Jeremy was ashamed of me for some reason.

We ran into Carrie, who was on her way back from the *dakshina* stand. Carrying a pineapple and a mango, she grimaced when she saw me. "Doug! I'm sorry I didn't think to get you something to give Baba. We'll wait for you while you buy something."

"It's okay," Jeremy said, tugging on her arm to head back in the direction of the hall. "We'll meet up after *darshan* to say good-bye."

"Yeah, it's no problem," I said, gesturing for them to go ahead without me. "I want to meet Baba on my own."

At the *dakshina* stand, there was a huge selection of fruit and flower bouquets. Prices ranged from two dollars for an apple to fifty dollars for an elaborate floral arrangement. "What do you recommend?" I asked the man behind the counter.

He scratched his nose and glanced behind him at the impressive display. "A lot of devotees give coconuts," he answered.

"Why?"

Before the man could respond, a familiar voice behind me answered for him. "With a coconut, we're symbolically asking the guru to break the hard shell of our ego to get at the sweetness within."

I turned around and was face to face with Paramananda, the female swami who had given the talk that morning. She seemed to be sizing me up with her small, dark eyes. I thanked her for the explanation, but decided on the fifty-dollar bouquet. Since I was just beginning my relationship with the guru, I wanted him to know I was ready to offer everything of myself to him, that I would hold nothing back.

The *darshan* line snaked its way from Baba's throne all the way out of the hall, through the corridor, and into the lobby. The word was they were allowing everyone at the ashram for Baba's *darshan*, not only those who were registered for the retreat. I marveled at the guru's generosity.

Bright, reedy Indian instrumental music played over the sound system. As I inched my way closer, I felt a fluttering in my stomach. *Will Baba make eye contact with me?* I wondered. *Will he speak to me?*

By the time I was about thirty feet from Baba's throne, the line was four abreast. Everyone who went before him placed an offering in one of the large wicker baskets at his feet, and then bowed down. Instead of giving fruit or flowers, some people placed empty bottles of alcohol, bottles of pills, or packs of cigarettes in the baskets. (I later found out that this was a way of asking the guru to rid them of their various addictions.) While the guru ignored some people, and had lengthy conversations with others, everyone who went before him received, at the very least, a loving tap on the head from his wand of peacock feathers. I drew nearer and my heart beat faster.

Glancing around, I saw Robert Cargill from Ithaca seated all the way up front, directly behind the swamis. I was surprised to see him sitting among the VIPs. No one had ever mentioned to me that he held such a prominent position in Baba's mission. Front and center on the women's side, I couldn't help but notice the angel Gopi. She was sitting at Baba's feet, next to Anjali on the dais that held Baba's throne. Behind them were the other princesses, Baba's female swamis, and the actress Sylvia Preston, along with other VIPs.

As far as I could tell, Gopi's *seva* was to monitor the baskets of offerings. As soon as one began to overflow, she'd replace it with an empty one, taking the full baskets through a side door near the throne. Meanwhile, Anjali's job, other than as translator, was to assist Baba. She determined whether anyone lingering before the guru should be encouraged to move on, or whether it was appropriate for them to crouch nearby until the guru was ready to speak to them.

There was only one row of devotees ahead of me in line now, and I was close enough to detect the sweet, grassy fragrance I'd smelled the day before, when Baba had given me *the touch*. The guru's field of energy was palpable and the *kundalini* energy that he'd awakened within me stirred in response. When it was time to receive his blessing, I bowed down before him and placed the large flower arrangement I had purchased on the platform next to one of the baskets. I felt a soft tap on the back of my head, and felt a faint popping sensation in my navel, heart, and throat. As I stood back up, I was face to face with the guru. My mind stopped. He was gazing directly into my eyes. Then he said something in an Indian language, which Anjali translated: "It's not enough for the guru to forgive you. You must forgive yourself."

I wanted to say something, but was unable to speak. All I could do was stand there in total amazement. This was further confirmation that Baba knew everything about me. He was aware of the guilt I was struggling with over my mother's death, and had heard my prayers for forgiveness. At the same time, he was acknowledging that he had already forgiven me. Then the guru spoke again: "You are a good boy. Very pure."

The next thing I knew, I was sobbing uncontrollably. Baba's eyes widened and a gentle smile spread across his lips. He held out his arms. I leaned forward and Baba wrapped his arms around me, giving me a powerful hug. A torrent of tears streamed down my face and onto the guru's shoulder. I felt as though the guru was absorbing all my pent-up grief and trauma.

Finally, after what seemed like an eternity, Baba released me from his embrace. But he continued staring into my eyes with an amused expression on his face. One of the male ushers rushed over to him with a cloth, presumably to wipe the tears I'd left on his shoulder. But the guru shooed him away. He said something to Anjali, which she didn't translate. Then they were both looking at me and smiling. I felt naked in front of the guru like this. He knew everything about me and could read my thoughts.

Baba wiggled his head from side to side. Then he motioned for me to crouch down next to Anjali, and the *darshan* line started moving again. "What is your given name?" she asked, turning to me.

"Douglas."

"Baba is giving you the spiritual name 'Deependra.'"

Baba's face lit up as he glanced in my direction. "Deependra," he repeated, as if pleased with his choice. "Very good name."

I bowed my head and thanked him. I returned to my place in the hall, where I continued to observe the guru and the *darshan* line from afar. Within seconds, I saw Anjali speak to Gopi, hand her something, and then point in my direction. A moment later, the angel was hurrying toward me. By the time she reached me she was out of breath.

"Baba wants you to have this," she said with a glowing smile. She knelt down and handed me a small, yellow card. Printed on one side was the name Baba had just given me: "Deependra." On the other side was written: "Lord of Light."

I looked at the girl kneeling in front of me, and thanked her. Then I noticed her eyes. They were like two precious jewels. Her left eye was sapphire blue, and her right eye was emerald green. Their beauty took my breath away and I was drawn in by them, unable to stop staring.

"Don't feel like you have to use it," she said. "Not everyone goes by their spiritual name around Baba." Gopi flashed her beautiful, wholesome smile at me again. Then she brushed a few strands of hair from her eyes, exposing the smooth, soft underside of her wrist. With her long, flowing hair, green silk sari, and golden jewelry, she looked like she was only visiting the Earth from a celestial realm.

I thanked Gopi again, and she returned to her place on the dais at Baba's feet.

In that moment I felt more loved than I'd ever felt at any time during my life. It was as if Baba had looked into my soul, had seen the *real me*, and had accepted me for who I was. He was aware of how I had caused my mother's death and the agonizing guilt I felt because of it. And he had forgiven me. With his divine power, he had reached into my heart and untied the knots that had been keeping me in emotional bondage.

The time had come for me to forgive myself. Through his command, he had empowered me to do it. I closed my eyes, folded my hands, and prayed: *With Baba's blessing, I hereby forgive myself for all the grief and misery I caused my mother.* Then, it was as if a great weight had been lifted from my shoulders. I sat up straight and opened my eyes.

I knew that from then on I would, of course, go by the spiritual name with which the guru had chosen to bless me. Douglas was dead.

12.
THE AVADHOOT

"GOOD MORNING, *DEEPENDRA*," CAME a voice from behind me. I was tying my shoelaces in the alcove outside the hall after the *Guru Gita*. I turned around to see the neckless swami, Akhandananda, smiling down at me. *That's me. I'm Deependra. Lord of Light!* The swami was the first to address me by my new name.

Akhandananda walked me down the long corridor that stretched between the meditation hall and the cafeteria. Soft, golden sunlight filtered through the trees outside and in through the large picture windows of the passageway. I felt deeply peaceful, at one with nature and the universe.

Over breakfast I told Akhandananda about my *kundalini* awakening in detail. The swami leaned forward, barely touching his savory porridge as I recounted my story of the explosions of energy in my spine and my vision of the blue pearl.

"All classic signs, my dear boy!" he said.

Then I explained how, ever since the retreat, I'd felt as though I were still in a blissful state of meditation. "I feel detached from everything happening around me—from my own thoughts and feelings, too. I feel like I'm sitting in a movie theater, watching a film in which I'm the main character."

Akhandananda brought a finger to his lips. "Shhh! Don't say another word, Deependra. If you talk about it, you'll lose it."

"I'm not sure I understand, Swamiji."

"The Buddha taught that an explanation of the Highest Reality is not that reality itself, just as a finger pointing at the moon is not the moon itself. A seeker who only looks at the finger and mistakes it for the moon will never see the real moon. Understand?"

I did not understand. During the retreat we'd been encouraged to share our experiences, but now the swami was telling me to keep mine to myself.

"The ego will always attempt to subvert any insight into the Supreme Truth for its own purpose. By talking about it, you're only helping it."

"And what purpose is that, Swamiji?"

"Survival," he answered. "*Kundalini* awakening is a death sentence for the ego."

As the days and weeks passed, my love of spiritual practice grew and my devotion to the guru deepened, but the bliss and the higher state of consciousness I'd experienced in the days immediately following *shaktipat* faded. Occasionally I still had visions of the small blue light, and I considered this a confirmation that I was getting closer to enlightenment. But to experience the bliss again, I realized, I'd need another infusion of spiritual energy from Baba.

I was beginning to understand why Jeremy had said, "You can never have too much *shakti*." But the retreats were expensive—they had already gone up another fifty dollars since the guru arrived. I prayed that my inheritance money would last long enough for me to take enough retreats to attain the ultimate goal.

My *seva* changed too. On a typical day I worked in Housing between breakfast and lunch, and then again between two in the afternoon and the evening *arati* in the Brahmananda temple. This schedule still left plenty of hours in the day for me to serve the guru, so I signed up for extra *seva*.

For a time, I woke up an hour earlier and meditated in the hall alone, so that I could chop vegetables in the kitchen before the *Guru Gita*. The kitchen was supervised by a strict, short-tempered woman named Yashoda Edwards. She'd spent a lot of time in Baba's ashram in India where she had picked up a little Hindi and Marathi. Slight, pale-skinned and thin-lipped, Yashoda wore wire frame glasses and had light brown stringy hair that she wore tied up in a bun. On her frail body she wore loose-fitting, frumpy blouses under her apron, and favored long, drab, denim skirts.

Everyone under Yashoda in the kitchen had to observe strict silence at all times, unless it was to ask Yashoda a question about *seva* or to chant. Only Yashoda was allowed to speak freely, and when she did it was either to give chopping instructions or to dispense spiritual wisdom: "Every activity has meaning and a vibrational effect on the food," she would often remind us. "Each movement of your knife counts. You must work joyfully and with complete concentration, as though you were meditating. Always remember: the *intention* with which we cook is the main ingredient. Everything we do is for the guru."

The precise way in which the ashram food was prepared was very important to Baba and he would often make surprise visits to the kitchen to check our work. For this reason, despite Yashoda's reputation for being strict, chopping vegetables was a coveted *seva*. One morning we were chopping turnips and chanting "Shree Ram, Jai Ram" when Baba appeared. I first detected his presence by the sudden stiffening of my fellow kitchen *sevites*' posture. I started when I saw him and nearly cut off the end of my index finger. I quickly regained my composure, however, and, like everybody else, went about my work pretending he wasn't there. He was accompanied by Suresh and Rashmi Varma—his personal attendant, a tall, thin, fair-skinned Indian man with droopy eyes, a big nose, and a long face shaped like a string bean.

He was also with the frowning man I saw during Baba's arrival, whom Yashoda introduced as Gajendra Williams, the ashram manager.

Gajendra Williams? I thought. Wasn't he the embezzler? What was that thief doing here? His presence caused me some alarm, but knowing that Baba could read my thoughts, I cleared my mind and focused all my attention on what I was doing. When we had finished with the turnips and were about to switch to broccoli, Baba came forward and told Yashoda that we had to keep chopping the turnips until all the pieces were the same size.

Baba held up a perfectly cut piece of turnip and spoke to us in Hindi. "Discipline and repetitive work," Suresh translated. "Through it, the mind becomes steady."

Later in the summer I heard Yashoda say the same exact same thing to newcomers, without attributing the quote to Baba.

Putting in shifts in the dish room after meals gave me an opportunity to get in another couple of hours of extra *seva* each day. Even though Baba rarely visited, I preferred working in the dish room to the kitchen. This was because Shankar, the man who ran it, had no rule against talking, and always shared fascinating stories about Baba. Not only had Shankar known Baba in India before the guru's first world tour, but he had also had the extreme good fortune of meeting Gurudev Brahmananda while he was still in his earthly body. Since he had been on the Raja Yoga scene so long, I was certain that Shankar must have already attained enlightenment. I was careful to watch my thoughts around him and treated him with the utmost respect.

We delighted in exchanging stories about the guru— where he had been recently sighted, what he was doing at the time, and with whom. Everybody wanted to hear all the details: Was the guru in a playful or fiery mood? Was he carrying a stick or was he dispensing chocolates and gifts? Which famous person had come to meet him? What kind of hat was he wearing?

I loved hearing about the latest Baba sightings, but what fascinated me most were the stories about the old days around the guru in the Ravipur ashram. I yearned to travel with Baba to his native land and to stay there for as long as he would let me. Devotees who had lived in Ravipur described the atmosphere there as ten times more powerful than any other ashram in the Raja Yoga universe. I figured that spending time in such a holy place would make me holy. In Ravipur, thousands of miles away from home and out of the reach of my deluded family, I would be free to live like a true renunciant and focus exclusively on my spiritual development. Far from the myriad distractions of the material world, I thought living in Ravipur would be like dying and going to heaven.

The highlight of every day was the evening program with Baba. The format was usually the same: the programs began with a philosophical discourse by one of Baba's senior swamis or an "experience talk" by a longtime devotee. Afterwards, we chanted a few rounds of *Om Namah Shivaya*. The lights were dimmed and Baba made his entrance. After a brief meditation session Baba spoke. One evening, he quoted the great poet saint Kabir: "All know that the drop merges into the ocean, but few know that the ocean merges into the drop."

The verse brought tears to my eyes, and helped me to understand the Supreme Truth: Although I was a tiny drop in the ocean of consciousness, I myself contained the entire ocean within me.

Back in my room, just before lights out, I took the vial of Baba's bathwater that Sita had given me, and in the privacy of the bathroom, poured a couple of drops of it into the palm of my hand. *These drops contain the entire universe*, I told myself. *They also contain the grace bestowing power of God.* I brought the palm of my hand to my lips and sucked the precious liquid into my mouth. My entire body shook with the force of its *shakti*.

As I lay in bed waiting for sleep, I had another fleeting vision of the tiny blue light, which appeared behind my closed eyelids. *The blue pearl is the seed that contains the entire cosmos,* I remembered Satyananda saying during the meditation retreat. Then I drifted off to sleep.

I am meditating with my eyes open, seated in the lotus position at the bottom of the ocean. I am surrounded by monster sharks with gaping mouths full of razor sharp teeth. They swim menacingly close, but I am unafraid. They do not attack me.

I was on my way to *seva* when Sita Perkins called out to me from the lower lobby. "Deependra, over here!" She and a tall man in his mid-thirties were standing next to the long gray curtain in front of Baba's house. The man was wearing a cowboy hat and a photographer's vest. Two professional-looking cameras dangled from his neck. He was Avadhoot Plotnick, the guru's personal photographer and one of his closest disciples. I knew this because I'd seen him make the rounds of the ashram with Baba and disappear behind the curtain with him many times. Today he looked agitated and seemed incapable of standing still.

"Listen," he said, sizing me up. "I want you to go down to the basement and get my Hasselblad and bring it to my room."

"Avadhoot is in room three," Sita said, thrusting the key to Baba's private storage unit into my hand.

I knew where Avadhoot Plotnick's room was—it was in the VIP dorm next to Suresh and Anjali's rooms—but I was worried about being late to *seva*.

Avadhoot clapped his hands together, startling me. "What are you waiting for, kid?"

"What about my regular *seva?*"

"Don't worry about it," Sita said. "I'll let them know you'll be a few minutes late. Baba's waiting. Go!"

I turned to leave, and then hesitated. I wasn't even sure what I was looking for. "What's a Hasselblad?" I asked, turning around.

Avadhoot was already hurrying toward the entrance to Baba's house. "It's a camera," he bellowed with a New Yorker's accent. "The case is marked. It's with the rest of my shit."

From his ten-gallon hat, snakeskin boots, and bolo tie, I assumed that Baba's photographer was a Texan. But this was before I'd heard him open his loud mouth. His accent and speaking manner gave him away. I was willing to bet that he'd grown up on "Lawn Guyland," and was Jewish, like me. I later found out that his spiritual name, "Avadhoot," referred to a kind of mystic who acted without consideration for conventional standards of behavior. The more I got to know Baba's eccentric photographer, the more I saw how well-suited he was to his name.

Down in the basement, I noticed that almost all the boxes labeled "Baba's House" were gone, along with the rest of the boxes that belonged to Suresh, Anjali, and Avadhoot. The boxes belonging to Sergio Casto, the broken Ganesh statue, the old throne, and the medical equipment were still there—except the examining table with foot supports.

I found the case labeled Hasselblad next to a tripod and some flash equipment. I lugged it up from the basement to the VIP dormitory next to Baba's house, and knocked on the door to the cowboy's room. There was no answer. Putting my ear to the door, I could hear Avadhoot talking inside. I knocked again. The door abruptly swung open, and there was Baba's photographer, glaring at me. In one hand he held the base of a telephone. Between his ear and shoulder he was cradling the receiver.

"Uh-huh," he said into the phone, impatiently motioning for me to enter with his free hand. I wanted to come in, but Avadhoot, distracted by his conversation and still in the doorway, was blocking my path. Irritated by my hesitation, he grabbed my arm and pulled me in, causing me to bump the case against the wall of his room.

Avadhoot's eyes bulged. "Easy!" he snapped. "No, not you," he said to the person on the phone. "I'm talking to the idiot carrying my Hasselblad."

I bristled at being called an idiot, especially by someone so close to the guru. But I accepted the insult as the bitter medicine needed to rid me of the disease of ego.

Like Suresh and Anjali, Avadhoot had a room all to himself. Instead of three cheap bunk beds crammed into one tiny room, his quarters were spacious, and furnished with a single queen-size bed adorned with a cotton red and black batik elephant bedspread. Like the rooms of Baba's young Indian disciples, his room had a telephone. But unlike the rooms of Anjali and Suresh, Avadhoot's quarters contained much more personal stuff. He had a high-end stereo system, an expensive-looking pair of headphones, and a large record collection. Glancing over it, I recognized the Andy Warhol banana from the album *The Velvet Underground and Nico*.

Who listened to worldly music in the ashram? I wondered. Even stranger, hanging on the walls was a collection of Stetson cowboy hats. Some of them were woolen, others were made of felt or straw. All were white, tan, or gray, except for one hung prominently in the center of the collection, which was black. Through the open door of his closet I noticed an array of leather and suede jackets. Also in the closet, on the floor next to a pair of snakeskin boots, were two small cases, a tripod, and a set of silver photographer's umbrellas.

All the other bedrooms I'd seen in the ashram displayed the same photos of Baba and Gurudev that were available in the bookstore. But Avadhoot's walls were covered with pictures of the gurus that I'd never seen before, all mounted in intricately carved wooden frames. I could have stared at them all day. One of the photos in particular caught my eye. It was of Baba and Avadhoot standing together with their arms around each other like they were best friends. Avadhoot towered over Baba, and they were smiling with their mouths wide open like they were laughing at something uproariously funny.

"No, fuck *you*, Gajendra!" Avadhoot hollered into the phone. He sat down on the edge of his bed and motioned for me to set the case down on the floor. I was about to leave when he tapped the spot next to him. "Sit, sit." I took a seat on the bed where I was told, and was now close enough to hear Gajendra Williams cursing on the other end of the line.

As I waited for Avadhoot to finish his conversation, I studied his unusual face: although he wasn't ugly, there was something vaguely grotesque about him. My guess was that he had once been in some kind of horrible accident and had needed extensive plastic surgery. The upper part of his left ear was missing. The small section that remained included only a partial earlobe. Even stranger, sections of his face were blotchy and unevenly stretched, as though the skin had been pulled too tightly in some areas, giving him an asymmetrical appearance. I looked up at the ten-gallon hat on his head, and then down at his buffalo skull tie. *What a freak!* I thought. *Why does Baba let him dress like such a buffoon?*

"That's not what *I* told that shit-for-brains asshole in Purchasing," Avadhoot grumbled. He eyed me as he continued to exchange obscenities with Gajendra on the phone. I couldn't be sure, but I had the impression he was trying to gauge my reaction. While I found his swearing and unspiritual manner unsettling—particularly because he was so close to the guru—I was determined not to reveal my true feelings. *If this is how Baba's people behave, so be it,* I told myself. *Who am I to judge?* I turned my face into a mask of detachment. "I'm doing portraits of Baba with the Hasselblad in half an hour, and I'm telling you I don't have enough of the right stock!"

Avadhoot turned red listening to Gajendra's response. I couldn't help wondering why he was subjecting me to this argument and keeping me from returning to my regular *seva*.

"I told that mental midget Ranjiv that I needed the medium format. And what does he order—thirty-five millimeter!"

Believing I was no longer needed, and anxious to get back to work, I got up from the bed to leave, but Avadhoot took hold of my arm again and yanked me back down. "*You* tell Baba we can do the pictures tomorrow!" Avadhoot shouted. Then he hung up the phone.

"Jesus Christ! Can you believe that *moron*?"

Unable to think of anything to say, I shrugged.

Avadhoot stomped over to the case I had just delivered, opened it, glanced inside, and then slammed it shut again.

"That *fucker!*" he shouted, making me jump. Then he looked in my direction, and again, I had the impression that he was taking note of my reaction.

"If you don't need anything else from me, I'll be going back to Housing now." I hesitated this time before getting up to leave.

Avadhoot ignored me and seemed lost in thought for a moment. "What's your name again?" he asked, regaining his composure.

"Deependra."

The photographer outstretched his hand for me to shake. "Good to meet you, kid."

I gave my hand to him and he turned it over so that his palm was facing downward over mine. His grip was firm at first, and then he relaxed it. I expected him to release my hand, but he held on to it with a maniacal grin on his face. I finally pulled it away after the awkwardness of the situation became unbearable. *Is he gay?* I wondered. Then I realized how preposterous the notion was. I understood that the photographer's odd behavior was yet another test from the guru.

"Sita tells me you're a bright kid. She says you have right understanding."

My mind raced. I wanted to respond in a way that seemed modest and, at the same time, confident, but the phone rang before I could say anything.

Avadhoot picked up and his demeanor changed instantly. His jaw dropped and his back went rigid. "Han ji," he said, lowering his head as he listened to the party on the other end. He was speaking in an Indian language. "Ji, Baba, sab theek hai." I knew he was talking to the guru.

How amazing to receive a call from Baba! I thought. *What would it be like to have a personal relationship with God?* I was also impressed Avadhoot had learned to speak to the guru in his native language.

He hung up the phone and turned to me. "Listen, the girl from the video department who usually helps me busted her leg, so you're going to assist me today, okay?"

"Sure!" Helping Baba's photographer sounded a lot more exciting than chopping vegetables.

Avadhoot told me that I would be helping him to adjust the flash, which would be set up on a stand, while he took pictures of Baba and a VIP from the Indian consulate who was up from New York City for the day. The guru would be receiving him in the Namaste room.

"This is a *gevalt* situation," Avadhoot said, opening the Hasselblad case. "You know what that means, right, kid?"

"I certainly do." *Oy gevalt* was a Yiddish phrase used to express anxiety or shock. His use of the word was confirmation that he was Jewish.

"What's your last name, kid?" Avadhoot asked, loading a film magazine into the big camera.

"Greenbaum."

Avadhoot smiled condescendingly. "Kid, you're alright!" Then he pinched my cheek, digging his nails into my flesh. "Come. Let's go. You take the Hasselblad."

Now that Avadhoot knew I was Jewish too, I hoped he might see me as a friend.

The Namaste room was adjacent to Baba's quarters off the lower lobby, and was a semi-private space where Baba received special visitors or conducted meetings with his staff. When we arrived outside the room, I could feel Baba's tremendous *shakti* through the closed door. The muscles in my arms and legs twitched in response, and I felt a popping sensation in the area of my solar plexus and heart. Avadhoot knocked on the door three times in rapid succession, and, a few seconds later, Suresh opened up and ushered us in.

Following Avadhoot into the chamber, I trod as lightly as possible, taking care not to bump the bulky camera case into any of the guests or inner circle people, who were seated before the guru on the carpeted floor. Baba sat cross-legged on a throne-like armchair. He was speaking

Hindi to a dapper Indian man sitting at his feet. The man was dressed in a mustard-colored business suit, had dark skin and a thin mustache, and was balding. A television crew was filming the exchange. Their camera was marked with the BBC logo.

I set the case down, and took a seat on the floor next to Avadhoot. When I looked up, Baba was staring in my direction. My stomach rolled. *Does the guru approve of my being here?* I wondered. He held me in his gaze. Then he turned to Anjali and said something to her in Hindi, which caused her to turn around and look in my direction. I half expected her to tell Avadhoot that Baba wanted me to leave, but the guru returned his attention to his guest, and I began to feel less like an interloper.

The angel Gopi was also there. She was seated in her usual spot, directly behind Anjali, and was watching Baba's every nod and gesture with laser-like focus. About ten minutes after we arrived, Anjali turned around to tell her something, which prompted her to dash across the room toward me. *That's it—I've overstayed my welcome,* I told myself. *She's going to ask me to leave.* I was wrong. Ignoring me, Gopi crouched down next to Avadhoot and whispered into his tiny, misshapen ear. I was close enough to hear: "Baba wants the video crew here right away."

"What for?" the cowboy asked too loudly. The guru glanced in our direction again.

"Baba wants them to film the television crew."

Avadhoot glanced over at the guru and nodded his assent. Gopi returned to her place behind Anjali, and Avadhoot sent me in search of Arjuna Weinberg, the videographer. "Tell him to bring extra lights."

Eager to prove myself worthy of the mission, I leapt to my feet, made a dash for the door, and raced toward the Audiovisual department. I wondered why the guru wanted footage of the camera crew, why he couldn't simply ask them for a copy of the interview on cassette later. Then I decided it wasn't my concern.

I'd gotten as far as the upper lobby when Gajendra Williams intercepted me. "Hey you! Hold on there a second!"

Stopping abruptly, I spun around to face the manager.

Gajendra frowned. "Where are you going in such a hurry?"

"Baba wants the video crew in the Namaste room ASAP!"

Gajendra's eyes widened in comprehension, and he waved me on. "Go! Go!"

I'd never spoken to Arjuna, but I had watched him closely ever since he had arrived from India with the rest of the tour people. Originally from Brooklyn, he traveled all over the world with the guru, videotaping all of his talks. Baba had named him after Arjuna, the hero of the Mahabharata, who was revered as a great archer, a peerless warrior, and the perfect disciple of Lord Krishna. The Arjuna Weinberg of Raja Yoga, however, was a diminutive, dark-haired man in his late twenties with a high-pitched voice, prominent nose, and small, tired eyes that were always watery and bloodshot. I found him in the video library, screening footage of Baba's pit bulls working with a dog trainer and another man wearing a protective gauntlet. I cleared my throat to make my presence known, but Arjuna remained engrossed in what he was watching. If he was even aware I was trying to get his attention, he was simply ignoring me.

"Avadhoot says you should come right away to the Namaste room with your camera. He says you should bring extra lights."

He was slow to respond. "I have no crew," he answered, without taking his eyes off the video monitor.

Kriyadevi, who had been at work in the editing suite with the door open, hobbled into the library on her crutches to join us. "He means he has no one to do *sound*. I'm out of commission."

Arjuna pressed stop on the VTR and the monitor went blank. He ejected the cassette, and wrote something on the label. I was baffled. He seemed to be in no hurry to come to the guru's service. I began to worry that Baba was being kept waiting. I didn't want Avadhoot to blame me for the delay. Then I had an idea.

"Maybe I could hold the microphone."

"You?" Arjuna scoffed, finally looking at me. The cameraman squinted as he sized me up. "Okay, why not?"

Kriyadevi explained the job to me as quickly as possible. As it turned out, doing sound was not as easy as I had thought. Pointing the microphone at whoever was speaking was only part of it. I also had to carry and operate the portable VTR. "The most important thing to remember is never to let the audio levels on the meter go into the red," she said. "When that happens, the sound gets distorted."

Arjuna hung the heavy deck around my neck and handed me a pair of large headphones. "Here," he said. "Try these on." I slipped the headset over my ears.

Kriyadevi picked up a long microphone and plugged it into the VTR. "This is a shotgun microphone," she said speaking into it. "Always hold it by the handle and listen carefully to make sure the sound is good."

"Pointing the microphone at the subject doesn't hurt either," Arjuna quipped.

Kriyadevi glared at him, and then turned back to me. "If you pay attention to what's going on and follow Arjuna's lead, you'll do fine."

I was excited and anxious at the same time. "How do I start and stop recording?"

"You don't have to worry about that," said Arjuna, hefting the camera onto his shoulder. He connected his camera to the recording deck with a thick, three-foot-long cable, and held it up for me to see. "The camera controls the VTR through this umbilical cord. You'll be tethered to me the whole time. All you have to worry about is getting good sound."

Just then the phone rang behind the closed door of Jake's office. A moment later, the door swung open, and the department head burst through. His eyes were wide with alarm. "They just called from the Namaste room. What are you still doing here?"

Taking care not to yank or snag the camera, I hurried back to the Namaste room behind Arjuna, maintaining as little distance between us as possible. When we arrived,

Baba was being interviewed by a journalist with the BBC crew. With all the bulky equipment hanging from me, I felt even more conspicuous than before, but no one seemed to notice when I came in this time—except Gopi. Turning her head to see who was at the door, she flashed me a radiant smile and gave me a thumbs-up. *She likes me!* I thought, and a warm feeling spread through me. In my state of distraction, I nearly stumbled over Rashmi Varma, Baba's personal attendant.

Luckily, Avadhoot was too busy taking pictures of Baba to scold me for taking too long to return with the cameraman. When he finally did become aware of our presence, he shot Arjuna—not me—a dirty look.

Don't mess this up, I told myself. In my mind, this was my big chance to demonstrate my dedication to the guru. If I came up short, I might never get a chance again.

Arjuna had me set the deck down on the floor next to his tripod. When Avadhoot saw where we had set up, he glowered at Arjuna and then motioned for us to move back.

"Make sure the entire BBC crew is in the shot with Baba at all times," Avadhoot said in a stage whisper. He seemed to want Baba to overhear him.

"What's the point of that?" Arjuna whispered back, tilting his head to meet the cowboy's glare.

Avadhoot towered over the cameraman. "That's what Baba wants."

Although I was pointing the microphone directly at the journalist, I could barely hear him over my headphones. Avadhoot must have noticed my concern because he stopped taking pictures to come find out what was wrong. Kneeling down on the floor next to me, he yanked the headphones off my head and put them on to have a listen. Curling his bottom lip over his teeth and squinting in concentration, he indicated for me to raise the audio level by pointing his thumb toward the ceiling. When I gained the right volume, he nodded and handed the headphones back to me. Then he cupped his hands around my ear and whispered so loudly it hurt: "Make sure you get clear sound from Baba, Anjali, and the schmuck. The microphone is hyper-directional. Just aim it at whoever's talking and you should be able to get decent sound, even from back here."

I assumed that the "schmuck" was the journalist from the BBC. He was a middle-aged man with a ruddy complexion and sandy hair, dressed in a tweed jacket and burgundy tie. He spoke with a posh British accent, and his tone with the guru was, at times, disturbingly condescending. From the way he kept shifting his legs during the interview, I could tell he was uncomfortable sitting on the floor. I wondered if he realized how blessed he was to be in the presence of such a great saint as Baba.

"Every weekend, hundreds of people come to see you here in your ashram," the journalist said. "All the people I've spoken to say they get something out of your teachings. Many of them have received your touch and claim to have had mystical experiences and profound feelings of love and inner peace. I've observed the effect you have on these people and have asked them to tell me about it. What do you have to say?"

"I have one simple teaching," Baba answered, through Anjali. "The happiness and love that you are all seeking outside of yourself and are unable to find is inside of you. I tell people to turn within and meditate. When they do this, they find the peace they are searching for within themselves. I don't preach religion. Just as breathing doesn't belong to any one faith, neither does meditation."

The journalist smiled politely. "Indeed, Swami. You tell people to look within themselves, but your followers dedicate their entire lives to you. You control every aspect of their lives. They've told me this."

Baba chuckled. "Maybe some say that. And perhaps some of them do give their lives to me. But I also give my life to them—as much as they are able to receive it. This is the nature of the guru-disciple relationship."

"But are you conscious of directing the activities of your devotees? Of controlling their lives?"

"It's not that I keep them next to me all the time. I send them back into the world to do their own work, too. I have ashrams all over the globe. If I tried to take all my devotees with me wherever I went, where would I put them? In my suitcase?"

Everybody in the Namaste room laughed, except the journalist and his crew.

"People come to me and spend some time in the ashram," Baba continued. "Then, after learning something, they return to the world. Some of them come back later."

"The guru-disciple relationship is an ancient institution in India, but here in the West the word guru is a newer term, and has developed negative connotations because of certain teachers who exploit their followers' naiveté. What makes you different?"

"Why are there so many charlatans posing as true gurus today? The blame for this lies with their followers. Americans choose their gurus the way they elect their presidents. Because of their ignorance, false disciples get trapped. And driven by selfishness and delusion, false gurus destroy the lives of their disciples. But a genuine seeker would never fall for a false guru."

"You insist that your followers observe celibacy. Why?"

"*Ojas* is a vital yellow fluid released and stored in the heart and serves as a fuel for meditation. It is derived from sexual fluid, and it gives mental strength and the physical endurance needed for yoga. If someone meditates a lot, but does not conserve his sexual fluid and provide his body with nourishing foods, his *ojas* will become depleted and he will lose all his radiance and energy for spiritual practice. If someone wants to live in the ashram and meditate for long periods, he should not only consume nutritious foods, but he must also practice abstinence."

"Does this apply to your married disciples as well, Swami?"

"This applies to everyone living in the ashram."

"Are you celibate, Swami?"

Everyone laughed again at the absurdity of the question.

"Yes, I have been celibate my entire life. A true guru must be immune to the temptations of the flesh. He must be free from desire."

"I'm told that through a look, word, thought, or touch, you can awaken a spiritual energy in people. Please tell me about it."

"Yes, that is my yoga—Raja Yoga—the *royal* yoga. The king of all yogas, an ancient tradition from the dawn of time. It is not a fad, like so many things that take people's fancy here in the West. Only a guru who has been a lifelong celibate, and has succeeded in reversing the flow of his sexual fluid in the most advanced stages of yoga, is able to give *shaktipat* and awaken the *kundalini* in his disciples."

"Some people seem to experience this awakening and others do not. Do you have control over this?"

"Certain people are aware that they have received *shaktipat* immediately because of their great faith. Others become aware of it only later, because it happens on a more subtle level."

"Will I experience this awakening as a result of having met you?"

"Yes, it is likely you will. The *shakti* is like a virus," said Baba, chuckling. "It is very contagious."

The room erupted in laughter—even the journalist laughed.

"Your followers worship you like a living god. What do you have to say about that?"

"The *inner guru* is not a person. He is the grace-bestowing power of God. The outer-guru is however you see him. If you see him as a god, he is a god. If you see him as a demon, he is a demon. If you see him as an ordinary man, he is an ordinary man."

"How do you see yourself, Swami?"

"I see myself as myself."

After the interview, Daniel Groza—the head of ashram construction—serenaded Baba with a few devotional songs he had recently composed. Daniel sang and played acoustic guitar, and his wife, Chamundi, accompanied him on the tambourine. Chamundi was the guru's personal cook. She and Daniel had been with Baba since his first visit to the States in 1970, and were members of his inner circle. I found all of Daniel's songs deeply inspiring.

When the Grozas' private concert was over, everyone was asked to leave, except the Indian man in the mustard-colored suit and a handful of Baba's closest people. Arjuna was also asked to take his camera and go, but Avadhoot told me to stay so I could help set up his Hasselblad and flash equipment.

The portraits were taken with Baba seated on his throne and the well-dressed Indian man kneeling next to him on the floor. The pictures only took a few minutes, and while I was extremely grateful to be able to stay, it was unclear to me why I was needed. All I did was stand next to Avadhoot and confirm that his flash was going off whenever he took a picture. The only time the flash failed to go off, however, Baba told Avadhoot himself. After the pictures, the Indian man presented Baba with a gold watch, which the guru regarded with indifference. Suresh showed him out, leaving me alone with Baba, Avadhoot, Anjali, and Gopi. With so few other people around to help drown out my thoughts, I became acutely aware of how active my mind was and how undisciplined it must have seemed to the Omniscient One.

Baba spoke for a long time in Hindi with Anjali while the rest of us sat on the floor at attention in case we were needed. Copying the others' perfect posture, I kept my back as straight as possible and my eyes glued to the guru. As hard as I tried to keep my mind free from thoughts, my attention wandered to Gopi. She was unbelievably beautiful. *A highly evolved being like Gopi could make me whole if Baba were ever to allow me to marry her,* I thought. Then, just as my mind began to wander to the pleasures of the flesh, the guru gazed in my direction and said something in Hindi to his translator. I was mortified by my impure thoughts.

"Deependra," Anjali said, turning around to address me. "Baba wants to know how long you will stay in the ashram."

"I want to follow Baba to India in September and stay in the Ravipur ashram until he returns to America."

"*Aacha, aacha,*" Baba said.

"Good, good," Anjali translated.

"How old are you?"

"Eighteen, Baba."

"What does your family think about your living in the ashram?"

"They would prefer I go to college."

I believed, of course, that Baba already knew the answers to these questions, and that the dialogue we were engaged in was benefiting me on a deeper level. The content of what we were saying to each other was unimportant.

"School is very good," Baba said. I was suddenly anxious. Was Baba going to send me away back into the world? Akhandananda once told me the guru did that sometimes when it became clear we no longer belonged in the ashram.

Baba continued to speak to Anjali, but he was no longer looking at me. When he finished, she turned around to address me again. Smiling, she said, "Baba says you should come to India with him at the end of the summer, and that you should arrange it with Gajendra."

I couldn't believe my ears. It was a dream come true. This was all the proof I needed that Baba loved me and valued me as a disciple. Baba stood up to leave, and as he did, everyone else sprang to their feet. Before exiting with Anjali through a second door that led to his private quarters, the guru gave me a big pat on the back.

Avadhoot said something to me, but I was too excited to listen. Then he also went out through the door to Baba's house, leaving me alone in the Namaste room with Gopi. She beamed her angelic smile at me.

"Did you even hear what Avadhoot just said to you?"

"No," I confessed, suddenly feeling too timid to make eye contact with her.

She laughed. "He told you to pack up all his gear and bring it to his office."

"Um, thanks." I forced myself to look at her. She was stunning. Her tan, freckled face glowed with the guru's *shakti*. Her lustrous blonde hair had been brightened by the summer sun, and her mismatched eyes were mesmerizing. Standing this close to her left me breathless.

"You did really well, by the way."

"You think so?" This was my chance to talk to her, but I was so overcome by my feelings for her I could barely speak. Finally, I blurted out the first thing that came into my head: "What exactly is your *seva?*"

As soon as the words had left my mouth I regretted the stupid question. Everybody in the ashram knew what Gopi did.

"I'm one of Baba's *darshan* assistants."

"What a great *seva*. It must be amazing to be so close to the guru all the time!"

Gopi smiled politely and nodded. "Being around the guru can get pretty intense sometimes. Baba has a fiery side he doesn't always show to the public."

13.
BROTHERS

"DO YOU HAVE YOUR passport with you?" Gajendra asked. He was sitting behind the desk that once belonged to Alan. I was suddenly seized by anxiety. I didn't have a passport. I didn't even know how to get one.

Gajendra narrowed his eyes. "You do have a valid passport, don't you?"

I confessed that I didn't.

"Better get one quick!" he growled. "You'll need time to apply for a visa."

I didn't care for Gajendra, and I was a little afraid of him. I missed Alan. I had looked up to him. He had been on track to become a swami, so I was shocked when one day I heard that he had "left and was never coming back." When I asked around about him nobody could—or *would*—tell me why.

Gajendra wrote down an address in Manhattan where I could apply for a passport in person. He said that I shouldn't waste any time, because the Indian government was slow to process entry visas. "You'll need to apply for *entry visa*," he said sharply. "It'll allow you to stay in India with Baba for up to a year. You only have to worry about getting the passport, okay? The ashram will take care of your visa and make all your travel arrangements. Got it?"

I nodded.

"I'll be giving you a bill for the ticket and the visa processing fee, too. You understand that, right, kid?"

I nodded again.

After the meeting with Gajendra, I called Melanie to ask her to send me my birth certificate. The need to involve my sister in my plans and the day trip I'd have to make to the Passport Agency in Manhattan stressed me out. I didn't want to interact with my family anymore. I didn't want to have anything to do with the world. I longed for the day when I'd be a swami and no longer have to engage in such mundane activities.

My stress about Melanie's reaction to my decision to go to India turned out to be needless. She agreed to send my birth certificate right away, and I got it in the mail a couple of days later. Predictably, she was against the trip, but conceded that I was now legally an adult and she had no right to stop me.

Ordinarily, the ashram shuttle was only available to Baba's personal staff or year-round ashram residents. But Gajendra said I could use it, since Baba had specifically invited me to travel back to India with him. I was dropped off with the other passengers in front of the Manhattan ashram, a converted brownstone in Greenwich Village. Jeremy had explained in detail how to find my way to the passport agency by subway, but I was nervous I'd somehow get on the wrong train and end up somewhere in Brooklyn. I decided to take a taxi instead. *Why not?* I told myself. *I'm rich. I can afford it.*

After applying for my passport, I consulted the information pamphlet that Gajendra had given me for first-time visitors to the Indian ashram. My next stop was a tropical disease center, where I could get a gamma globulin shot. After that, I went in search of a flashlight, insect repellent, toilet paper, and Birkenstock sandals, all of which were listed in the pamphlet. I was unable to figure out where to buy the Birkenstocks, but Jeremy agreed to meet me an hour earlier than planned at Bloomingdale's in Midtown, where we found them easily. Later we met up with Carrie at a vegetarian restaurant called Serendipity Three.

My brother and his wife had been up to Birchwood Falls a handful of times since Baba's arrival. But it seemed that whenever they came, my heavy *seva* schedule made it impossible for me to see them for more than a few minutes at a time. I was glad to be able to spend time with them over dinner, without the pressure of having to rush off to work. I told them I'd be going to live in India with Baba at the end of the summer.

"Any chance of your visiting Baba in India anytime soon?"

Jeremy smiled wistfully. "A trip to India would be our dream come true, but I won't be able to get away until I finish my internship. Even then, it will be tricky—I'll be starting my residency. I just don't know…"

I found it difficult to understand how Jeremy and Carrie could be at once so spiritual and devoted to the guru, yet at the same time so enmeshed in *Maya*—the illusion of this world. I spent the night on the sofa in the living room of their shoebox apartment, and then got a ride back up to Birchwood Falls on the ashram shuttle the next morning. I was astounded at how much money I'd spent just on taxi fares alone. It made me feel queasy. I made a mental note to study a subway map the next time I was in New York. The City turned out not to be as scary as I'd feared. The idea of running out of money someday and not feeling rich anymore was much more terrifying.

My passport came in the mail a couple of weeks later. It was a huge relief to turn it over to Gajendra, knowing that Baba would be taking care of everything else for me. All I had to do was write a check, and the ashram would do the rest. In just a few more weeks, I'd be on my way to Ravipur, the holiest place on earth.

During the period leading up to our departure, I was thrilled whenever I got a chance to be close to Baba. But I had to stand guard over my thoughts at all times. It was unnerving knowing that I was in the presence of someone who could hear everything I was thinking. Before long, I developed the ability to keep my mind a blank. This skill also served me during meditation. I believed I was making steady progress on the path to enlightenment. At this rate, I thought, I'd attain the ultimate goal by the time I was thirty.

The ashram was mobbed with devotees on the weekend of Baba's departure, and my brother and his wife had come to see Baba off. The theme of the guru's last public talk of the summer was unconditional love and devotion to the guru. Many in the audience had tears in their eyes, knowing it would be the last time they'd see their beloved Baba for at least a year. I was misty-eyed too, but for a different reason. I was overcome with gratitude for being one of the lucky ones who wouldn't be left behind.

"The connection between a guru and his disciple is sacred. It is deeper than all other relationships. It is comparable to the bond between a lover and his divine beloved," Baba said.

"An essential virtue for a true disciple is an unwavering devotion to the guru. All the disciple's flaws are burned away in the fire of this divine love. A worthy disciple must dedicate his life to the guru without any reservations or conditions."

Baba paused to let his words sink in.

"Kalyan was the favorite disciple of Swami Ramdas Samarth, who was a perfected master of Raja Yoga of the seventeenth century. One day, Swami Ramdas decided to put the devotion of his closest disciples to a test. Placing a mango on the joint of his knee and wrapping it in a bandage so that it looked like an enormous swelling, he summoned his students and pretended to be very ill and near death. Pointing to the bump, he said that it was a malignant tumor and that he would die unless someone sucked out the poison from the joint. He also warned that whoever sucked out the poison would die instantly.

"While the others hesitated, Kalyan instantly knelt and put his lips to the tumor. To his great surprise, instead of poison, Kalyan tasted sweet mango juice. Swami Ramdas revealed to his disciples that it had been a test, and praised Kalyan's perfect devotion and selfless love. To lay down one's life for the sake of the beloved in this way is true devotion."

I was amazed at Baba's words. With all my heart, I longed to be a worthy disciple like Kalyan.

"What inspires this kind of pure devotion?" Baba continued. "It is the superior love that the guru has for the disciple. The perfect faith and loyalty that Kalyan demonstrated can only come to the disciple through the grace of the master."

After Baba's talk, the *darshan* line stretched all the way back to the entrance of the cafeteria. "I have an idea," I said to Jeremy and Carrie. "Why don't we all go up to see Baba together as a family?"

Carrie's eyes sparkled. "That's a great idea, Doug!"

Jeremy looked less certain.

Ever since meeting Baba, I'd wanted to go up on the *darshan* line with Jeremy, but he had always made excuses not to go. This time he reluctantly agreed. When it was our turn to greet Baba, the guru smiled at us.

"Brothers?"

"Yes, Baba," Jeremy answered, trembling slightly.

Baba turned to Anjali and said something else, and then she translated for Jeremy.

"Baba says that Deependra is a good boy. His heart is very pure."

Jeremy looked away from the guru. "Yes, Baba."

"He is also very intelligent, no?"

Jeremy nodded.

Carrie glanced at me sideways, and then covered her mouth to stifle a giggle.

After blessing each of us with his wand of peacock feathers, Baba dismissed us with a nod of his head.

We ate dinner in the cafeteria, and afterwards, at Carrie's request, we had a sweet milky fruit salad called *kastarda* for dessert at Prasad. We sat outside on the deck, and the evening air was warm. Fireflies blinked on and off all over the ashram grounds. Jeremy, whose mood had darkened since *darshan* with Baba, barely said a word.

"Time to go," Jeremy said, standing up suddenly.

Carrie glanced at my half-eaten bowl of *kastarda*. "Deependra and I haven't finished our dessert yet."

Jeremy looked at his watch and frowned. Then he excused himself to use the restroom.

"Is everything okay with Shree Ram?" I asked Carrie.

She turned to watch Jeremy disappear into the men's room. "I think he's bummed out that the only time Baba ever spoke to him, it was about *you*."

I opened my mouth to say something, but no words came out.

"Your brother's always been jealous of you, you know."

Now, I couldn't help laughing. *With all his accomplishments—Jeremy jealous of me?* I shook my head. "That can't be true."

"Yes it is!" she insisted. "Never tell Shree Ram I told you this, but he's always believed you were your mother's favorite."

I folded my arms in front of my chest. "That's absurd."

"Your mother spoiled you rotten, Doug." Carrie's voice wavered as she spoke. "She always gave you way more attention than Jeremy, and if she didn't give you exactly what you wanted, when you wanted it, you'd throw a fit."

I felt a sharp pain in my gut. "That's so untrue!" I thought back to when my brother's personality had changed in high school. "So, am I supposed to believe that Jeremy's depression was my fault—because our mother loved me more? Well, that's bullshit!"

Carrie lifted a finger in front of her lips and looked around nervously. "Shhh! We're in an ashram, Doug!"

Then it hit me: *Baba's working on Jeremy's ego! Doesn't he realize that?*

"Harvey leaving you all his money didn't help either."

I massaged the back of my neck. Just then, Jeremy appeared behind us on the deck. Startled, Carrie began to fidget and run her fingers through her hair.

Jeremy scowled and slung his overnight bag over his shoulder. "Let's go, Carrie. We're leaving."

In the parking lot, Jeremy managed to give me a half-hearted hug and a tepid pat on the back. "Have a great time in India, Doug," he said without smiling.

Carrie threw her arms around me and squeezed me tight. When she let go, there were tears in her eyes. "Don't forget to write!"

PART TWO

14.
PROMISED LAND

I HELPED GAJENDRA UNLOAD the shipping container from one of the ashram pickup trucks that had followed us down to the airport. Gajendra told me to check it under my own name. It contained "essential supplies" for the Ravipur ashram that were unavailable in India.

"Won't the airline people be suspicious that I'm taking so much stuff to India? What do I tell them?"

"They probably won't ask you anything," he said, closing the tailgate with a loud clank. "If they do, just say *personal effects*. You'll tell customs the same thing when you get to Bombay."

I began to sweat. I didn't like the idea of lying, and doubted Baba would approve of it. "Wouldn't it be better if *you* checked it in under *your* name?"

"*Me?*" Gajendra said, thrusting his hands into his pockets. "I'm already taking as much as I can, believe me."

I felt a tingling in my limbs. *I should never have agreed to this*, I thought.

"Listen, kid. Everybody's carrying an extra suitcase for Baba. We do this all the time."

A suitcase was one thing; a shipping container was another. I couldn't help wondering: *Why me?* But I was afraid to ask.

Baba's Indian disciples—Suresh, Anjali Bhandary, and Baba's attendant, Rashmi Varma—rode together in a private car. The rest of us had been shuttled down to JFK in a rented motor coach. By the time we reached the international terminal, Baba and the others had already checked in and were waiting in a VIP lounge.

Within the confines of the ashram, I had never felt self-conscious around Baba's swamis. But here at the airport, I couldn't help seeing myself through the eyes of the public. To them, the American swamis in our group, with their shaved heads and orange robes, were probably indistinguishable from members of the Hare Krishna sect. They drew more than a few disapproving stares and raised eyebrows. I was afraid we looked like members of a cult—the furthest thing from the truth! I wished that everybody could know we were followers of a *true* guru.

While our fellow travelers might have thought we were a bunch of weirdos, the Air India reps treated us like royalty. They were Indian and must have known who Baba was.

Flying to India with Baba felt like accompanying a superior being from an alien civilization back to his home planet. The guru and his two Indian disciples sat in first class. The only times I got to see Baba were during boarding, as I passed him in the aisle on the way to my seat, and when he made a brief appearance in the economy section to talk to Avadhoot Plotnick. I wished I could understand them, but they were speaking in an Indian language. Whatever Avadhoot was saying, he sure knew how to make the guru laugh.

Baba didn't so much as glance in my direction the entire journey, but I didn't mind. I knew the only reason I was on this flight was due to the fact that the guru valued me as a disciple. I was filled with gratitude because of this and vowed not to disappoint him. Yet despite feeling closer to Baba than ever, on another level I felt lonely. This was because, from what I observed, the people traveling with him laughed and joked like they had known each other for years. Nearly all of them were members of Baba's personal staff. I was the only newcomer, and I felt like an outsider.

In the row in front of me were a couple of young men around my age. One of them was Poonish Davidson, the drummer who worked in the Birchwood Falls kitchen. Despite the fact that Poonish wasn't Indian, he was considered one of the best tabla players in Raja Yoga, second only to Suresh. From what I had heard, Poonish came from a middle-class family in Wisconsin. His parents weren't devotees. He had left home at the age of fifteen and had lived in Baba's ashrams ever since. Although he wasn't an official member of Baba's entourage, everyone on the flight seemed to know him and accept him as one of their own.

The young man seated next to him was Stephen Ames. He was even taller and more handsome than Poonish, but his pale complexion and widow's peak gave him the look of a youthful vampire. His parents, I was told, were wealthy devotees from Massachusetts. He and his siblings had grown up in the ashram around Baba. He was an official member of the tour, and responsible for setting up Baba's microphones. During Baba's talks, he always sat up front, behind a mixing board, as he was in charge of audio.

I was familiar with other people on the flight. Swami Akhandananda and Sita Perkins were coming to India, too. I had assumed Sita was a permanent staffer in Birchwood Falls, but apparently she traveled with Baba all the time. She had been in Birchwood Falls as part of an advance team. Gopi was also traveling home with the guru. She was sitting several rows ahead of me with the other *darshan* girls, but she may as well have been seated a million miles away. I would've given anything to sit next to her during the seemingly endless flights.

The food on the plane was delicious, and I looked forward to eating nothing but Indian cuisine during my long stay in Ravipur. After the meal service, the flight attendants pulled down a screen and projected an Indian movie. It was a musical with extravagant dance numbers and a cast of thousands. Although I couldn't understand the dialogue, I could tell it was a love story. I found it amusing that whenever the leading man and his love interest were about to kiss, the scene would cut away to footage of beautiful rolling hills, or close-ups of bees pollinating flowers.

A couple of hours into the first leg of our journey, Anjali appeared from behind the curtain separating first class from economy. After speaking to Gopi for some time, she gradually made her way down the aisle toward the back of the plane, stopping a few times to chat with other members of our party, including Poonish and Stephen. Then, much to my surprise, she spoke to me: "Ahhh, Deependra, how are you?"

"Feeling very blessed to be on this flight with Baba," I answered, too shy to look her in the eye. Something about her intimidated me, but she sure was beautiful: she had a big smile and the deepest brown eyes I'd ever seen. When she looked in my direction, I was certain that she, like the guru, could see into the deepest recesses of my soul and knew all of my deepest secrets.

"I understand your mother recently passed away," she said, tilting her head to one side and furrowing her brow.

"Yes. She died of cancer almost two years ago."

The plane lurched and began to shake as it entered a patch of mild turbulence. Anjali held onto the back of Poonish's seat to steady herself. "Gajendra tells me you're a good worker, and that you come to all the chants." I wondered how Gajendra could know that I went to all of the chants, considering that I almost never saw him at any of them. "We need more sincere seekers like you in the ashram. We'll be very happy to have you with us in Ravipur." She smiled so broadly that a dimple formed in her right cheek. Then she mussed up my hair with her fingers and made her way back up the aisle toward first class.

After changing planes at Heathrow, we made another stop in Dubai. While nearly everybody else in our party visited the duty free shops, I stayed behind and silently repeated the mantra to myself, hoping to demonstrate to

Baba that I was uninterested in material things—a true renunciant. When we were in the air again, Suresh made the rounds of the economy section with a box of Godiva chocolate. I accepted a piece from him as *prasad* from the guru himself, with my right hand cupped over my left in the traditional manner. This prompted a fit of laughter from Poonish and Stephen. I couldn't understand what was so funny about my heartfelt display of devotion.

After yet another stop in New Delhi, and nearly twenty-four hours after taking off from New York, our plane finally touched down in Bombay. As the plane taxied toward the terminal, a torrent of rain beat against the windows. I peered out into the pitch darkness. The captain informed us that the local time was 11:55 P.M. and the outside temperature was eighty-eight degrees Fahrenheit.

I'd been unable to sleep more than an hour or two during the entire voyage. I was tired and had a massive headache. As I inched my way up the aisle toward the open door of the aircraft, my sense of smell was assaulted by a powerful, pungent odor—a nauseating mixture of exhaust fumes, woodsmoke, and putrefying garbage.

Inside the terminal building, under the flickering light of fluorescent ceiling fixtures, we followed hand-painted wooden signs to Passport Control. There we found a uniformed immigration official asleep in a glass cabin. Suresh had to rap on the window to wake him up.

As I waited my turn to be interviewed, I dreaded being asked about the container.

"Why India coming?" the officer asked, studying my passport.

"Religious studies at Shree Brahmananda Ashram in Ravipur," I answered, remembering what Gajendra had told me to say. The officer tilted his head slightly, wobbling it from side to side. Then he stamped my passport, handed it back to me, and motioned for me to pass with a supercilious wave of his hand.

After what seemed like an endless wait in front of the luggage carousel, I spotted my duffel bag and grabbed it.

Fifteen minutes later, however, there was still no sign of the shipping container.

"Deependra!" I turned to see Avadhoot glaring at me. "What the fuck are you still doing here? You need to claim the container!"

I was embarrassed and confused. I thought that was what I was trying to do. I followed Avadhoot to another section of the baggage claim area where the shipping container was waiting.

"What is inside, inside?" barked a customs agent, striking the side of the container with a bamboo stick.

I swallowed hard then answered: "Personal effects." The agent eyed me suspiciously, and called for assistance. Two uniformed officers joined him and together they opened the container. Inside they found a large reel-to-reel tape deck, and other professional-looking sound equipment. The logo on the deck said "TEAC." My heart shot up into my throat, and my already aching head throbbed with pain. I prayed to the guru. *Please Baba, I don't want to go to jail!*

The customs agent shook his head disapprovingly. "What is this? What is this?"

I started sweating. I couldn't think of anything to say. I didn't want to let Baba down.

The customs agent struck the side of the container again with his stick, making me jump. "Yes, please!"

I glanced over at Avadhoot, who was talking to another agent with Poonish Davidson. They were going through the contents of Poonish's suitcase. At least I wasn't the only one carrying questionable items. I caught Avadhoot's eye. He must have understood from my pained expression that something was wrong, because he rushed over to me and confronted the agent. He spoke a mixture of Hindi and English. A moment later Stephen Ames joined him. Together they spoke to the airport official in his native language. I imagined what it would be like to serve time in an Indian prison. I had heard stories about the infamous lice-infested Arthur Road jail in Bombay, where prisoners were routinely beaten and forced to eat maggots. The thought of spending even one night there filled me terror. I could hardly breathe.

At first Avadhoot and Stephen seemed to be arguing with the man. Before long, however, the agent was smiling.

"Not to worry," Avadhoot said in a fake Indian accent. "He will be returning it to America when he goes home only."

"And he will revert back to you," Stephen said with a goofy smile and in the same fake accent.

I couldn't be sure, but I had the strong impression that Avadhoot and Stephen were mocking the man by imitating the way he spoke. But if they were, the agent took no notice of it.

"Okay, no problem," the agent said, wobbling his head from side to side. He wrote something down in my passport. The other two uniformed men put the tape deck back in the container and closed it up. My breathing slowly returned to normal. Avadhoot sent Stephen in search of a luggage cart, and then returned to Poonish, who appeared to be still in negotiations with another official.

The agent stamped my passport and handed it back to me. It was a huge relief. Once I was outside the terminal, under the shelter of an overhang, I opened my passport to the page with my Indian visa. The official had written the brand of the tape deck "TEAC," along with its model and serial number. Underneath, the words "To be returned" were stamped.

"Are you okay, man?" Stephen asked, grinning widely and resting a hand on my shoulder.

"Fine," I lied. Something about his wide grin made me doubt his sincerity. "I thought I was going to be carrying supplies for the ashram. What do you need that thing for anyway?"

"The TEAC? We need it to record Baba's talks and chants." Stephen searched my face, and smiled again. "Hey, don't worry about it. We bring equipment like that over here all the time. It's nothing a little *baksheesh* can't take care of."

I did worry about it. Lying had always made me feel uncomfortable, even when I had avoided telling the truth to Melanie about school. In this case, I'd just given false information to a representative of the Indian government. I wondered what the penalty would be if they found out that the reel-to-reel tape deck wasn't really mine.

As we waited for our transportation to the ashram to arrive, it occurred to me that I had just been tested by the guru. I resolved to face bravely any punishment that befell me. I remembered Baba's story about the disciple who selflessly sucked what he thought was lethal poison out of his guru's knee, and decided that if I did go to jail, I would view it as a blessing. As an opportunity to demonstrate my devotion. *This is right understanding*, I told myself, and I knew that the *inner guru* was pleased.

Despite my exhaustion and throbbing head, I was still intrigued by my new surroundings. The women were dressed in colorful saris or pajama-like pantsuits. Men wore polyester camp shirts and the kind of bell-bottom trousers that had gone out of style a decade earlier back in the States. Most of the automobiles were outdated, too. With the exception of a few luxury cars, they looked as though they were from the 1950s.

An Arab sheik and two women cloaked in burqas exited the terminal. A moment later they were picked up in a large, black Mercedes-Benz. I thought of the guru. "Where's Baba?" I asked Stephen. "How's he getting to Ravipur?"

"Baba was picked up a while ago. We'll see him later at the ashram."

A few minutes later, a trio of minibuses pulled up. Several dark-skinned Indian boys jumped out, and together they worked to stow our suitcases into the baggage compartments. They strapped some of the larger items to the roofs. The boys were so skinny and tiny, they looked like children. They handled our luggage roughly, and I was glad I had nothing fragile in my duffel bag. I wondered if the TEAC would make it to the ashram in one piece.

The ashram was located north of Bombay, in the Thane district of Maharashtra state. Since it was only fifty miles away, I assumed the journey would take one or two hours maximum. I was wrong. The trip from the airport to Ravipur took four long, grueling hours, and I drifted in and out of sleep the whole way there. The farther from the city we got, the bumpier the ride.

When we reached the countryside, I noticed the trunks of the trees lining the roads had been marked with broad bands of red and white paint, just above the roots. I wondered why the trees had been defaced in such a hideous manner. Perhaps the practice helped to repel insects? Maybe the paint acted as a reflector to mark the sides of the road at night. I couldn't imagine anyone doing such a thing in the States. It seemed like such a violation of nature.

I dozed off for what must have been an hour or two. When I awoke, the sky was beginning to lighten. Soon I was able to make out rolling hills, palm trees, and lush green fields of rice paddies dotted by black water buffalos. My head was still killing me, but I couldn't stop staring out the window at the alien landscape. At one point, we passed a man carrying at least a dozen mattresses on his head. *We could have used his help in Birchwood Falls!* I laughed inwardly. A bit later, our bus was overtaken by a small minivan with only three wheels. It was driven by a bearded man in an orange turban, and was carrying what looked like a large family, crammed into it like circus performers in a clown car. The road narrowed and we passed huge stacks of bricks from which plumes of gray smoke billowed. As the sun moved higher into the sky, the sights became more vivid: flocks of sari-clad women with heavy metal jewelry hanging from their noses, carrying impossibly large burdens on their heads; naked toddlers covered in mud, darting in and out of straw huts; and an old man squatting on the side of the road taking a dump. It occurred to me that these people were just as stuck in the illusion of the world as the people back home. What was special about India? How had it given birth to the most advanced system of philosophy and produced the greatest spiritual masters in the world?

I drifted off to sleep again, and when I awoke we were on the outskirts of a village. In the distance I saw what looked like a majestic palace. The building was pale yellow, with orange flags flying from its spires. I recognized the structure from the many photos I'd seen of it in *Raja Path* magazine. The beauty and serenity of the place left me in a state of awe and wonder. My headache was gone.

Our convoy pulled up alongside the palace, in front of a large circular gate. A colorful sign above it read "Shree Brahmananda Ashram."

I had at last reached the Promised Land.

15.
ASK NO QUESTIONS AND YOU WILL HEAR NO LIES

THE RAIN HAD STOPPED, but the ground was wet and muddy. Leaving our luggage in the hands of the Indian boys, I followed the rest of the group through the gate into a narrow antechamber. It led to a small temple, an office, and a glistening outdoor marble courtyard, where dozens of Western and hundreds of Indian devotees had gathered, closed umbrellas in hand. Garlands of tiny white star-shaped flowers hung everywhere, decorating the square and the buildings surrounding it. All these years later, I can still smell their heavenly fragrance—the sweet, intoxicating scent of jasmine.

Some of the men were dressed in traditional Indian garb, others in more Western-style attire. The women—Indian and Western—wore traditional silk saris or ghagra cholis. I immediately noticed that nobody was wearing a name tag.

Although Baba had left the airport before us, it was apparent from the looks of anticipation on the ashramites' faces that the guru had not yet arrived. Looking at the buildings enclosing the courtyard, I saw dozens of devotees expectantly peering down from open windows and balconies. I wanted to see Baba make his entrance too, but I was thirsty and tired. I wanted to be shown to my room so I could get some sleep.

A tall, attractive Western woman in a robin's egg blue sari appeared before me, bearing a tray of glasses brimming with steaming hot milky tea. She had long dark hair, pale skin, and liquid brown eyes, and her delicate features glowed. "Welcome to Shree Brahmananda Ashram," she said. "Please, have a cup of chai. You must be thirsty after your long trip." She was soft spoken, and her American accent was comforting. I took a cup from the tray and sipped the sweet, scalding hot tea. "My name is Indira St. John," she said.

"I'm Deependra."

"Whenever you're ready, just drop by the Housing office for your room assignment and linens."

"Thank you, Indira. I'll come by after Baba arrives."

"Of course! It shouldn't be long now." Indira turned to leave, and then gave me the once over. "You're going to need an umbrella, you know," she smiled. "Monsoon season isn't over yet."

I surveyed the crowd. Like in Birchwood Falls, it included swamis, single people, and married couples holding the hands of small children. It was easy enough to tell who was close to the guru. I recognized them not only from their expensive-looking clothing and the confidence with which they carried themselves, but also from the way they darted around the courtyard telling everyone else what to do.

Out of the corner of my eye, I spotted a familiar face. It belonged to Namdev Loman, whom I hadn't seen in many months. He was seated on a large marble planter under a mango tree, barefooted and dressed in a dirty white cotton kurta and lungi. His unkempt beard was longer than the last time I'd seen him, and his hair was matted into dreadlocks and bleached yellow by the sun.

"You're a long way from home," I said, greeting my friend. "How is Collegetown Bagels surviving without you?"

Namdev looked up. A smile of recognition spread across his face, but he didn't say a word. Lifting a finger, he pointed to a laminated cardboard tag clipped to the pocket of his kurta that said "Silence."

"He's not going to answer you, mate," came a voice from behind me. I turned and found myself face to face with a muscular young man around my age with short-cropped blond hair. He spoke with what sounded like an Australian accent. "He's taken a vow of silence. Baba told him he talked too much."

Suddenly there was a thunderclap. Seconds later, the sky opened and rain poured down as if a giant bucket of water had been turned upside down. Umbrellas sprang open in a burst of colors, and I ran for shelter under an open-air meditation hall. Then, as if on cue, car horns and cheers of "Jai Gurudev" sounded in the distance.

The honking and cheers gradually grew louder, and then came to a stop. The throngs of devotees in the courtyard began pressing toward the main entrance. Swept up by the excitement, and forgetting any concern I might have had about getting wet, I pushed my way toward the entrance until an Indian man in a uniform blocked my passage.

"Please to be Baba-looking here only," the man scolded, slapping a bamboo stick against the palm of his hand. A silver badge on his chest said "Ashram Security." On his hip was a holstered gun.

Heeding the guard's warning, I moved back from the entranceway, following the sound of jingling bells and the scent of camphor to a pair of open windows. There, I joined a mob of mostly Indian devotees, gently pushing and shoving each out of the way to get a better look at what was going on inside. Squeezing my way to the front of the crowd, I caught a fleeting glimpse of Baba prostrating himself on the floor before a life-size statue of Gurudev.

Next to him, a Brahmin priest was ringing a hand bell and waving a flaming, multi-tiered lamp.

When the ritual was over, the crowd did an about-face and I turned to see Baba making his entrance into the courtyard, shielded from the rain by an enormous bright orange umbrella held by Avadhoot. Suresh and Anjali followed closely behind.

"Jai Gurudev! Jai Gurudev!" the crowd cheered. Baba waved, and then greeted his adoring devotees with folded hands. In their efforts to get as close to him as possible, the mob of Indians behind me lurched forward, knocking me off balance. I slipped onto the hard, wet marble floor of the courtyard, landing on my elbow. A stab of white-hot pain shot up my arm, but I didn't cry out. I sprang back onto my feet and, using my good arm, pushed my way to the large planter where Namdev had just been sitting. Jumping onto an empty spot, I scratched the side of my head on a branch of the mango tree. Ignoring the pain, I exclaimed "Jai Gurudev!" From my elevated vantage point, I could see the glorious guru speaking with a middle-aged Indian couple. They bore a striking resemblance to Anjali and Suresh, and I guessed the man and woman were their parents.

Next Baba greeted Indira St. John with a beaming smile, and whispered something in her ear. The tall beauty burst out laughing, turning bright red. As they chatted, she shifted her weight from foot to foot like a little girl.

Baba worked his way through the crowd until he reached a door in the building opposite the open-air meditation hall. Rashmi Varma unlocked it and held it open for Baba, who turned to smile and wave one last time before crossing the threshold.

"Jai Gurudev!" called Anjali and Suresh.

"Jai Gurudev!" the throngs of devotees cheered. "Welcome home, Baba!"

Then the guru and his closest disciples disappeared into the building, pulling the door shut behind them.

The rain stopped as suddenly as it had begun. I set off for the Housing office to get my room assignment, locker key, and clean linens. Indira told me that my room was located on the second floor of one of the men's dormitories, *Bhakti Shayanagrih*. It was a three-minute walk from the central courtyard where Baba had made his entrance earlier.

"The courtyard is the heart of the ashram," Indira said, pointing to the location on a framed map of the ashram grounds. "Baba sits for *darshan* there almost every day."

My duffel bag was waiting for me just outside my dorm room. To my pleasant surprise, the room currently had only one other occupant, although he wasn't there when I arrived. Over the ashram loudspeakers, I could hear the recitation of the *Guru Gita* ending. He was probably at the chant.

Looking around my new living space, at its concrete floor and walls and noisy ceiling fan, I was struck by how different my accommodations were from my room back in Birchwood Falls. As I unpacked my bag, my eyes were drawn to my roommate's puja altar. At the center of it was an old black and white photo of a young Swami Rudrananda at the feet of a virtually naked Gurudev Brahmananda. *This was where it all happened*, I thought. *Right here in Ravipur, Baba received shaktipat from his guru and attained God-realization.*

At seven in the morning, the heat and humidity were already worse than I ever could have imagined. I switched on the ceiling fan. It provided little relief.

I was exhausted, completely jet-lagged. I made up my bed, stripped down to my underwear, and lay down on top of my sheets. As I drifted off to sleep, I remembered Indira St. John's advice: "Try to stay up until lights out tonight. That's the fastest way to adjust to the time difference."

I awoke several hours later, disoriented and groggy, wondering where the hell I was. I turned over on to my side to see a tall man sitting up in bed. He had closely-cropped silver hair and gray eyes, and was dressed in an immaculate white cotton *kurta* and *lungi*. Eager to make a good first impression, I shot up to a sitting position and introduced myself. "Hi! I'm Deependra."

"Claus," he said, staring back at me with a blank look on his face.

"I'm from the States—New York—well, upstate New York, really. Ithaca."

"*Ja*, stop talking now." From his accent, I could tell Claus was German. He was about as personable as a filing cabinet. "It's lunch time," he added, and then lumbered out of the room.

Unlike Birchwood Falls, silence was strictly observed at mealtimes in the Ravipur dining hall. It was also segregated into a men's side and a women's side. The food consisted of spicy vegetable curry, dal, and rice, served on disposable banana leaf plates. Seated cross-legged on the floor, we ate with the fingers of our right hands. The food was tasty and, I assumed, nutritious. I decided that, as a true renunciant, I would stay away from the fancy Prasad and eat all my meals in the cafeteria.

The heat and humidity, combined with the jet lag and the heavy meal, were making me feel lethargic. All I wanted to do was rest, but I needed to pay my rent and buy a bucket and dipper so I could take a bath. The bank and general store, I learned, were located just across the street from the ashram, so I decided to take care of business before having another nap.

The conditions outside the confines of the ashram walls stood in stark contrast to those within. Inside, the buildings were well maintained and freshly painted. The grounds were immaculate and extravagantly landscaped. Outside, the shops and dwellings were covered with mold and in a state of disrepair. The street was dirty and strewn with litter.

I gave the bank teller three thousand dollars in traveler's checks. After a few minutes of careful counting, he handed me an impossibly thick stack of rupee notes. Considering my rent was less than fifty dollars a month, I questioned whether I had made the right decision by converting so much currency.

I was impressed to find Gajendra Williams already at his post in the ashram manager's office only hours after stepping off the plane. He had shaved off his beard and was dressed in an immaculate yellow polo shirt, perfectly pressed khaki pants, and fine leather sandals. A Rolex watch glittered on his wrist. "Sign here, Deependra," he said, handing me a form stating the amount of my donation.

I was confused, and hesitated before writing a figure or signing my name. "Donation? What about the rent?"

Gajendra wrinkled his nose. "Technically we don't pay room and board at the ashram, we make *donations* to the Mission."

I still didn't understand.

"Donations to the ashram aren't taxed by the Indian government. With the savings, Baba has more money to give to the poor."

More than satisfied with his answer, I signed the paper, and then handed it back to him along with a fat stack of rupee notes. I paid for six months in advance.

I turned to leave, but Gajendra stopped me. "Your passport?"

I was confused again.

"Ashram rules," Gajendra frowned. He would hold my passport in the office for safekeeping. Hesitantly, I handed it over.

Back in the dormitory, I washed myself by filling up my new bucket with warm water and using the dipper to pour it over my head and body. The improvised shower was refreshing and it felt wonderful to finally get clean. But just as I was rinsing the shampoo out of my hair, an enormous cockroach landed on my arm. I let out a cowardly scream, prompting one of the ashram security guards to investigate. He arrived on the scene as I was toweling off. "Yes, please, hello," the guard said. I tried to pantomime what had happened with the giant roach, but he wasn't paying attention. I had the impression he was staring at my penis.

Back in my room, I got into bed. As soon as my head hit the pillow, I fell into a deep sleep. I awoke many hours later, when the overhead light was switched on. Claus was getting dressed, and through the window, I saw it was dark outside.

"What time is it?" I asked, still half asleep.
"Quarter to four. Time for meditation."
"What time is the *Guru Gita*?"
"After chai—five-thirty," he answered, slipping on his sandals. Then he ambled out of the room with his *asana* and prayer book.

I couldn't believe how unbearably hot it was, even at this early hour—at least eighty degrees. With the humidity, it felt even hotter. I decided to skip the meditation and go back to sleep. I was sure Baba would understand that I needed just a little more rest after my long journey. But after Claus left, I couldn't get back to sleep. I worried the omniscient guru would think I was becoming lax.

Then I remembered something Baba had said: "The more we give into laziness and other deplorable tendencies, the more we strengthen these tendencies and increase our likelihood of giving into them again in the future. On the other hand, the more we refrain, the sooner we will become free from their hold."

I threw on my clothes, barreled down the stairs, and headed into the darkness toward the courtyard. On my way I passed the kitchen dumpster, which was opposite my dormitory. Rats the size of cats were feeding from it, and the stench of garbage filled my nostrils. I shuddered at the thought of these oversize beasts scurrying across the open toes of my sandals.

Just then an older, shaven-head Indian man exited the kitchen through a screen door. He wore nothing but an orange lungi tied around his waist to cover his nakedness. He was sweetly chanting "Shree Ram, Jai Ram" and swinging an overflowing bucket of slop in his hand. "Namaste," I said, greeting him with folded hands.

The man didn't so much as glance in my direction. I figured he was too absorbed in God's name to notice me. Oblivious also to the rats surrounding him, he poured the refuse into the dumpster, and then returned inside.

I turned the corner and glanced up at the pre-dawn sky. The light of a million stars shone down on me. I remembered that everything in the cosmos was an expression of my innermost Self. Tears of gratitude welled in my eyes. *I'm finally here in Ravipur!* I told myself. *I'm really here!*

The "meditation cave" located beneath Baba's private quarters was accessible from the courtyard. According to Indira St. John, it was the only air-conditioned public space in the ashram. In the dim, flickering candlelight, I found a free spot on the carpeted floor and sat down to meditate. It was cool and refreshing inside the cave. Within seconds, I was fast asleep.

When the session was over, I woke up from my nap and followed the others to the dining hall for morning chai, served by Indira. There I saw the chanting, bare-chested Indian man again. He was supervising a group of *sevites* who were seated cross-legged on the floor chopping vegetables. Each was equipped with their own cutting board.

"Who's that?" I asked Indira.

She lifted a finger to her lips, glancing nervously in the direction of the man in question. "That's Prakashananda, the kitchen swami. Don't get on his bad side."

I turned to take another look at the man, just as he kicked one of the male Indian *sevites* in the side. The blow caused the ashramite to knock over his cutting board, spilling his vegetables on the floor. The strict swami reminded me of Yashoda Edwards back in Birchwood Falls.

Leaving the dining hall to finish my chai in the courtyard, I sat down on one of the large planters. The tea was sweet and delicious, but had a skin of buffalo milk floating on the top, which grossed me out.

I glanced around at the others. Drinking their chai in silence, their faces expressed an air of post-meditation serenity. Under the shelter of an overhang, next to the door through which Baba had disappeared the day before, I saw a sumptuous blue velvet throne mounted on a raised platform. A skinny Indian man in white cotton was polishing a pair of silver sandals on a small table in front of the platform.

Nearby, a hairy Western man shaped like a sack of potatoes was using a bucket of soapy water and a squeegee to clean the marble floor. No sooner had he finished his work than it started to rain, washing more mango leaves and debris to the ground. Following the others, I went under the shelter of the open-air meditation hall.

As the rain fell in sheets in the courtyard outside, we chanted the *Guru Gita*. After months of reciting the scripture faithfully every morning, I knew the entire text by heart and scarcely had to glance at my chanting book. In the shelter of the hall, I felt protected by Baba and enveloped in his love.

By the time the *Gita* was over, the rain had stopped. I went for breakfast in the dining hall, expecting to be served the same delicious savory porridge I had eaten every day in Birchwood Falls. Instead, I was given some kind of tasteless oatmeal. I was also surprised to be one of the only Westerners eating there. The only other person I recognized was Namdev Loman, from Ithaca. After the meal, I stopped by the Prasad before reporting to the *seva* office for my assignment. The mystery was solved. Everyone I had traveled to India with was there, along with all the other Western ashramites—even the swamis. On the menu was a variety of Indian breakfast dishes, coffee, and exotic fruit.

As I arrived at the *seva* office, the rain started up again. Sita Perkins smiled philosophically. "Monsoon season in India!"

I smiled politely.

"Don't worry, Deependra, we're at the tail end of it. In a couple of weeks, the rain will be over and it will start to get cooler."

I wasn't worried. I was here to attain enlightenment. The harsh conditions would only help me to turn within. "Oh, good," I replied.

Sita glanced down at a clipboard on her desk. "They need help in Housekeeping."

"Housekeeping?" I was unable to hide the disappointment in my voice. Did she expect me to work as a maid? "But I've been assisting Avadhoot and Arjuna in the Audiovisual department."

"Don't be silly, Deependra. Avadhoot won't be doing much photography while Baba is in India, and Arjuna is still in Birchwood Falls."

It felt like a demotion. "But—"

Sita thrust her bosom forward and her expression hardened. "Have you forgotten the meaning of *seva*? We're here to offer our service to the guru selflessly. It's not about your ego's personal preferences."

My cheeks burned with shame. "Sure, I understand that—"

Sita looked down at the clipboard again "You'll also be cleaning the courtyard. Pablo is going back to Spain tomorrow. We need someone to cover his two morning shifts. Report to Vinod Desai at three-thirty. He'll show you the ropes."

"This afternoon?"

Sita laughed. "You're funny, Deependra. Tomorrow *morning*!"

"What about meditation?"

Sita opened a filing cabinet behind her desk and began thumbing through it. "The cave is open twenty-four hours a day," she said, without looking at me. "You can meditate before your shift."

I tried to imagine waking up every day at two-thirty. I already felt tired. "Of course."

"Cleaning the courtyard is a wonderful *seva* opportunity," she said, taking a folder out of the cabinet. "And you'll *love* Vinod. He's a sweetheart."

I was about to set off for Housekeeping when Sita told me that new arrivals had a forty-eight-hour "grace period" before they were expected to report for work. "Take the morning off," she said. "Visit Gurudev's *samadhi* shrine in the village and order some more climate-appropriate clothes at the tailor. You can check in with Rohini after lunch."

"What's wrong with what I'm wearing?"

The *seva* coordinator glanced down at my legs and chuckled. "You're going to die of heat stroke in those heavy jeans of yours."

I left the *seva* office in a funk. Intellectually I understood that a true disciple should view all service to the guru equally, but I worried I might never get a chance to be up close to Baba again if I were cleaning toilets. I wondered why others were worthy of serving the guru more directly, but not me. I prayed to Baba to dispel my confusion and to bless me with right understanding.

As soon as I set foot on the street outside the ashram gate, rickshaw drivers called to me: "Yes please, hello! Railway station going? Village, sir?"

The *samadhi* shrine was only a couple of miles down the road, and a ride in an oxcart or three-wheeler looked like fun. But since it wasn't raining I decided to walk.

As I made my way down the muddy path to the village, I passed ramshackle homes and improvised storefronts, where tiny dark-skinned women hawked rice, vegetables, and garlands of flowers from their perches on rickety wooden platforms. "Hello please! You buy, yes?"

Men with red-stained hands and mouths stood in conversation, spitting betelnut on the ground in turn. Others lay sprawled on the side of the road in a state of oblivion.

I passed a post office, followed a bend in the road, and crossed paths with a group of school children who waved and smiled at me: "Hello! Hello! What is your name?"

"My name is Deependra," I replied, which they met with howls of laughter. I felt ridiculous. I couldn't tell if they were amused by my spiritual name or by my mispronunciation of it.

As I drew closer to the village, I could see Mount Paramita rising from the Agniparvata Valley. According to ashram literature, the mountain had been formed by volcanic eruptions, which were also the cause of the many natural hot springs in the area. Before Gurudev Brahmananda had settled in Ravipur in the early 1920s, the entire valley had been a jungle. After his arrival, Gurudev's reputation as a holy man attracted scores of seekers from nearby Bombay and beyond. Within a few short years, the obscure village of Ravipur was transformed into a site of spiritual pilgrimage.

Supplicants from all over India flocked here to receive his blessings and to bathe in the thermal hot springs, which were said to have miraculous healing powers.

I decided to finish my errands before paying my respects at Gurudev's tomb. My first stop was the tailor—a short, pot-bellied homunculus of a man who spoke ten words of English. He offered me a cup of tea the moment I walked through the door, and then sent one of his underlings across the street to the chai shop to fetch it.

He showed me a variety of fabrics in different colors and weaves, assuring me that everything in his shop was "best quality only." In the end, I ordered seven identical outfits—one for each day of the week—of pale blue, loosely-woven cotton.

As the tailor took my measurements, I looked around the shop. He had a number of old black and white photographs of Gurudev on the wall, but not a single picture of Baba. I found this odd.

I explained that I needed my new clothes as soon as possible because my clothes from America were all too heavy.

"No problem," the tailor said with a wiggle of his head. "Tomorrow only."

My next stop was the barber, a gentle, mustached, stick of a man with a gaunt face and an oily comb over. His shop was in a tiny, broken-down shack with a single height-adjustable chair held together with duct tape. On one grimy, mold-covered wall hung a framed poster of a blue-hued Lord Krishna playing a flute, surrounded by cow-herding girls vying for his affections. On the opposite wall were a few photographs of Brahmananda and another holy man I did not recognize. Again, no pictures of Baba. There was no mirror.

I thought about asking him to shave off all my hair like the swamis, which would have been a relief in the unbearable heat. But I was afraid I might be seen as some kind of wannabe around the ashram. I was also worried what my head might look like without any hair—some of Baba's swamis had odd-shaped pates and looked weird. I finally decided that with my worse-than-average teenage acne, I was ugly enough.

With my fingers I indicated to the barber how much to take off. Layers of my thick brown hair fell to the floor. When he was finished, he held up a mirror for me to see. I was horrified: the barber had given me a crew cut. I looked like I had joined the military!

Upset, I continued down the street. Before entering the *samadhi* shrine, I removed my sandals and left them with a toothless old man, who promised to guard them for a few *paisa*. The moment I stepped inside the tomb, I was blown away by the incredible force of Brahmananda's *shakti*. Ripples of blissful energy spread through my body, and my arms and legs shook and quivered in response. When I sat down at the feet of Gurudev's statue, I instantly fell into a state of profound meditation. I came out of it a couple of hours later, when a priest solicited me for a donation. I reached into my pocket for my wallet and took out a thick wad of rupees. The priest's eyes widened and his mouth went slack when I handed it to him. I might have given him the equivalent of fifty dollars, but I didn't know for sure because I didn't bother to count it. *Whatever I give away to God and the guru will return to me one hundredfold in the form of grace*, I told myself.

Leaving the shrine, I heard the nearby shouts and taunts of what sounded like an angry mob. I hurried to the other side of the building and came to a large square. There, at the center of a wild pack of men, stood a defenseless old woman. She was frail and stooped. Her skin was cracked and leathery. On her head was a shock of white hair.

I wished I could understand what they were yelling about. I couldn't imagine what crime the old woman could be guilty of to have elicited such a hysterical public condemnation.

I edged through the crowd, closer to the woman. While at first I had thought she was pleading with the men to spare her, I now saw she wasn't desperate or fearful at all. She was laughing. It was a creepy cackle that made the hair on the back of my neck stand up on end.

The old woman turned toward me, and looked directly into my eyes. I abruptly felt like I was going to throw up. Just then, a hand gripped my arm. I turned and was face to face with a smartly dressed Indian man. He had pale skin, bushy eyebrows, and a large, eagle-like beak of a nose.

"You mustn't look her in the eye!" he said, squeezing my arm tightly. "She can hypnotize you with one glance! Come with me! This gang is about to get ugly!"

"Are they going to hurt that woman?" I asked, hurrying after the man back toward the main street.

"It's entirely possible, I'm afraid," the man answered, panting a little. "They want to drive her out of the village."

"Who is she and why are the people so angry with her?"

The man curled his lower lip in disgust. "She's a *churel*—a sorceress—the witch from Surat!"

We turned the corner and stopped in front of Gurudev's *samadhi* shrine. "Palash Chaapkhanawala," said the man, catching his breath and extending a large hand for me to shake. "And what is your good name please?"

"Deependra."

An almost imperceptible smirk flashed across Palash's face. Then he turned away, covering his mouth with the back of his hand. "And from which country are you coming, Mr. Deependra?"

"America."

"*Bahut accha*! Very good!" Palash said, with a twinkle in his eye. "I invite you to take tea with me at my sanatorium."

I glanced at my watch. I still had a little time before lunch. "Is it far?"

"It is *there* only," Palash said, pointing in the opposite direction of the ashram. "Merely a hop, skip, and a jump."

I followed Palash for a couple of blocks until we reached a gated estate. A large hand-painted sign at the entrance read: "Chaapkhanawala's Thermal Spring Baths and Health Resort. Established 1936."

As we entered the compound I asked myself, *Do I even believe in witches?* A year ago, I would've laughed at the idea. Now I wasn't so sure. If a saint like Baba can exist, why not his opposite?

"The main attraction of the resort is the thermal hot spring," Palash said. Then he turned to me and grinned knowingly. "The water is slightly radioactive." He said this like it was a good thing. "It can cure many illnesses. Hydrotherapy at its best!"

At the end of a shady garden path, we reached a two-story building with a large veranda. The building was surrounded by smaller bungalows amidst lush flower gardens. Palash showed me to a seat at a table on the veranda, and then called out to someone inside the building. "*Don cup chaha aana!*"

"Is this your place?"

Palash sat down at the table with me. "Indeed, I am the proprietor of this splendid establishment. Many years ago, before the ashram was here—before anything was here—my grandfather's family had a vacation home on this very spot. After Baba passed away and the shrine was built, my father saw the commercial potential here and opened this resort."

"Uh, I'm sorry, but I don't understand what you mean, sir. Baba is still very much in his physical body."

Palash narrowed his eyes. "I'm not talking about Rudrananda," he said. Turning his head, he pointed to a garlanded photo of Brahmananda on the wall. "I'm talking about *my* Baba."

"Did you know Gurudev?"

Palash opened his mouth to answer, but was interrupted by the sound of a woman hollering from an upstairs window. The rattle of her Hindi sounded like a machine gun. I couldn't see the woman from where I sat, but she didn't sound happy.

Fists clenched, Palash rose abruptly to his feet and then bounded down the steps of the veranda. "*Ab kya chaahiye tumhein?*" he shouted back at the woman upstairs.

Just then a barefoot man with a bent neck and sagging posture shuffled onto the porch through an open door. He was dressed in a badly stained t-shirt and bell-bottom pants, and carried a tray of chai and cookies. Before setting down the tea, the man removed a filthy white towel from his shoulder and wiped some crumbs from the table.

The argument between Palash and the woman ended with the sound of a window slamming shut, and the servant went back inside.

"Please excuse my wife," Palash said, wincing as he returned to his seat at the table. His face was flushed. "She is in a foul temper today. Now, what was I saying?"

I took a sip of tea. "I asked if you knew Gurudev Brahmananda."

"Of course I did!" Palash answered with a gleam in his eye. Then he held his arm out in front of me. "Look at it!" he said, looking down at his bare arm. "Look at it! I have gooseflesh just thinking about him."

I couldn't see any goosebumps, but gave Palash the benefit of the doubt.

"Wow."

"You see that banyan tree?" asked Palash, pointing to a large tree with many secondary trunks arising from its branches.

I glanced at my watch again. If I left right now, I could still be back before they stopped serving lunch. "Uh, yes, very exotic."

"Unlike me, my father and grandfather did not believe in swamis or holy men— they were Parsis, not Hindus." Palash sipped his tea, and then bit into a cookie. "What's more, they were military men. But one day, several years before I was born, they had set off to a nearby village by motorcar when on the road they met a young *sadhu* by the name Brahmananda."

My interest was piqued. I wanted to hear Palash's story and decided to skip lunch at the ashram. "What happened to make them believe?"

"I'm getting to that," Palash said. "Brahmananda asked them for a lift. At first, my father flatly refused, but my grandfather insisted they oblige him. Respecting my grandfather's wish, my father grudgingly stopped the car and let him in. A few miles down the road, Brahmananda requested my father stop the car because he needed to urinate."

Suddenly, Palash's story was making me feel uncomfortable. I had never thought of holy men like Gurudev and Baba having bodily functions. But I wanted to find out what happened.

"My father again refused the *sadhu*, even after my grandfather insisted that they accommodate him. At that very moment, the car stalled and came to an abrupt halt. While Brahmananda went about his business behind a bush, my father tried to get the car started again, but was unable. So he and my grandfather got out to check the engine. In addition to being an army officer, my father was also a highly skilled auto mechanic. Yet despite all his knowledge and ability, he was unable to find anything wrong with it. When Brahmananda rejoined the men in front of the car, he placed a hand on the engine. A moment later, he asked my father to start the engine. Skeptical and irritated, my father turned the key and, *just like that*," Palash said, snapping his fingers, "the car started again!"

Now *I* had gooseflesh. "What about the tree?"

Palash rubbed his chin. "Tree? What tree?"

I gestured toward the strange tree Palash had pointed out to me earlier. "The banyan tree."

"Ah yes! My father and Gurudev had many philosophical debates under that tree."

I was amazed. I tried to imagine myself living in Ravipur during the days when Brahmananda was still in his physical body, receiving personal teachings from him. My skin tingled all over.

Checking my watch again, I saw that it was time for me to head back to the ashram to check in with Housekeeping. I made my excuses to Palash. I wanted to hear more about the so-called "Witch from Surat," but it would have to wait for a future visit.

Palash got up and walked me to the gate. "Do come back again to take a dip in one of our bubble baths!"

I shook his hand, and as I turned to leave, a burning question came to me: "Mr. Palash, one more thing. Why don't I see any pictures of Baba Rudrananda here in the village?"

Palash slowly folded his arms in front of his chest. A tight smile spread across his lips. "Ask no questions and you will hear no lies."

16.
AUSTERITIES

HOUSEKEEPING WAS LOCATED IN a small, stand-alone building located between the courtyard and Prasad. Rohini Brinkerhoff, the supervisor, was an older German woman with pale blue eyes, a full jaw, and closely-cropped silver hair. She was from Düsseldorf and spoke with a thick German accent which took me a few days to get used to.

Rohini took a step back and looked me over from head to toe, as though she weren't sure if I were real or just a figment of her imagination. "Mein koodness! Only eighteen years old und you haffe already found zee *guru*! I did not meet Baba until I vas fifty!"

Rohini assigned me the task of scrubbing the men's public restrooms, and showed me where to find the cleaning supplies.

"Do you have any rubber gloves?" I asked.

The German shook her head and laughed good-naturedly. "Welcome to India!"

In India, only Untouchables cleaned toilets, but the rules of the Hindu caste system didn't apply to foreigners.

Therefore, there was no reason why Western ashramites couldn't do the job. I was horrified. Not only was I humiliated to have such a "lowly" *seva*, it was also the most disgusting.

How could I have sunk so low? I asked myself. *What is Baba trying to teach me?*

A young, pleasantly plump French woman was responsible for the women's restrooms. She had cleaned some of the ashram's VIP quarters, and told me that most of them were equipped with Western-style bathrooms. All the other restrooms in the ashram only had squat toilets. Scrubbing lavatories back in the States would have been bad enough, but here in India the job was much worse due to the fact that nobody seemed very particular about where they did their business. Making a direct deposit in the hole in the floor, it seemed, was purely optional. As a result, urine and excrement were everywhere. The only thing worse than this god-awful sight was the stench: a spicy, pungent fecal odor unlike anything I'd ever encountered back home. My job was to make the men's rooms sparkle and smell clean and fresh.

Getting down on my hands and knees, I used a brush and a strong smelling disinfectant to wash the tiled floor. Before I even finished cleaning the first stall, I became nauseated and threw up.

Back in my room after an exhausting second day in the ashram, I set my alarm for two A.M. I needed to give myself enough time to bathe and meditate before reporting for courtyard-cleaning duty.

Sita Perkins had promised that my supervisor was a "sweetheart" and she was right. Vinod Desai was a disturbingly thin, dark-skinned Indian man with huge, bulging eyes. Despite my tremendous difficulty understanding him, I liked Vinod immediately. He was kinder than most of the Western *seva* supervisors. He didn't talk down to me like I was beneath him. If anything, he looked up to me because I was American. Sometimes, however, he was *too nice*, and made me feel awkward. On the morning we first met, I didn't know what to make of his odd behavior.

"You're coming from America proper?" he asked, taking my hand in his.

"Uh, yes, I guess." I eyed him uneasily. "I'm from the state of New York."

The Indian wiggled his head from side to side, and smiled approvingly. "New York is *too big* city!" he said. His eyes stuck so far out of his head I thought they might pop.

Vinod stroked my hand affectionately. *Is this guy coming on to me?* I wanted to pull away, but didn't dare. *Maybe this is how men speak to each other in this country.*

"New York City has many tall buildings," I said. I was unable to think of anything more interesting to say.

"Bombay same, same," he said with a frown and a dismissive wave of his hand.

"I beg your pardon?" I thought I might have offended him.

Vinod released my hand, and then looked down his nose at me. "Same, same."

While I squeegeed the fallen mango leaves and debris from the courtyard, Vinod cleaned and tidied the area around Baba's throne. Then he polished the pair of silver sandals that sat on a small table in front of it.

"What are those for?" I asked, pointing to the sandals.

Vinod creased his forehead and frowned. "Too many peoples Baba's feet touching," His eyes bulged out of his head again.

Clueless as to what he was talking about, I shrugged.

Vinod wiggled his head and flashed a toothy grin at me in response. Later, I saw what the sandals were for. In India, when approaching a holy man for his blessing, it was customary to touch his feet. During *darshan*, the silver sandals—called *padukas*—were put out in front of the guru's throne and served as a surrogate for his feet. They spared Baba the indignity of having his physical body touched a thousand times a day, but conferred the same blessing.

Despite Vinod's strangeness and the sleep I was missing, I was grateful to the guru for what my *seva* in the courtyard taught me about detachment and letting go. As soon as I finished clearing all the mud and leaves, the ashramites would track in new dirt and more leaves would fall. I got satisfaction out of getting the marble squeaky clean before the first meditators arrived, and then again an hour later before the recitation of the *Guru Gita*. For me, the Sisyphean task was a form of worship.

Later that day I took an auto rickshaw to village so I could pick up my order at the tailor's. The tailor greeted me with a warm smile and a cup of chai, but no clothes.

"My shirts and trousers?" I asked after a while. "Where are they?"

The tailor grinned broadly and wiggled his head. "Tomorrow only."

I was fuming, but hesitated to show it. I was in desperate need of cooler clothes.

"Tomorrow only?" I repeated.

"Yes, yes."

I went back to the tailor every day for three days in a row. On each occasion I was promised I could pick up my order "tomorrow only." But when I returned the next day, nothing was ready.

When I complained about the situation to Rohini Brinkerhoff, she explained that the communication problem was cultural: "Indians have a more flexible concept of truth than we do in the west." In other words, what she meant was that when the tailor said my clothes would be ready "tomorrow," he really meant at some unspecified point in the future. It was then I realized I had a lot to learn about India.

Finally, a week after they were originally promised, my clothes were waiting for me. Eager to try them on, I hurried back to the ashram. But I cringed when I tried them on and looked at myself in the mirror. I looked like a clown. The kurtas were not a complete disaster, but the trousers were ridiculously baggy. Instead of getting depressed about it, I reminded myself that I hadn't come all the way to India to win any fashion contests. I thought of Mahatma Gandhi in his simple homespun cotton. I convinced myself that dressing this way would be a profound act of renunciation.

The high point of every day at the Ravipur ashram was *darshan* in the courtyard with Baba. In Birchwood Falls, *darshan* almost always followed the evening program, and involved long lines. In Ravipur, *darshan* was less formal. There was never a long wait, except on weekends when hordes of visitors flocked to the ashram from Bombay. Baba might appear at any time of day, sitting for hours on his velvet throne under the shade of a mango tree, greeting devotees in the stifling heat. Whenever I had a free moment, I'd sit and gaze upon his divine form.

In India, *darshan* was a time when Baba took care of ashram business. Sometimes he'd receive special visitors, or converse with his swamis and close disciples. Other times, he'd sit for hours in a silent state of blissful absorption, without saying a word to anyone. He radiated a love and serenity so profound, it permeated the courtyard and spread throughout the entire ashram. Whenever I sat in his presence, I'd spontaneously enter into a state of meditation, identifying with my innermost Self.

When Baba went outdoors in India, he almost always wore dark sunglasses. This made it hard to tell exactly where he was looking, and I often had the impression that he was staring directly at me. At moments like these, I could feel him reading my thoughts, looking deeply into my soul. This experience was unnerving at times, but it was also comforting to know that the guru knew everything about me—even my deepest secrets. Thanks to these abilities, Baba was able to diagnose exactly what was holding his disciples back from attaining enlightenment, and prescribe the perfect remedy.

I felt good about my *seva* cleaning the courtyard, but my Housekeeping work would take me longer to get used to. For weeks I struggled with my aversion to cleaning up shit. To make matters worse, because of the constant rain during the last days of monsoon and the exposure to God-knows-what in the men's toilets, I developed a nasty fungal infection between my toes. Believing it would disappear on its own, I neglected the problem for as long as possible.

Eventually Rohini noticed my feet and convinced me to visit the ashram infirmary for treatment.

The ashram doctor was a Western swami by the name of Nirmalananda. He was a tall, spindly man with cold, joyless eyes and pale lips.

When I showed Nirmalananda my feet he blamed *me* for the condition, and admonished me for letting it get so bad. "You need to keep your feet clean and dry at all times," he said. But he never offered any suggestions on how to do this. Virtually everyone in the ashram wore the same Birkenstock sandals as I did. I wondered why more ashramites weren't afflicted.

The swami doctor gave me an antifungal ointment and a red substance called "mercurochrome" to apply between my toes. This had the effect of making my feet look as though they were constantly oozing blood—a shocking sight to some of the Western newcomers, who gasped when they saw my feet for the first time.

In order for me to have enough time to bathe, meditate for at least an hour, and arrive on time for my courtyard-cleaning shift, I needed to wake up every morning at two, even earlier than I originally thought. This would not have been a problem if I had been going to sleep at night by six or seven, but this wasn't the case. Determined to attend all the meditation sessions, chants, and rituals, I never got to bed until after the *Shiva Mahimna Stotram*—the last chant of the evening—which ended at nine. At most, I got only four or five hours of sleep at night.

I felt exhausted all the time, and would nod off in the middle of the chants and *seva* like a narcoleptic. Despite my renewed positive attitude about *seva*, I was angry with myself for needing so much rest. I had read that some yogis never slept—the profound states of meditation they had attained provided more than enough repose for their thought-free minds. According to Baba, this allowed them to dedicate every second of their lives to *seva*. *Why should I be any different?* I asked myself. It never occurred to me that it might take me a few more years of *sadhana* before I too could serve the guru twenty-four seven.

Remembering that Swami Akhandananda had once practiced medicine, I spoke to him about my problem.

"The fatigue is nothing to be concerned about, my boy," said Akhandananda. "Once you've adjusted to the incredibly high levels of *shakti* in Ravipur, you'll be full of energy all the time."

The difficulty of my *seva* hours, the strangeness of my new surroundings, the problems with my feet, and the constant exhaustion were beginning to get me down. In moments of desperation, I even had thoughts about leaving the ashram and going home to Ithaca. I didn't dare tell anyone about these feelings, however. I knew I just had to work through them. I did my best to keep in mind that whatever happened to me in the ashram was the will of the guru. Baba's *shakti* was working to purge me of both attachment and aversion. I had to let go of wanting a particular kind of *seva* and accept my new situation.

I was experiencing the first of what I had heard other devotees refer to as a "mental *kriya.*" Through these *kriyas* the guru's grace would eventually cleanse me of all my petty hang-ups and help free me from the shackles of ego. *Everything is equally a manifestation of divine consciousness,* I reminded myself. *From Gopi's mesmerizing emerald and sapphire eyes to the foul smelling shit on the floor of the public restrooms.* The more I strove to cultivate an attitude of gratitude, rather than one of self-pity, the cleaner I felt on the inside. Who knew how many lifetimes of evil karma I was washing away through this process?

Before long, my feelings of wanting to leave the ashram and return to what I now idealized as my carefree existence in Ithaca began to subside. They were soon replaced by an even greater spiritual zeal and a commitment to the practice of surrendering to the guru's will. This, combined with all the meditation and chanting I was doing, gave rise to feelings of euphoria. *This is it!* I told myself as it was happening. *I'm swimming in an ocean of bliss just as Baba promised!* I actually believed I was on the cusp of enlightenment.

But the ecstasy didn't last, and before long I was coming down from my mania-induced high.

Around this time, Baba gave his first public talk since my arrival in India. It was held in the open-air hall that opened onto the courtyard, where we chanted the *Guru Gita*. The theme was "delusion"—how easy it was to deceive oneself into thinking that one had already attained God-realization after a "minor mystical experience." As he spoke, the guru seemed to be looking directly at me, and I convinced myself that I was the intended recipient of his message.

"As long as there is a *you* attaining something," Baba said, "it is delusion you are experiencing, *not* realization. The ego is extremely subtle in its efforts to outsmart us and keep us from becoming truly free, like the guru."

I reflected on Baba's words: *If there is no I attaining enlightenment, then who attains the goal? If the ego just disappears, how is that different from death and eternal oblivion?* I struggled with these questions until I drifted off to sleep that night. In the morning, as I cleaned the courtyard, I reminded myself that this question could not be answered by the conceptual mind. I had faith, however, that through a combination of my effort and grace from the guru, the ultimate nature of reality would be eventually revealed to me.

Despite my constant fatigue, I felt good about my spiritual practice and believed that I had arrived at right understanding regarding my *seva*. I no longer wished I had a "more important" job in the ashram that would bring me into closer daily contact with Baba. I began to relate more and more to my *inner guru*. I let go of the idea that it was necessary to have a personal relationship with the guru in order to make progress.

On the other hand, it wasn't always so easy to maintain a positive attitude. I sometimes got discouraged when I saw some of the guru's closest people not living up to what I imagined were Baba's standards of the "perfect disciple."

Avadhoot Plotnick was a good example of this. His main *seva* at the moment was not at the guru's side or taking pictures, but taking care of Baba's elephant. In his white *kurta, lungi,* and cowboy hat, Avadhoot looked like even more of a freak than he had back in Birchwood Falls. On my way to clean the public restrooms on the far side of the ashram grounds, I'd often see him in the fenced-in area next to the elephant house, beating Baba's beloved pet with a stick and swearing at it like a sailor.

Once I saw him arguing with one of Baba's Indian swamis about his treatment of the animal.

"Mr. Avadhoot, you are not to be striking Baba's elephant in this manner."

The New Yorker's eyes bulged and his mouth fell open in indignation. "He started it! He keeps swatting me with his tail!"

"You must be patient and treat Raju with loving kindness," the swami admonished, wagging a finger in Avadhoot's face. "This is what Baba is teaching."

If Baba had ever taught about "loving kindness," it must have been before I arrived in the ashram, because I hadn't heard him mention it. In any case, Avadhoot didn't strike me as a particularly nice or caring person. As I cleaned the men's room behind the *mandap* pavilion, I thought about what I had witnessed at the elephant house: *Perhaps Baba has given Avadhoot this seva to teach him something about patience in the same way Baba gave me the seva of cleaning toilets to learn how to surrender.*

Although I was striving to lead the life of a chaste renunciant—practicing for the day when I would become one of Baba's swamis—I was never able to stop thinking about Gopi. She wasn't the only female distraction, of course. There were a lot of other pretty young "princesses" around Baba. Dressed in the finest silk saris, adorned with elegant gold jewelry and pearls, they were always at the guru's feet during *darshan,* and up front at all of his public talks.

Yet as beautiful and alluring as these other princesses were, the only one I was incapable of getting completely out of my mind was Gopi. If I let my guard down for a second, my head filled with romantic fantasies and impure thoughts about her. Despite all my hard work to rid myself of desire, I was still its slave.

Sometimes during *darshan*, Gopi would notice me in line and our eyes would meet. Whenever this happened, she would usually look away, but every once in a while she'd flash me an enormous smile. When she did, my mind would fly away to fantasyland: *Maybe instead of becoming a swami, Baba will command me to marry the angel. She and I will complete our sadhana together, as one. Our marriage will not be based on selfish motives, like ordinary relationships. Ours will be an ideal love. We will only have sex for the selfless purpose of bringing more highly evolved beings into the world to do Baba's work.*

Other times her behavior confused me. We passed each other in the courtyard or somewhere else in the ashram, and she completely ignored me. When this happened I fell into a funk. I chastised myself for allowing my mind to be led astray by desire.

Nonetheless, I believed I was leading the life of a true disciple: I had thrown myself wholeheartedly into the ashram routine, overcome my aversion to cleaning toilets, kept mostly to myself, and given up the hope of ever being close to the guru. Spiritually, I was on the right track. Yet I often found myself wondering: *If I'm such a good disciple, why am I so lonely and nostalgic about my miserable old life back in Ithaca?* I missed Mike and my other friends. I even thought fondly of Melanie and Lucy sometimes. And, although I had found the perfect parent in Baba, I still missed my mother.

I wished I could call home to check in with my family, but the ashram had no phone—only a telex machine that was for Mission business only. To make an international call, I'd have to go to the post office in Bombay and wait for hours for an available line.

"*Ach*! No one makes telephone calls in India," explained Rohini Brinkerhoff. "Much too expensive! We send aerogrammes instead." Aerogrammes were the cheapest way to send a letter. Rohini said I could buy them at the post office in the village. I wrote and told Melanie about my life at the ashram, how hard I worked, and how little sleep I needed. I also sent an aerogramme to Jeremy, describing my daily routine and the amazing mystical experiences I had been having in Baba's presence.

But writing home did little to help me overcome my loneliness. It might have even made it worse. What I needed was a friend. To fill that need, the first person that came to mind was Namdev Loman. He was around my age and we were both from Ithaca. On my way to and from *seva*, I'd often see him working in the field behind the *mandap* pavilion, barefoot and covered with sweat and sawdust, and operating a chainsaw. When I saw him taking risks like this, I thought he might be insane. No, I couldn't be friends with such a freak.

Of all the men around my age in the ashram, I liked and admired Suresh Bhandary the most. He was the friendliest member of Baba's inner circle and one of the only Indians. But despite my high opinion of him, I didn't always approve of his behavior. Often during my three A.M. cleaning shifts in the courtyard, I'd see him stroll in through the ashram gates with one or two other young Indian men. At first, I thought that they had just gotten out of bed and were on their way to the cave for meditation. But from the way they were laughing and joking, I soon realized that they were just returning from somewhere outside the ashram, and had probably been out partying all night.

One morning, I couldn't hide my disappointment when Suresh and his pals sauntered into the courtyard, clearly drunk off their asses.

"Hey, Deependra!" Suresh called too loudly. "Good morning!"

He stopped to chat with me. His friends continued on their way, leaving us alone together. "Is this your regular *shift?*" he asked. He was slurring his words.

I nodded.

"I see you every night at the *Shiva Mahimna*. When do you sleep?"

"Well, right afterwards," I said proudly.

Suresh grimaced in disbelief, and then took the stairs up to his room in the VIP dormitory. On his way out, he took special care not to step where I had already squeegeed.

I was confused. Suresh had seemed to imply I wasn't getting enough sleep. For the rest of the morning, I couldn't stop thinking about his question: "When do you sleep?" *Could my constant fatigue and drowsiness simply be the result of sleep deprivation?* To my naive, eighteen-year-old self, this was hard to believe, but I decided I couldn't rule it out. As soon as possible, I'd work up the courage to ask Baba about it directly.

Later that day at *darshan*, I got in line to greet Baba, but when it was my turn to bow down to him, I lost the nerve to say anything. When I stood up, Suresh was speaking to Baba in Hindi, and I had the impression they were talking about me. Baba looked at me and frowned. Suresh nodded his head encouragingly, and gestured toward the guru with a flick of his chin.

"Babaji," I began timidly. "I'm tired all the time, but I don't know why."

Baba turned to Suresh and the two again spoke together in Hindi. By the way Suresh kept looking in my direction, I was now certain they were talking about me.

Suresh translated the guru's words: "How many hours of sleep are you getting at night?"

"About four, Baba."

The guru's eyes blazed and his face tightened in anger. He turned to Anjali and spoke to her for a while.

"Sit, Deependra," Anjali said, motioning for me to take a seat next to Suresh. Then she turned to Gopi. "Go fetch Sita. She's in the *seva* office."

This was the first time I'd ever sat so close to the guru. I kept my back as straight as possible and tried to clear my mind of mundane thoughts. As we waited for Gopi to return with Sita, I watched Baba greet dozens of devotees and curiosity seekers who had come for his blessing. The strange circular motions of his hands and the way he kept pointing with his index finger in seemingly random directions fascinated me.

A few minutes later, Gopi returned with a sweaty and out-of-breath Sita Perkins. Even before she had a chance to bow down, Baba began to scold her.

"Why do you give this boy so much work that he has no time to sleep?" Baba asked through Anjali. The guru's nostrils flared and his eyes glared down at the *seva* coordinator, who was now kneeling and trembling.

"I don't know, Babaji," Sita croaked, her eyes welling with tears.

"I don't know!" Baba bellowed, speaking in English now. Turning to Anjali, he said something else in Hindi, which she then translated: "This boy is up every morning at two o'clock so that he can meditate and be at his *seva* to clean the courtyard on time. Give him a different job to do."

Just then Suresh, who was sitting next to me, tapped me on the knee. I turned to look at him and he winked, and then smiled mischievously.

I was grateful to Suresh for his concern, but couldn't help wondering why Baba, who was omniscient, hadn't known something was wrong and said something to me about it weeks ago. *The ways of the guru are mysterious indeed*, I reminded myself.

Later that afternoon, as I rested in bed, staring at the ceiling with the overhead fan on full blast, Sita appeared at the screen door to my dorm room. "Deependra? Are you decent?"

I sat up. "Yes, come in."

Hours after Baba had scolded her, she was still shaking. "I've given your courtyard cleaning *seva* to somebody else. You'll be washing dishes in Prasad after breakfast and dinner instead."

When I pointed out to Sita that working the evening dish room shift would make it impossible for me to get to the *Shiva Mahimna* on time, her temper returned.

"Don't be ridiculous! Nobody goes to *all* the chants!"

17.
ORPHANS

BY THE END OF September, as Maharashtra entered the post-monsoon season, the rain started to let up. Thanks to the change in my *seva* assignment, and skipping the evening chant, I was getting to bed earlier and waking up later, and I didn't feel exhausted all the time.

Even though I was still lonely and homesick sometimes, I had gotten used to my simple routine in Ravipur. The only thing I missed about the Birchwood Falls ashram were the regular evening programs with Baba. Although Baba held *darshan* in the courtyard almost every day, he had only given a handful of talks since our arrival, and hadn't come to a single chant. I prayed to the guru that this would soon change. I missed chanting with Baba and listening to him speak.

After the *Guru Gita* one morning, I questioned Akhandananda about the change.

The neckless swami chuckled. "Even a perfected master like Baba needs periods of rest. The guru's not on tour right now. He's home."

"Yes, of course," I said, scratching my head. "It's just that—"

"—you never thought of the guru as having any needs before, did you?"

Akhandananda's words stung. My cheeks burned and I felt pangs of guilt for having been so thoughtless. "I guess not."

A kindly smile brightened the swami's face and he tousled my hair with the palm of his hand. "Don't worry, my boy. The realization that the guru has a human body with human needs is all part of maturing in your spiritual practice."

I looked down. "I'm so ashamed of my selfishness—not thinking about what's best for Baba."

"Tut, tut, Deependra! Embarrassment is the purview of ego. An enlightened being knows neither pride *nor* shame."

I looked up and smiled at the swami and suddenly felt lighter.

"By the way, your color is much better now. Are you feeling less tired?"

"Oh yes, Swamiji! Baba—"

"You see, my boy. It didn't take long for you to adjust to the *shakti* here, now did it?"

I chose to remain silent, rather than disabuse the swami of his belief.

Baba must have heard my prayers, because later that day during *darshan* he asked for a microphone and gave an impromptu talk. Once again, I was astounded by Baba's clairvoyance. Without a doubt, he knew exactly what was on my mind, and addressed what I'd been struggling with since coming to India.

"Many of you have left your friends, family, and the comforts of home for the sake of your spiritual development," Baba said. He was looking in my direction. "But what do you do as soon as you arrive here? You search for new friends, for a husband or a wife, and sneak out of the ashram every chance you get to indulge in sense pleasures."

I wanted to disappear into the floor. I knew Baba was talking to me. I wasn't sneaking out like others, but I was constantly thinking of marrying Gopi.

"But if you continue in this way, you will attain nothing by studying with a guru. Your life will be a complete waste."

I clasped my hands together in prayer. *Please Baba, don't let my life be for nothing!*

"You must come to the ashram as an orphan, and become a lonely person who depends only on the guru. If you try to relieve your loneliness through idle conversation and superficial relationships, you will become distracted. To attain enlightenment, you must embrace loneliness. Only then will you know the supreme Self of all."

It had been easy to avoid Prasad before I had to report there twice a day for my dish room shifts. Now, after only a week of *seva* there, the tantalizing sights and smells were becoming irresistible.

"A renunciant should avoid all pleasurable experiences, especially tasty food," Baba had once said. "The dining hall food in Ravipur provides all the nutrition and sustenance an ashramite should need." Knowing this was the guru's view, I couldn't help wondering why all the swamis and inner circle people ate at Prasad.

I also wondered why the dining hall food never felt like it was enough for me—literally. Since my arrival, I had lost a ton of weight. For the first time in my life, I was able to see my ribcage when I took off my shirt.

The food on offer at Prasad made my mouth water: for breakfast they had traditional Indian dosa crepes and idli sambar, and Western-style oatmeal, granola, yogurt, and fresh hot croissants and scones. They also had a big selection of fresh fruit, including bananas, oranges, mangoes, and papayas. But the café was not cheap—even by American standards.

One morning I finally broke down and ordered a Swiss cheese and avocado dosa, and got a papaya for dessert. I paid for my food, took my tray outside to the open-air pavilion, and looked for a place to sit down. It wasn't easy.

Unlike the dining hall, Prasad was crowded. Here ashramites sat at tables and ate off Western-style plates with forks and knives. Conversation was permitted and everyone seemed to be eating with their friends. I looked around the pavilion to see if I recognized anyone. Gopi was there, but she was with the other princesses. I couldn't imagine fitting in with them. Poonish Davidson and Stephen Ames were eating together with some other *darshan* ushers I didn't know, laughing their heads off. There was a free seat at their table, but I didn't dare claim it. Swami Akhandananda was also there, but seemed to be in the middle of an important discussion with Gajendra Williams. I couldn't sit with him either.

I was about to give up, when I noticed Namdev Loman seated by himself at the very back of the pavilion. I remembered that he had taken a vow of silence, but thought maybe we could exchange a few friendly glances. "Hey, Doug, have a seat!" he said, greeting me with his signature shit-eating grin. He gestured to the empty seat across from him. I glanced at his shirt. The "silence" badge was gone.

"You're talking again?"

"I gave myself four months. My time is up."

I sat down and started eating.

"So, how's life treating you at the Ravipur ashram?" Namdev asked. "Is it everything you dreamed it'd be? I see they've got you cleaning toilets?"

I told him I felt like I'd died and gone to one of the celestial realms that Baba had written about in *Divine Dance of Consciousness*. I also explained I no longer went by Doug. "Baba gave me the spiritual name Deependra," I said, hoping to impress him. "It means 'lord of light.'"

Namdev was unimpressed. "Which dorm did they stick you in?" He spoke through a mouthful of cheese dosa. I couldn't believe how fast he was devouring his food. I thought he might choke.

"*Bhakti Shayanagrih.*"

"You're lucky," he laughed. "I'm in *Siddha Shayanagrih.* It's closer to the village. The noise sometimes keeps me up at night."

"Noise? What noise?"

"Oh, not now," he sneered. "But just you wait—during the month of May—if you make it here that long—there's a fucking wedding every night."

Namdev's swearing made me uncomfortable. I glanced around the pavilion to see if anyone had heard him, but no one seemed to be paying any attention to us.

"The princesses have it the best here, you know," he said, glancing in the direction of Gopi and her friends.

"How so?"

"If you're a young and pretty girl, they put you in the *Devi* dorm. It's connected to Baba's house. He treats them like royalty. It's not fair. They say the caste system doesn't apply in the ashram, but that's bullshit. You and me, my friend, are Raja Yoga Untouchables."

"That's ridiculous." I was beginning to wish I had sat by myself.

"You don't think so? Just look at where they sit at *darshan* and in the hall—right up front, at the guru's feet. You and me have to sit at the back of the hall with the Indians."

I thought about what Namdev said. I would've loved to sit up close to Baba and sleep in a dormitory adjacent to his private quarters. I also wondered why most of the Indian devotees were seated at the back. This seemed strange to me because, after all, we were in their country.

"The entire ashram is Baba's house," I said. "And we're always close to the *inner guru*, no matter where we sit or sleep."

"Oh yeah, how silly of me to forget," he sneered. Then he shoveled the rest of his breakfast into his mouth.

As I watched my ill-mannered friend finish his food, I remembered when I had first met him back in Ithaca, and how eager he had been to go to India. But now that he lived here, he seemed as dissatisfied as ever. I wondered why he stayed.

"You've been here—what—a year already?" I asked. "Aren't you happy?"

"Nine fucking months," he said. "You'll see—it's not so easy to live in Ravipur. I don't get to eat here often, you know. This is my first visit to Prasad in weeks. I can't afford it."

"What's wrong with the food in the dining hall?"

Just then our conversation was interrupted.

"Namdev! Didn't Baba tell you to stop swearing? This is an ashram, not a brothel!" I glanced over my shoulder to see Anjali Bhandary standing behind me, looking down her nose.

Namdev stared down at his empty tray and muttered something under his breath.

Anjali folded her arms and squinted. "What did you say?"

After a moment of reflection, Namdev responded so softly I could barely hear him: "Sorry."

Anjali turned her attention to me and smiled warmly. "Ahh, Deependra! How are you?"

"Fine —*great!*"

"Happy in the ashram?"

"Very happy!" I chirped.

"You see, Namdev," she said, jutting her chin out. "Some people are *very happy* in the ashram. You should try to develop right understanding like Deependra. He's grateful to be here."

Namdev angled his torso away from us and curled his shoulders over his chest. Anjali left us. Her next stop was at Gopi's table for a friendly chat.

"I saw you cutting down a tree with a chainsaw a few days ago," I said. "You were barefoot."

Namdev lifted his head to look at me. A few strands of his long yellow hair were dangling in his face. "I lost my sandals. I think someone stole them."

"Can't you get new ones?"

"With what money? Anyway, I don't need shoes."

"That's true. You never wore them in Ithaca either."

"Yeah, anyway. Cutting shit down is only one of my *sevas*." Namdev explained that Sita had sent him to work in the ashram generator plant to monitor the mains voltage, promising it'd be a temporary position. "Someone always has to be there to shut the generator down if the voltage gets too high, or the whole thing will blow up."

"That sounds like a good *seva* to me," I said. As far as I was concerned, it definitely beat cleaning toilets.

"Good *seva*, my ass. Have you seen that rat-infested hellhole? The walls surrounding the plant are covered with broken glass bottles. It looks like a prison."

Annoyed at Namdev's attitude, I set down my fork and knife. "You're free to leave the ashram anytime you want, you know."

"Free to leave? I just spent my last fucking rupee on this dosa. I'm on staff now, so I don't have to pay rent anymore, but unlike some people—" he gestured toward Gopi's table "—I get no stipend at all. At this point, I wouldn't even have enough money to get to the airport, if and when I ever decided to use my open-ended ticket."

"That's rough," I said, but I couldn't help wondering why he hadn't saved any money or planned better before coming all the way to India.

Namdev stood up abruptly. "Yep, I'm probably going to die in this place." Then he marched out of Prasad, leaving his dirty dishes on the table.

WASHING DISHES IN PRASAD was hot, wet, sticky work, but it was a welcome change. Part of my job was to bus dishes from the dining area in the pavilion to the dish room, which was on the second floor of the café building. The Prasad in Ravipur was equipped with a dumbwaiter that made the life of everybody who worked in the dish room easier. It was used to lift tubs of dirty dishes upstairs, and to bring clean dishes back down. The only drawback to this system was that the elevator in which the tubs of dishes sat didn't have a front or back. As a result, plates and utensils were always falling out and getting stuck between the shaft wall and the elevator. Whenever this happened, any time the machine saved was wasted trying to get it unblocked. Sometimes I thought we'd be better off just carrying the dishes up and down the stairs ourselves.

Working in the Prasad dish room gave me the opportunity to get to know some of the Indian devotees who visited regularly from Bombay, and I struck up a friendship with an adolescent boy named Ganesh Doodhwala. Small for his age by Western standards, Ganesh was a bright, happy-go-lucky twelve-year-old with dark skin, straight black hair, and curious big brown eyes.

"Babaji has given you this name, *Deependra?*" Ganesh asked. He was drying some plastic trays that had just come out of the industrial dishwasher.

"Yes, of course," I answered, loading a rack of clean dishes into the dumbwaiter.

"*Aacha, aacha!* Very auspicious! The name means *lord of light*."

"I know." I looked down at the floor and rubbed my forearm. I didn't want to appear too proud of the fact. I wanted to impress Ganesh with my humility.

"And do you know who is *Ganesh?*"

"Yes, *Ganesh* is the elephant headed god, the son of Shiva and Parvati."

"Precisely, my friend! I am thinking you are knowing all of our Hindu deities too well!"

I shrugged, and then lifted another tray of clean dishes to load into the dumbwaiter. "They're my gods too, you know."

An enormous grin erupted on the boy's face. "And don't forget," he said, bouncing on his toes. "Ganesh is also number one remover of obstacles! This is why I am expert-ed at unblocking this machine!"

Everybody in the dish room laughed, including the boy's father. It was true. Ganesh was quite skilled at climbing into the shaft and removing the various objects that got stuck between the dumbwaiter and the shaft wall. The dumbwaiter had built-in safety features, of course, but it always made me nervous to see little Ganesh practically disappear into the wall. I would've gladly gone in his place, but he was the only one small enough to fit into the shaft.

During the week, when Ganesh wasn't around, we sometimes had to wait hours before maintenance got around to fixing the blockage.

Later that day, I found a note on my bed from the manager's office saying that they were holding mail for me. When I went to pick it up, Indira St. John told me that Gajendra was irritated that I didn't stop by the office more often to check. "It's a waste of Baba's time when we have to go to the trouble of writing you a note and bringing it all the way to your dorm room," she said, blinking rapidly and holding a notebook up in front of her chest.

I hadn't gotten any mail before, so it was my first offense. I nevertheless apologized for being thoughtless. Back to my room, I saw I had a letter from Melanie, a postcard from Jeremy, and an invitation to my cousin Scott's wedding. *How sweet,* I thought, tearing up the invitation. *Two deluded souls joining together in miserable ignorance of the ultimate nature of reality. How pathetic! I won't dignify their invitation with a response.*

Melanie wanted to know how much longer I was planning on staying in India, and if I had given any more thought to going back to school. "If you apply now," she had written, "you might be able to attend TC3 in the spring." *TC3* was short for Tompkins Cortland Community College, a few miles northeast of Ithaca.

Her suggestion enraged me. I made a mental note to not write to her again for several months. *Silence will be my answer,* I thought. I would show her. Maybe then she'd finally get the message that Raja Yoga was my life.

All Jeremy had written on his postcard was the news that he'd been accepted for a residency at Long Island Jewish Hospital. He also asked how I liked the food in India. No comment about the sublime spiritual experiences I'd described to him in my letter, and not a word about how much he missed Baba. He obviously lacked devotion to the guru. Worse, he was uninterested in *me.* It was then I decided my family was dead to me. Even my brother and his wife.

That night I dreamed I was kissing Gopi, touching her beneath her clothing and underwear, while she moaned with pleasure. I woke up highly aroused, but deeply ashamed. I was angry with myself for having made so little progress in purifying my subconscious mind. I laid awake in bed for a long time, tossing and turning, burning with lust, my erection not going away. Unable to sleep, I went to the bathroom and dumped a bucket of ice-cold water over my head. It did nothing to make me less horny. I went back to my room and checked my watch. It was almost midnight. With no hope of falling asleep again without "relieving" myself, I decided to go for a walk.

With nowhere else to go at this hour, I headed for the courtyard. As I drew nearer, I heard an unfamiliar chant. I entered the square and saw no one in the hall. At first I couldn't figure out where the singing was coming from. Listening more carefully, I realized the guru himself was leading it. Looking up at the building that housed Baba's private quarters and the "princess dormitory," I noticed a light on. The chant was taking place in Baba's house. *Why in the middle of the night?* I wondered. *And why in private?*

Taking a seat on one of the planters, I listened for a while. Baba sounded ecstatic. I wondered who was lucky enough to be invited to this secret rite. I listened more carefully. The voices accompanying him were mostly feminine. Then it hit me: Baba was chanting with the *darshan* girls! Anger flared up inside of me. *Why do those spoiled brats get so much attention from Baba? It's not fair!*

As bitterness spread through my body, I tried to take control of my mind, as I had learned to do in meditation. I replaced negative thoughts with ones that reflected right understanding: *The guru has divinely inspired reasons for everything he does, even if I'm unable to understand them with my unenlightened mind. I should be grateful to be in his ashram at all. Things could be worse: I could be trapped in a mundane existence and a slave to my career, like Jeremy. Negative emotions like jealousy are my worst enemy.*

The chanting went on for another quarter of an hour. When it was over I could hear the distinctive sound of

Baba's voice intermixed with bits and pieces of Anjali's translation, and feminine laughter. This was followed by silence, and then the light went off in the room where they'd been chanting. A few seconds later, the door next to Baba's throne swung open, startling me. Avadhoot Plotnick stepped out with a tall, lean Mediterranean-looking man I'd never seen before. Avadhoot was dressed in his usual Ravipur ashram attire—kurta, lungi, and cowboy hat. But the other man looked like he was dressed for a night out on the town. He wore a chic white linen shirt and an elegant pair of gray linen slacks that fit him perfectly. His hair was dark and wavy, and his face was long and angular. Although the courtyard was dimly lit, he noticed me immediately and appeared to be scowling. Then he said something to Avadhoot while gesturing in my direction. He spoke too softly for me to hear, but if I had to guess it would be something along the lines of: "What is that piece of shit doing here?"

Now both men were glaring at me.

"Tell him," I heard the well-dressed man say to Avadhoot. Then, with an air of confidence and authority, the man crossed the courtyard and disappeared into the entrance of the VIP dormitory.

"What are you doing here at this hour?" Avadhoot demanded. "Why aren't you in bed?"

"I couldn't sleep." *Have I done something wrong?*

"Lights out is at ten," he barked, towering over me. "No exceptions!"

With my head hung low, I apologized to Avadhoot for breaking the rules, and then went back to my room. My roommate Claus was sleeping soundly, snoring his head off. I was still upset. I didn't see what the big deal was. Despite the reprimand from Avadhoot, and the awful feeling that I had somehow angered the guru, I was still intrigued to have overheard the secret ritual in Baba's quarters. I prayed that one day I could be part of it.

18.
WISH-FULFILLING TREE

THE NEXT MORNING, I found it impossible to meditate. I couldn't stop thinking about the secret ritual in the guru's house I'd seen the night before. *Why does Baba lavish those girls with so much attention? Why not me?*

During breakfast I considered asking Rohini, Sita, or even Swami Akhandananda if they knew anything about the chant, but decided against it. I didn't want anyone to think I was nosy.

My afternoon *seva* finished early that day, so I managed to get to the courtyard before *darshan* had started, before all the spots near Baba's throne were taken. One of the princesses let me sit directly behind the swamis. Within ten minutes the courtyard was full. Turning around, I looked at all the people sitting behind me. I felt blessed to be seated so close to the throne, and thanked the omnipotent guru. After a few more minutes, the door to the guru's house opened and Baba strode out, followed by Anjali and Suresh. As soon as the guru was seated, Stephen Ames brought him a microphone.

"Once, Mullah Nasrudin was wandering around all day in the hot sun, until he came upon a beautiful tree and sat down in its shade. He was very happy to have found such a lovely tree, but then he had a thought: 'Wouldn't it be much better if there were a beautiful cottage here for me to live in?' Nasrudin did not know it, but the tree he was sitting under was a wish-fulfilling tree. So the moment he made this wish it was granted and a beautiful cottage appeared just like that." Baba snapped his fingers.

"Nasrudin went inside the house and took a look around. It was exactly what he had wanted. He was elated. Then he had another thought: 'This is wonderful, but wouldn't it be even better if I had delicious food served to me on golden platters?' And, since no trick is too difficult for a wish-fulfilling tree, this desire was also fulfilled—not just one, but hundreds of delectable dishes on golden platters materialized. Nasrudin was surrounded by them, and their aroma was intoxicating.

"Still unsatisfied, Nasrudin wished for servants to wait on him. They also appeared and began doing his bidding. So, Nasrudin ate and drank very happily without having to lift a finger. Next, Nasrudin wanted a female companion." The courtyard erupted in laughter. First the Indians, then, after Anjali's translation, the Westerners. "How could he sleep all alone in such a beautiful house?" Baba continued. Again, laughter erupted.

"So, a moment later, a ravishing maiden materialized. Nasrudin couldn't believe his good fortune. But then, he began to have a doubt: 'This is all too good to be true. She must be a ghost because the moment I thought of her she appeared.'

"No sooner had the doubt occurred to Nasrudin, than the girl turned into a ghost. When he saw the ghost, he became afraid it would devour him, and this is exactly what happened. The ghost ate him up."

Baba paused for a moment to allow the moral of the story to sink in.

"So this is how poor Mullah Nasrudin's story ended under the wish-fulfilling tree. This was all he achieved in his life. He had acquired so much, and then, through the power of his own mind, he turned the woman into a ghost who destroyed him. Your own mind is a wish-fulfilling tree. It has enormous potential. But like Nasrudin, you create wonderful experiences for yourself with your mind, and then, because of your doubts, you are eaten up by them. This is why you practice Raja Yoga—through meditation, through self-inquiry, you are able to eliminate these self-destructive tendencies."

A *darshan* line formed immediately after Baba's talk. I got up to join it, leaving my *asana* on the floor to hold my place. As I waited my turn, I thought about the story he had just told about the wish-fulfilling tree. Like Nasrudin, I thought that I too should wish for something. I didn't have to think long about what I wanted. I would wish for enlightenment, obviously. Through the power of my own mind, and the grace of the guru, I would make it happen. Unlike Nasrudin, I was sure I'd never let my own mind destroy me in the process.

Yet in the instant that I bowed before the guru, a pitiful cry rose up from deep within my wounded heart. Instead of wishing to attain the most lofty goal of human existence, the lonely orphan inside of me cried out for what I needed more than anything else in the world: *Love me!* I wished to be close to Baba. I prayed for him to make me a member of his most beloved inner circle. When I stood up, my eyes met Baba's, and he held me in his gaze for what felt like an eternity. The guru had heard me.

As I turned to go back to my place on the floor, a small group of Indian men with their chins held high entered the courtyard and caught my eye. They weren't dressed like the typical devotees from Bombay, in polyester camp shirts and bell-bottom slacks. These men wore starched white Gandhi caps, lightweight cotton kurtas, and loose-fitting trousers.

Returning to my spot behind the swamis, I found my *asana* crumpled between two skinny Indian men. "Excuse me, I'm sitting here." I pointed to my woolen carpet. "That's mine."

One man ignored me. The other wiggled his head, waving his hand at me dismissively.

Fuck this! I thought. I flew into a rage. *They're not going to get away with it.* I wedged myself between the two men, expecting them to either put up a fight or cede the spot to me. I was astonished when they did neither. Oblivious to my aggression, they allowed me to sit on top of them. Then, after all that, one of the *darshan* ushers told me to move. I was outraged: I couldn't understand why he didn't make the Indians move. *I was there first!*

As I got up to leave, Anjali called out to me: "Deependra!" Her sharp tone struck me like lightning. I looked at Baba. He was staring back at me. *Shit! I've angered the guru!* I thought. Baba turned to Anjali and spoke a few words, and then she pointed in my direction and motioned for me to come.

I pointed to my chest. "Me?"

Anjali nodded her head vigorously. As I stepped into the aisle, I was almost knocked over by the men in Gandhi hats. Vinod Desai was leading them up the aisle to meet the guru.

Pushing my way to the front of the line, I knelt down next to Baba's translator. "I'm so sorry, Anjali. I wasn't sure you were talking to me, then—"

"Be quiet!" she snapped. "Go fetch Avadhoot. Baba needs him. Tell him to come quickly!"

I knew exactly where to find the photographer. Thrilled to have been sent on such an important mission for the guru, I ran to the elephant house as fast as I could. When I got there, Avadhoot was in the fenced-in area with Raju, patting him affectionately, and cooing sweetly into his enormous ear.

"Who's a good elephant? Is it Raju? Is Raju a good elephant? Yes he is! Yes he is!"

Just then, Raju snatched Avadhoot's cowboy hat with his trunk and waved it around in the air.

"Ho, ho, ho, Raju. Be a good elephant. Give Avadhoot back his hat."

The elephant brought the hat back down within Avadhoot's reach, and then lifted it up and away again just before Avadhoot had a chance to grab it.

"Give it back Dumbo!" Avadhoot hollered. "Or I'll rip your tusks out with my bare hands and sell them for ivory!"

Catching my breath from the run, I called out to him from the other side of the fence. "Excuse me, Avadhoot."

"Yeah. What is it?" he grumbled, struggling to get his hat back from the playful elephant.

"I'm sorry to interrupt, but Baba wants you to come to the courtyard, right away."

"Fuck! With my camera?"

My mind froze. "They didn't say!"

The photographer narrowed his eyes. "And you didn't even think to ask?"

I felt like a fool. I shook my head. *I've blown it!* I thought. *I've failed in my mission!*

"Idiots!" Avadhoot shouted. "The ashram is overflowing with idiots!" He hastily herded Raju back inside his house, locked the gate, and then, hatless, he tore down the garden path toward to courtyard, with me chasing after him.

I wanted to shoot myself for how poorly I'd handled the mission. I should've known to ask Anjali about the camera. Suddenly it occurred to me: *Of course he needs it. Baba probably wants pictures with those Indians in the Gandhi hats. Shit!*

"Avadhoot!" I called. But it was useless—he was too far away now to hear me. "I think Baba wants you to take pictures! Avadhoot, wait!"

Out of breath, and with no possibility of catching up to him, I slowed to a walk.

By the time I got back to the courtyard, Avadhoot was already posing the men around Baba's throne. I realized he must have raced to the Audiovisual office, grabbed his camera, and begun directing the visitors, all in the time it took me to walk to the courtyard.

From the back of the courtyard, I surveyed the area where I'd been sitting to see if I could spot my *asana*, but it had been swallowed up in the sea of devotees.

Curious about the important visitors, I looked around for someone to ask. Indira St. John was a few feet away. I approached her. "Who are those people with Baba that Avadhoot is photographing?"

"Oh, them?" said Indira, her eyes glued to the guru. "Just a bunch of politicians. They want Baba to endorse their candidate in the next election."

"I didn't know Baba was political."

"He's not—*obviously*. He gives them his blessings, like everyone else who comes to see him."

Baba was now laughing and joking with the men while Avadhoot continued to take pictures. When their audience was over, one of them placed an envelope in the basket at the guru's feet, and Suresh escorted them out of the courtyard in the direction of Prasad.

Just then I got a whiff of strong cologne. I turned and saw the well-dressed man from the previous night.

"Indira, I need to speak to you," he said in a strong Italian accent. He turned to face me, looking me up and down before locking eyes with me. "Alone."

The man creeped me out, but I was unable to look away. He dismissed me with a flick of his chin, and then turned to Indira.

I moved back to where I'd been standing and continued to look on as Baba greeted more weekend visitors. But my thoughts kept returning to the swarthy Italian man. *Who is he? And why haven't I seen him around Baba before?* I glanced back to see him walking away from Indira and toward the manager's office. Indira was now headed in my direction and I stopped her just as she was about to pass me. "Indira, who was that man?"

"Sergio," she muttered, without looking at me. Then she turned to walk up the aisle and took a seat behind the younger *darshan* girls.

Sergio Casto? Wasn't he the rapist? I was horrified.

As I dried dishes at Prasad that evening after dinner, I was in such a state of confusion I could barely focus on what I was doing. *Why? Why does Baba allow Sergio back in the ashram after what he did? And what was he doing in Baba's house in the middle of the night? Are rapists invited to the guru's secret rites?*

"Deependra, uncle, I have one doubt," said Ganesh Doodhwala, who had come for the weekend with his parents.

"A doubt about what?" I asked, absently feeding a tray of dishes into the machine.

"Something is weighing heavily on your good mind. What is wrong? Please tell me."

"No, I'm okay," I answered.

"Then why have you loaded the washer with the clean dishes which you yourself have only just now dried?" Everybody in the dish room laughed.

"How stupid of me!" I buried my face in my hands. I was *not* okay, but didn't want to share what was troubling me with anybody, least of all a twelve-year-old boy.

My head was spinning. The fact that Sergio was in the ashram disturbed me deeply. I needed to regain control of my thoughts. I went to the small Brahmananda temple off the courtyard, sat down in front of the life-size statue of Baba's guru, closed my eyes, and prayed: *Gurudev, please help me understand your successor Rudrananda's actions. They make no sense.*

I opened my eyes and looked up at the statue's impassive face. Silence.

Answer me Gurudev! Why would Baba do such a thing? Sergio's behavior flies in the face of Baba's teachings! We are meant to remain celibate in the ashram and rid our hearts and minds of lust. If I can do it, why can't one of Baba's closest disciples?

Again I gazed up at the statue of Brahmananda. Silence.

Then I had another thought. *Maybe silence is the answer!* Suddenly I felt lighter—almost giddy. *I must stop trying to understand the actions of an extraordinary saint with my ordinary mind.*

I guided my mind toward thoughts of Baba's tremendous compassion. I remembered my first *darshan* with him, when he had taken me in his arms, forgiving me for causing my mother's illness and giving me permission to forgive myself. *Didn't Baba also forgive me for my own sexual perversion? If Baba could forgive me, why not Sergio, or any of his other followers?*

I prostrated myself before Lord Brahmananda, and thanked him from the depths of my heart for granting me right understanding. I was so relieved I felt like dancing. On the way back to my room, I looked up at the millions of stars in the night sky. The heavens were smiling down on me. I had passed another of the guru's tests!

I thought about Baba's supreme love for his children. Tears of gratitude streamed down my face. *Baba has given Sergio a second chance,* I told myself. I was now more in awe of the guru than ever.

Jai Gurudev! I whispered out loud.

Jai Gurudev! Jai Gurudev!

19.
A Sacred Mission

GANESH AND HIS PARENTS stopped me on my way to the dish room. "Happy birthday, Deependra uncle!"

"I can't believe you remembered! Thank you!"

I was glad that *somebody* knew what day it was. I hadn't heard from anyone in my family for almost three months, and they had obviously forgotten my birthday. It hurt. Then I remembered that this boy and my other Raja Yoga brothers and sisters were all the family I needed.

"You are how old only?" asked the boy's father.

"Nineteen."

Ganesh's parents smiled and wiggled their heads approvingly. His dad reached for my hand and shook it. "*Aacha!*"

As time passed in the Ravipur ashram, my initial shock and confusion over Sergio's return to Baba's side gave way to a fascination. The man was always challenging my concepts of what it meant to be spiritual. Of all of the guru's Western disciples, Sergio and Avadhoot were undoubtedly the closest. But like Baba's cowboy photographer, Sergio couldn't have been more different from the typical devotee. For one thing, I never once saw him in the meditation cave, the dining hall, or at a chant, unless Baba was in attendance. For another, his appearance was as fashionable as Avadhoot's was outlandish.

Favoring chic linen shirts, slim slacks, and fancy leather dress shoes, Sergio also wore an intricate gold chain around his neck to match his expensive-looking gold wristwatch. He had the distinction of being the only man in the ashram to wear cologne, and he used a lot of it. You didn't need extrasensory perception to know when Sergio had just left a room or was lurking around a corner. What made him seem even more exotic were his deeply tanned olive skin and perfectly coiffed dark curly hair, which always appeared to be damp. Along with his squeaky clean appearance, his wet hair gave the impression that he had only just stepped out of the shower a few moments earlier.

Sergio had perfect posture and was in excellent shape. Even though he was in his thirties—which, to me at the time, seemed ancient—he was probably the fittest man in the ashram. Because I never saw him lift a finger, however, I couldn't help wondering how. It seemed like his only *seva* was to sit up front during *darshan*. I imagined him with a treadmill and weights, working out in the privacy of his room while the rest of us were meditating or at the chants. This would at least explain the permanently wet hair.

While Sergio more closely resembled a resident of the French Riviera than an ashramite, it was the way he spoke and behaved that made him so different. I hadn't spoken with him since our first encounter, but I was able to observe him during mealtimes at Prasad. The exclusive company he kept was no surprise: he only sat with other members of the inner circle, and enjoyed a close relationship with Anjali. It also didn't escape my notice that Gopi was all smiles whenever she sat with him. *Doesn't she know he's a rapist?* I asked myself again and again.

When I was lucky, I found a seat close enough to his table that I could overhear bits and pieces of his conversations. I liked his accent—the way he always added just the hint of a vowel sound at the end of every word, as if he wanted to pronounce it but was stopping himself.

Sometimes at night, when I was alone in the bathroom, I'd stand in front of the mirror doing impressions of Sergio's hand gestures and facial expressions. One of my favorites was when he'd smile, pinch his fingers, draw a straight line in the air with them, and then declare, *"Perfetto!"* I loved to imitate the way his lips curled into an ugly scowl when he got angry, or, when he was having a private conversation, how he sometimes looked furtively over his shoulder and stirred an imaginary bowl in the air with the tips of his fingers.

Despite the fact that I never actually saw Sergio do any physical work, he was a busy man. He was in and out of Baba's house at all hours of the day and night. During *darshan*, he always told everyone else what to do. Rohini told me that he was Baba's tour manager, but as far as I could tell, Sergio Casto was in charge of everything.

Around the same time I was becoming obsessed with the Italian, I began to notice that not only Sergio but all the men close to Baba dressed in conservative, Western-style clothing. The only exceptions were the swamis, of course, and Avadhoot, who always dressed like a wackadoo, even in the States. I started to notice that only ordinary devotees like Namdev Loman and me donned traditional Indian clothing. I realized that if I wanted to be close to the guru, I should start dressing like the people who were.

This meant I needed a whole new set of clothes. But Bombay was only place I could buy the Fred Perry polo shirts and straight-leg khaki pants favored by the men on Baba's staff. The prospect of traveling to the enormous city frightened me. I asked Namdev if he'd make the trip with me, but he declined. He was now on scholarship at the ashram, and he couldn't come and go whenever he pleased. Rohini was more than happy to give me the time off. She made some suggestions about what to do while I was there, including a visit to the Gateway of India and the caves on Elephanta Island. I thanked Rohini for her ideas, but knew I wouldn't be doing any sightseeing. I saw myself as a spiritual aspirant on a sacred mission, not a tourist.

Sita Perkins also gave her permission for me to leave for a couple of days, and found someone to cover my shifts in the dish room.

"Don't stay away too long, Deependra," said the *seva* coordinator. "Gurudev's *mahasamadhi* celebrations begin next week. There'll be a lot of *extra seva* for everyone, and you won't want to miss the *saptah*."

The *saptah* was a chant that went on twenty-four hours a day for seven days, culminating in the beginning of a holiday. In this case, we were commemorating Brahmananda's *Punyatithi*—the anniversary of his leaving his physical body to merge with the Absolute.

The day before my excursion, I went by the office to pick up my passport. Gajendra's reluctance to hand it over bothered me. He first wanted to hear why I needed it. When I explained that I needed new clothes, he was satisfied and wrote down a few addresses for me.

"I'd also like to call home," I added.

Gajendra folded his arms and eyed me cautiously. "Why? Is something wrong?"

"Wrong?" I felt a tightening in my chest. "No, nothing is *wrong*. I'd just like to say hello."

"Which hotel are you staying in?" he asked, handing me the paper with the addresses.

"I thought I'd spend the night at one of the guest houses on the list recommended by the ashram."

Shaking his head, Gajendra took my passport out of a file cabinet behind him and handed it to me. "Forget about those places. You should stay at the Taj."

"The Taj Palace? Isn't it expensive?"

The manager's permanent frown was momentarily eclipsed by a smile. "It's worth the money. You'll also be able to make an international call there. Anyhow, what's the big deal?" Gajendra said, wiggling his eyebrows. "You can afford it, right?"

THE NEXT MORNING, I didn't bother packing a change of clothes. I knew I'd be returning from Bombay with a brand new wardrobe. The *Guru Gita* was just beginning when it was time for me to leave. As I tiptoed past the open-air hall, I felt everyone's eyes on me. Outside at the bus stop, I could still hear the chant over the ashram loudspeakers.

I wasn't sure exactly when the bus to the railway station would arrive—no one in the ashram could say with any certainty—but forty minutes into the *Gita*, I boarded a run-down, dust-covered red and yellow bus.

As the bus crawled down bumpy dirt roads through the Maharashtrian countryside, I was fascinated by what I saw: men and boys walking alongside the road hand in hand, or sleeping on top of each other under the shade of trees; impossibly huge loads of sugarcane transported by rickety ox carts; trucks elaborately adorned with religious symbols and garlands, the words "Horn OK Please" or "Please Use Dipper At Night" painted on their back ends. I wondered what these instructions could possibly mean to other motorists, and why they were in English.

Suddenly I felt knuckles rapping on my head, knocking on my skull as if it were the front door of a house.

"Hello, please!" came a man's voice from behind me.

I whipped my head around and was face to face with a balding man with an oily comb-over and a shit-eating grin.

"Hey, cut it out!"

I wanted to smack him, but held back. I was in a foreign country, I reminded myself. For all I knew, maybe it was normal to greet people that way.

"So sorry," the man said, apologizing by quickly touching his hand to my arm and then touching his own head. "You are coming from which country?"

"America."

The man's eyes widened in alarm. "Iran?"

He had misheard me. "No, no! The United States."

"*Aacha! Aacha!*" the man exclaimed, wiggling his head and smiling again. "America proper?"

"That's right." I was unsure what *America proper* actually meant.

After what felt like an interminable journey, the bus finally arrived at a ramshackle train station. Half of the passengers got off the bus.

"Is this the Vasai Road station?" I asked a man sitting across from me.

The man smiled at me benevolently, but remained silent.

"Vasai Road?"

The man's grin widened and he wiggled his head ambiguously.

Again I felt the knuckles of the man sitting behind on my head. The heat of anger spread through me. I bit my lower lip and turned around again.

"What is it?" I demanded through gritted teeth.

"This one—Vasai Road railway station—here only," the man said happily.

Inside the station, the line for a ticket was so long I missed my train to Bombay. I had to wait outside on the platform for nearly two and a half hours until the next one came.

When the train finally arrived, it was packed with people. After a two-hour journey, we pulled into Churchgate Station. I was astounded when my fellow passengers began pushing and shoving each other, jumping out of the open doors of the train before it had even come to a complete stop.

The railway station in Bombay reeked of rotting fish—an even more unpleasant odor than the public toilets at the ashram. I nearly vomited. On the street, I was assaulted by hot blinding sunshine and the incessant cacophony of car horns blaring, the aggressive calls of hawkers, and the raucous conversations of pedestrians. I was also greeted by another familiar odor—the one I had first encountered on the tarmac at the airport months ago—a sickening combination of exhaust fumes, wood smoke, and putrid garbage. As much as my senses were overloaded, I was fascinated by the scene: men carrying dozens of tin canisters on their heads; women in elegant saris or shrouded in black burqas; old men in traditional Indian garb; businessmen in Western-style suits; teens in tight blue jeans; children with stumps for limbs begging in between traffic lanes; skinny men sleeping in the middle of the sidewalk; scrawny dogs everywhere. *I should be disturbed by the terrible poverty,* I thought. *But I feel nothing. What's wrong with me?*

I looked on in amazement at the chaotic ebb and flow of traffic in front of the station. Vehicles heedlessly swerved in and out of lanes, coming perilously close to one another in a perpetual state of near misses. I had no idea how to hail a taxi, but several drivers solicited me the moment I stepped to the curb. I hopped into the nearest car and asked the cabbie to take me to the Taj Palace hotel in Colaba.

At first, the seeming recklessness of my driver scared me—he came within millimeters of hitting a young couple sharing a motor scooter, and then narrowly avoided colliding with an oncoming double-decker bus as he passed an auto rickshaw. I felt safer, however, after I noticed a flower-adorned photograph of Gurudev Brahmananda fixed above his dashboard. *Baba's guru will protect me!*

"I'm a devotee of Brahmananda, too," I said from the back seat.

The driver squinted at me in the rearview mirror.

"I'm a disciple of Gurudev's successor, Swami Rudrananda. I live in the Ravipur ashram."

Ignoring me, the driver turned sharply onto a broad avenue with many shops, street vendors, and restaurants. I assumed he didn't speak English.

I stared out the window at a haggard man playing a reedy wind instrument, leading an emaciated cow by a rope. At his side was a small boy in filthy clothes beating an impossibly large drum that hung from his neck.

The taxi turned onto a side street, and then turned again onto a six-lane boulevard parallel to the harbor. A street sign identified it as "Marine Drive." In the distance I saw a great stone archway at the end of a large wharf crowded with people.

"What is that?" I asked, pointing to the archway in a last attempt to communicate.

"The monument, sir?" the driver said in perfect English.

"Yes!" I wondered why the man had previously pretended not to understand me.

"That is the Gateway of India. Erected by the British in 1911."

After passing a few blocks of badly weathered apartment buildings, we arrived at an enormous hotel with red domes and pointed arches. The entrance was guarded by two Sikh doormen, ceremonial daggers holstered at their sides. Their long hair and beards were tucked neatly into bright orange silk turbans that matched the sashes tied around their waists. The ends of their mustaches were waxed and twirled into points that curved upward toward their cheeks.

They're never going to let me in that place, I worried. *Not the way I'm dressed.* I was wearing one of my clownish blue ashram ensembles.

"Good afternoon, sir," one of the doormen said, holding a door open for me. "Welcome to the Taj Palace."

Stepping out of the sweltering heat, humidity, and glaring sunlight into the sumptuous, dimly lit, air-conditioned lobby was like entering an oasis of comfort and luxury.

Contrary to my fear of looking like a weirdo in such elegant surroundings, I fit right in. In addition to the Indian and Western businessmen, glamorous women, and Arab sheiks, there was a variety of white-skinned oddballs and freaks lounging in the lobby: a crazy-eyed man with a long beard and shock of white hair in the orange robes of a *sadhu* grasping what looked like King Neptune's trident; a barefoot, middle-aged lady in a pale yellow sari with a string of enormous rudraksha beads hanging from her neck; and a couple of young, long-haired backpackers in tie-dyed t-shirts and cutoffs who reeked of pot.

I was impressed by the elegance of the place: its Persian carpets, crystal chandeliers, onyx columns, and gigantic bouquets of fragrant lilies. I wished I could stay longer than just one night, but I knew it must cost a fortune. I decided to ask for the cheapest room in the house.

"Just you, your good self, checking in, sir?" the woman at reception asked in a British accent. Her hair was dark brown instead of black, and her eyes were an arresting shade of gray.

"Yes."

"I have a lovely single room for you, sir, with a splendid view of the Arabian Sea."

Suddenly I changed my mind about trying to save money. *After a year of austerities, I deserve the best!* "Do you have any *suites* with the same view?"

The clerk stared at me incredulously for a moment. Then she responded: "Yes, sir. However, we will require payment in advance."

I took a wad of traveler's checks out of my knapsack and, handing a small chunk of my inheritance money over to the woman, felt the walls of my throat begin to close.

"Very good, sir," said the clerk, handing me a room key. She struck a call bell on the counter with the palm of her hand, and a moment later a bellhop appeared beside me.

"Your luggage, sir?" he asked, looking around on the floor next to me.

I was confused. "What luggage?"

The bellhop's bushy eyebrows squished together. "Your valise?"

"Oh!" I handed the man my worn out knapsack. "This is it."

The woman behind the reception counter cringed, and then dismissed me with a disapproving wiggle of her head.

My suite consisted of a bedroom with a king-size bed and a living room with a large sofa. Both rooms had access to a balcony with a breathtaking view of the harbor and the Gateway of India.

After settling in, the first thing I did was to set up a *puja* to Baba with a small framed photograph of him and an incense burner I'd brought with me. Pleased with my makeshift altar, I lit a stick of sandalwood incense, and then prostrated myself before the guru's picture.

I stripped naked and drew a bath. As I waited for the tub to fill, I regarded myself in the mirror. I'd never been thinner in my entire life. I noticed something else: my acne had completely cleared up. It had must have happened gradually, but for some reason I hadn't noticed it getting better. This was further proof that the fire of *Raja Yoga* was burning away all of my imperfections, inside and out.

When the bathroom had filled up with steam and I could no longer see my reflection, I slid my aching body into the tub. The water was much hotter than the bucket baths I'd gotten used to in Ravipur, but thanks to the air conditioning, it felt wonderful.

Although I had a lot of shopping to do before the stores closed, it was difficult for me to drag myself out of the delicious hot water. I soaked until my fingers and toes became swollen and wrinkled.

Stretching out on the bed, I luxuriated in the firmness and enormous size of the mattress. *No crazy roommates. Alone at last!* But as I drifted off to sleep, another thought occurred to me: *Wouldn't it be perfect if Gopi were here with me?*

A loud knock came on the door. I shot out of bed, wrapped a towel around my waist, went to the door, and looked through the peephole. Outside stood a heavyset Indian woman and a tall Indian man in a hotel uniform. The woman scowled and knocked again. I unlatched the door and cracked it open, exposing only my head and bare torso.

"Good afternoon," the woman frowned, turning her nose up at me. "I am Mrs. C.N. Narendra —hotel security. Kindly to open the door please."

I glanced up at the tall uniformed man next her. He had a vacant look on his face, and although he was taller than me, he was even skinnier. He didn't seem particularly threatening. The fat woman looked a lot more dangerous, and I was afraid of her.

"May I please put on some clothes first?"

"Very well," the woman said, pursing her lips. I shut the door, and hastily got back into the same sweaty clothes I'd been wearing before my bath.

I opened the door again and Mrs. Narendra waddled into my suite to begin her investigation. While her assistant waited in the doorway, she checked all the rooms.

"May I ask what you're looking for?"

Mrs. Narendra turned around and regarded me suspiciously. "I'll know when I find it."

She let herself out onto the balcony. I couldn't imagine what they suspected me of. I couldn't help feeling like a criminal.

Satisfied that I had nothing to hide, Mrs. Narendra and her lanky assistant departed without saying a word, leaving the door to my suite open behind them.

I had wasted enough time. I'd skip lunch, hit the shops, and have a big dinner later. On my way out of the hotel I stopped at reception to drop off my room key. The light-skinned woman I'd spoken to earlier was assisting another guest, so I talked to a different clerk—an earnest-looking young man in thick-rimmed glasses.

"A Mrs. Narendra made a visit to my room earlier," I said, handing him my key. "She said she was from hotel security. She didn't find anything. May I ask why she was sent?"

"Ah yes," the clerk said, blushing a little. Then he opened his mouth again to speak, but nothing came out.

"Yes, *what?*" I insisted.

"Checking for *monkey business* only, sir," the clerk muttered, turning redder.

"Monkey business? What sort of monkey business?"

"Oh, you know, sir—" he began, looking away. "—the usual hanky-panky, mischief making, and what-all."

Out on the street I lost my way a couple of times before finding the Colaba Causeway, where Gajendra had told me the men who tour with Baba bought all of their clothes. After an hour or two of window shopping, I came upon a store called Arrow, where I found everything I needed: Fred Perry polo shirts—one in every available color, and half a dozen pairs of pants—khaki, white, blue, and charcoal gray. I was spending a small fortune, but I didn't care. I was doing this for Baba.

Before leaving the shop I changed into one of my new outfits and asked the shopkeeper to throw out my old Indian "clown suit." He was all too happy to oblige.

I left Arrow in my stylish new clothes with my head held high and a spring in my step. I felt like a new man. *What would Sergio think of me now?*

Above me I heard the sound of someone clearing phlegm from their throat. I looked up to see a man spitting out of an open window. I moved just in time to avoid getting hit.

"Please don't be afraid, sir," came a voice from behind me. I spun around and was face to face with a beautiful Indian girl in her teens. She was dressed in an indigo blue sari. In her hand she held tiny garlands of jasmine flowers.

"I don't want money," she said in perfect English. "But could you please buy me some food? I'm very hungry."

I looked the girl over: she was clean and well groomed. Her dark skin was radiant in the sweet light of the late afternoon, and her braided hair looked like black silk. There was an air of purity about her, and I guessed she was unmarried.

All she wanted was something to eat, she had said. I thought about inviting her back to my suite and ordering room service. We could eat out on the balcony and enjoy the sunset together. Afterwards, I would seduce her and make love to her in my big king-size bed. *When she sees how rich I am, how will she resist me?* I thought. *Perhaps I will make her my wife and take her back to the ashram. I wonder what our children would look like? Will they look Jewish or Indian?*

"Sir, perhaps you would like to buy some flowers? I just want to buy something to eat. Sir?...Sir?"

I snapped out of my reverie. *Am I insane? What am I thinking?* Then I remembered Baba saying that one should never give to beggars. I had no idea what his reasons were, but it didn't matter. I'd be damned if I disobeyed the guru.

I turned away from the girl and ran back toward the hotel as fast as I could.

"Wait, sir! Please! Don't be afraid!"

She chased me for a few blocks and finally gave up. I was relieved.

Feeling peckish myself, I looked for somewhere to eat an early dinner. After sticking my head into a few restaurants, I finally settled on a place called Café Leopold, where other Westerners were dining. One of the waiters seated me. There were so many vegetarian options, it was almost impossible for me to choose. I ended up ordering three paneer vegetable dishes, and was unable to finish them all. Leaving half my food uneaten, I asked for the check and returned to the hotel.

With nothing to do, I dropped off my purchases in my room and went back outside into the warm evening air for a long walk, giving both doormen generous tips on my way out. *Baba said not to give to beggars, but nothing about tipping,* I reminded myself.

Strolling down Marine Drive for a few blocks, I passed luxury apartment buildings, all of which were protected by stick-wielding security guards in ill-fitting uniforms. Some of them looked like they were on the verge of falling asleep and slipping from their chairs.

After wandering down random streets for a couple of miles, I came upon an area where dwellings were made of plywood, corrugated metal, and sheets of plastic. There I encountered more beggars, most of whom were children.

This must be a slum, I thought. I didn't know how to react to what I saw around me. Again, I was unable to feel anything. *This is their karma,* I told myself. *They deserve to live like this.*

Night fell, and as I made my way back to the hotel I was accosted by shifty-eyed men: "Yes, please, hello! Looking for smack?"

Smack? At the age of nineteen, I didn't even know what *smack* was. As they looked me up and down, trying to gauge how much money they could extract from me, I ignored them and avoided eye contact.

A few blocks from my hotel I heard what sounded like chanting. As I drew nearer, the singing got louder and I discovered its source: the music was coming from the open windows of a church. Curious about what an Indian church was like, I stopped and looked through the windows. The people inside were standing with their eyes screwed shut and their arms raised in the air, singing what sounded like a cross between a Hindu chant and gospel. To me, they were pathetic. Their hearts were full of devotion to God, yet they had chosen the wrong path. I was lifetimes ahead of them.

"Yes, sir—the post is the cheapest way to make a trunk call," said the earnest-looking clerk at the reception. "But it will be a very time-costing undertaking. The queue for an international line is too lengthy. Better to wait in the comfort of your suite. Kindly to be giving the number of the party you wish to ring in America. The hotel operator will revert to you when your line has been achieved."

I glanced at the clocks on the wall above the clerk—there was one each for Bombay, Hong Kong, London, and New York. It was eleven o'clock in New York. "Is it A.M. or P.M. in the States right now?"

"Most definitely A.M., sir."

I would only be able to call one sibling this time. I was about to write down Jeremy's number, but then I changed my mind and gave him Melanie's.

Up in my room, I was pleasantly surprised when the phone next to my bed rang within a few minutes. "Good evening, Mr. Greenbaum," came a woman's voice when I answered. "This is the hotel operator. I have your party in America on the line."

"Hello, Melanie?"

"Dougie, is that you?" My sister's voice was shrill. "Is everything alright?"

"Yes, yes—fine. I'm at a hotel in Bombay." There seemed to be a slight delay between the time I spoke and when she heard me.

"What happened? Did you leave the ashram? You sound so far away—like you're calling from the moon!"

"No, I didn't leave the ashram. I'm just doing some shopping. I'm going back to Ravipur tomorrow afternoon."

"When are you coming home?" I assured Melanie that I'd be returning to Birchwood Falls in the summer with Baba—unless he asked me to remain behind.

"What? You mean he might tell you to stay in India? They can't force you!" My sister was angry now and, as usual, jumping to conclusions. I'd forgotten how annoying she could be. "What about college? Are you going to apply to TC3 for the fall?"

"I'm thinking about it," I lied.

Mindful of the time, I asked about our other siblings and Grandma Millie. Lucy had started at Syracuse University and was dating a star player on the basketball team—a black guy named Henry. Aunt Gabby had moved down to Florida so that she and Grandma could have more time together to argue—a good distraction for both of them, we agreed. She had no news from our brother.

"Before you hang up, Doug, I think you should know that I've decided *not* to sell Mommy's house."

"What? Why?"

"I'm getting out of the nursery business—I'm going to teach horticulture at a correctional facility for girls in South Lansing. I'm putting the farm up for sale."

I wondered how teaching horticulture to juvenile delinquents could possibly benefit them, but didn't want to waste time and money talking about it.

"So, you and the girls are staying in the house? How exactly does that work? Are you going to be buying the rest of us out?"

"I'll write you a letter explaining everything," she answered. "You've got nothing to worry about."

I got off the phone with Melanie, and then stepped out onto the balcony for air. The cool sea breeze was a welcome change after the sweltering heat of the day. I looked over the harbor. The Gateway of India was all lit up for the night. I regretted I had no one to share the enchanting view with me. Again, I thought of Gopi and how romantic it would be to share my luxury suite with her. We would make love on the king-size bed, order room service, and dine together out here on the terrace. Then I reminded myself of Baba's recent talk, in which he said that we were not in the ashram to meet a husband or a wife or to make friends. I repeated the mantra silently to myself and tried to put the lustful fantasies out of my mind.

But it was impossible. I felt lonely and homesick. I missed my family and wished I were back in Ithaca.

AFTER A LATE BREAKFAST in the hotel restaurant, I took a walk across the street to the wide jetty that led out to the Gateway. There, men who barely spoke English solicited me relentlessly, offering their services as tour guides. Some of them were selling tickets for boat rides to and from Elephanta Island, where I could visit its famous caves and see the ancient Hindu and Buddhist sculptures cut from the rock. I would've liked to make the voyage. I wanted to learn more about India in general. But there was no time. I had come to Bombay on a mission for the guru: I had purchased the stylish clothes required to serve him more closely, but I still needed to find a pair of dressy loafers, like the ones Sergio wore. Then I had to get back to Ravipur as soon as possible. The chanting *saptah* was scheduled to begin that evening, and I'd be needed for extra *seva* in the week leading up to Brahmananda's *Punyatithi*.

At the suggestion of the concierge at the Taj, I looked for shoes in the hotel's shopping arcade. The stores in the arcade were fancy, but pricy. A gift shop offered a huge selection of decorative objects, bronze sculptures of Hindu gods and goddesses, shawls from Kashmir, and jewelry. Past the hotel swimming pool, I found a clothing store called Burlington's that sold traditional Indian men's and women's clothing.

This must be where the princesses do all their shopping, I mused. Then I couldn't believe it—I caught a glimpse of a familiar form in one of the stores. My pulse quickened. I turned my head and there, on the far side of the shop, was

Gopi. She was examining an elegant green and gold sari that another one of Baba's *darshan* girls was holding up for her. She didn't see me at first.

I continued to stare until, glancing in my direction, she noticed me and a bright smile of recognition dawned on her face. "Deependra! Hi!"

My breath caught in my chest.

As I approached, Gopi gave me the once over. "Hey, nice new threads!"

She noticed! My heart swelled. "Thanks!"

The other princess was a tall, curvaceous young woman with an olive complexion, long brown wavy hair, and an aquiline nose. I guessed she was Jewish or Italian. She was attractive, but nothing compared to the angel.

"This is Parvati," Gopi said, introducing her companion.

"I'm Deependra."

Parvati sneered. "I know who you are. I've seen you cleaning the courtyard. What's your *last* name?"

"Greenbaum."

Parvati laughed without smiling. "Of course it is."

"What's yours?" I asked, wondering what was so funny.

"Halabi," the girl said.

I turned to Gopi. "Yours?"

"Defournier. It's French."

Now all three of us were laughing, but I still wasn't sure why.

Gopi glanced at her watch. "Did you eat lunch yet?"

I shook my head.

"Parvati and I are going to get a quick bite. Then we're going to head back to Ravipur. Want to join us? The three of us can share a rickshaw from the railway station at Vasai Road to the ashram."

"Can three passengers really fit into one of those things?" I asked.

"It depends on how much stuff they're carrying!" Parvati chuckled, gesturing to the five or six fancy shopping bags at her feet.

Gopi smiled and blushed. "And we've got more in our room."

"So do I!" I said. Then we all laughed again.

Gopi and Parvati paid for their things, and then the three of us went to the hotel restaurant for lunch. The buffet was enormous and the food was fantastic. Nearly half of it was vegetarian.

To drink, Gopi and I ordered Indian colas. Parvati ordered a Kingfisher. She took a sip of her beer, and then offered me her glass. "Want to try it?"

"I don't drink," I said, wondering why she did.

Parvati jutted her chin out. "It's a lot better than the shit you're drinking."

"Deependra, how do you like living in Ravipur?" Gopi interrupted.

"It's a dream come true. I'm so grateful to the guru to be there."

Parvati smirked. "How do you like cleaning the courtyard? Weren't you working with Avadhoot and the video crew in Birchwood Falls?"

I explained that I'd been only filling in for a while for Kriyadevi Friedman after she broke her leg. "And I don't clean the courtyard anymore. I wash dishes at Prasad. I... also clean the public restrooms."

Both women leaned back and cringed. "Ewwwwwwww!"

Heat rushed to my face and I got a sharp pain at the back of my neck. *They are Baba's darshan girls because they are pure and innocent*, I thought, lowering my head in shame. *I am a worthless wretch.* I stared at the uneaten food on my plate.

A superior smile crept across Parvati's face. "I clean Baba's bathroom, sometimes."

I am out of my league with these girls!

"It's so full of *shakti*—" continued Parvati. "The second I go in there I slip into a state of meditation." For some reason I doubted Parvati's story. Not because I didn't believe Baba's bathroom wasn't a powerhouse of divine energy, but because I had the distinct impression that the girl never meditated.

I pushed the food around on my plate and sank lower in my chair. "You're really lucky to have that kind of *seva*."

Parvati took another swig of beer. "Of course, it's already perfectly clean before I even get started. The guru is completely pure in all respects."

When we were ready for dessert, Parvati left, saying that she'd meet up with us in the lobby. There was something else she still wanted to buy at Burlington's.

"Don't worry, *Greenbaum*," Parvati said, winking at me. "Gopi will pay my share."

For the next few minutes Gopi and I sat without saying a word to each other, eating sweet cheese dumplings smothered in rose syrup. Then I had a thought. Alone and away from the ashram, this was the perfect opportunity to get some answers. "Can I ask you something, Gopi?"

She straightened her back. Then she looked up at me and tilted her head to one side. "Um, sure. What is it?"

"Not long ago, I heard a chant coming from Baba's house. It was late—after midnight. Do you know anything about it?"

Gopi stared at me with her mismatched eyes. "What were you doing out of bed and wandering around the ashram at midnight?"

Remembering that lustful thoughts about her had driven me from my bed that night, my mind raced, searching for an excuse. "Sometimes I can't sleep because of the noise from the village. It seems like there's a wedding every night."

Her eyebrows drew together. "Weddings?" She carefully placed a tiny spoonful of *gulab jamun* in her mouth. "At this time of year?"

"Baba was leading," I said, pretending I hadn't heard her question. "But I'm pretty sure most of the others were women."

Gopi formed a steeple with her fingers and stared into her dessert for a long time before speaking. "Chants to Devi."

"What?"

"We recite mantras to worship the Goddess with Baba twice a week."

"Oh, so you were there?"

Gopi looked away, and then hesitated again before answering. "Yes."

"But why the secrecy? And why are they chanted in the middle of the night?"

Gopi turned her head back to look me in the eye. "Because they're not for everybody."

Neither of us said another word until the waiter brought the check. Then I asked him to charge it to my room.

"Room number, sir?"

I gave the waiter the name of my suite and signed the check. Gopi let out a short bark of laughter and stared at me in disbelief. "You're staying here? In a suite?"

"Yeah, aren't you?" I asked, trying to sound casual—as if I stayed in suites at fancy hotels all the time.

"Are you kidding? We're staying at the Apollo Guest House across from the police station. The Taj is way too expensive." Gopi reached into her purse and counted out some rupees, and then set them down on the table in front of me.

I shook my head and pushed the banknotes back in her direction. "Keep your money."

The angel looked nonplussed, but accepted my offer to treat. "Thanks, Deependra."

Gopi and Parvati accompanied me while I looked for shoes in the arcade, but I couldn't find anything that looked like Sergio's loafers.

"Forget it, Greenbaum," said Parvati. "If you want high quality shoes, you're better off waiting till you get back to the States." Gopi agreed and I gave up looking.

The girls waited in the lobby while I checked out of the hotel. When the clerk handed me my statement, I gasped. The five-minute "trunk call" to the States accounted for over twenty-five percent of the bill.

We stepped out of the climate-controlled hotel into the sweltering heat of the afternoon.

"Shall I call you a taxi, sir?" the Sikh doorman asked.

"Yes," said Parvati, before I had a chance to respond. "Make it fast, please."

By the time our train pulled into the Vasai Road station several hours later, it was dark. Parvati haggled with a few drivers in a combination of English and Marathi before finally settling on one. The girls climbed into the three-wheeler and I helped load their purchases onto their laps. I got in on the other side next to Gopi.

The ride across a seemingly endless series of dirt roads was bumpy, but I didn't mind because Gopi and I kept getting knocked into each other. Even better, whenever the rickshaw took a sharp turn, we were practically thrown into each other's laps. This was a thrill for me, and the physical contact made me long to take her in my arms and tell her how much I loved her.

The rickshaw hit a large pothole in the road and I awoke, disoriented. Someone's head was resting on my shoulder. Then I realized who it belonged to. Gopi had also fallen asleep. Meanwhile, Parvati was wide awake, watching the road like a bird of prey. *Where the hell am I?* It was dark, but by the buildings and shops along the side of the road, I could tell that we were on the outskirts of Ravipur. We would be arriving at the ashram in just a few minutes. Looking down at my feet, I was relieved to see that my shopping bags were still there and hadn't fallen out of the three-wheeler while I nodded off.

"Wake up Gopi, we're almost there," I said, gently shaking her.

Gopi opened her eyes, and then glanced up at me. She looked confused for a moment, but then a smile of recognition lit up her eyes. I wasn't one hundred percent sure, but at that moment I thought Gopi liked me.

For the rest of the ride, I reflected on my visit to the city. I'd miss the luxury and comfort of the Taj, but was glad to be returning home to the ashram and the safety of my familiar routine. I was also pleased with myself. Despite my anxiety and misgivings, I'd gone through with the trip.

Managing everything on my own made me feel grown-up. *There are probably a lot of other things I could do now that used to scare me,* I realized. *I have the guru to thank for that.*

By the time we pulled up in front of the ashram, it was late in the night. But over the ashram loudspeakers, we heard a rousing chant in progress. I listened closer—Baba was leading it!

"The *saptah*'s already begun!" Parvati said, scrambling out of the rickshaw with her belongings.

"You're going to love it," Gopi said, hopping out of the three-wheeler. "At the end of the *saptah* there'll be a huge feast and a celebration!"

Impatient to join the chant, we paid the driver without arguing about the price, and then rushed to the gate.

I tried to open it, but couldn't. "It's locked! How do we get in now?"

Gopi chuckled and playfully elbowed me in the side. She reached for a cord that rang a small bell hanging inside the gate. "Thought we had to stay out here all night, huh?"

A few seconds later, out of the darkness a groggy Indian guard emerged and let us in. I followed the girls into the courtyard, drawn by the hypnotic melody and rhythm of the chant. Then I caught sight of my guru: holding his tambourine high above his head and beating it in time to the music, Baba swayed from side to side on his throne. His eyes were rolled up into his head and his eyelids fluttered. I was enthralled.

The hall was packed with ashramites and devotees, overflowing into the courtyard. Not wasting any time, the girls raced off in the direction of their dorm, presumably to drop off their shopping bags. My room was much farther away, however, and I hesitated to leave the courtyard. I didn't want to miss anything.

Utterly transfixed by the chant, and oblivious to how much time was passing, I stood in the center aisle near the back of the hall, shopping bags and knapsack at my feet, gazing at my beloved guru and singing along: "*Om Namo Bhagavate Brahmanandaya! Om Namo Bhagavate Brahmanan-*

daya!" The same sacred mantra over and over. It meant: "I surrender to Lord Brahmananda."

At one point, Baba opened his eyes and seemed to be staring directly at me. Knowing he was watching, I threw myself even more deeply into the chant. I let the sound of Baba's voice and the sacred mantra purify my being and wash away the decadence of the past two days. I closed my eyes and allowed the chant to lift me away: "*Om Namo Bhagavate Brahmanandaya! Om Namo Bhagavate Brahmanandaya!*"

Baba's *shakti* coursed through my entire body.

Then someone grabbed me by the arm so forcefully I cried out in pain. Opening my eyes, I saw Sergio Casto standing two inches from my face, glaring at me. He smelled strongly of cologne, and his breath was minty fresh.

"Don't stand there like an idiot in front of the guru with all your shit on the floor!" he hollered, trying to make himself heard over the chant. "This is a place of worship, not an American shopping mall!"

Trembling all over, I shouted back an apology. "I'm so sorry, Sergio! I didn't mean to be disrespectful!"

"Let's go," he mouthed, gesturing for me to pick up my stuff. Grabbing my arm again, he led me into the courtyard. We drew stares from people on our way out of the hall. "You crazy or something?" he said, tapping the side of his head with his finger. "Have some respect! Bring these bags to your room, and then come back."

"Right away, Sergio!"

Looking me up and down, an amused smile spread across his face. "Hey, nice clothes."

"Thank you."

Sergio placed his hands on his hips and smiled again. "Arrow?"

I nodded.

"*Molto bello!* But next time you should shop at Maharaja's. You can tell 'em Sergio sent you."

"Thank you. I will!"

"Now go, Greenbaum. Take your things to your room and come back quick!"

Returning to my room, I found Claus snoring noisily in his bed. *Why would anyone rather be sleeping when they could be chanting with the guru?* I couldn't fathom it. As I put my things away I thought about my encounter with Sergio. His temper frightened me, but I understood that he could also be very nice.

Statutory rape is not really rape *rape*, I mused. I wondered what the age of consent was in Italy. Maybe Sergio was just ignorant of US law? I thought about it some more and decided that even if he thought it was legal, he was still too old to have sex with a sixteen-year-old. *Then again, everybody makes mistakes*, I told myself. *If Baba could forgive the Italian, why shouldn't I?*

Sniffing my arm where Sergio had grabbed me, I smelled traces of his cologne. I made a mental note to find out what it was called and where to buy it. I recalled how he had been impressed by my new clothes and felt elated. Then it hit me: Sergio had called me by my last name. And I thought he didn't even know I existed!

20.
SUPERMAN

AT FOUR THE NEXT morning, the chant was still going strong, even though there were only a handful of ashramites and musicians left in the hall. The door to the meditation cave was locked, and a handwritten sign was taped to the door:

CLOSED UNTIL AFTER THE SAPTAH.
BABA SAYS EVERYONE SHOULD GO TO THE CHANT.

Obeying the guru's command, I went directly to the hall and chanted with those already there. Within a few minutes, many others joined us. At five-thirty there was no break for the *Guru Gita*.

Later at *seva*, Rohini confirmed what I had suspected: "All the regular practices are suspended during the *saptah*. Everything will be back to normal next week."

During the *saptah*, when we weren't at the chant, we were expected to ready the ashram for the thousands of visitors who would come from all over the region for the celebrations. This meant that in addition to my regular duties in Housekeeping and the dish room, I also helped out by giving the ashram buildings a fresh coat of paint, weeding the gardens, and decorating the *mandap* pavilion with thousands of flower garlands. Sleep was frowned upon during the *saptah*. Day or night, if we weren't doing *seva* we were expected to be at the chant.

That afternoon at the *saptah*, the guru's mood was dark and his behavior was starkly different from anything I had seen before. I was finally seeing what Gopi had referred to as Baba's "fiery side." He kept complaining. First the overhead lights were too bright. Then they were too dim. Next the men were singing too fast, and the women too slow. At one moment, for reasons that were unclear to me, Baba became enraged. He shouted at one of the younger princesses, causing her to burst into tears. Nothing anyone did was right, and thanks to Baba's microphone and the ashram loudspeaker system, his harsh reprimands could be heard as far away as the village.

That evening the hall was packed, like every other night Baba had come to the chant. But because I had arrived before the guru, I managed to find a place up front, right behind the area reserved for the swamis.

I was dead tired, but wide awake. I was going on my third night in a row of less than three hours of sleep. But as they said in the ashram, during the *saptah* you didn't need any sleep. You could get by on the guru's *shakti* alone.

Gopi and Parvati were there, decked out in the high-priced saris they had purchased just a day earlier in the shopping arcade at the Taj. Swaying from side to side, striking their cymbals in time to the melody, they and the other princesses chanted with abandon. They seemed oblivious to Baba's bad mood. As they gazed up at him, tears of devotion streamed down their faces.

Seated up front next to Sergio, Avadhoot was by far the loudest chanter. Unfortunately, he was incapable of carrying a tune. Singing off key at the top of his lungs, his body convulsing, his hands twisted and turned endlessly, clumsily forming the gestures of an Indian classical dancer. I would've thought it was an affectation on his part, if I hadn't already seen and heard the often bizarre movements and sounds caused by Baba's *shakti* and *kundalini* awakening.

Sergio, by contrast, was in a state of agitation. While everyone else sat still, backs erect, attention fixed on the guru, Sergio glanced around the room and fidgeted constantly, scowling whenever he saw anything that displeased him. Suresh, who normally sat opposite Anjali, was on drums that night. It was always a treat to hear him play—through his music, I felt as though I were being transported to a higher realm.

While Baba led the chant from his throne, Suresh controlled the rhythm and tempo. Normally, master and disciple were in perfect sync, but tonight Suresh was having difficulty following the guru's lead. A few times I saw what looked like pure hatred flash across Baba's face, when Suresh, serene and poised as ever, and seemingly unaware of the problem, played slightly faster than the guru was chanting.

Just as Suresh was bringing the chant to a crescendo, Baba turned bright red and shouted at him in Hindi. A pained expression came over the young Indian man's cherub-like face, and he shifted to a slower tempo. But this only seemed to make the guru angrier. Beating his tambourine at the speed he wanted Suresh to play, Baba shouted insults at him until he adjusted the tempo again. Unfortunately, not everyone in the hall caught on at the same time—the people seated all the way in the back and in the courtyard were still singing, clapping, and playing their cymbals too fast, and the chant degenerated into a discordant free-for-all.

I thought the people in the back were idiots for failing to notice what Baba was trying to do, and, from the way Sergio was glowering at them, I could tell he thought so too. But the guru's rage was reserved solely for Suresh. Just as the chant was finally getting back under control, the guru drew his arm back, and then hurled his tambourine at his disciple's head.

The instrument struck Suresh with a cheerful jingle. He grimaced in pain, but didn't miss a beat.

A feeling of dread washed over me. I looked around. Mouths hung open in disbelief, and many people had stopped chanting and clapping. Gopi's eyes were squeezed shut. Baba again shouted at Suresh in Hindi, and then yanked the microphone off its stand and thrust it into Anjali's hands.

"Where's Poonish?" Anjali's voice reverberated loudly in the hall over the now almost inaudible chant. A few seconds later, Poonish Davidson appeared beside the guru with his own set of tablas, as if he'd been waiting in the wings.

"*Nikal jaao yahaan!*" Baba hollered, pointing at Suresh.

"Suresh, get out," Anjali translated for the rest of us. Her face was a mask of dispassion. "Poonish will take over on the tablas."

Without hesitation, Suresh ceded the drumming to the American. Lowering his head, he calmly rose to his feet, bent over to retrieve the tambourine from where it had landed next to the harmonium, and brought it back to the guru.

Curling his lip and shaking his head, Baba snatched the instrument out of his disciple's hands and shooed him away. Unperturbed, Suresh bowed down before him, collected his drums, and then nonchalantly sauntered out of the hall. Once he was out of sight, Baba leaned over to speak to Anjali, who immediately shot up, taking Baba's microphone in hand.

"Baba says everyone should be chanting." Her voiced boomed over the sound system. "Go on, chant—chant!"

Within seconds everyone was chanting again, and Baba smiled with approval at Poonish's drumming. "Acha, acha! Good drummer! Very good drummer!"

I prayed that I'd never cause the guru to become so angry.

On the last night of the *saptah*, I was working with a group of Indians and Westerners to string the dozens of flower garlands needed to decorate the *mandap*. After a couple of hours, Stephen Ames pulled me aside. "You'll be working with Govinda now," he told me.

Govinda Brown was a thin, spry Australian man with tattoos all over his body. He lived in the ashram with his wife and young daughter. Apparently, the Indian devotee who had been helping him to hang garlands had requested another *seva*. I soon understood why: his job required repeatedly scaling a rickety twenty-foot bamboo scaffolding with one hand, while carrying as many finished garlands as possible in the other. The work would have been scary enough, but the Australian's devil-may-care attitude made it terrifying.

"Ow!" I cried out, as my shoulder hit the marble floor of the *mandap*. For the first time in my life, I had fallen asleep standing up.

"You alright, mate?" Govinda called from the top of the scaffolding. Fortunately, I hadn't been up there with him when I collapsed.

"I think so," I said, rubbing my arm and willing myself back on my feet. "I fell asleep."

Govinda laughed hysterically, jumping up and down on the wooden platform as though it were a trampoline. Fearing the makeshift rig might come crashing down, I scrambled to get clear of it. This also struck Govinda as funny. He again laughed wildly, and then bounded down the side of the scaffolding, shaking it violently.

"Crikey! I'm knackered too," he said, jumping to the floor. He didn't look tired to me. Looking up at the high ceiling of the pavilion, he surveyed our work. "This section is done. Let's take a chai break after we move the rig."

The last thing Govinda needed was another cup of chai, but I wasn't in a position to stop him. He was a nice enough guy, but his manic energy was beginning to wear me out. Tomorrow was the last day of the *saptah* and I was desperately looking forward to a full night of sleep.

"Come on, mate!" said the Australian, gulping down his seventh cup of chai. "The sooner we finish, the sooner we can go back to the chant!"

As I climbed, the bamboo frame yielded under my weight and wobbled. I was sure one of the bamboo rungs would snap, or that the rig—held together with only a few strands of worn-out rope—would give at any moment and come crashing down.

"She'll be right, mate! That's it, bring 'em up to Govinda. I ain't got all night!"

I'd never worked with Govinda before, so I couldn't tell whether he was always like this, or if his reckless behavior was the result of an adrenaline rush and too much chai. The Australian's constant jabbering and sudden movements on the scaffolding were endangering both of us. I was afraid that if he didn't calm down he'd cause an accident. And that's exactly what happened.

Around two in the morning, Govinda accidentally dropped his hammer over the side of the platform. Reaching down after it, he lost his balance and slipped. He screamed as he fell, and his bones made an audible cracking sound when he struck the marble.

I ran over to him. He was unconscious. I thought he was dead.

Sergio, who had arrived just in time to witness the mishap, sprang into action. He immediately sent for Nirmalananda, the swami doctor, and cleared the *mandap*.

"Everybody get out!" he shouted, pointing to the exit.

"Can we go to bed now?" a woman asked, tearing up. Her face was drawn and her eyes were bloodshot.

"No! Everybody should go back to the chant!"

I followed the others down a dimly-lit garden path, until we arrived at a fork. I was shocked when almost everybody headed in the direction of the dorms, instead of the hall for the chant. I was tired too, but I would do as I was told. After all, an order from Sergio was as good as a command from the guru himself. The quitters had *wrong understanding*.

An older woman who had come to the chant with me from the *mandap* was crying over the accident. When she wouldn't stop, an usher finally had to ask her to leave. I felt bad about the accident too, but not *that* bad. I tried to see it in a positive light: the guru's *shakti* was purging Govinda of his evil karma.

Then I had a thought: *Isn't feeling sad when someone gets hurt a normal emotional reaction? Why don't I feel anything?* I remembered Baba teaching that the world and all phenomena within it were an illusion. I chose to believe the reason I didn't care was because I had already attained a higher state of consciousness. The universe I lived in was as unreal as a film projected on a screen. Why worry about "others" when I was merely asleep and dreaming?

An hour later, Sergio came to the hall looking for people to help finish decorating the *mandap*. I immediately volunteered. When I returned to the scene of the accident, I was surprised to find everything back to normal. There was no sign that anything bad had happened.

Avadhoot was there now, taking pictures of the flowers. His camera was mounted on a tripod and his eye was glued to the viewfinder. I approached him and asked about the Australian. "Is Govinda going to be alright?"

"He'll live," he muttered, changing lenses. "They took him to Breach Candy Hospital in Bombay. His wife's there with him. Now hold this." Avadhoot handed me a reflector, and then inched the tripod closer to his subject.

"Does Baba know about what happened?"

"Sure, sure, kid. Baba knows everything. Now shut up and let me work."

The *Punyatithi* celebrations were only a few short hours away and there were still many garlands to be hung. But after what happened to Govinda, nobody wanted to go anywhere near the scaffolding. I couldn't blame them. I was scared too, and was glad to be assisting Avadhoot on the floor instead. This didn't last, however. Before long, Sergio needed a volunteer to finish what Govinda had started. I hesitated at first, and then changed my mind. "I'll do it!" *This is how I will prove myself.*

"Grande, Greenbaum!" the Italian said, handing me a hammer and giving me a big pat on the back. "Indira will help you."

I was now starting to look up to Sergio as a leader. He was good at telling other people what to do, but what I liked most about him was that he valued me as a member of his team.

As the hours passed, and the sky began to lighten, my fatigue was replaced by a rush of blissful energy. Baba's *shakti* had turned me into a superman. By comparison, Indira St. John looked like a wilted flower. She could barely make it to the top of the platform. Toward the end, I was climbing down the scaffolding myself to get the garlands.

With the help of those I considered to be the guru's "hardcore" devotees, we were able to finish decorating the *mandap* and setting up Baba's throne before dawn. By the time I hung my last garland, I was no longer desperate for sleep. I was ready to do more *seva* or go to the chant.

In addition to the euphoria I experienced something else, and there was no denying it: overwhelming sexual desire. I wanted to have sex with every woman who came into view, even some of the older female swamis. If Indira were game, I would've fucked her right then and there on the hard marble floor of the *mandap*, in front of everyone. I knew these thoughts were impure and sinful, but I reached the point of no return. Desire had overtaken any sense of control I usually possessed. I was incapable of stopping myself from fantasizing.

"Looking good, Greenbaum!" Sergio called, from below. "*Finito?*"

"*Sì!*" I answered, speaking the only word of Italian I knew.

"*Benissimo!* Very good!" he said, beaming an enormous smile up at me.

Bounding down the scaffolding, I jumped to the floor right in front of him.

Gazing at the Italian's noble face, I had a realization: *Sergio is more than a man. He's a god.* I would do anything he asked of me. "What's next?"

"Now you take a rest, Greenbaum."

"Rest? I'm not tired!" I was pumped up and eager to serve. There was no way I'd be able to fall asleep at this point.

"*Sì, sì.* I have an important *seva* for you in a few hours. You need to be in good shape. You make a nap now and report to me in front of Baba's house at nine o'clock. *D'accordo?*"

"What about my regular *seva?*"

Sergio frowned. "You work for Baba now. Understand?"

"Got it!"

I turned to leave, but Sergio called out to me before I reached the exit. "Hey, Greenbaum!"

I turned around. He was smiling again.

"You did good. You make me very happy. When I'm happy, Baba is happy. Understand?"

"Totally!"

When I got back to my dorm, I took a bucket bath with ice-cold water, washing off the grime and dirt from the past week of nonstop *seva* and chanting. As I toweled off, I caught a glimpse of my reflection. I was glowing. I was not as good-looking as Sergio, of course, but for the first time in my life, I liked what I saw.

21.
BY ANY MEANS NECESSARY

"TURN IT OFF! TURN it off!" In the black depths of sleep, the angry voice of my roommate and the persistent whine of my alarm reached me. I forced my eyes open and slapped the off button, knocking the clock to the floor.

"Sorry, Claus," I said, rolling over to face his side of the room. But there was no answer. He was already asleep.

Dragging myself out of bed, I threw on one of my new Fred Perry polo shirts and a pair of khaki slacks. I skipped breakfast in the dining hall and hurried to the entrance of Baba's house off the courtyard. I didn't want to be late.

As I waited for Sergio, I admired the festive decorations in the courtyard, and inhaled the heady fragrance of the countless garlands of jasmine flowers that hung everywhere. In the hall opposite the guru's house, a few hardcore devotees were keeping the chant alive. Anyone not doing *seva* was still in bed, and the hordes of visitors expected for the celebrations were yet to arrive.

I glanced at my watch. It was nine-o-five, but there was no sign of Sergio. Nine-o-seven, still no sign of him. Then, after what seemed like ages, a rugged, powerfully built man in his mid-twenties rode into the courtyard on a bicycle, dismounting in front of Baba's house. I recognized him immediately. His name was Brian Pettigrew and he was from New Zealand. He often worked as an usher during *darshan*.

"Who are you?" he asked, furrowing his brow.

"I'm Deependra." *Where's Sergio?* I wondered.

Brian pulled out a small notepad from his pocket and studied it. "Greenbaum?"

I nodded.

Just then, two more men wandered into the courtyard and joined us. One was tall and balding. I didn't know him. The other was Namdev's friend from Down Under.

Brian glanced at his list again. "Names?"

"Andy Martin," said the Australian.

Brian nodded. "Right."

"Seth Gold."

Brian glanced at his watch. "Brilliant! Now that you're all *finally* here, we can get started." The New Zealander spoke with a lisp and, looking more closely at his face, I noticed the vestiges of a cleft lip.

"I love your accent," Seth said with a smirk. "Where do you hail from?"

Brian put his hands on his hips and puffed out his chest. "Christchurch, and you?"

Seth pursed his lips. "New York."

"I'm from New York, too!" I said. "Well, Upstate really."

Brian snorted. "Good on ya, mate." Pulling a set of keys out of his pocket, he unlocked the entrance to Baba's house. Then he disappeared within, shutting the door behind him. A minute later, he came back out with laminated badges that said "Shree Brahmananda Ashram Security" and a bundle of bamboo sticks, which he distributed among us.

Brian stiffened up. "Right. In another hour, there'll be a thousand people lined up outside. Every bloody Adivasi and his mother within a twenty-kilometer radius will be cued-up for a free lunch and a handout. The three of you will be stationed at the gates, helping the ashram guards keep order."

Seth studied his stick with the curiosity of an anthropologist examining an artifact from a primitive culture.

"Think you can handle it, ladies?"

Andy and I nodded. Seth was lost in thought.

"Seth?" Brian lisped. "Doctor Gold?"

Seth looked up at Brian. "Yes?"

"You reckon you're man enough for the job?"

A squiggly vein on Seth's temple began to quiver. "I'm here to serve the guru."

Brian grinned contemptuously. "That's the spirit!"

Suddenly, I got a strong whiff of cologne. A moment later, the door to Baba's house swung open and Sergio stepped out. Behind him was a young girl in pink pajamas. She must've been about twelve or thirteen. Her eyes were red and swollen, as if she had been crying. It took me a moment before I realized that she was Prema, Govinda Brown's daughter. It touched me knowing that Baba was taking such good care of the injured man's child.

"Go on, sweetheart," Sergio said, gently pushing the girl in the direction of the dining hall. "Come back later. Baba will have ice cream!"

Prema nodded blankly, and then took off. Sergio turned his attention to our group. "Okay, listen, after the *festa*, Baba's going to pay his respects at Gurudev's *samadhi* shrine in the village. It will be your job to protect the motorcade."

"How do we do that?" Andy asked, rubbing the back of his neck.

Sergio's lower lip curled down into a sneer. "You beat the shit out of anybody who gets too close to the car. Understand?"

I held up my stick. "You expect us to hit people with this?" I asked, my voice cracking.

"Don't worry, Greenbaum, we're not in America. Nobody's going to arrest you!" Sergio winked at Brian and they both burst out laughing.

What have I signed up for? The last time I had ever hit anyone was in third grade. *What does beating people up have to do with meditation and spirituality?* I was about to tell Sergio and Brian I wouldn't be able to be a guard, when a loud voice rose up inside of me: *This is another test from the guru. Another opportunity to prove myself.*

Before taking up our posts, we helped bring boxes from a storage room off the courtyard to the *mandap*. When everything was moved, Sergio opened a few of them. Some were full of American-style blue jeans, others contained t-shirts bearing Baba's picture and the ashram logo. Sergio took a pair of jeans out of a box and held it up for everyone to see. "Anyone want a pair?"

The jeans were ridiculously out of fashion: tight in the thighs and flared. I hadn't seen a pair of bell-bottomed jeans like that since the early seventies.

"Hey, Gold, Greenbaum—you like? They're free!" Sergio winked at Brian again. Everybody laughed except Seth and me.

"Who are they for?" I asked

"They're Baba's gift to the Adivasis," said Brian. "The feast they're preparing in the dining hall—it's all for them. He's also giving every family a new pot and blanket."

I was moved by the guru's profound generosity, but couldn't help wondering how the Adivasis would feel about the out-of-date jeans.

"They're going to love them, believe me," Sergio growled, reading my face. "The fashion here is ten years behind Europe and America."

On the way back to the courtyard, I asked Andy what he knew about the Adivasis. He explained that they were a tribal people like the aboriginals of Australia, and were considered to be the indigenous people of India.

"They're mostly hated by the general population. Brahmananda was like a father to them. He provided food and clothing, and even founded a school for them. Baba's been following in Gurudev's footsteps by employing them for construction work and gardening."

I scratched my head. "If the Adivasis are indigenous, where do all the other Indians come from?"

"Good question, mate," Andy laughed. "Beats the hell out of me!"

Seth, Andy and I followed Brian out of the ashram into the street, and took up our position in front of the main gate, where two armed Indian guards were already stationed.

"If you've already got them," Andy said, gesturing to the security men, "what do you need us for?"

Brian shot a cold glance toward the guards. "Sergio doesn't trust 'em."

As I stood guard in front of the ashram, the heat and the endless drone of the chant from the loudspeakers made me sleepy. Dark thoughts clouded my mind. I replayed the scenes of Baba throwing his tambourine at Suresh's head, and of Govinda falling off the scaffolding. I got a sinking feeling. I also had doubts about my latest *seva* assignment. *Would I really be able to hit someone with a stick?* To combat my negative feelings, I reminded myself that whatever happened in his ashram carried the guru's blessing.

Arriving on foot, the Adivasis began to form a line in front of the gate. With their happy faces and friendly demeanors, they were a beautiful people, much darker and smaller than the average Indian. The older men wore traditional garb, but some of the younger ones favored Western-style camp shirts and slacks. The women, young and old, dressed alike in colorful cotton saris. Many of them held the hands of small children or balanced babies on their hips.

Not long after the locals arrived, auto rickshaws began dropping off devotees from Bombay and beyond. In practically no time, the line was over two blocks long.

I couldn't stop yawning. Seth crossed over to my side of the gate, using his stick as a staff. "Tired?" he asked, with a smug grin on his face.

"A bit."

Seth sniggered. "Well, if you've been working as many hours as the rest of us, you should be."

I shrugged. "Brian called you 'doctor' earlier. Are you a physician?"

Seth shook his head and laughed again. "I'm a clinical psychologist."

"I see." I was unimpressed. Seth reminded me of Melanie's boyfriend, Herb, and he was beginning to get on my nerves.

Just then Brian rode through the gate on his bicycle. "Right, they've relocated the chant to the *mandap* now. We're going to start letting these drongos in. If anyone starts pushing or shoving, get rid of 'em."

Over the loudspeakers I heard Baba join the *saptah*, and soon the number of voices with him increased exponentially. An hour later, the chant reached a crescendo, and then came to an end.

"Jai Gurudev!" Baba called.

"Jai Gurudev! Jai Gurudev! Jai Gurudev!" the public roared.

"Today we mark the twenty-second anniversary of our beloved Gurudev's *mahasamadhi*—the day when he left his physical body to merge with the Absolute." Baba's and Anjali's voices sounded tinny over the ancient sound system.

"Those of you who knew Brahmanandaji will recall that he lived his life absorbed in the divine, and the legends of his miraculous powers are many. Hindu, Muslim, Christian, Buddhist, and Jew were equal in his eyes—all pilgrims on different paths to the same destination. In his company, ordinary beings were transformed into accomplished yogis, and seekers into enlightened sages. Through his teachings, misguided ascetics were able to see their own True Self reflected in the world.

"He was a master of all branches of yoga. Though he was a great being, he lived an ordinary life. Although he was all-knowing, his manner was unassuming. Many witnessed his awesome power: he had the ability to transmit his own spiritual energy to others with a mere touch, awakening them to their own sublime nature. He was kind and loving, but he could also be ferocious.

"The behavior of such perfected masters may seem strange and difficult to understand at times. Ordinary beings are bound by countless lifetimes of mental conditioning, but the actions of such liberated souls are the spontaneous expressions of the divine goddess herself! Therefore, if you live in the company of such a master, you must never criticize him."

After Baba's talk, the line outside the gate surged forward. Over the loudspeakers, one of the Indian swamis announced in Marathi and English that *darshan* would begin after the feast, and that everybody should take their turn eating in the dining hall.

I had been keeping an eye out for any disorderly conduct, but so far everything was going smoothly. Just when I thought I could start to relax, however, there was a commotion on the other side of the gate. Psyching myself up to do whatever was necessary to preserve order, I had to laugh when I discovered that the source of the disturbance was Namdev Loman. Moving against the flow of the line, he was trying to exit the ashram. "Let me pass! Get out of my way!"

The Indian guards were doing nothing to prevent Namdev from leaving the ashram, but they weren't doing anything to help him either.

"Stand aside!" I demanded, brandishing my stick, but nobody listened to me. "I said move! Make way for this man!"

I felt like an actor playing a part in a movie. While most of the visitors remained oblivious, at least a couple of them got the message—there was just enough movement for Namdev to slip out.

"Fucking cretins!" Namdev cursed, pushing his way through the crowd.

"Hey, watch your language," I said, tapping the stick against the palm of my hand.

Namdev lowered his eyes to read my badge. "What the fuck? Is this your new *seva?*"

"It's just for today, I think."

Namdev chuckled. "Beats the hell out of cleaning Indian toilets, I guess."

I bristled. I hoped now that I "worked for Baba," I'd never have to clean up shit again. "Why aren't you in the *mandap*?"

"I had to get out of there for a minute. Too many people." Something over my shoulder caught Namdev's eye and he licked his lips. "I'll be right back," he said, and then sprinted across the street and disappeared into the chai shop.

A minute later he returned with a bottle of Indian cola. It looked cool and refreshing, and I wished I'd asked him to get me one, too. I was getting hungry.

Namdev twisted off the top and drank it down in one gulp. He tossed the empty bottle onto a pile of garbage on the side of the road.

"Hey, Deependra," he said, wiping his mouth with the back of his hand. "Did you hear about Govinda Brown?"

"Yeah, I saw it happen," I said. Then I added, "He'll live."

"Yeah, but he may never walk again. It's not right—making people work for days on end without any sleep. An accident like that was just waiting to happen."

I shook my head. "You weren't there. It was his own fault. He was careless—acting like a clown."

"Sure, whatever you say," Namdev said, looking away. He didn't believe me. I didn't believe myself.

"Isn't it wonderful what Baba's doing for the Adivasis?"

"Give me a break, man—the whole thing's a publicity stunt. Did you know the ashram only pays them the equivalent of one dollar a day?"

"That can't be true," I said without conviction. I got an uneasy feeling in my gut.

"The ashram's excuse is that they don't want to distort the local economy, but that's a load of crap, if you ask me."

Righteous anger rose up inside of me. He was insulting the guru now, and if he kept at it I was ready to bring my stick down on his head.

"Let me tell you," Namdev continued, "these skinny little Indians are tough, and their working conditions are horrible. Once, when I was supervising some Adivasi laborers loading a truck, I cut my arm on a rusty old pipe—I was squirting blood all over the place. None of my fellow Raja Yogis gave a shit, but the Adivasis all came running to help me. Do you think anybody in the ashram cares about them?"

I swallowed my anger. "Are you still working at the generator plant?"

"As a matter of fact, I am. And it was supposed to be a 'temporary' position. The other day it got up to a hundred and fifty degrees in there!" I believed him—in India it could get up to a hundred and ten degrees in the shade. "I'm on call twenty-four seven. The generator automatically starts whenever the main power fails, and I have to be at the plant whenever it's running. Sometimes the power doesn't come back on for over a day. The hours I put in are insane. My record is a hundred and fifty-two hours of *seva* in one week!"

"Think of all the good karma you're accumulating."

"Yeah, sure," Namdev scoffed. "I complained to Sergio about it, and he said I should be grateful to live in the ashram for free. Then he told me some story about how his uncle Giovanni was taken prisoner by the Red Army in Poland and had to walk all the way back to Sicily after the war."

"World War Two?" I asked, remembering that Sicily was an island.

"I guess so. Anyhow, it's not fair—I can't even go to any of the programs or big events whenever the video crew is shooting, because the generators have to be running in case the power fails."

"Well, you can go today, right? There's no video crew in India right now."

"Wrong! Arjuna arrived yesterday. He's setting up in the *mandap* right now. The only reason I'm standing here talking to you is because Baba went back to his house for lunch."

If he's so down on the ashram, why does he stay? I wondered. Just then, there was a squeal of feedback over the loudspeakers and someone made an announcement in what sounded like Marathi. A look of mild panic came over Namdev's face.

"What are they saying?" I asked.

Namdev started to push his way back in through the gate. "I don't know, but if they're saying anything, it probably means Baba's on his way back to the *mandap*. I gotta go!"

The announcement was followed by a live performance of Hindu devotional songs. Moments later there was another surge and the line began to move more quickly.

Two more hours passed and my empty stomach was gnawing at me. I was afraid there'd be nothing left to eat by the time I was allowed to go to the dining hall.

Another group of musicians began to play Sufi devotional songs called *qawwalis*. Their music was hauntingly beautiful. I wished I could be in the *mandap* with everybody else. I wanted to complain to Seth, but held my tongue.

I must get a hold of my mind and remember that my purpose in life is to serve the guru, I told myself. *The hardships I go through now will only help to purify my soul and help make me strong enough to hold Baba's grace.*

Seth sauntered over to my side of the gate smirking. "You think they forgot about us?"

"Maybe Brian and Sergio did," I quipped. "But not Baba!"

He shrugged, and I noticed the squiggly vein in his temple was pulsating again.

"When Brian gave me this stick this morning I was afraid I might have to use it on somebody," I said. "But they seem pretty docile, don't they?"

Seth smiled philosophically. "The day isn't over yet."

As he strolled back to his post, I wondered why Sergio had assigned him to Security. I assumed he had chosen Andy for his muscles, and me for my loyalty. But Seth didn't strike me as either particularly strong or committed to the path. He was tall and towered over most Indians, which could be intimidating, I guessed, but I couldn't imagine him protecting his guru by *any means necessary*.

Down the street, well-fed Adivasis bearing gifts from Baba were exiting through the south gate. My stomach growled and I felt faint. It was nearly three-thirty, but the line of people waiting to get in still looked endless.

"Stand aside! Move it mister!" came a voice from the other side of the gate. I turned around to see Brian pushing his way out. This time he was on foot. "Right. Seth, Greenbaum, which one of you wants to eat first?"

Seth turned to me, and smiled insincerely. "You go, Deependra. You're a growing boy."

I didn't argue with him. I hadn't eaten anything since dinner the night before, and was beginning to feel lightheaded. Pushing my way through the masses of visitors crowding in the courtyard, I bumped smack into Gopi, causing her to drop the clipboard she was carrying. She burst out laughing.

"Whoa, Deependra!" Gopi's eyes and mouth were wide open in mock surprise. "Where you goin' with that big stick!" She was wrapped in a turquoise silk sari, which picked up the blue and green of her mismatched eyes perfectly. The outfit left her midriff and navel exposed and I couldn't stop staring. "Did you eat yet?" she asked.

"No. Do you know if there's any food left?"

"Tons. I just ate myself."

I wanted to keep talking with her, but she continued on her way to wherever she was hurrying.

When I got to the dining hall it was still crowded and I had to wait in line. Fifteen minutes later I was still nowhere near the front. I reflected on my encounter with the angel: *I think she might have been flirting with me! What I would give to hold her in my arms...* Someone grabbed me by the shoulder, interrupting my reverie. "What the fuck are you still doing in line, dipstick?" I turned around and was confronted with Brian's angry face. His eyes were wide and his nostrils flaring. "Go eat with the bloody VIPs!"

A small area of the dining hall had been reserved for members of Baba's personal staff, ashram trustees, and public figures, but by the time I was seated it was empty. The food was amazing and unlike anything I had ever eaten at the ashram. Prakashananda—the shirtless Indian swami—

served me himself: gourmet vegetable curries, basmati rice, pickled mango, puris, and a tangy taro leaf roll called elephant's ear. For dessert I received a sweet, milky banana dish with chopped almonds and cardamom. Everything was delicious. I ate greedily and as quickly as possible—I had kept Brian waiting long enough.

When I returned to the main gate, there were fewer people waiting to get in, and I didn't have to push my way to get out into the street. By the time I got to the other side, however, I was shocked at what I saw: all hell had broken loose. A band of angry Adivasi men were in a shouting match with some of the people in line, and the ashram guards were caught in the middle. Seth and Andy were frozen on the sidelines. Running over to where they were huddled together, I had to shout to be heard.

"What's going on?"

"Don't know, mate!" Andy said, his lower lip quivering. "The car across the street pulled up, and these hooligans jumped out and starting giving everyone bloody hell."

I glanced at Seth. He seemed calm, but the vein in his head looked like it was going to explode.

The argument escalated into violence. A couple of the troublemakers ran back to their vehicle and returned with wooden clubs. As women and children fled, Seth began to back away toward the gate. Before he was able to go back inside the ashram, however, he was knocked to the ground when another man was pushed into him. Leaping to his feet, he ran in the opposite direction and disappeared into the chai shop.

Andy was trembling. "What do we do?"

I pushed my fear aside and raised my stick in the air. "Let's get 'em!"

Just as we were about to charge the agitators, we heard shouting from inside the ashram. The next thing I knew, Sergio, Brian, and Vinod Desai stormed out through the gate. The Italian's eyes were wild.

Brian beat his stick into the palm of his hand, every fighting muscle in his body straining against his skin. "What the fuck is going on?"

"Union men, sir! Very bad!" Vinod said, shaking his head. The Indian's eyes were bulging so far out of his skull I thought they might pop.

I was shocked by what Sergio did next. Reaching under his jacket and behind his back, he pulled out a snub-nosed revolver and fired a shot into the air.

Stunned also, the union men dropped their weapons, and then made a run for their car. As they sped away, Sergio ran after them firing several more rounds at the back of their vehicle. "*Vaffanculo!*"

We all breathed a collective sigh of relief, and joined Andy and Brian at Sergio's side. Re-holstering his gun, the Italian spat on the ground. "Okay, the ashram is closed now. *Basta!* Vinod, tell all of these *contadini* to go home!"

Vinod translated Sergio's words for the guards, and then made a general announcement in Marathi to everybody who was still in line. Without protest, the Adivasis turned around and headed back in the direction of the village.

Brian gritted his teeth. "Where's Seth?"

Andy shook his head. "Don't know, mate."

"Me neither," I lied.

Sergio glanced at his watch. "Brian, Andy, go to *darshan* now." They nodded and started to leave. "And come back quick! Baba's motorcade leaves for the village in an hour. Greenbaum, stay here, I want to talk to you."

Is Sergio angry with me for happened? I braced myself for the worst.

"Listen, Greenbaum," Sergio said, lowering his voice. "After tomorrow, Baba makes a pilgrimage with a small group to Haridwar in the north—he wants you to come to help the video crew."

I suddenly felt lighter. This was good news—no, amazing news! I remembered that Haridwar was the holy city where Baba had spent three years in silent retreat and took the vows of a swami. I got even more excited.

"A pilgrimage with Baba? I would love to!"

The Italian lifted a finger to his lips. "Shhhhhh. It's a secret. You say nothing to nobody. You know how to keep a secret, don't you?"

"Of course I do. You can count on me!"

Sergio smiled broadly and gave me an affectionate pat on the cheek. "You know something, Greenbaum? I like you. You're okay!"

I went to the *mandap*, where the Sufi *qawwali* singers were still performing. They clapped and sang with an all-consuming yearning to know God that moved me beyond measure. I took a seat at the back of the pavilion and watched my beloved guru bestow gifts and blessings on the last of the visitors. Tears of gratitude gushed from my eyes. I couldn't believe my good fortune. I was going on a pilgrimage with Baba. I was one step closer to joining the guru's inner circle.

The procession to Gurudev's *samadhi* shrine in the village was slow, and I was grateful that it had been scheduled at the end of the afternoon, when the sun was lower in the sky.

The swamis and the members of Baba's personal staff led the procession, followed by the rest of the ashramites and dozens of Indian devotees. They sang, clapped, and danced to a recording of "*Om Namo Bhagavate Brahmanandaya*," which blared from the loudspeakers of an ashram van. Behind them, at safe distance, Baba rode in an air-conditioned sedan with Anjali, Suresh, and his valet. Brian and Andy guarded the front of the motorcade, while Seth and I took up the rear.

I had to hand it to Brian: he was good at keeping the public at bay. All he had to do was to lean his large muscular body into anyone who got too close, and they immediately backed off. Seth, who seemed to have recovered from the incident with the union men earlier, also proved effective. He kept people away by glaring at them with a crazed look in his eye. I was impressed. The shrink could be pretty scary when he wanted to be.

Arjuna Weinberg shot video from the sidelines. He was aided by an Indian man who looked clueless. Whenever Arjuna checked on the man's performance, he got a pained look on his face, and was clearly frustrated by the Indian's inability to follow his instructions or anticipate his movements. More than a few times I saw Arjuna yank the headphones off the Indian's head and readjust the audio levels.

While Avadhoot was not part of the procession, he was the most conspicuous member of our party. This was due less to his great height and eccentric attire than to his outrageous behavior. He would climb on anything or push anybody out of his way for a picture. He was careless, and had no respect for other people's personal space. When he wasn't intentionally making people move, he was bumping into them with the oversize camera bag that hung from his shoulder. Sometimes he even appeared to be blocking Arjuna on purpose. I couldn't tell whether this was the only way he could get a particular angle, or if he was intentionally trying to keep Arjuna from getting it. No one was safe from him, except the guru, of course. Remarkably, it was only the Western devotees who ever complained about him. Indians were oblivious to his abuse, as if being knocked to the ground during a parade were par for the course. Instead of provoking anger in them, his aggressive style elicited only big smiles, words of encouragement, and offers of assistance.

When Baba's motorcade arrived in the center of the village, Sergio and Vinod were already waiting in front of Brahmananda's *samadhi* shrine. As soon as the car pulled up, the Italian rushed to open the door for the guru. His eyes hidden behind dark sunglasses, Baba was beaming smiles in all directions. He was met at the entrance of the shrine by two sour-looking Indian men, who gave him a cool reception. I couldn't understand what Baba was talking to them about, but it seemed as though they hesitated before letting him in.

I asked Brian who the men were.

"Trustees, mate. They control everything that goes on inside the shrine."

As soon as Baba was inside, Avadhoot rushed in after him, ignoring the protests of the trustees and the temple's security guard.

"Photography is strictly prohibited!" one of the trustees shouted in English.

Arjuna was about to follow Avadhoot in, but seemed to change his mind, and remained outside.

Through the open entryway of the temple, I watched the security guard confront Avadhoot, who completely ignored him. When the cowboy wouldn't stop taking pictures, the guard grabbed him and tried, unsuccessfully, to pry the camera out of his hands. Oblivious to the altercation, Baba, Suresh, Anjali, and the rest of the swamis prostrated themselves in front of the statue of Gurudev, and then performed a puja.

Meanwhile, the guard was joined by one of the trustees in his efforts to stop Avadhoot. When the noise they were making reached an unacceptable level, Sergio intervened, shaking the trustee's hand and discreetly passing him an envelope. The slightest hint of a smile spread across the sour man's face, and he called off the guard.

"The pictures are for Baba's personal use only," Sergio said.

"Yes, okay," the trustee said, wiggling his head in assent. "No problem."

Sergio flicked his chin in the direction of Arjuna. "What about the cameraman?"

The trustee narrowed his eyes and frowned. "For American television?"

"But no!" Sergio laughed, holding his open palms.

The trustee wiggled his head again, and Sergio hurried to the entryway to tell Arjuna to come inside.

Arjuna mounted the camera on his shoulder and Sergio curled his lip down in disgust. "Hey, what kind of an asshole are you?"

The cameraman let out a long exaggerated sigh.

"Why you such a pussy? Why you wait outside? You should be more like Avadhoot!"

"The man said *no pictures!*" Arjuna protested.

"Who's your guru? Baba?" Sergio asked, and then gestured in the direction of the trustee. "Or maybe that asshole?"

Tired of arguing, Arjuna entered the shrine and positioned himself alongside Avadhoot. At Sergio's command, Brian, Seth, and I went in, too.

I found Avadhoot's disrespectful behavior and Sergio's use of profanities in Gurudev's tomb disturbing. I wondered how Baba could put up with them. But despite my nagging doubts about the guru's closest disciples, the awesome power of the shrine was enough to silence my agitated mind.

When the ritual was over, Baba turned to address the gathering. Anjali translated, and Suresh stood at his side. "Today is the anniversary of my beloved Gurudev's *mahasamadhi*—the day he left his physical body to become one with the Absolute. On such a uniquely auspicious occasion I have an announcement to make. This young man," Baba said, gesturing to Suresh, "will be my successor."

There was a collective gasp. Even Anjali, who was usually a picture of dispassion, had to pause to collect herself before translating. "Suresh still has much *sadhana* to do, and he will not take his place on the throne until after I pass away. But make no mistake, he will be the future leader of the world-wide mission begun here in Ravipur by my own guru. Today, I install Shree Brahmananda's *shakti* in him. In two days' time, we will leave on a pilgrimage to the banks of the holy Ganges, where he will be initiated as a swami. Jai Gurudev!"

"Jai Gurudev! Jai Gurudev! Jai Gurudev!"

22.
PILGRIMAGE

BABA, SURESH, AND THE rest of the innermost circle would fly to New Delhi, where the guru would meet local devotees to lay the cornerstone of a new Raja Yoga ashram. Everyone else was setting off by train a day earlier, and would arrive in Delhi in time for the ceremony. From Delhi, we would continue to the holy city of Haridwar, about a hundred and fifty miles north of the Indian capital.

From the moment we found our first-class cabin on the train, Arjuna Weinberg complained about how jet-lagged he was and how little sleep he had gotten since leaving Birchwood Falls. As always, his eyes were watery and red.

"I can never sleep on planes," he said. "I hate flying. And I've barely gotten any sleep since I got to India. I had to run all over Ravipur tethered to the village idiot with a twenty-pound camera on my shoulder. It was a nightmare!"

Within seconds of sitting down, Poonish Davidson retreated into his own world, mouthing the words to the music he was listening to on his Walkman. Although he was wearing headphones, the volume was cranked up enough so that I could tell he wasn't listening to anything remotely spiritual. Stephen Ames was also tuning Arjuna out, reading a book entitled *The Yoga Sutras Of Patanjali*.

After a few hours of nonstop chatter, Arjuna finally fell asleep against the window. I felt gratitude to the guru for including me on his pilgrimage, but with the cameraman dead to the world, Poonish listening to mixtapes and staring out the window, and Stephen absorbed in his book, I was beginning to feel rejected: *Why don't they want to talk to me? Do they consider me beneath them?* I reminded myself that it could have been worse. I could have been assigned to the cabin with Brian and Seth.

At the New Delhi railway station, hired cars picked us up and took us directly to the site of the future ashram. Arjuna filmed the guru performing various rituals while I held the microphone and operated the VTR. Afterwards, Baba gave a brief talk, which was followed by a sumptuous luncheon hosted by prominent local devotees.

The ashram had booked us rooms at the Hyatt Regency, which was even more luxurious than the Taj Palace in Bombay. Baba stayed in the Presidential Suite with his attendant Rashmi Varma. Everyone else was paired with a roommate on the floor below. I was assigned to a room with Poonish.

At a short staff meeting in the hotel lobby, Sergio told everyone that we should eat in one of the hotel restaurants and charge it to our rooms. With nothing better to do after dinner, Poonish and I went for a drink at the bar off the lobby. When no one came to take our order immediately, my new friend waved impatiently at a waiter to get his attention. "Garçon!"

"Good evening, gentlemen. What is your pleasure?"

"One fresh lime soda, please," Poonish said. "Sweetened."

I ordered the same.

"You don't drink alcohol?" I asked him.

"Of course not."

"Why?"

"Alcohol is toxic. I don't ingest impure substances for the same reason I don't splash mud all over myself."

As we sipped our refreshing drinks, Poonish told me about his passion for playing the tablas, and how before meeting Baba he had been a drummer in a rock band back in Wisconsin.

"What's your favorite group?" he asked, taking a swig of his soda.

"I'm not interested in popular music anymore. I only listen to Raja Yoga tapes."

Poonish leaned forward in his seat and looked at me expectantly. "Yes, but if you *had* a favorite, which would it be?"

"I don't know. The Stones. Or maybe The Who."

His face dropped. Then he smiled politely. "Cool."

"What about you?"

"Duran Duran!" he answered, with a delighted grin. "Simon Le Bon rules!"

Over a second round of fresh lime sodas, the conversation shifted to clothes. "I do all of my shopping at Barney's in Manhattan," Poonish said. "That's where Sergio goes." Then he pointed to his shoes. "You see these loafers? Sergio has the same pair."

"Italian?"

"No, they're *Bally*."

I had no idea where Bally shoes came from, but tried not to let on. I asked him how he was able to afford such expensive clothes and travel all over the world with Baba. At first he was reluctant to say. Then he explained that as a new member of Baba's staff, all his expenses were paid. He even received a "modest" stipend.

This disturbed me. "Wait—you mean that people's donations to the ashram are used to pay for your and Sergio's fancy clothes?"

Before Poonish could answer, the Italian himself stepped out of one of the elevators. I gulped—he was arm in arm with Gopi. They sat at the far end of the bar. She didn't even notice I was there. She was too busy gawking at Sergio.

As Poonish and I finished our sodas, I was unable to take my eyes off Gopi. She blushed, played with her hair, and smiled every time Sergio opened his mouth. She was obviously smitten. And the drinks they ordered looked like real cocktails.

Much to my embarrassment, Sergio noticed me staring. Then he said something that made Gopi look in my direction and laugh. They lifted their glasses to salute me. With blood rushing to my face, I lifted my lime soda in return.

Later that night in my room, I reflected on what I'd seen in the bar. Did Baba know that his closest disciples drank alcohol the moment they stepped out of the ashram? And where was Baba while Sergio and Gopi were getting cozy in the lobby? What did the Omniscient One make of their flirtation? Did he condone it? And did he know that money donated to the ashram was being spent at Barney's?

THE HOLY CITY OF Haridwar lay on the banks of the river Ganges in the foothills of the Himalayas. For the next leg of our journey, the staff drove in a convoy of hired 1950s-style Ambassador cars. Baba drove with Suresh, Anjali, and Rashmi Varma in a chauffeured luxury sedan, which had been put at his disposal by a wealthy devotee from New Delhi. An ill-tempered, scar-faced man named Hameed drove the car I shared with Poonish.

Hameed drove excessively fast up the narrow, winding mountain roads, taking his turns much too sharply. Guardrails were nonexistent in India and one second of inattention would have sent our vehicle tumbling off the side of the mountain. To make matters worse, Hameed was in the habit of randomly honking his horn every few seconds. His constant braking and sudden accelerations, along with the incessant beeping of his horn, were making me ill.

Poonish told me that Haridwar was one of the four sites of the *Kumbha Mela*, a religious event that happened once every twelve years and drew millions of Hindus to the banks of the Ganges to wash away their sins. The sacred ritual, however, was not the reason for our pilgrimage. We were on our way to the ashram of His Eminence Vedantananda Acharya, where Suresh would take the vows of a renunciant and become a swami.

"Why can't Baba just hold the ceremony himself in Ravipur?" I asked Poonish.

"The Acharya is the head of the *Smriti* order. Only he has the authority to ordain swamis."

I was skeptical. "He has more power than Baba?"

"Of course not! Baba is a *shaktipat* guru—a perfected master. The Acharya's role is purely institutional."

"Hey, do you think we'll get a chance to take a dip in the Ganges?"

Poonish winced. "I hope not. That's where they dump the bodies after they burn them."

I remembered Hindus believed that if they were cremated on the banks of the sacred river, they would attain liberation.

"Sometimes the bodies don't burn up completely," Poonish continued, "and the snapping turtles finish them off."

The idea of bathing in a river full of half-burnt corpses made me want to puke.

As we drove around a curve, our car nearly collided with an oncoming truck. The driver swerved, and we narrowly avoided driving off the edge of a cliff. Hameed slammed his hand down on the horn in anger. I broke out in a sweat.

"You want to give that thing a rest," Poonish scolded. The driver glared at my friend, and in defiance, honked the horn again.

My belly churned. I thought I might throw up at any second. "Can you stop the car a minute, please?"

The scar-faced driver frowned. "No stop."

"He can't—not unless Baba's car stops first," Poonish explained. Then my friend got a glint in his eye, and a mischievous smile played on his lips. "Hey, you want to hear something totally gross?"

I inched closer to the open window. "Not really."

Poonish ignored me. "There's a Shiva-worshipping sect of ascetics in Haridwar called the Aghoris. They're known for doing all kinds of disgusting stuff. They drink urine, eat shit, and practice ritual cannibalism using the partially-cremated remains of the dead. They live in the charnel grounds and smear ashes all over their bodies."

"What's a charnel ground?" I asked, unsure if I really wanted to know.

"It's like an above-ground graveyard, where they leave half-burnt dead bodies to rot. The Aghoris make bowls out of human skulls and eat their meals out of them."

I felt a wave of nausea. "You're going to make me puke!"

"Look at you!" Poonish hooted. "You're turning green!"

I didn't want to be sick all over the inside of the car, so I rolled down my window. Hameed the driver eyed me suspiciously in the rear-view mirror.

"Most Hindus are afraid of them," said Poonish. "They shun them."

"Understandably." I decided that if I had to throw up, I'd aim for my new friend.

"They're considered black magicians, but many of the local people in Haridwar revere them because of their supernatural powers."

"So they do all of these weird, gross things, but what do they believe in?"

"They have the same goal we do—enlightenment."

I was skeptical, and suspected that Poonish might be making the whole thing up.

"How does eating dead people and drinking piss help them achieve that?"

Poonish explained that the Aghoris believed that the greatest obstacle to attaining a state of perfect non-dualistic awareness was people's tendency to cling to concepts of right and wrong. For the Aghoris, this kind of delusional thinking was an even greater hindrance than an addiction to comfort and sensual pleasure. They achieved transcendence through self-degradation and the breaking of social taboos.

"They take drugs, eat meat, and engage in Tantric sex rituals."

"They sound totally insane. I can understand why decent people want nothing to do with them. I'd be afraid of them, too."

"Maybe they sound crazy to you," said Poonish, lifting his chin and sitting up straight. "But from the standpoint of an enlightened being, their view makes perfect sense."

I was beginning to think Poonish was nuts too, but wanted to understand what he was getting at.

"What do you mean?"

"You agree that Shiva is the cause of everything that occurs in the phenomenal universe, don't you?"

"Um, yeah," I said. "Everything is an expression of God."

"And God is perfect, right?"

"Yes, of course."

"Then logically, everything that exists must be perfect too. The Aghoris believe that to deny the perfection of anything would be to deny the sacredness of God as well."

"Agoris—very bad," Hameed growled, frowning at us through the rearview mirror.

I agreed with the driver, and wondered why on earth Baba chose Haridwar as a place to spend three years in silent retreat.

Hameed's constant horn honking irritated Poonish even more than it did me. Indian drivers, I noticed, had a tendency to use their horns as a way of making their presence known to other drivers. But Hameed's honking was gratuitous. He honked any time another vehicle came into view, and he honked whenever he saw cows or pedestrians in the immediate vicinity, even if they were nowhere near the road.

Despite Hamid's refusal to stop earlier, when we were about halfway to our destination, he pulled into a service station. A sign above the fuel pumps said "Indian Oil."

"What's wrong?" Poonish demanded. "Why are you stopping?"

"Petrol."

Three men attended to our vehicle. One pumped the gas while the other two cleaned our windshields. When they were finished, Hameed went inside to pay.

Fearing this might be my last chance to puke before we got to the Acharya's ashram, I got out of the car and walked a few feet to the side of the road. After a few painful dry heaves, I finally found relief. When I returned to the car, the hood was up and Poonish was bent over the engine with a hand on one knee. The other hand held a Swiss army pocket knife.

"What are you looking for?"

"The wire," he said, biting his lower lip.

"Which wire?"

"The one connected to that fucking horn."

I glanced nervously in the direction of the station office. Hameed was still inside. "Are you crazy?"

"Hel-l-l-l-o! What's this?" Poonish said, opening his knife. Before he could snip the wire, Hameed returned and started shouting.

"*Ae! Tu meri gaadi ke saath kya kar raha hai?*"

"Fixing that fucking horn hey!" Poonish hollered back. Then he cracked a wicked smile and doubled over with laughter.

Hameed turned purple with rage and slammed shut the hood of the car. "Foolish American boys!"

Poonish and I were both laughing now as we piled back into the car. Turning the key in the ignition, Hameed slammed his foot down on the accelerator. The tires on the car screeched as we sped back out onto the roadway. We didn't get even a tenth of a mile before Hameed's hand was back on the horn again.

The city center of Haridwar was crowded with ancient temples and shrines, and overflowing with pilgrims, tourists, hawkers, and saffron-robed monks. As we drove through, devotional songs in praise of the river goddess Ganges and Lord Shiva blared from loudspeakers. Looking out the window, I saw naked, trident-carrying holy men with long matted hair and bodies smeared with sacred ash.

They begged in the streets or performed rituals like street magicians. The Acharya's ashram was located on the outskirts of town.

Above the ashram gate, a banner in Hindi and English read: "Welcome Swami Rudrananda and His Disciples." Inside, Baba was received by His Eminence and a huge gathering of *sannyasins*—all of whom were Indian. Avadhoot was taking pictures everywhere at once.

Attired in the plain cotton robes of a simple renunciant, the Acharya was more modest and austere-looking in appearance than I had pictured. Like Baba, he was in his early seventies, but appeared much older. Our guru's full head of hair was lustrous, and had not yet gone completely gray. His Eminence's head and face were shaven. Baba's skin was golden-hued and radiated good health; the Acharya's complexion was pallid.

Hands folded in reverence, His Eminence greeted Baba with sparkling eyes and a warm smile before garlanding him with flowers. Patting the Acharya on the shoulder, Baba said something in Hindi, prompting laughter from his host and everyone else who could understand. I marveled at these two great beings exchanging pleasantries and knowing glances, as if they were both in on the same cosmic joke.

"Shouldn't we be filming this?" I asked Arjuna.

"Nah. When they want us to shoot, they'll tell us— believe me."

The Acharya escorted Baba and Suresh to a nearby temple, while the *sannyasins* led the rest of us to a grassy spot on the riverbank. Under the shade of trees, they served us water in crudely fashioned clay cups and a simple lunch on banana leaf plates. Sipping my water, I cringed, wondering where it came from. If it was from the Ganges, *anything* could be floating around in it. I reminded myself that the river was holy and washed away the sins of all those who came in contact with it. I had nothing to fear.

Most of the food was palatable. The only thing I couldn't eat were the chapattis— they tasted like concrete. Halfway through the meal, Poonish showed me what he had found embedded in one of his puris: a dead cockroach. My nausea returned with a vengeance and our lunch was over. Shooting up to our feet, we searched for a garbage can to dump the rest of our food, but were intercepted by Sergio.

"Act polite!" he scolded. "Go back and finish your food!"

When the meal was officially over, the *sannyasins* took our dirty leaf plates and clay cups and tossed them into the river. I watched as the banana leaves were carried downstream by the current.

"You think there're any corpses floating around in there?" I asked Poonish.

"That is not the Ganges proper," he said in a fake Indian accent. "That is a canal only."

From a dais in one of the ashram's many shady gardens, our guru and His Eminence held *darshan*. Suresh sat at their feet.

"Make sure you get good coverage of this," Avadhoot said to Arjuna, loading a roll of film into his camera. Then he pointed at me. "And make sure *he* gets usable audio. The sound at the shrine was a disaster!"

"Yeah, yeah," Arjuna answered, adjusting his tripod. "I get it."

"What's happening? Why is this so important?" I asked Arjuna, after Avadhoot was out of earshot.

"They set up Baba's throne higher than the Acharya's."

I glanced in the direction of the two holy men. Arjuna was right; Baba's throne was raised a few inches higher than the other guru's.

"That's very significant—it's an acknowledgement of Baba's superior attainment. We want it well documented."

Our guru may have been the guest of honor, but from the way Baba and His Eminence kept glancing down at Suresh and smiling, it was clear that Suresh was the center of attention.

"Tomorrow morning, Suresh will be taking the vows of *sannyasa* and will be ordained as a swami," Baba said through Anjali. "Later in the evening we will all go to the Hari-ki-Pauri ghat for the Ganga *arti.*"

"Great," Arjuna grumbled.

"What's wrong?" I whispered.

"You'll see. We're going to have to *kill* to get any decent footage next to the river. Too many pilgrims and tourists."

Darshan went on for hours. The sun fell lower in the sky. At one point, Baba turned to Avadhoot and spoke to him in Hindi. This time the photographer translated for us: "Baba says we should put our cameras away now."

The Acharya eyed Avadhoot with admiration. I could tell he was impressed by the American's fluency in an Indian language.

"His Eminence likes your big hat," Anjali said to Avadhoot. Everybody laughed, but I noticed that Baba's translator was not amused. Her expression was glum and her lips were pressed flat. I'd never seen her so sullen.

Avadhoot tipped his idiotic ten-gallon hat to the Acharya and spoke with a ridiculous Texas accent: "Why, thank you, Your Eminence! Whoo-whee!"

Everybody laughed again.

"Do the cowboy walk!" Suresh called.

Avadhoot swaggered away from the dais in an exaggerated bow-legged strut. Then he stopped and spun around with his index fingers aimed at Arjuna like pistols. "Stick 'em up, pardner!"

Arjuna sighed and shook his head. "What an asshole," he muttered.

Luckily for the cameraman, only I heard him.

Slapping his knee, the Acharya laughed heartily, and then turned to speak to Anjali.

"Avadhoot, His Eminence would like to try on your hat."

"Why certainly!" said the cowboy photographer, brimming with pride. With a bow and a flourish, Avadhoot handed the Acharya his Stetson.

His Eminence regarded the alien object with childlike curiosity, and then set it down on his own head. The hat proved much too large for him, however, causing it to slip down over his face, covering his eyes. While everybody else laughed and applauded, a quarrel broke out between Anjali and Gopi. I was unable to hear what they were saying, but I could tell Baba's translator was angry. Gopi was on the verge of crying. When their bickering became too loud to ignore, the laughter stopped abruptly, and all eyes were on the two women.

"Get out of here, you incompetent fool," Anjali scolded.

Gopi fled the garden in the direction of the river, tears streaming from her eyes, the back of her hand held against her mouth. For a second I thought about running after her, so she could see how much I cared. But I didn't dare move. I was on this pilgrimage to serve the guru. If Baba needed Arjuna to film, and I wasn't there to assist him, Sergio would be furious.

A moment later, Baba was blasting Anjali, I assumed for the disruption. If the scolding upset her, however, she didn't show it. When Baba dismissed her, she left calm and collected, shoulders back and chin up.

Baba's closest disciples were housed in newly constructed bungalows, but the accommodations for the rest of us were austere, even by Indian standards. The room I shared with Poonish was covered with dust. Cobwebs dangled from every corner of the ceiling. Two doors on cinderblocks served as beds, and a wooden crate between them served as a night stand. On the crate was an old lamp. A ceiling fan wobbled noisily, giving little relief from the heat.

"It's not so bad," I said, putting on a good face for my fellow Raja Yogi.

Poonish stood with one arm holding the other at the elbow. "We don't even have air conditioning. And the bathrooms are a hundred yards away."

"We don't have air conditioners or bathrooms in our rooms in Ravipur either."

Poonish bit his lip. "Some of us do."

I was envious. Baba's staff really had it made.

We stayed up late talking about Duran Duran, men's fashion, and whatever else popped into Poonish's head. When we finally switched off the light, it was a quarter to midnight. As I waited for sleep, I thought about how blessed I was to be in the holy city with Baba, and how happy I was to have made a new friend. I also thought about how Anjali had scolded Gopi at *darshan*. I wished I could've defended her. I was sure she hadn't deserved Anjali's harsh treatment.

Just as I was drifting off to sleep, Poonish cried out: "Aaaaaaaagh!"

"What's wrong?" I said, fumbling for the switch on the lamp between our beds.

Poonish was hopping around the room in his underwear, frantically scratching himself. His eyes were wide with dismay. "Bed bugs!"

Suddenly, I felt itchy too. "Are you sure?"

Grabbing his clothes off the top of his suitcase, Poonish quickly got dressed. "One hundred percent sure. I'm getting out of here!"

"Where are you going to sleep?" I asked, scratching my arm.

Poonish thrust open the door to our room with so much force he practically knocked it off its hinges. "In the car. You coming?"

"Yeah, but what if it's locked?" I pulled my clothes on as fast as I could.

"Then I'll break a window!"

I wasn't as convinced of the threat as Poonish, but he knew India much better than I did. If he said there were bedbugs, I wasn't going to argue with him.

The quickest path leading to the cars took us along the river. Luckily, we could see where we were going—the moon was full and cast an eerie, washed-out light over the water and the ashram compound. As we got closer to the main gate, I noticed that lights were still on in a couple of the bungalows. I wondered why they were still up at such a late hour.

The car wasn't locked, as it turned out. Inside, Hameed was asleep on the back seat, with his feet propped up in an open window. We looked around for an empty vehicle, but they were all already occupied by their drivers.

Poonish pounded a fist against the roof of Hameed's car. "Wake up, stupid!"

The scar-faced driver was unresponsive. Next Poonish tried whistling through two fingers. He was so loud the whistle hurt my ears, but still nothing. As a last resort, Poonish grabbed Hameed's legs and shook them.

"*Vakt kya hua hai?*" said the driver, rubbing his eyes.

My friend pointed to the back seat. "We sleep here!"

Hameed blinked his eyes a few times to check if he was really awake. Then he vigorously shook his head. "*Nahin! Chale jao!*"

"Yes, yes!" Poonish insisted, reaching for the door handle. Before he had a chance to open it, however, Hameed brought a fist down on the lock. Then he rolled up all the windows.

"What's plan B?" I asked, relieved not to have to share the back seat of a hot car with two other men.

Poonish went from car to car, waking up the drivers, demanding that we be allowed to sleep in their vehicles. The response from all of them was the same. They were off the clock and we should get lost.

"Listen, Poonish," I said, "maybe there weren't any bedbugs in our room and you just imagined it."

But he wasn't listening to me.

"I have a better idea," he said finally. "Let's sleep in the temple!"

I thought about it, but decided to pass. A temple was a sacred space—I didn't want to risk angering the guru. "I'll take my chances back in the room."

"Suit yourself," Poonish said. Then he hurried toward the temple.

On my way back to the room, I again walked along the edge of the holy river and remembered that we'd be visiting the Har-ki-Pauri ghat with Baba the next evening. I looked forward to participating in the Ganga *arati* ritual. Everyone said it was spectacular.

Just then, I saw something out of the corner of my eye that freaked me out. A large object—only a few yards away—was floating downstream toward me. *Could it be? Please God, no, not a dead body!*

I thought about the Aghori cult and a chill spread through me. I wondered if we were anywhere near a charnel ground. They could have been munching on half-burnt corpses just a mile or two upstream.

When the object was close enough, I saw it was only a log. But this did little to calm my nerves. Even if I couldn't see the dead bodies floating on the surface, I knew they were in there, probably just below the surface. I regretted my decision to return to the room without Poonish. I was alone, with no one to protect me. What if the Aghoris also ate people while they were still alive?

I was about to turn around and head for the temple, when I finally saw the lights of the bungalows up ahead. As I drew nearer, I saw something that shocked me. A man was standing in the open doorway of a bungalow, holding a woman in his arms. I was pretty sure it was Sergio and Anjali.

Unsure what to do, I ducked behind a bush and observed. Although the light coming from the open door was dim, I was almost certain I recognized the translator's long black braided hair, and the floral pattern of the sari she had been wearing earlier. Then I heard the man speak. I'd recognize that accent anywhere—it was the Italian. A moment later, he led the woman by the hand inside and closed the door behind them.

I was confused and angry. In the bar the night before, I'd seen him making bedroom eyes at Gopi. Now, he seemed to be canoodling with Baba's translator! I'd heard Baba say many times that everyone living in the ashram—even married couples—was required to observe strict celibacy. I was appalled by Sergio's immoral behavior. Not only was he hitting on the girl I loved, he was two-timing her!

Back in the room, I was now more afraid of being eaten alive by the Aghoris than of getting a few insect bites. After making sure the door to my room was securely locked, I inspected the flimsy pad that passed for a mattress on my makeshift bed. No sign of bed bugs. I checked Poonish's bed, too. Nothing. Stripping down to my underwear, I got back into bed, switched off the light, and pulled the bed sheet over my head. A few seconds later, I thought I heard a tentative knock on the door. Unsure if I'd imagined it, I didn't immediately respond. A moment later, the gentle knock came again. *It's Poonish*, I thought. *He must've forgotten his key.*

Turning the light back on, I thought about getting dressed, and then changed my mind: *It can only be Poonish.* I opened. To my astonishment, it was Gopi!

Her eyes were red and wet with tears. She glanced down at my bare legs, and then looked away. "Oh, sorry!"

I ducked behind the door. "It's okay. Just a second." My heart raced. "Let me put something on." I left the door slightly ajar, and scrambled to get dressed. I couldn't imagine what she could possibly want. As soon as I was decent, I went to the door again.

"I'm sorry to bother you," she said. "I saw your light on just a minute ago."

"It's no problem," I assured her, and invited her in.

Gopi glanced around the room. "Where's Poonish?"

"Sleeping in the temple. He thinks we have bedbugs."

Gopi laughed, wiping her eyes with the back of her hand. "That figures. He panics easily. I'm sure he's imagining it."

I studied her face. She looked so sad—but God, she was gorgeous. "Well, he *did* find a dead cockroach in his lunch."

Gopi laughed and cried at the same time. "I'm so sorry," she said, trying to pull herself together.

"Please," I said, gesturing toward Poonish's bed. I'd already forgotten about the imaginary bed bugs.

Glancing at the bed, she took a seat on the edge. I sat on my bed, across from her.

Gopi stared at the floor and twisted a strand of hair around her finger. I couldn't believe she was there, in my room. Of all the people making the pilgrimage with Baba, she had turned to me. I was thrilled, but couldn't help wondering why.

"What's up?" I asked her, trying to sound casual.

"It's Anjali. She's been in a horrible mood ever since Baba announced that Suresh would be his successor."

I found it hard to believe that Anjali could be jealous of her brother—she was too spiritually advanced for such a primitive emotion. But who was I to say? Gopi knew her infinitely better than I did.

"What were you two arguing about at *darshan?*"

Gopi looked at the floor again and continued to play with her hair. "Oh, that. She accused me of forgetting to bring a gold watch that Baba had intended as a gift for the Acharya. But it's not true. Baba gave it to her to pack, but she forgot. Now she's trying to blame the whole thing on me!" Gopi sniffled and wiped her eyes again. "I just don't understand it—she's not usually so mean."

"How unfair!"

Gopi's shoulders curled over her chest and she again began to cry. Even with her face twisted in sorrow, she was by far the most beautiful girl I'd ever seen.

When she finally stopped bawling and looked up at me again, her lips were slightly parted. They were full and sensuous. I wondered what it'd be like to kiss them.

What would Baba think if he knew I had a girl in my room at this hour?

"Listen, Gopi, I'm sure Anjali is just having a bad day. She's mad now, but she'll get over it. She definitely doesn't seem like the kind of person to hold a grudge."

Gopi looked away from me. She was quiet for a few seconds before speaking. "I'm not upset about the watch or Anjali—not really."

"You're not?" I couldn't imagine what problems someone as close to the guru as Gopi could have that would be worth getting so upset. "What's wrong, then?"

She began to sob again, even harder and louder than before. Brian and Seth were in the room next door. I was afraid they might hear her.

"I just can't understand what he sees in her!" she said abruptly.

"Well, she's been with him since she was a little girl, and she's obviously extremely devoted," I said. "I mean, he did make her his translator."

Gopi shook her head, sobbing. "I'm not talking about *Baba*."

"Wait—who—what—are we talking about then?"

She opened her mouth to speak, but said nothing.

"Gopi?"

I got up from the bed and looked for something to give her to wipe her tears. When I couldn't find anything, I took a clean t-shirt out of my duffle bag and handed it to her. She nodded in thanks, and then blew her nose in it. I decided I'd never wash that t-shirt again.

"You want to tell me?" I asked as gently as possible.

There was another long silence. Finally, she blurted out: "I'm talking about Sergio!"

A vision of the Italian having his way with the angel flashed through my mind, and every cell in my body burned.

"Oh—" I was unable to think of anything to say. Beautiful girls were the same in the ashram as they were in the ordinary world, I told myself. They always fall for the biggest jerks. What cruel game was Sergio playing with Gopi's feelings?

"They're together right now in his bungalow!" she said, confirming my earlier suspicion.

I suddenly felt a little better. Sergio was no longer interested in Gopi. He had moved on to someone else. "Are you sure?"

She nodded. "I'm sharing a bungalow with her and she's still not back yet."

I realized Gopi was totally hung up on him. I couldn't see why. He was handsome and a snappy dresser, but he was old—or so I thought at the time—and a convicted rapist!

Gopi pulled herself together and glanced up at me with her head tilted to one side. "What's wrong?"

"Me? What do you mean? *Nothing*."

"You look upset."

Am I that transparent? I wondered. I turned away. "I'm fine. I'm just concerned about you."

I didn't know much about Sergio, or how he had become so close to the Baba, but it was strange that the guru seemed to put up with all of his shenanigans. We were in a holy place. And the guests of another guru. How could he allow Sergio and Anjali to be alone together at this hour?

I looked back at Gopi. She was so vulnerable and sad. I wanted to make her smile again.

"You're a beautiful girl, Gopi."

She sniffed and dabbed her eyes with my t-shirt. "Thank you, Deependra. You're very sweet."

"Any guy would be extremely lucky to be with you."

Her face fell, and she began to wail again. "He told me he loved me!"

I couldn't stand to see her cry anymore. I took a different approach. "Well, if you like oily hair and shiny shoes, I can see why you're into him."

Gopi stopped crying for a second and let out a laugh.

"Hey, what kind of an asshole are you?" I said, perfectly imitating Sergio's voice.

Gopi's eyes widened in astonishment and an open-mouthed grin lit up her face. "Oh, my God—that's amazing! You sound just like him!"

"Don't worry, we're not in America," I said in the Italian's voice again. "No one's going to arrest me."

The smile vanished from Gopi's face. "That's not funny." Then her face screwed up and she cried again.

I stood up, and then sat down on the edge of Poonish's bed, next to her. Putting my arm around her, I softly kissed her on the top of her head.

She buried her face in my shoulder, wrapped her arms around me, and continued to cry. She smelled even better than I could ever have imagined—an intoxicating mixture of pheromones, shampoo, and a light floral perfume. I had to stop myself from burying my nose in her hair. Instead, I took her hand in mine and gently caressed the back of it with my thumb. Her skin was soft and smooth, and I found myself overcome with desire. I thought about trying to kiss her, but remembered where I was.

Baba would be angry.

Reaching up, I cradled the back of her head and stroked her long golden hair. If I could hold this beautiful creature in my arms for the rest of my life, who needed meditation and *sadhana*?

Then a dark thought invaded my reverie: *Has Gopi slept with him? Is that bastard doing it with Anjali right now? Is the guru onto him? Hasn't Baba ever heard of three strikes and you're out?*

I tried to apply right understanding to the situation: maybe Sergio and Anjali were only talking. For whatever reason, Anjali appeared to be troubled at the moment. Maybe he was comforting her.

Just then, I heard the sound of creaking wood outside. I turned my head to see a shadowy figure move away from the window. There was a pounding in my chest and any lust I felt immediately subsided.

"Did you hear that?" I asked.

Gopi lifted her head off my shoulder and looked at me quizzically. "Hear what? I didn't hear anything."

I thought of the Aghoris again and freaked out. "I heard a noise and thought I saw someone right outside the window."

Gopi shrugged. She seemed unconcerned. Not only that, but her tears had dried up. If I was going to make a move, it was now or never.

She glanced down at her watch and gasped. "Oh my God, I can't believe how late it is. I should be going."

We got up from the bed and I saw her to the door.

"Are you sure you're going to be alright? Do you want me to walk you to your bungalow?"

"Oh, no—that's okay. You're the sweetest, Deependra. Thanks for listening to my sad story." She laughed self-consciously.

"Anytime."

Gopi smiled and then leaned in and kissed me softly on the cheek.

"Good night, Gopi," I said, opening the door. She stepped out into the night and was gone.

For a few moments I stood in the open doorway, savoring the sweetness of the encounter. I was grateful that the Omnipotent One hadn't let anything inappropriate happen between us.

The sins committed in the world are washed away at an ashram, I remembered Baba saying in one of his books. *But those committed in the house of the Guru cling stubbornly. They are difficult to cleanse.*

I got undressed again, got back into bed, and switched off the light. Now it was ridiculously late, and I worried I might be too tired to carry the heavy VTR and do a good job with the sound all day tomorrow. I was desperate to sleep, but my visit from Gopi had left my mind racing: *She turned to me because she can sense how much I love and care for her,* I told myself. *Soon she'll forget all about Sergio and will be mine!*

If there was any chance I'd get to sleep, I had to get my mind under control. I repeated the *Om Namah Shivaya* mantra to myself and breathed deeply, but I was unable to focus—the room was still fragrant with her intoxicating scent.

Is Sergio trying to get under the sari of every cute girl in the ashram? If that's the kind of man she's attracted to, what hope do I ever have of getting under her sari?

STOP! shouted a voice inside my head. I had come to the ashram to pursue the loftiest goal of human existence, not to give in to my animal urges. *What must the omniscient guru think of me? He has brought me on a pilgrimage to the banks of the sacred river to bear witness to the ordination of his closest disciple, and I thank him by inviting a girl into my room?*

Suddenly the door to the room burst open. My heart thudded against the wall of my chest. *Aghoris!* I shot up to a sitting position. It was too dark for me to see who it was. I thought I'd piss myself.

"Poonish?" I croaked. There was no answer. I began to tremble. "Who's there?"

Again, my words were met with silence. All I could discern was a dark figure standing in the doorway. My mind went to the worst-case scenario: the Aghoris had come to eat me! There was an excruciating pounding in my ears. Holding my breath, I switched on the light.

The bright light stung my eyes, and all I could make out was a flash of orange. I screamed like a child.

A half second later, I realized how cowardly I'd been. The shadowy figure was not a cannibal, but my own beloved Baba! I was mortified!

For what felt like an eternity, the guru stood in the doorway, staring at me without saying a word. Then he stepped into the room and closed the door behind him. I couldn't believe it: Baba was actually in my room!

Then I saw he was holding a big stick. Now I was afraid for a different reason: the guru was here to beat the shit out of me for breaking the rules.

"Gopi is good girl, no?" he finally said, speaking English. His tone was gentle. He didn't sound angry.

"Yes, Baba," I said, shaking all over. "A very *nice* girl, too."

"Very pure," the guru added, pursing his lips and tapping the stick against the palm of his hand.

I swallowed hard and nodded.

Sauntering over to Poonish's side of the room, he regarded the empty bed for a few seconds. I wondered what he could see there. Maybe he was psychically replaying my conversation with Gopi in his mind's eye.

Baba lightly tapped the stick against the palm of his hand again, and then turned to face me. Sweat trickled down my temple. I was sure he was about to strike me with it. Instead, he sat down on the bed where Gopi had just been, and stared inscrutably into my eyes.

I felt naked in front of the guru—utterly exposed. This was partly due to the fact that I was literally almost naked—all I had on was a pair of briefs—but mostly because I knew I could hide nothing from the Omniscient One.

"Your brother—" Baba began, "—ashram finished?"

I hesitated before responding. I didn't understand what he meant. "Jeremy? I mean, *Shree Ram?*"

The guru stared back at me in silence.

"He just graduated from medical school, Baba. He's a doctor. Lives in the world."

Baba just gazed into my eyes without saying a word, or giving any indication that he understood me.

I couldn't think of anything to say. I knew Baba could read my thoughts, so why repeat them out loud? Instead, I tried to keep my mind as still as possible.

I no longer had the sense that he was angry with me. Maybe he didn't mind I had broken the rules, because I was with a member of his inner circle. Regardless, I was awestruck: Here I was, face-to-face and alone with the guru for the very first time!

Finally, Baba spoke: "Ashram, world—same, same."

Although I wasn't quite sure what he was talking about, I nodded in agreement.

The guru was silent again for a while.

"Coming, going," said Baba, swatting the palm of his hand with his stick. "Same, same."

"Um, yes, Baba."

"Birth, death,"—*swat*—"same, same." *Swat.*

Now I really had no idea what he was talking about. And I was too distracted by what he was doing with his stick to figure it out.

"Waking, dreaming,"—*swat*—"same, same." *Swat.*

I was utterly confused. I was about to ask him for clarification, when suddenly the door to the room swung open. Baba and I turned our heads to see a wide-eyed Poonish trembling in the entrance.

Baba frowned and looked my friend up and down. "Why not sleeping?"

"Bugs, Baba," Poonish rasped. "Insects in my bed—biting me."

"No bugs," snapped the guru, swaggering toward Poonish, slapping the stick hard against his hand now.

Poonish winced.

The guru regarded the side of my roommate's head for a while. "Bugs in here—" said Baba, lifting his stick and pointing it at Poonish's temple. "—*not* in bed."

"Yes, Baba."

The guru moved closer to my roommate. I held my breath—I was sure he was about to bring his stick down on Poonish's head. Instead, Baba strode straight past him, exiting through the open door. Before disappearing into the darkness, the guru turned around one last time to confront my friend. "Go to sleep!" he commanded. "Tomorrow, busy, busy." Then he was gone.

Carefully closing the door behind the guru, Poonish staggered over to his side of the room, collapsed into bed, and exhaled forcefully through puckered lips.

"What was *that* all about?" I asked.

Poonish shrugged.

"That's the first time I've ever seen Baba by himself. What was he doing at this hour walking around the ashram with a stick?"

Poonish was silent for a few seconds, and then shrugged again.

I scratched my head. I wanted answers, but my roommate was in no mood for a conversation. He was still shaking.

"I thought you were sleeping in the temple," I said, lying back down in bed.

"One of the temple priests found me and kicked me out."

I switched off the light, and then lay awake in bed, reflecting on the most bizarre night of my life. *First a visit from an angel, and then the guru himself! How would I be blessed next?*

MY ALARM CLOCK SOUNDED like a Mack Truck backing up.

"Shut it off!" Poonish moaned.

Groping for the clock in the darkness, my fingers came in contact with the snooze button. I desperately wanted to go back to sleep for a few minutes, but I had no time to spare. I switched on the light and Poonish shot up in bed, squinting and rubbing his eyes. Not wanting to risk falling back asleep, I dragged myself out of bed and immediately got dressed.

Something was wrong. I felt an intense itching all over my body and I began to scratch. I glanced over at Poonish on the bed. A look of horror was creeping across his face and he started scratching, too. Looking down at my arms and legs, I gasped. I was covered in rows of tiny red bites.

"I knew it!" Poonish shouted. "Fuck! Fuck! Fuck!"

I took a better look at my roommate. His face was covered with little red welts, too. I couldn't believe it. Baba had told Poonish that he'd been imagining them. It was unthinkable to me that Baba had been wrong. I racked my brain. The only explanation I could come up with was that this was yet another *test*.

Poonish carried on like a crazy person. I was afraid he might have a nervous breakdown, but then he surprised me. It was as though a switch had been flipped inside his brain. One moment he was freaking out, the next he was calmly getting dressed and reciting the *Om Namah Shivaya* mantra under his breath.

For me, meditation in the Acharya's temple that morning was impossible. The itching sensation all over my body was unbearable. Even when I was able to stop scratching my bites, I couldn't put the midnight encounter with Gopi and the surprise visit from Baba out of my head. Instead of focusing on the mantra, my mind alternated between visualizing Gopi naked and attempting to interpret Baba's latest test. Why, I wondered, hadn't the guru been angry with me for having a girl in my room after lights out? Was the stick some kind of unspoken warning? I was also confused by Baba's cryptic words: "Coming, going. Same, same." What did that have to do with Jeremy?

What perplexed me the most, however, was the question of why Baba had told us categorically there weren't any bed bugs, when he *obviously* knew that there were. Had he *wanted* us to get bitten? In the back of my mind, I also wondered if Baba was the shadow at my window when Gopi was in my room. But I immediately shot this idea down. What possible need could an omniscient being have to spy on people?

As if my turbulent mental state wasn't hard enough to cope with, the person sitting directly behind me was snoring his head off. Incapable of getting into meditation, I gave up trying. I opened my eyes and turned around to see which loser had fallen asleep. I should have known—it was Avadhoot Plotnick! The cowboy photographer's upper body was slumped over, with his head between his knees. *He's lucky Baba isn't here!* I thought.

I glanced over at Poonish, sitting a few feet away. The raised bite marks on his face were probably just as irritating as my own, but his face was completely serene. His legs were folded in the half lotus position, his eyes were gently closed, and his back was straight as a wall. Despite his unspiritual behavior at times, his ability to meditate under the circumstances was proof that he was secretly an accomplished yogi. Then it hit me: I too needed to learn to transform doubt into *faith*.

My eyes wandered to the women's side of the small Shiva temple, and I noticed Gopi was missing. I glanced back to the men's side. Sergio wasn't there either. *Are they together?*

Then I remembered that Sergio *never* came to meditation. Looking around some more, I realized that none of Baba's closest people were there, except for Avadhoot. They were all probably busy preparing for the ordination ceremony. The idea that they might all be sleeping never occurred to me.

The meditation session ended and was followed by the recitation of the *Guru Gita*. I had hoped the chant would be easier for me to get into, but it was useless. I remained completely unfocused. Thanks to Avadhoot, however, I soon forgot all about my doubts and confusion. Even if his deafening off-key chanting and mispronunciation of the sacred Sanskrit syllables didn't inspire me to delve one-pointedly into the ritual, it irritated me so much I was incapable of hearing or thinking about anything else.

Just when I thought the torturous chant would never end, Gopi appeared at the side entrance. She was glancing around the temple, looking for someone. The someone turned out to be me. When she saw me, she came over. *What now?* I wondered.

She crouched down next to me and whispered: "Baba says you, Arjuna, and Avadhoot must come to the garden immediately with your camera equipment. Tell the others."

Her gaze was alert, but emotionless. It was as though our intimate exchange last night had never happened.

Dejected, I rose to my feet. "Got it."

Gopi jerked her head back, and then studied my face with alarm. "What happened to you?"

"What do you mean?"

"Your face?" she said, covering her mouth with her hand.

"Bed bugs. Poonish wasn't imagining things."

Gopi bit her lip and shook her head. Then she turned to leave the temple.

We arrived in the garden where *darshan* had been held the day before. A group of Brahmin priests were chanting mantras and offering oblations at a fire pit. The pulsating flicker of the fire and the cadence with which the sacred syllables were recited was hypnotic. The mantras had a vibrational effect on me as well, causing the muscles in my arms and legs to twitch and a subtle energy to stir at my heart and throat chakras.

Arjuna tapped me on the shoulder, and then waved a hand in front of my eyes. "Are you going to stand there like a zombie, Deependra, or are you going to set up the VTR?"

"Oh, sorry," I said, snapping out of my trance. "What are the priests doing?"

"The fire ritual?" Arjuna said, attaching a tripod plate to the bottom of his camera. "It's called a *yajna*. It's part of the *sannyasa* ceremony."

I popped a blank cassette into the deck, and then did a sound check with Arjuna. While we waited for Baba, Suresh, and the others to arrive, Gopi appeared again at my side and handed me a tube of ointment.

"Use this stuff on your bites. I found it in Baba's first aid kit."

I was deeply touched—she cared. "Thanks, Gopi."

The prescription was for a steroidal anti-itch cream and it was in the name of "Walter Plotnick."

"Avadhoot's real name is *Walter*?" I asked, trying not to laugh.

Gopi nodded. She glanced in the photographer's direction and stifled a giggle.

When she was gone, I applied the anti-itch cream over the areas where I'd been bitten, and the irritation went away almost immediately. I thought about how Gopi had gone out of her way to help me. It made me love her all the more.

Then someone shouted: "What are you doing here?"

I turned to see Anjali hurrying toward Avadhoot, lifting her sari off the ground as she ran. There was a tightness in her eyes and her brow was furrowed.

"What do you mean *what are we doing here?*" he hollered back.

"You're missing everything! They're shaving Suresh's head right now behind the cowshed. Baba's very angry!"

Having delivered the message, Anjali did an about-face and rushed back in the direction from which she had come.

As soon as she was out of earshot, Avadhoot let me have it: "You're the one who said we should set up here!"

"But that's what Gopi told me—" He didn't want to hear my excuses. As far as Avadhoot was concerned, the miscommunication was *my* fault.

Grabbing our gear, we raced to the opposite end of the ashram. By the time we arrived at the cowshed, however, the ceremony was over. We found Baba chatting with his arm around Suresh, who was now shaven-headed and dressed in white robes. Avadhoot immediately started taking pictures.

I was expecting Baba to be angry, but he greeted us with a wide grin and beaming eyes, like a proud father at his son's high school graduation. Since we had "missed everything," Arjuna and I were sent to join the rest of our group for breakfast on the riverbank while Avadhoot joined the guru and his successor for a private meal with the Acharya.

The fire in the *yagna* pit hissed and flames leapt every time Suresh made an offering.

"*Jyotiham viraja vipatmam bhusam*," he recited.

Anjali translated: "May I become a being of light, free of dust, free of stain."

Baba and His Eminence were seated on their thrones, surrounded by their respective disciples.

"After today, the person known as Suresh Bhandary will be considered dead," said our guru through Anjali. "This morning, he participates in his own funeral. Bones, skin, and all the other constituents of the physical body are symbolically offered to the fire and are burnt as they would be in cremation. Through the fire, he will be physically and mentally purified," said Baba. "His soul will be set free, even while his body is still alive."

The ceremony dragged on for hours, and the heat next to the fire pit was unbearable. Arjuna had the luxury of filming from a tripod, but I had to handhold the microphone while squatting uncomfortably on the ground the entire time. When one arm got so tired that I could no longer hold the mic, I changed hands. After an hour of this, both arms began to ache, and I asked Arjuna if I could put the mic on a stand I'd seen earlier. The cameraman agreed, but Avadhoot, who had overheard our exchange, put the kibosh on it: "No way! He has to be able to move quickly in case something unexpected happens."

Arjuna shrugged. "Whatever."

The photographer glared at Arjuna, and then, reaching out to grab him by the arm, inadvertently knocked the video camera off-kilter.

"Hey, cut it out!" Arjuna scolded, readjusting his frame. The cameraman and the photographer's testy exchange drew angry stares from Sergio and Anjali, but Baba and the Acharya appeared oblivious.

"You can't shoot from a tripod all day," Avadhoot fired back. "You should be getting different angles!"

"Why don't *you* do *your* job, and I'll do *mine?*"

"Lazy dipshit," muttered Avadhoot. Then he stomped off to the other side of the fire pit and resumed taking pictures from every conceivable angle. After a few minutes of this, Baba became annoyed with Avadhoot's conspicuous performance and sent Sergio to deal with him. The moment Avadhoot realized Baba wanted him to stop, he immediately capitulated and sat down. Within five minutes, however, he was on his feet snapping pictures again. This time, instead of constantly changing his position, he stood directly in front of Arjuna.

"Pssst, Deependra," whispered Arjuna, tapping me on the shoulder. I turned around and was face to face with the cameraman, who had abandoned his post to communicate with me as discreetly as possible. His eyes were even more bloodshot than usual. "Go tell that nutcase he's blocking my shot."

"Don't you think he knows?" I whispered back.

"Just tell him."

Avadhoot's behavior was bizarre. He and Arjuna were both here to serve the guru, yet Avadhoot appeared to be intentionally sabotaging the cameraman's work.

When I reached the photographer's position, I gave him Arjuna's message. "Avadhoot, you're standing in front of Arjuna's camera," I whispered. "He says you should move."

"You tell that lazy fuck that he was right," the cowboy said, removing the camera from his face for a second. "This *is* the best angle. I'm going to stay *right here* until the end of the ceremony."

I turned around to face Arjuna and shook my head. The cameraman didn't waste any time. Turning scarlet, he marched right over to where Avadhoot and I were standing and yanked the photographer's arm.

"Move, you psycho!"

"You move, whiny little kike!" shouted Avadhoot.

This time Baba and the Acharya heard them—even the Brahmin priests noticed. The next thing I knew Sergio was on his way over.

"Hey, Arjuna, what kind of an asshole are you?"

The cameraman's eyes widened and his mouth fell open. "*Me?* What did *I* do? *He's* the one blocking my camera."

The Italian marched right up to Arjuna until he was towering over him. "Stop complaining all the time and get back behind the camera!"

Toward the end of the ceremony, Suresh, Baba, the Acharya, and all the witnesses set off for the bank of the holy river. Arjuna and I raced ahead of them to get a shot of their arrival.

The priests recited a text from the Vedas, and the guru's future successor was immersed in the Ganga. Afterwards, one of the Acharya's disciples led Suresh to a nearby building. When he returned he was dressed in the orange robes of a swami.

"Through the fire of his spiritual practice, a *sannyasi* must burn away all his impure qualities," Baba said through Anjali. "He must remain in a state of detachment from the distractions of this world and rid himself of desire forever. He must become a perfect example to others and work continuously for the enlightenment of humanity, striving always to relieve all beings of sorrow and never to become the cause of unhappiness in others. He must become a vessel of divine light and spread it everywhere he goes. Remember these precepts always and never stray from the true path!"

Baba placed his hands on Suresh's head and uttered a blessing in Sanskrit. Then he turned to address the gathering again: "The one known as Suresh is now dead to the world. The name of the swami you see before you is Brahmananda."

I got the chills and nearly let the microphone slip from my hand. *Did the guru just say what I thought he said?* I glanced around at the other members of our party. I had heard right. Everyone was in a state of shock. Baba had just renamed his closest disciple after his very own guru.

The new Swami Brahmananda dropped to his knees and prostrated himself before Baba. The rest of us cheered: "Jai Gurudev! Jai Gurudev! Jai Gurudev!"

Our convoy arrived at the Har-ki-Pauri ghat at dusk, just as the evening *arati* was about to begin. My microphone and VTR were tethered to Arjuna's camera. He began filming the moment we got there. Worshippers mobbed the great flight of steps leading down to the river, vying for the best place to sit or stand. Some succeeded in staking out places along the river's edge, cupping water in their hands and then letting it fall back into the river.

With bamboo sticks in hand, Sergio, Brian, and Seth cleared a path for the guru and Suresh to descend to the riverbank. Sensing his greatness, no doubt, most of the pilgrims immediately made way for Baba. Some, however, were determined to touch his feet first. My job, as usual, was to keep up with Arjuna and get good sound. Trying to walk backwards down a flight of stone steps in front of the guru, with thousands of people pushing and shoving around me, was nerve-racking. But this was not nearly as frightening as working alongside Avadhoot. He was hell-bent on getting the best pictures possible, even if this meant knocking me and Arjuna over in the process.

The closer we got to the bottom of the steps, the more crowded they were with worshippers, and the more the agitation of Baba's security team increased. While the guru and his successor appeared perfectly serene in the midst of chaos, Sergio's face was pinched tight. Brian had turned purple and his neck was corded. When a man refused to move out of Baba's way, the New Zealander swatted him on the shoulder with his stick.

Of everyone in our party, Seth seemed the most out of sorts. Sweat dripped from his face, and the squiggly vein in his temple was throbbing so hard I thought he might have a stroke.

As if on cue, the music which had been blaring over the loudspeakers abruptly stopped when we arrived at the bottom of the ghat, where the steps met the river. Moments later, hand bells rang out and multi-tiered lamps were lit and waved in the direction of the holy Ganges. Under the watchful eyes of Baba's security team, Baba and Suresh folded their hands and bowed their heads in prayer. Avadhoot feverishly snapped pictures, and Arjuna filmed.

Just then, a scarecrow of a man in ragged clothes with a crazed look in his eyes cried out something in Hindi and lunged at Baba's feet. Gopi screamed. I wanted to do something to help Baba, but before I could make a move, Suresh and Baba's bodyguards sprang into action. The first to reach the aggressor was Seth. He brought his stick down so hard on the man's back I thought he might have broken it. Then Suresh, Sergio, and Brian all tried to pull the man off of the guru. Wrapping his arms around Baba's legs, the deranged man put up a good struggle. They were unable to free Baba of his desperate hold. It wasn't until Seth again brought his stick down on the man's head that he finally let go. Sergio and Brian held the man at bay as he clasped his hands together in prayer and sobbed uncontrollably. Suresh, his demeanor calm as ever, tried to speak soothingly to the man. Meanwhile, Baba appeared unfazed by the drama unfolding around him. As Avadhoot, Arjuna, and I did our best to fend off curious onlookers, Anjali and Gopi led the guru away to safety.

Suddenly, I heard Seth shout, "I'll kill you!"

I turned to see him push past Sergio and Brian to swing his stick down on the man's head. The man screamed in pain and blood spurted from a gash at his temple. He tried to shield himself from further blows, but it was no use. Seth appeared to have developed superhuman strength, managing to beat Baba's aggressor half to death before the rest of the men in our party were able to subdue him. Even then, they couldn't hold him. Like a rabid dog, Seth turned on them, whacking Suresh a few times over the head. Sergio was able to wrest the stick from his hand, and Brian knocked the wind out of him with a blow to the stomach.

While Baba's aggressor lay unconscious and bleeding on the steps of the Har-ki-Pauri ghat, Sergio and Brian continued to beat and kick Seth into submission. Minutes later, the police arrived. After conferring with witnesses, they handcuffed Seth and hauled him away.

"Savages!" he shouted, struggling to break free. "I'll kill you! I'll kill you all!"

As soon as we were back in the Acharya's ashram, Baba spoke to the members of our party in the garden: "The *kundalini-shakti* is the most powerful force in the cosmos. It has the power to impart enlightenment—or cause insanity. Some deluded disciples believe that once they receive *shaktipat*, they no longer need anything from the guru—that the guru's job is finished. They abandon the guru and try to do *sadhana* on their own terms. This is very dangerous. Only a fool abandons the guru and rejects his guidance. Only a perfected master can control the awakened *kundalini* in the disciple. This evening, you saw the results of such arrogance."

I didn't understand how, or if, the guru's words related to Seth's violent behavior. But like many of Baba's profound teachings, I would have to meditate on them before meaning revealed itself to me.

Dinner was served indoors, under harsh fluorescent lights. I ate in silence, alone, and I thought about the man that Seth attacked. He was hurt badly. Anjali and Rashmi, Baba's attendant, had taken him to a local clinic. When they returned to the ashram, they reported that the doctors said he'd be alright. I wondered what he had done to deserve such a savage beating, and how the guru could have let it happen. Then I thought about Seth. When I finished eating, I approached Avadhoot and asked if he knew what the police would do with him.

"I don't give a shit what happens to that crazy motherfucker," he answered. "He can rot in an Indian prison, for all I care. He ruined what should have been an amazing shoot!"

Overhearing my exchange with the photographer, Sergio joined in. "It's like what Baba said about the *kundalini*. Seth turned his back on the guru and couldn't handle the *shakti*. It made him *pazzo*."

"How long are the police going to hold him?" I asked.

A vicious smile crept across Sergio's face. "Oh, they're not going to *keep* him. They're going to take him to a hospital. You know, for *therapy*."

The Italian glanced at the photographer and they exchanged grins of delight.

"Yeah, right—a *mental* hospital," Avadhoot said, and both men burst out laughing.

"What about the man who attacked Baba?"

Sergio's smile grew even wider. "If he ever wakes up, he's also going to the loony bin!"

Both men let out hoots of laughter, drawing disapproving glances from the Acharya's disciples, who were still serving dinner. The two men regained their composure, and then exited the building together, sniggering on their way out.

As soon as they were gone, Brian, who had been finishing his dinner and listening in on our conversation, rose to his feet and swaggered over to me.

"You don't mention a word of this to anyone back in Ravipur, Greenbaum. Understand?" The New Zealander stared at me searchingly.

I drew in a deep breath and then released it. "Got it."

MY SECOND AND FINAL night at the Acharya's ashram was less eventful—no midnight visits from the guru or girl of my dreams. The Acharya's swamis had been apologetic over the bedbug situation. They "shifted" Poonish Davidson and me to another "clean" room. Yet despite the lack of excitement and promise of a bite-free night, it took me ages to fall asleep.

Doubts haunted me. I was deeply troubled that Seth—a psychologist, no less—had gone off the deep end, practically beating a man to death. It also upset me that Baba's people didn't seem to care or want to do anything to help him. I thought about suggesting we help Seth find a lawyer or contact the American Embassy in Delhi, but held back. I didn't dare anger Sergio and Avadhoot. Instead, I convinced myself that Seth had let the guru down and had brought whatever happened to him on himself. He was on his own.

After trying for what seemed like hours to lull myself to sleep through repetition of the mantra, I finally gave up and allowed my thoughts to turn to Gopi. In my mind's eye I visualized her long golden hair and her mismatched emerald and sapphire eyes. I tried to imagine what it would feel like to have her all to myself, far away from the ashram, in a safe place, like my hotel room at the Taj. I fantasized about kissing her full lips and caressing her bare breasts—about doing everything with her without the fear of disobeying the guru's command or breaking any rules. I'm not sure what time it was, but I eventually drifted off to sleep sometime before dawn, without giving in to any impure urges.

23.

THE REAL JOB OF THE GURU

THE NEWS THAT BABA had named his future successor after his own guru reached Ravipur before us. It was all anyone wanted to talk about in the ashram. Wherever I went, a different theory was being discussed. The most common was that Suresh was actually the reincarnation of Gurudev Brahmananda, who had passed away only a year before he was born. Others held that by distinguishing the young man in this way, Baba was lending him the gravitas he would need to carry the lineage forward after Baba was gone.

Arjuna Weinberg was already on a flight back to Birchwood Falls with video footage and photo negatives from the *Punyatithi* celebrations and the guru's pilgrimage to Haridwar. Kriyadevi would be editing the highlights into a "newsreel," and the pictures would be featured in the next edition of *Raja Path* magazine. Soon the big news would be making waves in Raja Yoga centers and ashrams all over the world.

Everyone I spoke to asked me about the pilgrimage. "Extraordinary," I would tell them, or else, "It was sublime." I never breathed a word about the disturbing incident with Seth and nobody seemed to miss him. It was as if he had never existed. The only person to notice he hadn't come back with the group was Namdev Loman. When he asked me where Seth was, I was forced to lie.

"He was puking his brains out in Haridwar," I told him. "I think it was something he ate. Or maybe it was altitude sickness. I'm not sure."

Namdev scratched his head and wrinkled his brow. "Altitude sickness? Well, where is he now? In a hospital in Haridwar?"

"Um ... ah ... Repatriated."

"What?"

"He was *repatriated*. Sent back to the States for treatment."

I knew that *he* knew I wasn't being truthful. But instead of feeling bad about lying, a strange thing happened: my heart hardened with self-importance. I got a thrill out of withholding information and being trusted with one of the guru's secrets. I felt *special*.

This feeling of specialness, however, didn't last long. I had wrongly assumed that I'd be considered an official member of Baba's tour staff, sharing an air-conditioned room with Poonish Davidson and Stephen Ames in S*hanti Shayanagrih*. Instead I found myself back in my old room with Claus the snoring German, and sharing a bathroom with a dozen other men. But that wasn't the worst of it. With Arjuna on his way back to the States and no need at the moment for extra security, I was sent back to do *seva* in Housekeeping and the dish room.

After the honor of being included in the guru's entourage, cleaning toilets again was humiliating. Why had Baba drawn me in only to cast me back out? I wondered if I'd done something wrong? I asked Sergio if my return to Housekeeping was only temporary. He looked at me like it was the most absurd question he had ever heard.

"*Why*? What kind of *seva* do you think you *should* be doing?"

My face burned with embarrassment. *Sergio thinks I'm a bad disciple, that I don't know how to surrender to the guru's will.*

"I'm not sure—it's just that you said before, that I work for Baba now—"

Sergio chuckled and waved a hand dismissively. "Sita's in charge of *seva*, not me."

Nothing made sense. Baba had visited me in my room after lights out. A *darshan* girl had confided in me and let me kiss her on the head. I kept a secret! Didn't Sergio realize I was a VIP?

Anger and frustration swirled inside me. As I mopped up splattered shit from the tiled floors of the public restrooms, there was a pounding in my ears and my vision became clouded by rage. On my breaks I sat in the meditation cave, but was unable to enter into a meditative state. I was too distracted by thoughts of how unjust my situation was. *The guru's working on your ego,* I tried to reassure myself. *This is good for you!* But it was no use.

I knew the guru was testing me, but I didn't know how to pass his test. I needed help, and confided in Akhandananda. I found the neckless swami eating dinner alone at the back of the Prasad pavilion.

"It's a bitter pill to swallow, my boy, but it's for your own good."

"But why would Sergio tell me that I work for Baba now, only to send me back to doing the lowest *seva* in the ashram?"

Anger flashed across the swami's face. "Everybody in the ashram works for the guru, young man. There's no such thing as a lowly *seva*. Instead of complaining, you should be full of gratitude that you have an opportunity to serve him at all."

Tears welled behind my eyes. "I know…"

Akhandananda's expression softened. He reached for my hand and squeezed it gently. "There, there, Deependra. This is a good thing. You're *burning*. That's all."

"What does that mean?"

"Your ego, my boy. This is the way the guru rids you of it. The ego is just a collection of negative ways of thinking about yourself and reacting to the world. In Raja Yoga we call these tendencies *samskaras*. The guru is burning them away."

I swallowed hard and held back tears. I pulled my hand away from the swami's and wiped my eyes with my napkin. "I am grateful, Swamiji. It's just that I feel like I've let Baba down somehow..."

"That's just the ego talking, son. Let it go. Remember why you came to the ashram in the first place. Was it to work in the Audiovisual department, or to know God?"

As I plodded back to my dormitory I realized the swami was right, as always. I remembered the vial of Baba's bathtub water that Sita had given me back in Birchwood Falls. If ever there was a time when I could use some extra blessings from the guru, it was now. I found the little bottle in my locker, next to my traveler's checks and a stack of rupees. I prayed to Baba to help me have right understanding and to accept my new situation. Then I carefully unscrewed the lid, poured a few drops of the precious liquid into the palm of my hand, and licked it off. Moments later, the *kundalini* bubbled and popped in my heart center and throat. I immediately felt lighter and my head began to clear.

That night, Swami Brahmananda—as we now called Suresh—gave his first public talk as Baba's future successor. He addressed the audience from a podium, while Baba sat behind him on his throne. He spoke in English, and this time Anjali translated to Hindi for the Indian devotees.

"When we first meet the guru our motives are very pure. We come to the ashram to chant, to meditate, and to turn within. But after a while we begin to slip back into our old patterns of thinking, and the ego reasserts itself. In the ashram, even in the company of a saint like Baba, we begin to crave status and recognition. We pursue romantic relationships and treat the ashram like a social club. But we are not in the ashram to find a husband or a wife, or to have an important *seva*."

Everybody laughed. I glanced at Gopi, who was seated up front. She was giving Suresh her full attention. Then

Suresh looked in my direction. Heat flushed through my body. Had Akhandananda spoken to Baba or the guru's future successor about me? Was he giving this sermon just for me?

"When we start thinking this way," Suresh continued, "we lose sight of why we came here in the first place. Instead of serving the guru with a pure heart, all we think about is how near we are sitting to Baba at *darshan,* or how we can get a better *seva*—one closer to the guru. But having daily contact with the physical guru is pointless unless we have cultivated a relationship with the *inner guru.* If we give up our life outside only to transform the ashram into the world through our *wrong understanding,* our *sadhana* will be fruitless.

"As it says in the *Shiva Sutras,* 'The guru is not an individual. The guru is the grace bestowing power of God flowing through an individual.' This power manifests as the physical guru, but also as the very circumstances of our life. We call this divine force *the guru principle.* It always has a message to help us evolve, and it is our task to recognize and listen to that message.

"The guru principle builds up our ego, only to knock it down again. Until high and low, and praise and blame have become one and the same for us, we will never reach the goal.

"The job of the guru is not to hold our hand, look lovingly into our eyes, and tell us what a wonderful disciple we are." Everybody laughed again. "The real job of the guru is to insult the disciple."

My feelings of embarrassment subsided and I was in awe of Suresh. Clearly, Akhandananda hadn't spoken to him about me. There wouldn't have been a reason to. The guru principle was already working through him, and speaking directly to me, reminding me of the real reason I had come to the ashram. I was not here to marry Gopi, or to become an important person in the ashram hierarchy. I was here to become a swami.

In any case, Suresh's talk had put me at ease. I was able to meditate again, and while I cleaned the toilets I joyfully reminded myself that I was burning away lifetimes of evil karma and negative *samskaras*. I vowed inwardly never again to think romantically about Gopi. If Baba's closest disciples chose to entertain romantic fantasies and lead impure lives, so be it. I was a *true* disciple, even if I sat at the back of the hall.

THE DATE OF BABA'S return to the States was just around the corner. I'd been in India nine months already, and had three months left on my entry visa. It was time for me to ask Baba if I should accompany him back to Birchwood Falls or renew my visa for another year. I wanted nothing more than to be with the guru at all times, but the decision wasn't up to me.

When it was my turn to go before the guru at *darshan*, he was in a lively conversation with Avadhoot, who was seated at his feet. Avadhoot was speaking in English, Anjali was translating. "You are giving Raju too many sweets," Baba was saying. "They are not good for him."

"Yes, Baba," Avadhoot said.

"Sweets should only be given to an elephant occasionally. As a reward, or to motivate him. Not every time. You understand?"

"Of course, Baba."

I bowed down to Baba, and I hoped to catch his eye, but he was looking away. This didn't surprise me. The guru had been completely ignoring me ever since we got back from Haridwar. Remaining on my knees before him, I signaled to Anjali that I needed to speak to him. Just as I was about to open my mouth, Baba turned his head and glared at me.

"What do *you* want?"

"I would like to go back to the States with you."

The guru turned to Anjali and spoke to her in Hindi for much longer than it should have taken to translate an answer to my simple request. Feelings of inadequacy swirled inside me, and I had an empty feeling in the pit of my stomach. Then the guru spoke to Avadhoot in Hindi.

The photographer kept glancing at me and frowning. I thought maybe I was getting a performance review, and was glad I couldn't understand what they were saying. I prayed: *Please, please don't send me back into the world.*

"Baba says you should return to America with him," Anjali finally translated. "He wants Arjuna Weinberg to teach you how to use the camera."

I was breathless. *Did I hear correctly?*

"But Baba—"Avadhoot interrupted, switching to English. "Arjuna is a terrible cameraman. How can he teach what he doesn't know?"

Eying the photographer disapprovingly, Anjali translated his words for the guru. "Baba says you should *also* teach him."

Avadhoot switched back to Hindi and said something that made the guru laugh.

Anjali turned back to me. "Talk to Gajendra Williams. He will arrange it."

With a wave of his hand, the guru dismissed me. I was ecstatic. I thought I might float up into the sky. Not only was Baba sending me back to the Audiovisual department, he had arranged for me to be trained as a cameraman. This could mean only one thing: he wanted me to go on tour with him!

As I stood up to leave, I noticed Gopi was looking in my direction. She winked and beamed an enormous smile at me. I winked back. *Maybe the guru intends for me to marry the angel after all!*

The day before our departure, Indira St. John came by my room. She told me that Stephen Ames needed to talk to me, and that I should report to him in the Audiovisual office immediately. I found him in a small room off the courtyard, crammed with audio mixers, microphones, cables, and recording devices. He was seated at a long table cluttered with equipment and paperwork. He was tinkering with a consumer tape recorder. The monster TEAC reel-to-reel tape recorder I'd brought to India for the ashram was on the table next to it.

"You need me to take the TEAC back with me to New York tomorrow, don't you?" I said, remembering that the customs agent in the Bombay airport had written down the machine's make and serial number and stamped "to be returned" in my passport.

Stephen shook his head and smiled. "Nope. The reel-to-reel is staying here." He held up the consumer tape recorder he was fiddling with. "You're taking this sucker here."

I was confused. "What about the stamp in my passport?"

"Not to worry, my friend," said Stephen, wiggling his head and speaking in a fake Indian accent. He picked up the tape recorder and handed it to me. "Take a look."

I studied the device, but didn't find anything noteworthy. "What am I supposed to see?"

A smile spread across Stephen's thin, colorless lips. "That's just it. You *don't* see anything. I removed the old Panasonic logo and serial number, and replaced it with a TEAC logo and the serial number from the reel-to-reel you brought here with you last fall. The art department made the new logo. It's perfect!"

I was impressed with Stephen's ingenuity, but got a sinking feeling. "What happens if customs realizes that I'm carrying the wrong piece of equipment?"

Stephen laughed. "Relax. They're too stupid to figure it out. Even if they do—which they won't—we know how to take care of these things. Just stay close to me at the airport."

Dejected and confused, I trudged to Prasad for dinner. I tried not to worry about the trouble I might get into at the airport, but still, I didn't feel comfortable being asked to do illegal things. *This is yet another test from Baba*, I told myself. *It doesn't matter if I get caught. My motive is pure. The guru's grace will protect me.*

"Deependra, wait up!"

I turned to see Namdev Loman hurrying down a garden path in my direction. He was too thin. His long yellow hair was dirty and matted, and his eyes were tired, as if he hadn't slept in days. He was barefoot and carrying a chainsaw.

"One of these days you're going to cut your foot off with that thing."

Glancing down at the saw, Namdev shrugged.

I invited him to join me at Prasad for dinner. "My treat."

"Okay, but let's eat at the chai shop across the street from the ashram," Namdev said. "The two of us can eat there like kings for under a dollar."

Soon after we ordered our food, I understood that my friend had another reason for not wanting to eat at Prasad. He wanted answers about what had really happened to Seth.

"The rumor is he was deported after spending a few weeks in jail," said Namdev. "Is it true?"

"Sounds like you know a lot more about it than I do."

Namdev regarded me suspiciously. "But you were there. Did he really beat some Indian guy half to death?"

I remained silent. The muscles in my upper back and neck tightened. I was determined neither to confirm nor deny the story. I took a sip of my Indian cola through a cracked plastic straw.

"Well, did he or didn't he?"

"I don't know anything about it."

Namdev shook his head. "You've turned into one of *them*."

"One of who? What are you saying?"

He lifted his chin to look down his nose at me. "Like the people on Baba's tour staff. Full of secrets."

"Look, Namdev—you know gossiping is against the rules. I'm not here to satisfy your petty curiosity."

Just then, the waiter shuffled out of the kitchen and set our food on the table. When he was gone I changed the subject. "How's your *seva* at the generator plant?"

"Sucks," Namdev said, devouring his food like a starving animal. "But that's not all I'm doing. They also have me working in the garden, washing vegetables, and making the chai in the morning. I have to be in the kitchen by three am every day, and I don't get off until ten at night."

"I used to have a schedule like that until I spoke to Baba about it. He made Sita give me fewer hours."

"Of course he did. But you're not on staff."

"Um—not technically, no." I answered. "I pay for room and board."

"Yeah, well if you're on staff they make you do a lot more *seva*. All I do is work—seven days a week, nineteen hours a day. When I first got here, I had time to meditate and go to the chants. Not anymore."

"Think of all the negative karma you're burning."

Namdev sniggered. "Everybody on staff gets a stipend but me."

"Maybe there's a message in that."

Namdev narrowed his eyes and pinched his face into a knot. "Fuck you, Deependra."

"Look, if you're so unhappy here, maybe you should go back to the States—to Ithaca. Maybe you can get your old job back at Collegetown Bagels."

We ate the rest of our food in silence. I asked for the check and paid. As we crossed the street to return to the ashram, Namdev spoke again. "You know, a lot of people were disappointed when Baba chose Suresh as his successor. They say it should have been his sister."

I didn't respond.

"Some people—especially the women—are saying that Baba is sexist."

Anger burned like acid in the bottom my stomach. I had nothing but contempt for the so-called devotees who tried to second-guess the guru or were critical of him.

"Whoever said that should be booted out of Raja Yoga!"

I didn't want to be having this conversation inside the walls of the ashram, so I waited for Namdev to finish speaking his piece before stepping through the gate.

"Some of the Western senior swamis are also wondering why Baba passed them up for someone so young and inexperienced. He's only nineteen!"

"First of all, what does that even mean: *inexperienced?* You're either enlightened or you're not. It's got nothing to do with age. Secondly, I don't believe any of Baba's swamis would say that. If you're going to spread rumors, at least give me a name."

Namdev laughed bitterly. "You'd be surprised."

MORE THAN HALF OF the Westerners living in Ravipur left with Baba on his flight to New York. The ashram staff would be reduced to a skeleton crew until Baba returned to India, two years later. Only hardcore devotees would be staying on. The list included Brian Pettigrew, Rohini Brinkerhoff, Indira St. John, the swami doctor Nirmalananda, and, of course, Namdev Loman. I was grateful I wasn't on it. And to be honest, I was looking forward to getting out of India for a while. The place was getting exhausting.

As a newly trained cameraman, I expected to travel with Baba on his next world tour. After spending the summer in Birchwood Falls, I'd follow Baba out west to Berkeley, California, where he'd be spending several months in his newly renovated ashram. Afterwards, it would be on to London, Paris, Munich, and Barcelona, and then continuing on to New Zealand and Australia.

I realized that flitting all over the globe with Baba would be expensive—it would eat through my inheritance fast. But who was keeping track? I really believed that through the grace of the guru, I would never run out of money. As far as I was concerned, my money was Baba's money, even if to my unenlightened mind it appeared to come from a different bank account. For this reason, I told myself it didn't matter that I was still expected to pay rent and my own travel expenses. I was now a member of the guru's entourage—part of his immediate family.

The truth was, even though I'd spent relatively little up until that point, I had stopped reading my bank statements. So I didn't have a clear idea of how much I had left. The tiny part of me that was still in touch with reality was afraid to look.

24.
A Divine Plan

STEPHEN AMES HAD BEEN right: I was able to leave India with the fake TEAC. The customs agents at the Bombay airport hardly glanced at it before waving me on. I took this as a message from the guru principle that my anxiety had been for nothing.

As I stepped off the plane into the International Arrivals hall at JFK, it felt good to be back home in the States. I realized how much I'd missed the moderate climate of my native land, and the simple things I used to take for granted, like flush toilets and hot showers. At the same time, I had the oddest sensation that I was not merely returning home from another continent, but was an interdimensional traveler arriving back on earth after visiting a higher realm of existence. My stay in India already seemed as though it had taken place long ago in the distant past.

In a spiritual sense, I'd grown tremendously in India, but my stay in the Ravipur ashram had also opened my earthly eyes: I still had so much to learn about fashion. At the first opportunity, I wanted to visit Manhattan with Poonish Davidson. We had a lot of shopping to do!

When we arrived in Birchwood Falls, the ashram was packed with devotees. There were at least twice as many people waiting in the lobby to greet Baba as there had been the day I first met him. Some of faces were familiar, many others I'd never seen before. Devotees had come from all over the New York City area and beyond to greet their beloved guru. I was surprised that Jeremy and Carrie were not among them.

Mentally preparing myself to accept with gratitude whatever accommodations were offered to me, I was overjoyed to find I'd be sharing a room with Poonish and Stephen. I was less excited, however, when I realized that we hadn't been assigned to the VIP dormitory next to Baba's house, with all the swamis, *darshan* girls, and senior members of Baba's staff. I was back in a room in S*hiva Shayanagrih*, where I'd been housed the year before. On the plus side, our room had only three beds. This meant I wouldn't be forced to share it with year-round Birchwood Falls residents or weekend visitors, whom I now considered a lower class of *Raja Yogis*.

Poonish, Stephen, and I had a good laugh when I told them about the mysterious spoon that Shivadas, my old roommate, used to keep on top of the toilet tank in the bathroom. They had both lived in Raja Yoga ashrams much longer than I had, but were just as clueless about what it might be used for.

Although happy to be roommates with other VIPs, and excited to be working in the Audiovisual department again, I was irked by the name tag requirement at the Birchwood Falls ashram. Despite the fact that I was now a de facto member of Baba's tour, because I paid rent I was technically still considered a "guest." As such, I could be identified by the green sticker in the upper left-hand corner of my badge. (Year-round residents had red stickers, and those on tour with Baba had orange.) This meant that I'd have to go to the end of the line at meal times, and during public programs I'd be seated with the ordinary devotees, instead of closer to the front with the rest of the important people. I hated wearing the green sticker, but reminded myself that whatever I experienced in the ashram was the will of the guru and an opportunity to rid myself of ego.

I'd written to Melanie and Jeremy as soon as I found out I'd be returning to the States, but by the time I reached them by phone, neither had yet received my letters. They were surprised to hear from me and to learn I was already back. The conversation with my older sister was predictable. She wanted me to come home to Ithaca for a visit. I explained that the timing wasn't right. I promised to come as soon as I could get away. She also urged me again to consider going back to school. The call with Jeremy, on the other hand, didn't go at all as I expected. He was happy to hear from me, but said that he and Carrie had no immediate plans to visit the ashram.

"My residency is extremely demanding," he said. "I've got virtually no free time. You should come out to Long Island to see us."

"Don't you want to see Baba?" I asked in disbelief. "He's going to be in Birchwood Falls until September, and then I'm going with him out to California."

My question was followed by an uncomfortably long silence. "We can talk about Baba when you visit," he finally said.

My spirits began to deflate like a balloon. His evasiveness said everything: my brother had left Raja Yoga. He was no longer a devotee.

"Have you thought at all about going back to college?" he asked.

I felt betrayed. Anger rose up inside of me. "*I* live to serve the guru." I scoffed. "I'll go back to school if and when Baba commands it."

I suddenly felt depressed. I told Jeremy I'd let him know when I might be able to visit, but I had no intention of ever calling or seeing him again. I did *not* want to "talk about Baba." I had no interest in hearing anything negative my brother might have to say about Raja Yoga, or why he no longer wanted to visit the ashram. I slammed the payphone receiver down with a loud clang.

How is it possible that the very people who introduced me to the guru have now turned their backs on him? It was unthinkable.

The next day I reported to Jake Gooding in the Audiovisual department. My main duties were logging tapes, assisting on shoots, and monitoring the sound in the control room during Baba's talks. But because the guru had commanded that I learn how to operate the camera, Arjuna Weinberg and Avadhoot Plotnick devoted a couple of hours each day to giving me lessons.

Arjuna held up a white card and asked me to zoom in on it. "It's essential to white balance the camera every time you find yourself in a new lighting situation," he said. "Especially when you move from indoors to outdoors."

I pushed a button under the lens of the camera and a second later the words "AWB OK" flashed on the screen.

I removed my eye from the viewfinder to see Avadhoot frowning, his arms folded over his chest. "So, you're telling the kid that every time Baba changes location in the middle of a shot he has to adjust his color?"

Arjuna cleared his throat. "Well, yes. Some white balance problems are almost impossible to fix in post. For example—"

Avadhoot's jaw line hardened and he moved his hands to his hips. "What about the once-in-a-lifetime moment he's going to miss while he's looking for someone to hold up a white card?"

Arjuna exhaled in exasperation and he threw up his hands. "Well, if that once-in-a-lifetime moment is totally blue because he didn't adjust his white balance, what good is it?"

As Avadhoot contradicted everything Arjuna tried to teach me about setting up the camera, I wondered if we'd ever get out of the office for an actual lesson on camera technique.

"You see, Deependra?" Avadhoot said, turning to me in disgust. "This is a perfect example of wrong understanding. You and me only care about getting the best possible shot of the guru. All Arjuna cares about is good color."

By the end of my first lesson, I understood that Avadhoot had nothing to teach me about the technical operation of a video camera. He was a good photographer, but he only *thought* he was an expert on everything else. To make matters worse, his constant interruptions of Arjuna—who actually *did* know what he was talking about—made it almost impossible for me to learn anything useful. Even if Avadhoot did know a lot about frame composition and lighting, his teaching style was unbearable. When lessons were in the office, he'd speak in a loud booming voice, as if he were in a lecture hall with a huge audience. He'd constantly glance around the room to see if everybody else who happened to be there was listening. If they weren't, he'd interrupt whatever they were doing to quiz them. If they resisted, he'd badger them until they paid attention to him, or left. If I didn't immediately grasp whatever he was trying to teach me, he'd fly off the handle and insult me—or Arjuna, for "confusing" me.

Worst of all, some days I never even got a chance to take the camera out of its case. Instead, Avadhoot would spend hours showing me proofs and books of his own work—not only of Baba, but pictures he'd taken as a freelance photographer in Hollywood and for *Life* magazine. I'd try in vain to steer the conversation back to cinematography, but it was as if he didn't hear me.

"It's a beautiful day, Avadhoot," I once said when I was desperate to get out of the office. "Do you think we could go outside and practice with Baba's dogs?"

"Oh, wait!" the photographer said. Oblivious to my request, he opened another album he'd taken from his room to show me. "You have to see these amazing pictures I took of John Travolta and Olivia Newton-John on the set of *Grease*. You won't believe it!"

Whenever Arjuna reminded Avadhoot that they were supposed to be teaching me how to operate the camera, the photographer would curse him out: "Shut the fuck up, Arjuna! What did you ever do outside the ashram that anybody cares about?"

As insufferable as Avadhoot was, Arjuna wasn't always the easiest person to be around either. He was not only a crank, but a hypochondriac, constantly complaining about how he was "allergic to something in the ashram." Yet despite how annoying the cameraman was, it was hard for me to understand why Avadhoot was so contemptuous of him.

"Arjuna has a huge ego," Avadhoot said once when we were alone together in the office after one of my lessons. "Thinks he knows everything."

"Why do you say that?" I asked.

Avadhoot peeled his eyes away from a contact sheet he was studying and stared at me with an irritated look on his face. "You never noticed how that little fucker always needs to be right?"

From time to time, I got a break from the constant bickering between my two teachers by sitting in on editing sessions with Kriyadevi Friedman. She was a graduate of New York University's film school and had worked in TV before coming to the ashram. She taught me everything I needed to know about things like headroom, screen direction, establishing shots, the proper length of cutaways, and the importance of letting the subject leave the frame before terminating a shot.

But there was no doubt about it, Kriyadevi was an odd character. It was hard for me to understand why she chose to wear rags out of the ashram free box instead of spending her stipend money on new clothes. She seemed oblivious to the fact that all the women closest to Baba paid careful attention to their appearance and strove to make themselves as beautiful as possible. It irritated me that she wore baggy, ill-fitting clothes and ugly glasses that were too big for her face. And her hair was a disaster! I'd never seen her do anything with it other than pull it back into a messy ponytail. From what she told me, the guru had given her a clear message: she wasn't feminine enough. Yet she chose to ignore him. I was embarrassed for her.

"Wouldn't you rather be a cameraman than an editor, so you could travel with Baba?" I once asked her.

"I love my *seva*," Kriyadevi said. "I get to spend all my time with the guru right here in the editing room. Besides, Baba says carrying a heavy video camera around is no job for a woman," she chuckled. "Once, when I had to cover for Arjuna, Baba saw the camera on my shoulder and got angry. He said it made me look even less feminine than usual!"

"Didn't it upset you when he said that?"

The editor arched a single eyebrow and touched her fingertips together, forming a steeple. "The guru is always working on us, Deependra. The things we most need to hear from him don't usually come sugarcoated."

I bristled. Who was she to tell me this? Did she think I was still a newcomer? I changed the subject. "Avadhoot doesn't think Arjuna is a very good cameraman. What do you think?"

"It doesn't matter what I or anybody else thinks. Baba says he's excellent."

I didn't know enough about cinematography yet to be able to judge Arjuna's ability for myself, but one thing I'd noticed about his images was that they always made the guru look taller and even more imposing than he was in real life. I asked her how Arjuna was able to accomplish this.

"That's a good question," she said, rubbing her chin. "I never thought about it." Then her eyes twinkled with amusement and she smiled brightly. "I don't think Arjuna does it on purpose. I think it's because he's so short!"

"What do you mean?"

"He's always shooting Baba from a low angle."

"Of course!"

Then something occurred to me: I wanted Baba to think I was an excellent cameraman, too. I made a mental note to crouch whenever I filmed him.

Despite Avadhoot's constant distractions, by the middle of the summer I was shooting video like a professional. This prompted Jake to requisition a second camera to be used to film audience reactions during Baba's talks. When it arrived, it was time to put my training to the test. Both the old and the new camera were set up in the hall, wired to video monitors and a mixer in the control room located at the back of the hall. Jake functioned like a live TV director and was able to communicate with Arjuna and me through intercom headsets. The mixer enabled him to cut, dissolve, and wipe between our two cameras with the flip of a switch. The output was simultaneously recorded on a VTR in the control room and fed to a closed circuit television in the dining hall for overflow crowds on weekends.

In the beginning, Jake played it safe: while *camera one* (Arjuna's camera) was *live* and trained on Baba, Jake had *camera two* (my camera) pan the audience in search of people who looked particularly attentive, or who were having strong emotional reactions. Once he found what he was looking for, he'd cut from the output of Arjuna's camera to my camera for a few seconds before cutting back to the main action. After a couple of weeks of this, Jake was confident enough in my abilities to let me switch places with Arjuna.

"Stay wide as Baba enters the hall, *camera one*," Jake said over my headset. I followed the guru with my camera as he made his way down the center aisle toward his throne. My camera jerked slightly and my heart began to pound. This was my big chance to prove myself and I was already screwing up.

"Steady, *camera one*, steady. You want *fluid* movements. As Baba sits down you should start to zoom out until your shot includes Anjali in the frame."

I held my breath, carrying out Jake's directions as smoothly as possible. Meanwhile, he told Arjuna to get a wide shot of the entire hall, which was full to capacity.

"Pull all the way back, *camera two*," came Jake's voice over my headset. He was addressing Arjuna, but the intercom was set up so that both of us heard everything Jake said and knew what the other cameraman was doing at all times.

"What is the difference between extraordinary beings and ordinary beings?" began Baba. "Extraordinary beings have received the grace of the guru, and have dedicated their lives to spiritual practice. Ordinary beings, on the other hand, lead empty, meaningless lives, squandering their existence in the pursuit of sense pleasures and material possessions."

"Take *camera two*," came Jake's voice over my headset. "*Camera one*, zoom in on Baba's face. Let's see some of that fire in Baba's eyes."

"During the day they stuff their faces with delicious food, leaving an endless stream of waste behind them. At night they rub their bodies against each other and lose all of their vitality."

"*Camera two*, get a close up of that big fat guy with the pasty complexion."

"In the end they are nothing but feces factories," Baba continued.

"Perfect! Beautiful!" Jake said.

"An extraordinary being is a practitioner of Raja Yoga. Raja Yogis put the precious gift of this human body and the grace of the guru to the best possible use. They lead selfless lives of service to the guru's mission, and strive to attain God-realization—the highest goal of human existence. Sometimes, however, the behavior of extraordinary beings can be worse than the behavior of ordinary beings." The audience laughed. "These people bring all their negative tendencies with them from the world into the ashram. But the ashram is not a luxury resort, or a social club. It is a sacred place of spiritual practice.

The swamis and staff should not be eating every meal in Prasad. The café is for visitors and newcomers who are unable to survive more than a few hours without delicious food in their mouths." Everybody laughed again. "The dining hall food is pure and nutritious. The meals are planned to give maximum benefit to health, and to facilitate your spiritual growth."

"Pan over to Anjali when she begins to translate, *camera one*," Jake said. By that point, I was so absorbed in Baba's talk that I forgot that *I* was on *camera one*, and at first I didn't respond to Jake's direction. "*Camera one? Are you awake?... Deependra?*"

"Sorry!" I blurted out, beginning my pan too abruptly. My outburst caused some audience members in my immediately vicinity to jerk their heads toward me and glare.

"Easy, Deependra," Jake said. "Take it nice and smooth."

"In Raja Yoga, the guru is like the sun. The sun shines on everything and everyone without discrimination. In the same way, the guru bestows his grace equally upon everyone with whom he comes in contact, but only those who open their hearts to him fully can receive it. Moreover, only those disciples who serve him faithfully and follow his every command can contain it. For example, many people on staff have fallen into bad habits. They think that they are in the ashram only to perform *seva* and to go to *darshan*. They no longer attend the meditation sessions or the chants." The guru paused a moment and directed his gaze toward the people at his feet. "Did you hear me, Sergio?"

"Yes, Baba," the Italian replied. "I'll see that everybody meditates and goes to the *Guru Gita*."

"That's very good, Sergio, but I'm talking about *you*." Everybody cracked up and the Italian turned red. It was the first time I'd ever seen Sergio look embarrassed. "You too, Avadhoot." The audience laughed even harder.

The photographer rose to his feet. "I'll be at every chant, Baba!"

The guru motioned for Avadhoot to sit back down. "You know, some people in the ashram think that Avadhoot is not very spiritual." Again the hall erupted in laughter. "People wonder what such a crazy man is doing here." Now I was laughing, too.

"Pan the audience *camera two*," Jake said. "These reactions are great!"

"But what people don't know about Avadhoot is that his heart is the purest of the pure."

"Get a close-up of Avadhoot, *camera one*," Jake said. "Close down a little, focus...take *camera one*."

"His devotion knows no bounds. He would do *anything* for the guru. Such dedication and loyalty are extremely rare."

Avadhoot's face filled my viewfinder screen. Tears streamed down his face and his lower lip was quivering.

"Nice work, *camera one*," Jake said.

Avadhoot wiped the tears from his eyes with his sleeve, and then continued to bawl.

"Thanks," I whispered into the microphone on my headset.

"Okay, boys," Jake said. "It sounds like Baba is wrapping it up. *Camera one*, pan back to Baba, and then slowly pull out to include Anjali in the shot again."

"I bow to God within each and every one of you. Jai Gurudev!"

Jake gave me a big pat on the back when I returned to the control room with my gear. "Good job, *camera one!*"

My heart swelled at his praise. The time and effort the guru had invested to teach me how to operate the camera had clearly paid off. I was certain the Omniscient One was also pleased with me.

Arjuna was putting away his equipment. Jake turned to him and smiled encouragingly. "You got some great reaction shots too, by the way."

"Gee, thanks, Jake," Arjuna said. His tone was sarcastic. "I've only been a professional cameraman for the past ten years."

I collected the rest of the gear, and then labeled and shelved the cassettes. By the time I returned for *darshan*, the line, which usually extended all the way to the lower lobby, was much shorter. As I inched closer to the throne, I made every effort to clear my mind of prideful thoughts. Instead, I filled it with the pure aspiration to be forever of service to Baba.

I bowed before the guru and he bopped me on the back with his wand of peacock feathers. Then he tapped me again on the top of my head. I was about to stand up to face him when he brought the feathers down on my back again and let them rest there. As he held me in place with his wand, I froze, and the entire *darshan* line came to a halt. The *kundalini* energy at the base of my spine began to stir.

Then a wave of bliss washed over me. When Baba finally released me and I stood up again, he was gazing deeply into my eyes, as if he were taking stock of me. From the blank expression on his face, I was unable to tell whether he was pleased or unhappy.

Then he spoke. "After the summer, you must go," Anjali translated. "You must go to school."

I was too stunned to respond. "But Baba—" I croaked.

"This is what's best for you." The guru's face was a mask of dispassion. He dismissed me with a wiggle of his head and a discreet movement of his hand. As I staggered away from the *darshan* line, I caught Gopi's eye. She looked sad for me, and I felt the prick of tears behind my eyelids. *Did she know this was coming?* I wondered. *Why go through all the trouble of training me on the camera only to send me back into the world?*

"Deependra," called Anjali from behind me. I did an about-face and hurried back to Baba's side. I expected the guru to speak to me again, but he was greeting others, seemingly oblivious to my presence. Anjali motioned for me to kneel down next to her. "Baba wants you to make movies for him someday. He wants you to go to the same college as Kriyadevi to study filmmaking."

The additional information made me feel a little better.

"Please tell Baba I will do whatever he asks."

Anjali winked and smiled broadly so that a single dimple formed on her right cheek. "He knows."

"Movies," said the guru in English, causing me to turn my head toward him. He was staring down at me. "You will make movies for Baba. Talk to Kriyadevi."

The guru was not simply casting me out. He had a divine plan for me!

25.
CONFIDENTIAL

THE IDEA OF GOING back to school—even film school—and having to fend for myself out in the world was terrifying, but I had to be brave. The guru had given me a command and I didn't want to waste any time in fulfilling it.

Immediately after *darshan,* I set off to find Kriyadevi Friedman. I looked in the cafeteria, but didn't see her. I peeked in Prasad, but after what Baba had said during his talk about the staff eating there too often, she was the last person I expected to find there. I was right—the place was virtually empty. Even the visitors were eating in the dining hall tonight. The only people in the café were Sergio, Avadhoot, and Baba's Indian attendant Rashmi. I marveled at their privileged position in the ashram. I tried to imagine being so close to the guru that his edicts didn't even apply.

Skipping dinner, I went down to the basement in search of Kriyadevi in the Audiovisual office. I found her in the editing room, working on a newsreel.

"Baba is sending me back into the world," I told her. "He wants me to study filmmaking."

"That's great news! Why so glum?"

"I don't want to live in the world. I don't want to associate with ordinary people."

Kriyadevi shook her head and laughed. "Isn't it obvious? The guru's trying to destabilize your ego."

"How so?"

"By sending you back into the world, he's forcing you to confront your insecurities head on. Fear is just another manifestation of ego."

I knew she was right, but the intellectual knowledge of this didn't make me any less afraid. I felt infinitesimally small at the thought of having to find a place to live, going grocery shopping, and having to prepare meals for myself. I was also afraid I'd be lonely.

When I told Kriyadevi that Baba had commanded me to speak to her about school, she understood immediately that the guru wanted me to go to New York University Tisch School of Film and Television, where she had gone. She told me all about the program and how I could apply.

"You'll need to send them your high school and Cornell transcript."

A feeling of hopelessness came over me. "NYU sounds great, but I'll never get in." I explained how I'd blown off my last year of high school, and flunked out of college. "I haven't got a prayer."

"Nonsense, Deependra. Of course you'll get in! If NYU is where the guru wants you to go to school, NYU is where you will go. With Baba's grace behind you, you can't go wrong!"

The next day I called the admissions department and asked to be sent an application. Kriyadevi helped me to put together a show reel of some of the better footage I'd shot around the ashram, and to write a convincing essay about why I thought I belonged in the program. I mailed in my application, forwarded my transcripts, and placed the rest in Baba's hands. In a few weeks, I'd have my answer.

The Guru's Touch

ARJUNA AND I WERE setting up the cameras in the hall when Sergio came by the Audiovisual office to deliver a message. "Baba wants the cameramen to start dressing like the ushers for the evening program, in a coat and tie."

Arjuna threw up his hands. "No can do! I don't own any clothes like that."

"I don't either," I said, "but I'd be happy to go shopping for some."

Sergio gave me a warm smile and a thumbs up. "*Bene*! The two of you will go to the city tomorrow."

Arjuna crossed his arms and shook his head. "Sorry, I can't afford new clothes."

The Italian furrowed his brow and curled his lower lip in disgust. "What kind of an asshole are you?" he asked, poking a finger in the cameraman's chest. "What do you think your stipend is for?"

We got a ride into Manhattan with Avadhoot, who made regular trips to the city to purchase film stock and run special errands for Baba. We took one of the ashram sedans. Arjuna and I took the back seat, while Poonish, who was eager to come with us, got into the front seat next to the driver.

As he got behind the wheel, Avadhoot thrust his Stetson hat into my roommate's hands. Poonish looked nonplussed. Did the photographer really expect Poonish to sit with his hat on his lap for the entire two-hour journey? Based on Avadhoot's past behavior, it would have seemed so. In any case, Poonish never challenged him about it. He was too excited to be on his way to Barney's to care.

Arjuna, on the other hand, was not happy. His eyes were bloodshot and he was wheezing. "My allergies are getting worse," he said. "I have doctors' bills to pay. How do they expect me to live on a hundred dollars a month? I've gone through nearly all my life savings already!"

Riding with Avadhoot was so stressful, I swore afterwards I'd never again get into a car with him. Not only did he reach speeds of ninety miles per hour in a fifty-five miles-per-hour zone and steer with his knees while he consulted a map, but he also harassed other motorists relentlessly.

Any time he was unable to pass a slower driver, he tailgated them and flashed his brights. When they moved out of his way, he abruptly pulled alongside of them and honked his horn, mouthing obscenities and giving the finger.

"Cocksucker!" Avadhoot shouted, racing ahead of another vehicle and slamming his hand down on the horn as he passed.

Poonish found the photographer's antics so hilarious, he was convulsed with laughter.

"They were driving the speed limit, Avadhoot!" Arjuna scolded. Even though the air conditioning was running, beads of sweat had formed on the cameraman's brow.

"Fuck 'em!" the photographer cursed. "Doesn't mean I have to." Then he popped an audio cassette into the car stereo and sang along—at the top of his lungs—to the soundtrack of the popular Broadway musical *Evita* until we reached New York.

We got our first glimpse of the Manhattan skyline from the Palisades Parkway. For a moment I felt queasy. *This hellhole will be my home soon. I will have to fend for myself.*

"Yeehaaaaw!" Avadhoot exclaimed. "I love this town! It's just dripping with *shakti*!"

When we hit the morning rush hour traffic on the George Washington Bridge, his mood darkened. "This traffic is un-fucking-believable! It's worse than Bombay!"

An hour later we found an underground parking garage a few blocks from Bloomingdale's in Midtown. Nowhere near Barney's.

As we pulled into the garage, Poonish spoke up. "Deependra and I want to go to Barney's."

Avadhoot took exception. "Barney's? Forget about it. It's all the way downtown. Anything you can get at Barney's, you can find at Bloomingdale's."

Poonish let out a long sigh, but held his tongue.

Arjuna agreed to meet us in front of the garage at five o'clock. Then he promptly disappeared down the stairs of a subway station. Avadhoot shook his head and sniggered. "He's probably headed for K-mart."

Our first stop was the men's formal wear department. Poonish wanted to shop for an outfit like the ones he'd seen Don Johnson wearing on the new TV series *Miami Vice*. We tried on a couple of linen Giorgio Armani jackets and rolled up the sleeves. The style flattered my tall and lean friend, but made me look ridiculous. I cringed when I saw my reflection in the mirror.

Poonish disagreed. "Are you kidding? You look amazing! All you need is a pair of Ray-Ban Wayfarers, and people will start mistaking you for Sonny Crockett!"

I had no idea who that was, but from the sound of his name, I would've been willing to bet he didn't look anything like me.

I picked out several other outfits, and found Poonish in the checkout line holding a single black t-shirt with a large Giorgio Armani logo printed on the front. His eyes were downcast and his shoulders were slumped in dejection.

"Aren't you getting the jackets and pants?" I asked.

"Nope. Just this," he said, shaking his head dolefully. "It's all I can afford at the moment."

I hated to see my new friend looking so defeated. "Not to worry, my friend," I said in an Indian accent. "Take whatever you want. Uncle will pay for everything."

Poonish's face lit up and his mouth opened wide. "Really?"

I nodded and smiled reassuringly. "Yes, really."

Poonish returned a few minutes later with a couple of outfits. "I guess it's true what they say about you, Deependra. You really are rich!"

I suddenly felt anxious. *Am I?* I wondered. I made a mental note to check on my finances.

We set all the expensive items we had picked out on the counter. The clerk behind the register raised his eyebrows and eyed Poonish and me suspiciously. When he finished ringing us up he announced the total: "That will be six thousand, seven hundred eighty dollars, and fifty-one cents, please."

I swallowed. I took almost all the traveler's checks I was carrying out of my wallet and surrendered them to the clerk. His demeanor changed immediately after he checked my ID. He handed me my receipt and change and smiled appreciatively.

"May I ask what you do for a living, sir?"

"I—"

"He directs music videos for MTV!" interrupted Poonish.

"Anything I might have seen?"

"Yeah—Girls On Film—Duran Duran," Poonish said. Then he turned pink and let out a long cackle. I laughed too, and felt lighter.

Our next stop was the men's cologne counter. We wanted to buy the same scent that Sergio used. After sampling a dozen fragrances, we determined that the one we were looking for was Kouros by Yves Saint Laurent. Spraying a little of the cologne on my wrist, I spontaneously broke into an impression of the Italian. "Hey, what kind of an asshole are you?" I said, my lower lip curling in disgust.

Poonish's head jerked back in surprise. Then he broke into another fit of laughter.

"Oh my God! You're giving me the chills. Say something else!"

"Take your shoes off, fuckhead. This a holy place."

"No stop! Please! I can't breathe!" He was amazed at how I was able to "get inside Sergio's head" and imitate his voice and body language so well. "It's uncanny! It's as though you're possessed by him. Can you do anyone else?"

All too happy to show off my hidden talent, I did an impression of the lisping Brian Pettigrew from New Zealand, one of the Indian Vinod, and another of Stephen Ames.

Poonish slapped his leg. "Unbelievable! They're all perfect!"

We each bought the largest bottle of Kouros they sold, and then went in search of Avadhoot. When we found him, he was arguing with the same clerk who had helped us earlier at the register.

"Yes, they *are* on sale," insisted the photographer, thrusting the pile of clothes he had been holding into my arms. *Does he think I'm his valet?* I wondered.

"I'm sorry sir, but you must have misread the sign." The clerk led us to a rack of sport coats. A sign above it said "25% off."

"You see, sir, the sale only applies to these items. The sign is very clear."

Avadhoot widened his stance and moved closer to the clerk, so that he leaned over him in the same way I'd seen him try to intimidate Arjuna with his greater height. "No, on the contrary, it's very confusing!"

Only an idiot could have misinterpreted the sign, but Avadhoot was no idiot. I knew he was lying, but was sure he'd finally give up when even the clerk's supervisor refused him. He didn't. Instead, he insisted on speaking to the floor manager.

"Is this how Bloomingdale's treats all of its customers?" he bellowed. "I demand the discount *and* an apology!"

In the end, they gave him what he wanted, probably just to get rid of us. I was mortified.

After a quick lunch at a falafel joint, we followed Avadhoot on foot to 47th Street Photo, a no-frills camera shop run by Hasidic Jews in the diamond district.

"It'll only take five minutes," he promised. "I just need to pick up some stock."

After forty-five minutes of standing around while Avadhoot tried out different lenses for his camera, and haggled with a sales clerk over the price, Poonish and I decided to head downtown to Barney's and meet up with him later. He reluctantly agreed.

"Okay, but you'd better be at the parking garage at *five sharp*. I hate when people are late. We're going to hit rush hour traffic as it is!"

Poonish and I took the subway downtown. At Barney's I was excited to find Bally loafers like Sergio's. I bought a pair for myself and another for my friend. I also bought dress shirts, ties, khaki trousers, and Ralph Lauren polo shirts. In just a few short hours, I had gone through at least twice as much money as I'd spent during the previous two years. I never understood the value of designer clothes before coming to the ashram, and I had the guru to thank for it. I felt like a prince.

As promised, Poonish and I reached the parking garage by five o'clock, but neither Avadhoot nor Arjuna had arrived yet. We waited another fifteen minutes, but there was still no sign of them.

"Did Avadhoot say to meet him in front of the garage or at the car?" I asked.

Poonish glanced at his watch again. "In front of the garage. I'm sure."

On the off chance they were waiting for us in the car, we took the elevator down a couple of levels to where we had left it, but they weren't there either. I was annoyed but not surprised by Avadhoot's hypocrisy. I was used to it. But I did wonder about Arjuna. It wasn't like him to be late.

We waited outside on the street until six. When neither of them showed up, we decided to call the ashram to see if Avadhoot had left a message for us. Poonish stayed in front of the garage, while I crossed the street and called home from a payphone.

Mukti at reception answered. "Avadhoot? Yes, he called in about three hours ago. I put him directly through to Baba's house. He didn't leave any message. But I do have one from Arjuna. He says not to wait for him because he took a bus back to Birchwood Falls. I can try to page Avadhoot, but he almost always forgets to turn his beeper on."

I thanked Mukti for her help, and told her that if the photographer did call, she should tell him that we were still waiting for him at the garage.

"I could kill that jerk," grumbled Poonish. "Maybe *we* should get a bus back to the ashram, too."

At ten minutes to seven, just as we were about to hail a taxi to take us to the Port Authority Bus Terminal, Avadhoot finally showed up, his arms laden with shopping bags.

"Hey guys, can you take some of these? They're heavy." His manner was nonchalant. He didn't say a word about why he was late, nor did he apologize. I felt like strangling him and wanted to curse him out, but kept my mouth shut. Poonish didn't say a word either, but I could tell from the tightness in his eyes and expression that he was seething too.

When we got to the car, we dumped Avadhoot's shopping bags in the trunk and put ours in the back seat next to Poonish. This time I sat up front next to the crazy man.

I thought about relaying Arjuna's message that he'd taken the bus back to Birchwood Falls, but was curious to see how long it would take Avadhoot to notice he was missing. He never did. And it wasn't until we were halfway back to the ashram that he finally spoke: "Aren't you glad we're leaving the city *now* instead of being stuck in traffic?"

"You said five," Poonish said through gritted teeth. "You were very insistent that we should *not be late.*"

Avadhoot glared at my friend through the rearview mirror. "Oh, so you *wanted* to be stuck in traffic."

"Of course not," I said, butting in. "It's just that if you had planned on leaving later all along you should have told us. We could have done more shopping or gotten something to eat. Instead we waited for you on the street for—"

"—*two hours!*" Poonish growled.

I expected Avadhoot to fly into a rage at my roommate's outburst, but much to my surprise, he backed down.

"Look, I'm sorry you guys had to wait for me, but something unexpected came up for Baba. I had to take care of it."

Poonish was suddenly speechless.

"What did you have to do for Baba?" I asked, trying to hide my skepticism. As soon as I had spoken, however, I realized that I'd committed a Raja Yoga faux pas. Avadhoot didn't answer me with words, but took his eyes off the road for a second to glower at me. One didn't ask questions relating to the guru's personal business. Everything about Baba's private life was confidential.

26.

WHAT'S MINE IS YOURS

BY THE MIDDLE OF August, a letter came from New York University. My pulse raced as I opened the envelope. It contained a single sheet of paper. My spirits sank when I read the message: My application had been rejected.

I found Kriyadevi in the editing room. A pained expression came over her face when I showed her the letter.

When she finished reading it, she crumpled it up and tossed it into the wastepaper basket next to her desk. "This is a test from Shree Gurudev, Deependra."

Instead of being heartened by her words, I bristled. "A test of what?" I don't think she picked up on the negative tone in my voice.

Kriyadevi's eyebrows drew together and she looked pensive before responding. "You have a ton of options," she began.

The Guru's Touch

But it was difficult for me to listen. Instead I thought about how she had been so certain that with Baba's grace I was sure to get into NYU. I interrupted her to call her on it.

"But that's not what I said, Deependra." Turning away from me, she pushed the *power on* button on the editing system and fired it up. "I said that *if* NYU is where the guru wants you to go, that's where you'll go." She fiddled with the dial of the control panel so that the images on the screen began to move forward in fast motion.

Her words did not ring true. "But you said that with Baba's grace, I couldn't go wrong."

Kriyadevi turned her head to look at me and broke into a smile. "That's right!" she said, raising a finger in the air just as the guru did sometimes. "You can't!"

She told me about a school where I could study video production and editing in Manhattan called the New York School of Broadcasting—only a few subway stops away from the Raja Yoga ashram.

"That sounds great, but my sister will never go for it—NYSB sounds like a vocational school." I explained that Melanie controlled my trust fund and that the money in it could only be used for college tuition and living expenses while I was in an accredited program.

"What about the money you inherited from your uncle?" she asked.

"Cousin," I corrected, wondering how everybody seemed to know about my personal business. "But I shouldn't have to use that money for school. I want to save that money to travel with Baba for the rest of my life."

"Talk to your sister. Maybe she'll change her mind. The course is not cheap, but it's only three months—much less expensive than four years of college. You can live at the Manhattan ashram. You'll learn everything you need to know about video, and you'll be back on tour with Baba in no time."

When I called Melanie to tell her that I hadn't gotten into NYU, she wasn't surprised. I told her about the program at NYSB, but my enthusiasm was met with silence.

"Well, is the trust going to pay for it or not?" I asked.

"Listen, Doug. If you want to be a cameraman, fine. But you need to get a college degree *first*." As she lectured me, I felt my blood pressure rise. "A certificate from a three-month video production course is not going qualify you for a whole lot of jobs out there. If you want to live in New York, why don't you apply to City College?"

"I only care about qualifying for one job," I said through gritted teeth. "And that's serving the guru. I'm going to spend the rest of my life in the ashram."

Baba was holding a private *darshan*, a time when Baba met with ashram staff or VIPs away from the crowds of devotees. It was held in the Namaste Room, a small salon adjacent to the guru's living quarters. Arjuna was in the city for "personal business" that day, so I was on camera. Kriyadevi assisted me with sound. Avadhoot was taking pictures and was being even more of a pain in the ass than usual. Today, instead of Arjuna, I was the one who was always wrong.

"You're going to have to move," Avadhoot said, tapping his foot.

"But this is where you told me to set up yesterday," I protested.

"Precisely! Do you want to shoot from the same angle every day like Arjuna?"

Baba was meeting with the astronaut William Brady, who was telling him about a life-changing spiritual experience he had had on his way back from the moon. He hoped the guru could offer some insight.

"What you are describing is a state of consciousness called *savikalpa samadhi*," explained Baba through Anjali. "Many of my followers have had the same experience after receiving initiation from me. You should take a *shaktipat* retreat. You will have this experience again."

The astronaut chuckled, and then looked thoughtful. "Swami, can a mystical experience, like the one I had in space, lead to the development of psychic abilities?"

"The Hindu scriptures speak of many supernatural powers that come to seekers as they progress on the path to enlightenment. These include the power to see what is happening far away, knowledge of past lives, and the ability to read the thoughts of others. In Raja Yoga, however, these abilities are considered distractions from spiritual life. You cannot know God if you are craving supernatural abilities."

"Do you know what I am thinking right now?" the astronaut asked.

"Yes," Baba said. "You are wondering if I know what you are thinking."

The room erupted into laughter.

"One more question, Baba," Brady said, still chuckling.

"Of course."

"In your book, *An Introduction to Advaita Vedanta*, you state there is no difference between a dream and real life. But how can this be true? In the waking state there is continuity from day to day. On the other hand, our dreams are different every night. Could you please explain?"

"All phenomena, whether they take place in the mind as thought or in the so-called external world, are ever-changing and therefore illusory."

"Granted," said the astronaut. "But there's nevertheless a difference, right? If I die in a dream, I still wake up and go about my life. But if I die in the waking state it's all over. Am I wrong?"

Baba turned to Anjali and they spoke in Hindi for a while before she gave her translation.

Baba shook his head. "No difference. There is no difference between the dream state and the waking state. From the standpoint of the ultimate nature of reality, they are one and the same. They are both *Maya*—an illusion."

A few moments later, I felt a tap on my shoulder. Removing my eye from the viewfinder, I turned to see Kriyadevi holding the microphone in one hand and pointing toward the door with the other. When I saw who she was pointing to, I was stunned. Standing next to Mukti, waving and smiling at me, was my sister Melanie. A moment later, Gopi got up to greet her, had a word with Mukti, and then showed Melanie to a place on the floor near the throne.

"This is Deependra's sister, Baba," Gopi said. "Her name is Melanie."

Anjali translated: "Your brother is a very good boy," Baba said. "Very intelligent."

Melanie smiled politely. "Yes, I know."

From behind the camera, I cringed at my sister's words. *That's no way to talk to the guru!*

Baba motioned for Gopi to approach him and whispered something in her ear. Disappearing through a door leading to the guru's private quarters, the angel returned a minute later with a basket full of cowry shell necklaces.

Taking a necklace from the basket, the guru smiled at my sister and beckoned her to approach. "Welcome to the ashram," he said, handing her the string of shells. Through the viewfinder of my camera, I saw that at the moment Melanie's hand came into contact with Baba's gift, she shuddered, as if she were receiving an electric shock. As she turned around to face the camera on her way back to her spot on the floor, I noticed she had a dazed expression on her face.

Baba rose to his feet, signaling the end of *darshan*. On his way out he stopped to speak to me: "Your *seva* is over now until the evening program. You should show your sister around the ashram, and take her to Prasad for lunch."

Weeks had passed since Baba had criticized the staff for eating too many of their meals in the ashram café. This was the first time I'd been back since, but I'd already noticed a while ago that business had returned to normal—everybody who had been avoiding the place was back to eating nearly all of their meals there again. *Am I the only one who follows the guru's commands without question?* I wondered.

Melanie and I ordered our food and then found a table under a large, newly hung picture of Baba with his young successor. The photo had been taken by Avadhoot on the Har-ki-Pauri ghat in Haridwar. Master and disciple were the picture of serenity. It had probably been taken only moments before the crazy man had thrown himself at Baba's feet and Seth had gone apeshit.

I asked Melanie if she had recognized the famous astronaut who had been meeting with Baba. She hadn't and was unimpressed. She had not come for Baba's *darshan*. She was here with papers for me to sign relating to her eventual purchase of our mother's house. As she had mentioned to me on the phone when I was back in India, she had decided not to sell it after all and was hoping to buy me and our other siblings out. I told her I didn't care who bought the house, as long as I got my fair share.

Whatever her reason for coming, the timing of her visit was perfect. I would need to make a tuition payment to NYSB soon, and I wanted the trust to foot the bill. Now I could ask her again in person.

"So, what do you make of Jeremy's new lifestyle?" she asked.

"New lifestyle?"

"Didn't he tell you? He's born again."

"He became a Jesus freak?"

Melanie chuckled. "No, no. He's shomer Shabbos."

"What's that supposed to mean?" I suddenly felt confused and depressed at the same time.

"He's become an observant Jew," she said, rolling her eyes. "He met *The Rebbe*. Carrie is studying to convert."

"You've got to be kidding me. Who's *The Rebbe*?"

"The Lubavitcher Rebbe. You know, the famous rabbi in Brooklyn who gives everyone who comes to see him a dollar. He's not just a rabbi—he's considered a holy man—they say the prime minister of Israel never makes any important decisions without consulting him first."

I didn't want to hear any more. I squeezed my eyes shut, and rubbed the sides of my head with my hands.

"Doug? Are you okay?"

I opened my eyes again. "Yes," I lied. I wasn't okay. I had a sharp pain in the back of my neck. *How could Jeremy and Carrie have strayed so far?*

"I see they have you working as a cameraman. How much are they paying you for that?"

Her question infuriated me. "Paying me? I'm not getting paid for my *seva*. If I got paid it would defeat the purpose."

As I attempted to explain the concept of selfless service, Melanie grimaced, and absently covered her mouth with her hand. "And I'm burning off the bad karma from countless lifetimes in the process."

"How many hours a week do you volunteer here?" she asked when I was finished.

"Something between sixty and seventy," I said proudly.

"You're shitting me!"

"Shhhhh! *Please* don't use foul language like that in the ashram," I scolded, as if no one swore in Raja Yoga. "This is a holy place."

"Sorry, but don't you at least get weekends off?"

"Well, no," I answered, standing up. "Let's continue this conversation outside." Exiting the café, I took Melanie around to the front of the ashram to see the Brahmananda temple.

"Are they still making you pay for room and board?"

The pain in my neck spread to the side of my head and I thought I might be getting what my sister called a migraine. I was becoming flustered and was having difficulty expressing myself. "I don't think you understand—"

"Oh, I understand, alright! That jacket you're wearing looks expensive."

"It's by Giorgio Armani," I snapped. "Of course it's expensive."

Melanie clenched her jaw and shook her head at me. "You're squandering your inheritance, Doug! Do you know how long it took Harvey to save all that money?"

I kneaded the back of my neck. "It's *my* money, and I'll do whatever I want with it!"

"Think about it, Doug—even if you were only getting minimum wage, do you realize how much you'd be making with all the hours you're putting in?"

I threw up my hands. "You haven't heard anything I've said."

We reached the temple. It was empty at this hour, but the door was unlocked. We went inside and removed our shoes.

"Is that Buddha?" Melanie asked, looking up at the statue of Gurudev.

"Someone much greater than the Buddha. This is a statue of Baba's guru, Lord Brahmananda."

"Why's he so fat? I thought holy men in India were all skinny like Gandhi."

My head began to throb. I wanted to shout at her, but remembered I still hadn't asked her about the money.

I gritted my teeth. "Gurudev was a great yogi. He had a big belly because of a breath retention practice called *kumbhaka*."

Melanie raised her eyebrows and cleared her throat. I turned away from her and gazed up at the statue's impassive face. *Please Gurudev, help me to cope with my wretched sister, and get what I need from her to serve you.*

We put our shoes back on and exited the temple. Then I led her to a bench beside a fountain, where I could talk to her about my plans. I reminded her that in the fall I'd be taking a course in video production, and how excited I was about it. I asked her once again if the trust would pay for it, but she acted like she hadn't heard me. Instead, she reiterated her argument that I needed a college education. Nothing else would do.

Listening to her, I got a bitter taste in my mouth. When I couldn't stand to hear one more word I cut her off: "Do you want to listen to me for a change!" An ashramite pruning a nearby rosebush turned to look in our direction, and I lowered my voice. "Maybe you think working for free here makes me some kind of sucker—"

"I didn't say that—"

"I know it's hard for you to understand, but I'm getting something out of it too—and not just spiritually—I've been getting free camera lessons from another devotee who used to work as a cameraman for WPIX, and Baba's personal photographer has been teaching me a lot too. These are marketable skills."

"Doug, listen—"

"Did it ever occur to you that maybe I'm not ready to go to college now? You seem more concerned about my obtaining a worldly credential than in my studying something that actually interests me. I hate farming, and I don't give a flying fuck about fruit! Is that what you want me to study? Maybe *you're* the crazy one!"

"Doug, that was just a way for you to get into Cornell, and you know it."

"Yeah, but I still had to sit through all those boring classes. Anyway, it doesn't matter anymore. Baba wants me to make movies for him someday, so I'm going to study video production. All I'm asking for is a few thousand dollars from the trust to pay for the course."

"So this was Baba's idea! I should have known!"

"Keep your voice down!" I scolded, glancing around. The ashramite pruning the hedges was shaking his head in disgust.

I was getting nowhere with Melanie. She refused to budge. If I wanted to go to "vocational school," as she put it, I'd have to pay for it out of the money I inherited from Harvey. I did, however, convince her to stay for the evening program, before she headed back to Ithaca.

When I took my place behind the camera for Baba's talk, I was stunned to see my sister sitting way up front on the women's side, just behind the lady swamis. I knew that Baba must have given the command to seat her there. It moved me that the guru was giving special attention to a member of my family, even though he must have known she hated him.

That night Baba spoke on a theme I'd heard many times before: the tendency of worldly people to search for love and happiness outside of themselves, instead of turning within and finding everything they need inside.

"*Camera one*, get a close-up of the attractive woman with the thick brown hair sitting behind Paramananda," came Jake's voice over the intercom. He was talking to me. While *camera two* was live with a two-shot of the guru and Anjali, I panned the audience until I found the person Jake was talking about.

"Yep, that's her," Jake said. "Get a nice close-up."

Much to my annoyance, I realized the person Jake wanted me to film was my sister. I zoomed in until Melanie's face filled the entire screen of my viewfinder. I did not like what I saw, and I doubted that Jake would either: the right corner of her upper lip was raised slightly in a sneer.

"Forget it," Jake said. "Take *camera two*." I hoped Jake wouldn't realize that the woman with the contemptuous expression on her face was related to me.

"*Camera one*, pan right to the pretty girl with the red hair instead." I zoomed into a close-up of a beautiful young woman with auburn hair, penetrating green eyes, and pouting lips. She was sitting in the same row as Melanie. I'd never seen her around the ashram before, but knew she must have been important, or related to someone important to be seated so close to the throne. She was giving Baba her undivided attention. Her name tag said "Cassandra."

"Okay, *camera one*," Jake said. "Pan back to Baba now."

"The true purpose of the physical guru is to acquaint the disciple with the *inner guru*, otherwise known as the Inner-Self," Baba said. "My most important teaching is to look within and know your own Self, for the true guru abides within you as you."

When the program was over, I offered to take Melanie up to see Baba again, but she declined under the pretense that it was getting late and she had a long drive back to Ithaca.

"So, what did you think of Baba's talk?" I asked, walking her to the car.

"I'm sorry, Doug, but I think the whole thing stinks."

I felt defeated. How could she have heard the words of a living saint and yet remain so closed-minded?

"Your swami is right: everyone has to be their own guru. But I don't need a charlatan like Rudrananda to tell me that."

The frustration I felt at my sister's wrong understanding was becoming more than I could bear. I scolded her about it: "First of all, you should never say such a thing about a great being like Baba! Secondly, you misunderstood what he was trying to say—"

"Just who does he think he is? Messing with people's lives?"

"Melanie—"

"You should be in college—not a vocational school!"

Anger rose up inside of me like a tidal wave. "Are you going to let me have the money or not?"

My sister crossed her arms in front of her chest and shook her head *no*.

"It's *my* money, Melanie!" I shouted. Luckily, everyone was still at *darshan* and the parking lot was full of empty vehicles.

My sister turned her back on me, opened the door to her car, and got in. "I'm sorry, Doug, I can't agree to that," she said, turning the key in the ignition.

"My name isn't Doug anymore, it's Deependra. Baba named me after one of the greatest saints of India! He thinks very highly of me—*unlike* you!"

"That's not true—"

"Baba cares more about me than you ever did! He took me on a pilgrimage, and gave me an important *seva* in the ashram! He wants me to make movies to spread the teachings of his guru all over the world! You have no idea what amazing spiritual experiences I've had since coming here. College is bullshit compared to the opportunity of being part of his sacred mission!"

Melanie's shoulders slumped forward and she turned away from me to stare blankly through the windshield of her car.

"Well?"

She let out a long sigh, and then turned her head back to face me. "Use some of Harvey's money to pay for the course. If and when you complete it, the trust will reimburse you." Then she turned the key in the ignition and drove away.

I didn't go directly back to the hall for *darshan*. I first made a stop in my room. I went to my dresser and took out the little bottle of Baba's bath water that Sita Perkins had given me last year.

"Save this for difficult times," I remembered her telling me. I put the bottle to my lips and drank down most of its contents. I fell to my knees and began to sob. *Thank God you found me, Baba.* I prayed. *I owe you my life. I owe you everything!*

Years later, I still can't believe what I did next. I went back to my dresser, found my checkbook, and wrote a check in the amount of ten thousand dollars to the Raja Yoga Mission of America. I put the check in an envelope, wrote "For my beloved Guru" on the outside of it, and then sealed it closed.

As I waited my turn in the *darshan* line, I gazed upon the guru's divine form while he blessed the other devotees in front of me. When it was my turn to greet him, I placed the envelope in the basket at his feet, my hand trembling, and performed a full prostration. I stood up, looked Baba directly in the eye and spoke silently to him with my thoughts: *My beloved guru, what's mine is yours.*

27.
THE MAN BEHIND THE CURTAIN

THE END OF THE summer had arrived. The Mission's renovations at the newly acquired property in the Berkeley Hills were complete, and the guru would be leaving for California to inaugurate a new Raja Yoga ashram at the end of the week. Sadly, I wouldn't be going with him. I was filming my last evening program with Baba, and the next day I'd be leaving Birchwood Falls to begin my three-month video production course in New York.

The guru was scheduled to remain in Berkeley until the spring, when his tour would continue on to Europe. I had no idea how long Baba intended for me to remain in school. Only the guru knew when I'd be allowed to rejoin him.

"Stand by *camera one*," came Jake's voice over my headset. "Go in for a two-shot of Baba and Anjali, *camera two*."

"A perfected master of Raja Yoga has passed beyond ego-consciousness, duality and common worldly concerns," Baba said.

"*Camera one*, get a medium shot of Baba," Jake said. I zoomed in on the guru. Jake cut to my camera as soon as Anjali had finished translating his last sentence. "Take *camera one*."

"Such a being, like my own guru, Lord Brahmananda, roamed free upon the earth like a child," Baba continued. "He acted without consideration for social etiquette. Ordinary boundaries of human behavior did not apply to him.

"The actions of saints like my Gurudev may seem crazy to ordinary beings, but everything they say and do, no matter how bizarre, is for the edification of their devotees, and is informed by their enlightened state and the highest wisdom."

"Tilt up and zoom in on the photograph of Gurudev above Baba's throne *camera two*," Jake said, "and stand by…"

"My guru was born an enlightened being. He lived his entire life immersed in the bliss of God consciousness."

"*Camera one*, get an audience shot," Jake said. I tilted down from Baba to Gopi, who was sitting at his feet, and zoomed in for an extreme close-up.

"That's a nice shot, *camera one*, but let's avoid staff for now and focus on regular devotees."

I carefully panned left until a familiar face caught my eye.

"Nice one," Jake said, "Stand by…"

I slowly zoomed in on the attractive young woman with shoulder-length auburn hair and the name tag "Cassandra."

"Take *camera one*."

"When Gurudev was a young man, he could sometimes be seen along the side of the road catching the droppings of cows before they landed on the ground," Baba continued. "He would smear the dung all over his body and refrain from bathing for many days."

Cassandra suddenly made a face as though she were sucking on a lemon. Definitely not the kind of reaction shot Jake was looking for.

"Take *camera two*," Jake commanded. I could hear the tension in his voice. "*Camera one*, forget the audience for now and try to get a three-shot that includes Baba, Anjali, and Suresh."

"Instead of a throne, he would sit on a heap of garbage. However, even though he was surrounded by impure things and covered in shit, he did not emit a foul odor. On the contrary, he was as fragrant as a festoon of flowers."

"And ... take *camera one*," Jake said.

"So, you see, my guru was no ordinary being. It is impossible to understand or judge the outlandish behavior of such masters with an unenlightened mind."

As I later broke down my gear after the program, I thought about Baba's talk. I tried to understand its meaning and what Baba was trying to teach us. *Is Baba like his own guru?* I wondered. He did wear a variety of eccentric hats, but up until then I hadn't seen him surround himself with garbage or smear shit all over his body. I could see that Gurudev's behavior had often been strange, but I failed to see the wisdom in it. As usual, I'd have to keep meditating on Baba's words until I arrived at right understanding.

"Surprise!" Jake, Kriyadevi, and Arjuna cried as I opened the door to the control room. On the counter next to them was a chocolate cake from Prasad.

Jake and Kriyadevi had big smiles on their faces, but Arjuna looked horrible. His eyes were severely bloodshot, and he couldn't stop sneezing.

"Are you okay?" I asked him.

"My allergies are flaring up again. I'm allergic to—"

"—something in the ashram," Kriyadevi said, finishing his sentence. "We know."

Jake served me a slice of cake. "Well, Deependra, it's going to be much harder to get good coverage of Baba's talks with only one cameraman."

Arjuna narrowed his eyes. "Yeah, and I'm kind of pissed you're leaving after all that time we spent training you."

I took a step back and let out a short bark of laughter. "Don't look at me—I don't want to go anywhere. I'm simply following the guru's command."

Jake closed his eyes and waved his hand in the air. "Don't listen to Weinberg, here—he's just a big crank." Everybody laughed but Arjuna.

"In any case, you won't be gone long, Deependra," Kriyadevi said, cutting herself a second slice of cake.

Arjuna frowned. "And you know this how?"

Kriyadevi arched a single eyebrow and looked at Arjuna cryptically. "I just know."

I thought about how her last prediction turned out and felt depressed. I hoped she wasn't jinxing me.

After the little going away party for me in the control room, I joined Poonish Davidson and Stephen Ames in Prasad for another round of dessert, and we said our goodbyes. "Don't forget," Poonish said, "always iron a shirt with the buttons face down."

Stephen rolled his eyes.

"I won't," I laughed.

"And a sharp crease down the front of your pants—very important."

"Got it!"

Before heading back to my room, I visited the Brahmananda temple to pay my respects to Gurudev, and meditated until lights out. As I traversed the deserted lobby, I saw a light on in the Housing office behind the reception area. I admired the devotion of these ashramites—they were working around the clock to prepare for the influx of visitors that were expected at the ashram before Baba's departure. As I drew closer to the guru's house, I got a whiff of a familiar scent. It was Sergio's cologne.

"Psst!"

I stopped where I was and listened.

"Psst! Greenbaum!" Sergio whispered from behind the long gray curtain. I stepped behind the drape and was face to face with the Italian. I wondered why he was hiding there in the dark.

"I need you to do something for me," he said.

"Of course, anything."

"You know the new girl who works in the kitchen?"

"I'm not sure I know which one you mean, Sergio."

"Yes, you do," he insisted. "She's the pretty one. Red hair...green eyes...nice—" he finished his thought by drawing an hourglass in the air with his hands.

"Cassandra?"

"*Sì*. Go find her and bring her here."

"What, now?"

"Yes! Baba wants to see her."

Just as I was about leave in search of the girl, I became aware of another presence standing behind Sergio in the dark. Adrenaline rushed through my veins and I gasped—the figure was Baba! He had an eye pressed up against the curtain and was peering through one of the pinpricks in the fabric that I had first noticed almost two years earlier. "Hello Baba," I said, folding my hands, and tilting forward slightly in a bow.

The guru turned to face me, took a couple of steps toward me, and gave my shoulder an affectionate squeeze.

"Ahh, Deependra, you go tomorrow, yes?"

"Yes, Baba. I'm starting video school this week. I'll be living in the Manhattan ashram."

Even though it was dark, I could tell the guru was smiling. "School, very good!"

"With your grace I—"

"Okay, *basta*!" Sergio interrupted. "Now you need to go find the girl."

I had no idea which room or even which dormitory Cassandra was staying in, but I remembered seeing the light on in the Housing office. I knocked on the door and a moment later Mukti opened. "We're closed."

"I know, but I was hoping you could tell me which room a newcomer named Cassandra was staying in."

Mukti stared at me like I was nuts.

"First of all, I have no idea who you're talking about. Secondly, we don't give out that kind of information."

I thought about telling her that Baba had sent me, but something in my gut made me stop. "*Sergio* needs to talk to her right now," I said instead.

It was as if I had said the magic word. Mukti nodded obligingly, and then went to a filing cabinet on the far side of the office. "Red hair, right?" she asked, opening one of the drawers.

"Yes, that's right."

Mukti pulled out a folder and thumbed through it until she found the sheet she was looking for. "Here you go: Cassandra Hayes. *Dhyana Shayanagrih*, Room 321."

I sprinted back through the lobby. As I passed Baba's house on my way to Cassandra's dormitory, I got another whiff of Sergio's cologne. Although I realized it was none of my business, I couldn't help wondering why Baba wanted to see her. I thought maybe she had done something wrong, or that maybe he wanted to offer her a job as a *darshan* girl.

I found the right room and knocked tentatively. A moment later, a middle-aged woman in a tattered bathrobe with a cloud of silver hair cracked open the door. She stared at me with an alarmed expression on her face.

"Is Cassandra there?"

"It's past lights out. Who are you and what do you want?"

"I'm Deependra," I answered, pointing to my name tag.

Just then, Cassandra appeared from behind the door in teddy bear pajamas. She was a beautiful girl in her late teens or early twenties, with a head of thick, lustrous auburn hair, delicate features, pale skin, and stunning green eyes.

"I'm Cassandra," she said, squinting. The older woman eyed me suspiciously before retreating back into the room.

"I have a message from Sergio for you."

"Who's Sergio?" she asked, wrinkling her nose, and pushing a few strands of hair from her face.

I was taken aback. I thought everyone in the ashram knew who Sergio was. "He's the tour manager. He wants me to bring you to the guru's house right away. Baba wants to see you."

"*Me?*" she asked, jerking her head back in surprise. "Okay, sure. Hang on a sec." Cassandra closed the door, and then reemerged a couple of minutes later in a pair of tight blue jeans and a snug forest green cotton sweater. I noticed she had fantastic breasts, but I pushed the obscene thought out of my mind. Letting Cassandra walk ahead of me on our way to the lobby, I couldn't help admiring her heart-shaped ass. This ignited long-repressed feelings of lust inside me. Again, I struggled to drive the impure cravings away.

When we arrived in the lobby in front of Baba's house, Sergio was out from behind the curtain, sitting on a bench waiting for us. "*Ciao*, Cassandra!" he said, greeting the girl with what looked to me like a phony smile. He ignored me entirely—it was as if I weren't even there.

"Come, Baba is waiting for you."

The redhead stiffened and scratched the back of her head. "Are you sure you have the right Cassandra?"

"Don't be ridiculous," laughed Sergio. "Please, follow me."

Without so much as a thank you, or a nod in my direction, Sergio disappeared with Cassandra behind the thick, vault-like metal door to Baba's house. My service to the guru was finished for the evening.

On my way back to my room, it troubled me that Baba would summon such an attractive girl to his living quarters at night. I immediately pushed the disloyal thought out of my mind. I focused, instead, on what troubled me even more: I wanted to know why a newcomer like Cassandra deserved an audience with the guru in his private quarters, while I, who had been serving Baba faithfully for the past two years, did not.

Then I remembered the teachings: Everyone was living out the fruit of lifetimes of positive and negative karma. *I should be grateful for the countless blessings I have already received.*

THE EARLY MORNING SUN cast a soft light over the ashram grounds. The staff shuttle that would take me to the Manhattan ashram pulled into the driveway. With a hollow feeling in my chest and my head hanging low, I tossed my bag in the back of the van and climbed in. I was miserable to be leaving Baba and Birchwood Falls, but tried to stay positive. Studying video production was what the guru had commanded. The day I returned to his side, I'd be better equipped to serve him than ever.

I wasn't the only ashramite going to the city today—the shuttle was nearly full—but I was the only one who wouldn't be returning later that evening. *What if no one likes me in the Manhattan ashram?* I worried. *What if I hate NYSB?* I swallowed hard as the driver started the van and began to pull out of the driveway. *Why is Baba sending me away?*

Just then, a fist pounded against the window next to me, and the van lurched to a halt. I turned to see a wild-eyed girl with an overnight bag slung over her shoulder circling around the vehicle to the driver's side. Her face was puffy and her beautiful auburn hair disheveled. It was Cassandra, the girl from the night before. The driver lowered his window.

"Are you headed to the city?" the girl asked, her voice quavering.

"The shuttle is for ashram *staff only*."

A second later the automatic doors of the main entrance opened and Sergio came bounding out of the lobby toward the van.

"It's okay," Sergio said, catching his breath. "Take her wherever she wants to go."

The driver pushed a button and the doors unlocked with a loud click. Pulling the sliding door of the van open, Cassandra jumped in.

"Don't forget your gift from Baba," Sergio said, thrusting what looked like a jewelry box into Cassandra's hands before closing the door behind her. She sat in my row, placing her bag between us.

The girl was trembling. Something had shaken her up badly. Then it occurred to me: Baba was sending her away, too. That was certainly why he had asked to see her so late at night. Maybe he wanted her to go to school like me. If not, I wondered what she could have done that was so egregious. I wanted to ask her, but stopped myself. She didn't look like she was interested in making conversation.

The driver popped an audio cassette into the car stereo and pressed play. A recording of Daniel Groza playing acoustic guitar and singing devotional songs to Baba in English came over the sound system. A quarter of an hour later, curiosity got the best of me. I turned to Cassandra and reintroduced myself.

"Hi, I'm Deependra. We met last night."

She turned to face me and a look of disgust spread across her face. She glared at me before unclipping her seatbelt. Collecting her bag, she got up and moved to an empty seat in the back of the van.

What a bitch! I thought. *Who cares about her private darshan with Baba, anyway!* To me, the girl was obviously an ingrate and incapable of appreciating anything he might have given her. Then I remembered something Baba had once said about grace: "If the vessel is cracked and full of holes, it doesn't matter how much grace the guru pours into you. You will not be able to hold it."

Several minutes later, I heard whimpering coming from the back of the van. I turned my head around to see who it was. As I expected, it was Cassandra. Before long, the sniveling turned into sobbing. An older women sitting next to me, who I recognized from the public relations department, turned to me. "Poor thing," she whispered. "Not everyone can handle the *shakti*."

I nodded in agreement. "She'll be alright," I said. "The guru is helping her work through something."

The traffic was horrendous, and it took ages to reach Manhattan. By the time we were over the George Washington Bridge, the sky had darkened with clouds, and it had begun to pour.

"Stop the car!" Cassandra hollered from the back of the van. "I want to get out!"

"Are you kidding?" the driver said. "This is Washington Heights—it's one of the most dangerous neighborhoods in New York."

"STOP—THE—FUCKING—CAR!"

The driver abruptly swerved to the side of the road and skidded to a stop. Cassandra shot up, grabbed her bag, and yanked on the door handle, but was unable to open it.

"Let me out! Let me out!"

The driver pushed a button and there was a loud click. Sliding the door open, Cassandra jumped out into the rain, and, without looking where she was going, dashed across the street. A car's horn blared and she narrowly missed being hit. Within seconds she disappeared down a side street, leaving the door to the van open behind her.

"Yeesh!" the driver said. "What a mouth on her. Good riddance."

By the time the shuttle pulled up in front of the ashram, the rain had stopped and the sun had broken through the clouds. As the ashramites piled out of the van, I noticed something wedged between the upper and the lower seat cushions. It was the jewelry box from Baba that Sergio had handed Cassandra earlier. When I was alone in the van, I opened it and peeked inside the little red box. It contained a golden chain necklace with a diamond-encrusted, heart-shaped pendant.

What an ungrateful wretch! I thought. *How could anyone forget a precious gift from the guru?*

Cassandra was obviously beyond saving.

PART THREE

28.
EXILE

THE MANHATTAN ASHRAM WAS located on a quiet residential street in Greenwich Village. Although on the outside it looked like a typical New York City brownstone, on the inside it was a spiritual oasis, with life-size photos of Baba and Gurudev, and the familiar smells of basmati rice and Nag Champa incense.

A young woman named Nitya with a head full of dark frizzy hair greeted me from behind a window in the reception area. When I tried to introduce myself, she smiled brightly. "I know who you are, Deependra."

Nitya gave me the tour of the ashram and showed me to a room on the third floor, which was already occupied by three other men.

"We all share rooms here," she said. "Everyone but Swamiji, of course."

Satyananda was the resident swami and spiritual director at the Manhattan ashram. He had been the master of ceremonies at my first *shaktipat* retreat with Baba. I recalled how gushingly Jeremy and Carrie had spoken of him, saying how highly evolved he was.

"It can get pretty cramped around here during weekend retreats. When the bunks are full, we put mattresses on the floor." Nitya explained that unlike the Birchwood Falls ashram, there were no married couples living here. "All the residents work in the world, or go to school."

"What do you do outside, Nitya?"

"I work at The Gap. I'm trying to save money to go to India."

I followed Nitya back downstairs into the office. She gave me the same pamphlet of rules I had received when I first moved into the Birchwood Falls ashram, and made up a name tag for me. "Any questions?"

"Do I have to wear the tag all the time?"

"Only at evening programs, and when you're doing *seva* in the office."

According to Nitya, the daily chants and evening programs were well attended by long-time devotees, as well as newcomers. They were led by Satyananda and held in a grand, high-ceilinged hall on the ground floor. Like every other Raja Yoga ashram, the hall contained a throne like the one in the meditation hall in Birchwood Falls, with a large framed portrait of a serious-looking Baba sitting in it. The hall abutted another large room that doubled as a spiritual library and dining area. In addition to Baba's books, the library boasted a huge collection of esoteric Yogic texts and Hindu scriptures.

The evening program on my first day was an "experience talk" given by Satyananda himself.

"I had the exceedingly good fortune of meeting Baba in Woodstock, New York, back in 1971. But unlike most people who come to the guru, before that blessed day I had already trained at a Buddhist monastery in Thailand. After years of meditation and a burning desire for enlightenment, I began to enjoy a deep stillness and unity with the cosmos, which culminated in a direct realization of the ultimate nature of reality."

He explained that although this experience had awakened him to his own true nature, he knew that he still needed time to become worthy of teaching others.

"While staying with relatives here in New York, I visited a spiritual book store and found a copy of the autobiography of the then little-known Swami Rudrananda. I was not looking for a guru, but by the time I finished reading *Divine Dance of Consciousness*, I understood that Baba was a fully realized master who would be able to help me deepen my experience of the divine.

"Not long after reading his book, I had the opportunity of attending one of his public talks. I was enthralled by Baba, who seemed to be speaking directly to me. When I went up on the *darshan* line to meet him, he took my hands in his and whispered in my ear: 'I have been expecting you,' and my heart exploded with bliss."

After the public program, Swami Satyananda invited me to join him for a cup of chai in the library, where he welcomed me to the ashram and let me know he was always available if I should ever need spiritual counseling. He was aware that I had been living in the Ravipur ashram, and was here now to study video production with Baba's blessing.

"Thank you, Swamiji. By the way, I think you may know my brother and his wife, Shree Ram and Anshika Greenbaum."

Satyananda scratched his shaved head and stared thoughtfully into the middle distance. "Yes, I do remember Shree Ram and Anshika. But I don't think I've seen them for at least a year now."

I was too embarrassed to tell him that they had left Raja Yoga.

As Satyananda and I spoke, other ashramites and visitors joined us in the library.

"I enjoyed your talk very much, Swamiji," said a man dressed in a business suit. "But how is it possible that you could have had a realization of the Inner-Self before meeting Baba and receiving *shaktipat?*"

"That is an excellent question," Satyananda said, rubbing his nose. "In a past life I was the disciple of a great *shaktipat* guru in India."

I wondered how he could know about his past lives, but I didn't dare ask. Everybody else seemed satisfied with his answer. I told him how deeply inspiring I had also found

Baba's autobiography, and that one day I hoped to take the vows of *sannyasa* too.

"Has your spiritual practice changed since you became a swami?" I asked.

"Well, obviously I was already leading the life of a monk long before I took the vows, but since putting on the robes I've noticed a tremendous increase in *shakti*. I've become an instrument of the guru's grace, able to give *shaktipat* on Baba's behalf."

"How does it work?" asked a young black woman who had sat down next to him. She was gazing at the swami with the kind of awe and reverence that, up until then, I had seen reserved for the guru alone.

Satyananda smiled knowingly. "For example, right now, as I speak to you, I can see pulses of pure consciousness shooting from my eyes into yours."

The woman stared into the swami's eyes searchingly. I looked too, but was unable to detect rays of light or anything else unusual.

Smiling beneficently, the swami reached over and gently touched the woman's arm. "Did you feel that?"

"I think so," the woman said, taking a deep breath and closing her eyes.

My conversation with Satyananda left me inspired, and strengthened my determination to become a swami in the future. Yet, although I admired him, there was something about the swami that gave me pause. I couldn't put my finger on it at first, but then I realized what it was: I didn't care for the way he tended to speak about himself more than he did about Baba.

THE NEW YORK SCHOOL of Broadcasting was located in neighboring Chelsea, just a five-minute subway ride or a twenty-minute walk from the ashram. I was in a class of about thirty students, half of whom were college kids taking the course for elective credit. Our days were divided between field production, TV studio operation, and post production (editing). The equipment was less professional than that used by the ashram, but for the purpose of the course it was perfectly adequate. Our instructor was a short, silver-haired man with a New York accent named Eric Lewis.

"Okay, people, I want all of you to get one thing straight from the beginning. I'm *not* a nice person. I only pretend to be."

Eric's deadpan delivery made me chuckle, but no one else in the room was laughing. Eric smiled and winked at me.

Unlike my experiences in high school and college, I found the course at NYSB interesting and engaging—not only because I was eager to serve the guru, but because it turned out I had a passion for broadcasting. My favorite part of the course was when we were teamed up in groups of three and were able to take the cameras and portable VTRs out onto the streets of the city. We took turns operating the camera, recording sound, and playing journalist, as if we were a professional news crew.

While I loved the class, I soon discovered I had little in common with the other students. I couldn't help pitying them: their professional goals were trivial, and their lives devoid of meaning. They would end up working for local TV stations as camera operators and editors. I, on the other hand, would one day help to establish an international Raja Yoga TV channel that would reach thousands, if not millions of seekers all over the globe. I hoped that with Baba's blessing, I'd end up running the network and serving as one of Baba's senior swamis at the same time. Maybe I'd even be able to give *shaktipat* one day like Satyananda.

Returning to the ashram after school one day, Nitya greeted me from behind the window at the reception. "You have a message, Deependra." She handed me the note and I read it as I climbed the stairs that led to my room. It said: *"Please call Jeremy."*

I would *not* be calling Jeremy and Carrie. I would not be visiting them on Long Island anytime soon. They had turned their backs on the guru and were doomed. As far as I was concerned, they could both go fuck themselves.

ALTHOUGH THE ROUTINE AT the Manhattan ashram was very similar to Birchwood Falls and Ravipur, I missed living in the presence of the physical guru and being surrounded by people who had turned their backs on the world to immerse themselves in Raja Yoga. In the Manhattan ashram, where all the residents either went to school or held jobs outside, I felt like I was living in limbo. Yet at the same time, even though I missed Baba and longed to return to his side, as the days passed I surprisingly found myself beginning to love school. I gave it my all, and never missed a class. I think at least some of my enthusiasm for the course was thanks to the encouragement I got from my instructor.

"You have a real talent for camera work and storytelling," Eric told me after screening a piece on the homeless I had shot and edited myself. "You should definitely stick with it."

The other students in my course respected my work too. A short piece I directed on Vietnam veterans and post-traumatic stress disorder got a big round of applause.

A few weeks into the course, something unexpected happened. A girl in the class showed interest in me. The conversation began with a note, which she wadded into a ball and tossed onto my desk while Eric had his back to the class. She was a pretty girl with big brown eyes, dark curly hair, and enormous breasts. I knew her name was Rachel—Rachel Hershkovitz. I remembered her last name because it rhymed with tits. Even though I knew it was wrong, I had secretly dubbed her "Hershkotits" after everyone introduced themselves on the first day of class. She was a sophomore at Stern, the women's college at Yeshiva University. She dressed more modestly than most girls her age. Her standard outfit was a charcoal gray sweater and a long black skirt that reached her ankles. She would have fit in perfectly at the ashram.

"Open it," she mouthed.

Straightening out the piece of paper, I read the message:

Imagine a day when your search for the meaning of life ends, because you find yourself at your spiritual center.

She obviously doesn't know who she's dealing with, I thought, chuckling to myself.

I glanced over at Hershkotits and waved. She waved back and grinned. When Eric turned his back to the class again to write something on the board, I again looked in her direction. She was busy writing another note. When she was finished, she crumpled it up and then flung it onto my desk:

Please join me for a Shabbat dinner this Friday evening at the Chabad house in Midtown.

Rachel was referring to the Jewish Sabbath, something my own family had never observed. Shabbat was a sacred day of rest when religious Jews were forbidden to do any work, drive a car, build a fire, or even turn on an electric light. Rachel was attractive, but I couldn't imagine a bigger waste of my time than spending a Friday night reciting Hebrew prayers. Even so, after class I struck up a conversation with her.

"I'm taking the course for elective credit," she said. "Stern is a liberal arts college. It doesn't offer any classes in video production and broadcasting." She explained that she planned to move to Israel after graduation and seek a job in television.

I walked her to the subway. "How did you know I was a member of the tribe?"

Rachel smiled proudly. "A Jewish woman knows these things. Have you thought about joining me at the Chabad house for Shabbat?"

"What's the Chabad house?"

"Think of it as a safe, cozy place where non-practicing Jews like you can learn more about their own faith."

I thought of my infidel brother and sister-in-law and the Jewish holy man they now followed. "Does this have anything to do with the Lubavitcher Rebbe?"

Rachel's eyes lit up. "Why yes, it does!" She explained that Menachem Schneerson—the Rebbe—was the founder of the movement. "How did you hear about him?"

"My brother and his wife are followers," I said, remembering their disloyalty to Baba.

"Wonderful, wonderful!"

"So, what's the big deal about your Rebbe? Is he supposed to be the Messiah or something?"

Rachel looked thoughtful for a moment. "Let's just say he's *eligible*."

We took a urine-soaked flight of stairs into the subway. I thought of telling her about Baba and how *he* could change *her* life. But I didn't think she'd understand, and I didn't want to put her off.

"So will you come?" she asked, lightly tugging on my upper-arm.

I had absolutely no intention of ever setting foot inside a synagogue, or a "Chabad house" for that matter. But I could tell Rachel was a nice girl, and I didn't want to insult her, or hurt her feelings.

"I would love to, but I'm a vegetarian. I doubt they'll have anything for me to eat."

Rachel laughed. "Orthodox Jews eat vegetables too, you know!"

"I have an idea," I said. "Why don't I take *you* out sometime? How about a movie?"

Rachel giggled and swatted my arm. "I'm not interested in dating you! If you're so worried about the food, eat before you come."

"I don't know—"

"Shabbat is a time for friends and family to relax and enjoy each other's company. You don't have to be observant to appreciate it."

The word "family" triggered a feeling of longing deep inside of me. I almost accepted her invitation, but then immediately changed my mind: *Baba is my real father.* I reminded myself. *Raja Yoga is the only family I will ever need.*

"Thanks, but no thanks."

As we waited on the platform for her train, I took another gander at Rachel. She looked like a chaste, wholesome young woman, and I could picture her as a *darshan* girl in a sari. *What harm could it do to get to know her better?*

"Want to catch a movie sometime?" I asked.

Before she could answer, her train pulled into the station. The train doors opened and she stepped inside.

"So what are you doing Saturday night?"

She smiled. "I guess I'll have to say thanks, but no thanks too."

I took the IRT to West Fourth Street, the closest station to the ashram. Walking the rest of the way home from my stop, I did a double take when a familiar face in the window of a diner caught my eye. I recognized the shoulder-length auburn hair and pouting mouth. They belonged to Cassandra, the girl Sergio had asked me to bring to Baba's house—the one who had made a scene on the ashram shuttle and carelessly left her gift from the guru behind. She appeared to be arguing with a bald man seated across from her. Crossing in front of the window, I turned discreetly to see if I knew him. Much to my surprise, it was Swami Satyananda! He was nursing a cup of coffee. Dressed in street clothes instead of his usual swami robes, he had been unrecognizable to me from the back. His brows were drawn in, and he was holding one of his elbows while the opposite hand was balled into a fist against his mouth. Neither of them noticed me.

Back in the ashram, I reported for my afternoon *seva*. As I dusted and vacuumed the meditation hall, I couldn't stop thinking about Cassandra and wondering what had happened to make her so upset that day. Then it hit me. The explanation was obvious and had nothing to do with Baba: Cassandra was a beautiful woman. Sergio must have been unable to resist hitting on her. Maybe he even tried to have sex with her! She was probably in the middle of telling Satyananda the whole story right now. I had confidence that Swamiji would know what to do. He'd call Baba and tell him everything.

The following Monday, I found another note on my desk from Rachel:

Hi Doug! I changed my mind. I think it would be fun to see a film together.

After class, Rachel and I made a date for the following Saturday evening, after the Jewish Sabbath, which ended at sundown.

She suggested I pick her up at her dormitory on East 34th Street, near the Empire State Building. "Be sure to wear a yarmulke."

"But I don't have one."

Rachel's big brown eyes widened, and she laughed. "I'll bring one to school for you tomorrow."

"Um, okay." I was beginning to think this date was more trouble than it was worth. What if we ran into someone from the ashram while I was wearing a Jewish skullcap?

"Don't worry," she smiled. "You won't have to wear it all night. Just when you come to get me. I don't want my friends to think I'm dating an apostate!"

"As a matter of fact, I am an apostate."

She laughed. "I like you, Doug. You're funny!"

On Saturday, I stood outside Rachel's building and took the yarmulke she had lent me out of my pocket, and then fastened it to the crown of my head with the accompanying bobby pin. In the lobby, a tall black man in a security guard uniform intercepted me.

"Where do you think you're going, young man?"

"I'm here to see Rachel Hershkovitz."

"You keep your shirt on, son. I'll let her know you're here."

I gave the guard my name and he called up to Rachel's room from his desk. When he was off the phone, I asked for her room number.

The guard shook his head, slapped his side, and laughed. "You can take a seat with the others, Casanova.

If you boys were allowed upstairs, those girls would all be pregnant in two minutes."

I sat down in the lobby with several other young men in yarmulkes. Soon Rachel came downstairs and after we had walked a few blocks, I started to take the yarmulke off.

"You can leave it on if you want," Rachel smiled. "You look good in it."

"No thanks," I said, and stuck the skullcap back in my pocket.

We took the subway uptown a few stops and got off at East 59th Street, near Bloomingdales. The theater was just around the corner on Third Avenue.

One of the films playing was *Terms of Endearment*, starring Shirley MacLaine, Debra Winger, and Jack Nicholson. Rachel had heard it was good. The movie was supposed to be funny and I liked Jack Nicholson, so I agreed to see it.

Unfortunately, I was in for an unpleasant surprise: the film started out as comedy, but it ended in tragedy. Toward the end, the character played by Debra Winger was diagnosed with cancer and eventually died. This brought back memories of my mother's illness. By the time the movie was out, I wanted to ditch Rachel and get back to the safety of the ashram as soon as possible.

"What did you think?" she asked, pulling a tissue out of her purse to wipe her eyes.

"Pretty good," I said. My eyes were dry. I was determined to keep my feelings to myself.

"You want to get a drink?" she asked. "I know a place on Lexington."

"Sure." I didn't want to be impolite.

We walked a couple of blocks and I followed Rachel into a smoke-filled restaurant. We sat down at the bar. Rachel ordered a single-malt whiskey. I ordered a coke.

Rachel eyed me incredulously. "You don't drink?"

"Nope."

"Any special reason?"

I tried to think of something to say without revealing too much about myself. "Alcohol is a toxin," I said, remembering what Poonish Davidson had told me when I asked him the same question.

"Oh, I see, you're into health food," she said. "I get it."

"Actually, I'm surprised that *you* drink."

Rachel laughed and pretended to take exception. "Why? Because I'm orthodox?"

"Well, that, and, I guess I didn't think Jews were big drinkers." I couldn't recall ever seeing my mother or elder siblings drinking alcohol, except on the High Holy Days.

"You mean, because it might prevent us from suffering?"

I had no idea what she was talking about. "Sorry?"

"It was a joke!"

The drinks came and we clinked glasses. I took a better look at my date: she was not unattractive, but she was nothing compared to Gopi. Rachel might have been considered pretty on Planet Earth, but Gopi was a yogini—a celestial being. She radiated the guru's *shakti* from every pore.

"Why do you want to move to Israel?" I asked.

Rachel's face brightened. "The Jews have dreamed of returning to the Promised Land for two thousand years."

"Well, speaking for myself, it hasn't been this Jew's dream. Why do *you* want to live there?"

"I've wanted to make *Aliyah* ever since my parents first took me to Israel when I was twelve years old."

The Hebrew word *Aliyah* meant *to ascend*. That's what Zionists called the act of moving permanently to the Holy Land.

"I guess I have a lot of reasons, but what I love most of all about Israel is how much emphasis is put on family and the strong sense of community."

At the time I didn't understand why, but after the upsetting movie and what Rachel said about Israel being family-oriented, I almost lost it. I had to excuse myself to use the restroom so that I wouldn't cry in front of her. As I took a leak, out of nowhere the oddest idea popped into my head: *I should find a nice Jewish woman to take care of me.* Maybe moving to Israel wouldn't be such a high price to pay for the right one. Maybe that's why Jeremy was trying to change Carrie into a Jew.

As I headed back to the bar, Rachel caught my eye and waved coyly. In that moment, something about her turned me off. I couldn't put my finger on it.

I paid the tab and, because it was a warm night, offered to walk Rachel back to her dorm. When we were halfway there, she started to talk about her parents. Her father was a doctor and her mother was a housewife.

"What do your folks do?" Rachel asked.

I always found it embarrassing having to tell people my parents were dead, as if it was somehow a poor reflection on me. "Both my parents are deceased, actually. My dad was a CPA, and my mother was a housewife, too. They both died before I was seventeen."

"Oh, Doug!" Rachel said, stopping in the middle of the sidewalk on 42nd Street. She turned to face me and grabbed my two hands. "I'm so sorry to hear that!"

She was crying. I couldn't believe it. Rachel didn't even know me, yet she was so affected by my sad story that there were actually tears in her eyes. I began to tear up as well.

She looked searchingly into my eyes. "I can't even imagine what it must have been like to lose both parents at such a young age."

In that instant, I wanted to spend the rest of my life with this woman who seemed to care so much. I would follow her anywhere. I would make *Aliyah* if I had to. She took me in her arms and began to kiss me.

I should have gotten excited. After all, I'd gone without any physical contact with the opposite sex for ages. And I was still a virgin. Yet although Rachel was pretty and nice enough, she didn't do it for me. As she kissed me, I barely opened my mouth.

"Get a room, for Christ sakes!" cursed an older man, irritated that he had to walk around us.

We stopped kissing and laughed. Then she stared up at me bashfully. "Do you want to?" she asked.

"Want to *what?*"

With a nod of her head, Rachel gestured toward the Grand Hyatt Hotel across the street. "Get a room somewhere?"

I was intrigued. But it made absolutely no sense. The idea that an orthodox girl would suggest getting a room in a hotel on our first date—or any date, for that matter—seemed so farfetched. *She must be testing me,* I told myself.

I took a good look at the woman in front of me and thought about what I wanted. In my mind's eye I tried to picture her naked and I thought back to the time I'd been lonely in my hotel suite at the Taj in Bombay. *It might be nice,* I told myself.

Then it hit me, what it was about Rachel that turned me off: the idea of being intimate with her seemed like incest. She looked and behaved like a close relative. *She could be one of my sisters!* Something else occurred to me: it wasn't Rachel testing me, but Baba himself! Besides, I only wanted my beloved Gopi.

"Um, thanks," I said. "I'm really flattered, but ... there's somebody else."

Rachel jerked her head back and released me from her grip. "What?"

"I'm sorry."

Her face distorted into an ugly mask. "Why did you ask me out then? Why did you kiss me?"

"I don't know..." I said, reflecting on the fact that it had been *she* who kissed *me*. "I guess I made a mistake."

"I'll say!"

"You wanted me to come to your Shabbat dinner. I didn't want to go, but I didn't want to hurt your feelings either. You seem like a nice girl."

"Up yours, Doug!" Rachel snapped, stepping to the curb to hail a taxi.

BY THE SECOND WEEK of November, only two weeks remained of my program at NYSB. For the first few days after our disastrous date, Rachel avoided me, but after a while it was as if our awkward evening together had never happened. Although it was clear she was no longer interested, she did occasionally smile at me when we ran into each other at school.

After covering the basics of studio operations and field production, the focus of the course shifted to post-production and the completion of our final projects. Mine was a five-minute report on the gentrification of the neighborhood of Morningside Heights on the Upper West Side. Studying the basics of journalism had stimulated my curiosity. While shooting video for my project, I visited Columbia University, located in the area. I passed through the campus gates and found myself in a vast courtyard surrounded by impressive old buildings that reminded me of Cornell. To my left, at the top of a grand flight of steps, was Low Memorial Library. With its Greek columns, it reminded me of photographs I'd seen of the Pantheon in Rome. Midway up the steps was a sculpture of Alma Mater, the mother goddess. Her arms were raised in benediction, beckoning me to mount the steps, granting admission to the temple.

I surveyed the campus, nostalgic about my brief time at Cornell. *Maybe I did throw out a great opportunity*, I thought. *There are so many things I would like to study and learn about.* I regarded the students with their backpacks full of textbooks, sitting on the steps and chatting with one another, and I wished I could be one of them. Suddenly, I yearned to be back in school. *I missed my chance...*

I was laying down a narration track when Eric stuck his head into the editing suite to see how I was doing.

"No question about it, Doug," Eric said watching the segment I was working on over my shoulder. "You've got a real talent for filmmaking."

I thanked my instructor for his words of encouragement, but inwardly offered my gratitude to the guru for blessing me with talent.

"You should really think about applying to film school. NYU has an excellent undergraduate program."

The mention of New York University soured my mood. Months after being rejected, I was still smarting.

"If you ask me, a bright kid like you belongs in college."

When I returned home to the ashram later that day, I was overjoyed to find Gopi. She was seated at a table in the library, slumped over a cup of chai, and wearing tight jeans and an oversize Guess sweatshirt. A stylish overnight bag rested on the floor beside her.

"Gopi!"

"Hey, Deependra," she said, lifting her head wearily. Her eyes were puffy and she looked tired, but I sensed something more was wrong.

I pulled up a chair and sat down opposite her. I welcomed her back to the East Coast and asked her about the new Berkeley Hills ashram.

"Baba's very pleased with the renovations," she said. Her voice was flat. Emotionless. She took another sip of tea. "You'll have to excuse me. I took the red eye from San Francisco last night and didn't get much sleep on the plane. How's school?"

"Great. I'm learning a lot about video production, but I really miss Baba, obviously." Gopi nodded politely, then stared down into her cup. "Has the Audiovisual department found a replacement for me on second camera yet?"

"Nobody's on camera at the moment."

"*Nobody*? What about Arjuna?"

"Left," she said, looking away.

"Left what?" I asked. "The tour?"

Gopi was silent for a moment. Then she turned to me and answered. "No. He left Raja Yoga."

Powerful emotions whirled inside me. *First my brother, now Arjuna—a member of Baba's tour staff. How is it possible?* I was too afraid to ask her why. "Can I take your bag up to your room?" I asked instead.

Gopi shook her head glumly. "No, thank you."

Just then, Swami Satyananda appeared in the doorway of the library. He looked paler than usual and had dark circles under his eyes. "I can meet with you now, Gopi."

The angel stood up abruptly and, without saying a word to me, slung her bag over her shoulder and strode past the swami in the direction of the ashram office, with Satyananda on her heels.

"Fuck Jeremy and Carrie!" I muttered under my breath as I cleaned the meditation hall. *"Fuck Arjuna!"* The vacuum cleaner accidentally caught the fringe of the Persian carpet under Baba's throne and I swore out loud: "Fuck!" Whipping my head around, I double-checked to make sure I was alone. I sat cross-legged on the floor and, as carefully as possible, extracted the border threads of the rug from the bristles of the vacuum. "Fuck! Fuck! Fuck!" I was angry and wanted the guru to hear me. I raised my head and glared at the large framed photo of Baba resting on the throne. The guru in the picture glowered down at me.

"Why?" I asked the guru. "Why, Baba? Why did they leave you? What do they know that I don't know?"

The expression on Baba's face in the picture softened. *Baba loves me*, I thought. Tears welled behind my eyes. *Baba loves me. I don't give a shit about why the others left. I will remain loyal until the day I die.*

It was my turn to help serve dinner. There was no program that evening, so the line was short. When Gopi passed through the kitchen on the meal line, she seemed to be in better spirits.

I ladled soup into the bowl on her tray. "Feeling any better?"

"Much better," she said with a forced smile. "Gotta hate the red eye."

After everyone was served, I joined Gopi at a table in the library, and asked what she was doing back in New York, away from the guru.

"I'm here on ashram business," she said, and left it at that. I knew enough not to ask any follow up questions.

We spoke more about my course, and the final project I was working on. Just as we finished eating, Gopi got a mischievous look in her eye. "Hey Deependra, what do ya say we blow this joint?"

My pulse quickened. "Sure! What do you have in mind?"

Gopi bit her lower lip and thought about it for a second. "Put on something spiffy and meet me in the reception area in thirty minutes."

Breathe deeply, I told myself as I changed into a coat and a tie. *Don't be nervous—she obviously likes you.* I threw on a contrasting pair of wool trousers, and sprayed copious amounts of Kouros cologne on my neck and wrists.

Waiting downstairs in the reception, I tried to clear my mind of impure thoughts by repeating the mantra.

I glanced at my watch. It had already been more than thirty minutes. *Remember, don't let her see how excited you are*, I told myself. *It will turn her off.*

"Going out?" came a whiny voice from behind the reception window. I looked up to see Sol, the night watchman, standing behind the counter.

"Um, yeah," I answered, eyeing the exit. Sol Berliner had lived in the Manhattan ashram since it first opened back in 1971. He was a fat, balding man in his mid-fifties who wore the same badly-worn blue and white striped sweater and sailor's cap every day. His ashram *seva* was to sleep on a foam mat in the office every night and open the door for residents who came home after lights out. Only Swamiji and Kalidas Smith, the ashram manager, had keys.

"I lock the door at ten," he warned. "If you're coming back later, you gotta ring the buzzer to wake me up."

I had never returned to the ashram after lights out, and wondered if it was frowned upon. Then I remembered I'd be with Gopi—one of Baba's people. The rules didn't apply to her.

She appeared at the top of the stairs in a red pea coat, low-cut black dress, and high-heeled black patent leather shoes. The transformation from chaste *darshan* girl to city sophisticate took my breath away. She was so irresistible to me in that moment, I would have given anything to have her.

"Gopi, you look...amazing."

Descending the stairs, she blushed and smiled shyly.

Sol Berliner eyed her disapprovingly. "Don't stay out too late," he grumbled.

We stepped out of the ashram into the bitter cold November night and hailed a taxi. "Where am I taking you?" I asked, opening the door for her.

Hopping into the cab, Gopi smiled and winked at me. "You'll see," she said, then leaned forward to speak to the driver. "Thirty Rockefeller Plaza, please."

The taxi sped up Sixth Avenue, and then made a right on West 23rd Street. "How long are you in town?"

"Just a couple of days," she answered, looking out the window. Then she turned to me. "Deependra, what do you think of Satyananda?"

"Swamiji? I like him. I mean, everybody likes him. He's very...inspiring."

Gopi tilted her head to the side and stared back at me skeptically. "Don't you think he has a big ego?"

The cab turned up Madison Avenue. I thought about her question and remembered Satyananda's claims about the blue rays of light shooting from his eyes, and his ability to give the touch like Baba.

"Well, I did hear him imply that he was already enlightened when he met the guru, and that he has the power to give *shaktipat*."

Gopi frowned. "Have you ever heard him speak critically of Baba?"

I shook my head. "No, never."

The taxi turned left onto East 49th Street, and then pulled up in front of the RCA building, home of the NBC television studios. Below was a sunken ice-skating rink and an enormous bronze gilded statue of the Titan Prometheus. The flags of countries from all over the world surrounded the recessed plaza. I paid the driver and we hopped out of the cab.

"Lead on, Mademoiselle Defournier," I said, beaming a smile at Gopi and making a grand gesture toward the entrance of the art deco-style skyscraper building. I had the feeling my first date with the angel was going to be expensive.

We rode the express elevator up to the sixty-fifth floor. "Welcome to the Rainbow Room," the host said. Because we were just having drinks, he escorted us to the bar and grill area.

"Could we be seated next to the window, please?" Gopi asked. After a moment's hesitation, the host showed us to a table with a spectacular view of the Empire State Building and the rest of the Manhattan skyline shimmering below.

"Well, Deependra, what do you think?"

I was breathless. "Amazing! You've been here before?"

Gopi's shoulders drooped and a look of sadness came over her. She nodded. "In the dining room they have a rotating dance floor," she said without enthusiasm.

"Wow!" I pictured her at the same table with Sergio, staring into his eyes like a love-sick school girl, and felt pangs of jealousy. I was about to ask her if something was the matter, but a waitress came to take our order.

"What can I bring you tonight?"

Gopi turned to me. "Have you ever had a Long Island Iced tea?"

"I don't think so."

"I think you'll like it," she said, the smile returning to her face. "Two Long Islands, please."

I was relieved she hadn't ordered any alcohol. I was still unclear about whether Baba approved of it or not.

A few minutes later, the waitress returned with two of the largest glasses of iced tea I'd ever seen. Each glass came with a thick slice of lemon and a plastic straw.

When we were alone again, Gopi looked me squarely in the eye and raised her glass. "Salud."

I clinked my glass against hers. "L'chaim." I took a sip and was so surprised to taste alcohol, I nearly spit it out.

Stifling a laugh, Gopi nearly lost hers too. "How do you like it?"

I took a second, smaller sip. The drink was sweet and lemony, but it didn't taste anything like tea. "Strong," I answered, my throat burning. "But yes, it's good. How much of this is actually *tea*?"

Gopi smiled playfully. "None of it. It's made from five different kinds of alcohol."

"Does Baba know you drink?"

"Baba teaches that everything is consciousness."

I took another long sip of the concoction. "What about the ashram rules?"

Gopi rattled the ice in her glass. "We're not in the ashram now, are we?"

I gazed into the angel's mismatched blue and green eyes. I'd never seen anyone with such unusually beautiful eyes before. They fascinated me, and it was all I could do to stop staring.

"Baba speaks very highly of you, you know," she said.

A tingling warmth spread through my body. "He does?"

Gopi nodded. "He says that your heart is very pure."

I filled with gratitude. *Baba knows me better than I know myself*, I mused. I took another sip of my drink. As the alcohol began to take effect, I felt warm and cozy.

"I've read Baba's *Introduction to Kashmir Shaivism*," I said. "So I understand that everything is an expression of the same divine energy."

Gopi nodded in agreement. "It's one thing to understand that intellectually, Deependra. It's another to have a direct, intuitive realization of it, like Baba."

"But I have. When Baba gave me *shaktipat* I had an experience that confirmed that everything the scriptures say is true. The guru is consciousness, I'm consciousness, you're consciousness, the building is consciousness—" I raised my drink in the air and spilled a little in the process. "This so-called Long Island Iced Tea is consciousness too."

Gopi giggled.

"So, if I pull out a gun and shoot somebody, it's just consciousness shooting consciousness?"

Gopi jerked her head back and narrowed her eyes. Then she tilted her head to the side and became lost in thought. I couldn't blame her for being taken aback—the boldness of my words surprised me, too.

"Well, yes."

The muscles tightened in the back of my neck. I took a big swig of my drink. "So, nothing we do matters?"

She shook her head. "Baba doesn't teach that—"

"There's no such thing as good and evil? Right and wrong?"

"From the point of view of an enlightened being, there is only Shiva. But you and I are *not* enlightened beings. We still have to live with the consequences of our actions."

"But an enlightened being doesn't?"

Gopi looked thoughtful again for a moment before responding. "Not exactly, but I guess you could say that they see the consequences of their actions as Shiva too."

"But if that's what Baba believes, why does he also teach *Advaita Vedanta?*"

"What do you mean?" she asked, using her straw to play with the ice in her drink.

"According to *Vedanta,* everything is an illusion—only the Inner-Self is real."

"That's right."

"But if everything is consciousness then everything is real. How can both of these philosophies be right?"

"*Kashmir Shaivism* and *Vedanta* only seem contradictory. They're just different ways of talking about the same Truth. The more we advance on the path, the more clearly we see this. In any case, the ultimate nature of reality can't be grasped by the conceptual mind. It can only be realized in a state of transcendence. That's why we meditate."

"So, if everything is consciousness, why are some thoughts and actions considered *pure* while others are considered *impure?*"

Gopi smiled, and brushed a few strands of her hair from her eyes. "This is really a better question for a swami, but in my understanding of *Shaivism,* there is no such thing as an impure action, only an impure way of looking at things. If you view everything you think, say, or do as an expression of Shiva, then your vision is pure."

"So we can do anything we want, as long as we have the *right view?*"

Gopi chuckled. "Let's not get carried away! We're not enlightened beings yet. Baba teaches *Vedanta* to beginners, but he emphasizes *Kashmir Shaivism* to his more advanced disciples."

I took a big swig of my Long Island Iced Tea. "So which are you, Gopi? Beginner or advanced?" I noticed I was slurring my words.

She smiled knowingly. "I am pure consciousness. Whether I realize it or not."

"I'll drink to that," I said, raising my glass.

We ordered another round of drinks and I asked for the check. I considered asking Gopi what she knew about why Arjuna had left Raja Yoga, but didn't want to upset her again.

Gopi tilted her head to the side and furrowed her brow. "What's on your mind? You look like you have another question."

Instead of returning to the subject of Arjuna, I shifted gears. "Do you think Avadhoot is crazy?"

Gopi laughed so hard she sprayed some of her drink back into her glass.

"Why ever would you ask such a question?"

I raised my hands in the air and gave an exaggerated shrug.

"Did he ever speak to you in the voice of Professor Karofsky, and tell you about his theory of *irrelevant relativity*?" she giggled.

"The Russian physicist? Yes! Hilarious! But I thought it was *relative irrelevancy*."

Gopi rolled her eyes. "That's a different one."

I shook my head and laughed. "What a nutcase!" It felt good to laugh. "By the way, what happened to his face? Was he in some kind of accident? He looks like he's had plastic surgery."

Gopi's expression became more somber. She told me that when Avadhoot was a baby he had been left unsupervised on a bed next to a boiling hot radiator. He had rolled over on his side, bringing the left side of his face in contact with the searing heat. The accident left him disfigured and in excruciating pain.

"They had to give him something like twenty operations to reconstruct the left side of his face," she said. "Supposedly his parents left him alone in the hospital for days or even weeks at a time. A thing like that can really mess a person up."

I stared into my drink for a moment before speaking. "I think I can relate."

Gopi slowly reached across the table and took my hand in hers. "I know you can."

Our eyes locked and the angel stroked the back of my wrist. My breath caught in my chest. "You know about my father and mother passing away?"

Gopi nodded and squeezed my hand.

"How did you hear about it?"

"The ashram manager always briefs Baba about all the new people staying in the ashram. I was there when Alan told Baba all about you."

Why does the guru need briefings if he's omniscient? I wondered.

The waitress brought the second round and handed me the check. I peeked at it and was stunned. I had no idea that drinks could be that expensive, even in a place as fancy as the Rainbow Room.

Gopi raised her glass. "I don't know about you, but I'm already three sheets to the wind."

I raised my glass and clinked it against hers. "L'chaim."

I gazed deeply into her sapphire and emerald eyes. She stared dreamily back into mine. "May I ask you a personal question, Gopi?"

She flashed me a knowing smile. "It's called heterochromia of the eye. I was born with it."

"Pardon?"

"I knew you were going to ask me about my eyes."

"Yes, I was. Sorry."

"It's okay. Everybody does. I get them from my father. He also has two different colored eyes. When I was little I hated them. I thought they made me a freak. But now that I'm older I like them."

"I think they're amazing. Like two precious jewels. They're one of your best features."

Gopi's lips parted and her eyes widened. "Oh really? What are my other good features?" I noticed Gopi was now slurring her words, too.

"Everything about you is gorgeous," I said, reaching across the table to take her hand in mine again. "Your hair, your face—I think you're the most beautiful girl I've ever seen."

Gopi smiled self-consciously. Then her face suddenly went slack.

"What's wrong? Is it something I said?"

She shook her head and pulled her hand away from mine. Tears escaped her eyes. I glanced around the restaurant. I wanted to get up from my seat and give her a hug, but my gut told me she didn't want one in that moment—at least not from me. I handed her my napkin instead.

After an uncomfortably long time, Gopi finally stopped crying and used my napkin to wipe away her tears.

"Are you okay?" I asked.

She stared down into her drink. "Baba always says, 'If you see me as a god, I am a god. If you me as a demon, I am a demon. If you see me as an ordinary man, I am an ordinary man.'"

My mind froze. "Why are you telling me this?"

"There are people who want to hurt Baba."

Her words set off an alarm in my head. "Who? What people?"

"Some people who were close to Baba," she said, looking away. "They left and now they're telling lies about him."

"Who could possibly want to hurt Baba?"

"Worthless jerks," she answered, her jaw line hardening. "Old-timers with sour grapes."

I felt a tightening in my chest. Gopi's words upset me, but they didn't shock me the way they would have in the past. I already knew that people made up stories about Baba and the people around him. My own brother had turned his back on him. People were fickle, and many people came to the guru seeking enlightenment only to lose sight of the real goal along the way. When they didn't get the position they wanted, or felt they weren't being treated fairly, they left. I assumed this had been the case with Arjuna.

I paid the check, and we took the elevator down to the lobby.

"I don't know what to think, Deependra," Gopi said. "Some people can spend half their lives around the guru and never *get it*. Others, like you, understand everything immediately."

"What are these traitors saying about Baba?" I wasn't sure if I really wanted to know, but felt compelled to ask.

The elevator doors opened and we stumbled out into the lobby. I took Gopi by the arm to steady her and nearly fell over myself in the process.

"Lies so awful they should never be repeated," she said.

It was still early, so we decided to walk part of the way home before getting a taxi.

I took her arm. "You were practically born into Raja Yoga I hear, is that true?"

"Uh-uh. My parents were among the first visitors to Baba's ashram in Ravipur in the late sixties. Some of my earliest memories are of sitting in Baba's lap in the courtyard of the ashram. I've been traveling with him ever since."

"What about school?"

"All the kids around Baba are home-schooled. Some of the swamis are excellent teachers."

I commented on how lucky I thought she was to have parents who supported her choice to be with Baba. Then I told her about the problems I was having getting Melanie to release funds from my mother's trust to pay for my tuition and living expenses.

"Don't worry about it too much," Gopi said. "The guru's grace will take care of everything. Baba loves you. We're your family now, Deependra."

Hearing these words from someone so close to the guru melted my heart and filled me with gratitude. Stopping in the middle of the sidewalk, I took the angel in my arms, and pulled her close.

"I love you, Gopi. I've loved you since the moment I first saw you on my first day at the ashram."

She leaned in and gently kissed me on the cheek, near the corner of my mouth. She was close enough so that I could smell her sweet, fragrant hair, and I thought back to the last time I was this close to her—the night she had visited my room in Haridwar.

"You're my angel," I whispered, kissing her on the nape of her neck. She moaned softly, and then suddenly our lips were touching. As we kissed, Gopi let her tongue slip into my mouth. Suddenly I wanted to run away with her. We'd get a taxi to the airport and hop on the next plane to Hawaii or somewhere in the Caribbean. We wouldn't tell anyone where we were going and we'd never look back. In that moment, I thought all I needed to be happy was this astonishingly beautiful, previously unattainable girl. I would have given anything to be with her for the rest of my life.

I hailed a cab, and the next thing I knew we were making out in the back seat. As I tasted the inside of her mouth, I forgot all about Baba. There were only two people on the entire planet: Gopi and me. There was an urgency to our kissing—as if we might never get another chance again.

The ride back to the ashram didn't last long enough. Before I knew it, we were stumbling out of the taxi and kissing on the street. Then she pulled away and rang the buzzer to wake up Sol.

"You'll have to sign in," said the night watchman, bleary-eyed and yawning. Catching a whiff of my breath, he grabbed his nose and exaggeratedly waved a hand in front of his face.

Gopi frowned and rolled her eyes. "Is that really necessary?"

"Anyone who comes in after lights out has to sign the book," he whined. "Put the date and time, and print your name under your signature." Sol obviously didn't know who he was dealing with.

A life-size picture of Baba in the reception area caught my eye. It was the same photograph that welcomed me home every day with love and compassion. But now it was glaring.

Gopi and I climbed the staircase to the residential floors of the ashram. We came to my room first, and I stopped in front of my door. I turned to kiss her one last time when, to my surprise, she continued up the stairs without saying a word.

"Good night, Gopi," I whispered.

"Good night, Deependra."

I heard a door open and shut on the floor above me, and, for the first time in my life, I wished I had my own place.

29.
SOONER IS BETTER THAN LATER

THE SCREAM OF MY alarm clock penetrated the depths of my slumber, jolting me awake. My head throbbed in pain. My mouth and throat were parched. I rolled over onto my side to check the time. It was five A.M., time for morning meditation. Reaching for the snooze button, I accidentally knocked my clock off the nightstand and practically fell out of bed trying to silence it. Luckily my roommates were already awake and getting dressed. I went to the bathroom down the hall, took four aspirins with a tall glass of water, and then went back to sleep. When I awoke again a couple of hours later, my head was better, but I felt bad about neglecting my spiritual practice. I had missed both morning meditation and the *Guru Gita*. If I hurried, I could still catch breakfast and see Gopi before I had to leave for school.

By the time I made it downstairs, they were already putting the food away in the kitchen, but grudgingly served me a bowl of savory porridge and a cup of chai. The library was empty when I sat down to eat. There was no sign of Gopi. I thought about our conversation the night before, and wondered which people wanted to hurt Baba, and what they were saying about him.

Nitya popped her head into the library. She told me that Kalidas Smith, the ashram manager, was looking for me. Her manner was terse. My face flushed with heat. I was afraid I was in trouble for missing the chant. Then I remembered my late night with Gopi. Sol Berliner had smelled alcohol on our breath. Maybe he had reported us.

On my way out the door I stopped by the reception to look for Kalidas, but no one was behind the window. Hearing voices coming from the office, I stuck my head in the door to see if he was there. But instead of finding the ashram manager, I found Gopi and Satyananda, who were seated across from each other at Kalidas' desk. They were in the middle of a conference call with the guru himself. Gopi's shoulders were tight, and her expression was deadly serious. The swami's eyes were wide with fear, and his visage ashen. Baba's voice thundered out of the speakerphone. I had never heard the guru sound so angry. Even Anjali, ever dispassionate, sounded shaken. Her voice sounded shrill, and her translation was missing its usual confidence: "This woman—this whore—and all the others—they are liars and traitors! Stop returning their phone calls!"

"Yu—y-e-s, Baba," stuttered Satyananda.

Just then Gopi became aware of my presence in the doorway. She shooed me away with her hand. "Not now, Deependra!"

I backed away, shutting the door behind me.

My mind reeled on the way to school. I had witnessed the guru's anger before, but this was different. The rage in Baba's voice had frightened me. He sounded out of control.

No lectures were scheduled at school that day. Instead, we screened final projects, including my piece on the gentrification of Morningside Heights, and the displacement of its poor, minority population. When my video was over, the class gave it an enthusiastic round of applause.

Glancing around the room, I noticed Rachel Hershkovitz was staring at me and clapping loudly. When our eyes met, she beamed me a smile and nodded knowingly. I guessed all had been forgiven. By the middle of the next screening, a note from her landed on my desk: *Fantastic work! Very moving! You're such a talented, sensitive guy. Let's get coffee together sometime soon!*

After class, I used a Betamax machine in one of the editing suites to copy my final project onto the end of my showreel. My instructor Eric poked his head in. He complimented me on my video and struck up a conversation about my future plans, again suggesting that I strongly consider applying to college.

"If you don't feel ready for school, I think I might be able to help swing you an internship or a job in production," he said. "CNN opened a bureau in the city and they're looking for cameramen."

"What's CNN?" I asked.

"Cable News Network is an all-news station that's on the air twenty-four hours a day. It's a totally new concept in broadcasting."

Eric had piqued my interest. I thought maybe I could work for this cable news channel and take a few college courses at the same time. After a year or two, I could try applying to NYU again.

On the subway ride home I remembered that Kalidas Smith, the ashram manager, had been looking for me, and that I still hadn't spoken to him. I dreaded finding out what he wanted, but what awaited me was even more unsettling. I entered the ashram to find Sergio and Avadhoot sitting in the reception area. Avadhoot was cleaning the lens of his camera. He was wearing a shirt with a Nehru collar and a black Stetson hat. Sergio was seated next to him, dressed in an elegant dark gray suit, with a purple tie. Their overcoats and Avadhoot's camera bag were resting on a free chair next to them. When I realized Sergio was studying the logbook that Gopi and I had used to sign in after lights out the night before, I freaked.

"Deependra, baby!" Avadhoot exclaimed when he noticed me in the entrance. Setting his camera down on the chair next to him, he rose to his feet and pinched my cheek like a Jewish grandmother. "How ya doin', boychik?"

I shrugged. "I'm learning a lot at video school, but I miss Baba."

Sergio looked up from the logbook and lifted his chin in my direction. "Greenbaum," he said by way of greeting.

"What ya got there?" Avadhoot asked, eyeing the Betamax cassette I was holding.

"It's my showreel."

Avadhoot jutted his lower-lip out, furrowed his eyebrows, and then released them. "I'd like to take a look at that," he said. "We can watch it in the library later."

Maybe I'm not in any trouble after all, I thought.

Just then the door opened, and Satyananda entered the ashram behind me. He was casually dressed in an orange down vest, yellow shirt, and a pair of red sweatpants. Sergio dropped the book and sprang to his feet. The swami went pale.

Sergio flashed the swami an enormous phony smile. "Satyananda, *come stai?*"

"Sergio, Avadhoot," the swami responded, shaking his head. "This is unexpected."

"Let's take a walk," Avadhoot said, as he and Sergio pulled on their coats.

Satyananda's knees buckled as he backed up against the exit. "Why don't we talk in the office?" The swami turned to me, beseeching me with his eyes. I remembered how angry Baba had been with him on the phone earlier and got a sinking feeling.

The Italian frowned. "Nah, we hear you like coffee. Avadhoot knows a great place for espresso, don't you, cowboy?"

Avadhoot pursed his lips, and nodded absently. Then he turned to me. "Hey, boychik, hang onto my gear for a while, will ya?" Thrusting his camera into my hands, he and Sergio escorted Satyananda out of the building.

I took Avadhoot's equipment up to my room for safe-keeping, and then reported to the meditation hall for my afternoon *seva*. I wondered why Avadhoot and Sergio were in town. I knew that it couldn't have been a coincidence that they had flown in only a day after Gopi.

At dinnertime, Swamiji and the three visitors from the California ashram were conspicuously absent. I ate alone. As I got up to bus my tray, Avadhoot appeared in the entrance to the library.

"Deependra. Let's see that video of yours now."

Avadhoot checked the kitchen to see if there was anything left to eat, while I fetched the audiovisual cart from the utility closet and wheeled it into the library.

Standing beside me in front of the large television set, Avadhoot dunked a piece of bread into the bowl of soup he held in his hand. At first I had a problem with the Betamax player—it was old and needed to be replaced. As I struggled to get it to work, the photographer sighed heavily. After fiddling with it for a while, I finally got it to play my cassette. The opening clip on my reel was of a homeless man pushing a shopping cart full of cans and bottles and other scraps of junk through Central Park. His clothes were black with dirt. The next shot was of the same man sitting on a park bench speaking directly into the camera.

"I'm a Vietnam veteran," he said. "All I want is a chance to earn an honest dollar."

As the next segment began, I felt a presence behind me. I turned to see Sergio watching the video over my shoulder.

"You filmed this yourself?" he asked.

I told him that I had, and that I had also edited it. The Italian jutted his lower lip out, and nodded in approval. A minute later he complained that the audio was "too quiet." He reached for the volume knob on the monitor, and I noticed his knuckles were swollen, and that he had blood on one of his shoes.

After he had seen most of my reel, Avadhoot commented. "I see that you've been applying a lot of what I taught you. I'm sure you were much better prepared for this course than the rest of the bozos in your class."

"Um, yeah," I said, wondering about what had happened to Sergio's hand, and why he had blood on his shoe.

"When do you finish school?" Sergio asked.

"I've already completed my final project, but I have a theory exam in two weeks. After that, I'm done. My instructor thinks he could help me find an internship, or maybe even a paying job in broadcasting. I'm also thinking about taking some college courses."

Just then Gopi stormed into the library, screaming and pointing a trembling finger in our direction.

"How could you? Baba said to *talk* to him!" Her eyes were wild.

"*Sta 'zitto!*" Sergio shouted. "Keep quiet!"

Gopi covered her mouth with her hand, and burst out crying.

Sergio stared back with his mouth agape.

"*Ma cosa vuole dire? Non ci credo!* Why are you so upset?"

"You're an animal! I hate you!" Gopi cried. Then she turned around and ran from the room. Meanwhile, Avadhoot, seemingly oblivious to the altercation, continued to eat his soup and give the video his full attention.

"Clara, come back here!" the Italian called, and ran out of the library after her.

Clara? Clara, I realized, was Gopi's given name. When they were both gone, Avadhoot, who hadn't taken his eyes off the video once, finally spoke.

"This is pretty good, kid. Got anything else?"

I was worried about Gopi, and even more concerned about *why* she was so upset. But I decided it wasn't the right time to get involved.

"I have a couple of short studio projects I collaborated on, but they're at school."

At that moment, Satyananda stumbled into the library. One of his eyes was swollen shut, and he was bleeding from the mouth. He could barely stand on his feet. I knew then exactly how Sergio came to have blood on his shoe.

I rushed toward him. "Swamiji! Are you alright?"

Ignoring me, he addressed Avadhoot who was staring at him blankly. "Tell Baba I'll go."

"Will do, Swamiji," Avadhoot said, wiping his mouth on the sleeve of his shirt. "You're going to love Wichita."

"Can I help you, Swamiji?" I asked. I offered him my hand, but he shook his head and waved me off. Then he did an about-face, and staggered back out of the room.

"What happened to Swamiji?" I asked.

"None of your fucking business," Avadhoot said matter-of-factly. "Come on. The chant is going to start in a second. Let's go."

After the evening *arati*, I found Gopi downstairs in the reception area. Her eyes were red, and her face was puffy. I persuaded her to take a walk with me. We turned up West Fourth Street, and ducked into the diner where I'd seen Satyananda having coffee with Cassandra. We got a table and ordered milkshakes.

"Your given name is Clara?"

Gopi took a long sip from her straw. "Yeah, but nobody calls me that except Sergio—not even my parents."

I nodded. "You want to tell me what's going on?"

She stared into her shake, and took another big sip. After letting out a long sigh, she turned to me and spoke: "Baba sent me here to check on Satyananda."

"Is that why you were questioning me about him last night?"

"Yes. Baba says that Satyananda's got a big ego and that it's getting bigger. He sent me to find out what he's been saying to people."

"What did you learn?"

"Well, for one thing, he's completely deluded—thinks he's already enlightened."

"Baba sounded really angry on the phone this morning."

Gopi looked me squarely in the eye and glared. I got the message: it was none of my business.

I turned away from her and took a sip of my milkshake. "What are Sergio and Avadhoot doing here?" I turned my head to look at her again. Her expression had softened. "Why aren't they in California with Baba?"

"They're here to make sure Satyananda leaves," she answered. Then she explained that the guru was reassigning the swami, sending him to Wichita, Kansas, to open a new Raja Yoga center. "Baba will be appointing another swami to take his place here in Manhattan."

"Did Baba tell Sergio to beat up Satyananda?"

Gopi shook her head vigorously. "No! Of course not! It's just that Sergio is so protective of Baba. He goes *nuts* whenever he thinks anyone has been disloyal."

It didn't ring true. The swami was delusional perhaps, but how had he been unfaithful to the guru? "Are you going to tell Baba what happened?"

"I already have."

"What did he say?"

Gopi frowned and looked away.

She took another long sip of her milkshake and a tear ran down her cheek. I wiped it away with my napkin.

"You ask too many questions, Deependra," she scolded, brushing my hand away.

On the walk back to the ashram, she told me she'd be flying back to California with Sergio and Avadhoot the following morning.

I turned to her as we reached the door. "I'll miss you."

She acted as if she hadn't heard me. When we were inside, she vanished into the office. I had more questions for her about Satyananda, but I didn't dare push her too far. I wanted to ask her about the girl Cassandra—if she knew anything about what happened the night I brought her to Baba's house in Birchwood Falls, and why she had been so upset the next morning. But for now, the incident would have to remain a mystery.

On the way up to my room, I crossed paths with Kalidas on the stairway.

"Deependra, may I speak to you a moment?"

I suddenly felt unbearably hot. I'd completely forgotten that the ashram manager wanted to speak to me. I hoped it had nothing to do with my staying out late and returning to the ashram drunk with Gopi.

"I'd like to purchase a new video cassette player for the ashram," he said. "I wanted to know if you had any thoughts about VHS versus Betamax?"

I took a deep breath and exhaled. "No question about it—Betamax, definitely. It's much better quality. VHS has no future."

Two days after the incident with Satyananda, I was helping serve breakfast in the kitchen when Nitya came looking for me. She told me I had a phone call from the Berkeley Hills ashram, and that I should follow her back to the office. A feeling of dread came over me. I was afraid I might be in trouble for something. Maybe Gopi had told Baba I was asking too many questions. My hand trembling, I took the receiver from Nitya, who left me alone in the manager's office to speak privately.

"Ahhh Deependra, how are you?" came a familiar feminine voice on the other end of the line. It was Anjali—I would know her soft, Americanized Indian accent anywhere. "Baba wants you to come to California and join the tour."

My first reaction was elation: Baba wanted me back! My exile was about to come to an end, and I'd be reunited with Gopi! But my excitement was short-lived. If I rejoined the tour, I could forget about the job at CNN, and I'd have to put off going back to college indefinitely.

"Do you think you can be here by Friday?"

"*This* Friday?"

"Yes, this Friday. Is there a problem?"

"Um, ah—no. No problem. If that's when Baba wants me to come, that's when I'll come. Of course. It's just that I still have another two weeks left of my video production course, and I have a final exam coming up."

Anjali's voice became muffled for a few seconds as she spoke to someone else. I assumed it was the guru, because she was speaking in Hindi. "Baba says you should come by

Friday." Then I heard the guru speak in the background. "He says, sooner is better than later."

My call with Anjali and the guru ended and I was happy again. I realized Sergio and Avadhoot must have told Baba how professional my video project looked. Who needed college or a stupid job at a cable news station that nobody's ever heard of? I was about to become God's very own personal cameraman!

But I had a problem: I remembered Eric's announcement to the class that the final theory exam was mandatory. He had said that anyone who didn't pass it would automatically fail the course. If that happened, I realized, Melanie would never reimburse me for my tuition and living expenses from the trust.

I decided to call my older sister and explain the situation. I hoped that maybe, just maybe, she would understand. But my conversation with her went even worse than I had feared. When she heard I was dropping the program only two weeks before it ended, she was livid.

"Out of the question!" she shouted over the line. "We had a deal. You're not getting a dime from the trust. Did you even go to classes this time?"

I defended myself as best I could, telling her I hadn't missed a single lesson, and that my instructor loved my work. But the fact that I'd been doing well in the program only made her more angry.

"You're telling me Baba can't wait another two weeks? What could possibly be so important? Don't you see that con man doesn't care about you at all? That cult is destroying your life!"

"You have no idea what an honor and a privilege it is to be invited to join Baba's tour. You should be proud of me!"

Later at school, Eric was reviewing the logarithmic scale of exposure intensity on the camera lens. I didn't bother taking any notes. My mind was on my future with Baba. After class I informed Eric that it was my last day, and that I wouldn't be sitting for the final exam. I explained that I'd landed a job as a cameraman out in California, and that they needed me to start immediately.

"Well, okay then," he said with a forced smile. "Congratulations, I guess. If you ever come back east, give me a call and I'll try to hook you up."

When I turned around, I was surprised to see Rachel standing behind me. She was alarmed to hear I was leaving. Before returning to the ashram to pack, I had coffee with her at a diner down the street from the school. I decided to tell her about my involvement in Raja Yoga.

"I've been studying video production in order to be of service to my guru. I'm leaving before the end of the term because I'm urgently needed by him out in California."

"So, just what are the tenets of this Raja Yoga?" she asked, folding her arms in front of her massive boobs.

"We believe that at their core, all religions worship the same God. Each has a mystical tradition—a path to unity with the divine. What makes Raja Yoga unique is what's called *the guru's touch*. Through it, Baba's disciples are able to have an effortless experience of the divine."

"Interesting, interesting," Rachel said, lifting a finger to her lips. "But let me ask you a question: what kind of spiritual leader encourages one of his followers to be a quitter?"

The muscles in my neck and back tensed. "It's not like that. You have to understand, this is the way the guru tests his disciples. I view it as an opportunity to practice detachment and demonstrate my faith."

"So, let me get this straight. If this Baba character asks you to jump off a bridge, you'll do that too?"

I clenched my teeth. "I knew you would ask me that. First of all, the guru would never test me like that. What would be the point? But yes, if he did, I would obey him. I would do whatever he commanded."

Rachel squeezed her eyes shut and shook her head. "But why?"

"Because I trust him with every fiber of my being."

"I want you to know this, Doug: there's absolutely no chance of you and me ever dating again, but it will *never* be too late for you to come home to Judaism. The covenant between God and his chosen people is eternal. Even if you turn your back on God, he will never turn his back on you."

30.
BABA'S COMMAND

ON THE FLIGHT TO California I reflected on the incident with Satyananda. I'd been shocked and saddened at first, but then I remembered Baba's teachings: the guru's grace didn't always come in the form of sweet words of encouragement or gentle taps on the head with his wand of peacock feathers. Sometimes what a disciple needed was a good kick in the ass.

I understood that even if Baba hadn't ordered Sergio and Avadhoot to beat up the swami, whatever happened in the ashram was the will of the guru, and came about through his *shakti*. I vowed that I would be ready on the day Baba showed me his fiery side. If a whack from the guru's stick or a slap in the face was what I needed to cure me of the disease of egocentric existence, I would accept his medicine gratefully.

In the baggage claim area of the San Francisco airport, I was met by a gloomy-looking man with wiry gray hair holding a laminated sign: "*Raja Yoga Mission*." His name tag said: "Bill."

"I think you're waiting for me," I said.

"That depends. Are you Dee…" He glanced down at a piece of paper.

"Deependra—yes!"

I retrieved my bag from the carousel, and then followed Bill out of the climate-controlled terminal building. The sight of green trees refreshed my eyes, and the warm breeze against my face reminded me of India. It filled me with joy to know that I would soon be in the presence of the guru again. I took off my winter coat and carried it under my arm as we walked to the car.

The ashram was located in the Berkeley Hills, about a half hour east of San Francisco. On the way there, Bill the driver—a newcomer to Raja Yoga—filled me in on the history of Baba's new West Coast meditation Mecca.

"You should have seen the place before. It was an old broken-down lodge that the Mission bought at auction for peanuts. Now, thanks to Daniel Groza and his crew, it's even more beautiful than the Birchwood Falls ashram."

"Thanks to Baba's grace, you mean," I corrected.

Bill took his eyes off the road for a second to take a good look at me. Then he shrugged.

The sparkling new ashram was everything I had heard: lavish gardens, neatly manicured grounds, and stunning views of the San Francisco Bay and the city's skyline. It was smaller than the Birchwood Falls ashram, but thanks to its spectacular surroundings, it was even more impressive.

When my car pulled into the ashram driveway, I was met at the curb by Anjali, who greeted me like an old friend. We entered the main building of the compound through automatic sliding glass doors—like the ones in Birchwood Falls—that opened onto a plush lobby. The familiar Raja Yoga aromas of incense and Indian spices instantly made me feel at home. An enormous portrait of Baba, wearing a red ski hat and a blissful expression on his face, hung in the lobby. Under it were the words: "God lives within you, as you."

Anjali had Bill bring my bags to my room. "You'll be roommates with Poonish and Stephen," Anjali said with a big smile.

I couldn't have been more pleased. "Great!"

"And Baba would like to see you in his quarters as soon as you get settled in," she added casually. *Me? Summoned to the guru's house?* I didn't know whether to be excited or afraid.

I went by reception to pay my first month's rent. The woman behind the counter handed me my room key and name tag. I glanced at the plastic badge, and was overcome with joy: an orange sticker was affixed just above my spiritual name, indicating that I was now an official member of Baba's tour staff!

I was about to set off in search of my room, when a familiar voice called to me from the far side of the lobby. "Deependra! You're here!"

I turned to see Gopi rushing toward me with a wide, open-mouthed smile. I was so happy to see her I threw my arms around her. I could barely resist the urge to plant a big sloppy kiss on her lips.

Gopi gave me a quick tour of the ashram, starting with the dazzling meditation hall and its ornate crystal chandeliers and sumptuous new carpeting.

"It's not as large as the Birchwood Falls ashram, but it's a lot cozier. You're going to love it here. Baba's been coming to all the chants for the past few days, and Suresh—I mean Swami Brahmananda—has been playing the drums. They've been ecstatic!"

Gopi showed me to my room in the "VIP wing," which housed Baba's tour staff and any celebrity visitors to the ashram. The room was painted a cheerful shade of yellow, and contained three single beds, two of which were made up. I claimed the free bed by the window, where my driver had already deposited my bag.

"Isn't the view of the bay amazing?"

I turned to admire the vista through the large window above my bed. It left me breathless, my heart overflowing with gratitude to the guru.

When Gopi finished showing me around, I summoned the courage to ring the doorbell on the wall next to the vault-like door to Baba's private quarters. Rashmi, Baba's Indian valet, opened the door, and regarded me suspiciously. "Who are you?"

"I'm Deependra. Anjali told me to come."

Rashmi was quiet for a moment, staring at my face searchingly through big droopy eyes.

"I'm the cameraman."

Baba's attendant scratched his head and yawned. Then he looked up as though he were remembering something.

"Come along, young man," he said, motioning for me to enter. "Take off your shoes and follow me."

He led me down a long corridor, where we passed a man on a stepladder repairing a light fixture in the ceiling. I recognized him—it was Daniel Groza.

"Baba wants you to have a look at the Jacuzzi again," Rashmi said, looking up at Daniel. "He says the bubbles are not coming like before."

"It's probably air in the plumbing lines again. I'll take care of it."

Baba's Berkeley residence was even more splendid than his apartment in Birchwood Falls—black lacquer furniture with gold trim, life-size photographs of Gurudev Brahmananda interspersed with silk wall hangings, leather sofas and loveseats, thick white carpeting, modern light fixtures, and the largest television set I'd ever seen. Yet as I looked around the room I felt uneasy. *Why would a swami and an enlightened being choose to live in such opulence?* I wondered how the devotees would feel knowing that their "donations" were used to buy luxury goods for a renunciant.

I pushed the disloyal thoughts out of my mind and remembered something Baba had once said: "Some saints live their whole lives in poverty, others live in the lap of luxury. How they lead their lives depends entirely on their karma. I myself was a ruler in India in a previous incarnation. Many of you were loyal subjects and members of my court."

Judging from Baba's position as the world's most respected spiritual master, and the splendor in which he still lived, it was clear that the guru must have accumulated a tremendous amount of good karma over countless lifetimes.

Rashmi showed me into Baba's study, where the guru was seated cross-legged on a richly upholstered, armless chair under a portrait of Gurudev. Anjali and Suresh were seated next to him on a matching sofa. Ravana and Yama, Baba's pit bulls, lay prone at his feet. This was the first time I'd ever seen Baba sitting on the same level as any of his devotees.

I bowed down before him, and as I stood up, he reached toward me, and motioned for me to approach. Wrapping his arms around me, the guru pulled my head against his chest. Time stood still as Baba held me in his arms and kissed the top of my head. I couldn't remember ever being held in such a tender, loving embrace. I didn't have a care in the world. I was home again with my father, and felt cared for and protected. I prayed that I'd never be separated from him again.

Baba gently released me from his embrace and stared lovingly into my eyes. Then he looked me up and down and addressed me in Hindi. Anjali translated: "Baba missed you very much and is very happy to see you, Deependra."

"I also missed you, Baba," I said, tearing up.

The guru asked me if I was comfortable in my new room. I replied that I was, and he told me that if I was not, other arrangements could be made for me.

"Please, have a seat," Anjali said, gesturing to the loveseat opposite her and Suresh. Unable to bring myself to sit at the guru's level, I sat down on the floor next to Baba's dogs.

Suresh informed me that the mayor of Berkeley would be visiting the ashram tomorrow, and meeting the guru for the first time.

"Baba wants full coverage, so make sure you have enough videotape stock and that all your batteries are fully charged."

I assured him that I would, and thanked the guru for his confidence in me. Now I understood why Baba had needed me to come to California immediately, and why it hadn't been possible for me to finish my course.

Baba's successor smiled and winked at me. "Baba wants to put you in charge of the video department on tour. Do you think you can handle that kind of responsibility?"

I swallowed. "*Me?* I mean, of course—I'll do any *seva* Baba wants. It's just that I don't have any experience managing anything. I thought Jake was the head of Audiovisual."

"Jake will still be in charge of the editing in Birchwood Falls," Suresh explained.

"On tour you'll be reporting to Avadhoot," Anjali added.

All the more reason to worry, I thought.

The guru spoke again through his translator. "Baba says that video is vital to the mission of spreading Gurudev's teachings around the globe."

"I understand," I said, beginning to tremble a little. *What if I fuck up?*

Anjali and Suresh exchanged knowing glances and laughed. "Relax, Deependra," the guru's successor said. "You'll do fine!"

"May I ask a question?"

Baba turned to me, narrowed his eyes, and lowered his brow. "Yes."

"Will I be working alone, or will Arjuna be coming back at some point?"

As soon as the words had left my lips, I regretted bringing up the subject of my predecessor. The guru's eyes became cold and hard. One of his dogs lifted his head and growled at me. Baba's voice became agitated, his face reddened, and his arms flailed as he responded. Anjali translated his words calmly and dispassionately.

"Baba says you should study the *Guru Gita*, so that you will understand what happens to those who contradict and betray their spiritual master."

I knew exactly to which verses Baba was referring:

The Guru's Touch

One who speaks to the Guru in rude or insulting terms or who wins arguments with him is born as a demon in a jungle or in a waterless region.

If Shiva is angry with you, the Guru can save you, but if the Guru becomes angry with you, even Shiva cannot save you. Therefore, by all means, take refuge in the Guru.

"Don't worry, you won't have to do everything yourself," Suresh said. "There's one boy who will assist you. He's a professional cameraman, and was helping while you were away at school."

As Anjali reached down to pet Yama and Ravana, she addressed me on her own behalf. "You should understand that people come and people go, Deependra. Some come to the guru and expect instant enlightenment. When they don't get it, they blame Baba. There can be no progress on the path without the guru's grace," she continued. "But the disciple must also put forth an effort."

Baba turned to me and spoke through Anjali. "Do not listen to gossip. Stay focused on your spiritual practice. And *stop dreaming about girls!*"

I lowered my head in shame and my face burned with embarrassment. The guru knew everything that went on in my mind and heart. I felt utterly exposed.

"I will, Baba," I said, unable to meet his piercing gaze.

At that moment, a tall, imposing woman wearing an apron and accompanied by a young, pretty girl of around twelve or thirteen entered the guru's study. Baba's eyes widened when he saw the girl. He greeted her with an enormous smile. I noticed the woman had an orange sticker on her name tag. She was a member of the tour staff, like me. Then I remembered she was Chamundi, Daniel Groza's wife and Baba's personal cook. The girl's name tag had a green sticker indicating she was a visitor. She was a pretty young thing, with large brown eyes, a nub of a nose, and a tiny mouth. Her light brown hair was pulled back in a ponytail.

"This is Priya, Baba," the woman said, introducing the girl. "She's Sanjula Brenan's girl."

Baba smiled, wiggled his head from side to side, and waved a hand in the air in approval. "Acha, acha!"

"Priya helped prepare your lunch today." The girl cautiously approached the guru, dropped to her knees, and bowed down before him. Baba smiled lovingly, and then called for Rashmi, who appeared moments later. He had a box of fancy chocolates, which he handed to his master. The guru studied the box thoughtfully for a moment, and then plucked out a piece of chocolate and offered it to Priya. Cradling her right hand in her left, the girl reached out to receive it. The girl popped the rich looking bonbon in her mouth, savoring it slowly. Baba watched her eat with delight.

"Very good chocolate," Baba said in English. "From Belgium." The girl knelt and bowed again. The guru laughed heartily and patted her head.

Anjali exchanged glances with Chamundi and chuckled affectionately. "It's okay, Priya. Once is enough."

The rest of us laughed too, and the girl blushed. Baba handed the box of chocolates back to Rashmi, who offered some to the rest of us. My piece was cream-filled and had a richer flavor than any other chocolate I had ever tasted.

"You will cook for Baba, yes?" the guru asked, speaking to Priya in English. "Every day in Baba's kitchen."

The girl bit her lower lip and nodded.

"I'll see to it, Baba," Chamundi said.

A bright smile lit up the girl's face.

"Come back to Baba's house tomorrow morning after the *Gita*, Priya," Chamundi instructed. "We'll prepare Baba's lunch together."

At dinner I was tempted to sit with Gopi. When I got through the serving line, I saw her seated with Parvati and the other princesses. When she noticed me, she grinned and waved. Remembering the guru's command that I "stop dreaming about girls," I wondered: *Did Baba mean that I should stop fantasizing about girls, or avoid them altogether?* Deciding it was better to err on the side of caution, I looked away without returning her smile. Then I marched straight past her table. I found my roommates and sat with them instead.

"Deependra, do your impression of Sergio," Poonish Davidson asked, already laughing in anticipation. "Stephen, you've got to see this!"

Stephen Ames raised his eyebrows, and formed a steeple with his hands on the table. "Let's hear it."

I pointed a finger at Stephen and channeled the Italian's voice and facial expression. "Hey, you—get back to work!"

Poonish laughed like a hyena.

Stephen's jaw dropped. "That's uncanny! Say something else."

"Why don't you and me go somewhere more... *private?*" I said, speaking in Sergio's sexy accent.

"Hahahahahahahahahahaha!" Poonish cackled.

Stephen laughed too. "Incredible!"

Just then, from behind me I heard the sound of single pair of hands coming together in a slow clap. I turned to see Gajendra Williams. He was applauding in mock appreciation of the performance. I was surprised to see him. I'd heard he was away in Switzerland on ashram business.

"Nice, nice," he said with heavy sarcasm. "You should do that for Sergio sometime. I'm sure he'll love it."

It occurred to me that making fun of Baba's closest people might be considered more than a little disrespectful.

"Now do me," said Gajendra.

I hesitated for a moment, unable to decide if I should do an accurate impression of the manager or something more flattering. I didn't want to get on Gajendra's bad side. "I don't know if I can do you. I never tried."

"Give it your best shot," the manager said. I couldn't tell whether he was encouraging or challenging me.

Pushing my anxiety aside, I hardened my face and wrinkled my brow. "Listen up everybody," I said, imitating Gajendra's clipped speech and gruff manner. "I've got zero tolerance for this kind of shit."

My roommates hooted in laughter. Gajendra's eyebrows squished together and his head flinched back. "That doesn't even sound like me!"

Poonish clutched his belly and his face turned pink. "It's perfect!"

On the way back to my dorm room, I crossed paths with Gopi in the lobby. I wasn't sure if I should say hello to her. I was shattered when she made the decision for me. She quickened her pace and hurried past, avoiding eye contact and pretending I didn't exist. I felt miserable for hurting her, but knew in my heart that I was facing yet another test from the guru. I was determined to prove to Baba that I would obey his every command. Even if it meant letting go of my angel.

31.
THE TEST

MAYOR CLARK AND AN aide arrived in the late afternoon. They were given a tour of the ashram by Suresh and Sergio, followed by private *darshan* with Baba. I was nervous on my first day on the job as the guru's main cameraman, but confident in my abilities, thanks to everything I'd learned in New York.

The meeting lasted thirty minutes, but by the time it was over, Clark was smitten with Baba and decided to stay for the evening program.

As soon as the mayor was gone, Sergio came by the Audiovisual office with a shipping box from Federal Express under his arm, ordering me to hand over all the cassettes I'd shot that day.

"But I haven't even had a chance to label any of them yet."

"No time," he said, shoving the tapes into the box. "These are going by overnight express to Birchwood Falls. They'll figure it out."

My new assistant was a newcomer to Raja Yoga named Patrick Kelly. At the age of twenty-three, he already had several years of experience as a cameraman.

"I work freelance for a video news service in Los Angeles," he said.

"They're an independent production company that monitors police and fire radio calls. Whenever something newsworthy goes down, like an accident or a crime, they send a video crew out to get footage. They specialize in the stuff that local stations want but don't have the manpower to cover."

"Cool," I said, thinking I might enjoy a job like that myself.

"Yeah. I used to shoot a lot of corporate events and parties in Hollywood, too. I've seen a lot of crazy stuff."

Patrick was a well-built, deeply tanned, good-looking guy with a freckled face and shortly cropped hair the color of bright copper. Clearly, he had tons more experience than I did, which made me wonder why Baba hadn't put him in charge of video. I asked Stephen Ames about it when Patrick was out of the office.

"That surfer dude?" laughed Stephen. "Are you kidding? He's got no loyalty. Baba is his fourth guru already."

When Patrick was back, he told me about his experiences with other spiritual groups.

"In high school I read *Dianetics* by L. Ron Hubbard, and it blew my mind," he said. "In college I was big time into Maharishi and Transcendental Meditation. Later I got turned on to the higher teachings of Bubba Free John. But two months ago I took a *shaktipat* retreat with Baba, and BAM! I've been like totally blissed out ever since."

While I was away at school, the ashram had acquired two new state-of-the art Sony Betacam cameras. They were called "camcorders," and it was the first time I ever heard the term. The camcorder combined a video camera with an audio recorder into a single shoulder-mounted unit. It eliminated the need for a second person to record sound and operate the VTR. Patrick trained me to shoot with it.

"This baby is the most light-sensitive video camera ever made," he said, placing the heavy unit on my shoulder. "Here, give it a try."

"It weighs a ton," I said, searching for the power switch.

"Here, let me help you with that." Patrick flicked a switch on the front of the camera under the lens, and it fired up. "Yep, she's heavy—but it's a pretty sweet trade off. The Betacam gives the operator complete autonomy. You don't have to depend on some jackass to keep up with you. I'm tellin' ya—once you shoot in Betacam, you can never go back."

Avadhoot Plotnick was even more excited about the new cameras than Patrick. "You have me to thank for them, boychik!"

I took the camera off my shoulder, and put it down on my desk. "They don't give you much control over sound though, do they? The camera mike only picks up whatever's directly in front of you."

The photographer sneered. "What the fuck else do you need?"

I kept my mouth shut. It was pointless to argue with him.

Avadhoot turned to my new assistant. "Look, I want to get one thing straight: Deependra is your supervisor, but both of you answer to me. Understand?"

Patrick and I answered in unison: "Got it!"

Baba's evening programs were attracting larger and larger crowds from the San Francisco Bay Area and beyond. His most recent *shaktipat* retreat was attended by a record-breaking fifteen hundred people. On weekends, the crowds became so large the ashram had to rent a circus tent to accommodate them. The new spiritual center and its guru became the talk of the town. TV news crews were becoming regular fixtures, and Baba was written up in the local papers several times. New centers were springing up all over the country, in places Baba had never even visited. A Raja Yoga revolution was sweeping the globe, and I was right in the middle of it.

One of the perks of being the guru's cameraman was being able to attend the *Shaktipat* retreats for free. Like me, most of the devotees who attended the weekend-long programs were not taking them for the first time. While the public evening programs were free, the *shaktipat* retreats were expensive. They had already doubled in price since my first one. I now understood where the Mission was getting most of its money, and how it was paying for all Baba's luxuries. The fancy rooms, the first-class international flights, even Sergio's clothes. *Was this right?* I wondered.

"I don't get it," Patrick said. We were setting up the cameras. "Most of the people in line this morning were at the retreat last weekend. If they already got *shaktipat*, why do they need to get it again?"

"There's no such thing as too much *shakti*," I answered, remembering that I'd asked the very same question only a couple of years earlier. I adjusted the white balance on my camera. "Baba says it's good to take the retreats as often as possible as a way of recharging our spiritual batteries and deepening our relationship with him."

Patrick shrugged. "As spiritual paths go, Raja Yoga isn't cheap. And I'm not just talking about the retreats. The ashram rent, the courses, books, tapes, and even the fruit to give to Baba at *darshan*. You have to be rich to spend any serious time around Baba." He looked squarely at me. "Rich or on staff."

I felt a rush of anger. *How dare he question Baba's advice or criticize Raja Yoga!* I wanted to tell him off, but held back. True, we were in a circus tent, but I still considered it sacred space.

When I handed Patrick his intercom headset, I noticed an orange sticker on his name tag. I felt another stab of anger. It had taken me almost two years of selfless service to earn my orange sticker. This newcomer with wrong understanding didn't deserve it.

My favorite part of the retreats were the meditation sessions, when Baba gave the touch. Meditation was always deepest for me after receiving an infusion of Baba's grace. I also loved the experience talks given by long-time devotees about their "life-transforming" relationship with guru. One of these was given by a young woman named Sridevi, who worked in the kitchen and had lived in Raja Yoga ashrams for several years. She gave an emotionally charged talk about meeting the guru when she was a homeless teenager, strung-out on heroin. Her voice was thick with emotion.

"Baba was the first person—if I can even call him a "person"—to love and accept me for who I was without judgment. He made me see that I wasn't some sinful, wretched girl—that my *true nature* was pure and divine. Through his grace, I was able to overcome my addiction and the behavior that was destroying me."

Sridevi described how Baba had taken her under his wing and healed her with his boundless compassion. At one point, she choked up and could barely speak. "The guru is not an ordinary man," she explained, weeping. "He is—" I zoomed in to get an extreme close-up the girl's face, which was wet with tears. "He is—the incarnation of love itself!"

The tent erupted in applause and Sridevi turned around to face Baba, who was seated on his throne behind her. The guru smiled at her approvingly, which made her sob even harder. The retreatants gave her a standing ovation.

"Her heart is very pure," beamed Baba. Sridevi was so overcome, she almost fell down. "A very good girl." Sergio and Brian escorted her out of the tent.

Seeing Sridevi melt into a puddle of tears speaking about the guru had an unexpected effect on me. Rather than lifting me up, it left me feeling depressed and questioning the depth of my own devotion. I wondered why I wasn't reduced to tears every time I spoke about Baba. What was wrong with me?

As Patrick and I broke down the equipment after *darshan*, I reflected on the meaning of love in the guru-disciple relationship. Members of the inner circle were presumably Baba's most devoted disciples, but few of them exhibited the qualities that came to mind when I thought of a "model disciple." For one thing, I rarely saw any of them meditate. If they meditated at all, they must be doing it in the privacy of their own rooms. For another, most of them only came to the chants when Baba was in attendance. Yet these lousy practitioners of Raja Yoga were closer to the guru than I was. The deepest character flaws and most outrageous behavior had no bearing on their relationship to him. All that seemed to matter in Raja Yoga was how much you loved Baba.

I had yet to find out, however, that how much you loved Baba was only part of it—what mattered most was what you were willing to do for him.

I found a place at the back of the cafeteria to eat alone and wallow in self-doubt.

"Feeling unworthy again, Deependra?"

I looked up from my bowl of soup to see Akhandananda standing in front of me, holding a tray of food. I'd seen him around the new ashram, but hadn't had a chance to talk with him yet. His bottom lip jutted out in a sulky pout.

My face tingled and burned with embarrassment. *Akhandananda could read my mind!* "How could you possibly know that, Swamiji?"

The neckless swami's head jerked back, and a braying laugh erupted from his belly. "Your posture, my boy!" He took a seat in the empty chair across the table from me. "You're slouching again!"

I told Akhandananda about the self-doubt I was struggling with, after hearing Sridevi's experience talk. I said my piece and the swami listened pensively. When I was through, he spoke his mind.

"Devotion arises in the heart spontaneously after our loyalty to the guru has been put to the test, young man." The swami took a long, noisy slurp of soup from his spoon. Then he looked away and wrinkled his brow. "And that test may come sooner than you think."

MY FIRST BIG TEST as a cameraman for Baba came during the filming of a public ceremony. Mayor Clark, who was now coming regularly to hear Baba speak, saw fit to honor him with the key to the city.

The ceremony took place on the steps of City Hall. This was the first time I'd ever seen the guru on the streets of an American city, and it felt strange. In India, even people who didn't know Baba recognized right away that he was a great saint and an enlightened being. Here in California, the passers-by seemed oblivious to him. They walked straight past without giving him a second glance.

"Baba Rudrananda, welcome to City Hall," the Mayor said, holding an oversize golden key embedded in a wooden plaque. Patrick was stationed on a high platform several yards away, with another local news crew. Avadhoot and I were up close, positioned side by side, only a few feet from the action. "Please know that all of Berkeley's doors are open to you. Lest there be any doubt of that fact, I'm very honored to present you with the key to the city."

Just as Mayor Clark was about to hand Baba the plaque, Avadhoot stepped directly in front of me, blocking my shot. *This can't be happening!* A wave of anger rose up inside of me. I felt like punching him, but I had no time for an argument. I jumped out from behind him, and lunged forward just in time to capture the historic moment on tape.

For the rest of the ceremony, I remained where I was, leaving only enough distance to include both the guru and the mayor in the shot. If the lunatic wanted to block me again, he'd have to physically push me out of the way.

After the ceremony, Patrick and I loaded the equipment back into an ashram van. I noticed that across the street, Avadhoot and Sergio were in a heated discussion. They were too far away for me to hear them, but I could see Avadhoot making his usual sweeping arm gestures, his face only inches from Sergio's. Just as I started the van to head back to the ashram with Patrick, Sergio appeared at my window and rapped his knuckles on the glass. I rolled down my window.

"Why do you always have to film so close?" he demanded, glaring at me.

"I—"

"Avadhoot says you were standing in front of him the whole time and ruined his pictures!"

Hatred for Avadhoot spread through me like a poison. "But —"

"Don't you have a—what do you call it?" he asked, making a turning motion with his hand.

"A zoom lens?"

"*Sì!* A zoom!"

"But Avadhoot was in front of me!" I protested.

Sergio drew his upper lip up toward his nose in disgust. "Just what kind of an asshole are you, Greenbaum?"

I wanted to defend myself, but realized it was useless. Avadhoot and Sergio were always right. They could do no wrong.

"You pull any shit like that again, and I'll smash that camera of yours over your fucking head! Understand?"

On the way back to the ashram, we stopped at Federal Express and arranged for the footage of the ceremony to be overnighted to Birchwood Falls. A few days later I got a call from Jake.

"Great job, Deependra! I think you're an even better cameraman than Arjuna. Kriyadevi added the ceremony to the end of the newsreel. It's already on its way to you."

When I got off the phone I took a deep breath. I felt proud of my work, and I took Jake's approval as a sign that I had acted appropriately during the shoot, even if I had pissed off Avadhoot and Sergio in the process.

Later that evening, I was summoned to the guru's house. Worried that Avadhoot had complained to Baba about me, I was apprehensive. When I arrived at the entrance to the guru's quarters, I was surprised to find the door ajar. Letting myself in, I traversed the long corridor to the inner sanctum, where I found the guru waiting for me in his study. He was seated cross-legged on a loveseat, dressed casually in a silken, burgundy-colored bathrobe.

The Guru's Touch

Rashmi was bent over a VCR, fiddling with its controls. I was about to prostrate myself before him, when Rashmi startled me.

"You—cameraman!" the Indian said, pointing a finger at me. "I can't get this bloody thing to work. See what you can do."

After a quick check, I discovered that the video player was working fine, but that Baba's enormous television had been set to the wrong channel. Just then, Avadhoot appeared in the doorway with a young, pale-skinned woman with short dark hair and freckles. The girl bit her fingernails. Her large, round eyes darted around the room, and then looked down at the floor. From her tight jeans and baggy Oakland Raiders sweatshirt, I could tell she was new to Raja Yoga.

"*Babaji, usaka naam Jenny hai*," Avadhoot said, speaking to Baba in Hindi.

The guru smiled warmly at the girl. "*Aacha, aacha!*" Baba answered, before saying something else to Avadhoot in Hindi.

"Baba is giving you the spiritual name *Jaya*," Avadhoot said through a toothy grin. "It means 'victory.'"

The young woman's eyes shone, and she returned the guru's smile.

"Come, Jaya, sit here," Baba said, speaking in English, and patting an empty spot next to him on the loveseat.

Jaya bit her fingernails again, taking small, tentative steps toward the sofa.

Baba chuckled. "Sit, sit!"

When the girl was close enough, the guru took her arm and gently pulled her down onto the loveseat next to him.

An image flickered to life on the big screen. "It's working again," I said.

"Deependra, come," Baba said, patting the free spot on the other side of him. I sat down and the guru put his arms around me too. The video opened with lively music and a montage of images of Baba and Suresh showing the mayor of Berkeley around the ashram grounds. *This is the moment I've longed for*, I thought. I felt like a small boy curling up with his father and sister on the sofa to watch television. Meanwhile, Avadhoot was hovering in the doorway like a bellboy waiting for a tip.

The next part of the video was devoted to Mayor Clark's first visit to the ashram—the event for which I'd blown off my last two weeks of video school. It was followed by a recent talk Baba had given on "selfless love." Apparently uninterested in hearing himself speak, Baba called for Rashmi. The guru's attendant appeared at the door and, after a brief exchange in Hindi, Rashmi went to the kitchen and came back with a big bowl of buttery popcorn, and set it down on the glass coffee table in front us. He then left Jaya and me alone with Baba again. At this point, Avadhoot ventured from the open doorway into the room again. Just as he was about to take a seat, however, Baba raised a hand, blocking him. Like a three-year-old being ordered back to their room after bedtime, Avadhoot dropped his chin to his chest, turned around, and stomped back out the door.

"Take, take!" Baba said, gesturing to the popcorn after Avadhoot was out of sight. I leaned forward and helped myself. When I sat back again, I could no longer feel Baba's arm resting against me. I reached for more popcorn and glanced in the guru's direction. Both of his arms were now wrapped tightly around the girl. A wave of jealousy washed over me. *Who is this newcomer and why is Baba showing her more love and affection than me?* I glanced at the guru again. His eyes looked cold, vacant, and unfeeling, like those of a shark. My breaths came coarser and faster. If I hadn't known any better, his embrace of the girl looked almost lustful—he appeared to be fondling her upper arms.

Baba's talk ended and the video faded to black. The picture came up again, on a wide-angle shot of the steps of City Hall, where the mayor was welcoming Baba to Berkeley and presenting him with the key to the city.

"Rashmi!" called Baba. *"Aao!"*

When Baba's attendant reappeared in the doorway, the guru pointed excitedly at the screen. Rashmi nodded his head in approval.

I looked again at the guru and felt ashamed. Baba had crossed the ocean of worldly existence and was a liberated being. He abided in a state of absolute perfection, devoid of all craving. I had been, of course, projecting my own impure desire for the girl onto him. The guru was simply expressing his tremendous love. Obviously, Jaya needed it more than me.

The video came to an end and Baba said something to his attendant in Hindi. Rashmi translated: "Baba wants you to rewind the cassette to the bit when the mayor of San Francisco gives him the key."

"The mayor of Berkeley, you mean."

Baba's Indian attendant grimaced. He eyed Baba furtively, and lifted his forefinger to his lips.

We watched the ceremony again, and when it was over Baba spoke to me through Rashmi: "Baba says that you make very good movies."

I lowered my head in modesty, but my ego puffed up with pride. "Thank you, Baba."

The guru said something else.

"And now you go."

As Jaya and I rose to our feet, Baba grabbed the girl's arm and pulled her back down onto the sofa. "Not you," Baba said to Jaya. "You stay."

I burned with jealousy and seethed in anger. *I'm the one who made the video—why does she get to stay?* Catching myself once again in delusional thinking, I bowed and left the guru alone with the girl.

The next morning, I woke up feeling hollow inside. Doubts about Baba's love for me filled my head. *Did Baba summon me to watch the video with him, or to just to fix the VCR? Why did he send me away and ask the girl—a newcomer—to stay?* I felt worthless.

At *seva*, I logged cassettes of Baba's talks and boxed them up for shipment to Birchwood Falls. By lunchtime I was still miserable. Preferring to be by myself, I steered clear of the cafeteria where Poonish and Stephen were eating, and treated myself to a veggie burger and fries at Prasad. There, much to my surprise, I saw Jaya, the girl from the night before, seated with Gopi and the other princesses. Gone were her baggy sweatshirt and tight-fitting jeans. Decked out in a silk sari, a string of pearls, and matching earrings, she looked as though she'd been a member of the guru's entourage her entire life. I assumed her new clothes had been a gift from the guru. *Why doesn't the guru shower ME with gifts?* I wondered. Gopi noticed I was staring in her direction, and I looked away.

When my food was ready, I searched for a place to sit as far away from Gopi and the *darshan* girls as possible. I found an empty table on the opposite side of the café, next to one where Chamundi and Daniel Groza were eating with Priya, the young girl I'd first seen with Chamundi in Baba's apartment. Her mother, Sanjula Brenan, was also seated with them.

"The Mission has its sights on a property in Portland, Oregon," Daniel was saying to the others. "The location is perfect."

This was the first I had heard anything about the exciting news that Baba planned to open another ashram on the West Coast. As I listened I noticed something odd about Priya. She was sucking her thumb with a vacant look on her face. She was definitely the oldest girl I'd ever seen do that.

"Priya, how many times do I have to tell you?" the girl's mother frowned. "Take your thumb out of your mouth."

Priya obeyed.

"And eat your food, sweetheart. You haven't touched a thing on your plate."

Chamundi gently patted Priya on the back. "You know, I didn't stop sucking my thumb until I was quite a big girl myself. My parents had to put a nasty-tasting ointment on it to get me to quit."

Sanjula rolled her eyes. "Yes, but *you* were probably no more than five."

I felt bad for the girl. If Sanjula wanted her daughter to stop sucking her thumb, maybe she should stop treating her as though she were a baby. It also bothered me that she was talking about the girl as if she weren't even there.

"I just don't understand it," Sanjula sighed. "She stopped sucking her thumb when she was five or six. Then she suddenly started up again a few weeks ago."

"Isn't that right about when she started helping Chamundi in Baba's kitchen?" Daniel asked.

"Well, yes," Sanjula said. "It's a lot of pressure for her, I know. But I'm so grateful for all the attention Baba is giving her."

"It's a blessing," Chamundi said.

Daniel and Sanjula nodded in agreement. Chamundi took Sanjula's hand in hers and squeezed it tightly.

Sanjula teared up. "It's been difficult, you know—with her dad out of the picture."

"You should talk to Baba about the thumb sucking," Daniel suggested.

Chamundi agreed. "Yes. Talk to Baba."

Later that evening, as I panned the audience during the guru's talk, I noticed Sanjula and Priya seated up front, just behind the lady swamis. Zooming in for a two-shot of the mother and daughter, I quickly changed camera angles when I noticed that Priya was sucking the thumb of one hand and clinging tightly to her mother's arm with the other. *What a peculiar girl,* I thought.

I observed that Jaya had already been promoted to *darshan* girl. Seemingly overnight, she had gone from a nobody to a bejeweled princess. Again, I was jealous. *It isn't fair,* I thought. Then I caught myself. *This is ego—the enemy—up to its old tricks.* How many times would I need to remind myself that this was yet another test from Baba? He *wanted* me to burn with envy. The guru was at work on my ego, purifying me of negative emotions.

"Sometimes the guru's medicine takes the form of a bitter pill," I'd heard Baba say many times. "The real job of the guru is to insult the disciple."

DESPITE CALLS FROM THE California devotees for the guru to stay longer, Baba's plan to leave for the European leg of his tour at the beginning of May remained unchanged, and I was expected to go with him. As exciting as this was, I couldn't help feeling nervous about money.

Even when I had written the tuition check for NYSB, I couldn't bring myself to look at my latest bank statement to see how much I had left. I knew I was burning through my inheritance fast. The only question was if I should wait until I ran out of money to ask the Mission to pay my way, or if I should mention something to the management now. I kept hoping for a sign from the guru about which was the most appropriate course of action, but none came. Finally, when my anxiety became too much for me to bear, I took my concerns to Gajendra Williams.

From behind the large wooden desk in his office, the grumpy manager looked down his nose at me. A file folder with my name on it was open in front of him.

"What can I do you for, Mr. Greenbaum?"

I wanted to talk to him about my financial worries, but couldn't bring myself to do it. If I asked the guru for money, my labors would no longer be selfless. I was also afraid of appearing presumptuous. So, instead, I talked to him about the first thing that popped into my head.

"I'm finding it harder and harder to provide good coverage of Baba's talks without a third person on our crew," I told him. "Two cameramen aren't enough."

"Uh-huh," Gajendra mumbled. He seemed a lot less surprised by my bold assertion than I was.

"The only way we can be sure that Patrick and I are getting complementary footage is with a director."

The manager frowned and stroked his chin. "Are you getting complaints from Birchwood Falls?"

"Well, um, not as such..."

Gajendra's eyes narrowed. "You are or you aren't?"

"I'm not."

"So, in reality, it doesn't sound like much of a problem."

"Perhaps not," I said. "But our coverage could be so much better. A two-camera shoot is pretty pointless without a director."

"I'll see if I can find somebody already on tour in another department," he said. "But I'm not promising anything."

"No!" I blurted out. "It can't be just *anybody*. They have to have experience!"

"Look, Spielberg," scolded Gajendra, closing my file and rising to his feet. "The Mission doesn't have that kind of budget. We can't bring somebody else on tour right now."

I felt the sting of rejection. If the ashram didn't have money for a director, they obviously didn't have money to pay my way either.

"I understand."

"It's bad enough we have to start paying your way now."

"What?" I wasn't sure I had heard right.

"Yeah, the word just came down from Baba's house. The Mission is going to start picking up the tab for you."

My heart overflowed with gratitude to the guru. Baba was aware of my anxiety over money matters. This was only more proof that the guru was truly omniscient.

"Frankly, I don't get it," Gajendra said, shaking his head. "Everybody knows you're rich."

To celebrate the good news, I invited Poonish for lunch at Prasad.

"You'll probably be getting a stipend too," he said, pouring half a bottle of ketchup on his fries. "All of us do."

Just then, we heard the crash of dishes breaking. Poonish and I turned our heads to see what happened.

"You idiot!" Chamundi shouted.

Behind the counter stood Baba's personal cook, trembling with anger, and a young African American woman frozen in shock, staring at the floor in disbelief.

"Don't just stand there! Go find a broom and dustpan, and clean it up!"

"I'm so sorry, Chamundi!" the young woman cried, before making a dash for the kitchen.

"Cripes!" Poonish said under his breath. "Do you know who that is?"

"Daniel Groza's wife?"

"No, the cute black chick. That's Tabitha Beaumont."

I scratched the back of my head. "Who?"

"The actress," Poonish said, blushing and grinning broadly. "Chamundi just called her an idiot in front of everybody in Prasad!"

The woman didn't look familiar, and the name "Tabitha Beaumont" meant nothing to me. According to Poonish, she was the star of a hit sit-com.

"She's been a devotee for a year or two. Whenever she stays in the ashram, she helps Chamundi in Baba's kitchen."

Later that day I came across Chamundi again, on the way back to my room. She was crying in the arms of her husband Daniel in the corridor of the VIP dormitory. I wondered if word had gotten back to Baba about how she yelled at the TV actress. Perhaps Baba had scolded her about it.

I didn't give Chamundi another thought until a few days later, when Poonish shared some disturbing news with me.

"Did you hear about Daniel and Chamundi Groza?" he asked. The color was drained from his face. His tone was unusually serious.

"No. What about them?"

"They left."

"Left? What do you mean *left*?" I asked, even though I knew exactly what he meant.

"Left Baba," he said, unable to make eye contact with me. "Without any warning. They packed their bags and took off in the middle of night. Sanjula Brenan and her thumb-sucking daughter went with them."

"Why?"

"No clue."

I would've given anything to be as close to Baba as the Grozas had been. It was unthinkable they could throw all that away. I also couldn't understand how Sanjula could separate Priya from the only real father her daughter ever had. They would all be lost without the guru.

The Guru's Touch

"Do you have any of his music tapes?"

"Yeah," I said, swallowing hard. "I have one of Daniel singing the *Guru Gita* in English, and lots more."

"Baba says they should all be destroyed."

The following morning, I was boxing up cassettes to overnight to Birchwood Falls when Sergio Casto came by the Audiovisual office looking for me. His face was pulled tight with anger, and he had the wild look in his eyes that I'd seen before.

"Greenbaum, come with me."

I began to tremble a little. *Had I done something wrong?* I racked my brain trying to remember, but couldn't come up with anything.

"Is something the matter?"

"Baba needs you," the manager said, giving me an impatient push out the office door.

I was so relieved not to be in trouble with the guru that all the muscles in my body went limp. I had to catch myself before falling over. *Baba needs me!*

I sprinted after Sergio toward the lobby. "What does Baba want?"

He was either too lost in thought to hear me, or was ignoring me on purpose. As we hurried past the guru's quarters, I glanced at the Italian. His forehead was beaded with sweat and his hands were balled into fists.

"Where are we going?"

Again, my question was met with silence. His face was blank now, as if his mind were a million miles away.

I followed Sergio to Avadhoot's room. Without knocking, he opened the door and we let ourselves in. Baba's photographer was seated in a swivel chair, with a telephone cradled in his lap. His expression was grim.

"What took you so long?" he asked.

Sitting on the edge of Avadhoot's bed, Sergio frowned.

The cowboy pointed to the bed with his chin, and I took a seat next to Sergio. Avadhoot stared at me as if he were trying to size me up. Then he glanced down at the phone in his lap. Looking up at me again, his mouth opened as if he were about to say something, then, pursing his lips, he turned to Sergio, who closed his eyes and nodded in response.

The photographer turned back to me and squished his eyebrows together. "You know there are people who want to hurt Baba, right?"

I felt a tightening in my chest. "Um, yeah. I guess so."

"We need to know if Baba can depend on you to protect him," Sergio said.

"Of course he can," I said, sitting up as straight as possible.

"You know that ungrateful cunt who was cooking for Baba?" Avadhoot asked.

"And her cocksucking husband," Sergio added, practically foaming at the mouth.

"You mean Chamundi and Daniel Groza?"

"*Si!*"

Avadhoot stood up suddenly, and handed me the telephone. "They're spreading lies about Baba. We need to make them stop."

I fidgeted in my seat, unable to understand how they thought I could help. "Okay, what can I do?"

"How well does Daniel know you?" the photographer asked.

"I don't know—we've spoken a couple of times, I guess."

Sergio folded his arms across his chest. "Do you think he'd recognize your voice on the phone?"

I swallowed hard. "I doubt it."

Satisfied with my answer, Avadhoot explained the situation to me. According to their "sources," after "fleeing the ashram" the Grozas had checked into a motel in Oakland.

Sergio smirked. "We have them under twenty-four hour surveillance."

"Right now, Chamundi's out running errands," the photographer said. "Daniel's alone in their room."

Just then, there was a light knock on the door.

"Who's there?" Avadhoot called. When there was no answer, he got up and opened the door.

Stepping into the room was Anjali. Her jaw dropped when she saw me.

"He knows?" she asked, turning to Sergio.

The Italian nodded.

"Baba wants to know if you've called yet," she said.

"We're about to," Avadhoot answered.

Anjali winced when she noticed the phone in my lap. "Deependra, you understand they're telling horrible lies about Baba, right?"

I nodded. I had no idea what the Grozas were telling people about the guru, but I knew that if they were saying bad things about Baba, they could only be lying.

Anjali let herself out, and Sergio and Avadhoot told me, word for word, exactly what they wanted me to say.

Holding my breath, I dialed the number of the Groza's motel.

"Is this Daniel Groza?" I asked, after an operator connected me to their room.

"This is he."

"I'm calling from Highland Hospital," I said, trying to sound as official as possible. "We have your wife here in the ER. I'm afraid there's been an accident."

"Oh my God! What happened?"

The fear in Daniel's voice made me realize the awfulness of what I was doing. It took every ounce of my loyalty not to hang up. I wanted to tell Daniel that he was just the victim of a cruel prank. But my relationship with the guru was on the line. I had no choice but to stick to the script.

"Someone threw acid on her face."

I heard the phone drop on the other end of the line. Sergio stifled a laugh, and Avadhoot nodded encouragingly.

"Mr. Groza, are you there?" I shouted, causing my co-conspirators to frown. "Mr. Groza?"

"Yes, I'm here."

"She's badly hurt—"

"Jesus!"

"—but she's going to be alright!"

Sergio's face twisted in anger, because I'd gone off script. Avadhoot looked like he was about to take a swing at me.

"I mean, she's in *critical condition!*"

Avadhoot and Sergio nodded.

"Disfigured..."

The two men grinned with duping delight.

"I'll get there as soon as I can," Daniel said before disconnecting.

I squeezed my eyes shut and hung up the phone. I felt as if I'd just committed murder.

Sergio and Avadhoot laughed so hard I thought they'd choke. I wanted to vomit.

"It's true what they say about you, Greenbaum," Sergio said, slapping me on the back. "You're quite an actor!"

I felt an overwhelming urge to run. I needed to get out of Avadhoot's room. I needed to get out of the ashram. I needed to get outside so I could breathe.

"What are the Grozas saying about Baba?" I asked, wheezing.

Avadhoot stopped laughing and shot me an angry look. "What fucking difference does it make? Anyhow, you don't want to hear their lies—believe me."

Sergio flashed me a phony grin. "You done good, Greenbaum. Now, go back to your *seva*."

I stumbled toward the door. I wanted to get as far away from Baba's men as possible. As I stepped into the corridor, the Italian stopped me.

"And don't say nothin' to nobody," he warned.

"Yeah, Deependra," added Avadhoot. "Keep that big mouth of yours shut!"

I felt as if the wind had been knocked out of me. Not just the wind, but my faith. *What have I done?* I asked myself. *That poor man must be beside himself with worry!* I couldn't fathom what the Grozas could have possibly said or done to justify such brutal retaliation.

There was no way I could return to *seva*. I needed to be alone with my thoughts. As I passed through the lobby on my way to the Audiovisual office, I noticed a taxi waiting outside the main entrance. Suddenly, I knew what needed to be done. I left the building and jumped into the back seat of the cab.

"Take me to Highland Hospital in Oakland as quickly as possible, please."

When I arrived at the ER, I found Daniel Groza hunched over the front desk, pleading with the receptionist.

"But there must be a mistake! I got a phone call from the hospital just a few minutes ago telling me she was here."

Picking up the phone, the receptionist shook her head. "I'll check again."

The knowledge that I was the cause of Daniel's torment was too much for me to bear. But to tell him the truth would be a betrayal of the guru. I was also afraid of what Daniel might do when he realized I was the one who had tricked him.

I summoned the courage to speak to him. "She isn't here."

Daniel whipped around to face me. "What?"

"Nothing bad happened to Chamundi."

Daniel stared at me in confusion for a few seconds. Then a look of comprehension spread over his face.

"I know you," he said, looking me up and down. Then he grabbed me by the shoulders. "You're from the ashram. You're the cameraman."

Unable to meet his eyes, I nodded.

"It was *you* on the phone," he said, shaking me. "Wasn't it?"

"Excuse me, gentlemen," a security guard said, tugging on Daniel's arm. "I'm going to have to ask both of you to leave."

Daniel's face was flushed with anger. His eyes filled with rage. "Sergio put you up to it, didn't he!"

"Let's go," said the security guard. I knew the second we were outside the building, Groza would take a swing at me. We exited the hospital, and I braced myself for a blow. But what happened next made me feel worse than if he had broken my nose. Burying his face in his hands, Daniel began to sob.

"Mr. Groza—Daniel, I'm really sorry for what I did, but—"

Daniel raised a hand to silence me. "He's got you brainwashed, you know."

My mind froze. "What?"

"You're under his spell. Just like we were."

"You've got to stop saying bad things about Baba."

Daniel clenched his fists and his nostrils flared. "Now you listen to me, you little punk. You tell Rudrananda we're not afraid of him. We've spoken to other devotees, and there's an investigative reporter working on a story about Baba and the Mission. He's not going to be able to get away with it anymore!"

"Get away with *what?*"

"You don't know anything, do you?" he said, shaking his head in disbelief. "A thirteen-year-old, for God's sake! And all the other women!"

"What are you talking about? Sergio raped a thirteen-year-old girl?"

"Not *Sergio*," Daniel said, raising his voice. "*Baba!*"

32.

NEVER GO TOO CLOSE TO A HOLY MAN

RUNNING FROM THE HOSPITAL, the world caved in around me. Images of Baba touching little girls took form in my mind's eye. I tried in vain to drive them away. *It's not possible!* a voice screamed inside of me. *Baba is pure—a celibate yogi and a perfected master, immune to desire and the temptations of the senses!*

A car's horn blared, followed by the screech of tires.

"Watch where you're going, you fucking idiot!" someone shouted.

I barely registered it. I just kept running. I didn't care where I was going. I was desperate to outrun my own thoughts. *Baba behaving like some depraved dirty old man? Impossible! Unthinkable! A disgusting lie!*

Or was it? That night Jaya and I watched the video with him, he couldn't keep his hands off her. *Did he ask me to leave them alone together so that he could have his way with her? Was the silk sari and jewelry I saw her wearing the next day a reward for putting out? No, no, no! It can't be true!*

"Deependra, stop!" someone called.

I kept racing straight ahead. Tears streamed down my face.

"Greenbaum, stop for a second! I just want to talk to you!"

I turned my head to see Gajendra Williams, craning his head out the window of a car, driving alongside of me.

Refusing to listen, I kept running. I ran until my lungs burned and my legs turned to rubber. Gasping for air, my hands met my knees and I doubled over in exhaustion.

Gajendra pulled the car next to me. "Get in!"

I shook my head. "No!"

How the fuck did he know where to find me? I wondered. Then I remembered Sergio bragging that they had the Grozas under surveillance. I guessed that he'd probably seen me talking to Daniel.

Gajendra pleaded with me. Then he got out of the car. Afraid that he might try to take me by force, I took off again. He chased after me on foot for a few more blocks, and then finally gave up.

For the next few hours I walked and thought about the guru. Everyone in Raja Yoga knew that it was only through Baba's lifelong commitment to celibacy, and the power of his upward-flowing sexual fluid, that he was able to give *shaktipat*.

"An enlightened being lives in a state of unimaginable ecstasy," Baba had told us many times. "This state is both permanent and ever new." What possible need would such a being have for the inferior and short-lived pleasures of the flesh?

I told myself there had to be an explanation, because that's what the mind does when it chooses to believe—when it *needs* to believe. Whatever Baba was doing with the girls, there had to be some higher yogic purpose behind it.

Why am I so quick to believe Daniel? I don't even know the Grozas. On the other hand, I do know Baba. I know in my heart that he is a true guru. The extraordinary experiences I've had since meeting him are all the proof I need.

I glanced at my watch. It was late. I'd need to get back to the ashram soon to have enough time to set up the cameras for the evening program. Up ahead I saw taxis queuing in front of a hotel.

As I rode back to the ashram, I felt a dull pain in my chest. Sergio and Avadhoot would be furious with me for going to the hospital to tip off Daniel, and I was sure they would tell Baba about it.

The guru will forgive me, I told myself. I had helped send the Grozas a message. They would think twice about spreading rumors about Baba again. By returning to the ashram, I would show the guru that I passed his test. Through my silence, I'd prove that I could be trusted.

Back at the ashram, faces were long and the mood was dark. I saw Stephen Ames in the lobby. He looked as though his dog had just died. When I arrived in the Audiovisual office, I found Sergio sitting at my desk talking to Patrick Kelly. Muscles tightening, I braced myself for the barrage of insults and recriminations I knew were coming.

"Welcome back to the ashram, Greenbaum," Sergio said, grinning insincerely. "Your colleague here was worried. When you didn't come back to *seva*, he thought maybe you quit."

I glanced at Patrick. He smiled nervously and shrugged in response.

Sergio let out a hollow laugh. "Me too, I was worried!"

I thought about apologizing or making an excuse, but kept my mouth shut.

"Patrick, go to Prasad and bring me back a *Raja* coffee. You want a coffee, Greenbaum?"

I shook my head.

"Maybe an espresso?"

"No, thank you."

As soon as Patrick was gone, Sergio's face twisted into a scowl. "You wanna tell me where you've been all day?"

"I went for a walk."

"*Sì*, a very long walk. All the way to the hospital in Oakland!"

"I—"

"What did that cocksucker tell you?"

I couldn't bring myself to say the words aloud. I looked away from him and covered my mouth with both hands.

"Well?"

"He said Baba was having sex with women in the ashram," I blurted out. "And that he molested a thirteen-year-old girl."

"Anything else?"

"He also told me that there was a journalist working on an exposé on Baba and the ashram, and that they were going to tell him everything."

Sergio swore in Italian and brought his fist down on the desk. He collected himself and spoke again. "Don't worry, Greenbaum. They're not going to talk to no reporters. Not after today. Trust me."

We were both silent for a long time, until a question forced its way out of my mouth.

"Is it true?"

Sergio drew his upper lip toward his nose in disgust. "You learned nothing since coming to the guru?"

I looked down at my feet. "I guess not."

"Whatever the guru does is to teach us something."

Sergio's words stung my ears. "I know," I said, blinking away tears.

Baba's tour manager studied my face. Then he rose to his feet and stepped out from behind the desk to approach me.

"Listen, Greenbaum—you're just a little bit confused right now." He reached for my shoulder and gave it a firm squeeze. "But I promise you, it's gonna pass. The Grozas are worse than rats. Baba gave them everything, and look how they repay him."

Patrick returned from Prasad with Sergio's *Raja* coffee on a tray, and handed it to him. The tour manager took a small sip of the hot spicy beverage and his face contorted in revulsion.

"*Merda!* They call that coffee?"

Patrick glanced at his watch, and eyed me nervously. "Shouldn't we be setting up the cameras now?"

Before I could answer, Sergio told us both to take the evening off. "Baba doesn't want the program to be recorded tonight, but be sure not to miss it. Swami Brahmananda is going to give a very important talk."

Ever since I started working in the Audiovisual department, I never needed to think about where to sit during the programs. My place was behind the camera. But tonight, with no work to do, I wasn't sure what was expected of me. I didn't know whether to sit up front, close to the guru with the other tour people, or further away with the ordinary devotees. Not wanting to appear presumptuous, I found a place toward the back of the hall. I spread my *asana* on the carpet, draped a shawl around my shoulders, and waited for the guru.

As I waited for the program to begin, I remembered Baba saying: "In order to make progress in the practice of meditation, you need the strength and seminal vigor that can only be attained through complete abstinence from sex... a true guru always practices what he teaches. He never wavers from his own discipline."

Hypocrite! shouted a voice inside my head. *Liar! Phony!*

The lights dimmed and we began to recite the *Om Namah Shivaya* mantra. In an effort to silence my mind, I chanted along at the top of my lungs. But it was futile. I continued to be tortured by doubts, and my mind was caught in an endless loop of treacherous thoughts.

After what felt like years, a door at the back of the hall finally opened, and Baba made his entrance. Following closely behind were Suresh, Anjali, and Sergio. Although it was dark, I could see that the guru was making his way down the center aisle more quickly than usual, the fingers of his hands interlocked behind his back. As always, before taking his seat he bowed to the enormous portrait of his own guru hanging above the throne.

Baba chanted a few more rounds of the mantra with us. Then the lights came back on, and he introduced his future successor. Standing behind a podium to the right of the throne, Suresh addressed the devotees.

"Never go too close to a holy man," he began, pausing for a beat or two to let the words sink in. "Ranganath was an enlightened being—a great saint of the seventeenth century. For many years he led the life of an ascetic, until one day he had a vision of his late guru, who commanded him to abandon his life as a renunciant and to accept whatever material things that might be offered to him.

"As time passed, his devotees made generous offerings to him. He was given a fine horse, a splendid house, servants, and beautiful clothes. He began to lead a life of luxury, which many of his devotees found confusing.

"One day, a pious king came to see Ranganath, whom he believed was still living the life of a renunciant. He found the great yogi in bed with two beautiful women who were massaging his feet. When the king saw Ranganath enjoying the attentions of these women, he began to have doubts about his saintliness. Sensing that the king was ill at ease, Ranganath dismissed the women and ordered one of his servants to bring him a silver bucket. With the door to his bedchamber closed, and in the presence of the king, Ranganath ejaculated all his seminal fluid into the bucket, filling it to the brim before the eyes of the astonished king.

"Immediately afterwards, using the advanced yogic practice of *maha vajroli mudra*, he re-absorbed all of the semen back into himself from where it had come out. Then he went back to sleep and the two women returned and resumed their massage."

As Suresh paused again for effect, I looked around at the other people in the audience. I wanted to see if they were as confused as me. Some of the devotees looked as serene as always. Others seemed pensive, or wore quizzical expressions on their faces. A few of the newcomers looked appalled. I thought they might walk out of the young swami's talk at any moment.

"When we say the guru is 'perfect,' it's not because he conforms to some preexisting concept we have about what that means. A yogi is said to have attained perfection when he has transcended the ego and become permanently established in God consciousness.

"Whatever a being like this thinks, says, or does is informed by this state of perfection. His actions are unencumbered by the mental conditioning that ordinary beings like us are subject to. His every movement is a spontaneous expression of the *kundalini-shakti*, and is for the upliftment of his devotees. Therefore, it is impossible for ordinary beings like us, who see everything through the veil ignorance, to understand the actions of a perfected master of Raja Yoga. He cannot be judged by our standards of conventional behavior."

Suresh sat in his usual place at the guru's feet, and then Baba addressed the devotees through Anjali.

"Faith should arise from a direct experience of the master's grace. A true disciple pays no heed to the vicious rumors he might hear. But what can I say? This kind of persecution is nothing new. Mansur Al-Hallaj was hanged, Haridas Thakur was beaten, and Jesus was crucified. Just as the *shaktipat* gurus are established in their lineage, the Judases of the world are established in theirs. You should be happy that no one has tried to assassinate me yet."

I glanced around the hall. Some people were leaving. The mouths of others were hanging wide open.

"But what surprises me is how quickly so many of you have rushed to judgment, forgetting all the divine experiences you have had in the ashram. Sadly, it doesn't matter how much grace is showered upon ingrates like you. Because of your flawed minds and inflated egos, you will not be able to hold it."

By the time Baba finished, only a few people were left in the hall.

When I returned to my room after the evening program, I found Stephen Ames and Poonish Davidson lying flat on their backs in bed. Poonish was listening to a recording of Baba reciting the *Guru Gita* on his Walkman, and Stephen was staring blankly at the ceiling.

I was unable to sleep that night, and from the sounds of my roommates tossing and turning, I knew I wasn't the only one. As I lay awake, I reflected on Baba's talk, trying to remember all the amazing experiences I had had since meeting him. I thought back to how mind-blowing my first read of *Divine Dance of Consciousness* had been, and how it had inspired me to change my life. I reflected on the higher states of awareness, and the feelings of love, oneness, and peace I had experienced after receiving *shaktipat*. In my mind's eye, I replayed the moment when I had first met Baba in Birchwood Falls, and recalled how he had singled me out of a crowd of hundreds to take my hand and speak to me. I remembered how Baba had chosen me to join his closest disciples and to accompany him on his pilgrimage to Haridwar. I thought about all of these moments, and felt truly blessed. The guru had saved countless souls from self-destruction, and I was certainly one of them. If it hadn't been for Baba's unfathomable compassion, I probably would have ended up at the bottom of a gorge back in Ithaca.

But it was hopeless. Again and again, my mind returned to unanswered questions: *How could the guru be susceptible to the temptations of the flesh after attaining a state of uninterrupted bliss? If he had transcended the ego, and attained a state of eternal peace, why did he react angrily to detractors and need to use scare tactics to silence them?*

My thoughts drifted to Suresh's talk. *What does the bizarre story of Ranganath reabsorbing his semen back into his penis have to do with anything? Was the guru's future successor implying that Baba had the power to do this?*

After what must have been half the night torturing myself with unanswerable questions, I resolved to remain loyal to the one who had lifted me out of darkness and given my existence meaning. *No matter how confused I am right now, I cannot deny Baba's divinity. When I attain enlightenment, the veil of ignorance will be lifted. I will see that everything the guru does, no matter how strange or disturbing, is for the sake of his disciples.*

What choice did I have other than to think this way? The guru was my only lifeline in an ocean of misery. Without him I would surely drown.

Sleep finally overtook me. When I woke up the next morning, I was too late for morning meditation. But I had just enough time to make it to the *Guru Gita* before it started. When I arrived in the hall, I was startled to find Baba already seated on his throne. I immediately felt self-conscious. Sergio had undoubtedly told him what I'd done, and it'd be impossible to hide my inner turmoil from the Omniscient One. Hoping Baba wouldn't notice me, I found a place at the very back of the hall. But it was no use. As I took my seat on the floor, I felt the guru's eyes on me.

"Deependra!" called Baba, beckoning for me to approach the throne.

Dreading the scolding I assumed was coming, I made my way down the center aisle. Bracing myself for the guru's wrath, I prostrated before him and held my breath.

"Deependra, sit, sit," Baba said in English.

My knees buckled, and I exhaled long and hard. I saw a free spot on the floor behind the swamis and staggered toward it. Then Baba spoke to me again.

"No, not there."

I turned around to face him.

"You sit here," he said, pointing to a nonexistent spot between Suresh and Sergio. As I approached the throne, the men immediately moved a few inches to the side to make room for me to sit down. Baba locked me in his gaze and I was unable to look away. We sat in silence, staring at each other for what seemed like ages, until the faintest of smiles crept across Baba's mouth. Right then the guru's tremendous compassion spread through me, enveloping me in its warm glow. I'd never felt more special and loved in my entire life. I didn't care what anybody else had to say about Swami Rudrananda. I would never leave him.

Over the following weeks, no one spoke of the lies that the Grozas had been spreading. Despite a slight decrease in the number of people coming to the evening programs, life in the ashram went on as usual. I was beginning to think I could put the whole miserable chapter behind me. Then, about ten days before we were to leave for the European leg of Baba's tour, I was summoned to Baba's house late one night for more upsetting news.

Baba had sent Stephen Ames and Gopi to Wichita, Kansas to pay a surprise visit to Swami Satyananda. They had just returned from their trip, and Baba wanted his entire tour staff to hear their report.

Rashmi escorted me to the guru's study, where Baba was seated on an armchair surrounded by his tour staff. Squeezing into a free space, I took a seat on the floor with the others. As we waited for the rest of the staff to arrive, we were entertained by a demonstration from Baba's dog trainer, showing the new tricks that Ravana and Yama had recently learned.

"Roll over Ravana," the young woman said.

The dog turned over onto his back and let his four paws wave.

"Good boy!" the trainer said, and then fed Baba's pit-bull a dog biscuit.

Baba laughed with delight, and everyone applauded.

"Beg, Yama."

Yama sat up on her back feet, with her front paws up in the air.

The room broke into applause again, and this time Baba fed the dog a treat, giving her an affectionate pat on the back.

When the last of the tour staff had arrived, the guru's demeanor grew stern. He spoke to us through Anjali.

"In the past, Swami Satyananda disappointed your Baba. Despite this, I was ready to give him another chance to demonstrate his loyalty and commitment to the path.

But once again, he has proven only that he has a huge ego, and is completely deluded."

Turning to Gopi, who sat on the floor next to Anjali, the guru nodded, prompting her to stand up and speak.

"Instead of opening a new center," Gopi said, "we found Swamiji living with three slutty women. I talked to these girls myself. They aren't even devotees of Baba, and have nothing to do with Raja Yoga. Stephen followed them one night and discovered that they work in a strip club. Any fool can see Satyananda has been breaking his vows."

As I listened to Gopi's obvious attempt to discredit the swami, I felt my faith and devotion for the guru drain out of me.

Next Stephen stood up and spoke. "From my conversation with him, it's clear he has a bad case of sour grapes. He's angry at Baba for removing him from his position as director of the Manhattan ashram, and for sending him away."

"We think he's going to try to get even by spreading more disgusting rumors about Baba," Gopi said. "If you receive a phone call from this man, do not speak to him."

Then the guru spoke through Anjali again: "Baba forbids it."

After the meeting was over, we filed out of the guru's house. I knew Gopi had been lying when she gave her report on Satyananda. The things she said about him were totally out of character for him. She and I crossed paths out in the lobby. I tried to look away, but for a fleeting moment our eyes met. She squinted and folded her arms when she saw me, and then turned around and walked in the opposite direction. Even though I knew I was forbidden to talk to her, it hurt more when she was the one doing the rejecting.

I can get away, I thought once again. *I could pack my bags and leave right now.*

Silencing the cowardly voices in my head, I thought: *Only the ego wants to run away. The true disciple in me will not allow it.*

The day before our departure for London, word spread through the ashram that Satyananda was now in the San Francisco Bay area, and was meeting with other disgruntled devotees. The rumor I heard at lunch was that he'd written an open letter to the guru, leveling new accusations against him, and complaining about how he'd been mistreated in the ashram. He'd sent copies of the letter to all the Raja Yoga ashrams and centers.

When I returned to the Audiovisual office after the meal, Patrick told me that Jeremy had called for me.

"Did he leave a message?" I asked.

"Yeah, he said it's important that you call him back *before* you leave for London."

I got change at the reception desk and used one of the phone booths in the lobby. I didn't want to talk to my brother, but his message sounded urgent, so I felt I had to. But when I heard the sound of Carrie's voice on the other end of the line, I chickened out and hung up before she figured out it was me. I assumed that they had heard the rumors about Baba and were trying to stop me from leaving the country with him. I didn't want to hear what they had to say. The truth was, I was afraid they might convince me.

Later that afternoon they tried to reach me again, but I refused to take their call. After that, I told the people at reception that if they called again just to hang up on them.

Of course, I wasn't the only one receiving calls from family members and former loved ones. At eleven o'clock at night, the ashram phone was still ringing off the hook. Many of the calls were from ashram managers and center leaders who had read Satyananda's open letter and were demanding answers. They all received the same orders from Baba: They should burn every copy of the letter they could get their hands on, and were never to speak of Satyananda again.

In the evening, Poonish and I were packing our bags when Stephen returned from Baba's house. He was trembling, and said the guru was in a rage. As he spoke, I could hear the faint sound of a siren in the distance.

"I've never seen him this angry before," Stephen said. "This morning he was shouting at Anjali and Gopi at the top of his lungs. He had them both in tears. Even Avadhoot and Sergio are afraid to speak to him."

"That's nothing," Poonish said, folding a pair of slacks. The sound of the siren drew nearer. "I saw Rashmi in the manager's office today, and his shirt was covered in blood."

"What happened?" I asked.

The siren sounded close to the ashram now. Poonish hesitated before answering.

"A devotee who works as a nurse was treating him for a wound in his side."

"What does that have to with Baba?" I asked.

"They say Baba stabbed him with a fork."

The source of the siren turned into the driveway of the ashram and through the glass we saw flashing red lights. The three of us ran to the window. An ambulance pulled up in front of the main entrance. A second later, two paramedics jumped out with a gurney and rushed into the building.

Leaving the door to the room wide open, we ran to the lobby, where we were joined by the rest of the ashram residents, some of whom were in various stages of undress.

Gajendra Williams stood guard in front of the open door to Baba's apartments. His eyes were wide with fear, beads of sweat formed on his forehead, and the tendons in his neck stood out so that I could see his pulse.

"What happened?" Stephen asked him.

Gajendra looked at the floor and shook his head.

After waiting for what seemed like an eternity, paramedics appeared through the door of Baba's house, wheeling our beloved guru on the gurney. An oxygen mask was strapped to his face and an IV ran into one of his arms. Rashmi, Anjali, Suresh, and Sergio followed closely behind.

What if Baba dies? I thought. *There will be no one to take care of me.*

As worried as I was about the guru's fate—and how it might affect *me*—I was equally disturbed by how suddenly human and vulnerable he looked. He no longer seemed like an all-powerful god. He looked like a very frail, very sick old man.

The paramedics transferred Baba to the ambulance.

"Everybody, go back to your rooms!" Sergio shouted. Then he directed his attention at the *darshan* girls. "I'm talking to you!"

Gopi was on the scene as well, tears streaming down her face. While the other princesses obeyed Sergio and headed in the direction of the dormitories, she stayed put, as if the manager's orders didn't apply to her.

The Italian eyes were wild with a combination of fear and rage. "I said, back to your rooms!"

I was about to do what Sergio said, when I noticed that Stephen and Poonish were also ignoring him. *They're right*, I told myself. *Who is Sergio to tell us what to do at a time like this?* I too, resolved to stand my ground.

Just then, Avadhoot burst into the lobby, dressed in nothing but a pair of boxer shorts.

"Baba! My Baba!" he cried, running outside toward the driveway. "Let me ride with him!" he implored the paramedics. "He needs me!"

Anjali and Rashmi climbed into the back of the ambulance with the guru. The driver pushed Avadhoot out of the way and closed the doors, making his way to the front of the vehicle to take his place behind the wheel. The ambulance sped away and we rushed outside to get answers from Suresh.

"What happened to Baba?" Stephen asked, his voice wavering.

"Another heart attack," Suresh answered. "It's better that everyone return to their rooms now. I'm going to the hospital to be with Baba. I'll call with news as soon as I have any." Then he turned to Avadhoot, who was bawling like a baby. "Avadhoot, put some clothes on, and come ride with me."

I followed Stephen and Poonish back to our room. Just as we reached our door, Gopi called out to me.

"Deependra, wait!"

I turned to see her standing in front of the door to her room.

"Can I speak to you for a minute?"

Leaving me out in the corridor, my roommates went inside the room and shut the door behind them.

I joined Gopi in front of her room. Standing in front of her, I was unable to think of anything to say. When the silence between us became too much for me to bear, I took her in my arms. Burying her head in my shoulder, she began to cry.

"I'm so afraid, Deependra," she said, gently pulling away and looking up at me. "I'm worried about Baba."

"So am I," I said, but the truth was I didn't feel anything. I desperately wanted to feel *something* for the guru, but I was numb. After trying so hard to rid my mind of doubts about him, the situation with Satyananda had been steadily eroding my faith. The open letter felt like the last straw.

Gopi unlocked the door to her room and invited me in. The room had only one bed, so I sat on it beside her.

"Can I ask you to do something for me, Deependra."

"Of course, anything."

"Can you stay with me a while?"

Lying together in the bed, I held Gopi and stroked her hair until she fell asleep.

I SCOWLED AT POONISH, and then, after a pregnant pause, tapped my forehead with my hand and spoke in Sergio's voice. "What kind of an idiot are you?"

Baba burst out laughing. This triggered more laughter, until everyone in the Namaste room joined in. Poonish laughed so hard he turned pink. Even Sergio pretended to find my G-rated impression of him funny.

"*Merda*! You call this coffee?"

Anjali translated my words for Baba, after which the guru slapped his side and guffawed even louder than before.

"Easy, easy, Deependra!" Anjali croaked, laughing so hard she could barely speak. "Baba's still recovering!"

"Do your impression of Avadhoot!" Kriyadevi called from the back of the room.

"Yes!" called Suresh. "Do Avadhoot!"

"Pleased to meet you," I said with a flourish and a small bow to the future guru, imitating Avadhoot's own version of a fake Russian accent. "I am Professor Boris Koreoffsky—author and sole proponent of theory of irrelevant relativity."

The audience cracked up again, and this time gave me a round of applause. Even Avadhoot, who'd been snapping pictures of my impromptu stand-up routine, was laughing so uncontrollably he had to put down his camera. When he regained his composure, he strutted over to me in his cowboy persona, whipped the ten-gallon hat from his head, and crowned me with it.

The informal gathering of Baba and his staff was the first of its kind since his heart attack. On the strict orders of his doctors, the guru had canceled the European leg of his tour, and had returned to his North American headquarters in Birchwood Falls to convalesce.

Later that evening, Parvati Halabi came to my room after lights out, with the message that Baba wanted to see me. I followed her to Baba's house, where I found the guru sitting up in bed. Suresh sat on a chair by his side.

Baba's face brightened when he saw me. I still felt nothing.

"Ahh, Deependra! How are you?"

I bowed down before him. Then he spoke to me in his native language.

"Baba wants you to make a 'best of tape,'" Suresh said, interpreting for the guru.

"Of course, Baba," I said. Then I turned to the young swami. "A best of what?"

"Baba wants you to take all the film clips of his appearances on American television and splice them together on one tape."

"Yes, Baba. I will have Kriyadevi get started on it right away."

The guru dismissed me, and Suresh walked me back to the lobby.

"When do you expect Baba to start touring again?" I asked him.

The young swami was silent for a few seconds, and then spoke. "He won't be touring again."

I was taken aback. Baba seemed to be doing much better.

"We're going to make the announcement tomorrow. Baba will return to Ravipur as soon as the doctors think he's well enough to travel all the way to India."

"I see." I was disappointed. I had wanted to visit Europe and Australia.

"Baba wants you to come back to Ravipur with him."

"Oh." I knew I should've been happy to hear that the guru wanted to keep me with him, but all I could think about was how I'd already been to India, and was afraid I'd be bored. "For how long?"

"Indefinitely. You should apply for a one-year entry visa again. Talk to Gajendra. He'll arrange it."

"Great news," I said, trying my best to sound enthusiastic. For the first time since I'd joined Raja Yoga, I didn't want to travel with the guru. Especially not back to hot, smelly India. Then a longing rose up from somewhere deep inside of me. I wanted to go home. Home to Ithaca.

Suresh studied my face and then looked concerned. "Deependra, are you okay?"

"Yes, very happy!" I said, forcing a smile. "But I was wondering—would it be alright if I went back home for a short visit before we leave for India? I have some personal business I need to take care of."

Baba's future successor smiled reassuringly. "Certainly. Take all the time you need. We're not leaving before several weeks' time."

33.
RETURN TO ITHACA

I HAD EXPECTED THE sight of the town I grew up in to be comforting, but as my bus rolled down State Street toward the Ithaca Commons, my heart was heavy with forgotten grief and shame. *This is where my mother died, and I became the freak with no parents*, I reminded myself. *This is the place where I permanently fucked up my life by dropping out of college.*

When my bus pulled into the Greyhound station, Melanie and my two nieces, Leah and Corinne, were there to greet me. My sister threw her arms around me, and looked me up and down. "Dougie! Oh my God, you're so skinny!"

Corinne dug the toe of her shoe into the asphalt of the parking lot and smiled at me shyly. Leah tilted her head to the side and squinted. "Hi, Uncle Dougie."

I made an effort to sound cheerful. "Wow, you two sure got big!" I was unable to think of anything else to say.

Leah stiffened and folded her little arms across her chest. "Maybe *you* got smaller."

I followed my sister and nieces through the parking lot toward the car. "Still driving the Volare?"

Melanie chuckled. "You haven't been gone that long, Doug."

As we approached my sister's car, I noticed a young woman seated in the driver's seat. She was dressed in a pink sleeveless halter-top, revealing a flat midriff and the tops of her small, pale breasts.

"Who's that?" I asked.

Melanie beamed a smiled in the young woman's direction. "That's Heather!"

As I climbed into the back seat between my nieces, Heather grinned self-consciously. My sister sat up front and introduced us. I smiled politely. I couldn't help notice that the roots of Heather's short blonde hair were brown, and that her ears had multiple piercings. She wasn't unattractive, but her skin lacked the luster of the Raja Yoginis, which I'd come to take for granted. From the dark circles under her eyes, I could tell she was tired and depressed.

Melanie twisted around to talk to me. "Heather just got her driver's license," she said proudly. Then she turned around again and spoke to the girl. "I taught Doug how to drive in this car, too."

I was hoping Melanie would explain who Heather was, but she was acting as if I should already know.

Heather pulled the car up in front of my mother's house, and when we all got out I got a good look at Heather's ass. *Round and firm,* I noticed, and remembered how good ol' Mike McFadden would've described her: "Eminently fuckable."

Then I caught myself. I couldn't allow myself to sink back into my old impure ways of thinking. *Om Namah Shivaya.* I repeated inwardly. *Om Namah Shivaya.* But I couldn't stop staring at Heather.

I followed the others into the house. Heather and the girls rushed upstairs, leaving me alone with Melanie. The familiar, pleasant smell of the house brought back memories of my mother.

"Who is she?" I asked, sitting down at the kitchen table.

Pouring me a glass of lemonade, Melanie's eyebrows drew together.

"Didn't I tell you about Heather on the phone? She's been with us for six months now."

"Six months? No, you didn't. Why?"

"She's my foster child."

"Isn't she a bit old to be a *foster child?* Where does she sleep?"

"She's seventeen. In your old room."

This news did not sit well with me. What right did Melanie have to rent my room out to a stranger? "Where do the girls sleep?"

"In Lucy's old room. I've made up the bed for you downstairs in the playroom."

Old, familiar anger began to bubble up, but I swallowed it back down. I hadn't been there long enough to pick a fight. "I see you've made yourself quite comfortable here. Taken over the whole house."

My sister just laughed. Then she filled me in on everything that was going on in the family since we had last spoken. I didn't ask about our younger sister, but Melanie reminded me that Lucy was now in her second year at Syracuse, and had transferred into the nursing program. I remembered the frequent visits from nurses during my mother's illness and felt horrible. *Why on earth would anyone want to spend their life taking care of sick people?*

"Any news from Jeremy? Is Carrie an official Jew yet?"

Melanie chuckled. "No. And I don't think she ever will be. Actually, they're into something else now."

"Something else? Something else like what? Another religion?"

"Not exactly. They've been going to these self-help training seminars. I think it's called EST."

I shook my head in disbelief. *Jeremy and Carrie don't know the meaning of the word loyalty. They turned their back on the true guru.* They were doomed to stray from one religious group to another for the rest of their lives.

The news from Florida was that Grandma Millie had recently won a bridge tournament, and was written up in the *Palm Beach Post*. Aunt Gabby had also made it into the paper, for donating an ambulance to a hospital in Jerusalem. The article was accompanied by a photograph of my aunt standing in front of the ambulance, holding a plaque honoring my late cousin Harvey, in whose name she had made the donation.

In my utter self-absorption, I thought about how much an ambulance cost, and all the nice clothes and meals in Prasad I could have bought with my aunt's money. I wished that she'd given it to me instead of wasting it on Israel.

"You really ought to give them a call, Doug. They worry about you."

I promised that I'd get around to it, and then changed the subject.

"How did you end up with Heather?"

"Most of the girls at the South Lansing Center where I teach are from New York City and are in for drug use or prostitution, but not Heather. She grew up only an hour away from here, in Auburn." Her only crime, according to Melanie, was borrowing her mother's car without permission. "Heather's mom reported it stolen to teach her a lesson. Can you believe it? What a bitch!"

"So what does she do all day?"

"She's studying for the GED, and has a part-time job at Burger Town."

I asked my sister about her love life. She was no longer seeing Herb. I was relieved I wouldn't have to be subjected to him during my visit. She had broken it off with him when she learned that he'd been using her as a "case study" in the Abnormal Psychology course he was teaching.

I burst out laughing. "That's hilarious. How'd you find out?"

Melanie was not amused. She explained that she'd dropped by Herb's office after class one day, and introduced herself to one of his TAs. When the student realized who she was, he became excited. "So, *you're* the *Melanie* Professor Moskovitch keeps talking about. I didn't realize Melanie was your real name!"

"What an asshole!" I said, laughing inwardly. Melanie felt betrayed by Herb and was angry with him, but it turned out she had another reason to dump him. She had met somebody else. His name was Marco.

"He's closer to my age and is more my type," she said. "What about you, Doug? How's life in the ashram these days?"

I thought of telling Melanie about Baba's heart attack, but then thought better of it. I didn't want to have to explain how a perfected being could also have health problems like everyone else. If I didn't understand it, how would she? I also considered telling her about the rumors going around about Baba. I knew they were lies, probably, but part of me was still trying to figure it all out. In any case, my sister would've been incapable of being objective. It would've only given her another reason to believe the worst about the guru.

"Life at the ashram? Fantastic!" I lied. "I'm only twenty years old, and I'm already a department head."

"That doesn't surprise me. Baba's lucky to have you."

"He's invited me to return to India with him. I'll be staying in Ravipur indefinitely."

I expected Melanie to launch into her usual tirade about how the guru was ruining my life, but her response surprised me.

"You already know what I think about that, Doug. It's your life. I can't stop you."

I suddenly felt heavy and profoundly sad. Melanie didn't seem to care about me anymore. I felt the prick of tears behind my eyelids. I was truly on my own now.

Springing to my feet, I slung my duffle bag over my shoulder, and quickly downed the glass of lemonade she had poured for me.

My sister stiffened. "Going somewhere?"

I wiped my mouth with the back of my hand. "I'm going to get settled in downstairs."

What I found in the basement upset me even more. My stereo and record collection were gone. The teenage

The Guru's Touch

hangout my mother had always referred to as the "playroom" was now an actual playroom for Leah and Corinne, cluttered with children's books and toys.

I couldn't bear to see my old hangout in its altered state. I decided to take a ride to Collegetown to see if I could find any of my old high school friends.

I went to the garage to look for my bike, but I couldn't find it. Thinking I might have missed it on my way downstairs, I looked for it in the boiler room. It wasn't there either. I got a sinking feeling. I remembered Melanie's warning. She had said that when we sold the house, she'd get rid of anything I left behind or would keep it for herself.

But we hadn't sold the house. As far as I was concerned, Melanie had stolen it along with all my other stuff.

I went back into the playroom and collapsed on the sofa bed. *Ithaca is no longer my home*, I thought. *I will never be able to return to my old life here.*

I dug into my duffle bag and pulled out one of Baba's books that I'd taken with me: *The Path of Perfection*. Opening it to a random page, I decided that whatever passage I read from would be a message from the guru. At the top of the page was a quote from the great poet saint Kabir:

Guru and God both appear before me. To whom should I prostrate? I bow before Guru who introduced God to me.

I set the book on the bed, clasped my hands together in prayer, and gave thanks to the omniscient guru for providing me with precisely the message I needed. *I don't need a home or possessions, or someone to love and take care of me*, I told myself. *I don't even need God. All I need is the guru!*

Later at dinner, Leah grimaced when she tasted her food. "I don't like these enchiladas. They don't have any taste."

"That's because they're vegetarian," Melanie explained, passing me the casserole dish. "Uncle Doug doesn't eat meat."

"Why not?" Corinne asked.

"I don't eat meat because it's full of impurities that interfere with the practice of Raja Yoga."

Melanie sighed heavily.

I thanked my sister for the vegetarian meal, but inwardly I was seething. Although I was committed to the life of a renunciant, I was still outraged that she'd gotten rid of my most precious possessions.

Heather looked amused. "You know how to tie yourself up in knots like a pretzel and do all of those funny exercises?"

"That's *Hatha* Yoga," I said. "That's only one kind of yoga. There are many. The kind of yoga I do has more to do with meditation and selfless service."

"Whatever floats your boat," Heather said with a wink. Then she turned to Melanie and asked if she could be excused.

After dinner, I lingered in the kitchen while my sister cleaned up and told me all about her new boyfriend.

"Marco owns his own construction company," she said, loading the dishwasher. "He drives a Corvette."

As I pretended to listen, I grew increasingly agitated, thinking about my missing bike and record collection.

"He wears a cross on a gold chain," she laughed. "Can you believe I'm dating someone who wears a cross? What would Mommy say!"

"Where's my stuff?" I finally blurted out.

Melanie's back stiffened. She turned off the water at the sink, and sat down at the table across from me.

"Which stuff?" she asked, lowering her brow and squinting.

I gritted my teeth. She knew very well *which stuff*. "My records, my bike."

"I told you when you left that I would not be storing any of your things."

Tears of frustration rimmed my eyes. "Yes, but I thought you meant *after* you sold the house. But you're still here, and you've taken over the place."

Melanie glared at me. "I thought I made it very clear that I would be buying you, Jeremy, and Lucy out."

"So buy us out already!" I hollered.

"I'm not giving you any more money until you come to your senses and go back to college."

"It's *not* your money! The house belongs to me just as much as it belongs to you! And I want to be reimbursed for the video course—"

"—which you never finished!"

We argued until we were both out of breath and red in the face. But Melanie wouldn't budge.

Before calling it a night, I went upstairs to the second floor to take a shower. When I was finished, I gathered my clothes under my arm, wrapped a towel around my waist, and stepped out of the bathroom into the hall. At the same time, Heather appeared in the open doorway of my old room. She was in a pair of white cotton panties and an AC/DC t-shirt. She gave me a knowing smile. I tensed with lust as she brushed past me on her way into the bathroom. I turned to follow her with my eyes, and admired the way her underwear hugged the curve of her ass.

When I was alone in the hall again, I poked my head into her room. Posters of hard rock bands covered the walls, clothing was piled on top of her dresser and spilled over onto the floor, and there was an unfamiliar musky smell mixed with the odor of stale cigarettes in the air. Gone were any signs that the room had once belonged to me.

Downstairs in the playroom, I tried to get into *The Path of Perfection*, but an image of Heather's butt kept popping into my head, making it impossible to focus on the guru's words. Before turning in, I went upstairs to take a leak one last time. But instead of using the nearest bathroom on the ground floor, I made the trip up an extra flight of stairs to use the one on the second floor. When I reached the top of the stairs, I was disappointed to find the door to Heather's room closed.

When I came out of the bathroom, however, Heather was standing in the doorway of her room waiting for me. Her t-shirt and white panties now glowed violet in the eerie cast of a blacklight. I swallowed as my eyes traveled from her delicate pink mouth to the swell of her small pert breasts. Her bare legs were smooth and toned.

"Wanna hang out?" she asked, inviting me in with a flick of her chin. For a split second I hesitated. *What would Baba think? What about Gopi?* Then, stepping into her lair, I gave in to temptation.

Heather offered me a seat on the bed next to her. Reaching into one of her dresser drawers, she produced a bottle of Bacardi rum and took a long swig from it. Then she offered it to me.

I tried not to wince as the sweet alcohol burned my throat.

Heather laughed. "Don't do much drinking in the ashram, do ya?"

"You'd be surprised."

I glanced around at posters of bands I despised. I barely recognized the place. Blobs of bright red wax rose, fell, and changed density in the lava lamp on the table at the foot of her bed.

"If you stare at it long enough," Heather said, "it'll hypnotize you."

"Cool." I took another swig from the bottle. "I've strengthened my mind through all the chanting and meditation I do at the ashram. I doubt it's even possible for me to be hypnotized."

Heather drank from the bottle again, and squinted as she studied my face. "So, what's it like being in a cult?"

"A cult?" I snapped. "I'm not in a cult! Is that what my sister told you?" I thought about going back downstairs to the basement. Then I glanced at her slender bare thighs. *I may never get a chance like this again,* I thought, and let the slight go.

"Jeeze! Sorry—I didn't mean nothin' by it."

"I'm the disciple of a perfected master of Raja Yoga—a member of his tour staff. I don't dance in the street and sell flowers at airports."

Melanie obviously considered me the family joke. Now I had another reason to be angry with her. I was about to ask Heather if she knew what Melanie had done with my bike and record collection, when, without any warning, she leaned over and kissed me. She tasted like a boozy ashtray. I cupped one of her breasts with my hand.

As I explored Heather's mouth with my tongue, I couldn't help thinking about Gopi. The night of Baba's heart attack, I had held her in my arms until morning. Nothing had happened between us. I was still in love with her, but was confused about how she felt about me.

I pulled Heather's hand to my crotch. I wanted her to feel how big I was underneath my jeans. If Gopi loved me, she should've shown me when she had the chance. Now it was too late.

Heather sucked on my earlobe and undid my belt buckle. Within seconds, both of us were out of our clothes. I had a raging hard on, and she was staring right at it. I felt self-conscious. No one had ever seen me this naked before.

While I hesitated, unsure of what my next move should be, Heather curled up next to me on the bed and put her head in my lap. She gave me a couple of soft, exploratory kisses before taking me into her mouth.

The sensation sent waves of ecstasy throughout my entire body. I looked down at her pretty face and watched as I slid in and out of her mouth. Her muffled groans added to my excitement. I felt as though I owned this girl, and she would do anything I wanted.

The pleasure was like nothing I'd ever experienced before. *Who needs the ocean of bliss when I can do this?*

"Okay. Now fuck me!" Heather demanded.

I couldn't imagine anything would feel better than what she was already doing to me, but I was eager to lose my virginity. I climbed on top of her and searched for her with my fingers. Suddenly I was gripped by anxiety. *What if I get her pregnant?*

"Do you have a condom?" I asked.

Heather looked up and grinned. Her teeth and the whites of her eyes glowed purple in the cheesy light.

"You're sweet. Don't worry about it—I'm on the pill."

I entered her and a jolt of electricity shot up my spine. I wondered how I could possibly be having an experience of the divine *kundalini* at the same time I was completely debasing myself. *What does Baba think of me now?*

Heather gasped and puffed as I lunged into her. "Turn me over."

"What?"

"Screw me from behind."

I was anxious again as I helped her roll over. *Can the girls hear us? What would Melanie say?*

The position was awkward, but I quickly got the hang of it. Before long, Heather began to thrash around beneath me. "Yes! Yes! I'm coming!"

A current of electricity flowed between us. I stopped moving for a moment so that I could pay closer attention to the sensation.

"Do you feel that?"

"Yeah, I feel it," she murmured through the side of her mouth. Most of her face was buried in the pillow.

"I mean my spiritual power. Can you feel my energy flowing into you?"

Heather grimaced as she lifted her head off the pillow. "Say what?" she barked.

"Never mind. Give me your tongue," I whispered.

Heather stuck out her tongue and turned her head up toward me. As her tongue entered my mouth, another bolt of lightning shot up my spine. My entire body convulsed as I climaxed.

I remained inside of her, motionless for a while, until I began to feel queasy. *What have I done?* I thought, pulling out of her. The vital *ojas* I needed to attain higher states was now depleted. Everything I worked so hard to attain over the past three years was lost in an instant of weakness. I could sense the guru's profound disappointment with me. *How will I ever be able to look Baba in the eye again?*

As wretched as I felt, another part of me was proud—I had lost my virginity! I was finally a man. I knew that Baba wouldn't approve of my behavior, but at least Sergio would be pleased.

"Want to do it again?" I asked hopefully.

The Guru's Touch

Heather sat up and lit a cigarette. "You should get out. I have to work in the morning."

Harsh sunlight filtered in through the small dirty windows of the finished basement windows, stinging my eyes. A glance at my alarm clock told me it was eleven in the morning. *Impossible,* I told myself. *It can't be.* I rubbed my eyes and looked again. I was astounded—I hadn't slept so late since high school.

Dragging myself out of bed, I trudged upstairs to the kitchen and brewed myself a cup of coffee. A quick check of the upstairs confirmed that no one was home. I took my coffee into the living room and, as the caffeine circulated through my bloodstream, took stock of my encounter with Heather the night before.

I was glad to be no longer a virgin, but at the same time I felt remorse for sullying myself and squandering my spiritual vitality. I'd behaved like an animal in heat. I resolved never to have sex again—unless the guru commanded me to get married. In time, I'd regain my seminal vigor, and I'd be able to think of myself as a yogi again.

I took a long sip of my coffee and let its heat radiate through my body. It felt good to have no chant to be at, and no *seva* to run to. For the first time since joining Raja Yoga, I had the day off. The only problem was, I had no idea what to do with myself. I decided I'd try to find out where Mike lived and go pay him a visit.

After a half-hour shower, I got dressed and threw a linen sports coat over my jeans and t-shirt and rolled up the sleeves. *This should impress McFadden,* I thought. In the back of my mind, I also hoped Heather would like what she saw and want to fuck me again.

I rang the bell at Mike's parents' house, but no one came to the door. They were obviously at work. I set off on foot for the Cornell campus, where I hoped to find him studying for finals at the library.

As I ambled toward Collegetown, I thought about my other childhood friends. Most of them were now seniors in college. In a couple of months, they would graduate and start looking for jobs. If I ever decided to go back to school, it would take me years to catch up. Then I realized it didn't matter. *I will never leave the ashram,* I told myself. *Who cares if I don't have a college degree? I don't need an expensive piece of paper to prove my worth. I am Shiva, the Inner-Self of all.*

On my way to campus, I stopped at Collegetown Bagels for a quick breakfast. A tall skinny kid with acne took my order, and I remembered when Namdev used to work there. He had lived in the Ravipur ashram for three years already, and had no college degree either. I wondered what he'd do if he ever decided to leave the ashram. At least I had learned a trade. I could always get a job as a cameraman. But what would Namdev do?

I finished my bagel and went to look for Mike at the Uris library. At the door, a security guard wouldn't let me in without a Cornell ID. Frustrated, I went by Willard Straight Hall, but ran into the same problem.

I wandered aimlessly around the Arts Quad for a while, hoping to run into Mike or somebody else I knew. But I didn't see anyone. Finally, I gave up and took a walk to the Raja Yoga Center. It would be nice to see Menaka Atkins or Robert Cargill, if they were home.

When I arrived in front of the old Queen Anne-style mansion where I first began my spiritual quest, the first thing I noticed was that the Raja Yoga Mission sign was missing. I rang the bell. As I waited for someone to come to the door, I peeked through the windows. Gone was the large portrait of Baba that used to hang in the front hallway, and all other signs that a Raja Yoga center had once been located there.

I rang the bell again, and knocked on the door. This time I heard heavy footsteps from within the house. Through a pane of glass in the door I saw Menaka descending the stairs. When she saw me through the glass she stopped abruptly and appeared to gasp.

"Menaka, hi!" I said through the glass. "It's me—Deependra Greenbaum—Doug."

After a moment's hesitation, she opened the door. She was not smiling.

"What are you doing here?" she snapped. Her head was tilted back, and the corners of her mouth were turned down in an ugly grimace.

I started to get a bad feeling. Something was wrong. "I'm in town visiting my sister. I'm going back to India with Baba in a few weeks. I thought I'd stop by to say hi."

"This isn't a Raja Yoga center anymore! We got the letter from Satyananda, and we know all about Baba. We know all about *YOU* too!"

"*Me?* What did I do?"

Menaka sneered. "That's a nice jacket. You look like one of his henchmen now."

"How can you believe the lies they're telling about the guru?" I shouted. "I thought you were a true devotee."

She barked with laughter. "You've got to be kidding! Baba is the biggest liar who ever lived! He betrayed all of us!"

Heat flushed through me and my mind raced, searching for something to say in defense of my guru. At the same time, I wanted to slap her across the face. "You'll burn in hell forever for saying that!"

"Screw you, you pathetic little bastard! Get out of here before I call the police!"

Menaka slammed the door in my face, and I nearly fell backwards down the steps.

I was badly shaken. I felt like the universe I lived in was being turned upside down. Menaka had said she knew all about me. I couldn't imagine what she was talking about. Unable to think clearly, I ran back up Buffalo Street in the direction of the campus. I crossed Eddie Street, and when I reached College Avenue, I sprinted toward the stone bridge that spanned Cascadilla Gorge. Sitting down on the edge of the parapet, I stared at the rushing stream far below, and I tried to picture what my lifeless corpse would look like after it had been bashed against the stone floor of the gorge.

First Jeremy and Carrie left. They had left even before the rumors. Next was Arjuna, followed soon after by Satyananda and the Grozas, who had succeeded in turning many others against the guru. I pulled at my hair. *How can it be? How can it be?*

The way I saw it, if Baba was a false guru, that meant that everything I'd come to believe about him was a lie. If everything was a lie, my entire life was meaningless!

"Faith should arise from a direct experience of the master's grace," I remembered Baba saying. "A true disciple pays no heed to the vicious rumors he might hear."

Yes, my direct experience: the explosion of kundalini at the base of my spine and the expanded state of consciousness I entered when Baba first gave me shaktipat, the guru's ability to read minds, and the countless stories from other devotees of the miraculous experiences they've had in his presence. This was all the evidence I needed that Baba was a true guru.

I continued to gaze into the gorge, remembering how three years earlier I had stood right there and considered throwing myself into it. Now I was considering it again. *I'm just as miserable now as I was the day I left home for the ashram. Where is the ocean of peace that Baba promised?*

This question was followed immediately by a feeling of remorse and shame. *How can I doubt the guru?* Even if I hadn't attained permanent spiritual bliss, I had still achieved so much in the ashram. Baba had transformed me from a nobody into a member of his personal staff. I was a star cameraman and the head of the video department.

I've made real friends in the ashram, like Poonish and... and...and... Kriyadevi! Menaka, and all the other losers who believe the lies, have no faith. They don't even know the meaning of the word disciple!

Then it hit me: A *real* disciple didn't care if the rumors were true or not. A *genuine* disciple sees *everything* as a test. *Everything* the guru did was an expression of his compassion, and was intended to teach us something.

I decided that if the rumors were true, then Baba's actions had a higher purpose—even if that purpose was too obscure for me to understand with my ordinary mind.

Instead of doubting the guru, I should be grateful. I told myself. For all I knew, Baba had sacrificed his reputation in order to expose his false disciples. Perhaps his actions pointed to a higher teaching: we must stop clinging to the relativistic concepts like "good" and "bad," and "right" and "wrong." It occurred to me that maybe this was what his closest people understood and I still didn't get.

Well, I too can be a bastard like Sergio or lunatic like Avadhoot, if that's what it takes to prove myself. Right then and there I made a pledge to live more spontaneously.

"Are you okay?" someone said behind me. I turned around to see a young woman staring at me with a worried look on her face. She was wearing a knapsack on her back. I assumed she was a student.

"Yeah, fine," I answered, looking her squarely in the eye. I knew what she was thinking and I didn't like it. I sprang to my feet, stood as straight as possible, and puffed out my chest.

The girl took a step backwards and let out a huge breath. A smile slowly brightened her face. "Phew! Sorry! You scared me. It's just that we've already had two suicides on the bridge this semester. You really shouldn't sit there. You could lose your balance and fall."

"Thanks," I said, lowering my chin to look down on her.

Having given up on trying to find Mike, and with nowhere in particular to go, I cut across campus and headed down East Hill in the direction of the high school. As I approached Lake View cemetery, I could hear the taunts and laughter of teenagers. A small pack of them were congregating in front of the Cornell family mausoleum, sharing a joint. A girl with a whale spout ponytail looked familiar.

As I entered the grounds, one of the boys called out to me. "Hey you!"

I continued my descent down the hill, but turned my head in the direction of the group.

"Yeah, you! Don Johnson! Come over here a sec!"

I realized he was mocking my outfit, but decided to take his comparison of me to one of the stars of *Miami Vice* as a compliment. With nothing better to do, I joined them.

"You're Lucy Greenbaum's brother, aren't you?" the familiar girl asked.

"That's right."

"Cool," the girl said, passing me the joint. "She used to hang out with my older sister."

My first impulse was to refuse. But then I remembered my earlier resolution to live more spontaneously. *No right, no wrong. Only Shiva.* I took a long drag, coughing violently as I exhaled. I passed the joint to the kid standing next to me.

"Yeah, you're Doug," a boy said with a safety pin stuck through his ear. His hair looked like it had been lightened with hydrogen peroxide.

I nodded.

"I heard you joined a cult," the girl who knew my sister said.

I bristled at the word "cult."

"Do I look like somebody in a cult?"

The girl regarded me through bloodshot eyes and a haze of smoke. "I don't know. Maybe."

I wandered past the high school in the general direction of downtown Ithaca. It felt strange to be high. It was nothing like the transcendental states I'd experienced around Baba. I wasn't sure if I even liked the sensation. I remembered Namdev Loman telling me that Baba used to smoke ganja. At the time, I was angry that he could repeat a lie like that about guru—it sounded so preposterous. Now I wasn't so sure.

My head in a fog, I had a strong craving for French fries. I was also feeling horny. I hoped Heather would be home from work by the time I arrived back at my mother's house. I thought about dropping in on her at Burger Town and getting something to eat, but that was too far away, and I wanted to eat right away. I went to McDonald's on the Commons and ordered three large packets of fries with extra salt and ketchup.

I arrived at my mother's house at the same time Heather returned home from work. She was dropped off in a beat-up pickup truck. The driver was a burly man in his early twenties with curly brown hair.

Climbing out of the truck, Heather greeted me with a flick of her chin. "Hey." She was dressed in a Burger Town uniform, and suddenly I was hungry for fries again. "This is my boyfriend, Bear."

"Um, hi, nice to meet you, Bear," I said, trying to hide my surprise.

"Who the fuck are you?" Bear growled. He took a step toward me and balled his fists.

"I'm Deependra."

Bear frowned. "What the fuck kind a name is that?"

"He's Melanie's brother," Heather said. "He's in a cult. His real name is Doug."

"Oh." Bear shrugged and had a confused look on his face. "Come on Heather, let's go. My lunch break's only half an hour."

"That's okay, Bear," Heather smiled, giving me a wink. "You only need five minutes."

I suddenly wished I never left the ashram.

Heather and her boyfriend headed upstairs to be alone together in my old room. I found Melanie in the kitchen preparing dinner.

"Oh, Doug. Someone with an Indian sounding name and an American accent called from the ashram."

The muscles in my neck and back seized up. "Really? They called here, for me?"

"Yeah, a couple hours ago. Someone named Godrenja—or something like that—"

"*Gajendra?*"

"Yeah, that's it."

"He *is* American. *Gajendra* is his spiritual name. He's one of Baba's managers."

"Whatever—he called from Birchwood Falls. Said it's urgent, and that you should call him back as soon as you can."

I got an uneasy feeling. I hoped I wasn't in trouble for being away from the ashram too long. Maybe Suresh had forgotten to tell Gajendra I was going away. I hurried downstairs to the basement, where I could call him back in private.

"Bad news," Gajendra said, after Mukti finally tracked him down and connected me to him. "Indira Gandhi was assassinated this morning, and the Indian government has put a hold on issuing any long-term visas. Right now Americans are only being granted three-month tourist visas."

Because I was still high, I at first thought that Gajendra was talking about Indira St. John from the Ravipur ashram. Then I remembered that Indira Gandhi was the name of the Prime Minister of India.

"Oh no!" I said, trying to sound upset. Part of me was relieved. *I'll only have to stay in India for three months.* "So, I guess I should tell them that I don't want the student visa anymore, and apply for a tourist visa instead?"

"I'm afraid it's not so simple. You see, you've already requested an entry visa. You're not allowed to change the stated purpose of your visit after you've already applied."

"Bummer," I said. "Why not?" I was beginning to worry that Gajendra might be able to tell that I was stoned.

"You can't just say you want to come to India for a year to study Hindu philosophy, and then change your mind the next day and tell them you only want to come for a few weeks to go sight-seeing."

"So how long do you think I'll have to wait before they start granting student visas again?"

"Difficult to say. No one really knows. Could be weeks, months—maybe years."

"I guess this means I won't be able to go back to India with Baba." Another part of me was upset at the prospect of being left behind. At the same time, I wondered if it would be too late for me to apply to some colleges for the spring semester.

"We may have a way to get around the visa problem," he said. "But I don't want to talk about it over the phone. You should get back to the ashram as soon as possible so we can take care of this. Baba needs you in India."

Baba needs me! I repeated inwardly, as I hung up the phone. *I won't let him down!*

I explained to Melanie that something had come up at the ashram, and I'd need to cut my visit short. I hoped she'd put up a fight and try to convince me to stay, but instead she told me that she understood, and that she wished me well. Her reaction made me miserable. It was further proof she didn't care about me anymore.

In the morning Melanie dropped the girls off at school, and then drove me to the Greyhound station. We arrived a few minutes early, and she stayed with me while I waited for the bus.

"Doug, before you leave there's something I wanted to tell you."

"Okay."

"Remember when I came to visit you in the ashram last summer?"

"Yeah, I remember. We had a big fight."

"Right. But after that visit I got to thinking. I realized that you're not a kid anymore."

"Okay..."

"My point is, I realized that I have to let you make your own decisions, even if I don't approve of them. But at the same time, you're going to have to live with the consequences of those decisions and learn your own lessons from them."

I thought about my bike and record collection and seethed.

"I want you to know that I love you very much, Doug. If you ever decide to come home to look for a job, or to take some courses while you're getting on your feet, I'll always be here to support you."

"I appreciate your saying that, Melanie," I said, suddenly feeling better.

"By the way, there's something else I've been meaning to tell you."

"I'm listening."

"Something that happened when I met Baba."

"Tell me," I said, hoping the bus wouldn't come before she had time to finish.

"Remember the necklace he gave me?"

I nodded.

"When he handed it to me, I felt a burst of energy."

"Like an electric shock?"

"Yes!"

Just then, my bus pulled into the station. Melanie gave me a big hug, and squeezed me tight. "I love you, Dougie."

"I love you, too," I said, though I didn't actually feel any love for her. But it did feel good to know she still cared.

34.
ABOVE THE LAW

MY TAXI DREW CLOSER to the ashram. As the main building came into view, I remembered the throngs of devotees who had come to see Baba in the past, and it disturbed me to imagine the place empty and deserted. If Menaka had turned against the guru, and Robert had seen fit to close the Ithaca center, I assumed that many others had turned their backs on the guru too. So when I saw what looked like hundreds of people in the lobby waiting to check in for the weekend, tears of relief welled in my eyes. So many people couldn't be wrong about Baba.

"Not everyone believes the lies, Deependra," Poonish said in the privacy of our room. "Far from it. Most of the devotees still have faith in Baba. I heard that this might be the biggest weekend in the history of the ashram."

I glanced at my watch. I had an appointment to discuss my visa situation with Gajendra in a few minutes, but wanted to hear my roommate's take on what was going on in Raja Yoga.

"Why do you think so many people are coming to see him now?" I asked.

"Baba's leaving for India in only a month. Everybody knows about his heart attack in Berkeley, and they're afraid he might never be well enough to travel again."

On my way to Gajendra's office, I was headed off by Sergio. I followed him into the Namaste room for a word in private. He wanted to warn me about the investigative reporter who was snooping around the ashram. The one Daniel Groza had told me about at the hospital in Oakland. The man's name was Christopher Walsh, and he was the publisher of a quarterly journal called *Veritas*. He had come to stay at the ashram a few days earlier, saying he was writing a piece on Baba and the Mission. Suresh had agreed to an interview with him, but ended it abruptly when the reporter started asking too many "inappropriate" questions.

"This asshole might try to contact you," Sergio said.

"Me? Why me?"

"Because that loser Satyananda mentioned you in his letter as one of the people who harassed the Grozas after they left."

I understood then what Menaka had meant when she said that she knew all about me. My first reaction was embarrassment—I was infamous.

Sergio chuckled, and gave me an affectionate slap on the cheek. "Don't look so upset, Greenbaum—you're in good company. He wrote about me too."

The Italian actually made me feel better when he said that. *I'm proud*, I told myself. *Yes, proud to be known as such a loyal defender of the guru's honor.*

"What do you want me to say if I hear from him?" I asked.

"Don't say nothing. Don't talk to that fucker. If he calls, you hang up—understand?"

I arrived at Gajendra Williams's office at the same time as Patrick Kelly, who had the same visa problem. We found Gajendra counting a mountain of cash piled high on his desk. A framed poster of the goddess Lakshmi sat propped up against the wall under the open door to a large safe behind him.

"Good, you're both here. Sit down, boys."

Patrick and I took a seat. I remembered that it was in this very office that I had first caught wind of the rumors about "Baba and little girls." Something Madhu had said about Gajendra and Sergio had upset me. Alan Jones had mistakenly assumed the *something* was about Baba, and unwittingly said too much. Madhu was gone now. And so was Alan.

"We need you to go down to New York to get your passports back."

"Where are they now?" Patrick asked, eying the money and frowning.

"They're sitting in the Indian consulate in Manhattan gathering dust. The status of your entry visas is pending, but we have no idea when or even *if* they'll be granted. You'll be better off applying for tourist visas in D.C."

Patrick looked confused. "But if they won't give us a tourist visa in New York, what makes you think they'll give us one in Washington?"

Gajendra smirked. "Well, they won't—not with *those* passports."

"Why not?" I asked.

"Because they've already been stamped by the consulate. They just haven't been signed yet."

I was beginning to understand. "You want us to destroy our passports, and report them lost or stolen."

Patrick stiffened and pressed his lips together.

Gajendra raised his palms in the air. "I didn't say that, *you* did."

"We apply for new ones," I continued, "and then go to the Indian embassy in Washington, where they don't know us, and ask for three-month tourist visas."

"Sounds like a plan," the manager said.

He and I both glanced over at Patrick, who was looking increasingly nervous.

"But it's *your* plan," Gajendra said. "The ashram doesn't want to know anything about it."

Patrick wrinkled his brow and scratched his neck. "But won't they know in D.C. that we already applied for entry visas in New York? Don't they have a central database or something?"

Gajendra folded his arms behind his head, leaned all the way back in his chair, and laughed. "That's a good one! You think the Indian government is that well organized? The consulates don't share that kind of information with each other—believe me."

First thing in the morning the next day, Patrick and I took the ashram shuttle down to the city to get our passports back from the Indian consulate. We explained that we had changed our mind and that we no longer wanted to study in India. Our next stop was the New York Passport Agency, where we reported our passports stolen and applied for new ones. We requested expedited service, which would still take up to three weeks, even with an extra fee.

A week before Patrick and I were scheduled to leave for India, our new passports finally arrived in the mail. I immediately burned the old one in the ashram parking lot, and then set off for D.C with Patrick in an ashram vehicle.

Baba may not have verbally given me the command to lie to the US government, but he had made his will known to me. Watching my passport go up in flames made me feel powerful. It made me feel that I was above the law. *The rules that ordinary people have to follow don't apply to me,* I told myself. *A Raja Yogi transcends conventional notions of right and wrong. The guru is the ultimate authority.*

Patrick and I switched off driving to Washington, where we spent the night at the D.C. ashram in Georgetown. The next morning, we were waiting outside the door of the Indian consulate when it opened, and they processed our tourist visas the same day. As soon as we had our passports back in hand, I called Gajendra in Birchwood Falls.

"Good work, Deependra. We're going to book you and Patrick open-ended round-trip tickets."

That evening, Patrick and I went out for a drink to celebrate getting our tourist visas. We found a bar near the ashram. Patrick complained it was "swarming with yuppies." I thought it looked nice. Looking around the place, I wondered if Gopi would have liked it too. We sat down at the bar, and I ordered for both of us.

"Two Long Island Iced Teas, please."

"Not for me," Patrick said, shaking his head. "I'll have a Heineken." When the bartender was gone he turned to me. "Are you crazy? That drink is way too strong!"

His resistance annoyed me, and I didn't like his tone. I was his *seva* supervisor.

"Relax, Patrick! What do you think? They're going to give us a breathalyzer test at the ashram?"

The drinks arrived and our conversation lightened. I did my impressions of Sergio and Avadhoot for Patrick, and we both had a good laugh.

"Out of curiosity, what did you do with your old passport?" I asked. "I burned mine."

Patrick slumped over his beer, and his mood darkened. "Deliberate destruction of a passport is a felony, you know."

"A felony?" I glanced around to make sure no one was listening. "Give me a break! I did what I had to do to be with Baba." From my point of view, it was a victimless crime. "Besides, the Indian government left us no choice. They're a bunch of jerks for not granting us our entry visas."

"It's not right, I'm telling you!" Patrick said too loudly. "The ashram shouldn't be asking us to do things that are against the law. We could go to jail if anybody found out we lied to the US government like that."

"Shut up!" I growled. "Keep your voice down! The ashram didn't ask us to do it—remember?"

"Well, not in so many words—"

"So, how did you get rid of it?" I insisted.

"How did I get rid of what?" Patrick asked, looking away.

"Your passport."

Patrick hopped off his bar stool and began rifling through the pockets of his knapsack. "You really want to know?" he scolded.

"Keep your voice down!" I warned again.

The cameraman produced one and then a second US passport from his bag. He held them above his head and waved them around in the air. "Check it out everybody! I've got *two* passports!"

It was loud in the bar, and most people were ignoring him. But a couple of women seated nearby turned their heads in our direction and regarded us with mild amusement. Wanting to avoid an even bigger scene, I snatched the passports out of Patrick's hands. Then I grabbed him firmly by the arm.

"What are you? Some kind of asshole?" I cursed. "You're drunk! Sit down and shut up!"

Patrick finally quieted down, and I asked for the check. When we were outside on the street, I gave him back his new passport with the valid tourist visa, but held on to the old one. I would burn it later myself.

In the morning I felt hungover, so I let Patrick do most of the driving on the way back to Birchwood Falls. He was sullen the entire trip, and we barely spoke a word to each other.

He didn't show up for *seva* the next day, and I was irritated. I assumed that he was still angry and was acting out. By lunchtime, however, I learned from Gajendra that he had left. I was on my way to the cafeteria when he found me in the lobby, pulled me into his office, and gave me the news.

"He'll be back," I said. "He's just pissed." Then I told the manager what happened in D.C.

Gajendra slid his hands into his pockets and pursed his lips. "I don't think he'll be back." His tone was matter-of-fact. "He took all of his personal belongs with him, except his pictures of Baba."

I was furious. At lunch I sat with Avadhoot and Stephen Ames, and gave them the news about Patrick. Neither of them looked surprised.

"Well, it's much better that he freaked out now, before we flew him all the way to India," Stephen said.

Avadhoot chuckled. "Yeah, remember Seth?"

"The psychologist that went berserk?" I said. "How could I forget him!"

We all had a good laugh.

"But seriously," I said. "We need a second cameraman. Is there anybody on staff who could be trained to replace him?"

Stephen smiled as if an idea had just occurred to him. "What about Kriyadevi?"

I had never seen Kriyadevi Friedman's camera work, but she was an excellent editor. I remembered her mentioning that Baba had once told her that camera was "no job for a girl."

"I don't think Baba wants a woman doing that kind of *seva*," I said. "Besides, we need Kriyadevi here in Birchwood Falls. She's the only experienced editor we have."

"I don't know," Avadhoot said, stroking his chin. "I'll talk to Baba. Maybe he's changed his mind since the last time anyone suggested it. You can never predict how the guru will react to an idea, guys—he flows with the *shakti*. What was true yesterday is not necessarily true today."

Later, I was with Avadhoot in Baba's house when he spoke to the guru about Kriyadevi. Baba approved of the idea of her serving as second camera operator and made no mention of his previous objection. Kriyadevi would return with the rest of us to India and work as my assistant. When Avadhoot pointed out that all the editing equipment was in Birchwood Falls, and that there would be no one to edit the monthly newsreels, Baba had a simple solution. He told us to buy a second editing system and have it shipped to Ravipur.

Preparing for the guru's return to India was a large-scale operation, and everybody on tour was given extra *seva* to do. Sergio put me in charge of distributing Baba's personal effects to the other devotees who were also making the journey. Everyone on the flight was expected to carry one suitcase of their own, plus an additional bag for Baba.

"Don't they ever get suspicious at customs in Bombay?" I asked.

Sergio tucked his thumbs into the tops of his pockets. "We have a system," he said. Then a fleeting smile played on his lips. "Tell all the women to pack their underwear on top of Baba's things."

I scratched my head, and tried to picture myself passing along the manager's orders to the guru's female devotees.

"Indians get embarrassed easy," he said. "If they find a pair of women's panties or a bra, they'll shut the suitcase immediately."

As I expected, some of the women—especially newcomers to Raja Yoga—were shocked with Sergio's instructions. Kriyadevi, on the other hand, was only too happy to comply. She proudly showed me how she had hidden a gold-plated water faucet for Baba in the cup of her bra.

The airline had a two-bag limit per passenger, but anyone traveling to India on a one-year entry visa could also check a trunk. Poonish Davidson was lucky enough to have been given his entry visa before the Indian government had stopped granting them. I assigned him a suitcase full of extra soft, two-ply toilet paper, and a trunk containing two hundred pounds of food for the guru's pit bulls, which were already in Ravipur with their trainer. The customs agents became suspicious of him, however, when he arrived in Bombay with dog food and no dogs.

"What is this? What is this?" an official asked, pointing at the food for Yama and Ravana inside Poonish's open trunk.

"Dog food," my friend said.

"For you?"

Poonish blushed almost imperceptibly. "No, I'm a vegetarian. This is dog food."

"Where is your dog?"

My friend's face turned pink, and the corners of his mouth threatened to curve into a smile. "I don't have a dog. It's for a friend's dog."

"What sort of dog does your friend have? A big dog, yes?"

"Oh, yes! A very big dog!" answered Poonish, now speaking in a fake Indian accent.

I wanted to laugh, but too much was at stake. If customs refused to allow Poonish to bring the food into India,

Baba's dogs would be forced to eat Indian dog food, and I wasn't even sure there was such a thing.

The agent wiggled his head, and waved Poonish through.

Next in line was Avadhoot. The men at customs seemed to know him and went through each of his cases one by one. They examined all of his cameras and lenses, and made notations in his passport. One of his bags, however, was full of bottles of prescription medication instead of photography equipment. I was as surprised as the agent when he discovered them.

The official glowered and pointed to the drugs. "What is this?"

"Medication," Avadhoot said. "I'm not well."

"Too many pills," the official said, shaking his head and making a tsk-tsk sound. Suddenly, the agent looked alarmed. He took a step backward. "For which illness?"

"I'm not sick," Avadhoot explained. "This is pain medication. I have a chronic condition."

"Okay, no problem," the official said, and then stamped the photographer's passport and waved him on.

When the rest of us had cleared customs and were safely out of earshot of the authorities, Poonish, Avadhoot, and I began hooting with laughter.

"A big dog, yes?" Avadhoot asked in a fake Indian accent.

"Oh yes, very big!" I said, slapping Poonish on the back.

We waited for the ashram shuttle buses outside the terminal building, under a protective overhang, as the monsoon rain fell like a curtain around us. It was two A.M. already, and I looked forward to sleeping on the long drive to Ravipur. Gopi waited only a few feet away with the other princesses, and I caught her staring in my direction a couple of times. Even after a twenty-four-hour journey, she still looked fresh and radiant. I wanted to be close to her, hold her in my arms again. But I reminded myself of the guru's command to stop thinking about girls, and I looked away.

Avadhoot was waiting next to me. I found myself curious about all the pills I'd seen in his bag.

"You suffer from chronic pain?"

"Yep," he said, staring into the middle distance and yawning.

"What hurts?"

"Everything."

PART FOUR

35.
Pezzo di Merda

WE ARRIVED IN THE Ravipur ashram a few minutes before the guru. The courtyard was decorated and suffused with the fragrance of a thousand white jasmine garlands, like it was on my first visit to India. The intoxicating scent evoked another time in my life, when I was pure of heart, a sincere seeker—and I felt sad. That person was gone. Could I ever find him again?

Baba's car pulled up in front of the ashram gates, and he was met with the usual fanfare. Sita Perkins, along with the other members of Baba's personal staff who had stayed on in India during the guru's long absence, performed an elaborate *puja* to him in the Brahmananda temple.

Baba seemed much more tired after his long journey than he had at his last homecoming. Even though the rain had let up, instead of lingering in the courtyard to greet and chat with ashramites and long-time devotees, he proceeded directly to the entrance of his private residence. As he traversed the courtyard, he gave only the most perfunctory waves to his suppliants.

"Jai Gurudev!" roared the crowd. "Jai Gurudev!"

From the back of the courtyard, I watched as Baba folded his hands and smiled faintly at everyone who had come to welcome him home. With a final wave to the devotees, Baba crossed the threshold of his house, and Rashmi closed the door behind him.

"Welcome back to Shree Brahmananda Ashram, Deependra."

I turned and was face to face with a gaunt, yellow-faced woman I barely recognized. In her hands was a tray of steaming hot chai.

"Indira—hello!" I said, trying not to stare. The tall, raven-haired beauty had been transformed into a living skeleton. Her hair was unwashed and disheveled, and the bottom of her sari looked as though it had been dragged through the mud. But it was her yellow complexion that disturbed me the most. I knew exactly what it meant: Indira St. John had jaundice. My mother had looked the same only a few weeks before she died.

I took a cup of chai from her tray. "Are you okay?"

"Me? I'm fine. The *shakti* was very strong during Baba's absence. I've been going through some heavy purification."

"I'll bet." I was about to take a sip of tea, and then changed my mind. I wondered if she might be contagious. "Maybe you should see a doctor."

"Don't worry about me, Deependra," Indira said, laughing weakly. "I'm fine. You'll be sharing a room with Poonish and Stephen in *Shanti Shayanagrih*. Your bed is already made up. Just come by Housing later to pick up your key."

The rain started up again and the crowd began to disperse. I wanted to run for cover, but Indira was still talking and I didn't want to be impolite.

"Oh, Deependra, it's so wonderful to have Baba back with us again." She was oblivious to the downpour that was drenching both of us. "We've missed him terribly."

"It's good to see you, Indira," I said, setting my cup of chai now overflowing with rainwater back down on her tray. Then I made a break for the shelter of the open-air hall.

My room was a significant upgrade from what I'd been assigned during my last stay in India. Located in a four-story building opposite the courtyard from the guru's house and in the floor immediately above the open-air hall, *Shanti Shayanagrih* housed only VIPs, the tour staff, and Baba's closest disciples.

Our next-door neighbors were Sergio and Avadhoot. Further down the hall were the rooms of Anjali, Suresh, and Gopi. In my new dormitory, the rooms were not only larger and more comfortable than everywhere else, but each had air conditioning and boasted its own private bathroom with a Western flush toilet. Not even the rooms in the "princess dormitory" that abutted Baba's house were air-conditioned. I felt valued and loved, and even ashamed for having thought about leaving the ashram and going back to school.

On my first day back in India, I was tired from the long flight. There was a lot of gear to sort through and unpack, however, and it couldn't wait. The Audiovisual department needed to be ready in case Baba gave a talk or wanted an event videotaped. I was also determined to stay awake until nightfall. I didn't like feeling jet-lagged, and wanted to adjust to the time difference as quickly as possible.

At lunchtime I crossed paths with Namdev Loman. He was alarmingly thin and limping badly.

"Hey, Namdev!"

"Welcome back to Oz," he said with a crooked smile.

I glanced down at his feet. His left foot had a swelling the size of a plum. It was bright red and oozing pus.

"What's the matter with your foot? It looks really nasty!"

"Not sure," he answered. His tone was matter-of-fact. "I've either got tetanus, or some kind of nasty infection."

I asked him if he'd been to see Nirmalananda about it. He said he had, but that the swami doctor told him there was nothing he could do about it.

"He didn't give you anything? No antibiotics?"

Namdev shook his head. "It started with a small cut on my foot. I didn't pay much attention to it at first. Then it started swelling up like a balloon. I have to keep my foot up or it kills like a motherfucker. Do you have any idea how hard it is to take a shit in a squat toilet on one leg?"

"You've got to go back to the doctor. That thing is out of control!"

Namdev shrugged.

Curious to hear about what life had been like at the Ravipur ashram while I was away, I invited Namdev to have lunch with me at Prasad. I lent him my arm for support as he hopped and limped to the café.

Waiting in line to place our order, I was startled when someone threw their arms around me from behind, giving me a big hug. I spun around, and was greeted by the teenage Indian boy, Ganesh, and his dazzlingly bright smile.

"Welcome in India! How are you, Deependra uncle?" He was much taller than the last time I'd seen him.

"I'm happy to be back in the holy land, and glad to see you again, Ganesh. You must have grown a foot!"

The boy laughed from his belly. "I am already as tall as father!" he said. Then the smile vanished from his face and his eyes grew wide with horror as he noticed Namdev's infected foot. "Oh my goodness! Not good!"

"See that?" Namdev said, turning to me. "If an Indian thinks it's bad, it must be fatal."

Namdev scarfed down his second dosa like a starving animal.

"You got really thin," I said, sipping my Indian cola.

Namdev's expression soured. "After Baba left for America, they changed the menu in the dining hall. They fed us nothing but rice, chapattis, and disgusting watered-down squash every day instead of dal."

"Maybe you should eat some of your meals at Prasad," I said.

Namdev narrowed his eyes and frowned. "Oh yeah? With what money? Everybody on staff gets a stipend but me! I can't afford the prices in here! How do they expect me to do hard physical labor on that kind of diet?"

I suddenly felt a dull pain in my chest. At first I didn't understand what I was experiencing. Then it hit me: I felt sorry for him.

"You're right, it's not fair." As soon as the words left my lips, however, any sympathy I felt for Namdev was replaced by anxiety. The last thing I wanted was to be overheard being critical of the ashram. I quickly surveyed the pavilion to see if anyone might be listening. An unfamiliar Western swami with a perfectly shaved oval head and pallid lips was staring scornfully in my direction. He was a spindly man with wire-frame glasses, dressed from head to toe in canary yellow.

"I don't understand it," I said. "I've often heard Baba talk about how rich and nutritious the dining hall food is—that it contains all the nutrients we need for meditation and yoga."

Namdev forced a smile. "Maybe he was talking about the food in Prasad."

After lunch, I talked Namdev into going back to the ashram infirmary with me. As we waited for the doctor to see him, I asked him about the swami in yellow.

"That's Swami Chinmayananda, from Spain. He's a creep. I'm surprised he wasn't taking notes."

The swami doctor examined Namdev's foot, and sighed heavily. "I see the swelling hasn't gone down by itself. Have you been keeping it raised?"

"All the time," answered my friend.

Nirmalananda frowned, and then glanced at his watch. "I'll have to drain it."

I nearly threw up watching the doctor cut open and then drain the pus out of the lump on Namdev's foot. When he was satisfied that he had gotten most of it out, he stuffed the abscess cavity with gauze.

"The gauze will keep the incision open, which will allow the pus to continue to drain," explained Nirmalananda. Then he took a box of medication from a shelf on the wall and handed it to my friend. "These are antibiotics. Make sure you finish the entire course. Otherwise the infection could come back." Nirmalananda went behind his desk and wrote something on a piece of paper, and gave that to Namdev too.

"I can't afford this. I don't have any money."

The swami looked away, shook his head, and glanced at his watch again.

"It's okay," I said. "I'll pay for it."

Nirmalananda raised his eyebrows and smiled at me tentatively. "Fine. Good."

I paid the doctor, and then helped Namdev back to his room.

Later, I went by the *seva* office to speak to Sita Perkins. I told her about the large abscess on Namdev's foot, and suggested that he be given some time off. Sita was not pleased.

"Namdev is always trying to get out of his responsibilities," the *seva* manager said, placing her hands on her wide hips and thrusting her chest out. "The problem with his foot is just another excuse. Don't be so easily taken in by him, Deependra. He senses you're a nice guy and is trying to take advantage of you."

"I'm sure you're right," I said. "But I saw his foot with my own eyes. He can barely walk. If the power goes down, it will take him forever to reach the generator plant to do anything about it. Can't you find someone else to cover for him?"

Sita looked thoughtful for a moment. "I'll tell you what. He can take the rest of today and tomorrow off, and I'll temporarily reassign him to a job that doesn't require him to spend too much time on his feet. He can chop veggies in the dining hall."

In the Ravipur ashram, vegetables were chopped by *sevites* seated cross-legged on the floor. I agreed this would be a good temporary assignment for my friend.

The corners of Sita's mouth turned down in a determined frown. "But as soon as the bandages come off, he's going back to his regular *seva*."

The next day, while I was repairing cables with Stephen Ames and Kriyadevi Friedman at the long worktable in the Audiovisual office, Sergio came looking for me. He was scowling, as usual.

"Hey, Greenbaum—what kind of an asshole are you?"

I didn't know how to respond. I couldn't think of anything I might have done wrong.

The manager tilted his head to the side and looked me up and down as though he were reconsidering my usefulness. "Who are you to give orders? Sita told me you came to her office demanding that she change Loman's *seva*."

"He's a friend—his foot is infected."

"That *loser* is your friend?" Sergio said, curling his upper lip in disgust. "You shouldn't even be talking to that *pezzo di merda!*"

Every muscle in my body tensed with anger. What came out of my mouth next surprised me as much as it did Sergio.

"Have you even seen Namdev since we arrived? He looks like he's lost half his body weight. Do you even know what they were serving in the dining hall while Baba was away? He's the only person on the ashram staff who doesn't get a stipend, so he can't afford to eat at Prasad."

Sergio's face hardened, and his hands balled into fists.

I glanced over at Stephen and Kriyadevi, who were still assembling cables. Stephen was absorbed in his work and appeared to be oblivious to our conversation. Kriyadevi was slumped forward in her chair, staring at the cable she was soldering.

Then the tension suddenly left Sergio's body, and his face broke into a wide grin. "I can't believe what I'm hearing," the Italian said, reaching toward me to give my shoulder an affectionate squeeze. "You got a screw loose, or something?"

I remained on guard and kept my mouth shut. I looked over at Stephen and Kriyadevi again, hoping for some sign of support. But they were now glaring at me in disapproval.

"Listen, my friend. All that boy does is complain. We're trying to discourage him from staying in India. Baba doesn't need ungrateful losers like him in the ashram. So, stop giving him a shoulder to cry on. Understand?"

I swallowed my anger like a bitter pill. If the awful treatment Namdev was receiving in the ashram was really the guru's will, then I told myself there must be a higher purpose in it. I agreed with Sergio that Namdev didn't belong in Ravipur. He was a hard worker, but had a terrible attitude, and clearly didn't have faith in Baba. But it was hard for me to understand: if the guru didn't want him in the ashram, why they didn't just ask him to leave? I thought about suggesting it to Sergio, but stopped myself. I knew he wouldn't be interested in my opinion.

Sergio left. I continued my work, and we pretended that nothing had happened. I thought about Indira St. John. She was thinner than Namdev, and obviously ill. I couldn't help wondering if they were trying to discourage her from staying in the ashram too.

36.
DULL NIGHT OF THE SOUL

OVER THE NEXT FEW weeks, Baba made only a handful of public appearances. This was difficult for the devotees who had stayed behind in Ravipur while the guru was abroad, but it was also hard for me. The only reason I'd come to India was to be with Baba, but like most of the other ashramites, I barely saw him. At least back in the States, the guru would occasionally send for me. But in all the time I spent in Ravipur, I'd never once set foot inside his private residence.

Some of the devotees worried the reason Baba spent so little time in public was because his health had declined. Others believed he was simply getting the rest he needed after his heart attack, and were quick to point this out to anyone who complained about not getting to see him enough. I wasn't sure what the real reason was, and no one who might have been in a position to know would say.

Even if I didn't get to see Baba during this period, I did sometimes get a chance to *hear* him. Soon after our arrival in India, the mysterious "*devi* chants" started up again. As before, they took place every night in Baba's private quarters, and only those who received an invitation from the guru were allowed to attend. This included my roommates Stephen and Poonish, but not me.

On the nights I worked late in the Audiovisual office, on the way back to my room I'd sometimes hear Baba chanting with his inner circle, through the open windows of his house. If my timing was right, I'd finish *seva* just as the chant was beginning. I'd take a seat on one of the marble tree planters in the courtyard and listen. Then I'd return to my room just as the chant was ending, to avoid being seen. As before, most of the voices in the chant were feminine.

I hoped that one day soon I'd be invited to the midnight ritual as well.

Since Baba hardly made any public appearances, there was nothing to film, and we were running out of *seva* to do in the Audiovisual department. There was a limited amount of basic maintenance we could perform on the equipment, and we had already made enough new cables to last us for at least a couple of years. Avadhoot didn't have much work either, and was taking care of Baba's elephant again. I knew it was only a matter of time before I was also reassigned.

With so much free time on our hands, I offered to teach Kriyadevi what I'd learned about camera technique during my stint in Manhattan at NYSB. She good-naturedly accepted my offer, but from the first lesson it was obvious that she had a lot more to teach me than I had to teach her.

This quiet period in Ravipur gave me more time for meditation and chanting, but it also gave my mind more time to wander. As hard as I tried to turn my attention within to reflect on the Inner-Self, I couldn't stop thinking about the incident in California with the Grozas and the ugly exchange with Menaka in Ithaca. Even more painful was my inability to forget the rumors about Baba, which continued to haunt me. Instead of finding peace at the ashram, I grew increasingly agitated.

Another distraction was my increased interest in sex. Part of me wished I'd been able to stay longer in Ithaca and had gotten another chance to do it with Heather. But more troublesome was my inability to stop fantasizing about Gopi. She was unfriendly on the few occasions I ran into her at Prasad. Ever since we had returned to India, she seemed to have eyes only for Sergio. Whenever he did his daily rounds of the ashram, she was by his side. They ate all of their meals together. I never saw him with Anjali anymore, so I assumed the feeling was mutual.

JUST WHEN KRIYADEVI AND I were beginning to think the cameras would be obsolete by the time we got to use them again, word came from Sergio that Suresh would start giving talks while Baba was "resting," and that the video department should record them.

For the first few days of the young swami's public programs, I let Kriyadevi operate the main camera in the front of the hall while I got the audience reaction shots. One evening, Sergio noticed this and came by the Audiovisual office after the talk to scold me. "You're the boss, the girl is your *assistant*. You should always do the main camera!"

He visited the office again the following morning, demanding to see the footage from the night before. Gopi was with him. She was dressed in an elegant silk sari, and her golden hair was braided and rolled in a bun at the back of her head. She stiffened when she saw me, and lifted the clipboard she was carrying tightly against her chest. My warm greeting to her was met with a curt nod of her head.

As we screened the rushes, Sergio grimaced and tapped his foot on the floor.

"Why do you zoom in so quick?" he asked Kriyadevi. "Your movements should be more smooth, like Greenbaum."

Kriyadevi rubbed her nose. "Actually, you're looking at Greenbaum's footage."

My face tingled with embarrassment. "We fix all of that in the editing room," I told Sergio.

Kriyadevi nodded in agreement.

The Italian turned to glare at me. "This is what you learned in New York?"

I rubbed the back of my neck. I wasn't sure how to respond. "I'll try to do better next time, Sergio."

"Don't try," Sergio said, shaking a finger at me. "*Do!*"

"We'll *do* better next time!" Kriyadevi said, smiling good-naturedly.

The Italian turned to my assistant, and looked her up and down.

"You should dress like a girl," he said. "You look like a dyke in those clothes."

Kriyadevi wrinkled her brow, lifted her chin, and stared back at him. I wasn't sure how a "dyke" dressed, but he was right that there was nothing feminine about the carelessly made, loose-fitting cotton pants and shirt she was wearing. I cringed, remembering I once dressed like that too.

"Go see Gajendra," Sergio said. "He'll give you some money to go shopping in Bombay." The Italian turned to admire Gopi and smiled proudly. Then he turned back to Kriyadevi and frowned. "And put on some makeup. *Mi fa cagare!*"

ONE MORNING AFTER BREAKFAST, I was on my way from Prasad to the Audiovisual office when my old *seva* supervisor Rohini Brinkerhoff called out to me.

"Yoo-hoo! Deependra!"

The German was standing in the doorway of the Housekeeping building. I felt a pang of guilt. I hadn't stopped by to see her since returning to India. She greeted me with a big hug, and asked me to step inside her office to chat a minute. Glancing around the room at the cleaning supplies, I had the oddest feeling. It took me a minute to understand what it was. The feeling was nostalgia. Not for cleaning toilets or squeegeeing the courtyard. The nostalgia I felt was for the *old me.*

"You've gotten taller!" Rohini said, looking me up and down, beaming with the pleasure of a grandmother. She gave me another hug. Then something on the top of my head caught her eye.

"Hello, what's this?" she said, squinting. Without warning, Rohini plucked a hair from my head. She held the strand up to the light for me to see—the hair was gray!

"Very auspicious!" Rohini declared. "You've obviously gained much wisdom since coming to the ashram!"

Just then, two young women came in through the open door of the building. One was a skinny blonde with a mild case of acne, and the other an olive-skinned beauty with jet-black hair. The blonde's eyes opened wide when she saw me. She stifled a giggle with the back of her hand, and playfully elbowed her companion in the side. They were new arrivals—I could tell by the way they dressed. Short-sleeved shirts and tight-fitting blue jeans. Inappropriate ashram attire.

"Come girls," Rohini grinned. "Look at this! The fire of yoga is turning this boy's hair gray!" The girls came over to inspect the strand of hair held between her fingers.

The blonde spoke with an Australian accent. "Crikey! Have a look, Gili! He *is* going gray!"

The blonde was cute, with long hair and bright blue eyes. I noticed she was missing one of her front teeth, however, and didn't have much of a chin. She looked around my age or a little younger. The beautiful dark-skinned girl was slender, with an athletic build, short straight black hair, dark penetrating eyes, and an aquiline nose. She had smaller breasts than her friend, but the confidence with which she carried herself made me guess she was a couple of years older.

"Isn't it sexy, Gili? I like older men!"

Gili rolled her eyes.

"And where are you ladies from?" I asked, straightening my back and puffing out my chest a little.

"Melbourne," the blonde answered.

"New York," the dark-haired girl said. She spoke with a familiar accent, but I couldn't place it.

"You don't sound like you're from New York," I teased.

"I'm originally from Tel Aviv."

"A-ha!" I laughed. "Well, I'm from New York, too!"

"Deependra used to work in Housekeeping," Rohini said, handing the girls cleaning supplies. "Now he's on Baba's tour staff."

In mock awe, the Australian girl opened her eyes wide and formed an 'O' with her mouth.

"Stop, Katie!" Gili laughed. "Stop poking fun at him. You're going to make him cry!"

The girls gathered their cleaning supplies, and set out for their assignments. I was also about to leave, when Rohini stopped me. Her face grew serious.

"Tell me, Deependra—do you have any news about Indira?"

"News? About Indira St. John?" At first, I didn't know what she was talking about. Then I remembered how yellow and sickly Indira looked the last time I'd spoken to her. "Come to think of it, I haven't seen her lately."

The German eyed me skeptically. "She's at Breach Candy Hospital in Bombay. You're *such* an important person in the ashram now, I'm surprised you didn't hear about it?"

"No, definitely not. What's wrong with her?"

"She worked herself half to death, that's what's wrong with her. Then she came down with hepatitis."

"How awful!"

"While Baba was away there weren't enough people left in the ashram to keep up with all the *seva*. Everyone took on extra work, but Indira did much more than her share."

I wondered if the rumors about the guru had reached India. "Did people leave while Baba was away?"

"*Ja*, of course they did. You left, didn't you?"

I was confused. I couldn't tell if we were talking about the same thing.

"Everybody always wants to be with Baba. No one wants to stay behind to do the hard work of taking care of the guru's house while he's away."

I was relieved I didn't have to get into an awkward conversation with Rohini. She obviously hadn't heard the rumors. "Tell me more about Indira."

"Foolish girl," the old lady said, shaking her head. "I told her she should see the doctor, but she refused. Said it was the guru's *shakti* purifying her. Finally, when she was too weak to report to *seva*, the manager forced her to go to the infirmary. I went with her. Nirmalananda scolded her for not coming sooner, then the swami doctor asked her when she had had her last gamma globulin shot."

"Why?"

"Nirmalananda said the shot might have caused it."

"Caused what? The hepatitis?"

"*Ja*," she said. "Hepatitis C."

An alarm went off in my head. I had also gotten a gamma globulin shot just before the first time I came to India. The ashram had recommended it!

"The manager made me disinfect her sheets and her clothes with bleach," she added. "The bleach was so strong, some of her clothes completely disintegrated!"

I shook my head and kneaded the back of my neck. I couldn't understand how such a sincere devotee like Indira could have so much negative karma.

Anger flashed across the old German woman's face. "It's just not right. They can't expect people to work twelve hours a day, seven days a week without destroying their health."

Rohini made me think about Govinda Brown, the Australian man who'd fallen from the scaffolding and broken his back during the *Punyatithi* celebrations the last time I was in Ravipur. I wondered what had become of him and his family. I hadn't seen them around the ashram since my return. Rohini had a point, I realized. I accepted and understood that the guru was always testing his followers by pushing them to their limits. But I couldn't help wondering: *When ashramites get hurt or sick from exhaustion, is Baba going too far?*

Then I caught myself: *What am I thinking? The guru is infallible!* I refused to become one of those people who tried to second-guess Baba or were critical of the ashram.

"I don't think I'm comfortable with this conversation, Rohini."

The German was speechless.

"It's very nice to see you again," I told her, "but I have to get back to my *seva* now."

37.
Fall from Grace

ANOTHER MONTH PASSED, AND in all that time I saw Baba only once. I'd caught a glimpse of him in the dining hall chatting with Prakashananda, the shirtless Indian swami. That had been three weeks earlier. Even the nightly "devi chants" had come to a stop.

Poonish thought Baba might actually be gone. He'd seen the guru's car pull up alongside his residence in the early morning hours. Baba and his attendant, Rashmi, got inside and drove out through the gates of the ashram. We speculated that he was away seeing specialists in Bombay for his heart condition, and spending time in various clinics for treatment.

"If Baba is really away, why the secrecy?" I asked Poonish.

"He probably doesn't want to worry the devotees unnecessarily."

Whether Baba was away receiving treatment or resting in his bed in the ashram, the result was the same: I missed him, and my enthusiasm for my spiritual practice was waning. These days, instead of springing out of bed for meditation when my alarm clock went off at four in the morning, I'd sleep in—a habit that I picked up from Poonish and Stephen. I needed Baba for inspiration. I wanted him to make me a sincere seeker again. I yearned to experience the wonder of meditation and the chants as I had in the beginning. I longed to be in constant awe of the guru and to feel the enchantment of living in the Ravipur ashram again. But what I felt was boredom. Instead of longing for liberation, I longed to visit Bombay to go shopping. If I never got to see Baba, what was the point of being in India?

Hoping to recharge my spiritual batteries, I decided to take a walk to the *samadhi* shrine of Gurudev Brahmananda in the village. I'd make a generous donation to the temple, and would pray to Baba's guru for his blessing during this dry period in my *sadhana*.

I got less than a half-mile down the road when I heard the sound of laughter and an approaching ox-cart behind me. Turning around, I saw the blonde Australian girl and the Israeli I'd met in the Housekeeping building a few weeks earlier. They were seated in a small wagon drawn by an emaciated, mud-covered ox, which was being driven by an even skinnier, dirtier man. Between them sat the pretty Australian boy I'd worked in Security with during the *Punyatithi* celebrations. I couldn't recall his name. Back then he had been dressing in traditional Indian clothes. I saw that he'd since graduated to spiffy Western clothes likes me.

"G'day, mate!" the blonde called. "Yeah, you!"

I gave the threesome a half-hearted wave hello.

"Stop!" commanded the Australian girl. "I said stop!"

The driver brought the ox-cart to an abrupt halt in the middle of the road.

The blonde smiled mischievously, revealing a gap between her front teeth.

"Where are you nicking off to, old man?"

"There's only one place to go to around here," I answered. "I'm headed to the *samadhi* shrine in the village."

"Not the only place, mate," she said. "We're going for a dip at Chaapkhanawala's hot springs. Wanna come?"

I thought back to the day I'd met the spa's owner, Palash, and the bizarre incident with the angry mob of villagers and the old lady who had been accused of being a witch. It all felt like a hundred years ago.

"Yeah, come with us," the Israeli girl said.

I remembered enjoying Palash's stories about his father and Gurudev, and how I'd promised to come back again for a dip in the thermal baths. I eyed Katie and Gili and thought that a visit to the hot springs with two cute girls seemed like a lot more fun than meditating in a hot, stuffy temple. But I already had a plan and didn't want to disappoint the omniscient guru.

"Get in, mate!" the Australian boy said. "We'll drop you off at the shrine."

I climbed in the cart and sat behind the others. The driver gave the ox a prod and we were on our way again.

"I'm Katie," the blonde said. "Katie Harris."

"Andy Martin," the boy said, extending me a hand to shake. "We worked in Security together for a day or two a while back."

"How could I forget?" I said, giving his hand a firm grip. "That was the day Baba announced that Suresh would be his successor. I'm Deependra Greenbaum."

Andy reeked of pot and his hand was clammy. I wondered how and where he managed to get high in the ashram.

"And this is Gili," Katie said, introducing the dark-haired girl. "Her surname's Ben Ami. She's a wog."

Gili rolled her eyes. "I told you before, I'm from Israel."

"Are you a wog, too?" Katie asked me, ignoring her friend. "You look like a wog. Andy, is Greenbaum a wog name?"

"No idea, Katie. Sounds German."

"I'm not sure I know what a *wog* is," I said

"Wog's Aussie for *Italian*," Katie said.

"That's rubbish!" Andy scolded.

Katie elbowed the boy in the side and giggled. "Shut ya gob, Andy!"

"In any case, I'm not Italian," I said, catching Gili's gaze. Her dark eyes were big and round, and they spoke to me: *Can you believe this idiot?*

"Not a wog?" Katie said. The hint of a smile played on the corners of her small mouth. "What are you then?"

"I'm American." My answer made Katie and Andy burst out laughing.

"We can tell you're a Yank by the way you talk, mate," Andy said, patting me on the back.

"I mean, *what* are you?" Katie insisted.

Gili frowned. "He's a Jew, like me."

The Israeli girl had full, sensuous lips. I thought about what it would be like to kiss her. She may have been a Jew, but she was not a Jew like me. My ancestors had spent two thousand years in Eastern Europe. I suspected Gili was a Mizrahi Jew, descended from members of the tribe who had settled in the Middle East. Unlike Rachel back in New York, Gili didn't remind me of any relatives.

"That's right," I said. "I'm Jewish."

Katie gave me an exaggerated wink. "Good onya, mate. It's like I said: you're *both* wogs."

When we arrived at the village, the others let me off in front of the *samadhi* shrine, and I paid the ox-cart driver.

"What a gentleman!" Katie laughed.

"Don't mention it," I said, with a wink like the one she'd given me. "See you in a few minutes."

I could tell Katie liked me, but I was more interested in the quiet Israeli girl. "I'll catch up with you guys later."

As the ox-cart carrying my new friends drove off in the direction of Chaapkhanawala's, I noticed a familiar figure in dark sunglasses and canary yellow robes staring at me from the other side of the square. It was Swami Chinmayananda, from Spain.

"Hello Swamiji," I called with a tentative wave.

Chinmayananda nodded his perfectly shaved head in response, and again I got a bad feeling from him.

Inside the temple, I prostrated myself before the life-size statue of Baba's guru. Then I stuck a large wad of rupee notes inside the donation box at its feet, and took a seat on the cool marble floor.

Unable to pray or meditate, I found myself daydreaming about Gili Ben Ami. I liked her dark hair, olive complexion, and lean body. I didn't remember ever seeing her at the Manhattan ashram or in Birchwood Falls, and wondered if she was new to Raja Yoga. She didn't seem to have much in common with Katie, and I thought it was odd they hung out together. Then I realized it probably wasn't easy for them to get to know other women their own age in the ashram. Most were in the exclusive princess club, and its members didn't socialize with ordinary ashramites.

As if the distracting thoughts of the Israeli girl weren't making it difficult enough for me to meditate, the temple was full of noisy Indian tourists. Even with a quiet mind, it would've been next to impossible to meditate there. The last straw came when a toddler tripped over me and started to cry. I was done trying to meditate. I bowed to the statue of Baba's guru, and left in search of my new friends at the health spa.

When I arrived, Palash the innkeeper was sitting on the veranda, sipping a cup of tea. He got up to welcome me. I could hear raucous laughter coming from the direction of the baths.

"Welcome to Chaapkhanawala's Thermal Spring Baths and Health Resort!" Palash said, shaking my hand. "Are you here for a bubble bath?"

"Yes, sir."

"Good, good!"

"Don't you remember me, Mr. Palash? We met in the village a couple of years ago, and you invited me back here for chai. I'm staying at the Rudrananda ashram again up the road."

"Yes, yes, of course!" he said, scratching his nose.

"There was an angry mob in the village harassing an old woman. You told me she was a witch."

"Ah yes, a nasty business, my young friend. A very nasty business."

I nodded in agreement.

"She's back, you know."

"Who's back?"

"The Witch from Surat."

Again, shrieks of laughter could be heard coming from the baths.

My face tingled with embarrassment. "Those are my friends from the ashram," I said with a shrug. "I'm afraid I don't have a bathing suit."

"Not to worry, my friend. Not to worry!"

Without warning, Palash shouted something in Hindi, and I was startled.

At first I thought he was yelling at me. A moment later, one of his servants emerged from the darkened interior of the Inn, limping out onto the veranda and carrying a fresh towel.

"Go with him," Palash smiled. "He will show you to your bath."

Palash's servant handed me the towel, and I followed him to a single-story concrete building, with small windows and doors at regular intervals. From inside I could hear the sounds of splashing water and the voices of Katie and Andy lobbing insults at each other.

The baths were not what I expected. I thought I'd be sharing one large Jacuzzi-like pool with the others. Instead, Palash's servant let me into my own private chamber. The room was dark and cheerless, containing an oversize concrete bathtub, which reminded me of a Roman sarcophagus. Before leaving me alone in my cell, Palash's servant opened a tap, and the tub filled with scalding hot water.

Adjusting the temperature by opening a second tap of cold water, I got undressed and slowly eased myself into the rejuvenating and "slightly radioactive" water. Considering the high temperature outside, the hot bath was much more enjoyable and relaxing than I expected. I could have soaked in it all day.

As I let the mineral-rich water do its work on my body, I eavesdropped on Katie and Andy. From the way they were shouting to each other, I could tell they were also in their own individual cells.

"It's not a rumor," Andy was saying. "It's a well-known fact that Baba used to smoke ganja. He even talks about it in one of his books."

"Right, mate, sure he did," Katie called, her voice echoing in her chamber.

"It's true!" Andy cried. "I heard an American once placed a joint at Baba's feet, you know, as a symbol of giving it up. But Baba didn't keep it. He picked it up and said, 'The problem with you Westerners is that you don't know how to use this stuff.' Then he gave the joint back to the bloke and told him that to have good meditation, he should soak it in milk for a three days before smoking it."

"Sounds like a crock of shit to me!" Katie said.

"I heard he used to smoke cigarettes," Gili called. Her voice sounded farther away than the others. "They say he had to stop after too many Americans asked him to help them quit."

I was disappointed by what I heard. I could understand why Katie and Andy would believe such stupid lies about the guru, but I'd been hoping Gili was smarter than that.

"You think that wog is gonna rock up?" Katie called. "Or is he gonna meditate in that stuffy temple all day?"

Andy laughed and it reverberated throughout the building. "You fancy him, don't you?"

"Do not!" Katie shouted.

I decided it was time to break my silence. "I'm not a wog!"

The others burst out laughing.

"You've been spying on us!" Katie cried.

"Afraid so!" I called back.

I heard water sloshing around, followed by the sound of it dripping on the floor.

"I've had enough," Andy announced. "I heard it's not safe to stay in too long."

I heard more splashing and dripping, and I also dragged myself out of the soothing hot water. Toweling off, I threw my clothes back on, and then stepped outside into the blinding hot sunlight. Much to my surprise, I was the only one dressed. Gili and Katie had their towels wrapped tightly around their upper bodies in a way that flattened their breasts and left their bare legs exposed. Andy had his towel wrapped around his waist lungi-style, exposing his ripped, hairless chest and abs.

I gave Katie the once over. Her acne looked much worse in the harsh daylight.

Noticing my eyes on her, the Australian girl winked back. "In a hurry to get dressed, are we?"

"Ladies! Ladies—please!" We turned toward the main building of the resort to a see a rotund Indian woman hurriedly waddling in our direction. "Nakedness is strictly forbidden on the grounds!" She was huffing and puffing so hard I thought she might keel over. "Please to be undressing inside only!"

"Oh my!" Katie exclaimed in mock alarm, covering her mouth with her hand. Turning to face me, she began to seductively shift her weight around from side to side. "I've been a naughty girl. Are you going to punish me, Deependra?"

Just as the woman reached us, Katie's towel slipped, exposing a pair of perfectly round milky white breasts and pink nipples. Andy, Gili, and I exploded in laughter as Katie's face turned scarlet.

"Inside only!" shouted the woman, whom I now recognized as Palash's wife. Frantically opening the door to one of the cells, she herded Katie and Gili inside. She then pointed a finger at Andy. "You too!" she scolded, opening another chamber and pushing him through the door.

After Andy and the girls were properly clothed, Palash invited us to "take tea" with him on the veranda. Looking around the place, I was once again surprised to see only pictures of Gurudev, but not a single one of Baba.

The four of us listened as the innkeeper repeated the same story he'd told me on my previous visit to the spa, of the day his grandfather and father had first met Gurudev—how his father had not wanted to stop the car to let Brahmananda pee, and how the holy man had miraculously gotten their car started again merely by placing a hand on the engine. He seemed to have no memory of having already shared this tale with me before.

"Mr. Chaapkhanawala," Andy began, "I notice you have many pictures of Gurudev Brahmananda on the walls of your establishment, but none of Swami Rudrananda."

The innkeeper's visage darkened instantly. He opened his mouth to respond, but was interrupted by the now familiar cries of Mrs. Chaapkhanawala, calling down from a second story window. Springing to his feet, Palash stepped off the veranda, tilted his head back, and shouted at his wife. At the exact same moment, one of Palash's servants arrived with a platter of sliced papaya and mango, and set it down on the table in front of us. The fresh fruit looked appetizing, but after reading a warning in the ashram information pamphlet, I made it a rule in India never to eat any peeled fruit or uncooked vegetables outside the ashram. The others helped themselves.

"I wouldn't eat that if I were you," I warned. "You could get sick."

Katie put a slice of papaya back down on the platter, but Andy and Gili kept eating.

"No worries, mate," Andy said, through a mouthful of fruit. "I've got an iron stomach. I eat *whatever* I want, *wherever* I want, and I haven't been sick once."

Gili picked up a slice of juicy-looking mango and popped it in her mouth. "If you never eat anything a little questionable, how do you expect to build up your immunities?"

I looked at the platter of fresh fruit. A perfectly ripe piece of mango caught my eye. *Maybe I've been too careful,* I thought. I reached for the slice of mango and bit into it. The tangy flavor exploded on my tongue.

"Well done, mate!" Andy said, chuckling.

The sun dipped below the horizon. Andy slapped his arm.

"Got the little blood sucker!"

I glanced at my watch and saw that it was nearly dinnertime. Palash brought us the check. Glancing down at it, I was astounded at how inexpensive our visit had been. I insisted on paying. I hoped Gili was impressed.

We took an auto rickshaw back to the ashram. The driver dropped us off in front of the main gate. Making the excuse that I needed to buy something at the general store across the street, I let the others go in ahead of me. I didn't want to be seen hanging out with girls or with an ashramite reeking of marijuana.

Just as I stepped into the courtyard, Brian rode in on his bike. When he saw me his face became flushed with anger. "Hey, Greenbaum! You're crusin' for a bruisin'!"

"Me? What did I do?"

"Baba's furious with you! Where the hell you been?"

Fear struck me like lightning. *Baba angry with me?* I began to tremble. "Baba's out? In public?"

"He's been making rounds all afternoon, and he wanted you to film. There are at least ten people looking for you!"

"Where's he now?" I asked, my knees shaking under me. "I'll get the camera and catch up with him."

"Forget it," frowned Brian. "They've got Kriyadevi on it."

Unable to bear the idea that I had disappointed the guru, I ran to the Audiovisual office, grabbed my gear, and took off in search of anyone who could tell me where to find Baba.

"There you are!" Jaya cried, rushing toward me. "Baba's at the *seva* office. Run!" Jaya had only been in Raja Yoga a few months, but was already telling me what to do. If I hadn't been so upset with myself for letting the guru down, I would've been even more irritated.

By the time I reached Baba, sweat was dripping down my forehead into my eyes. I found him between the *seva* office and my old dormitory, surrounded by ashramites and visitors from Bombay. He was in the midst of an animated conversation with Sita Perkins, which Anjali was translating. He was holding a big stick and, even though it was now after dark, he was wearing sunglasses. Chinmayananda, the Spanish swami whom I had crossed paths with earlier in the village, was by his side. Avadhoot was also there, taking a thousand pictures and barking orders at Kriyadevi, who was shooting video. She was calm and confident, and looked like she'd been doing it her whole life.

As discreetly as possible, I approached Avadhoot from the rear and tapped him on the back. Glancing over his shoulder, he glared at me. "Oh man, are you in trouble now!"

Before I could explain to him where I'd been, someone poked me in the back. I turned around and was face to face with Brian again.

"You'd better back off! I told you, you aren't needed!"

At this point, Chinmayananda noticed me too, and alerted Baba to my presence. Whipping his head in my direction, the guru shouted something at me in Hindi.

"Baba says you should go back to your *seva*," Anjali translated. The tone of her voice was harsh.

Everybody's eyes were on me, and from the looks I was getting, you'd think I had just murdered the guru's dog.

"But my *seva* is to film Baba," I protested.

As Anjali translated for Baba, the guru pointed his stick in my direction. "Go on, get out of here! And stay away from girls!"

I raced in the direction of the Audiovisual office, but by the time I reached the courtyard, I found that I barely had enough strength left to stand. I was suddenly burning up with fever, and felt queasy.

How is it possible? Baba hadn't been out in public for weeks, and there'd been almost no *seva* for me to do during that entire time. What were the odds that on the one and only day the guru needed me, I hadn't been there to answer his call?

I burst into the office and startled Stephen, who was seated at the table, repairing a microphone. His eyes grew wide with alarm when he saw me.

"Deependra, what is it? You look horrible! Are you okay?"

"Baba's angry with me. I'm not feeling so great."

"Maybe you should go up to the room and lie down before the evening program."

"No, I don't dare. I've missed enough *seva* for one day already."

A few minutes after I arrived at the office, Avadhoot exploded through the door, demanding to know where I'd been all afternoon. I began to explain, but he interrupted almost immediately.

"I don't give a flying fuck where you were or what you were doing. You could've been getting a happy ending massage, for all I care. The point is, you weren't here when Baba needed you, and there's never any excuse for that!"

Just then, the door swung open again, and Kriyadevi blew in with the camera still slung on her shoulder. An enormous, triumphant grin was plastered on her face.

"I think I have some great footage!" she announced.

"Let's see it!" Avadhoot said, displaying uncharacteristic interest.

Kriyadevi ejected the cassette from her camcorder, popped it in the VTR, and rewound the tape to the beginning. As we watched her rushes, I saw she was right. Her footage was excellent. Her framing was better than mine, and so were her camera movements.

I sat behind Avadhoot and Kriyadevi as he lavished praise on her. He turned around from time to time to gauge my reaction to what he was saying.

"This is beautiful! Amazing stuff! Baba is going to love it!"

Kriyadevi beamed with pride. "Thanks, Avadhoot!"

Ordinarily, I probably would've been jealous, but at this point I was too sick to care.

"If I have one criticism—and it's not really a criticism, mind you," Avadhoot said, "it's that you should stop recording when you change angles. We don't need hundreds of miles of tape of people's feet."

"With all due respect, Avadhoot, that would be a mistake," Kriyadevi said. "Shooting video is not like taking a still photo. In video, you need to preserve continuity on the audio track. Baba was in the middle of a conversation. I didn't want to stop recording in case he said something interesting while I was changing angles. We can always cover up the images of feet with the strong reaction shots I got later."

As Kriyadevi explained herself, Avadhoot's eyes began to close and he slumped over in his chair. Meanwhile, my nausea was getting worse. I'd broken out in a cold sweat. I thought I might throw up, but was afraid to leave. I continued to watch Kriyadevi's rushes until the photographer began to snore. I was about to leave, when the phone rang and woke Avadhoot.

Stephen picked up. It was Sergio calling from the guru's house. He said Baba would be giving a talk after dinner, and that it should be filmed and recorded. The urge to vomit became impossible to ignore. I leapt to my feet and ran to the door.

"Where the fuck are you going in such a hurry?" Avadhoot demanded. "You and Kriyadevi need to start setting up the cameras."

"I'm going to be sick," I blurted out. I ran as fast as my weakened condition would allow, but only got halfway to the restrooms before I started puking behind a coconut tree. A couple of young male Adivasi workers saw me and laughed.

"It was the fruit from Chaapkhanawala's!" I moaned. I felt like I was going to die. "I knew it! I knew this would happen!"

My self-pitying monologue made the Adivasi boys laugh even harder.

Climbing the stairs to the second floor of *Shanti Shayanagrih* took every ounce of strength I had left. I was sure I'd never felt sicker in my entire life, and that I was burning up with fever. When I finally reached my room, I put the air conditioner on full blast. I desperately wanted to lie down, but thought it'd be safer to hover over the toilet bowl in case I needed to throw up again. Catching a glimpse of myself in the mirror, I was even more alarmed. I was disturbingly pale, as if all the blood had been sucked out of me.

Staggering out of the bathroom, I fell into bed. It wasn't long, however, before I had to crawl back to the bathroom for another round of vomiting. This time I experienced painful cramps in my gut and an overwhelming urge to shit. As if the fever, nausea, and puking weren't enough, I now had diarrhea.

If there had only been a phone in my room, I could've called down to the Audiovisual department to tell them what was wrong with me and why I hadn't returned after my sudden, oddly-timed departure. But short of hauling my incapacitated ass back downstairs, there was no way I could let them know.

At a certain point I realized that the constant vomiting and diarrhea were dehydrating me, and that I needed to drink some water. I was too afraid to drink from the tap, for fear that it would only make me worse. I prayed to the guru that Avadhoot or Stephen would come looking for me soon, but I passed out long before anybody arrived.

The sound of my roommates' voices in the darkness woke me up.

"Deependra, are you alright?" Poonish asked, switching on the light. The weak glow from the overhead forty-watt bulb felt like a thousand tiny daggers stabbing me in the eyes.

"Food poisoning," I groaned. "I need water."

"I'll go get some in the dining hall," Poonish said, hurrying out the door.

"Kriyadevi had to film Baba's talk by herself," Stephen said. "Avadhoot went nuts when you never came back."

"Too sick," I answered weakly. "Couldn't get out of bed."

"Don't worry about it. Baba didn't even notice."

As if on cue, the door to our bedroom abruptly swung open, and the guru blazed in like a fiery comet. He had a wild look in his eyes, and in his hand he gripped the walking stick he'd been carrying earlier. Before I had a chance to say anything, Baba lunged at me. Using the weight of his entire body, he brought his stick down on my chest so swiftly it made a high-pitched whistle as it cut through the air. *Thwack!*

I cried out in pain.

"Lazy boy!" Baba shouted in English, his eyes bulging with what looked like pure hatred. Again, he struck my upper body. *Thwack!*

"No Baba! I'm sick!"

The third blow was to my shoulder and sent a wave of searing, white-hot pain through my entire body. *Thwack!*

I screamed. "Baba please!"

The guru hit me on the head so hard I saw stars. *Thwack!*

"Sleeping all day!" Baba yelled, the spittle spraying from his mouth. *Thwack!*

Blood oozed from the gash on my head and stung my eyes. The pain was so excruciating I thought I might pass out.

Doesn't the Omniscient One know I'm unwell? Why is he so angry? This can't be happening!

Using a combination of English and Hindi, Stephen was pleading with Baba to stop beating me. The guru ignored him at first, but after the seventh blow he slowed down and began to listen.

"*Krpaya, Baba! Bure bhojan ne use beemaar banaaya!* Bad food made him sick, Baba!"

Suddenly, a look of comprehension spread across Baba's face and he stopped beating me.

The guru backed away from my bed. It took him a moment or two to catch his breath and regain his composure. When he did, he spoke in English again. "See Nirmalananda. Get medicine."

With that, the guru turned to exit through the open door at the precise moment Poonish returned from the kitchen with my water. Poonish was so stunned to see Baba, he nearly dropped the pitcher.

The guru didn't offer any apology for the misunderstanding, nor offer any words of kindness before leaving. He simply vanished as abruptly as he had appeared only a few moments earlier.

I sat up to sip the water Poonish had brought for me, and my beaten body screamed in agony. Somehow I managed to get to the bathroom to wash the areas of broken skin. In the places I wasn't bleeding, the marks where Baba had hit me were purple and raw.

"Is it true that you went to the village today?" Stephen asked, as I collapsed back in bed. "Did you eat any outside food?"

Dazed and writhing in pain, his questions stung my ears and throbbing head. As best I could, I explained to my roommates where I'd been and with whom, and about the platter of fruit.

"You should stay away from Andy," Poonish said. "I hear he's a drug dealer. They're going to kick him out of the ashram for smoking pot on the roof of *Bhakti Shayanagrih*. I don't know anything about the Israeli girl, but I hear Katie Harris is a slut."

"Neither of them are Baba's girls," Stephen added. "And there's probably a good reason for it."

The following morning I slept in, missing the *Guru Gita* and breakfast in Prasad. When I finally woke, I was still in terrible pain, feverish, and nauseated. I lay in bed staring at the ceiling for at least an hour. I couldn't decide which was worse: Baba was omniscient and had known I was in bed because I was sick and had beaten me anyway, or that he was ignorant of my condition and had assumed I was just being indolent. In either case, it was unthinkable that the guru didn't know me well enough to realize I'd never miss *seva* simply because I didn't feel like working. I began to wonder if I could've been wrong about him. Maybe he was an ordinary man after all. In as much physical pain as I was from the food poisoning and beating, it was nothing in comparison to the emotional agony I felt over being doubted by Baba.

Dragging my savaged body to the infirmary, I waited for what seemed like an eternity before Nirmalananda called me into his examining room.

"Deependra, I can see you now."

The American swami doctor was almost as pale as I was. Living for as long as he had in India, I wondered how he managed never to get any sun.

As he applied iodine to my gashes, he neglected to ask me how I'd come to be injured. However, he did take it upon himself to scold me for not being on hand the night before to film Baba's talk. When I explained how I'd been too sick to get out of bed, he berated me for eating "outside fruit" and diagnosed me with an acute case of "Delhi belly." He gave me an injection of some sort and a course of strong antibiotics.

"You should start to feel better pretty soon," he said. "You should spend the rest of the day in bed and try to get some rest."

On the way back to my room, I saw Andy and the girls laughing it up outside Housekeeping. They looked fine to me. I was obviously the only one who'd eaten a contaminated piece of fruit. I wanted to ask if any of them had gotten sick too, but didn't dare being seen talking to them in public again.

As Nirmalananda predicted, my fever abated and the nausea went away almost immediately. By the end of the day, the only places that still hurt were where Baba had wounded me, both inside and out.

38.
A DENIAL

FOR DAYS I WAS black and blue, and sore from the guru's beating. But this was the least of my suffering. I constantly wrestled with doubts about Baba's omniscience and psychic abilities. When I couldn't stand to live with the doubts anymore, I convinced myself that the guru had engineered the entire incident as a test of my faith, and to purge me of my evil karma from willfully disobeying him and spending the day in the village with the girls. I vowed that from then on, I would resolutely follow his command to stay away from the opposite sex. I threw myself into the daily routine of the ashram, getting up early every morning for meditation and going to as many chants as possible. To avoid socializing, I ate all my meals in the dining hall where talking was not permitted.

Avoiding Gopi in the ashram wasn't easy. I saw her everywhere, and these days she was inseparable from Sergio. Wherever he went, Gopi was either by his side or running interference for him. At meal times, I often saw them sitting alone together in the Prasad pavilion. Once after dark, I spotted the lovebirds sitting together, holding hands on one of the marble tree planters in the courtyard. The angel was gazing dreamily into the Italian's eyes the way everyone else looked at Baba. Seeing them together like this made me miserable. The most painful moment of all, however, was the time I saw them leave together in one of the ashram vehicles. I knew they were headed for Bombay.

Desperate to confirm my hunch, I went by the ashram manager's office, pretending to be looking for Sergio. Indira St. John, who was back from her two-week stint at Breach Candy Hospital in Bombay, was behind the counter making photocopies.

"Have you seen Sergio?" I asked her, trying to sound casual.

"He went to Crawford Market in Bombay."

"Do you know when he'll be back?"

The photocopier jammed with a screech. Indira opened the paper drawer to remove the sheets that were stuck. "I think he said he'd be staying overnight in the city."

Images of Sergio and Gopi in bed together flashed across my mind, and my stomach went into a free fall.

Indira pressed a button on the machine and it started up again with a racket. Then she turned to face me. "If you need to get a message to him, I can telex him at his hotel." I couldn't hear her. I was deep in thought.

"Deependra? Are you alright?"

As if shell-shocked, I staggered all the way back to *seva*. I wanted to know how Gopi could allow herself to be defiled in this way. Couldn't she tell he didn't respect her? He was just using her. He wasn't worthy of her love! I was the one who worshiped and adored her! Didn't she know he was a rapist?

Upset as I was over Gopi's romance with Sergio, I felt just as bad about Baba's double standard. Why had he forbidden me to talk to girls while turning a blind eye to Sergio?

A little while later, Indira stopped by the Audiovisual office. She had forgotten to give me my mail. There was a letter from Jeremy. I wasn't sure I wanted to read what he had to say. Still, I was heartened that he'd been thinking of me enough to write. After *seva*, I sat down in the shade on one of the marble tree planters in the courtyard and carefully opened the envelope.

> *Dear Doug,*
>
> *I'm sorry we didn't get a chance to speak before you left the country. There's no easy way to tell you this, so I'm just going to say it: As the person who got you mixed up in Raja Yoga, it pains me to tell you that Baba is not what he pretends to be. You should know—*

"Where you been at, mate?" I looked up to see Andy Martin staring back down at me. "Haven't seen you since we took the girls to Chaapkhanawala's," he said. "What you got there? Bad news?"

"What?"

"The letter. Your hands are shaking. You look pretty upset."

I stood up, crumpled the letter from Jeremy, and stuffed it into my pocket. "It's nothing," I said, and then answered his first question. "After we got back from the spa that night, I was sick. I think it was the fruit. Spent the whole night barfing my brains out in my room. The rest of you were okay?"

"Yeah, mate. I told you before—I've got an iron stomach."

"Guess so," I said, turning to head up the stairs to my room.

"Hang on, mate," Andy said. He climbed the stairs alongside of me. "I wanted to ask you something. Do you think Gili fancies me?"

His question irritated me. Blind to my own hypocrisy, I wanted to tell him we were in the ashram to meditate on God, not women. "*Fancies* you?"

"Yeah. I think she might be keen on me, but I'm curious to know what you think."

"I don't know, Andy," I said, stopping in front of the door to my room. "To be honest, I haven't the slightest idea. But let me ask *you* something—why are you in the ashram?"

The Australian took a step backwards, and then looked me up and down with a puzzled expression on his face.

"To attain enlightenment?" I asked. "Or to meet girls?"

Andy thought about my question for a couple of seconds, shrugged, and turned around to go back downstairs.

In the privacy of my room, I took the letter out of my pocket to finish reading. But then I changed my mind. *I won't let Jeremy contaminate me with his doubts and false information*, I told myself. The way I saw it, I had more than enough misgivings of my own to deal with. I didn't also need to hear his. I tore the letter into shreds and flushed it down the toilet.

AS THE DAYS PASSED, Gopi and Sergio carried on in plain sight of everyone in the ashram, and the guru's command that I stay away from girls bothered me more and more. Yet despite my persistent doubts about Baba's fair-mindedness, and my feelings of resentment in the aftermath of the beating, I still managed to convince myself that the problem lay in my bad attitude or wrong understanding. The guru was blameless. *I* was a bad disciple. To contribute to my low self-esteem, my libido was in a state of rebellion. I found myself ogling every attractive woman in the ashram. Instead of making progress on the path, I was moving backwards! I prayed to Baba about my shortcomings.

Oh Guru, why is my mind plagued with doubt and my heart so full of anger and lust when it should contain nothing but pure love for you?

Whenever I sat for *darshan*, I gazed upon the guru's divine form and inwardly begged him for guidance. But for the longest time, none came.

Then, finally, he sent a messenger. As I stood in the back of the courtyard with my eyes fixed on Baba, I felt a hand resting on my shoulder. I turned and was face to face with the neckless swami, Akhandananda. His head was tilted to the side, and the expression on his face was one of sympathy.

"It's not always so easy, is it, my boy?"

"Swamiji?"

"Surrendering," he said, turning his head in the direction of the guru.

"What do you mean?"

"I'm talking about learning to let go, Deependra. It's part of the purification process. Sometimes the guru's commands may seem arbitrary, unfair—even cruel at times. But if we truly yearn for liberation, we must surrender to his will. It's the only way."

I remained silent. Did the swami know what I was going through? Could he read my thoughts like Baba?

At that moment, the guru directed his gaze in my direction. Even though his eyes were hidden behind dark sunglasses, I could feel his x-ray vision burning into me. I was deeply ashamed, and remembering the beating he had given me, I trembled.

Baba is keeping me away from the opposite sex for my own good, I reminded myself. The things I need to work on are not what Sergio and Gopi need to work on. *Only by letting go and faithfully following the guru's command can I ever hope for the seeds of lust and worldly desire in my unconscious mind to be burned away forever.*

Now that Baba was making public appearances and giving talks almost every evening, the workload in the Audiovisual department was back to normal. But ever since the day I had gone AWOL, Sergio didn't seem to trust me anymore. His visits to the office became more and more frequent, and he was constantly second-guessing me. Most humiliating, however, was his new instance that Kriyadevi operate the main camera.

"It's good practice for the lesbian," he'd tell me when she was out of earshot. But I didn't find his words reassuring. Whenever I became upset about Sergio's interference like this, I tried to remember what was really going on: the guru was presenting me with another opportunity to *surrender*.

One morning on my way to Prasad, I ran into Namdev Loman. His foot had healed, but he was still far too thin, and had some nasty scabs on the right side of his face. He seemed to be in better spirits though, so I invited him for breakfast. I watched uneasily as my fellow Ithacan devoured three cheese and avocado dosas and a side of home fries in the time it took me to eat one scone.

"Are you still chopping vegetables in the kitchen?" I asked.

Namdev answered through a mouth full of food. "Well, I was. After my foot got better, Sita Perkins sent me back to the generator plant, but told me I also had to keep helping in the kitchen."

"Shit—that's a lot of *seva*," I said, buttering my scone.

"Tell me about it. I came down with a nasty case of shingles. The swami doctor said I needed to get some rest."

"So, did you?"

He laughed bitterly. "Sure! You know what Sita's definition of rest is? Only working sixty hours a week instead of my usual eighty."

"You should've come to me. I would've said something to her."

"When I couldn't get up out of bed one morning, Sita went to Nirmalananda—I guess to make sure I wasn't faking being sick. He convinced her to give me a few days off, followed by a month or two of less demanding *seva*."

"I'm impressed," I chuckled. "Nirmalananda's less of an asshole than I thought he was."

Namdev managed a spiteful smile. "He's still an asshole."

"So what do they have you doing now?"

There was a faint glimmer in his eye. "I'm organizing the ashram library."

"I didn't even know the ashram had a library."

"It's new. For years now, Rohini Brinkerhoff has been collecting books left behind by visitors and stashing them in a closet in Housekeeping. She didn't have the heart to throw them out."

"You mean Baba's books?"

"No, all kinds of stuff: English translations of Hindu scriptures, Balzac, the complete works of William Shakespeare, murder mysteries, trashy romance novels, comic books. I've organized and shelved nearly a thousand books already!"

"Comic books? You mean like Batman and Superman?"

"No, Indian comics—religious stories—like the Ramayana and the Mahabharata. Some of them are about historical figures like Mahatma Gandhi. Kids love 'em, but so do the adults. They're so popular, I can't lend them out. Sometimes I've got up to ten kids at a time on the floor reading. Your friend Ganesh from the dish room comes by almost every weekend."

"Did Baba give his blessing for this library?" I asked, wondering what the guru thought about the trashy mystery and romance novels.

Namdev shrugged. "Not exactly, but I can't see why he'd object. Gajendra gave me permission to set it up in an unused office on the ground floor of *Bhakti Shayanagrih*."

"So, that's your *seva* now? You're a librarian?"

Namdev leaned back and laughed. "Are you joking? As soon as I started feeling better, Sita sent me back to the kitchen to chop vegetables. I'm also still manning the generator plant."

"So you take care of the library in your *spare time?*"

"Yeah, right—in my *spare time*. Did you know that despite the fact that I work more hours than anyone else in the ashram, I'm still the only person on staff who doesn't get a stipend?"

I thought about the unfairness of Namdev's situation, and then remembered Sergio saying they were trying to discourage him from staying in the ashram.

"Yes. You've mentioned it before. Several times, actually. Have you ever considered the possibility that there might be a message from the guru in that?"

Namdev's eyes flashed with anger. "Go fuck yourself, Deependra."

With Baba giving regular public talks, I had little free time. But I always tried to find a few minutes a day to sit for *darshan*. As a member of the guru's tour staff, no matter how late I arrived, I was always given a place up front near the throne, usually right behind Sergio, Avadhoot, and the male swamis.

Despite my unresolved feelings toward Baba and the heavy purification I was going through at the time, I enjoyed observing the guru's interactions with other devotees. This was especially true when they were with Westerners and I could hear Anjali's English translations. It fascinated me to see how different Baba was with one devotee to another. With some people he was fatherly, affirming, or affectionate. With others he seemed hostile, fiery, or coldly indifferent. *The guru always gives his disciples exactly what they need, when they need it,* I reminded myself. *And that includes me.*

One afternoon, as Baba chatted with a longtime devotee from Bombay seated at his feet, his attention suddenly shifted to Rashmi Varma, who was hurrying toward the throne with a large leather-bound book in his hands. The guru's eyes widened with delight as his attendant handed him the hefty tome. Baba leafed through the book until he appeared to find the page he was looking for. Then he held the book up for everyone to see.

"This is a picture of the great Utpaladeva giving *darshan* at his ashram," said Baba through Anjali. "All the swamis should get a copy of this book and study it very well."

I had never heard of Utpaladeva, but I assumed he was some great guru or saint in the Raja Yoga tradition, and that the book was some esoteric piece of writing of his. I made a mental note to find out who Utpaladeva was and why Baba was so enthusiastic about this book.

A few days later, at *darshan* again, I saw a side of the guru I'd never witnessed before: He looked afraid. He was afraid of a woman.

As she waddled into the courtyard, she looked like a typical elderly Indian woman. But something about her gave me the creeps, and when I realized who she was, the hair on the back of my neck stood up. She was the Witch from Surat!

Black eyes protruded from her ghoulish face, and her long black and silver hair was unkempt and greasy. Wrapped around her skeletal body was a blood-red sari. Her misshapen bare feet were badly calloused, and her hands were withered and claw-like. As she drew nearer, I noticed she carried an offering for Baba—a crudely made earthenware cup, like the ones we had drunk out of at the Acharya's ashram in Haridwar.

When it was her turn to come before the guru, she didn't bow down or touch her head to the pair of silver sandals set out in front of him. Instead she began to slowly wave the clay cup at the guru in a circular motion, as if she were performing some kind of puja. Meanwhile, Baba stared vacantly at the old woman's hands and hardly blinked. As she performed her strange ritual, she recited an incantation that was eerily melodic. The only thing I could understand of it was "Gopal Rana"—a name that sounded familiar to me, but I couldn't place it.

Each time the witch said "Gopal Rana," the guru's response was the same: he shook his head and said, "*Nay-hee*," which meant "no" in many Indian languages.

I glanced at Stephen, who was sitting next to me. His eyes and mouth were as wide open as mine. I leaned over and whispered in his ear.

"What the fuck is happening?"

"No clue," he whispered back, "but I think she's speaking to Baba in Gujarati."

"Who's Gopal Rana?"

Stephen turned his head and regarded me with disbelief. "You don't know? Gopal Rana is Baba. It was his name before he became a swami."

The old woman turned away from Baba and pointed a bony finger at Anjali, who winced before looking away. The witch then held the cup out to give to Baba, but he refused it.

I was beginning to wonder how long Suresh and the others would allow this to continue. Finally, after what seemed like ages, Suresh and Rashmi leapt to their feet and grabbed the old woman.

"Deependra!" Suresh called, signaling for me to come.

I shot up and ran to the aid of Baba's future successor.

As the old woman struggled to break free of his hold, Suresh grabbed the cup from her hands and held it out for me to take. It was warm to the touch and contained what looked like milky chai.

"Get rid of it!" Anjali commanded.

While Suresh and Rashmi dragged the witch out of the ashram, I ran toward the kitchen with the old woman's cup. Pouring its contents into a sink, I gagged when I saw what had not been visible below the surface of the warm liquid—a tangled ball of human hair.

Later that evening, Suresh made an announcement before the guru's talk.

"Baba says the strange old Indian lady who came to *darshan* this morning is forbidden from entering the ashram. If you see her outside on the street or in the village, you are forbidden to speak or to make eye contact with her. She is a *churel*—a practitioner of black magic, and she is very dangerous."

A few days later, I heard a rumor that a band of Adivasi men in the village had apprehended the old woman, stripped her naked, and run her out of town.

Poonish told me that on the first moonless night after the witch's visit, Baba and some Brahmin priests from the village had performed a ritual on an old banyan tree near the elephant house. The rite involved the guru striking a nail into the trunk of the tree at the stroke of midnight. The purpose of the ritual, Poonish explained, was to lift a curse the *churel* had placed on the ashram.

It was hard for me to understand how some witch's curse could possibly pose a threat to a perfected master of Raja Yoga like Baba. When I asked my roommate how he thought this could be, he quickly reminded me that it wasn't our place to second-guess the guru.

"Baba doesn't owe us any explanations for the why, where, and how he does things," Poonish said. "The burden is on *us* to have right understanding. If we don't, it's because we're still stuck in our ordinary minds."

UNFORTUNATELY, THE "EXORCISM," IF that's what it was, didn't succeed. Tragedy struck the ashram only a week later. I didn't witness the accident myself, but I got a blow-by-blow account of what had happened from Andy Martin, who was on duty in the dish room when everything went down. I was laying audio cable in the *mandap* when he gave me the bad news.

"The dumbwaiter got jammed with a knife, and was stuck on the upper level of Prasad," Andy explained. "The supervisor tried to get the lift to come back down to the lower level by repeatedly pushing on the down button, but the carriage wouldn't budge. So then this cheeky Indian kid from Bombay said that it happened all the time and that he knew exactly what to do."

I got an awful feeling in my gut. "Was his name Ganesh?"

"Yeah, that's the one."

I was afraid to hear any more.

"So the Indian kid reaches all the way in, finds the knife stuck at the back of the lift, and yanks it out."

I was very familiar with how the dumbwaiter worked at Prasad, and Andy only confirmed what I knew must've gone wrong. He explained that because the supervisor had kept pressing the down button, the elevator cable fully unwound, so that the only thing holding the carriage in place was the knife. When Ganesh pulled it out, the dumbwaiter, which weighed several hundred pounds, went into a free fall and landed on the boy's back, snapping his spine and crushing him.

I suddenly felt lightheaded and dizzy. *It's can't be true. Ganesh, dead?*

"Are you alright, mate?"

I couldn't form any words.

"Deependra?"

My throat swelled shut.

"The kid was a friend of yours, wasn't he?"

Tears pricked my eyes I nodded.

Andy looked nonplussed. "I liked him too, mate," he said, and then reached for my shoulder and gave it a tentative squeeze. "We all did."

I wiped the tears from my cheeks with the back of my hand.

"Look, if it's any consolation, he was killed instantly. At least he didn't suffer."

I thought of Ganesh's radiant smile, and the way he used to brighten everyone's mood in the dish room with his laughter. I thought of his parents and how they must feel. I couldn't begin to fathom what they were going through.

When I was ready to hear more details, Andy told me it took over an hour to remove the body from the elevator shaft.

"When did this happen?" I asked.

"About ten days ago."

"How is it possible that this happened over a week ago and this is the first I'm hearing of it?"

"Sergio told everyone on duty at the time of the accident to keep our mouths shut, and not to gossip about it."

My grief was turning to rage. A sharp pain pierced the back of my neck. I knew it was the beginning of a massive headache.

"Not a trace of blood the next day, mate. It was like nothing ever happened."

"But why the secrecy?"

"Not sure, but I've got a theory."

"I'm listening."

"I read in one of Baba's books that no one should ever be born or die in an ashram. My guess is that Baba doesn't want to look bad."

Anger flashed like lightning through my thoughts. I wanted to punish someone for what had happened to Ganesh, but I didn't know whom to blame. Instead, I lashed out at Andy for speaking ill of the guru.

"How dare you talk about Baba like that?" I shouted. "I'll have you kicked out of the ashram if I ever hear you say anything like that again!"

Andy stepped back and held his hands up. "Get a woolly dog up ya, mate!" He looked me up and down as if he were assessing whether or not he could take me. "Who the fuck d'ya think you are? The thought police?"

It was all I could do to resist the urge to punch Andy right in his pretty face. I invoked what I imagined to be my superior ashram status instead. "Don't you have any *seva* to do?"

"Get stuffed, Deependra."

By the time *seva* was over, I had a painful migraine. I skipped *darshan* and went back to the dormitory. Alone in the room, I stretched out on my bed and sobbed into my pillow. I wanted to know why there hadn't been some kind of an announcement about Ganesh's death—why Baba hadn't mentioned it at *darshan* or during one of his talks.

I couldn't stop crying. I wasn't only crying about Ganesh. The news of his death was a shock to my system, releasing pent up emotions I didn't even know I had. I cried about the death of my father and mother, about flunking out of college, about not getting into NYU, and about being prevented from finishing the video course I started. I cried because Melanie had thrown out my bicycle and record collection, and given my old room to a stranger. I cried because Gopi preferred Sergio to me. And, most of all, I cried because Baba wasn't really my father, and never would be.

The Guru's Touch

A FEW DAYS LATER I summoned the courage to speak to the guru about my sadness over Ganesh's death, and my confusion over the silence surrounding it. He'd just given a talk on devotion and was holding a late evening *darshan* in the open-air hall. When it was my turn to go before him I bowed, and then waited off to the side while he finished speaking to another devotee. When the other devotee went back to her seat, and there was no one left in line to talk to Baba, the guru ignored me and struck up a conversation with one of the female swamis who was sitting nearby. Ordinarily, I would've taken the hint—I would've understood that Baba didn't wish to speak to me, and gone back to my seat and meditated on the higher teaching contained in the guru's silence. This time, however, I stayed where I was and spoke up.

"Babaji—" I croaked. "I'm very sad about the death of my friend, Ganesh, who was killed in the ashram dish room a couple of weeks ago."

The guru's placid expression twisted into a scowl. But he still didn't look at me or acknowledge my presence.

"I don't understand why you haven't mentioned it in any of your talks, or why nobody says anything about it."

Anjali began to translate my words for Baba, but he responded before she had spoken even two words. "No one died in the ashram," growled Baba, turning to glare at me. His eyes were cold and hard.

Remembering the recent beating he'd given me, I began to tremble. "I'm talking about the Indian boy from Bombay."

"I know who you are talking about. This boy did *not* die in the ashram!"

Seated nearby, Sergio was staring and frowning at me now too. His posture was even straighter than usual, and his eyes were two narrow slits.

"But I heard he was killed—"

"The boy died in the car on the way to the hospital," scolded Anjali, speaking for herself. "Now go!"

Powerful emotions swirled inside of me. Baba didn't seem to care at all about Ganesh or the fact that I was grieving. His only concern was that I accept his version of what had happened.

I needed to be alone. Instead of returning to my place behind the swamis, I decided to get a head start breaking down the equipment.

As I stomped back to the Audiovisual office with the gear, I had another thought: *Maybe Andy didn't have his facts straight. Perhaps Ganesh hadn't died instantly and had, in fact, died on the way to the hospital.* Was I jumping to conclusions, trusting the word of some pothead over the word of my guru?

Then something else occurred to me: it didn't matter where the boy had died. The problem was that nobody seemed to care that he was gone.

Unlocking the door to the office, I spotted Gopi up ahead on the path, heading in my direction. For once, she was by herself. Sergio was still seated for *darshan* with Baba. In defiance of the guru's command, I waited until she was close enough, and then approached her.

As she drew nearer she looked straight ahead, as if she didn't see me. "Gopi, can I speak to you a minute?"

She looked over her shoulder and then stopped. "I'm not supposed to be talking to you," she said with a nervous grimace.

"Not supposed to talk to me? Who said that?"

Gopi turned her head away with a look of determination. "What do you want?"

Opening the door to the office, I reached for the light switch on the wall and the overhead fluorescent light flickered on. "Come in."

Gopi glanced around again, and then ducked inside. I closed the door behind her. "Well?" she said, standing with her back against the wall.

"An Indian kid was killed in the dish room a few days ago. Did you hear about it?"

Gopi stared back at me blankly. Then she swallowed hard before answering. "I was sitting next to Anjali when you spoke to Baba about it earlier. Didn't you hear what he said? The boy died in the car on the way to the hospital."

I felt my face getting hot. "What difference does it make where he died?"

"Okay, okay. Calm down!" she said, taking a seat at the worktable.

I sat down across from her.

She was quiet for a moment. Then she spoke again. "Baba says no one should ever be born or die in an ashram."

"I understand that," I said, kneading my forehead with my hand. "But that's not what happened in this case. Why the cover up?"

Gopi's lower lip began to quiver and her eyes became moist.

"I'm not having this conversation with you," she said. Then she stood up. "I know only *one* Truth."

"And what truth is that?"

Gopi opened the door to leave. "Whatever the guru says it is."

39.
THE SECRET PATH

THE ACTIONS OF AN enlightened being are impossible to understand with an ordinary mind.

This was my mantra. It had to be. Otherwise, there was no way I could stay in the ashram. Weeks had passed since I tried speaking to Baba about Ganesh's death, and in all that time the guru didn't so much as glance in my direction.

My *seva* changed too. Kriyadevi Friedman was the now the de facto head of the Audiovisual department. The shift of control from me to her was gradual. Although guarded with her "constructive criticism" of my camera work when we alone together, she was always sure to point out my mistakes and areas of weakness whenever Avadhoot or Sergio were present. In this way she undermined my authority. Whether she was consciously doing it or not, I'll never know.

After repeated prodding from Sergio, she finally acquired a new wardrobe for the part as well, no longer "dressing like a dyke." She had taken him up on his offer for the ashram to pay for new clothes, returning a new woman after a weekend in Bombay with a few of the princesses. So extreme was her transformation from ugly duckling to beautiful swan that even the guru appeared not to recognize her.

When she went before him on the *darshan* line for the first time after her makeover, Baba greeted her with big eyes and an enormous grin, the way he often greeted new devotees for the first time. I had only learned a few dozen words of Hindi, but as the new Kriyadevi prostrated herself before him, I was nearly positive I heard him ask Anjali, "Who's the new girl?"

Kriyadevi was the new rising star in the Audiovisual department. She did almost all the filming, and my responsibilities were fewer and fewer. My status in the ashram changed too. Instead of being seated up front in the hall, I was now routinely seated way in the back.

The news of the change in my "job description" came in the form of a message from Sergio, who sent Brian to deliver it.

"Sergio says that since you're only needed an hour or two a day in the Audiovisual department, you should report to the *seva* office for reassignment."

I was upset, but it didn't come as a shock. I had been expecting the change for a while. The only thing that surprised me was that I hadn't been sent back to my old dorm room in *Bhakti Shayanagrih*. Why? Because I'd confronted the guru about the death of Ganesh. In Raja Yoga, questioning the guru's actions was the ultimate sin. Verse one hundred and four of the *Guru Gita* came to mind as I dragged my feet toward the *seva* office:

One who speaks to the Guru in a rude or insulting manner or who wins arguments with Him is reborn as a demon in a jungle or in a waterless region.

The party line in Raja Yoga was "All *seva* is equal," but everybody knew that those in favor with the guru were given more prestigious jobs. My new assignment made it clear I'd sunken very low. Sita sent me to work in the kitchen.

My first shift started at three o'clock in the morning. Prakashananda, the shirtless Indian swami, handed me a dull knife and a deeply scratched wooden cutting board. He led me into the dimly-lit dining hall, where several rows of Indian and Western devotees were seated cross-legged on the floor chopping eggplants. The strict rule against talking in the dining hall was observed at all times—we had to work in absolute silence.

My last shift in the kitchen finished as late as ten o'clock at night. This meant that I was now only getting about five hours of sleep a night—if I was lucky. To make matters worse, I began suffering from insomnia, and often found myself lying awake half the night wondering what I'd done to deserve such harsh treatment. After weeks of constant sleep deprivation, I became completely worn out. On the rare occasions I was required to help with video, I found myself falling asleep behind the camera. Eventually, Kriyadevi stopped asking for me and started training someone else to replace me.

Worse than the humiliation I felt at being given such a lowly job, my new *seva* no longer brought me into regular contact with Baba. Desperate to get on Baba's good side again, I decided to telex my bank in Ithaca to ask them to wire me a large sum of money. I hoped that another sizable donation to the Mission would help me win back Baba's trust. But I couldn't go through with it. Somewhere in the back of my mind I must've suspected I'd be needing the money for something else.

ONE NIGHT AS I laid awake feeling sorry for myself, I had a breakthrough. I thought about the teaching I'd heard so many times before, but seemed so hard to put into practice: *If I truly yearn for liberation, I must surrender to the guru.*

As difficult as it was, I had to let go of the past, accept my new situation, and remind myself constantly: *Whatever I experience in the ashram is the will of the guru and is for my spiritual upliftment.*

I was still wide awake when my alarm clock went off at two-thirty. I sprang out of bed, took a quick bucket bath, and marched to the kitchen with a renewed sense of purpose and dedication to my *sadhana*. As I sat on the cold marble floor of the dining hall performing my humble *seva*, I continued to wage war with my inner demons. Despite the sadness I felt knowing that I'd probably never be a member of the guru's inner circle again, I realized there was a message in it: I had to give up trying to get closer to Baba. It was time for me to cultivate a relationship with the guru principle.

As right understanding took hold in my mind, I was able to become absorbed in my work and let the mind-numbing, repetitive sound of dull metal against wood lead me into a state of deep concentration.

Just then, the choppers in the row in front of me straightened their backs. I knew immediately what this meant—Baba had just entered the building. In the doorway of the kitchen, he and Anjali were in the midst of a conversation with Prakashananda. He was carrying the same stick he had used to beat me. My hands began to shake.

Even if I hadn't noticed the others correcting their posture, the sudden surge in the guru's divine energy was unmistakable. *Will Baba notice me? Will he recognize what a faithful disciple I am?* These thoughts fought to take shape in my mind, but I was determined to rid myself of any shred of expectation, and to keep my mind a blank slate. I wanted the Omniscient One to be proud of me.

As I kept my eyes on the eggplant I was slicing, my nose detected the familiar fragrance of sweet, grassy hay. Lifting my head, I saw the guru beaming a warm, benevolent smile down at me. Tears rose in the back of my eyes. It seemed like it had been a thousand years since he had even acknowledged my existence.

Baba reached down and stroked my head. "What are you doing here in the kitchen, silly boy?"

"They told me I was no longer needed in the Audiovisual department," I said, rising to my feet.

Anjali translated my words.

"Who is your guru?" Baba asked, his face growing stern. "Avadhoot? Sergio? Or Rudrananda Swami?"

"You are my guru, Baba. Only you."

"*Haan!*"

Baba gave me an affectionate pat on the back, exchanged a few words with Anjali, and then left the dining hall, leaving his translator to finish his conversation with me. She stood only a few inches from me, gazing with her big brown inscrutable eyes into mine.

"Baba wants you to return to the Audiovisual department," she said. "He has an important announcement for the entire world, and he wants you behind the camera when he makes it. After that, we will all have much work to do."

"Will Baba be touring again?"

The hint of a smile played at the corners of Anjali's mouth. "We shall see."

The following morning, Baba caught the video crew off guard by showing up in the hall just before the start of the *Guru Gita*. Kriyadevi, her new assistant Frank Barbetti, and I had to scramble to get the cameras set up.

After the chant, we followed the guru as he made rounds of the ashram with Anjali and Suresh. By the time we had put away the equipment, the Prasad kitchen was about to close. We got our dosa orders just in time, and sat with Poonish, who was lingering in the open-air pavilion over an extravagant breakfast.

"So what 'big announcement' do you think Baba is going to make?" Frank asked, addressing all of us.

Arching a single eyebrow, Kriyadevi smiled cryptically at the newcomer. "I guess we'll just have to wait and see."

It was difficult to believe that the well-dressed new head of our department was the same woman whose wardrobe used to consist exclusively of the discarded old clothes she found in the Birchwood Falls ashram free box. The elegant new Punjabi-style suit flattered her. Even her face was different. In addition to helping Kriyadevi pick out new clothes, Baba's girls had obviously encouraged her to use make-up.

Poonish stared into his plastic cup of chai. "Have you all heard the latest about that journalist who's writing about Baba and the ashram?"

I remembered Sergio's warning about the investigative reporter who wanted to interview me about the role I had played in the ashram's alleged harassment of the Grozas. I hadn't thought of it in months. "You mean the exposé Christopher Walsh is writing for *Veritas*?" I asked.

"Yeah, that's the one," Poonish said, looking up at me.

Frank suddenly made a gurgling noise. I thought he was about to barf, until I realized he was choking.

Unsure of what to do, Poonish slapped Frank on the back.

"Are you okay?" I asked.

Frank regained his breath. "Exposé?" he croaked, taking a sip of water. "What's *Veritas*?"

Kriyadevi smiled knowingly. "It's nothing to worry about, Frank," she said cheerfully.

"*Veritas* is a quarterly journal that investigates claims of paranormal phenomena," said Poonish. "You know—ghosts, UFOs, Bigfoot, fringe-science. They expose hoaxes, and that sort of thing."

"How could that possibly relate to Baba?" Frank asked with a frightened look in his eyes. I suspected the rumors going around about the guru were getting to him.

"Exactly," I said. "It doesn't." I was trying to sound casual in front of the others, but the situation troubled me deeply.

Frank rubbed his temple and winced.

"So, what's the latest news?" I asked Poonish.

"Walsh was here, snooping around the ashram, asking questions. Sergio and Brian kicked him out. People say he's staying in the village at Chaapkhanawala's."

I began to lose my appetite. "I guess he's pretty determined."

Kriyadevi laughed deeply from her belly. "You know what Baba says, don't you?"

The three of us turned to Kriyadevi and looked at her expectantly.

"What?" Frank asked hopefully.

"The truth is fearless. Lies are without legs."

Frank looked confused. Poonish and I nodded in agreement.

The others got up to bus their dirty trays to the dish room. I stayed behind to finish my chai. I thought about Christopher Walsh. The fact that he had followed Baba all the way to India meant he was probably onto something. Part of me wanted to talk to him. I didn't have anything to tell him, of course, but I was curious to learn what he had found out.

The pavilion was almost empty now. A Western man dressed in a grimy white kurta and lungi began putting the chairs up and wiping down the tables. He had long matted hair and a beard. On the far side of the pavilion, near where the man was cleaning, Gopi and Sergio were sitting alone together. They were deeply engrossed in a conversation and were unaware of my presence. I couldn't hear what they were saying to each other, but their conversation appeared to be escalating rapidly into an argument. Gopi was frowning, with her arms folded across her chest, and repeatedly shaking her head. The Italian was leaning forward in his chair, turning red, and gesturing angrily.

As the man cleaning the tables inched closer to the couple, Sergio's attention shifted from Gopi to the encroacher.

"Hey, you, hippie!" Sergio shouted. "Get out of here! Can't you see we're trying to enjoy our breakfast in peace?"

Jerking his head back in surprise, the man dropped the rag on the ground, and took a couple of steps back. "Sorry, man, but I'm just doing my *seva*."

This only made Sergio angrier, and he got a crazed look in his eye.

"Get out!" shouted the Italian, pointing toward the exit.

Glancing around, Gopi noticed I was sitting less than twenty feet away, and we exchanged a fleeting glance. Then she turned to the hippie. "Do you think you could give us some privacy please?"

"This is an ashram, not a resort!" the man shot back, picking up his rag off the ground and resuming his work. "If you want privacy, go to a hotel! Prasad is closed now. *You get lost!*"

"*Ti ammazzo!*" Sergio shouted. Then he leapt to his feet and lunged at the man, punching him in the face.

"Sergio, no!" Gopi cried.

I was sure the hippie would immediately back down. But he swung back, landing a blow on Sergio's jaw.

Touching his mouth, Sergio saw blood on his hand and went berserk. He reached for the nearest chair and brought it down over the hippie's head, knocking him to the floor. Then Sergio repeatedly kicked the man in the side. Gopi tried to pull him away, but it was no use. In his rage, Sergio pushed Gopi back, and she fell over.

"Gopi!" I called. I ran to her side and helped her up. "Are you hurt?"

She might have heard me, but her mind didn't register my questions. Her face contorted in horror as the hippie appeared to lose consciousness.

"Sergio, stop!" she shrieked.

Sergio turned around and glared at both of us. "*Vuoi rompermi i coglioni, eh?*" he shouted, pointing at me. I had no idea what he said, but I could guess he didn't appreciate my interference. I held on to Gopi. Sergio again shouted at me in Italian, and again I didn't move. Reaching under his jacket, he pulled out his gun and pointed it at me.

"Get your hands off her, *sporco ebreo!*" he shouted.

I was so scared I nearly pissed my pants.

Beads of perspiration had formed on Sergio's brow, and his eyes were on fire.

"You want to live or die?" he asked, waving the weapon in my face. "Get the fuck out of here!"

My heart thudded against the wall of my chest. I couldn't move.

"Sergio!" Gopi cried. "Are you crazy?"

The hippie moaned in pain.

I raised both hands in the air, the way I'd seen it done on television. I wanted to speak, but was unable.

"*Fanculo!*" the Italian shouted. He cocked the pistol and I started crying.

Gopi covered her mouth with both hands. "Stop, Sergio!"

Sergio shoved me with his free hand. "Get the fuck out of here, Greenbaum!"

I wanted to bolt, but I wouldn't leave Gopi. Sergio was out of control. Who knew what he was capable of?

Gopi fixed her eyes on me. Her chin and her lips were quivering. "Just go, Deependra! Go!"

Taking care not to make any sudden movements, I began to back slowly away toward the closest exit, and then made a run for it.

"That's right, you Jew coward, run!" the Italian shouted. "Run!"

Later that morning, I was still in shock from the incident with Sergio when Rashmi Varma came by the office with a message from Baba. The guru wanted us to film an important interview with *Raja Path* magazine during *darshan*. Despite the dismay I felt at what had happened earlier, my curiosity was piqued. I wondered if Baba would make the "big announcement" we'd heard was coming.

As we set up the cameras, I told Kriyadevi about how Sergio had beaten up the hippie and pulled a gun on me after she and the others had left Prasad.

I thought she'd be horrified. Instead she shook her head and laughed. "That Sergio is so moody! What a character!"

"A character?" I asked, rubbing my ear. "I'd use a different word to describe him."

Kriyadevi smiled good-naturedly. "Oh yeah? What's that?"

The word I was thinking of was *psychopath*, but I pretended to laugh instead—some things were better left unsaid.

Just then, the door to Baba's house opened and Parvati Halabi stepped out and closed the door behind her. When she saw me taping down a cable, she smirked.

"I thought you worked in the kitchen now?" she said, placing her hands on her curvaceous hips.

"Sometimes I do. I serve the guru wherever I'm needed."

Parvati tilted her head and laughed. "Of course you do." Then she moved closer to me and spoke softly, so that only I could hear. "I heard you were there this morning."

"Where's there?" I answered, playing dumb. I loaded a cassette into the camera, and then adjusted the tension on my tripod.

"You were there when Sergio kicked the shit out of that hippie in Prasad. I heard he pulled a gun on you."

"You heard right. What happened to him? Is he alright?"

"Yeah, he calmed down."

"I'm talking about the hippie."

Parvati jutted out her lower lip and shrugged.

"What's wrong with Sergio, anyway?" I asked. "I know he's a hothead, but I've never seen him so angry—over nothing."

Parvati smiled in the way that people do when they take pleasure in the misfortune of others. Glancing over her shoulder, she moved even closer to me. "He's upset because Gopi broke it off with him."

Suddenly I felt hopeful. "Broke it off with him? Why?"

The princess frowned. "Because he's a cheating bastard, that's why. Anyhow, it's nobody's business. You didn't hear it from me."

"Whatever," I said, feigning indifference.

Parvati regarded me incredulously. "Whatever?" Parvati smiled her wicked smile again. "Come now, Deependra—I know you're excited. You're thinking you might have a chance with her again!"

I looked away. "I don't know what you're talking about."

"You're not fooling anybody. We all know you're in love with Gopi—even Baba!"

I was mortified. I wanted to sink into the marble under my feet and disappear. I understood that the omniscient guru knew *everything*, but that he would discuss my feelings for a girl with other disciples filled me with shame.

"Baba *knows* that I'm in love with Gopi? Why do you say that?"

"Because I was there when Gopi told him."

A feeling of dread seized me.

"She told Baba that I was in love with her? What was his reaction?"

Parvati's expression turned serious. "He forbade her to talk to you."

I had the impression the walls of the courtyard were closing in on me. "*Forbade* her to speak to me? But why?"

"That's exactly what Gopi wanted to know," she said, grinning again.

"So what did he say?"

"He told her to forget about you. He said she deserved to marry a *prince*."

"Baba said that?" I felt my legs begin to buckle. I almost fell over.

I heard someone call my name, but I couldn't register it. The words *Baba thinks I'm worthless!* lit up like a neon sign inside my head.

"Deependra!"

There was a tug on my arm. I didn't feel it at first. I wished I were dead.

"Deependra!" Kriyadevi scolded.

I shook myself out of my painful reverie.

"I just got the signal. Get behind your camera. Baba's going to come out now."

I couldn't think straight. *Where is my camera?* I surveyed the courtyard for a couple of seconds. Then I realized I was standing right next to it.

Sensing the guru's imminent arrival, the devotees began to cluster around the throne like bees in a hive. I fired up the camera. Frank counted into the microphone and I adjusted my audio levels.

Parvati took her spot on the floor, next to the throne with the other *darshan* girls. I glanced in her direction and we locked eyes. A sadistic smile played on her lips. *Could she have been making the whole thing up just to fuck with me?*

"Deependra!" Kriyadevi called from her position behind the other camera. "Move your camera closer to the throne so you can get a two-shot with Baba and Tejasa."

Tejasa Klein was the editor of *Raja Path* magazine. She'd be interviewing Baba. Hitting the quick-release latch on my camera, I removed it from the tripod and fought my way toward the throne through a sea of devotees, trying to avoid injuring anyone in the process. But in my state of shock and confusion, I accidentally stepped on the bare toes of Swami Chinmayananda. He cursed me under his breath in Spanish.

Just as I reached my new position, the door to the guru's house swung open and out popped a cheerful Baba, followed by Suresh and Anjali. Bowing to the photo of his own guru mounted on the wall behind him, he smiled mischievously to himself, and then took a seat on his throne, folding his legs in front of him. Suresh and Anjali took their usual places at his feet. A moment later, the door to Baba's house opened again. Avadhoot flew out and immediately started taking pictures.

Putting my eye to the viewfinder of the camera, I froze. I couldn't remember what to do next.

Baba thinks I'm worthless.

Just then, someone tapped my leg. It was Frank. He was holding up a thick, black cable for me to take from him.

"What's this?" I whispered impatiently.

"You want sound, right?" muttered Frank.

It was the output from his audio board. I snatched the cable out of his hand and connected it to the back of my camera. If Frank hadn't reminded me to do this, the sound would have been unusable.

Bringing my eye back to the viewfinder, I got a wide angle shot of Baba and the people seated closest to him.

Tejasa asked her first question. "Babaji, do you still expect to make another world tour? If so, when do you think you might be well enough to return to the West?"

There was another tap on my leg. I pulled my head away from the camera and looked down at Frank.

"Your tally light's not on."

Jesus Christ! I had forgotten to hit record. I broke out in a sweat. Hands trembling, holding my breath, I groped the side of my camera until my fingers finally came into contact with the record button. I pressed it in, and locked it in place. Three agonizingly long seconds later, a little red light appeared at the bottom of my viewfinder, and I could breathe again.

"Everything that happens in this world takes place through the will of Gurudev Brahmananda," Baba said. "And he has made his will known to me."

For the first time, it was not Anjali translating, but one of Baba's Indian swamis. I glanced over at Anjali with my free eye. I wondered if she might be ill, but she was sitting in her usual spot, on the floor below the throne, and looked fine.

"Just as Gurudev passed on the power of the Raja Yoga lineage to me, I am passing the torch to the next generation of teachers."

"You say *teachers*, Baba, in the plural," Tejasa said. "Last year you named Swami Brahmananda as your successor. Are you implying that you will have more than one successor?"

"Because there are two groups of people in this world—men and women, it is appropriate that the lineage be passed on to members of both these groups. Therefore, today I announce that Anjali Bhandary will also be my successor."

There was a collective gasp from the public, followed by an enthusiastic round of applause.

I was so shocked by Baba's announcement, I momentarily forgot how horrible I felt. I thought about it: *Two successors. A man and a woman. A brother and sister.* It made sense.

Tejasa asked the guru some follow up questions, and as I continued to film the interview I became distracted by my own thoughts. *The job of the guru is to insult you,* I remembered Suresh saying. *Baba is working on my ego. That's why he told Gopi to forget about me, and that she should marry a prince. He knew I'd eventually hear about it.* Then doubt crept in. *If his intention was to insult me, why didn't he just say it directly to my face?* Then I remembered my new mantra: *Everything that happens in the ashram is a manifestation of the guru's will, and happens for the sake of my spiritual development.* But doubt fought back. *Baba said I was unworthy of the angel. Perhaps on a cosmic level, the guru principle is working on my ego, but on a personal level, Baba still thinks I'm inferior!*

Someone grabbed my free arm. I turned around to see Avadhoot standing over my shoulder. He was glowering.

"Are you getting a close up of Anjali?" he whispered. It was a question, but it sounded like he already knew the answer.

"No, I'm getting a two-shot," I whispered back. "Kriyadevi's getting the reaction shots. Talk to her."

"Don't you have an intercom?" His whisper was getting louder. "No monitor?"

"Not today."

Avadhoot's eyes flashed with madness, as if the *crazy switch* in his head had just been tripped. He grabbed my arm again and pulled me away from the camera so that he could see what I was shooting for himself.

"How do you zoom in on this thing?" he asked, verging on hysteria. "How do you zoom?"

"Let me do it!" I said, wrestling with him to get back behind the camera. He pushed me away. "Okay, film it yourself," I scolded, "you stupid asshole!"

I glanced around the courtyard. People were staring at us. The photographer noticed too, and made an effort to compose himself.

I hastily zoomed in on Anjali and got an extreme close up. Her face was a mask of dispassion. As distraught as I was, in that moment I admired her. She was the *perfect disciple.*

Then I felt a hand against my ear and the moist hot breath of Avadhoot whispering in my ear. "The most important announcement Baba ever made and you don't even have an intercom set up! You're all a bunch of incompetent amateurs!"

I didn't care that Avadhoot was angry. He was *always* angry. It didn't matter what anyone did or said, I was always *wrong.* I was tired of his abuse. I was sick of Sergio and his self-importance. I hated all of them!

"Back the fuck off, Avadhoot!" I blurted out before I could stop myself.

I expected the photographer to shout back, or punch me in the face. But he did neither. Instead, he just stared back at me blankly, as if my sudden outburst had shorted a circuit in his brain.

Avadhoot wasn't the only one who had heard me. Glancing around, I saw that several people up front had turned around to see what was going on. Baba had heard me too, and was now staring in my direction. Instead of looking angry, however, he smiled and winked at me approvingly.

Before bringing my eye back to the viewfinder, I glanced over my shoulder to check if Avadhoot was still behind me, but I didn't see him. He had moved to the other side of the courtyard and was busy taking pictures again.

"Will Anjali be initiated as a swami, or will she become a householder-guru in the tradition of Lahiri Mahasaya?" Tejasa asked, continuing her interview.

"She will be initiated into the *Smriti* order of monks by His Eminence Vedantananda Acharya, and will take the vows of a sannyasin," Baba answered.

"Does this mean you will be retiring, and that your successors will take over your role as guru?"

"As long as I am in my physical body, the power of the lineage will stay with me, and only I will sit on the throne. Nevertheless, I will let the younger generation do more of the hard work." Baba laughed and so did the audience.

"These two," Baba said, gesturing to Anjali and Suresh, "have been admitted into Gurudev's university. Now it is up to them to pass or fail. Jai Gurudev!"

While the rest of the crew put away the equipment, I was logging the tapes from Baba's interview with Tejasa, when Avadhoot sauntered in through the door of the Audiovisual office. I expected him to chew me out for talking back to him during Baba's interview, but he behaved as if nothing had happened. Instead he boasted about the "amazing" close-ups he'd taken of Anjali's face right after Baba made his big announcement about her. He emphasized that he'd gotten *close-ups* of her several times.

"One of them will be on the cover of the next issue of *Raja Path*," he predicted. "You can bet on it!"

When Avadhoot finished bragging, he turned to me and was unusually friendly. "Boychik, when does your tourist visa expire?"

"At the end of the month, but my ticket is open-ended."

"Perfect! The *pattabhishek* will be over by then."

The *pattabhishek*, Kriyadevi had explained, was the ceremony to officially install Anjali and Suresh as Baba's successors.

"Have you asked Baba if he wants you to stay on after your visa is up?"

Wants me to stay? The question reverberated in my head. It had never occurred to me that Baba might not want me to remain in India after my visa expired. My plan was to fly to Kathmandu at the end of the month, apply for a new one, and then fly back to Bombay as soon as it was granted. I'd repeat the process as many times as necessary. That's what everyone did who stayed in the ashram on a tourist visa. But maybe Baba would want me to return home to the States? He had sent me away before, he could do it again. And now that I knew what he really thought of me, it was even more likely.

"Go talk to him now," Avadhoot said. "He's still giving *darshan* in the courtyard."

I was about to approach the throne when something occurred to me. Before I could ask Baba what he wanted me to do, I had to ask myself what *I* wanted to do. Did I want to stay? I wasn't so sure. I bowed to the guru and returned to the office.

Avadhoot poked me on the shoulder and waved a hand in front of my eyes. "Well?"

I'd been lost in thought. "Well, what?"

"Did you ask Baba if you could stay?"

"I'll ask him tonight," I answered firmly. "After the evening program."

I can still remember all the excitement. Everybody was talking about Baba naming Anjali as Suresh's co-successor. At lunchtime, I saw her in Prasad, surrounded by people who wanted to congratulate her. I imagined an ordinary person would have become puffed up with pride under the circumstances, but not Anjali. She remained completely humble. This made me think that maybe she had already attained enlightenment.

I wasn't so sure about her brother. Granted, he was an excellent speaker and a nice guy, but he seemed too down-to-earth and easygoing to be a perfected master of Raja Yoga. Maybe he still had a little ways to go.

Baba didn't come to the evening program in the hall that night. So I didn't get a chance to speak to him. Gajendra Williams made a general announcement that the ashram would be shifting into high gear to handle all the preparations for the *pattabhishek*. The ceremony, he said, would be held in the *mandap* pavilion at the end of the month, and presided over by Vedantananda Acharya himself.

Gajendra's words were followed by a rousing call-and-response chant led by Anjali, with Suresh on the drums. Her voice was deep, powerful, and brimming with devotion. Suresh's steady tabla playing was precise, complex, and melodious. As I looked around, everyone seemed to be chanting with abandon. Some had risen to their feet and were dancing in place—something I had never seen in the ashram before. Tears of love streamed down their faces. The chant filled me with a longing to break free from the hard shell of my ego and to join the brother and sister duo in whatever realm they were visiting us from.

But something held me back. I couldn't feel the bliss. I couldn't let go. Baba told Gopi to avoid me. She'd never marry me now. I wasn't highborn—no matter how devoted I was to the guru, or how much *sadhana* I did, there was nothing I'd be able to do to change my caste.

By the time the chant ended, it was already time for lights out. As I passed through the courtyard on the way to my room, I saw Stephen and Poonish disappear with the rest of Raja Yoga's royalty behind the closed door of Baba's private quarters. I felt sad and jealous, but at least I now understood the reason for my exclusion.

I tried to sleep, but it was impossible. I thought about the implications of what the guru had said about me. Then it hit me: Baba wasn't following his own teaching, to see everyone and everything equally as divine consciousness—an expression of the Inner-Self of all.

I needed answers. I decided that rather than toss and turn all night, I'd return to the courtyard and listen in on the *devi* chant. I'm not sure why I did this. Maybe I thought if I listened carefully enough, the hidden meaning behind the guru's actions would be revealed to me.

When I returned to the courtyard, I was surprised to find Kriyadevi seated in my usual spot on the tree planter. Her eyes were closed, and she seemed to be in a state of meditation. On the planter next to her was a flimsy cotton bag with broken handles, and a commercial tape recorder. Connected to the recorder was a directional microphone from the Audiovisual department, aimed at the open windows of Baba's private quarters.

Sitting next to her, I cleared my throat to make my presence known. When she opened her eyes and saw me, she smiled self-consciously.

"What are you—" I started to say, but Kriyadevi lifted a finger to her lips with one hand and pointed to the microphone with the other.

I stayed with her until the chant was over, and then, before anyone from Baba's house came out and saw us, we made a dash to the Audiovisual office. When we were safely inside, Kriyadevi locked the door behind us.

"So, you aren't invited to the chants either," she said without a trace of rancor.

"I'm afraid not," I said.

Her eyes shone with spiritual zeal. "Do you know what they're for?"

"Hymns to the goddess?"

"Precisely!" Reaching into her bag, she pulled out a thick, leather-bound book, which she handed to me. It was entitled *Utpaladeva: An Historical and Philosophical Analysis* by C.N. Gupta. I recognized it as the book Baba had told the swamis to study during *darshan* a few weeks earlier.

"Utpaladeva was one of India's greatest philosophers and mystics," Kriyadevi said, speaking rapidly, bouncing from foot to foot. "He lived in the tenth century. I've read this book from cover to cover."

"Okay," I said, taking a seat at the worktable.

Kriyadevi quickly opened the book to an illustration. It depicted a guru from Utpaladeva's lineage that reminded me a little of Baba. He wore flowing silk robes and was seated in the lotus position on a golden throne decorated with flower garlands, crystals, and strings of pearls. The scene took place in a courtyard—like the one in the Ravipur ashram—and was crowded with both male and female disciples.

"See how he has three stripes of sacred ash on his forehead?" Kriyadevi asked, tapping the picture of the guru with her forefinger. I found her intensity a bit unsettling. "He was a devotee of Lord Shiva, just like Baba!"

I looked at the book more closely. The guru in the picture was immersed in a state of bliss, with his eyes rolled up toward the center of his forehead.

"What does this book have to do with the *devi* chants?" I asked.

"Everything!" She sat down at the table across from me. "According to the book, Utpaladeva was an exponent of *Vamachara Tantra*."

"What's *Vamachara Tantra?*"

"In Yoga, *Vamachara* is known as the *secret path*, and it's only practiced by the most advanced yogis and yoginis." Kriyadevi went on to explain how *Vamachara* denied the duality between sensual pleasure and divine ecstasy, considering the former to be a vehicle to the latter. Pulling out another leather-bound book from her bag, she read me a passage from it.

"*Vamachara* is intended for only the most advanced practitioners of the Raja Yoga. They must have achieved such mastery over the mind and senses that they are able to redirect their attention from the stimulating object, even at the moment of greatest pleasure."

I was utterly confused. "What does that even mean?"

"It means true masters of *Vamachara* never lose a drop of semen."

The conversation was becoming awkward and I broke eye contact with her. "I still don't understand."

"They never ejaculate because they're not engaged in sex for the sake of sensual enjoyment."

My mind immediately jumped to the Aghori sect in Haridwar that Poonish had told me about. I also remembered the bizarre talk that Suresh had given back in Berkeley, about the yogi Ranganath who absorbed all of his semen back into his penis after getting a sensual massage from two beautiful women.

"Don't you see, Deependra?"

I shook my head. "What are you saying—that Baba is like Utpaladeva? That he's a secret practitioner of *Tantra*?"

"That's exactly what I'm saying! Utpaladeva was one of the greatest gurus of the *Tantra Shaiva* lineage, and so is Baba!"

"But Baba never mentions Utpaladeva or *Vamachara Tantra* in any of his books."

"Of course he doesn't!" she chuckled. "It's not something they teach to newcomers in the *shaktipat* retreats. *Vamachara* is only for the most advanced disciples. The rest of us are taught to abstain from sex and to conserve our energy for meditation and chanting. It makes total sense that Baba would keep these practices a secret!"

"But why would anyone who already attained the highest state of consciousness need to engage in such a practice? What would they have to gain from it, even if it were a legitimate form of yoga?"

Just then, someone outside the office began to unlock the door. Kriyadevi grabbed the books and stuffed them back inside her bag. The door swung open and in walked Anjali and Sergio.

The Italian was surprised to find us still in the office at this late hour, and he frowned disapprovingly. "What are you two still doing here?"

Anjali interrupted before we could explain. "Sergio, it's okay," she said. "How are you, Kriyadevi?"

"Wonderful!" she replied, her eyes shining again.

Anjali turned to me. "Deependra, you should be in bed."

"I couldn't sleep."

Her eyes narrowed and I felt she could see right through me. "What did Baba tell you about talking to girls?"

Something inside of me snapped. *The sheer hypocrisy of it!* Here was one of Baba's successors, about to take a vow of celibacy, hanging out alone in the middle of the night with this homicidal anti-Semitic rapist! Was I supposed to believe they'd come to watch videos together? I used every ounce of willpower I'd developed through meditation to remain calm.

"Kriyadevi and I work together," I said. "I didn't think the rule applied."

"Don't talk back!" Sergio growled. "Go to your rooms! Both of you!"

Kriyadevi and I were about to leave when Anjali stopped us. "Before you go, could you please cue up the footage from Baba's interview with Tejasa this morning?" They wanted to watch a video together after all. Anjali asked to see the moment when Baba announced her as his successor. She was particularly interested in the audience reactions. They watched it a few times.

How do I know? They made me stay to operate the VTR.

40.
A CHANGE OF HEART

PREPARATIONS FOR THE *PATTABHISHEK* were in full swing, especially in the *mandap*. Western ashramites and weekend visitors from Bombay alike were working long hours to get everything in the ashram ready for Anjali and Suresh's coronation ceremony, a little over two weeks away.

Sergio had purchased several new loudspeakers for the pavilion, and assigned me to install them. To get the job done, I used the same rickety bamboo scaffolding from which Govinda had fallen and broken his back a couple of years earlier.

Andy Martin, who was down below, passed a speaker up to me. As I mounted it on a rafter, I reflected on how little I knew when I first came to the ashram, and how many skills I had acquired since. I knew how to assemble a bunk bed, repair a broken microphone, operate a professional video camera, and dress for success. I felt my mother would've been proud of me.

But I'd also learned how to smuggle contraband into a foreign country, and defraud the US government. I wasn't sure my mother would've been proud of that.

Ever since I discovered that Poonish and Stephen were participants in the midnight *devi* chants with Baba, I was spending less and less time with them. People who were close to Baba served as a reminder of the guru's low opinion of me. Instead of sitting with my roommates at mealtimes, I hung out with Andy. In my demoralized state, I'd linger with my new Australian friend in the Prasad pavilion, long after the café stopped serving.

"I resent the rumors," Andy said, jutting his lower lip out in mock petulance. "I am *not* a drug dealer. I'm happy to give my dope away free to anyone who asks!"

I'd recently taken the Australian up on an offer to get high with him on the rooftop of *Bhakti Shayanagrih*. It helped me to forget.

"Good stuff, isn't it, mate?" Andy said, passing the joint back to me.

"Yeah, who needs *samadhi* when you can smoke grass instead?"

I was joking, of course, but for the first time since joining Raja Yoga, I had stopped meditating and attending the chants. I was also less strict in following Baba's command that I stay away from girls. Ever since Kriyadevi had shared her theory about Baba being a secret practitioner of *Tantra*, I stopped caring. I think part of me thought the rumors might be true. In any case, I believed the time had come for *me* to get laid again. With this in mind, I began inviting Gili Ben Ami and Katie Harris to join Andy and me for meals at Prasad.

"Do either of you girls know what you're going to wear to the *pattabhishek?*"

Katie and Gili turned to each other and shrugged.

Slipping off my left Birkenstock under the table, I lightly placed a bare foot on top of one of Katie's open-toed sandals. I thought this was a good way to make an overture. At first she acted as if she hadn't noticed. She and Gili were sitting opposite Andy and me, and it was possible she couldn't tell which one of us was responsible.

"What's wrong with what I'm wearing now?" Gili asked with a wry smile. She was dressed in tight jeans and a black t-shirt that revealed too much cleavage to be considered appropriate for the ashram.

Katie squirmed a little as I began to rub the top of her foot with the bottom of mine, but she made no attempt to move it away.

"I haven't thought about it, really," Katie said.

I gently massaged the top of the Australian's foot again. Taking a deep breath, she stared at me searchingly. A second later, her eyes darted to Andy, and then back to me again.

"Well, you know, all the princesses will be shopping in Bombay this week for new saris," I said, turning my head and winking at Andy.

"That's right, ladies," Andy chortled.

Gili sneered at Andy and me. "Do you really think I care what those stuck-up bitches do with their time?"

"What about you, Katie?" I asked, sliding my foot slowly up her leg and tickling her outer thigh with my toes. "Don't you want a pretty new sari to wear on the big day?"

The Australian girl's eyes widened and her mouth dropped open. Reaching down, she grabbed hold of my foot and twisted it so that I cried out. This prompted surprised looks from Gili and Andy.

Katie gave me the evil eye. "Sorry, *Deependra*, it was an accident."

"Well, don't you?" I said, regaining my composure.

"Don't I what?" the Australian girl snapped.

"Want a new sari to wear to the *pattabhishek*?"

"Maybe."

Andy scratched his head. "What do you have in mind, mate?"

"I have some personal business in Bombay to take care of. How does an overnight in the city grab you?"

I slipped the sandal off my right foot now, and then went to work on one of Gili's feet.

Eyebrows raised, Gili and I locked eyes. She slipped her other foot on top of mine, sandwiching it between the two of hers. "Sounds like fun," she said dryly.

I turned to the Australian. "How about you, Katie?"

"Sure!" she said, with a conspiratorial wink.

"Andy?"

"You bet your arse, mate. I know a clean, proper guest house on the Colaba Causeway that's popular with Westerners."

"Nah, I know a better place," I announced proudly. "You're all going to be my guests at the Taj."

SINCE BABA HAD MADE his big announcement about Anjali, and set the date for the *pattabhishek*, center leaders, Mission trustees, celebrities, devotees, and swamis from the guru's many ashrams all over the world began arriving every day by the dozen. They were all here to bear witness to the passage of the power.

One of the new arrivals was Jake Gooding from Birchwood Falls. Sergio had sent for him after Kriyadevi convinced him that we absolutely needed someone to direct the video recording of this once-in-a-lifetime event. Jake had been on staff in the Birchwood Falls ashram for many years, but this was his first trip to India. He had never been able to afford to come before and, until now, the Mission never had a compelling enough reason to fly him over. He spent the first couple of hours after his arrival exploring the ashram grounds with wide-eyed wonder. I promised to accompany him to Gurudev's *samadhi* shrine in the village whenever he was ready.

"Did you check with Baba if you could stay on after your visa expires?" Avadhoot asked.

I was helping the photographer unpack a large shipping box in the Audiovisual office. It contained blank videocassettes and film stock that Jake had couriered over with him.

"Um ... not yet," I answered.

"You're kidding me, right? Your visa's about to run out!"

"I just haven't gotten around to it."

The truth was, I didn't know what I wanted to do.

"Better do it now," he warned. "Baba just came out for *darshan*. There's a big line forming. Cut to the front and get back here as fast as you can. You need to show Jake the *mandap*. He needs to decide where to set up the camera platforms."

As I headed out the door, Avadhoot had one more thing to tell me. "By the way, I spoke to Indira St. John. She's got a new room assignment for you. Go see her after you talk to Baba."

This news didn't surprise me, but it sapped all my energy. A lot of important Raja Yoga personalities were arriving from all over the world. They couldn't be expected to sleep in non-air-conditioned rooms with a bunch of nobodies as their roommates. I had to free up my bed in the VIP dorm to make room for them.

I tried to cut to the front of the *darshan* line as Avadhoot had asked, but it was impossible. Brian, one of the *darshan* ushers, saw me trying to sneak in and sent me to the back of the line. I tried to explain that Avadhoot told me to skip to the front, but he didn't care. I wasn't important enough to receive special treatment. I wasn't a prince.

As I waited my turn to pay my respects to Baba, I prayed inwardly to the guru:

Dear Baba, my mind and moods change like the wind. One minute, I am your faithful servant, the next I am breaking the ashram rules and disobeying you. Please bless me with a strong, stable mind, and keep me on the right path.

"What the fuck are you doing all the way back here?" Avadhoot scolded when he found me. "I told you to cut in line! We don't have all day!"

Herding me to the front, Avadhoot interrupted Baba as he was greeting some new arrivals. I cringed as the photographer misrepresented the situation to the guru.

"Excuse me, Baba, Deependra has something he insists on asking you right now."

The guru gazed deeply into my eyes. I felt the *kundalini* stir at the base of my spine, as blissful energy spread throughout my body.

"Babaji, my tourist visa will expire right after the *pattabhishek*. Do I have your blessing to apply for a new one?"

"Talk to Sergio," Baba said, wiggling his head from side to side. Then, with a wave of his hand, he dismissed me.

"Does that mean I can stay?" I asked Avadhoot as we headed back to the office.

"You heard Baba. He said talk to Sergio!"

After our meeting in the *mandap*, Jake and I rode to the village together by oxcart.

"I'm going to run a quick errand while you're visiting the shrine," I told him, speaking loudly to make myself heard over the rattle of the cart. "I'll meet up with you later."

I didn't tell Jake, but my "errand" was a visit to Chaapkhanawala's. I was hoping Christopher Walsh, the investigative journalist, might still be around. I had some questions for him, and was curious to hear directly from him why he wanted to talk to me. When I arrived at the main building of the resort, the veranda was empty, and there was no one in the office. With a few minutes to kill, I took a seat on the terrace and waited to see who would turn up.

A few minutes later, one of Palash's servants came shuffling out of the main building. He was surprised to find me there, but then beckoned me inside. I followed him up a cool, dark flight of stairs to the Chaapkhanawalas' private residence, where I found a shirtless Palash at work behind a desk.

"Hello, my young friend!" the innkeeper said, standing up to greet me. "I'm very pleased to see you again! Have you come for a bubble bath?"

"Um, not today, Mr. Palash."

"I'm afraid my memory isn't what it used to be. Kindly remind me of your good name?"

I was about to say "Deependra" when, much to my surprise, the name "Douglas" came out instead.

"*Bahut aacha*! Welcome! Welcome, Mr. Douglas!"

"Actually, I'm looking for an American by the name of Christopher Walsh. Do you have anyone by that name staying here?"

Chaapkhanawala regarded me suspiciously. "Did the ashram send you?"

"No, sir. I'm here on my own. Nobody sent me."

"Such as the case may be, Mr. Walsh is no longer here. He checked out a few days ago."

I couldn't tell if I was disappointed or relieved that the journalist was gone. Part of me wanted to hear what he had to say, but another part of me felt it would be disloyal to talk to him.

"I see," I said turning to leave. "Well, thank you anyway." Before I reached the stairs, I turned around again to ask another question. "Mr. Palash, sir, I'd still like to know why you have so many pictures of Lord Brahmananda on the walls of your resort, but none of Swami Rudrananda, his successor."

Palash let out a bark of laughter. "Gurudev had many disciples, you know. Not all of them attract wealthy benefactors from America and Europe, and drive fancy cars. I can tell you all about Swami Rudrananda and his origins—"

"Deependra! Are you up there?"

Someone was calling my name from the outside of the building.

Palash hurried to an open window, and motioned for me to join him. Looking down, I saw Jake talking to the servant.

"Jake!" I called. "I'll be down in a second."

Once again, I left Palash without hearing his explanation.

Back at the ashram, I found Sergio and Anjali in the manager's office. *Does she know he pulled a gun on me and called me a Jew coward?* She was busy photocopying documents. I thought it was strange to see a future Raja Yoga guru doing something as mundane as office work, and even stranger when I realized she was doing it for Sergio.

The Italian greeted me with a huge, insincere grin. "Greenbaum, what can I do for you?"

I explained that my visa was about to expire, and I needed to fly to Nepal to apply for a new one. But he knew all about it. He told me where to go in Bombay to buy my ticket, where I should eat, and even made a couple of suggestions about where I could stay overnight in Kathmandu. After our recent altercation, I found his friendly behavior creepy. I wanted to get away from him as quickly as possible. I turned to leave, but Anjali stopped me.

"How does your family feel about your living in India and being so far away from home?" she asked, handing Sergio a stack of copies.

"They realize I'm an adult, and can make my own choices."

Sergio leafed through the papers. Baba's future successor gazed deeply into my eyes, the way Baba sometimes did. It was impossible for me to look away. I felt the overwhelming urge to stare back into her eyes until I became completely lost in them.

Nodding thoughtfully, she broke eye contact, picked up another stack of documents and returned to the photocopier. *Can she read my mind?* I wondered.

"Go to Bombay and take care of your ticket soon, Greenbaum," Sergio said, looking up at me. "Don't waste no time. A lot is going to happen in the ashram over the next few days, and you won't be able to leave."

As our train pulled into Churchgate Station, we were greeted by the familiar stench of rotting fish. The heat and humidity was more brutal in the city than in the shady gardens of the Ravipur ashram. The midday sun's rays burned mercilessly. We hailed a taxi and told the driver to take us to the traditional Indian women's clothing store, Kala Niketan, which turned out to be only a few blocks away. According to Katie, Kala Niketan was where all of Baba's *darshan* girls shopped. When we arrived at the store, Gili pulled a few rupee notes out of her purse.

"Let me give you something for the fare," she said.

"Not necessary," I said, holding the door open for her as she stepped out of the cab. I told the driver that we'd be at least half an hour, but that he should wait.

"I know!" Katie exclaimed, locking elbows with me. "Let's pretend we're married!"

Inside the store, a man was waving incense and ringing a hand bell in front of a framed poster of Lord Krishna. The god was depicted in his incarnation as *divine lover*, serenading a group of beautiful young women known as the gopis.

"G'day, my good sir," Katie said to a man behind the counter. "My husband would like to buy me the most beautiful and therefore most expensive sari in the shop." The man's eyes darted to me for a moment, and then back to Katie. "Wouldn't you, darling?"

"Um ..."

Katie elbowed me in the ribs.

"Yes, that's right. Please show my wife your finest silk saris."

The man looked me up and down for a moment before responding. "Very good, sir. Madam, won't you please follow me?"

After the girls browsed for what seemed like hours, Andy and I were thoroughly bored.

"Could be worse," Andy said. "At least it's air-conditioned in here."

In the end, Katie picked out an elaborate ghagra choli ensemble, instead of a traditional sari. Despite her initial lack of interest, Gili also ended up finding something—a bright blue sari with genuine gold thread.

Katie's mouth dropped when she heard the price.

"Don't feel bad, Katie," Gili said. "Mine is also too expensive."

"Do you have anything a little cheaper but also nice?" the Australian girl asked.

"I assure you, madam—these are *top quality* items. How much you want to pay, sir?"

The girls followed an underling to another section of the store, and I made a quick calculation of how much the shopkeeper was asking in dollars, and then reached for my wallet. "We'll take them."

"You're a nutter, mate," Andy said as I paid.

Of course, I knew he was right. I was totally insane to spend that kind of money so frivolously, but I wanted to impress my new friends.

Gili scolded me when she found out. "Are you *meshuga*, or something? It's too expensive. I don't want it! Take it back!"

Katie felt differently, and she showed it by jumping into my arms and giving me a sloppy kiss on the mouth.

The door to the shop opened and two Western women entered. When Katie was finished thanking me with her lips, I realized the women were Gopi and Parvati.

Parvati laughed and smiled cruelly when she saw the girl in my arms. Gopi's mouth fell open, and the color drained from her face.

"What did you buy?" Parvati asked, turning to Katie.

"It's a ghagra choli. I'm going to wear it to the *pattabhishek*!"

Parvati sneered. "You can't wear that to a religious ceremony."

"Can too," Katie said, releasing me from her embrace. "I can bloody well wear whatever I want to! Come on, Gili, I want to show you something."

Gili followed Katie to the other end of the store. Andy raised his eyebrows and tapped the face of his watch at me.

"What are you doing in Bombay, Deependra?" Gopi asked.

"I came to book a flight to Kathmandu. My visa is about to expire."

"I see," she said, looking away.

Returning to my side, Katie and Gili erupted in giggles.

"Where are you staying?" asked Parvati.

"The Taj Mahal Palace Hotel," announced Katie, puffing out her chest and looking down her nose at the princesses.

Gopi's shoulders drooped and her face went slack. "Of course you are."

Andy, Katie, Gili, and I piled back into the taxi. Andy sat up front, and I sat in between the two girls in the rear.

"The Taj Palace in Colaba, please," I told the driver, and we were on our way.

"Did you see Gopi's face?" Katie asked. "She was dying of jealousy!"

Gili frowned. "I doubt that very much."

"It's bloody obvious," Katie insisted. "She's got a huge crush on him."

I felt a headache coming on. "Can we talk about something else?"

"Good afternoon, sir!" the Sikh doorman said with a warm smile. "Welcome back to the Taj!"

I felt a surge of pride. "I was here so long ago—you still remember me?"

"Of course, I do, sir."

I tipped him extravagantly.

I checked into the hotel while the others waited in the Harbor Bar. Having just shelled out a lot of money for the girls' new outfits, I decided against a suite, booking a single room instead. *It will be more cozy,* I told myself.

"Just you yourself personally checking in, sir?"

"That's right," I said to the clerk. I couldn't look him in the eye.

The room had a king size bed, a large sofa, and a balcony with a spectacular view of the sea. I hoped the girls would find it romantic. I hadn't given the sleeping arrangements much thought, but figured with enough grass and booze it would all work out nicely. I tipped the bellboy, used the can, and then went back downstairs to find the others.

I found Katie and Gili at a table in the bar sipping soft drinks.

"Where's Andy?" I asked.

Katie glanced around the room. "He went to find *something* for later."

"*Some*thing?"

"You *know!*" the Australian girl teased, batting her eyes at me over a raised shoulder.

"Oh, yeah ... *something*."

Gili rolled her eyes. "He said he'd meet us later at the restaurant."

I suggested we take a stroll across the street to see the Gateway to India, but Katie insisted on seeing the room. In order to avoid suspicion, I went up first. Five minutes later there was a knock on the door, and I let the girls in.

"It's splendid!" Katie said, looking around the room with big eyes.

Gili stared at the big bed and frowned. "It's a hotel room. What's so *splendid* about it?"

"Look, it's got a balcony and a view of the sea and everything!" Katie continued.

Gili folded her arms across her chest and glared at me. "There's only one bed. Where are Katie and I supposed to sleep?"

"We'll figure it out," I said, massaging the back of my neck.

There was a knock on the door. I rushed over and looked through the peephole. I immediately recognized the heavyset Indian woman from my last stay.

"Hotel security!" I whispered. "Get in the shower, you two."

There was another knock.

"Just a minute, please!" I called through the closed door.

The girls made a dash for the bathroom, hopped into the tub, and I pulled the shower curtain closed behind them.

I opened the door.

"Good afternoon," the woman said curtly. "I am Mrs. C.N. Narendra from hotel security."

I opened the door wider, and stood aside so that the woman and her assistant could enter. Unlike the Sikh doorman, Mrs. Narendra didn't seem to recognize me from my last stay.

After glancing around the room, she let herself onto the balcony. I coughed and scratched the back of my head. I knew they'd kick me out of the hotel if they found Katie and Gili.

"Please excuse the intrusion, sir," the woman said, skipping the bathroom on her way out. "Enjoy your stay at the Taj Palace."

Closing the door behind them, I waited a few seconds, and then called for the girls to come out of hiding.

"What were they looking for?" Katie asked, stepping out of the bathroom.

Gili answered for me. "Us."

I dropped the room key off at reception and took a short walk with the girls to Leopold's Cafe, where we met Andy for lunch. On the way, we passed the Bowen Memorial Church. Through its open windows came strains of beautiful singing that sounded like a cross between Hindu chanting and gospel music. Inside, worshippers stood with their arms raised in the air and their eyes screwed shut. They sang with tremendous passion, swaying from side to side in time to the music.

"What's going on in there?" Katie asked, gesturing toward the church.

"Christians," Gili said. "Bombay has a couple of synagogues, too."

When we arrived at the restaurant, Andy was already seated. But he wasn't alone. Avadhoot was sitting across the table from him, sipping a soft drink. I got a sinking feeling when I saw him.

"Boychik!"

I swallowed hard. "Avadhoot, fancy meeting you here."

His thirty-five millimeter camera and ten-gallon hat were on the empty chair next to him. He knew very well that I'd be in Bombay, arranging my trip to Kathmandu. I wondered why he hadn't told me he was also coming to the city. In any case, the guru would be furious when he found out what I was up to with Andy and the girls. Then I had another completely radical thought: *Do I care?*

"Sit, sit!" Avadhoot said. "Andrew here was just telling me that you're all staying at the Taj together. An excellent choice! I'm at the Oberoi—the ashram gets a discount."

Avadhoot's eyes followed Gili's breasts as she sat in the only free chair. Katie and I waited a moment for Avadhoot to remove his property from the empty seat. When he didn't, we pulled up chairs from another table.

"Have you been here before?" the photographer asked.

"No," the girls said.

"You're gonna love it! I eat here whenever I'm in Bombay."

The waiter came and we ordered. Avadhoot continued to dominate the conversation.

"So, listen guys, I have an incredible idea for a new restaurant. It's a totally new concept!"

"Let's hear it, mate," Andy said, sipping his beer.

"It's gonna serve food from a made-up country."

"What do you mean, a made-up country?" Katie asked, wrinkling her nose.

"One that doesn't actually exist. The dishes will be totally unique. Like nothing anyone has ever tasted before."

"What about the decor?" Gili asked. She was playing along.

"Generic European—nothing anyone can pin down to a specific place."

"You know what, mate?" Andy said. "As insane as your idea sounds, I think it's pretty clever. It could work in a town like Sydney."

Gili smirked. "I think it's the stupidest idea I've ever heard."

"Do you?" Avadhoot said, reaching for his camera and taking a few pictures of the beautiful Israeli. "What do you know about business?"

"More than you, obviously," Gili laughed.

"Oh yeah? Who do you think came up with the idea for the *shaktipat* retreat?"

"I don't get it," Katie said, tilting her head to one side and squishing her eyebrows together. "Is the restaurant thing supposed to be a joke?"

Ignoring the Australian, Avadhoot turned to me. "You're rich, Deependra— want to invest?"

"I'm afraid my money's all tied up for another couple of years. I can only use it for college."

Avadhoot furrowed his brow. "I'm only joking. Lighten up, man. Stop being so serious all the time!"

When lunch was over, I told the others I'd meet up with them later at the hotel. I had to get to the Thomas Cook office to book my travel to Nepal before it closed for the day. Avadhoot convinced Gili to do a little sightseeing with him. Andy wanted to score some more "stuff" for later, and Katie wanted to come with me.

Our taxi slowed to a crawl as we hit the late afternoon traffic.

Katie let out an exaggerated sigh. "We could've probably walked there faster."

She was right.

"I know—I'm sorry."

Even with the windows down, we were unbearably hot.

I thought about all the money I was throwing around, trying to impress everyone with how rich I was, and felt like a fool. At the rate I was spending, all my inheritance money from Harvey would probably be gone in a matter of days.

"What are you thinking about?" Katie asked, taking my hand in hers. Her palm was sweaty, and warm to the touch.

I was thinking about how conflicted I was. How I longed to go back to school, and how my doubts about Baba and the Mission were growing. But I couldn't bring myself to tell her about it. "I'm thinking about how beautiful you are," I said instead.

Katie smiled, turned her head toward me, closed her eyes, and puckered her lips expectantly. I leaned over and kissed her. Her mouth tasted like curry, and her face smelled like the acne medication I used in high school. She was a good kisser. I hoped my lack of experience didn't show.

Katie and I climbed two flights of stairs to the travel office in the Thomas Cook building. My legs felt like they weighed a ton. I didn't want to buy a ticket to Nepal and renew my visa. I wanted to go home.

"He'd like a round trip ticket to Kathmandu, please," Katie said to the woman behind the counter.

"Very good," the woman said. "May I see your passport, sir?"

I reached into my knapsack for my passport, and held it out for the woman to inspect. But when she reached to take it from me, I couldn't let go of it.

The woman narrowed her eyes and frowned. "Sir? Are you going to let me have your passport?"

I froze.

Katie look confused. "Deependra? Are you okay?"

A line was beginning to form behind us.

I dug into my knapsack again and pulled out my open-ended ticket back to the States, and handed it along with my passport to the woman.

"This is a ticket to New York," the woman said, growing impatient. "What would you like me to do with this?"

"Forget about the ticket to Nepal. I want to go home."

"Home, sir?"

"Back to New York."

"I don't understand," Katie said, when we were out on the street again. "I thought you were getting a round trip ticket to Kathmandu so that you could renew your visa."

"Oh, I'll be back in a couple of weeks. I just need to take care of some things in the States."

Of course I was lying. I had no plan to return to India, and I was suddenly eager to get away from the ashram as soon as possible. I had booked my travel on the first available flight—the day after *pattabhishek*. I felt lighter already.

We got a taxi back to the Taj, where I received another warm greeting from the Sikh doorman. Reaching into my wallet, I handed him another generous wad of rupee notes. *I won't be needing these anymore,* I told myself.

We found Gili sitting in the lobby. The corners of her mouth were turned down, and her arms and legs were tightly crossed. On the seat next to her were a couple of fancy shopping bags.

"Where's Avadhoot?" I asked her, hoping we were rid of him.

"Thrown out of the hotel," the Israeli grumbled.

"What happened?"

Gili told us that Avadhoot had taken her to see the Gateway of India across the street from the hotel.

"Then we did some shopping. The pervert couldn't keep his eyes off my boobs for even two seconds! When we were finished, he wanted to go upstairs with me to the room—for a *drink*, he said." Gili shook her head in disbelief. "When I told him I didn't have a key, I thought that would be the end of it, but the schmuck wouldn't take no for an answer. Instead he goes to the reception and asks for the key, pretending to be you. A minute later they kicked him out of the hotel."

Katie burst out laughing. "Crikey! What a perv!"

When I went to pick up my room key at the reception, I was told the hotel manager wanted to have a word with me. A moment later, a short, dapper man appeared behind the counter. His badge said: "P.T. Gupta – Manager." He recounted the incident with Avadhoot, whom he referred to venomously as "the impostor." He gave me a description of the photographer, and asked if he was an acquaintance of mine.

"Sorry, he doesn't sound familiar," I lied. I didn't want it to get back to the ashram that I reported him. I'd be in enough trouble when I got back to Ravipur as it was.

"Not to worry, Mr. Douglas!" the hotel manager said, brimming with confidence. "Hotel security is on high alert. If this miscreant should so much as set foot on the premises again, we will have him arrested."

"I appreciate that," I said, turning to leave.

"This isn't the first time this scoundrel has been up to his tricks at the Taj."

I turned around again. "Oh, really?"

"Yes, this very same foreigner and his band of hoodlums were here in the lobby harassing another guest only a few days ago."

Upstairs in the room, we took turns using the shower. Andy had been able to score some decent grass on the street. As each of us waited our turn for the bathroom, we passed a joint around. At dinnertime, wanting to avoid crossing paths with Avadhoot again, I called for room service, ordering almost everything vegetarian on the menu, and a bottle of champagne.

"Don't you think you're exaggerating a bit?" Gili asked when I was off the phone. "We just ate a couple of hours ago."

Katie giggled. "But I'm starving!"

Gili took a long drag on the joint, held it, and then exhaled a large plume of smoke. "You're not starving. You're stoned."

Still laughing, Katie picked up a pillow from the sofa and buried her face in it.

By the time the food came, we all had the munchies. Andy and the girls hid in the bathroom, and I opened the door for room service. Our meal was delivered on two overflowing carts, by a crew of four. I was ready with a lame excuse for why a man staying in a hotel room by himself would order so much food, but none of the attendants so much as raised an eyebrow.

As ravenously hungry as we were, we barely made a dent in the food. There was enough jalfrezi, gobhi charchi, aloo choley, korma, and naan bread left over to feed a hungry Ravipur ashramite for a month.

"Is it okay if I ring my mom in Melbourne?" Katie asked, taking a sip from my glass of champagne.

I thought back to how expensive my call to Melanie was and felt anxious.

"Of course," I answered. I didn't want Katie and the others to think I was cheap. "Are you crazy?" Gili scolded, grabbing my glass of champagne out of Katie's hand and putting it down on the dresser. "Call from a post office tomorrow! You know how much an international call will cost from a hotel like this?"

"You're no fun," Katie said, falling backward onto the king size bed.

I picked up the phone. "It's okay, don't worry about it."

The hotel operator booked the call and advised me the wait would be at least a couple of hours. They'd call up to the room as soon as it went through.

Katie took a remote from the nightstand and aimed it at the large screen TV.

"Let's see what's on the telly," she said.

The girls wanted to watch an Indian musical. Andy wanted to keep smoking pot. He sat outside on the balcony, while the girls and I sat up in bed watching the movie. We had a good laugh by supplying our own dialogue to the Hindi-speaking actors and actresses on the screen.

I was sitting between the girls, and as we watched Katie snuggled closer to me. At the same time, Gili inched away. After a while, Katie surprised me by switching off the light and kissing me. We began making out, and at this point Gili let out a sigh of disgust and relocated to the sofa.

A few minutes later, the door to the balcony opened, and Andy came back inside. A few moments later, I heard Gili start to argue with him.

"Hey!" said the Israeli. "I said *stop it!*"

"Come on, babe," whined Andy.

This was followed by a loud slap.

"Ouch! What the fuck d'you do that for?"

"No means no, asshole!" shouted Gili.

"Everything alright over there?" I asked.

"No worries, mate. She'll be right."

"Tell this jerk to keep his hands off me!"

Katie switched on the light next to our bed. Andy was hovering over us. His cheek was red. "I don't reckon I can sleep here with you folks, can I?"

Before I could answer, the telephone rang, making me start.

"Who the bloody hell could that be?" Katie demanded.

My mind immediately went to the worst-case scenarios: *It's hotel security! They're on to me and they're going to kick us out of the hotel. Or maybe it's Sergio. He found out I booked a flight home without permission from Baba. Maybe he's downstairs right now to bust me for hanging out with girls!*

"It's your trunk call to Australia, obviously," Gili said.

Meanwhile, the phone continued to ring loudly.

Katie shot up straight in the bed, and pulled the blanket over her boobs. "It's me mum! Answer it! Answer it!"

"Hello, Mr. Greenbaum?" a woman with an upper class Indian accent said on the other end of the phone. "I have Melbourne, Australia on the line for you. Go ahead please, madam."

"Hello? Who is this?" a woman with an Australian accent asked.

"Just a moment, ma'am. Your daughter's here, and she wants to speak to you."

Katie jumped out of the bed to take the call, pulling the top sheet with her to cover her bare chest.

"Mummy, hi!...No, I'm not at the ashram. I'm staying at a fancy hotel in Bombay...No, I'm not with Durga, but she knows where I am. I'm with a very nice Italian boy from the ashram."

Gili and I exchanged knowing looks.

There was a longer pause as Katie listened.

"Okay," she said finally, "put him on ... Hello, Daddy! ... No, it's not like that! What?"

Katie took the phone away from her head and handed it to me. "He says he wants to speak to *you*."

The man on the other end of the line made it abundantly clear that he would get on an airplane, come find me wherever I was, and beat me to within an inch of my life if I so much as touched a hair on his daughter's head. Then he hung up.

"Who's Durga?" I asked.

Katie stared back at me with guileless blue eyes. "She's my guardian. She's looking after me at the ashram."

"Guardian?" I repeated, "Why do you need a guardian?" Then comprehension dawned on me. "You're under eighteen, aren't you?"

Katie nodded.

"You're seventeen?"

Katie smiled. "I will be in June!"

"Fuck! Fuck! Fuck! Did you know she was underage?" I asked Gili.

Gili frowned and folded her arms across her chest. "Under age for what?"

Andy went back to the sofa and covered his head with a pillow. Gili and Katie got into the bed together and I went into the bathroom to take a cold shower. When I came back into the room, the television was switched off and all the lights were out. The shower did nothing. I was still incredibly horny.

Desperate for sex, I went to back into the bathroom to relieve myself. I tried to stop short of ejaculation, but it was no use. The need for release was too strong. The intense pleasure that accompanied orgasm, and the tremendous feeling of relief that followed it, however, soon gave way to remorse. The last time I had debased myself in this way was with Heather. *How could I have been so weak?* I thought of the countless times I had heard Baba say that in order to practice Raja Yoga, one must remain celibate. I needed my sexual energy for meditation. Then the new voice inside my head spoke up again: *Do I still care?*

With the bed and the sofa spoken for, and nowhere to sleep comfortably, I decided to go downstairs for a drink at the Harbor Bar. Feeling like I'd already had enough to drink *and* smoke for one evening, I took a seat at the bar and asked the bartender to make me a fresh lime soda, instead of a cocktail.

"Did you know that the Harbor Bar is the oldest bar in Bombay?"

The question came from a forty-something, rugged-looking white man seated next to me. He was dressed in a tweed sports jacket, white shirt, and mustard-colored tie. At his feet was a beat-up leather briefcase. He spoke with an American accent.

"No, I can't say that I did."

"Jamsedji Tata, the original owner of the Taj, was a wealthy Parsi who got the idea to build the hotel after he wasn't allowed to enter another of Bombay's grand hotels—it was restricted to whites only."

"You don't say," I said, making a minimal attempt at being polite. "The story I know about the Taj is that supposedly the construction people got the plans confused and built the place backwards, facing away from the harbor. When the architect came to inspect the site and saw what they'd done to his masterpiece, he was so upset he committed suicide by jumping off the tower."

The man laughed and shook his head. "That's a good story, but it's just a myth. Tata deliberately built the Taj facing inland so that horse carriages bringing guests to the hotel could more easily approach it from the city."

"Oh," I said, taking another sip of my soda.

"I'll take another Scotch on the rocks," the man said to the bartender. "Would you like another one, Doug?"

"No, thank you," I answered. Then I did a double take. "How do you know my name?"

"I'm very pleased to finally meet you," he said, extending a hand for me to shake. "I'm Chris Walsh."

41.
SATYANANDA'S LETTER

DESPITE MY PREVIOUS INTEREST in talking to Walsh, my first instinct was to get away from him. I stood up and reached for my wallet to pay for my drink.

"I'm sorry, Mr. Walsh," I said. "I shouldn't be talking to you."

Walsh was the enemy. I had been explicitly told *not* to talk to him. If Avadhoot was still lurking around the hotel and saw me speaking to the journalist, he'd tell Sergio and Baba. My life in Raja Yoga would be over, and I wasn't yet sure if I wanted it to end. Still, part of me wanted to hear him out.

"I want you to know, Doug, I think your going to the hospital to talk to Daniel Groza back in Oakland was really brave. It took a lot of guts."

"How do you know who I am?"

"Are you sure you wouldn't like another drink?"

"Alright, fine," I answered, sitting back down. I glanced over my shoulder. I didn't see anyone from the ashram. "What's that you're drinking? I'll have one of those."

Chris got the bartender's attention and ordered me an Old Fashioned instead.

"Everything on the up and up, Mr. Walsh?" the bartender asked.

"Yes, thank you, Vikram, everything's fine now," Chris said, raising his drink to salute the bartender.

"What did you mean by fine *now*?" I asked.

"A few days ago we had a bit of a scene here at the hotel, with some of your coreligionists. The management informed me earlier that someone from the ashram was here again this afternoon." The bartender set our drinks down in front of us. "Vikram here is just looking out for me."

"What'd they do?"

"Rudrananda's right-hand man, Sergio Casto, and that freak who dresses like a cowboy, tried to intimidate me into not publishing the piece I'm writing on the Mission."

I tried my drink. The concoction tasted like liquid smoke and fermented fruit. It stung my throat going down. I took another swig of it.

Walsh told me he'd been investigating Baba and the Mission for the past year and a half. He had interviewed over two dozen current and former devotees.

"To you and to most of his followers, Rudrananda is a great saint with tremendous spiritual power," Chris said. "But to others, he's a very flawed and ordinary man who doesn't practice what he preaches. He's repeatedly broken his vows of celibacy, and has had relations with dozens of his female devotees—including underage girls and married women. He's made millions of dollars from the blood and sweat of his followers, and has allowed guns and violence in his ashrams."

"Why do you want to interview me?" I asked, taking another swig of my cocktail. "What can I tell you that you don't already know?"

"I've wanted to speak to you ever since the Grozas told me how you showed up at the hospital to tip off Daniel that

Chamundi hadn't really been attacked. To me, you sounded like someone with a conscience. From the moment I heard about you, I knew you wouldn't last long as one of Casto's lackeys."

I didn't know what to say. I swirled the ice around in my glass, and then took another sip.

"Palash Chaapkhanawala came to see me here at the hotel the other day. He told me you had come around the spa looking for me."

"I still don't understand how you recognized me," I said.

Chris explained that someone had pointed me out to him back in Birchwood Falls. "Do you have something you want to tell me, Doug?"

Do I have something to tell him? I asked myself. No, I did not. I'd never directly witnessed anything in the ashram that would corroborate what his supposed witnesses had told him about Baba.

"Not really," I muttered.

Chris took another sip of his drink. "How do you like the Old Fashioned?"

"Okay, I guess." I took another sip and decided to take a chance. "I want to ask *you* something. Baba awakened a spiritual energy in me called *kundalini*. I know without a shadow of a doubt that this really happened. If Baba isn't what he says he is, how would that have been possible?"

Chris was thoughtful for a moment, and then spoke. "Have you ever heard of Franz Mesmer?"

"I don't think so."

"The word *mesmerize* comes from his name and Mesmerism later came to be called hypnotism. Mesmer was a German physician who lived in the eighteenth and early nineteenth centuries. He claimed he'd discovered an invisible force flowing through channels in the human body. He believed rare individuals, such as himself, could control the flow of this energy through the power of their will. He called this power 'animal magnetism' and he developed an elaborate theory of its effect on health."

"Sounds like acupuncture or something. What does this have to do with Baba?"

Chris nodded confidently. "He used to receive all his patients together in a dimly lit room, play spooky music, and move around mysteriously in a purple cloak, administering his 'treatment' with a touch of his hand, a penetrating look, or a tap from a metal wand."

"And what happed to his patients?"

They had all kinds of amazing reactions. Some fell into a trance, others cried out, some had convulsions, others experienced odd bodily sensations. Whatever manifested, however bizarre, Mesmer claimed, was exactly what the sick person needed to make a full recovery. Sound familiar?"

"It sounds like these people had a genuine experience of the divine, even though Mesmer was a false prophet," I said. "Is that your point about Baba? Are you saying that even though he may be an imperfect vessel, the grace-bestowing power of God still flows through him?"

"No, actually," Chris said. "I don't believe that for a second. Mesmer was a master hypnotist, and so is Rudrananda. And they both used many of the same techniques. Mesmer also used to attract a lot of rich people and high society types, and charged a lot of money for his 'treatments' to rule out skeptics."

"What are you saying?"

"If a *shaktipat* retreat is expensive enough, you ensure that everybody attending is already heavily invested in receiving this so-called '*kundalini awakening.*' The chanting, the incense, the votive candles—all of these things help to induce a highly suggestible state."

"No, but you're wrong," I said. "When I received Baba's touch I had a classic *kundalini* awakening, with all the signs and symptoms. I felt a powerful energy moving up my spine and explode when it reached the *chakra* in my heart. I saw lights—I entered a higher state of consciousness. All of that really happened to me!"

Chris shrugged and took another sip of his drink. "People experience all kinds of crazy stuff when they're under hypnosis, Doug."

Anger surged inside of me. "Sorry, but I don't buy it. I wasn't hypnotized! I can still feel Baba's *shakti* working inside of me."

Chris tilted his head to one side and his eyes grew sympathetic. "Post-hypnotic suggestion."

I had heard enough. Who was this interloper to tell me whether I had experienced divine awakening or not? I got up to leave. This time, I didn't take out my wallet to pay.

"I know it's a lot to digest all at once, Doug." Chris reached for his briefcase, opened it, and pulled out a few sheets of paper. "I'd like you to take this with you and read it when you have a chance."

"What's this?" I snapped, snatching the document from his hand.

"It's Swami Satyananda's open letter to Rudrananda. The one your Baba told all the ashram managers and center leaders to burn."

"Satyananda? Are you kidding? I know him—the man is an egomaniac and a traitor. Thinks he's already enlightened!"

"I've spoken to him at length," Chris said, "and that's not how he sounded to me."

The journalist gave me his card. He urged me to contact him when I was ready. He wanted to hear in my own words how Avadhoot and Sergio had convinced me to help intimidate the Grozas, and why I got cold feet.

"Read the letter, Doug. Draw your own conclusions."

When I returned to the room, everyone was sound asleep. I felt emotionally drained and exhausted. I went into the bathroom, switched on the light, and closed the door. I thought about tearing up the envelope with the letter and flushing it down the toilet. But I couldn't bring myself to do it. My longing to know the truth was too powerful.

OPEN LETTER OF CONDEMNATION

FROM SWAMI SATYANANDA TO RUDRANANDA

Dear Rudrananda,

It is with the most profound sadness and regret that I must now bear painful witness to you and to all my dear brothers and sisters in the Raja Yoga movement.

In Manhattan, in the summer of 1983, a young woman named Cassandra Hayes came to me claiming that you, Rudrananda, had taken advantage of her sexually in your private quarters in the Birchwood Falls ashram. I doubted her outrageous allegation. She stated that you summoned her to your chambers, asked her to remove her clothes, sit on a table, and spread her legs for you, while you took liberties with her under the pretense of verifying her purity. Initially, I was angry with this young woman. I was certain she was lying. "How could Baba, a perfected master of Raja Yoga, ever do such a thing?" Then I told myself that even if you had touched her, she misunderstood your motives and that there must have been some reason for your actions. At the time, I dismissed her account as the confabulation of a disturbed mind, and kept my conversation with the young woman to myself.

Not long after this incident, I received a phone call from my dear friend, Swami Krishnananda, from Melbourne, Australia, to inform me that he had left Raja Yoga and why. He said that a devotee by the name of Nathan Brown, a.k.a. Govinda, had come to him with a grievance: after falling from a scaffolding in the Ravipur ashram, he broke his back, and was bedridden in a Bombay hospital for several weeks. He told Krishnananda that during this period you took his wife and his fourteen-year-old daughter under your wing, and made sure that they were comfortable in the ashram. He said you doted on his daughter and received her on several occasions in your private quarters. At the time, he was extremely grateful. Later he discovered, to his horror, that you had been sexually molesting his child—touching her inappropriately and probing around inside her.

After hearing from Krishnananda, I could no longer keep silent. When I reported to you what I heard from him and from Cassandra Hayes, you screamed and cursed at me over the telephone like a madman.

You subsequently began your campaign to discredit the Browns, along with the swami, so that no one would believe their story. Krishnananda, you told me, was "a piece of excrement" who had left the ashram because he was a "loathsome homosexual" and wanted to have sex with young boys. The Browns, you said, were drug smugglers and spies for another guru who had planted them in the ashram to destroy your reputation.

You ordered me to make collect phone calls to Krishnananda and the Browns in Australia, and instructed me to tell them that you were "all-powerful and all-knowing" and that they should stop spreading lies about you or your loyal followers everywhere would silence them one way or another. You also ordered me to spread false rumors about Cassandra Hayes, to tell people that she was a whore who had undergone multiple abortions, and to lie saying that she had tried to seduce me in the Manhattan ashram.

Despite your numerous attempts to enlist me in your crusades of slander and intimidation, I proved uncooperative. In an effort to bully me into submission, you flew Sergio Casto and Walter Plotnick, a.k.a. Avadhoot, to New York to assault me. They threatened further brutality if I did not toe the line. Yet even after the revelations about the dark side of your character, and the physical violence wrought upon me by your henchmen, I continued to hold out the desperate hope that there was some method to your madness. I continued to believe in you as my Guru, and as a perfected master of Raja Yoga.

Fearing that sooner or later I would talk, you removed me from my prominent position as spiritual director of the Manhattan ashram and sent me into exile in Wichita, Kansas. My mission, you said, was to establish a new Raja Yoga ashram. Despite my growing doubts about you and your motives, I willingly went there as your devoted servant. Unbeknownst to me, however, you had set me up for failure from the outset. You sent me to a region where you had never visited, and where no one had even heard of you. Instead of providing me with enough funding for publicity or to purchase a suitable property for a future ashram, you sent me to Kansas virtually penniless. Even more curiously, you sent Craig Williams, a.k.a. Gajendra, to Wichita in advance of my arrival with the instructions to rent a two-bedroom apartment in a dilapidated building, which he arranged for me to share with three young women who had no connection to Raja Yoga. Not only did the women have no interest in meditation or spirituality, I later found out that they worked at a local strip club.

With everything in place for you to launch a smear campaign against me, you flew Stephen Ames and Clara Defournier, a.k.a. Gopi, to visit me on a fact finding mission, with the results of their investigation predetermined. When they returned to California they told anyone who would listen how I had done nothing to establish a Raja Yoga presence in Wichita and was squandering the Guru's money. They claimed that I knowingly set up house with prostitutes and had most certainly broken my vows as a swami.

Shortly after this watershed event in my relationship with you, I heard still more horrors. A former mission trustee and long-time disciple of yours called me from Berkeley to tell me that you, Rudrananda, had enlisted a young member of your tour staff by the name of Douglas Greenbaum, a.k.a. Deependra, to impersonate an emergency room employee. According to the devotee, you had Deependra call Daniel Groza, who had recently left your services, with the false news that his wife had been attacked with acid and lay in the hospital badly disfigured and in terrible pain. Your goal, presumably, was to keep them from talking. Daniel and his wife, it turned out, had been close dis-

ciples of yours for many years and were in a position to corroborate many of the outrageous stories already circulating about you. Rather than silence them, your threats of violence only served to embolden them. They told everyone they knew about your sexual exploits with young girls in your chambers, and contacted an investigative reporter. You, in turn, stepped up your intimidation tactics and sent your goons to warn them that if they spoke to any reporters about you they would be "taken care of." Fearing for their safety, they turned to the district attorney in Berkeley. Remarkably, even after the couple filed a lawsuit against you and the mission, you continued to threaten them with castration and other violence.

Knowing in my heart that it was my duty to uncover the truth, I abandoned my post in Kansas and flew to California to investigate the allegations about you myself. In Berkeley, I met personally with the Grozas. They confirmed that the previously mentioned events had actually occurred. They also told me that dozens of girls in their early to middle teens had spoken of having sexual relations with you over the years in the name of Tantric initiation. Many of these girls and their parents are ready to speak the truth about you—and have agreed to meet with the journalist who is planning to write an exposé.

In the past, Rudrananda, I was able to excuse most of your outlandish behavior. "The actions of an enlightened being are impossible to understand with an ordinary mind," I heard you say time and again. But now, after everything that has come to light, I can no longer find a way to rationalize the treachery and exploitation that you have visited upon your faithful devotees. I can no longer find a way to expand my vision of an enlightened being to include the monster you have become. You believe you are above morality, treating your followers as objects for your own gratification and destroying the lives of others for your own selfish ends. It is therefore my duty to leave your service, and to warn others about you. I end my discipleship to you with heartfelt anguish, Rudrananda. May God have mercy on your soul.

*Sincerely,
Harold L. Frost a.k.a. Swami Satyananda*

"DEEPENDRA... DEEPENDRA." MY EYES cracked open. Andy was standing above me. I had fallen asleep on the bathroom floor. It was morning.

"Sorry, mate, but I've got to drain the lizard, and I can't hold it in any longer."

We ate breakfast in the hotel restaurant. The Taj had an enormous buffet, with both traditional Indian and Western options. I felt awful. Like I was dead inside. Andy looked as jolly as ever, and Katie was annoyingly cheerful. Gili, however, looked miserable. Her eyes were red and she looked like she'd been crying.

At the buffet I ordered an omelet with cheese. I checked out the vegetarian items on offer, and eyed some delicious-looking sausage. The new voice inside me spoke again. *Go ahead, you know you want them.* It was the first meat I had eaten in almost four years.

"Bugger me dead!" Andy exclaimed, staring wide-eyed at the sausage links on my plate. "What's gotten into you, mate?"

"They look good, don't they?" I said. "Want one?"

"Not on yer life."

Katie covered her mouth and laughed at Andy. "What? It's okay to smoke dope in the ashram, but it's not okay to eat some meat when you're fifty miles away from the place?"

Andy grimaced. "Animal flesh is disgusting."

I cut off another morsel of one of the links and popped it in my mouth. It was delicious, but too rich for me. *I'll have to get used to eating meat again slowly,* I told myself.

I looked up from my enormous plate of food and noticed Gili wasn't eating. "*Kol beseder?*" I asked her, remembering the two of the few words of Hebrew I knew. It meant: "Everything alright?"

"*Lo! Lo beseder!*" she snapped.

I knew that meant: "No, not okay!"

She kicked me under the table, got up, and stomped out of the restaurant into the lobby.

Katie's mouth dropped in mock surprise. "I'll be stuffed! What's her problem?"

"She's a moody one, that Israeli," Andy said. "No wonder they make so many enemies."

I got up from the table and went to look for Gili. I found her sitting on a sofa in the lobby. Tears of frustration were rolling down her cheeks. I sat next to her. She pretended I wasn't there.

"What's the matter?" I finally asked. "Did something happen?"

"Did something happen?" she repeated, her eyes glaring. "You turned out to be a jerk—just like everyone else in the ashram. That's what happened!"

"Me? What did *I* do?"

"Playing the game with my feet under the table in Prasad. You pretend you like me—and then you spend the day with that little blonde bitch, and try to fuck her right in front of me. She's not even a grown woman. Is that what you want—a little girl?"

I thought of the things Satyananda had accused Baba of in his letter, and felt nauseated.

"Look, I had no idea she was only sixteen! She never told me her age. I just—"

"Whatever!" Gili snapped, wiping the tears from her face with the back of her hand. "I don't care anymore. I'm done with all of you!"

"Listen, I really do like you. I'm sorry for the misunderstanding. I'm not interested in Katie at all—was just fooling around."

"Just fooling around?" She shook her head in disgust. "Didn't nobody ever teach you not to fool around with other people's feelings?"

The four of us rode the train and bus back to Ravipur. Katie and Andy slept most of the way, and Gili refused to speak to me. I had totally blown it with her.

42.
Trespassers

BACK AT THE ASHRAM, I didn't feel like socializing. I went for supper to the dining hall, where I could eat by myself. The austerity of the place, and its cool marble floor, complemented my mood. Almost as soon as I sat down, Namdev Loman spotted me from the other side of the hall, and came over to sit next to me.

"What's a big shot like you doing in a place like this?" he asked. "I thought you only ate in Prasad."

We weren't supposed to talk in the dining room, but I didn't give a shit anymore. "You're right. I usually do. The food sucks in here."

Namdev started to laugh, but ended up in a coughing fit. "You okay?"

He nodded, and then finally stopped coughing. His face was drawn, and he was thinner than ever. *I have to get him out of this place before he drops dead of exhaustion*, I thought.

I didn't feel much like talking, but listened as Namdev went off on one of his rants against the ashram. He told me he was still doing *seva* in the generator plant, but that the ashram library was closed down.

"What happened?" I asked him.

"I arrived at the library to find a big pile of books on the floor, and Sita Perkins pulling more books off the shelves and adding to it with a big shit eating grin on her face. Then she told me to take all the books in the pile to Housekeeping to be burned. I looked through the books she wanted to get rid of and couldn't believe my eyes: they included a bunch of crappy novels, but also the *Bible*, and other spiritual books by Indian saints that Baba reveres—anything that had not been published by the Mission had to go!"

Part of me was outraged, but nothing in Raja Yoga surprised me anymore. I just felt sad.

"What did you do?" I asked.

"When no one was around, I went to Housekeeping before they had a chance to burn them, sorted through the pile, and took a bunch of the better books back to my room."

"Wasn't it locked?"

An enormous smile spread over Namdev's face. Then he dug into his pocket and pulled out a big key ring, like the ones the ashram security guards carried.

"I've got a master key to all the buildings," he whispered, before stuffing it back into his pants. "I haven't tried all of them, but I'm pretty sure one of them opens the door to Baba's house."

"Where the fuck did you find it?" I asked, speaking a bit too loudly.

Prakashananda, the shirtless Indian swami, glared at us from the door to the kitchen and went, "Shhhhh!"

"I found it on one of the garden paths coming back from the generator plant," Namdev said, when the swami was out of earshot again. "One of the guards must have dropped it."

I nodded and continued eating.

"You think I should turn them in, don't you? Isn't that what you're going to tell me?"

"You want to know what I really think?" I said, no longer whispering. "I think we never should have left Ithaca."

"Deependra?"

I looked up. Gajendra Williams was staring down at me, frowning. I wanted to disappear into the floor. I was afraid he had heard me.

"I need your passport back. Bring it by the office before the chant tonight."

"Oh yeah," I answered. "Sorry, I forgot."

Indira St. John was alone in the office when I came to return my passport, and she greeted me with a pleasant smile. She was using the telex machine. She had been back from the hospital for a while now, and had recovered from her bout of hepatitis. The color of her face had returned to normal, but she was still much thinner, paler, and older looking than when I had first met her.

With an uneasy feeling, I handed her my passport.

WHEN I REPORTED TO *seva* in the Audiovisual room the next morning, Avadhoot was friendly—too friendly.

"Back from the big city already? Where are your lovely friends?"

"I'm not in the habit of bringing my friends to *seva* with me," I answered.

"Friends like that? You should, you should! Feel free!"

"Maybe tomorrow," I said, going along with his stupid joke.

I sat at the table to clean the heads of the VTRs and Avadhoot spoke to me again. This time he was more serious.

"Actually, I've spoken to Baba about the Israeli girl—Gili. He wants her transferred to the princess dorm. She'll be helping out with *darshan* now."

"Lucky her," I said, making no effort to hide my sarcasm. Then I put down what I was doing, stood up and faced the photographer. "Avadhoot, why did you ask for my room key at the Taj?"

"*Excuse me?* Ask for your room key? I don't know what the fuck you're talking about!"

"I think you do. Gili was there when the manager spoke to you. She said they kicked you out of the hotel."

Avadhoot denied the whole thing. "There must have been a misunderstanding," he said. "The girl told me she was tired of schlepping her shopping bags around. When I suggested she put them upstairs in the room, she complained that only you could ask for the key. Not very cool, by the way. You didn't think your friends were entitled to a key? Some friend *you are!*"

"The point is," I interrupted, "you were pretending to be me and were unlawfully trying to gain access to my room."

Avadhoot laughed. "Un*law*fully? What are you, a lawyer? Ask your girlfriend, she'll vouch for me."

He was so convincing I began to think that maybe Gili had wanted to get into the room, and made up the part about how Avadhoot wanted to have a drink with her up there. *Who knows? Who cares?* I told myself.

I was about to call him out on the altercation he supposedly had with Walsh, but decided to drop it. I didn't want anyone to know I'd spoken to the journalist.

Baba sat for *darshan* in the courtyard that afternoon, and was unusually quiet. I looked for Gili among the other princesses sitting up front. But she wasn't there. I did see Gopi, however. She was sitting directly behind Anjali at Baba's feet, and as painfully beautiful as ever.

I thought about getting in line and bowing down before the guru as usual, but decided to go back to my room instead. I caught Gopi's eye as I left the courtyard. She looked sad.

That evening, Suresh announced that we would begin a non-stop chanting *saptah* until the *pattabhishek*, which was scheduled one week from that day.

"As the preparations intensify," he said, "there will be extra *seva* for everybody."

At the Audiovisual office, Kriyadevi reminded me to report to Sita first thing in the morning to receive an additional assignment. Hundreds of people, mostly from the

West, were yet to arrive for the ceremony. Extra mattresses had to be brought to all the rooms to accommodate them, the grounds and gardens needed work, and the decoration of the *mandap* still needed to be finished.

I didn't attend the *saptah* the first night. Instead I stood on the far side of the courtyard next to the entrance to Baba's house, listening and observing for a while. As I watched the believers chant their hearts out, I realized that only a few days earlier I would've been one of them.

But I'd never be one of them again. I felt angry and betrayed. I didn't want to meditate, I didn't want to chant, and I didn't want to pray. I wanted to get out of the ashram. The sooner the better.

Suddenly the door to the guru's house opened, and Baba stepped out into the courtyard, only a few feet from me. I was startled, but not as nervous as I would've been in the past. He was accompanied by his two successors, Suresh and Anjali. By force of habit, I tried to quiet my mind and hide my thoughts from the guru, even though I was beginning to suspect he couldn't read my mind at all.

Baba stood facing me with his hands behind his back, looking me up and down. Then he spoke to me through Anjali. "Baba asks why you are not at the chant."

"I was right about to go to the chant, Babaji," I lied, and then closely observed his reaction to see if he could tell I was not being truthful. "*Aacha, aacha,*" was all he said in response. "Good, good."

There was nothing in his expression to indicate that he doubted me. Taking it a step further, I tried to send him a message telepathically: *Maybe you can't hear my thoughts, after all,* Rudrananda. *Maybe you're a big fat phony!*

Again, he gave no sign he heard me. I folded my hands and bowed my head in respect.

The guru smiled, and I felt nothing. Then he crossed the courtyard to the open-air hall, where throngs of adoring devotees were waiting for him.

I SLEPT IN. I didn't go to meditation or the chant, and I failed to report to Sita at the *seva* office by eight a.m. as I'd been ordered. Not only that, even though I received my new room assignment a few days before, I still hadn't moved back into my old dormitory.

Why? I wanted to see how long I could get away without doing any of these things before I got into trouble.

At lunch I sat with Katie and Andy in the Prasad pavilion, where we lingered over ice-cold *Thumbs-up* colas. *Soon I'll be enjoying Coke again,* I told myself. *The real thing.*

Gili sat alone on the other side of the pavilion. I invited her to join us at our table, but she declined. So I went over and sat with her instead.

"I heard you were transferred to the Princess dorm."

"Ha!" Gili exclaimed. "That's a laugh! I wouldn't be caught dead sharing a room with any of those spoiled brats."

"So, you're not helping with *darshan* either?"

"That Italian guy—what's his name? Spazzio? Silvio?"

"Sergio."

"He offered me the job. Told me Baba said that I was 'very pure' and should be sitting up front."

"And you said no?"

"Of course I said no."

"What was Sergio's reaction?"

"He didn't say nothing, but a few hours later that miserable man—Gajendra Williams—the manager—told me he thought it was best if I didn't stay in the ashram anymore. He said the ashram and I 'weren't a good fit.'"

"So, when are you leaving?"

"He said I could stay until the *pattabhishek*."

"And are you?"

"Well, I don't really have a choice: I've already booked my flight home and my room and board are paid up until the end of the week." The Israeli smirked. "Anyway, I don't want to miss the *big show!*"

I returned to my table, and Andy and Katie convinced me to do my impressions of famous ashramites. I started with the lisping Brian. This time, with nothing to lose, I held nothing back. Katie laughed so hard she cried.

Waving my hands around, and speaking manically of "my" idea for a new restaurant concept, I imitated Avadhoot. People in the immediate vicinity applauded, and Andy nearly fell off his chair.

"This isn't a comedy club, Deependra!" shouted Sita, who was seated at the next table. "This an ashram!"

Katie got up and bussed her tray. Andy giggled.

Sita glared at him. "And why aren't you at *seva*, Andy?"

Without responding, the Australian shot up, bussed his tray, and rushed out of the pavilion in the direction of the ashram gardens.

Sita trained her sights back on me. "Didn't Kriyadevi tell you to come by the *seva* office this morning? Everyone is doing extra work this week."

"Oh yeah," I said, yawning and scratching my head. "As soon as I finish moving into my new room, I'll drop by."

The *seva* manager eyed me dubiously. "You're going to be working in Housing. VIPs are still arriving, and we have a lot of furniture to shuffle around."

I didn't have a lot of stuff, so changing rooms only took a few minutes. All I had to move were my clothes, Raja Yoga books and tapes, and my framed pictures of Baba and Gurudev Brahmananda.

As I set the photos of the gurus on the altar shelf above my new bed, my eyes lingered on the picture of Baba I had purchased four years earlier, at the center in Ithaca. I was struck by how different he looked to me now. The face of the benevolent father who once stared back at me with limitless compassion had been replaced with the face of a con man.

Who are you? I asked the stranger in the photo.

Baba's words came back to me: "The guru is however you see him: If you see him as a god, he is a god. If you see him as a demon, he is a demon. If you see him as an ordinary man, he is an ordinary man."

I see a fraud and a pervert!

Leaving the pictures of Gurudev where they were, I snatched Baba's photos off the shelf and stuffed them back in my bag.

I needed to use the toilet and remembered I no longer had the luxury of a private bathroom. I found one of my new roommates in my floor's communal bathroom—a tall beefy man from Argentina. He was shaving with one hand, and holding his penis and peeing into the sink with the other.

One more week! I told myself.

I relieved myself in one of the squat toilets. Before heading over to the *seva* office, I stuck my head into Namdev Loman's library, on the off chance he was in there. I found him sitting on the floor, against the wall, his face buried in his hands.

"Excuse me, sir," I said. "Do you have *The Catcher in the Rye* by J.D. Salinger?"

"Hilarious," Namdev said, standing up. He looked even more miserable than usual.

"Are you okay?"

"Kicked out," he mumbled.

"What?"

"I'm getting kicked out of the ashram. I have to leave right after the *pattabhishek.*"

"You're not the only one. If it's any consolation, I'm leaving too. But please keep it to yourself. I haven't told anybody yet."

You don't understand," he said. "My parents don't answer my letters or take my phone calls. I've got no money, nowhere to go—I've got nobody."

"It'll all work out," I told him. "You'll see. I'm sure it's for the best."

Namdev slid back down to the floor in a heap and burst out crying.

Then an unfamiliar feeling came over me: it was as if his suffering were my own suffering. I think I was starting to care.

"Hey there! It's going to be okay," I said, getting down on the floor next to him.

Namdev sobbed like a little kid, and I took him in my arms.

"My life is over," he kept repeating. "My life is over."

I began to tear up too. "No, it isn't. Your life is just beginning. And so is mine."

When Namdev finally pulled himself together, I promised I'd check in on him later. I left him with a crushing feeling in my chest. Looking back, I wish I'd thought to lend him some money.

When I reached the *seva* office, instead of going inside to get my extra assignment from Sita, I had a change of heart. I marched straight past it, and then ducked out the gate of the ashram. The oxcart drivers and rickshaw-wallahs called out to me, but I ignored them. I wanted to take a walk, and set out in the direction of the village. When I reached Gurudev's *samadhi* shrine, I thought about going inside to pay my respects, but changed my mind. *If Baba's a fake,* I thought, *what makes Gurudev any different?*

"Mr. Douglas?" someone called.

I turned to see Palash Chaapkhanawala waving to me. He was sitting alone at an outdoor table of a chai shop across the street.

I sat across from the innkeeper and ordered tea.

"Would you care for some fresh fruit?" he asked.

I told him, "Thanks, but no thanks. Please tell me everything you know about Rudrananda, and why people in the village don't have photographs of him."

He was hesitant and looked away.

"Please. I need to hear it now."

He looked at me and sighed. "The trouble started a few years ago, when the ashram burned down the huts of the Adivasi union leaders. The people reviled Rudrananda after this."

"Why did the ashram do that?"

"Rudrananda ordered the attacks in retaliation for union leaders stirring up trouble, demanding higher wages for ashram laborers."

As Palash spoke, I sank lower in my chair. At first I couldn't believe it—an enlightened being behaving like a mafia boss? Even with everything I now knew about Rudrananda, it still seemed inconceivable. At least now I understood why there weren't any pictures of him on the walls in the spa or anywhere else in the village.

"Are the Adivasis better compensated now?"

"Better compensated?" Palash laughed. "They are still paid less than one dollar a day!"

I asked why I'd never seen him once at Baba's ashram.

"I will tell you the same thing I told Mr. Walsh. Anyone who was around at the time of Gurudev's passing was banned from Rudrananda's ashram. I haven't set foot in there since the 1960s."

"But why?"

"Because we know too much," he said, lowering his voice like a stock character in a TV thriller. "We know there was no 'passing on of the lineage.' Gurudev had many disciples, but there was never any formal succession to any of them. Rudrananda's claim is a fiction!"

"But what about all the pictures?" I asked.

"Pictures? What pictures?"

"The pictures of Baba Rudrananda at the feet of Gurudev."

"Let me show you something," Palash said. He stood up, leaving money for our tea. He led me across the street to a shop where they sold color posters of Indian gods as well as old black and white photos of Gurudev Brahmananda and other Indian saints. Palash said something to the shopkeeper in Marathi, and a few moments later the shopkeeper produced several old pictures of Rudrananda and Gurudev together.

"What do you see here?" asked Palash holding up a photograph.

It was a black and white picture of Baba standing like a humble servant behind Gurudev Brahmananda, who sat cross-legged and naked on an ornate throne.

"This is a picture of Rudrananda and his guru."

"False!" exclaimed the innkeeper, pointing a finger in the air. "This is not one photograph, but two distinct photos which have been cleverly melded into one!"

I looked more closely, but couldn't see what Palash was talking about.

"This is a genuine photograph of Gurudev," he said, pointing to the naked holy man in the picture. "And this is also a real picture of Rudrananda. But the image you see before you, my young friend, is a *composite!*"

Inspecting the photograph more carefully, I could see how the film grain between the two parts of the photograph were different, and how they might have been combined into one.

"I know the gentleman who crafted this image. He is a darkroom specialist with all of the latest optical gadgetry. Look at this one!" Palash cried, thrusting another picture in my face. "They're all fakes, I assure you!"

"If your friend is such a *gentleman*, why would he do such a thing?"

"Put it this way," Palash said, looking around and speaking more softly, "Rudrananda made him an offer he could not decline."

Becoming animated, Palash ranted to me about what a fraud Baba was. "He never ever dared to wear the orange robes of a swami as long as Gurudev was still in his physical body. The man was never officially ordained! His best-selling spiritual autobiography—dreamed up by American public relations experts!"

"With all due respect, Mr. Palash, I find all that a little difficult to believe."

"He claims to have wandered all over India and studied at the feet of many illustrious masters of yoga and philosophy. I tell you, he gleaned everything he knows from books! I grant you, he may have spent a long time sitting, but it was not in a straw hut meditating as he claims. It was on the inside of a jail cell!"

"Jail? What was his crime?"

"Black magic! Unspeakable acts! Nasty tricks he picked up in Haridwar a long time ago."

Had Baba once been an Aghori? That would have explained a lot. I wasn't sure I really wanted to know.

I SPENT THE REST of the day relaxing in the thermal baths and lounging around Chaapkhanawala's resort. I returned to the ashram in the late afternoon. Strolling into the courtyard, I saw Baba seated on his throne next to the Acharya. They were laughing and joking. Like the last time they were together, the visiting holy man's throne was smaller and lower than Baba's.

Avadhoot was taking pictures in ten places at the same time. Kriyadevi Friedman, assisted by Frank Barbetti, was shooting video. Once again I'd been AWOL from the ashram when I was needed behind the camera. But this time I wasn't afraid of the consequences.

What more can they do to me? I thought. *Demote me to a lowly seva? Send me to an inferior dormitory?* They'd already done all of that. All they could do to me now was kick me out of the ashram, and that would have suited me fine. I was going home in a few days anyway, and I was never coming back.

As it happened, they did none of those things to me. I was still needed behind the camera for the big event.

On the eve of the *pattabhishek* I filmed the ritual shaving of Anjali's head, and the ceremony during which she took lifetime vows of poverty and chastity. Her voluminous jet-black hair fell to the ground in thick, lustrous clumps. But even now, in her simple orange frock and shaven head, she was still a beauty.

The fire ritual, like the one I'd filmed for her brother in Haridwar, seemed to go on forever. I thought I might collapse at any moment from dehydration and heat exhaustion. When she was finally ordained by the Acharya, Baba gave her the monastic name, "Leelananda," which meant "the bliss of divine play" in Sanskrit.

After we put away the equipment for the night, Jake advised the crew that the next day the Acharya would preside over two important ceremonies. In the first, Baba would be ritually bathed, like a Hindu statue of a god, or like an Indian king at his coronation. He explained that this was to honor Baba as the head of the Raja Yoga lineage. The second ceremony would be similar to the first, except that it'd be to consecrate Suresh and Anjali as the guru's co-successors.

That evening my camera work was not needed. My new room in *Bhakti Shayanagrih* was deserted. All five of my roommates were at the *saptah*, where I was supposed to be. Around midnight, the sound of Baba's voice joining the other devotees over the ashram loudspeakers pulled at my heartstrings. Despite all the anger I felt toward the guru and Raja Yoga, the chant called to me. I was unable to resist it.

Dragging myself out of bed, I headed out into the night toward the chant. A few feet before the entrance to the courtyard, someone called out to me from the shadows:

"Hey, asshole!"

I turned to see Sergio and Brian Pettigrew emerge from the darkness.

Before I had a chance to say anything, Brian belted me in the jaw. I thought he might have broken my tooth.

"What did Baba tell you about talking to girls?" Sergio demanded. "Hit him again!"

Brian dealt me another blow. This time to the gut. I doubled over in pain. I brought my hand to my mouth, and then glanced down at it. It was smeared with blood.

I tried to get up.

"We know all about your orgy at the Taj!" the Italian shouted.

As if on cue, Brian smacked me again, and I collapsed to my knees.

"Then you disappear from the ashram for the entire day when Baba needs you the most? Think you're too good to do extra *seva*?"

I was too stunned to respond. Instead I just groaned in pain, lying in a heap on the path.

"And another thing," said Sergio. "The next time I hear you've been doing any more of your fucking impressions of people, I'm going to beat the shit out of you myself! You like making fun of people, don't you?"

"I like making fun of you, asshole," I said, closing my eyes and bracing myself for a kick to the side. But nothing happened. When I opened my eyes again, Sergio and Brian were gone. I tried to get up, but my body protested.

Despite the agony, I was strangely unafraid. They could try to beat me into submission again, but my mind was free now. And soon I would be going home.

"Deependra! Oh my God, what happened?"

I looked up and saw Gopi's angelic face leaning over me.

"You'd better get out of here. I'm not supposed to talk to girls."

Gopi helped me up and walked me back to my room, which was fortunately still empty. Then she left me alone. But she returned a few minutes later with a small first aid kit marked "Baba's house." I lay down on the bed and she cradled my head in her lap. I winced in pain as she dabbed the cuts on my face with rubbing alcohol. When she was finished, she leaned down and kissed me on the forehead. After that, both of us were silent for a while. Then it was Gopi who spoke first.

"How's the patient?"

"Alright, I guess."

"How was your stay at the Taj with *Katie?*"

"Nothing happened. Believe me."

She seemed to soften. I decided to tell Gopi about my meeting with Christopher Walsh at the Harbor Bar. I repeated everything he told me. When I finished, she sat back against the wall on my bed and frowned.

"I've heard all those allegations before. You're not telling me anything new."

I got up off the bed and went to my locker. I reached in and took out the open letter to Baba from Satyananda.

"Read this," I said, thrusting it into her hands.

Gopi snorted in disgust. "I don't need to read this to know it's bullshit."

"Could you do me a favor and just read it? If you still think it's bullshit, I'll never mention it to you again."

Gopi's neck stiffened as she began to read. By the time she got to the last page, her shoulders drooped and her mismatched eyes were wet with tears. She handed the letter back to me and stared blankly into the middle distance.

"He makes it sound so sordid. But...it wasn't like that."

An alarm went off in my head. I hesitated before speaking again.

"Do you know...what it was like, then?"

"I was one of these girls," she said, drawing her knees to her chest. "It began when I was thirteen. At first I didn't understand what Baba was doing." She was unable to look at me. "I remember what he said to me: 'Don't try to understand what is happening with your mind. Just know that today is the best day of your life.' As strange as the experience was for me at first, I told myself that whatever the guru was doing to me was a precious gift. It was Baba's way of showing me how much he loved me."

As I listened to Gopi's confession, a deep sorrow enveloped me.

She started crying, and wiped her eyes.

I should have guessed—probably months ago. But in all this time, I had no idea Gopi was one of Baba's victims.

"Did you ever tell anyone about it?" I asked.

She shook her head. "Not a soul until now. Baba told me I had to keep it a secret. That we were practicing sacred *Tantra*, and that I should tell no one, not even my parents."

"You're telling me nobody ever suspected anything?"

"I never spoke to any of the other girls about it. But I knew that they knew, and they knew that I knew. Anyone who got a new sari or jewelry was going to Baba's bedroom a lot."

"Did you even know what *Tantra was* when you were thirteen?"

"I only knew what Baba told me. Once he said, 'I don't have sex for the same reasons that ordinary people do—because it feels good.'"

I felt anger spread through me like poison. "Oh really? Did he say why, then?"

Gopi's bottom lip trembled. "He said that pure young girls like me had a lot of *shakti*, and that he needed to borrow it so that he could awaken the *kundalini* in many others."

As enraged as I was, somewhere in the back of my mind, what Baba had told Gopi about "borrowing her *shakti*" made at least a little bit of sense.

"How long did it go on for?"

"Off and on for a few years. Then one day he stopped inviting me to his room at night. Then he never asked for me again."

"Why?

Gopi looked away. "I don't know."

"Were you sad about it?"

"Sometimes. But even though there's no touching anymore, I feel like I have a powerful bond with him. I'm immensely grateful for that."

"Can I ask you something else, on a different subject?"

Gopi finally looked up, and met my eyes.

"Did Baba ever tell you that you should stop talking to me because you should marry a prince?"

Gopi's eyes narrowed. "Is that what Sergio told you?"

"No, actually it was Parvati."

"What a fucking bitch! Yes, Baba really said that. But I knew he was just testing me."

"Testing you?"

"That's how it is when you're close to the guru, Deependra. Everything—everything is a test."

"That night in Manhattan after the Rainbow Room, when we kissed—the night we spent together after Baba's heart attack—did any of it mean anything to you? Did you—*do you* have any feelings for me?"

Gopi tilted her head down. "Yes, I did—*do*. But I also had feelings for someone else."

"Sergio?"

She hesitated before answering: "Yes. But now it's over."

"I don't understand—how could you ever have had any feelings for that psychopath?"

"I know he seems crazy sometimes, but he can also be very gentle and loving." Gopi started to cry again. "He made me feel… special."

Gopi stayed in my room for another hour, until the chant reached a crescendo and we could no longer hear

Baba's voice over the loudspeakers. The *saptah* would continue with a handful of people until morning, right up until the beginning of the *pattabhishek*.

"Your roommates will be back soon," she said. "I should go."

I wanted to tell Gopi that I was leaving the ashram and going back to the States for good, but felt I couldn't risk it. I was afraid she might tell my plans to someone close to Baba and they wouldn't let me go.

Before Gopi left she turned to me and looked me in the eye. "You have to have faith that Baba is a perfected master of Raja Yoga. He is the *guru*—the grace bestowing power of God. Whatever he does is an expression of God's will."

I thought about what she said for a moment, and then spoke. "How can that be true? Can't you see how Baba *and* Sergio have been exploiting you, and all the others? Do you honestly believe there could ever be a justification for a man in his seventies to be having sex with a thirteen-year-old child?"

Gopi teared up again. "You must never compare Baba with an ordinary person. Baba is a great mystic, an enlightened being—a saint!"

Her words lacked conviction. I could tell she was no longer sure she believed what she'd been brainwashed to think.

"He may be a great mystic, but he's definitely no saint."

Gopi wiped the tears from her face with her sari. "You can only know by your own inner experience of him," she said before turning to leave. "There's no other way."

She's definitely had an inner *experience of him*, I thought.

Just as she was stepping out through the door, one of my roommates stepped in with a blissed out expression on his face. I jumped out of the bed, and rushed through the door, almost knocking him over in the process.

"Gopi!" I called, as she was about to go down the stairs. She turned around and waited. I caught up with her, and then I took her in my arms. "What if he's both?"

"Both what?" she asked, furrowing her brow.

"Both a flawed man and an enlightened being."

Gopi shook her head forcefully, pushing me away. Then she disappeared into the darkened stairwell.

When the rest of my roommates had returned from the chant, we turned out the lights and went to bed. But I was unable to sleep. Obsessive angry thoughts tormented me. *How can she not see the truth about Baba?*

Hatred welled up inside of me. Hatred for Baba for what he had done to Gopi and the other girls, and hatred for Sergio and Avadhoot and all the others for protecting him.

Something else occurred to me: by remaining silent, and not doing anything to stop it, I was participating in the abuse. Rage rose up inside of me like a tidal wave. It lifted me out of bed and onto my feet. I touched the corner of my mouth, and could feel that I was still bleeding a little. My gut was also sore as hell, but I was too mad to care.

I needed to do *something*. I would confront Baba face to face. I wouldn't waste another minute!

I threw on my clothes, and rushed to Namdev's room in *Siddha Shayanagrih*.

"Namdev," I whispered through the screen door of his darkened room. "Namdev!" I said louder. No answer. "Namdev!"

"Are you crazy?" came an angry response from someone inside the room, who was *not* Namdev. "We're trying to sleep!"

"Where is he? It's an emergency."

"The generator plant—where else!"

The ashram grounds were dark. But thanks to moonlight I was able to find my way to the plant. When I arrived, I found Namdev sleeping on a thin mattress pad on the floor. His back was curved forward and his arms and legs were folded in front of his body.

"Namdev," I said, softly. "Namdev."

He snuffled once, but didn't wake up. I grabbed his shoulders and shook him gently. "Namdev, wake up!"

He shot up to a sitting position as if waking from a nightmare.

"What? What?" he gasped.

The Guru's Touch

"Take it easy—it's only me."

"Deependra?" Namdev stood up and switched on a light. Then he squinted and rubbed his eyes. "What happened to your face?"

"Brian beat the shit out of me. Do you still have that ring of keys you found?"

"Yeah, I do."

"Did you check to see if they open any of the doors to Baba's house yet?"

Namdev shook his head with a tight expression on his face. "No." A moment later a smile spread across his face. "I'm in," he said. "Let's go."

Namdev grabbed a flashlight, and we set off for the guru's quarters. As we wound our way down a garden path toward the heart of the ashram, Namdev was uncharacteristically quiet.

"Are you okay?" I asked.

"No man, I'm not. I'm not at all okay."

"You're going to be fine," I told him. "The ashram is doing you a big favor by kicking you out."

My words of encouragement were met with silence.

We went around to the back kitchen entrance of Baba's house, across from the main dining hall, where we'd be less likely to be seen. Randomly choosing a key from the loop, he tried it in the lock. It didn't fit. As he tried another, I thought about what Sergio might do to us if he caught us.

"Let me try," I said.

Namdev handed me the keys. I tried a couple more with no luck. Just then, there was noise. Namdev started and I nearly fell over. We turned in the direction the sound was coming from. A rat the size of a small cat scurried out from under a wooden box next to the entrance to the dining hall. I tried a few more keys, but none of them fit the lock.

"They open all the other doors in the ashram—even the manager's office," whispered Namdev. "Sorry, man."

Then I had a thought. I'd often seen members of the inner circle simply open the door to Baba's house and step inside. Maybe they didn't always keep it locked. Reaching for the knob, I turned it. The door opened!

Pushing my fear aside, I put Namdev's key ring in my pocket, and then stepped across the threshold into the inner sanctum.

The light was on in Baba's kitchen. It was immaculate, and smelled like saffron and cumin.

"Can you tell me why we're doing this?" Namdev whispered from just outside the door. He was looking around nervously, and his hands were jammed into his armpits.

"Maybe it's better I do this alone."

"Are we looking for something specific?"

"I'll know when I find it."

"I'll wait for you out here," he said. "Good luck!"

Namdev gently pulled the door shut again, and I was on my own.

I exited the kitchen and crept up a staircase, which I assumed led to Baba's chambers. There was just enough light from the kitchen for me to find my way. At the top of the stairs, I paused in front of a closed door. I held my breath and opened it as quietly as possible.

Inside was an ornate and luxurious bathroom, with the same gold faucets I had helped Kriyadevi smuggle into India in her bra. The bathtub was enormous and the toilet was state-of-the-art. I pictured Baba sitting on it, taking a dump like an ordinary person. I wondered if it was true that a fully realized being's shit was fragrant like roses.

I opened the medicine cabinet above the sink and found an array of prescription medication. I took one out and read the label. The prescription was for oxycodone, which I knew was a highly addictive painkiller. It was in the name of Walter Plotnick. It had been filled by a pharmacy on Third Avenue in Manhattan. I remembered that Avadhoot's last name was Plotnick, and I remembered him answering questions about the medication at the airport in Bombay. I took another bottle off the shelf and examined it. It was also a prescription for oxycodone in Avadhoot's real name. I looked at another, and then another. They were all the same.

Baba's an addict! a voice screamed inside my head.

The Guru's Touch

I tiptoed back into the hall. I noticed a light spilling out of a door ajar at the end of the corridor. As I crept nearer to it, I could hear the hum of an air conditioner running inside. I reached for the knob and slowly opened the door. My heart pounded. What I saw on the other side of the door made me take a step back and turn away. I couldn't look. In an instant, my worst fears about Baba were confirmed.

I looked again. I thought I might throw up.

Inside the room, Baba lay asleep in bed. He was completely naked, and sprawled out on his back. He lay between two sleeping girls, who were also naked. Neither of them could be much older than thirteen or fourteen. On the other side of the room, on the floor, in front of what looked like an examining table with stirrups, the girls' nightgowns and panties were strewn in a heap. At the side of his bed, within easy reach, a shotgun was propped against the wall.

Adrenaline pumping through my entire body, I stepped into the guru's lair. It smelled like sex. I could hear the faint strains of the chant over the din of the air conditioner. I looked at the girls sleeping next to Baba. Their names were Lakshmi and Sharmila. Like Gopi, they were *darshan* girls.

Something was different and disturbing about Baba's appearance. Then I realized what it was. The guru's mouth was sunken in where the outline of his teeth should have been. I noticed his false teeth soaking in a jar on top of a dresser. The guru's flaccid penis was shrunken. Did he invite only one girl at a time to his bedroom? I wondered. Or did he put one of them up on the table and fuck her while the other watched?

Although I'd come to confront Baba, I was speechless and paralyzed. All I could do was stare at the naked truth before my eyes.

"Holy fuck!" exclaimed Namdev, who'd just joined me inside the open door to Baba's bedroom. He was shaking all over and his knees looked like they were about to give way. Baba didn't awaken immediately at the sound of Namdev's voice, but the girls did. Sharmila gasped and both girls scrambled to cover themselves.

"What are you doing in here?" Lakshmi shrieked.

At this, Baba also woke up and shot up to a sitting position. The guru seemed startled at first, but he relaxed almost immediately when he recognized it was me.

"Deependra, you are not chant going?" Baba asked in his broken English. His question took me aback. *Wasn't he angry or afraid that his dirty secret had been found out?* Next Baba turned to Namdev. "Get out stupid boy! You don't belong here!"

For the first time since I'd met Namdev, he was speechless. As he slowly backed out of the room, the color drained from his face. A moment later, I heard him run down the stairs and slam the door behind him.

"Girls, you go now," Baba said. Lakshmi and Sharmila sprang to their feet, and pulled their nightgowns down over their heads as quickly as possible. Lakshmi gritted her teeth and sneered at me as she pulled her panties back on over her skinny legs. Sharmila avoided making eye contact with me. Her ears had turned bright red and she trembled while she got dressed. A moment later they were gone.

"Why does Deependra disturb Baba?" the guru asked. "Baba did not call for you."

I was speechless. The guru made no attempt to cover his nakedness. Wasn't he the least bit embarrassed about what I had just witnessed? Then I had a realization: *Baba's high—zonked on painkillers! He doesn't give a shit about anything right now.*

"Why you come too late in the night and bring foolish boy with you?" With his dentures in the jar on the dresser, Baba's mouth appeared crooked and his speech was slurred.

"Why?" I asked, all the muscles in my body beginning to tremble in rage. "Why did I come?" I spoke louder this time. Tears rolled down my face.

"*Babaji, kya baat hai?*" someone said behind me. I turned. It was Rashmi, Baba's Indian attendant, rubbing his chin and yawning. He was wearing a robe and slippers, and looked as if he'd just dragged himself out of bed.

"*Sab theek hai,* Rashmi," Baba answered. I knew enough Hindi to understand that Baba was telling his attendant everything was under control.

"No, Baba! *Sab theek nahi hai!*" I spurted out. "Everything is *not* okay!"

"Now look here, young man," Rashmi scolded. "Baba has a big day tomorrow. We *all* do. Right now you should be in your bed, at the chant, or doing *seva.*" Rashmi clapped his hands and motioned for me to leave. "Run along now," he said, yawning again. "Scram!"

Just then, the sound of a woman screaming at the top of her lungs pierced the night. It sounded like it was coming from the courtyard. A moment later the chant came to an abrupt halt.

Next Baba hollered something at Rashmi in Hindi. The servant nodded in acquiescence, and then rushed out the door and made for the stairs.

I could hear a commotion outside in the courtyard. Then I heard someone call out: "He jumped!"

Comprehension dawned within me and there was an excruciating pounding in my ears.

I pointed a finger at Baba and shouted, "You caused this! You're a monster! I don't love you anymore!"

Baba's misshapen mouth fell open and he jerked back in surprise.

I ran from his bedroom, but instead of taking the stairs and leaving his quarters through the kitchen, I took another door and found myself in the princess dormitory, which was connected to his house through a well-hidden narrow passageway. The lights were on and all the beds were empty. I went to an open window and stuck my head out of it, to get a look at what was going on in the courtyard. A crowd of people were standing around what looked like a body.

"Is he still breathing?" I heard someone ask.

"I can't tell," someone else said.

"Somebody get Nirmalananda!"

"Who is it? Who jumped?"

I found a staircase and took it down to the ground floor. At the bottom of the stairs was a door that opened onto the courtyard. I exited the building and joined the crowd of people gathered around the body.

"Everybody get back!" Gajendra was hollering. "I said, get back!"

I pushed my way to the front of the crowd to confirm what I already knew must be true. Namdev Loman lay crumpled on the cold marble floor of the courtyard. His eyes were open, and lifeless. He had jumped from the roof of *Shanti Shayanagrih*.

43.
THE GURU'S TOUCH

I KNEW I HAD to get out of the ashram immediately, but I wasn't going to leave without Gopi.

"Everybody, please return to your rooms," Suresh said, his voice choked with emotion.

"Go back to your rooms or return to the chant," Anjali added.

The crowd began to disperse and I caught sight of Gopi. She was headed out of the courtyard in the direction of the *mandap*.

"Gopi, wait up!" I called.

She turned around to face me. "Oh, Deependra, isn't it awful? Does anyone know why he did it?"

"I know why—he was kicked out!"

"Kicked out? When?"

"This morning. He totally freaked out. He had nowhere to go and no money."

"Nowhere to go? What about his family?"

"They didn't want anything to do with him."

"Oh my God, that's horrible!"

"You think so?" I said, unable to hide my contempt. "That's not the worst of it. I was with him just before he jumped. We were in Baba's house."

"Baba's house? What were you doing there?"

When I didn't answer, she understood.

"We found Baba in bed with two girls. Fourteen-year-olds! Namdev was totally shocked. Maybe he hadn't heard any of the rumors. Then Baba shouted at him—called him a stupid boy and told him he didn't belong here. It was more than he could bear!"

Gopi covered her mouth with her hands and shook her head in disbelief.

"Look, Gopi. I'm getting out of here. I'm not going to Nepal to renew my visa. I'm going home to New York and I'm not coming back. I'm through with Baba."

Gopi started crying tears.

"I want you to come with me."

Gopi shook her head. "I can't! I won't!"

"Do you honestly still believe everything that happens in the ashram is thanks to the grace of the guru? Namdev is dead! Baba and this place drove him to it!"

She gasped at something she saw behind me. I turned around to see Namdev's lifeless body being carried away on a plank of wood.

"When are you leaving?" she asked.

"First thing in the morning," I answered. "During the finale of the *saptah*, before the *pattabhishek*. Everybody will be at the chant with Baba—no one will notice."

"Who will film the ceremony?"

"I don't give a shit!" I hissed, grabbing her shoulders and giving her a shake. "Are you coming with me or not?" The choice was obvious to me. I couldn't understand her hesitation. "Are you?"

Gopi took a deep breath, and then looked me in the eye. "Yes."

I told Gopi when my flight was leaving, and that she was welcome to stay with me at the Taj before we left. I also offered to pay for her ticket, but she said she had enough money to buy it herself. We agreed to meet in front of the ashram at six-thirty in the morning. We'd then get an auto rickshaw to the train station.

"Where are you going now?" I asked.

"Back to the *mandap*. Sergio is supervising the final preparations. He'll be suspicious if I don't come back." She turned to leave.

"Gopi, wait!"

She stopped and turned around to face me again. Tears were streaming down her face and she was trembling.

"I love you," I said. Then I leaned in to kiss her, but she pulled away. "Tomorrow at 6:30. In front of the ashram."

She nodded and hurried off in the direction of the *mandap*.

BACK IN MY BED, I was unable to sleep. I wanted to pack, but didn't want to risk waking up my roommates by making noise or turning on the light. Instead I lay awake until dawn, waiting for my roommates to leave for the chant.

Then I remembered: I didn't have my passport! It was in the manager's office, which was closed at this hour and surely locked. I broke out in a sweat.

I had to think of something. Sitting up in bed, I racked my brain for a solution. *Gopi and I will have to go to the American Consulate in Bombay and plead our case*, I told myself. *They will have to help us. We're American citizens!*

As soon as my roommates left for the chant, I packed my duffel bag. Going through my locker, I found the little bottle of Baba's bath water that Sita Perkins had given me when I first came to the ashram. I took it to the bathroom and spilled it out into one of the squat toilets and tossed the vial in the trash. Returning to my room, I packed everything but my framed photos of Baba and Gurudev Brahmananda, which I left in place on the altar shelf above my bed. I didn't want them. And it was better that way: if anyone came looking for me and checked my room, no one would suspect I had left. Who would leave without their precious pictures of the guru?

As more and more voices joined the chant, it got louder and faster over the loudspeakers. But by six fifteen I still didn't hear Baba. I knew the *saptah* would have to wrap up soon, because the *pattabhishek* ceremony was scheduled to begin at eight. They needed to allow time for breakfast and the change of venue from the open-air hall off the courtyard to the *mandap*.

Six twenty, still no Baba.

At six twenty-five I decided to head for the gate for my rendezvous with Gopi. As I guessed, no one saw me on the path on the way to the courtyard. Almost everyone was at the chant. *Will Baba or Sergio notice Gopi is missing?* I worried. *If there aren't any rickshaws waiting outside of the ashram, we will have to walk or take an oxcart to the village to find one? We won't be able to risk waiting outside the ashram gates with our suitcases. Someone is bound to spot us.*

I knew Baba would be exiting his house at any moment to join the chant. I began to panic: What if he crosses the courtyard on his way to the hall at the precise moment I'm crossing it to get to the gate?

I'd have to risk it. There was no other way in or out.

I got lucky. Just as I was about to turn the path and enter the courtyard, over the loudspeakers I heard Baba's voice and Suresh's distinctive drumming style. I knew there was a risk that someone close to Baba would spot me with my bag and go after me, but I had no choice. I had to make a break for it. As I bolted across the courtyard, I glanced down at the spot where just a few hours earlier Namdev's broken body had lain. The marble had been wiped clean. No sign of the horrible tragedy remained.

"He died on the way to the hospital," is what they would say. *No one is born or dies in an ashram.*

Exiting through the main gate, I could feel the sweat trickle down my back. I held my breath.

Will Gopi be waiting for me as we agreed?

There was no sign of her. I glanced at my watch: it was six thirty-two.

The Guru's Touch

Maybe she's just delayed. Perhaps Baba sent for her just as she was about to leave.

The chant would continue at least another half hour, now that Baba and his successors had joined it. I'd wait another few minutes. In any case, there were no rickshaws outside the gate. It was still too early.

At six fifty-five the chant reached a crescendo. Still no sign of her. A rickshaw approached the ashram from the direction of the village. It pulled up alongside of me.

"Railway station going?" the driver asked. I was heartbroken to leave without Gopi, but what choice did I have?

"Yes, take me to Vasai Road." I threw my duffel bag on the passenger seat and climbed in. As we pulled away from the ashram, I turned around to look in the direction of the gate and was overcome with an unbearable feeling of loss.

"Stop!" I shouted. The driver slammed on the brake.

"Yes please, what problem?"

"Yes, a problem," I said, grabbing my bag and jumping out of the vehicle. "I'll be back in a few minutes."

Now I was screwed. The chant was over, Baba had gone back inside his house, and the crowd was dispersing. How would I explain the bag?

Just as I feared, Kriyadevi spotted me as I entered the courtyard. I could only have been coming in from the street.

"Deependra!"

I pretended I didn't hear her and continued on my way. I had to drop my bag off in my room and search for Gopi. She needed my help!

"Deependra!" Kriyadevi called again and then caught up with me. "Are you serious?" she said looking down at my duffel bag. "You're doing laundry today of all days?"

"I, um—"

"I don't know what's gotten into you lately, but you've been letting the team down," she said, shaking her head. Her tone was sharp. "Jake, Frank, and I were up in the *mandap* setting up half the night. We could really have used your help."

I didn't know what to say, so I said nothing.

"Get something to eat fast," she said. "You need to be behind your camera in twenty minutes. We have no idea what time Baba or the successors will show up at the *mandap*. Jake and Frank are already in place."

I ran back to my room, shoved my bag under my bed, and hightailed it for the *mandap*. If I wanted to leave with Gopi, I'd have to stay and film at least part of installation ceremony. Gopi and I would be able to sneak out toward the end of it.

How will I get word to her of the new plan? I wondered.

When I arrived at the *mandap*, Avadhoot was waiting outside the main entrance with a bulky camera bag hanging from his shoulder and two thirty-five millimeter cameras dangling from his neck. When he saw me approaching, he widened his stance and thrust out his chest. He was dressed in a white, lightweight linen suit, snakeskin cowboy boots, and a white Stetson hat. Around his neck he wore a silver and turquoise bolo tie. He looked like a freak, and I was itching to tell him so.

"Well, hello there, boychik!" he said, baring his teeth in a mocking grin.

"Morning," I muttered.

"Sleep well?" he asked, standing menacingly close.

"Um, not really."

"Of course you didn't," he said. His breath was sour.

"You were a very busy boy last night. But we're not going to talk about that just now. You need to get behind the camera. Think you can handle that, partner?"

I nodded. "I'll go to my station. Camera two, right?" I asked.

"Yes, but now we have another assignment for you. Since you already know very well where Baba lives, I want you to take the camera from the *mandap* and get some behind-the-scenes shots of Baba with his successors. They're going to perform a short ritual in a few minutes."

I couldn't believe he was serious. *After what I did and said last night, he wants me go back to Baba's house?*

"Go on!" he snapped. "Baba's waiting for you! I'll be along shortly."

The inside of the *mandap* was spectacular, with fragrant garlands of white and red flowers hanging from every rafter. The Brahmin priests had already gathered around the fire pit and were performing a ritual. Sergio was busy putting the finishing touches on Baba's majestic throne, with the aid of a few of the *darshan* girls. Gopi was not with them. The cameras were set up on tripods on raised platforms. Hoping to avoid being noticed by Sergio, I rushed to the camera two station, disconnected it, and made a beeline for the exit.

"Hey! Asshole!" I heard Sergio call behind me. I knew he was addressing me, but I pretended not to hear.

Standing outside the entrance to Baba's private quarters, my pulse quickened. I tried the door. This time it was locked. I found a doorbell and rang it. A few moments later, a forlorn Suresh opened up and let me inside. Like his sister, his face and head were clean shaven.

"Deependra, how are you holding up?" he asked in his lilting Indian accent.

Is this some kind of test? I wondered. I shrugged

"Bad timing, isn't it?" he said.

"I guess so."

"Such sad news about Namdev," he said. "But as they say, 'the show must go on.' Weren't you and he from the same village?"

"Um, yeah, Ithaca, New York."

"Just terrible," he said, shaking his head. "Come on, I believe you know the way."

Why does the show have to go on? I wondered. *Can't they postpone it out of respect?*

In a room just off the top of the stairs, Anjali, Rashmi, and a stern-looking Baba were waiting for us. The room appeared to be the guru's study. Rashmi was lighting the ghee-soaked wicks on an *arati* tray on a small table in the corner. The guru gave me the once over and grunted something in Hindi.

"Baba says you should start filming now," Anjali said.

I grudgingly hefted the camera to my shoulder, put my eye to the viewfinder and composed a three-shot of the guru and his two successors. I didn't want to be there. All I could think about was how I would get a new message to Gopi. Rashmi handed the *arati* tray to Suresh, who began to wave it in front of Baba. Anjali lowered her head in prayer.

Suddenly, Avadhoot rushed into the room and started taking pictures. "Film, film!" he hissed. In my state of distraction, I'd forgotten to push the record button. Avadhoot could see this because the red tally light on the back of my camera was off. As I began rolling tape, I recoiled at his angry tone. I'd heard it one too many times.

Screw Avadhoot! I thought. *Screw all of them!* What would they do if I just dropped the camera and ran? Then I got a better idea. With my free eye, I noticed that Rashmi was picking his nose just outside of the frame. I zoomed out to include him in the shot.

Not bad, I told myself, *but it doesn't quite capture the moment perfectly.* Zooming in now, I got a close-up of the tip of Rashmi's finger disappearing into a nostril. *Much better!* I thought. I felt a new rush of adrenalin.

For the next quarter of an hour, Baba performed various sacred rites with his successors while Avadhoot snapped photos and I shot footage of everything in the room that caught my fancy, except what I was supposed to be recording. No one noticed my errant filming because I made sure to aim my camera in the general direction of whatever action was unfolding. I was burning my bridges in Raja Yoga for all time, and there was no turning back.

By the end of the rituals, both future gurus were shedding tears of devotion and prostrating to Baba, who was all smiles now. I noticed that Avadhoot had stopped taking pictures, so I took the camera off my shoulder for a moment to take a break. Just then Baba turned to me and smiled warmly.

"Deependra is a good boy, isn't he?" Baba said in English, giving my shoulder a firm squeeze.

"Yes, Baba," Anjali answered.

Then he turned to Avadhoot and spoke again. "A very good boy, no?"

"Yes, of course he is, Baba."
Is Baba onto me? Sweat dripped down my forehead.
"Don't you think so, Rashmi?"
"Most definitely, Baba—a very, *very* good boy!"
"Yes, yes! A very, very, very good boy!" Baba laughed, slapping me on the back.

I remembered the shotgun in Baba's bedroom. My knees buckled, and I almost dropped the camera. Baba's eye's widened in response and he began to laugh even harder. Then everyone was laughing except me. The guru turned to me, gazed deeply into my eyes, and touched the top of my head. Just then, I felt a sharp pain at the base of my spine, and a sensation like an electric current shot up my back. A wave of blissful energy washed over me and my sense of self expanded to encompass everyone and everything around me. As this happened, I continued to hear Baba and the others laugh and talk, but their words were distorted and unintelligible. It was as though I were seated at the bottom of a swimming pool and they were having their conversation above me on the surface.

"Deependra," Baba said. The guru came into focus again. He gently stroked my cheek. "You are very tired. Take rest." Then Baba turned to Rashmi and said something in Hindi I couldn't understand.

"Come with me, young man," Baba's attendant said, motioning for me to follow. I glanced over at Avadhoot.

"It's okay, man," the guru's photographer said. "Take a break. We've got a long day ahead of us."

I followed Rashmi into the living room, and took a seat on a plush sofa. He left me alone and rejoined the others. My sense of self dissolved. All that remained was pure, luminous awareness. Limitless, divisionless, and infinite.

I wasn't sure how much time had passed when I heard Baba and the others outside in the hall, and then descending the stairs. *Are they leaving me alone here? Who will film the ceremony?* A moment later, Anjali joined me in the living room and took a seat on the couch opposite me.

"What is the guru?" she asked, gazing into my eyes. Her expression was impassive, inscrutable. "Who is this man who appears like an ordinary human being, yet has the ability to transmit knowledge of the ultimate nature of reality with the mere touch of his hand?"

She continued to stare at me blankly. I was silent.

"A great master once said, 'Praise and blame, deprivation and gain, all thoughts disappear into the infinite as a wave merges back into the ocean.'"

Her words penetrated to the center of my being, and some part of me, deep inside, understood.

Anjali stood up to leave, but before she did she spoke again. "The truth cannot be grasped in words, nor can it be understood by thinking. It is only in the not knowing that we can know."

I sat on the sofa, alone in the guru's house. A clock on the wall ticked loudly. It was eight twenty-five.

Have I been drugged? I wondered. Impossible. I hadn't had anything to eat or drink in hours. No, there was no denying that Baba had caused the experience I was having. But I didn't want to feel blissed-out or at peace. I wanted to feel the anger and the hatred again. As seductive as the experience was, I had to fight against it. I reminded myself that Baba was a despicable pervert, and that my friend was dead because of him.

The clock on the wall said nine-thirty. *How long have I been here?*

The solemn, monotonous recitation of Vedic mantras by Brahmin priests could be heard over the loudspeakers. The chanting triggered a state of blissful absorption in me again, and called to me:

"*Om Namo Bhagavate Rudraya Vishnave Mrityume Pahi.*"

I remembered the meaning of the first Sanskrit verse. We chanted it every evening in the ashram: "*Om. Salutation to the omnipresent Lord Rudra. Protect me from death.*"

Then I remembered something else: *Gopi! I can't leave without Gopi!*

If I wanted to make a new plan with Gopi, I had to get back to the *mandap* and get to my post. I shot up from the sofa, grabbed the camera, flew out of Baba's house, and ran all the way to the pavilion.

I have to get Gopi alone for a minute to talk to her. But how, and when?

By the time I got to the *mandap*, I was dripping with sweat. I rushed to the camera platform, mounted my camera on its tripod, and put on the intercom headset.

"Deependra? Where have you been, for Christ's sake?" came Jake's voice over the intercom.

"I'm here now," I answered, without apology.

"Connect the monitor cable to your camera so that I can see what you're getting," he scolded. "Hurry!"

In the *mandap*, Baba was seated high on a grand throne under an enormous portrait of Gurudev Brahmananda. Baba's successors were ritually washing his feet.

Kriyadevi was stationed on a platform up front, close to the action. She was operating the main camera, and was supposed to capture most of the close-ups and principal action. The platform I was shooting from was situated at a forty-five-degree angle from hers. It was higher and farther back, affording me the best vantage to get wide angle and audience reaction shots.

Over the intercom, Jake told me to get a static three-shot of Baba and his successors. I did as directed, and locked my tripod head in position. I now had a few seconds to take my head away from the viewfinder and look for Gopi among the *darshan* girls. I spotted her up near the front. She was dressed in a stunning new indigo sari.

Has she even had time to pack yet? I wondered.

"Okay, Deependra—you're up," Jake said. "It's time to get some footage of the audience. See if you can get a few VIP and celebrity shots."

That would be easy. The front rows were full of big donors, movie stars, pop singers, and famous academics. Sylvia Preston was there with her husband, the film director Richard Foxman. Tabitha Beaumont, the TV actress, was seated with the princesses. The astronaut William Brady was also there. Everyone who was anyone in the Raja Yoga community was here for the big event.

Now it was time to perform the installation ceremony of Anjali and Suresh. Like Baba, their feet were ritually washed, but in their case, by Brahmin priests. Just when Baba began to perform a blessing, there was a tremendous thunderclap. A few moments later it sounded like a million golf balls suddenly dropping onto the metal roof of the pavilion. It was raining in the middle of the dry season. What were the odds that it would happen today?

"Baba says the rain is a most auspicious sign of a shining future for the Raja Yoga lineage," announced one of Baba's Indian swamis, translating for the guru. Everyone clapped and Baba smiled triumphantly.

"Wake up Deependra!" came Jake's voice over the intercom. "Kriyadevi's getting a three-shot of Baba and the successors. Get some audience reaction shots."

I trained my camera on the *darshan* girls and panned the front row. When I got to Gopi I stopped.

"Nice one, Deependra. Now get somebody else."

I couldn't hear Jake, except on the periphery of my consciousness. I couldn't hear Sergio either—he took the intercom away from Jake and started barking orders at me himself. I couldn't hear them because I chose to block them out. I did so because, looking at the close-up of the angel's face, I knew it was the last time I'd ever see her. She didn't look like someone plotting an imminent escape. She was beaming at Baba with an expression of unwavering love, loyalty, and devotion. I realized at that moment that Gopi wasn't going anywhere. She would never leave the guru. When she had said she would, she was merely placating me. If I wanted to get away before they saw the footage I'd ruined in Baba's house, I had to leave now.

I left my headset hanging on the tripod, but Sergio was cursing so loudly into the intercom I could still hear him as I climbed down from the platform. With Sergio and Jake behind the video monitors on the far side of the *mandap*, I was safely out of their line of sight. I managed to run to the nearest exit before they even realized I'd abandoned my post. The rain outside was coming down in sheets and within seconds I was completely drenched.

The Guru's Touch

Just as I reached my dorm room, Baba began to address the assembly. Despite the din from the rain, I could hear him over the ashram loudspeakers.

"I bow to God in each and every one of you. Today marks a very auspicious occasion. Today I pass the torch of the Raja Yoga lineage to these two most worthy of disciples..."

I grabbed my duffel bag, which I'd hastily stored under my bed, and started for the door. Then I remembered that I'd left the open letter from Swami Satyananda to Baba in my locker. For some reason, I suddenly felt it was important to hold on to it. I took the letter and stuffed it into my bag.

Nearly everyone in the ashram was at the *mandap*. Anyone who wasn't had taken refuge from the rain indoors. Nobody noticed me running through the ashram with my bag. Even if they had, they probably assumed I was looking for a place to get out of the rain. When I reached the courtyard, I remembered again that my passport was locked up in the manager's office. I began to panic: *What if the US consulate gives me a hard time about replacing my passport? What if they make me return to the ashram to retrieve it?*

Then it hit me: I still had Namdev's keys right in my pocket. He had said one of them opened Gajendra's office!

"...today, I am installing the great *shakti* of the Raja Yoga lineage within both of them," Baba continued over the loudspeakers. "It will be up to them to maintain what they have received..."

I tried every key on the ring, but none of them opened the door to the office.

"...today *only* they will sit on the throne. From tomorrow on, until the day they assume power, they will sit on the floor with all the other disciples..."

Just as I was about to give up, I heard someone walk up behind me. I turned around to see one of the professional ashram security guards frowning.

"*Tumhi kaye karit ahata?*" he said. I didn't know him by name, but I'd known the man for a long time, and he knew me.

"Do you think you could help me, sir?" I said. "My key doesn't seem to work."

"Why office going?" He looked down at my bag and frowned again.

I had to think of an excuse fast. "Um, ah—I need to make photocopies," I said. I put my duffel bag on the floor and took out the manila envelope containing Satyananda's letter.

"Baba needs many copies of this right now in the *mandap*. It's extremely urgent!"

The guard frowned again, and I wasn't entirely sure he understood me. Then he swiveled his head from side to side acquiescently, took a ring of keys from his own belt, and motioned for me to step aside. A moment later, the door was open and I was inside.

I hoped the guard would leave me on my own, but I had no such luck. Instead he hung around to supervise. I had no choice but to go through the motions of making the copies until he either became distracted and I could grab my passport, or he left me to my own devices.

I'd never used the copier before, but it wasn't complicated. After a few seconds of trial and error, I got it to work. I set the machine to *collate*, and began to print a dozen copies. When the machine finished spitting out the last of them, the guard tapped the face of his watch at me.

"Finish?" he asked.

Again, I had to think fast. "No, not finished. Baba needs *many* copies."

This time I set the machine to print a hundred copies, and pressed *start* again. By the time the machine had spit out fifty, the guard finally left me alone. As soon as he was out of sight, I went to the cabinet where Gajendra kept the passports and grabbed my own. I was home free!

Just as I was about to pull the door to shut behind me, the copier suddenly stopped. Given the time it had taken to print a dozen copies of the letter, I doubted it had finished all one hundred copies. Then I had a terrible, wonderful, wicked idea.

I could hear that the rain had stopped. Baba was winding up his talk. Soon *darshan* would begin, and devotees would start trickling toward Prasad and the dining hall for lunch. I would have to act fast. I rushed back to the photocopy machine. A light next to the words "out of paper" was blinking. It didn't matter—I had more than enough copies.

With the duplicates of Satyananda's letter in hand, I ran to Prasad and left a copy on each of the tables. I ran to the public toilets I had cleaned so many times, and left one in each stall. I ran back to the courtyard and stuck a dozen or two in the shoe rack outside of the open-air hall. I glanced around. The courtyard was still empty. I had some time left. I dashed up the stairs of *Shanti Shayanagrih*, and stopped when I got to the floor where I knew all the VIPs and celebrities were staying. I stuck a copy under every door.

Now I had to get out. With the ceremony over, Sergio would be sending someone to look for me. I didn't want to get the shit beaten out of me again. I was still smarting from the previous night.

When I got downstairs to the courtyard, I headed for the main gate where, hopefully, I'd find a rickshaw to take me to the train station. Suddenly, someone called out to me.

"Deependra! Where ya off to, mate?"

I turned, and heaved a sigh of relief—it was only Andy.

"What the fuck did you do to your face?" he asked.

I didn't have time to explain. I could see other people heading down the path from the *mandap* toward the courtyard. "Read this," I said, handing him the rest of the copies of Satyananda's letter. "And if you feel it's the right thing to do, circulate as many of these as you can."

"What's it all about?" he asked, with a confused expression on his face.

"Just read it."

At that moment I saw Kriyadevi heading down the path with a tripod slung over her shoulder. She hadn't seen me yet.

"But where are you going?" Andy asked.

"Home."

44.
THE HYMN THE BRAHMIN SINGS

FOR OVER AN HOUR and a half, I waited anxiously at the Vasai Road railway station. I held my breath with each car that passed from the direction of Ravipur. I knew it was only a matter of time before they came after me.

Although it might take them a while to figure out who made and distributed the copies of Satyananda's letter, and they might not see the footage I ruined until later, surely they were already furious with me for abandoning my camera during the ceremony.

I couldn't help feeling that I made the wrong decision about leaving Gopi. Maybe when she looked at Baba with so much devotion, she still wanted to leave but was temporarily swept up in the emotion of the moment. Maybe she was hurt that I left without her. In any case, there was nothing I could do about it now. If Gopi wanted to join me, she knew where I was staying and when my flight left.

"Good afternoon, sir," the Sikh doorman said, holding the door open for me. "Welcome back to the Taj!"

"Thank you. Nice to see you again," I said, reaching for my wallet.

"Everything alright, sir?" The doorman looked alarmed.

"Yes, why do you ask?"

"Your face, sir."

"Oh that!" I answered, handing him a wad of rupee notes. "You know what they say? You should've seen the other guy."

The man at the reception also looked concerned. He did a double take when he saw me. I checked in and immediately booked a trunk call to the States. I wanted to talk to Melanie and let her know my plans.

Up in my room, I collapsed on the bed and let out a deep breath. It felt good to be in comfortable surroundings. In the bathroom, I was confronted by my reflection in the mirror. I looked worse than I thought. My left eye was bruised and my lip was swollen. I regretted not having gotten in a swing at Brian, but congratulated myself on managing to do substantial damage before leaving the ashram.

My call went through faster than I expected. By the time I shaved and had a long hot bath, the hotel operator had Melanie on the line for me.

"Melanie, I'm coming home."

"That's wonderful news!"

"I want to get a part-time job and start earning some money. I plan to go back to college as soon as possible."

"I'll do what I can to help you get back into Cornell, but don't get your hopes up. It's a long shot."

"Actually, I was thinking about going to school in New York. I hear Columbia has a special program for adults returning to school."

Melanie laughed on the other end of the line.

"What's so funny?" I asked.

"You think you're going to get into Columbia after flunking out of Cornell? You weren't accepted at NYU, remember?"

"This time it will be different. I'm just the kind of student they're looking for."

"I suppose anything's possible—the important thing is you *want* to go back to school. And you're coming home!"

"Any news from Jeremy?" I asked.

"Jeremy—let's see—I don't hear from him that often, but I understand that he and Carrie have a new guru."

"A new guru!" I groaned. "Which one?"

"Some Vietnamese Buddhist monk in France—Tic Tac Toe, or something like that."

"Thich Nhat Hanh?"

"Something like that. By the way, Dougie, I want you to know that I realize I've been too judgmental of you. I've been giving it a lot of thought. Meeting Baba was very powerful, and I've been doing a little meditation since then. I was hoping you could take me to see him again next time he comes to New York."

"Sure. That'd be great," I lied. I knew if I told her I was done with Baba and Raja Yoga and why, I'd be on the phone all night. I'd tell her the whole story when I got home.

"I love you, Dougie."

"I love you too, Melanie," I said. And I meant it.

After the call with my sister, I was hungry. I realized I hadn't eaten lunch, and decided to take a walk to Leopold's on the Colaba Causeway for an early dinner. As I was about to exit the hotel, I remembered that I hadn't checked to see if Christopher Walsh was still staying there. I wanted to tell him what I'd witnessed in Baba's house. I also wanted him to see what Brian had done to my face.

"I'm sorry, Mr. Greenbaum, but Mr. Walsh checked out several days ago," said the man at reception. I was too late. I still had his business card, however. I'd contact him as soon as I was stateside.

I kept thinking of Gopi. Maybe she managed to get a message to me here at the hotel. I asked the hotel clerk to check. He disappeared into an office behind the reception and returned a moment later with an envelope addressed to me. "This telex message came for you just a moment ago, sir."

My breath hitched. Gopi had reached out to me after all! I opened the envelope. The message was from Shree Brahmananda Ashram in Ravipur. My hand began to tremble as I read the message:

> *He who speaks to the Guru in rude or insulting terms or wins an argument with him will be reborn as a demon in a jungle or a waterless region.*

I could feel the hair on the back of my neck stand up on end. It was verse one hundred and four of the *Guru Gita*. I knew the text well. I scanned the hotel lobby, but didn't see any familiar faces.

Perhaps they are just trying to rattle me.

Then I remembered Sergio's gun. Not long ago he pulled it on me for merely not minding my own business. After everything I'd done at the ashram, he had more than enough reason to use it on me now. I decided to skip the restaurant and return to the safety of my room.

On the elevator ride up, I wondered how they knew to reach me at the Taj. Had Gopi betrayed me and told them where I was? Then I remembered that Avadhoot knew I stayed at the Taj last time I came to the city. He must've told them! It wasn't Gopi! There was still a chance she was planning to meet me.

I had over twenty-four hours until my flight. I didn't dare leave the hotel. They could be waiting for me outside on the street, or even in the lobby. I was better off lying low in the room. I had until noon the next day to check out. In the meantime, I ordered room service.

Forty-five minutes later, a knock came on my door. Looking through the peephole, I saw the hotel porter and opened the door. Three room service attendants were standing outside with a cart. I motioned for them to enter. The first held the door open, the second pushed the cart into my room, and the third removed the fancy silver dome that was keeping my dinner warm.

The food was delicious and was a good distraction. I was finally able to calm down. I'd certainly miss eating Indian food every day. But before I even had a chance to finish my meal, another knock came on the door.

"I'm sorry, but I haven't finished eating," I said, opening the door.

To my horror, it wasn't the room service attendants again, but Brian from the ashram! He lunged at me, but I reacted just as quickly, slamming the door on his shoulder. His face twisted in pain and he cursed me.

"Fucking little cunt!"

To prevent him from forcing his way into the room, I repeatedly kicked him in the shin and pushed against the door with all my might. With strength I didn't know I had, I managed to force him back out the door, which I slammed shut and locked.

"Just you wait, faggot!" Brian shouted from outside in the corridor. "You're going to pay for what you did!"

"Get out of here!" I hollered through the locked door. "I'm calling security!"

"I am security, you little shit!"

"Get lost!"

There was silence.

I looked through the peephole. Nobody.

I called downstairs to the reception and asked to be connected to Mr. Gupta, the hotel manager.

"I'm sorry, Mr. Gupta is presently unavailable," an assistant said.

I explained what had happened, and he connected me to security.

"Taj security," came a man's voice on the other end of the line. I reported the incident and told him that Mr. Gupta was familiar with the history behind it.

"We will launch a full investigation!" the man on the other end of the phone promised. "The hotel detective is now just coming, sir. He will drop by your room in a few minutes' time."

After what seemed like hours, a knock finally came on the door. Not taking any chances, I looked through the peephole before opening. Three Indian men were standing outside.

"Good evening, sir. My name is Mr. Farooq. I am the hotel detective." Farooq was dressed in plain clothes, but the two men accompanying him were in uniforms and looked like security guards. "I am here to escort you off the premises. Kindly collect your belongings and come with me."

"You're throwing me out of the hotel! What did *I* do?"

"We received a complaint about a disturbance."

"I know you did, because *I'm* the one who made it!"

"*You*, sir?" Farooq looked incredulous.

"Yes, *me*! I called security just a few minutes ago."

I tried to explain the situation to the detective, but it was no use. He either didn't believe me or didn't care.

I could probably find another hotel nearby to stay in, even at this hour. That didn't concern me. What terrified me was being put out on the street where I'd be an easy target, if Brian was still hanging around the hotel.

"Please to collect your personal items and follow me," repeated the detective.

"But I'm the victim here! If you will just call Mr. Gupta, he will explain everything."

Farooq stared into my eyes and pursed his lips in thought. Then he went to the telephone by my bed and made a call.

"*Gupta kahan hai?*" the detective said into the phone. "*Ji haan.*" Farooq hung up the phone and turned to me again.

"Yes, please. Come with me."

"Did you speak to Mr. Gupta?" I asked, my voice becoming shrill. The detective didn't answer my question. Instead, he gestured toward my duffel bag.

I hastily packed up my things, and followed the three men down to the lobby. One of the uniformed men carried my bag. The situation was incredibly unfair, but I was helpless to do anything about it.

To make things worse, they asked me to pay my bill in full before leaving.

"I'm telling you, Mr. Gupta knows me! He'll explain everything,"

At that moment, another man came out through a door behind the reception area. His employee badge said "Night Manager."

"May I be of assistance?" he asked. His tone and demeanor were supercilious.

While the detectives stood by impassively, I explained the situation to the night manager. When I was finished, he told me to wait, and went back into the office. Five minutes later he returned and dismissed the detective and the security guards.

"My humblest apologies, Mr. Greenbaum, for the misunderstanding. Mr. Gupta has instructed me to refund your money and to let you know that your stay at the Taj tonight is on the house."

FOR HOURS I TOSSED and turned in my bed, thinking about the events of the last few days. I had been fooled and had wasted four years of my life following a charlatan. But then I remembered the first *shaktipat* retreat I'd taken with Baba. When I received the guru's touch, something extraordinary had happened. I had felt the kundalini moving up my spine, and entered into a profound state of consciousness. I also had many similar experiences since. Even that morning, despite how angry I was with Baba, when he touched me it was like getting *shaktipat* again. I didn't buy Chris Walsh's theory that Baba was merely hypnotizing people.

I thought about Namdev Loman and all the things I might have said or done differently that could have stopped him from killing himself. *If only I had offered to lend him money...*

I thought about college and what I might like to study. Maybe I'd become a filmmaker, or a journalist. Maybe even a lawyer. The future held endless possibilities. I thought about Katie Harris and Gili Ben Ami and how stupidly I had behaved with her. Gili was smart and beautiful. I admired her self-confidence and the fact that she had never been taken in by Baba. I could see myself being with her. I wished I'd made an effort to get to know her better. I felt like a jerk to have made out with her insipid, underage friend. Gili lived in New York City and I didn't have her phone. I had no way to find her. Like everyone else in Raja Yoga, I'd probably never see her again.

Before finally drifting off to sleep, I thought about Gopi. Maybe she'd still show up at the hotel or the airport. Then I remembered the look of adoration on her face as she gazed up at Baba during the *pattabhishek*.

No, I told myself. *She's not going anywhere. She'll be in the ashram for the rest of her life. That's all she's ever known.*

I FEEL INTENSE HEAT. I am alone with Baba in the Ravipur ashram courtyard. Baba sits naked on his throne and holds a trident. A cobra is coiled around his neck. The guru is scowling at me and I am afraid. He speaks to me without opening his mouth: "The serpent has been awakened and can never go back to sleep. There is no turning back."

"I know, Baba."

"You may try to leave the guru, you may run from him lifetime after lifetime, but the guru can never leave you."

"Why, Baba?"

"Because the guru is in everyone and everything. The guru is YOU."

"No, Baba. I'm not you! You're evil! You hurt people!"

"Evil?" *Baba's tone is indignant.* "Hurt people?"

The guru's body grows larger and larger until he towers over me. He transforms into a living statue of Nataraja, the Hindu god Shiva as the cosmic dancer.

I look up at the enormous statue, but I don't see the face of Shiva or Baba. I see my own face. The statue brings his mighty fist down on my head and I fall to the ground. He continues to beat me as the heat inside my body becomes so intense I fear I'll be incinerated.

"Baba does not hurt people!" thunders the statue. "He sets them free!"

The statue of Shiva and I are enveloped in white light. We merge into one. No thoughts remain, only the mantra: Soham—*"I am that."*

I woke up drenched in perspiration. My sheets were soaked and I was burning up as if I had a fever. But I didn't feel ill. The muscles in my arms and legs were twitching as they sometimes did when I chanted or meditated.

I was groggy, but it felt good to have slept so late. The digital clock on the nightstand said eleven a.m. I had one hour to vacate the room. My flight wasn't until midnight, and I didn't need to be at the airport until eight that evening. Where in Bombay could I be safe from Brian?

I checked out and saw Mr. Gupta, the manager. I thanked him for the complimentary night at the Taj. I told him about my concerns after the night's incident with Brian.

"You are most welcome to wait in the lobby until it is time for you to leave for the airport," he said. "Otherwise, feel free to take a dip in the pool."

"Thank you, Mr. Gupta," I said. "You're very kind."

The hotel manager slowly stroked his well-manicured mustache. "I have an even better idea!" he said. "You should take the ferry to Elephanta Island. Spend the afternoon there and visit the caves! No one will think to look for you there. And when you return, it will be time to leave for the airport."

Elephanta Island was located nine miles across the sea from the Gateway of India. The island was famous for its ancient stone sculptures of Hindu and Buddhist deities cut directly into the walls of its caves.

Mr. Gupta assured me that the hotel would keep my bag while I visited the caves, and he gave me a ticket with which to retrieve it later on. I was careful to keep my wallet, passport, and airplane ticket with me on the excursion.

"Oh, and Mr. Gupta," I said before turning to leave, "if a young American woman with blonde hair comes around the hotel looking for me, would you please tell her that I'll meet her at the airport?"

The hotel manager wiggled his eyebrows, gave me a knowing look, and chuckled.

"I most certainly will, young man! And I must say, you lead quite a life of adventure—I envy you!"

The crossing to Elephanta was not as pleasant as I'd imagined. Every time our little boat crossed the wake of a large military or cargo vessel, it rocked violently and I became seasick. Once we were hit by a wave so large that everyone on board was drenched. But the Indian sun was incredibly strong, and within an hour of my arrival on the island, I was completely dry again.

The heat was unbearable, and I didn't have a moment of peace, after I thought I saw Brian lurking in the shadows of one of the caves. It wasn't impossible—he could easily have seen me leave and come after me on the next ferry.

As I entered the largest of the island's caves, I was awestruck by a colossal, three-headed sculpture of the Supreme Being. Each head represented an aspect of the ultimate nature of reality: Brahma was the creator of the universe, Vishnu the protector, and Shiva the destroyer. As I contemplated the sculpture's symbolism, someone behind me spoke:

"If the red slayer think he slays,
Or if the slain think he is slain,
They know not well the subtle ways
I keep, and pass, and turn again.
Far or forgot to me is near;
Shadow and sunlight are the same;
The vanished gods to me appear;
And one to me are shame and fame.
They reckon ill who leave me out;
When me they fly, I am the wings;
I am the doubter and the doubt,

I am the hymn the Brahmin sings.
The strong gods pine for my abode,
And pine in vain the sacred Seven;
But thou, meek lover of the good!
Find me, and turn thy back on heaven."

I turned to see an old man staring at me. From his appearance and the way he spoke, I guessed he was American. "Emerson," he said, and then walked away.

After two hours of sightseeing, I took the ferry back to Bombay. On the crossing I thought about the meaning of the poem the old man had recited in the cave. I couldn't remember the precise words, but I knew the poem was about how everything was Shiva:

They reckon ill who leave me out;
When me they fly, I am the wings;
I am the doubter and the doubt,
I am the hymn the Brahmin sings.

Everything is Shiva or consciousness: the doubter, the object of doubt, and the doubt itself. I accepted that. *But if everything is just some cosmic dream, then we can do whatever we want. Nothing we do matters.*

No! I rejected this nihilistic view that Baba obviously subscribed to. There was more to reality than this! *Even if everything is consciousness, here on planet Earth, people still suffer when you hurt them.* I concluded that if immorality was the price of Baba's version of "enlightenment," I was better off living in ignorance.

By the time I got back to Bombay, it was only six p.m. As I walked up the pier toward the Taj, I kept an eye out for Brian. But there was no sign of him. I guessed he'd gone back to ashram. If his goal had been to scare me, he hadn't succeeded. I still planned to contact Christopher Wash as soon as I was back in the States. I was going to tell him everything.

As I crossed the street in front of the hotel, I noticed that my favorite doorman was on duty.

"Good evening, sir!" said the Sikh, holding the door open for me and greeting me in his usual affable manner.

I was about to tip him when Sergio, Brian, and the neckless swami, Akhandananda, exited through the other door. With the sound of my own heartbeat thrashing in my ears, I turned to run.

"Deependra, wait!" Akhandananda called after me. "We just want to talk to you!"

Akhandananda had always been kind to me, but in light of recent events, I had every reason to fear him. I ran as fast as I possibly could in the direction of the Colaba Causeway. As I was about to turn the corner onto Mahakavi Bhushan Road, I heard Sergio shouting in Italian. I turned to see my friend, the Sikh doorman, wrap his massive arms around Sergio, while the other, equally large doorman, detained Brian. I knew the doormen wouldn't be able to hold them for long. I needed to get a taxi to the airport fast, even if it meant abandoning my duffel bag at the hotel.

But it was rush hour and I couldn't find a free cab. I continued to run until I heard the faint but familiar strains of Indian "gospel" music up ahead of me. It was coming from the open windows of the Bowen Memorial Church. Desperate for a place to hide, I found an open door and ducked inside. As soon as I crossed the threshold, I was met by an Indian man and woman wearing big, syrupy smiles.

"Welcome, brother!" the man said.

The ceiling of the church was high. At the altar, a benevolent-looking man in white robes was leading the chant. High on the wall above the altar were painted the words: "Holy is the LORD of hosts; the whole earth is full of his glory!"

"Take one," the woman said, handing me a tract. It said: "The Gospel is not good news if it does not reach you in time." I wasn't sure what *they* meant by "good news," but it sure was good news to me that the door to the church was open.

"Come in, come in," the man said, taking me by the hand and leading me to the front of the congregation.

Apparently, I was the only Westerner, but I was made to feel more than welcome. Nearly everyone in the churched beamed a benevolent smile at me. The man stood me in front of a chair next to the window, where, I feared, I was too visible from the street. Just as I was about to leave my assigned spot, in search of another on the other side of the hall, I saw Sergio, Brian, and Akhandananda hurry by. They didn't even notice me in the window, so I decided to stay put.

Grateful for my reprieve, I threw my hands up in the air, and began to sway in time to the gospel music like everyone else. This spurred even wider smiles of approval from the rest of the congregation.

I glanced at the cross above the altar and thought about Jesus. *He was probably a charismatic guru like Baba.* Then I wondered if he also had a dark side that his followers were forbidden to talk about.

After a while the singing came to an end, and the priest in white robes began to give a sermon in Hindi. Reasonably confident that enough time had passed, I decided it was time to leave. As I made my way toward the back of the hall to the door, I was intercepted by the man and woman who had greeted me. Blocking my exit, they asked me where I was from, and what I was doing in India. They wanted to get to know me. At first I politely answered their questions, but when my anxiety about making a getaway to the airport became unbearable, I bolted passed them for the door.

Out on the street, my pulse raced. I looked both ways—there was no sign of my pursuers. A taxi barreled up the street in my direction. I held my arm up to hail it. Already taken. Another cab shot passed me. Also taken. I looked down the street in the opposite direction. Another was coming. I frantically waved for it to pull over. I was in luck. It was free.

"You are flying to New York, JFK via London Heathrow, sir?" the Air India representative at the check-in counter asked.

"Yes, that's right," I answered, still looking over my shoulder.

"No baggage, sir?"

"No, no baggage."

I regretted leaving my bag at the hotel. It was full of all my expensive designer clothes. Then I thought again: *Who needs them?*

With hours to go before I had to pass through security, I found a snack bar. I sat down and got a cup of chai while I waited. As I sipped my tea, I contemplated the fresh start I was about to make in my own country, far away from the ashram and the psychos that ran it. With nothing to read, I people-watched instead. A young woman with her back to me caught my eye. She had long blonde hair and was in line at the Air India counter. *Could it be?*

"You are so dead!"

My breath caught in my chest. I turned to see Brian, Sergio, and Akhandananda glaring down at me. I didn't know whether to scream for help or run. It was Sergio who had spoken. His fists were clenched and his eyes were wild, like the time he pulled the gun on me. Brian's face was beet red and he was baring his teeth. I thought he might have a stroke. The neckless swami was as stern-faced as ever. He was impossible for me to read.

Looking around, I reminded myself that I was in a public place. They wouldn't dare attack me.

"If you're here to bring me back to the ashram, you can forget it," I said. "I'm not going."

"Take you back? We wouldn't dream of it," Brian sneered. "We're the farewell committee—come to see you off." I noticed his arm was bruised from when I'd slammed the door on it.

"Brian, please," Akhandananda scolded. "We're here to talk to you, Deependra."

"Taking your medication, Greenbaum?" Sergio asked.

"My medication?"

"You know, for your head," he answered, tapping his temple. "You're completely *pazzo*, no?"

"Look who's talking!" I shot back.

"Would you mind leaving me alone with Deependra, boys?" Akhandananda asked.

"You're going to pay for what you did, fucker," Brian said, wagging a finger at me.

They left me alone with the swami and waited on the other side of the departure hall, where they could still keep an eye on me.

"May I?" Akhandananda asked, gesturing to the empty seat across from me.

I nodded.

Sitting down, the swami linked his fingers together and rested them on the table. Then he cocked his head to the side and stared at me searchingly for an uncomfortably long time before speaking.

"You do realize, of course, that you have no hope of survival."

"Are you threatening me, Swamiji? Is Baba going to have me whacked?"

"My boy, if Baba gave the word, these loyal disciples would follow you to the ends of the earth."

I glanced across the hall at Sergio and Brian. They were leaning against the wall and glaring at me.

"But Baba would never ask such a thing," he said, shaking his head and smiling, as if the very notion of the guru retaliating against a detractor were absurd. "In any case, I'm not talking about your physical body, I'm talking about your *ego*."

"With all due respect, Swamiji, I think my ego has an excellent chance of survival. I'm taking steps to ensure that."

Akhandananda leaned forward and furrowed his brow. "It's too late for that, my young friend. You have received the touch. The *kundalini* has been awakened. Even if you never meditate, or chant the name of God, or see or talk to Baba again as long as you live, the very circumstances of your life will conspire with the guru principle to undermine your ego and show you the truth of what you really are."

"A slave?"

The swami laughed ruefully. "A slave is what you are now, Deependra. You're a slave to your desires, to your aversions, to your pride, and to your concepts of the way you think things should be. Combined, these things make up your ego and prevent you from knowing the bliss of your own true nature."

I shook my head. "I'm sorry, I just don't buy it anymore."

"The energy that Baba awakened within you can never go back to sleep. Why fight it? *Shaktipat* is a death sentence for the individual self. It can be a slow painful death that takes many lifetimes of immeasurable suffering. Or the compassionate guru can put you out of your misery in just a few years. Why put off the inevitable?"

"If the goal of Raja Yoga is egolessness, why all the catering to ego that goes on in the ashram?" I asked.

"I don't know what you're talking about," he said unconvincingly.

"The VIP seating at the programs, the air conditioned rooms for Baba's special people. While others are treated like dirt. The ashram worked Namdev Loman to death. He worked over eighteen hours a day, seven days a week, but was the only ashramite on staff who didn't get a stipend, or Prasad passes. The other ashramites had nothing but contempt for him. No one even cared if he was getting a bare minimum of sleep or enough nourishing food to eat. That was for his spiritual upliftment?"

The swami opened his mouth to speak, but I cut him off.

"The ashram milked him for everything he had, and when he had nothing left to offer he was disposed of like human garbage. That's why he jumped. That's why he's dead!"

The swami's eyes widened and his nostrils flared. "The guru's *shakti* is ruthless, Deependra! No one said the path was easy. This boy that you speak of—he had extremely negative karma, which Baba was working to cleanse. Not everyone can take what the guru dishes out."

"So it cost him his life?"

"That boy was already deeply disturbed when he came to the ashram. Like everyone who has received the guru's grace, his journey is not over. It will continue into his next life."

"And what kind of a so-called 'enlightened being'—one *free from the shackles of desire*—needs to molest little girls?

Every decent person knows, regardless of what culture they come from, that the sexual abuse of children is evil."

"To suggest that Baba does anything for his own personal gratification is a gross distortion! If Baba ever did anything to hurt these women, as some have claimed, why haven't any of them spoken out? To have relations with a perfected master of Raja Yoga is the highest blessing. Don't attempt to judge Baba by the conventions of Western culture."

Behind me a voice said, "Why don't you ask Govinda Brown's daughter if she felt it was a blessing to be used repeatedly as a sexual object by Rudrananda?"

Akhandananda's mouth fell open.

"Chris Walsh. How do you do?"

The journalist pulled up a chair from an empty table and sat down with us.

"I know who you are," Akhandananda snapped.

"Prema was only thirteen when Rudrananda first summoned her to his chambers," said Chris. "Her story and many others are about to be told in next month's issue of *Veritas*."

The swami gritted his teeth and tapped the table with his forefinger. "You're traveling together, I take it?"

"No, we're not," I said.

"But it's no coincidence I'm here," Chris said. "I went by the Taj today and the manager told me that Mr. Greenbaum here was looking for me, and that he was flying home tonight."

"I'm ready to have that conversation with you now, Mr. Walsh."

Chris smiled. "I'm pleased to hear that, Doug." Then he turned back to Akhandananda. "Let me ask you something, Swamiji. Was it also a blessing when Sergio Casto raped Julie Kessler in New York? Is Casto also a master of *Tantra*? Does it help him to give *shaktipat*?"

"You know very well that was not a legitimate case of rape!" Akhandananda growled. "Besides, it was settled out of court. I would be extremely careful if I were you not to slander the Raja Yoga Mission."

"Libel," I corrected.

The swami, who was now red in the face, looked confused. "What?"

"When you print slander it's called *libel*," I answered.

"I know that! Don't patronize me!"

"You do realize that the Mission is about to face a criminal investigation," Chris said. "Some of the parents of the girls Rudrananda molested are going to press charges. You may imagine you're above the law, but you're not. Rudrananda will probably never be able to set foot on American soil again without getting arrested."

"Let me tell both of you something," Akhandananda said, jabbing a finger in Chris's face. "Before I became a swami, I was a medical doctor. For years I've seen Baba interact with his devotees and their children, in public and behind closed doors. And because I am a physician, I understand human behavior. If Baba had ever done anything harmful to any of these girls, I would have seen something in one of those children's eyes—I would have seen something wrong in the expression on one of their faces that would indicate to me fear, apprehension, depression, or something unsavory!" The swami's eyes were bulging and spittle was building up in the corners of his mouth. "I would know that something was wrong because of my years of training and experience! Can't you understand that?"

"According to my sources, just before you became a swami you lost your license to practice medicine for overprescribing painkillers to your patients," Chris said. "So, not only would I question your lack of bias, I would also question your credentials."

The swami was quiet. Then a smirk played on his lips as he let out a slight scoff.

"You know, a certain devotee was killed in a plane crash after spreading false rumors about Baba."

"Is that a threat, Akhandananda?" asked Chris. "Are you going to sabotage my flight back to the States and kill everyone else on board too?"

The neckless swami turned to me and his expression softened. "Deependra, Baba wants you to know that he loves and forgives you. He asks that you return to Ravipur with me now."

Baba said he loved me. I thought back to the day I first met Baba and he squeezed my hand in the lobby. I thought of the day Baba gave me *shaktipat* and took me in his arms on the *darshan* line and I cried on his shoulder. I could go back to the ashram. It wasn't too late. *Baba forgives me.*

"No," I said, looking the swami squarely in the eye. "I'm never going back to the ashram. Baba is a tyrant, a hypocrite, and a child molester!"

The swami rose to his feet and a moment later Sergio and Brian returned to his side.

"Ahh, everybody's here now," said Chris, leaning back in his chair. "Are you here to drag Douglas back to the ashram? Shall I call for help? There are three policemen standing right over there."

Brian's jaw clenched and his muscles flexed under his shirt.

Sergio drew his upper lip up toward his nose. "Be careful, Walsh."

"And if I'm not? What? I might have an 'accident?'"

"Deependra is free to go wherever he wants," the swami told Chris. Then he turned to me. "Just remember, young man, if you choose the wrong course of action, the guru might not be so welcoming should you ever change your mind and wish to come back."

With that, the swami turned to leave. Reluctantly, Sergio and Brian followed behind him.

"You think they're really gone?" I asked after Baba's thugs exited the terminal.

"I think so, but even if they're not, I wouldn't worry. They may be angry that you're talking to me, but they're not going to try anything at an international airport. They're fanatics, but they're not stupid."

"Oh, they're mad at me alright, but my talking to you is the least of it," I laughed. "I left quite a paper trail on my way out."

"Is that why they messed up your face?"

I laughed again.

Chris asked what time my flight left, and I told him I had to leave for the gate soon.

"I'll be back in New York in a couple of weeks," Chris said. "I hope you'll still be willing to sit down for an interview with me."

I swallowed hard. "Okay."

"Look, Doug. You started out in Raja Yoga as a sincere seeker with the noblest aspirations. Predators like Rudrananda take advantage of people like you."

"I feel like I've wasted so much time."

"Look on the bright side: You're young. You can go back to school. You're just beginning your life. Some people, on the other hand, spend their entire lives in cults."

FINALLY SITTING ON THE plane that would take me home, I heaved a sigh of relief. I looked around the cabin. The flight was practically empty, and I was the only one in my row. It was crazy, but I still had hope that Gopi would turn up.

Why had I been such a coward? Instead of running away from the *mandap*, I should have shouted Gopi's name from the camera platform at the top of my lungs, like Dustin Hoffman in *The Graduate*. Baba would have been stunned and embarrassed in front of the Acharya and all his celebrity devotees. The Brahmin priests would have been so surprised by my outburst, they would have stopped chanting. Using my camera tripod as a weapon, I would have fought off Sergio and Brian, and anyone else who stood in my way. We would have escaped Baba and the ashram together. If I'd been brave enough, Gopi and I would be sitting together on the plane right now.

Waiting for take off, I kept looking down the aisle toward the front of the aircraft, hoping I'd see her. There was still a possibility Gopi would come. But in my heart I knew I'd never see her again.

Glossary of Sanskrit and Hindi Terms

Advaita Vedanta a non-dualistic philosophy. The universe that we see around us has only relative reality, and it is Brahman alone at the base of the universe which has absolute reality.

Acharya a religious instructor; founder or leader of a sect of Hinduism.

Aghori a sect of Shiva-worshipping ascetics known to engage in post-mortem rituals and other taboo practices.

Arati a Hindu ritual in which light from wicks soaked in purified butter or camphor is offered to one or more deities. Aratis also refer to the hymns sung in praise of the deities during this ritual.

Asana a posture adopted in performing Hatha yoga. Also, a mat upon which one sits for meditation.

Ashram a monastic community or place of religious retreat under the direction of a guru.

Avadhoot a mystic who abides in a state of non-dual awareness and acts with the freedom and spontaneity of a child without consideration for social mores and etiquette.

Ayurveda a three-thousand-year-old system of medicine with historical roots in India.

Bhakti devotional worship directed at one supreme deity.

Brahma the creator god in the trinity of supreme divinity in Hinduism. See Vishnu and Shiva.

Brahman a member of the priestly caste in the Hindu caste system.

Chakra a center of spiritual energy located in the human body. Chakras are usually considered to be seven in number.

Churel a female ghost in South Asian folklore; also used colloquially to refer to a witch.

Dakshina an offering made in gratitude to the guru.

Darshan an occasion of being in the presence of a holy person or the image of a deity.

Deva or **Devi** a god or goddess.

Diksha initiation by a guru into a spiritual practice.

Ganesh the elephant-headed god, son of Shiva and Parvati. The god of wisdom and learning, as well as the remover of obstacles.

Gita   "Song of God."

Guru   a spiritual master, especially one who gives initiation.

Gurudev or **Gurudevi**   a term of address for a spiritual master recognizing him or her as an embodiment of God.

Hatha Yoga   a branch of yoga that emphasizes physical exercises.

Jai Gurudev   "Glory to the eternal guru."

Ji   a gender-neutral honorific used as a suffix in many Indian languages.

Karma   the law of cause and effect. The intent and results of a person's actions in the present and in previous states of existence influence the future of that individual.

Kashmir Shaivism   a non-dualist philosophy that views the entire cosmos as a manifestation of consciousness.

Kali Yuga   the final of the four stages the universe undergoes as part of a cycle of yugas, or epochs. The other stages are the Satya Yuga, Treta Yuga, and Dvapara Yuga.

Krishna   one of the eight incarnations of Vishnu, the Hindu god of love and compassion.

Kriya   a spontaneous physical or mental expression of the awakened kundalini in a practitioner of yoga.

Kundalini   the evolutionary energy that lies dormant at the base of the spine in most people.

Lakshmi   the Hindu goddess of wealth, fortune, and prosperity.

Mahasamadhi   the great and final samadhi, when an enlightened being leaves his or her physical body to merge with the absolute.

Mandap an outdoor pavilion for public religious rituals.

Mantra a sacred utterance.

Maya the illusion of the exterior world.

Paduka India's oldest and simplest form of footwear, consisting of a sole and a post and knob.

Nirvikalpa samadhi the highest stage of meditative absorption in which the distinction between the knower, the act of knowing, and the object known dissolves.

Ojas a vital fluid in the human body derived from sexual fluid.

OM the primordial sound.

Om Namah Shivaya a popular Hindu mantra meaning "Salutations to Shiva."

Prasad a gracious gift, typically an edible food, that is first offered to a deity, saint, or guru, and then distributed in his or her name to their devotees.

Paramahansa a title of honor applied to Hindu gurus who are regarded as having attained the highest state of consciousness.

Puja the act of worship.

Pattabhishek a coronation.

Punyatithi a death anniversary.

Rama the seventh incarnation of Vishnu and central figure in the Sanskrit epic the Mahabharata.

Rudraksha a seed traditionally used for prayer beads in Hinduism.

Sadhana spiritual practice with the goal of enlightenment.

Sadhu a holy man, sage, or ascetic.

Sahasrara the seventh or "thousand-petaled" chakra located in the crown of the head.

Samadhi the final stage of union with the absolute, attained during meditation or at the moment of death.

Samskaras the psychological imprints or mental impressions accumulated over many lifetimes and stored deep within the unconscious mind and subtle body.

Sannyasa a form of asceticism marked by renunciation of material desires with the purpose of devoting one's life to spiritual practice.

Sannyasin one who has taken the vows of sannyasa.

Saptah a week-long ashram chant or program.

Satsang a sacred gathering.

Savikalpa meditation with the support of an object.

Seva selfless service or work offered without thought of reward or payment.

Shakti the divine feminine energy.

Shaktipat the transference of divine energy from guru to disciple to awaken the kundalini.

Shanti peace, tranquility, or bliss.

Shayanagrih a dormitory.

Shiva the all-pervasive supreme Self in Shaivism. Shiva is the transformer and destroyer god in the trinity of supreme divinity in Hinduism. See Brahma and Vishnu.

Shiva Mahimna Stotram a hymn in praise of Shiva.

Shree or **Sri** a polite form of address equivalent to the English "Mr." or "Mrs." Also, a title of respect prefixed to the name of a deity or sacred text.

Shushmna nadi the central subtle energy channel that travels the full length of the spine.

Soham a Vedic mantra meaning "I am That."

Swami an ascetic or yogi who has been initiated into a Hindu monastic order.

Tantra a Hindu or Buddhist mystical or ritual text, dating from the 6th to the 13th centuries. A spiritual practice.

Upanishads a collection of Hindu religious and philosophical texts dating sometime between c. 800 BCE and c. 500 BCE.

Utpaladeva (ca. AD 900–950) one of the great teachers of the philosophy of Kashmir Shaivism and an influential philosopher-theologian of the Pratyabhijna school of Tantric Shaivism.

Vamachara the "Left-Hand Path." A mode of spiritual practice that is at odds with standard Vedic injunction and extreme in comparison to the status quo.

Vishnu the protector and sustainer god in the trinity of supreme divinity in Hinduism. See Brahma and Shiva.

Yagna a ritual sacrifice performed in front of a sacred fire.

Yoga an umbrella term for a group of mental, physical, and spiritual practices or disciplines with the goal of enlightenment.

I WISH TO THANK the following people:

My editor Randy Rosenthal trimmed thousands of words from these pages, giving a sharper focus and smoother flow to my prose. He not only helped me to write a better book, but taught me to be a better writer in the process. My dear friend Sophie Bland and my sister Mimi Trudeau believed in me and finally convinced me to pick up a pen. My sister Marta Brody created the cover illustration and worked tirelessly with me on two complete rewrites. Without her constant encouragement, I never would have made it to the finish line. Nate Davis, Emily Jeffries, Bethany Powell, and my daughter Melissa Schneider also read early drafts of the manuscript and gave me valuable advice.

I am also indebted to my dharma brother, the legendary Gorakh Silvester, whose heartrending yet fascinating accounts of his years in an Indian ashram inspired many of the scenes in this novel. And most of all, I am grateful to my beloved wife and editor-in-chief, Manette Pottle, who supported me through all my manic ups and downs during five years of writing The Guru's Touch.

ROBERT G. SCHNEIDER WAS born in Bayside, Queens, in 1964, and raised in Ithaca, New York. He left college to follow the India guru Swami Muktananda, living and working in the guru's *Siddha Yoga* ashrams in India and the US for four years. He is a graduate of the New York University Tisch School of Film and Television, and for many years was a commercial filmmaker in Belgium. He lives in Maine.

Made in the USA
Middletown, DE
01 September 2017